Geoffrey's arms went around Joanna and pulled her down onto his lap. He kissed her hungrily, her lips and throat. "God knows when we can marry," he groaned. "The war may continue for years." She pulled her face away enough to take in Geoffrey's hungry eyes, his usually flexible thin lips, full and rigid now with desire. The thin silk night robe she wore was little protection against the rings of steel that bruised her arms and back. She did not know what to say but her treacherous body was urging her to yield, desire already overriding discomfort, dulling the pain his fierce embrace gave her. A cry in response to a pleasure nearly as agonizing as pain rose in her throat. *"Geoffrey—"* she whispered, having not the faintest idea of what she would say or do next.

io the third book of the magnificent four-volume saga, THE ROSELYNDE CHRONICLES. A richly detailed and panoramic story set in medieval England, the novel weaves a romantic tale of power and passion, danger and desire—and the poignance of tender young love.

Joanna

Roberta Gellis

PLAYBOY PRESS
PAPERBACKS

JOANNA

PRODUCED BY LYLE KENYON ENGEL.

Copyright© 1978 by Roberta Gellis and Book Creations, Inc.

Cover illustration by *San Julian:* Copyright © 1978 by Playboy.

Published simultaneously in the United States and Canada by Playboy Press, Chicago, Illinois. Printed in the United States of America. Library of Congress Catalog Card Number: 78-59971. First edition.

This book is available at quantity discounts for promotional and industrial use. For further information, write our sales-promotion agency: Ventura Associates, 40 East 49th Street, New York, New York 10017.

ISBN: 0-872-16490-x

Other books by the author:

BOND OF BLOOD
KNIGHT'S HONOR
THE DRAGON AND THE ROSE
THE SWORD AND THE SWAN
ROSELYNDE
ALINOR

CHAPTER ONE

Lady Alinor bit her lip and stared upward at her daughter, who was standing before her. Any mother would have been proud of such a daughter. Lady Joanna, at fifteen, was exceptionally beautiful; her flaming hair was, of course, braided and hidden quite properly under a wimple, but its color could be assumed from the fine, bright red brows that arched over her large gray eyes and from the dark red lashes which were thick and long. Alinor was distracted momentarily from her main purpose by thinking how fortunate Joanna was. Usually red-haired people had pale, scanty eyelashes, which made their eyes seem inflamed rather than lending beauty to them.

The rest of the face was perfectly in harmony, oval, with a fine nose and a pretty mouth, a short, well-shaped upper lip and a full sensuous lower. In more than her beauty, Joanna was an ideal daughter. She was intelligent and capable, well-able to operate Roselynde keep, control the servants and men-at-arms, do the accounts, even sit and give justice when necessary. To top all those virtues, she was good humored, gentle, and biddable. Indeed, any mother would have been proud of such a daughter — any mother except Lady Alinor, who was tempestuous, passionate, and authoritarian.

"Joanna," Alinor said, trying earnestly to keep her voice gentle, "I ask again who you wish to marry. There are men and men and men. Between the times you have been at court, the times you have traveled with us, and the times there have been visitors to this keep, you have met nearly all of those suitable to your rank and dowry. Do you mean to say there is not *one* among them all that you like?"

"I like them all—nearly all, mother. I say again also that I will marry any man you choose for me."

Alinor impatiently closed her eyes and swallowed. Shrieking at Joanna never did the slightest good. The large gray eyes would open wide. Color would stain the delicate white skin. And that was all. The pretty mouth would remain closed. The eyes would show neither fear nor anger. Joanna could be angry; Alinor had heard her flay a servant with her tongue and had seen her lay on with a whip also, but Joanna never quarreled with her mother.

"But surely," Alinor suggested quietly, having regained control of her own temper, "you like some better than others."

"Yes—" The word was drawn out doubtfully. "But usually that is because I know them better. I like people I know well. I am more comfortable with them."

"Joanna," Alinor began for the third time. "Sit down. Did you understand what Ian told you last night?"

"Of course I understood it, mother. It is quite mad, though. How can the king or Lord Llewelyn be angry at Ian because he cannot split himself in half?" The misty gray of Joanna's eyes brightened and her soft mouth curved upward. She had a very ticklish sense of humor. "After all, whether he split himself lengthwise—sending one arm and one leg to each—or split himself crosswise—arms to one and legs to the other—he would not be much use that way."

"Joanna!" Alinor exclaimed, and then broke into laughter herself.

That was how her quarrels with Joanna usually ended. Joanna would make her laugh, and the matter would be put aside to resolve itself with time. Simon, Alinor thought, with a sudden sharp pang at heart. Simon was Joanna's father; he had been Alinor's first husband, many years older than her, and he had managed her in much the same way. Usually the thought of Simon would soften Alinor completely. Usually whenever Joanna recalled Simon to her mother's mind, Joanna's cause was won. This time, however, it did not work. Alinor had loved Simon with a hot and consuming passion. She had wheedled and connived so that she could follow him all the way to the Holy Land, accompanying King Richard's wife and sister on the Crusade. Joanna had been named after Richard's sister, who had been godmother to Alinor's first child. And Simon had been as passionately in love with his wife as she was with him.

Two strong and determined natures, two violently passionate people, could not produce a milksop, Alinor thought. In fact, she knew Joanna was not a milksop. Outwardly she was more placid than her mother, but she could love fiercely—as she did that damned dog. Alinor glanced briefly across to the hearth where something that looked like a shaggy gray pony lay curled before the fire. Instantly, a bedraggled and unkempt tail, thick as Alinor's wrist, began to thump the ground. Alinor laughed again and looked away. To look at Brian too long generally induced him to rush over and try to sit in your lap. Sturdy as she was, Alinor did not relish nearly fifteen stone's weight of dog climbing on her.

It was very hard not to love Brian, but Alinor had contended that anything that size must be banished to the kennel. Joanna did not argue; she merely went to the kennel with the dog, Alinor reasoned, then pleaded, then whipped her daughter soundly. Joanna returned to the kennel, was whipped again, returned to the kennel—and Brian came to live in the chambers of the keep with his mistress. Suddenly Alinor's eyes returned to the dog. Perhaps there was a clue in Brian to Joanna's preference that Joanna herself did not suspect or would not admit.

"Yes," Alinor said, "you can make me laugh, but it is not really funny at all. I do not know whether you remember, my love, but when Ian married me he gained the enmity of the king. John still does not love him, but a truce has been patched between them by Salisbury. It would be very dangerous for Ian to break that truce by going to serve Lord Llewelyn in Wales. Yet, Ian cannot serve with the king. He is clan brother to Lord Llewelyn—and he loves him."

"I see that. I see what you have decided is best, but. . . . Oh, mother, are you *sure* there will be war between Llewelyn and the king? Llewelyn has not really done anything to offend John, and he is married to John's daughter."

"Since when is it necessary to *do* something in order to offend King John?" Alinor asked tartly. "It is enough that Llewelyn has gained what John considers too much power." Then she bit her lip. "That is not fair. I like Llewelyn and dislike the king, and that was my heart speaking. In truth, even Ian agrees that John is not all wrong this time. Llewelyn has eaten nearly all Wales. There can be little doubt that he will next begin nibbling on the borders of England unless he has a sharp lesson. It is all the more dangerous because he is a good lord. Men are none so unwilling to swear to him instead of to the king."

"Would it be so ill if Llewelyn ruled England?"

"Not ill, just not possible. He has not the right. There are still men of honor in this land who would oppose him— Pembroke, Salisbury, Arundel, Ian, too, no matter how much he loves his clan brother. John has the right to rule England; Llewelyn has not. To a good man right and honor—as I have often told you—have nothing to do with best and easiest. Sometimes, by accident, they coincide; that is all."

"Yet you have persuaded Ian to do what is best and easiest—have you not?"

Alinor's hazel eyes lit with anger. "Do you impugn Ian's honor or courage?"

Joanna did not seem to notice the danger signal of green and gold sparks in her mother's eyes. She shook her head. "No. I was not thinking of that at all, only how love can make a person—make a person different from what is his nature."

There was a moment's silence while Alinor absorbed what her daughter had said. "I suppose that is true," she admitted slowly, "but a true love does not permit bending that love's partner all awry."

"Instead one tears out one's own heart."

Again there was a silence. Alinor studied Joanna's face with a new, shocked understanding. In general, love and marriage had very little to do with each other. Men and women were mated to make political alliances, to increase or join estates, to provide security for a woman, and, if a woman was an heiress, to provide a livelihood for her husband. Alinor's grandparents, married against both their wills for political purposes, had fallen deeply and sincerely in love. Alinor had been raised in that atmosphere, for her parents had been drowned when she was two. She had seen the joy with which love can invest everyday life. She had seen the pain also; the quarrels and the tears, the terror her grandmother endured when her grandfather rode out to war. Adventurous by nature, Alinor had thought the pain a small price to pay in exchange for the joy.

It had never occurred to her that Joanna could feel differently. But Joanna *was* different. She did not lack courage—not in the least. Like her father, she had the strong, deep courage of ultimate endurance. She also had Simon's caution. Whereas Alinor rushed headlong to meet danger, impatient for the conflict and the decision—Joanna waited for trouble to come to her. She never retreated from it, but she did not seek it out either.

She does not wish to permit herself to love, Alinor thought. It was perfectly logical. Joanna had also been raised in a household where love reigned, but perhaps she had seen—or remembered—more of the pain than the joy. She was eight when her father sickened; for more than a year she had watched him die inch by inch and had watched her mother's heart die with him. Then she had lived through the first tempestuous years of Alinor's second marriage. Alinor loved Ian as deeply and perhaps even more passionately than she had loved Simon, but what Joanna had seen was their difficult adjustment to each other and then her mother's constant fear for her stepfather's safety.

Yet it was impossible for Joanna to avoid love, Alinor thought. There was a passion in her as hot as her fiery hair. Alinor's eyes flicked across the room to the dog. Look how easily she had fallen into love for that silly animal and how strong she held to it. And Joanna was no fool. She knew Brian would not live long. Dogs did not, and a dog that size more especially had a short life. The knowledge of grief to come cannot defend the heart. Then there was no reason to wait. Joanna had a strong sense of right and duty. If the man were well chosen, if he treated her well, entreated her softly, and, above all, loved *her,* she would tumble into love with him as she had into love for Brian.

Perhaps the love was already there. Perhaps Brian was a safe substitute for the young man who had given the dog to Joanna. Alinor stared at Joanna's slightly downcast face. There was both good and ill in that chance. On the one hand, the seeds of love already planted might more easily grow into a blooming tree; on the other, half aware of their presence and fearing their growth, Joanna might more fiercely resist. Between the two chances there was no way to judge. Such things were truly in the hands of God.

"It is because the only honorable path is to give exact due and favor neither side that Ian has chosen to go to Ireland," Alinor said at last, ignoring the personal note and resuming the conversation on the political level. "For his lands in Wales, Ian has done Llewelyn homage. He owes him the service of the Welsh vassals and their men. For his northern properties, Ian has done King John homage and also as Adam's guardian he has sworn the service of Adam's men. I, too, have sworn fealty for my lands and, as I cannot lead men to war, it is my husband's duty to do so for me."

A fine red brow quirked upward. "Perhaps Ian would not need to split himself in half. Perhaps, since the due to the king is so much greater, only one leg or one arm would content Llewelyn."

"I will murder you, Joanna," Alinor exclaimed, half-irritated, half-laughing. "This is a serious matter."

"Oh mother, I know that, but I do not see what it has to do with me or my marriage."

"It has this to do with your marriage. The Welsh vassals are no problem. Ian has ordered them to obey Lord Llewelyn in his stead while he is away. However, Ian does not dare trust his men, my men, and Adam's men to the king's governance. Either John would try to steal them from us, seducing them to swear directly to him and thus rob us of our rents and our power, or he would thrust them into the greatest danger so that they would be killed and he could control their heirs. We must have a man who can take Ian's place as leader. We must have a man who has the *right* to take Ian's place, a right the king cannot dispute. Your brother is too young—"

"Not Adam!" Joanna cried, almost starting out of her chair. Fear clouded her eyes. "I will marry anyone you say, anyone. Do not let Ian send Adam to war."

Alinor laughed, although her eyes filled with tears. "Ian—Ian would die ten times over to save any of you a prick of the finger. I said Adam was too young. Nonetheless, Joanna, soon he will not be too young. You must know that you cannot protect him from danger, and to show him your fear can only hurt him. Men must offer their bodies to hurt, and women must offer their hearts." Alinor's voice faltered a trifle. Perhaps it was better that Joanna should not love. "In any case," she went on more firmly, "Adam is not in question. If you marry, your husband will have a blood bond with us and thereby blood right to lead the men in our absence. We—Ian and I—will take oath of them to obey him."

"Mother, do you know what you are saying? You are telling me to choose the man I like best so that he may be laid down as a sacrifice in the king's war."

"Nonsense!" Alinor rejoined tartly. "Your father died of sickness in his bed, yet he had fought all of his life. My grandfather, who lived to be four score years, died in his bed also. Ian is near forty years of age. He, too, has seen much of war—and much of treachery also—and he is hale and hearty. Men do die in war. Women die too, in childbearing. Is that a reason to stop having children? What I am telling you is that you must choose a husband, a man with whom you wish to spend your life, whose children you wish to bear, to whose interests you believe you can devote yourself.''

Stubbornly, Joanna shook her head. ''I cannot choose. I have said, and I say again, that I am willing to marry any man you name to me.'' Suddenly her expression lightened. ''Your reinforcements are here.''

Alinor turned her head toward the doorway. She did not speak but her eyes lit and her color rose a little. Her husband hesitated in the doorway, his intense brown eyes looking from mother to daughter. It would not have been surprising if Joanna had refused to marry because no man she had seen could measure up to her stepfather. Alinor said often that Ian had the face of a black angel, and God had seen fit to preserve his dark masculine beauty. His battle scars were all on his body. Perhaps Ian's looks had made Joanna's friends pale in comparison, but it was useless to worry about that. Simply there was no one available to match Ian for looks, and there might never be.

''Well,'' he said when neither woman spoke, ''what have you decided?''

Alinor shrugged. Joanna said, ''I will be obedient to your will, my lord. I will marry any man you and my mother decide is fitting.''

Instead of looking satisfied, Ian looked appalled. ''My love,'' he said gently, ''we will not force you. I will sooner stay and—''

''No, no.'' Joanna protested, getting up and going over to him. ''I am not unwilling, really I am not. I know it is time, and past time, for me to be married.''

Ian put his arm around Joanna and drew her close. Over her head he looked doubtfully at his wife.

''She does not fancy any man she knows,'' Alinor remarked neutrally, as if a husband was a dish laid on the table.

''We have been too sudden,'' Ian said. ''There is time enough. Do you think again, love—''

Alinor cast an exasperated and affectionate glance at her husband. One would think he had not a bone in his body and his blood was milk and water when he had to deal with Adam and Joanna. And it was not only because they were Simon's children. He was just as bad with little Simon, his own son. He could never bear to see any of them sad, even when the sadness was their own fault.

"One does not need to think about such things," she said sharply. "Either one desires a man or one does not. If Joanna has no preference, it is better for us to choose."

The first reaction Ian had to that was surprise. Years before, he had suggested contracting Joanna in marriage when he had received a most favorable offer for her. At that time, Alinor had flatly refused, insisting—in defiance of all reason and propriety—that Joanna must choose for herself. It was not like Alinor to do an about-face in such matters. Then Ian's arm tightened protectively around his stepdaughter, and a wary look came into his eyes. When Alinor was angry, she could be very severe with her children. Ian often found himself pleading their cause. Sometimes he saved them a whipping, sometimes he did not, but this was not a matter so easily healed as a few wheals. Still, Alinor did not look angry. Her eyes were meeting his purposefully, but there were no sparks of rage in them; she was trying to tell him something.

"Joanna, my love, is this really what you desire?" Ian pleaded. "Do not let your mother frighten you. There is time enough to think, and if you do not wish to marry— well, I will find another way to settle the matter of the men. My troubles must not come upon you. They will be easily overcome by some other device."

When Ian started to speak, Alinor had opened her mouth to protest, but she shut it again. Nothing could better draw an opinion from Joanna, if she had one concealed, than Ian's offer to sacrifice himself—not, of course, that he thought of it as a sacrifice. He would regard it as a welcome excuse to stand his ground. Ian was not inclined to back away from trouble. The retreat to Ireland had been Alinor's idea and at first scornfully rejected by him. It had been adopted only after the earl of Pembroke had written to say that Ian's presence was really necessary to him in Ireland and the earl of Salisbury had pleaded, almost in tears, that he should leave England. Joanna, however, would believe that Ian was endangering himself to gratify her whim.

"You do not understand," Joanna replied firmly, gently freeing herself so that she could look up at her stepfather. "It will be a great relief to me to have the matter settled. I *have* thought of marriage. Every girl who does not wish to give herself to God must do so. I just do not prefer any particular man. I trust you and mother to choose well for me, and I will be a good and faithful wife—I swear it."

That was settled, Alinor thought. If Joanna could have named someone, she would have done so to ease Ian's heart. "Then we come to the meat of the matter. Sit down, Ian. And you too, Joanna, take a stool." When the girl was settled, Alinor said to her seriously, "It is your whole life, child. I beg you, if you have the smallest, faintest doubt, that you speak out at once. Perhaps you have guessed that Ian and I do have a preference for your husband. Nonetheless, there are many other men, equally suitable. If you feel a shadow of distaste—no matter how vague, no matter how foolish it seems to you—tell me at once. Above all and beyond all—immeasurably above and beyond all—I desire that you be content. Now I say this. More grief can come upon me, and upon Ian too, by your unhappiness than by anything else."

"I will try to be honest, but mama—"

"You do not need to answer now," Ian suggested. "Let us suggest a few—"

"No," Alinor objected, "to name more than one would make the problem worse. But Ian is right on the other matter. You do not have to answer now. We will suggest one man. You may refuse outright. If you have a doubt as to your ability to share a whole life with him, do so. You may accept outright. Or you may think it over and tell me later, or tomorrow. Remember, there are others. That we name Lord Geoffrey FitzWilliam to you now does not mean there is any need for you to take him."

The name was slipped in very naturally. Alinor had been holding her daughter's eyes steadily all the while so that there was no need to seek to catch her expression. In fact, there was no change in her face. Perhaps a fleeting emotion flickered in her eyes—relief?—but it was so brief that Alinor could not really read it. Joanna said nothing and a silence fell, broken after a moment by the sound of Ian shifting uneasily in his chair. Alinor turned toward her husband. When her eyes came back to Joanna, the girl was looking at Brian. The dog lifted his head, then rose and came to his mistress. Joanna braced herself. Brian sat, with a thump that shook even the solid hardwood floor, and then leaned heavily against Joanna. The stool began to tilt. Joanna hastily moved her feet to brace herself better. Alinor smiled. Geoffrey had brought the puppy that grew into Brian from Ireland where he had been serving as Ian's squire. Called back to action, he had given the still-blind, gangling, emaciated creature to Joanna.

"Now Joanna," Ian went on. "It is true that we all love Geoffrey, but if you feel—if perhaps you think—"

"Tush!" Alinor exclaimed impatiently. Men were always accused of coarseness because they cursed and spat and pissed in odd places, but they really were afflicted with the silliest delicacy of mind. "What Ian wants to know, Joanna, is whether you will feel as if you are bedding your brother when it comes to coupling with Geoffrey."

"Alinor!"

"Well, that is what you meant, is it not?"

Instead of replying, Ian rose and walked to the window in the antechamber, where he stood staring out at the walls and, beyond them, to the little whitecaps that showed on the swells of the sea. Joanna and Alinor looked at each other with identical expressions of amusement, each biting her lips to restrain giggles. Each knew that it was not especially the mention of incest that troubled Ian but the idea of Joanna's mating. His reaction was fortunate, however, in that it broke the tension.

"Well, Joanna?" Alinor insisted, but she was smiling.

"No," Joanna replied, "I do not feel that."

"Think about coupling with him, child," Alinor urged. "Is there anything distressing to you in that idea? Think about children that look and speak and move like Geoffrey. Would you prefer your children to be different? Like unto someone else?"

It was a great relief to Alinor to see the expression of interest on Joanna's face. Obviously her daughter had never considered Geoffrey in the light of lover and husband. That was reasonable. For a girl to allow such thoughts about her father's squire to get into her head was dangerous and might lead to great unhappiness. Joanna was too practical to fall into such a mistake. Alinor, far more headstrong than her daughter, had not taken that into consideration enough, she realized now. Fortunately, it was equally obvious that there was nothing displeasing to Joanna in the notion. Now, if only the girl did not come to realize that thinking about such things would swiftly lead her down the path to love. Alinor rose and shook out her skirts.

"When you have decided, come and tell me. Whatever you say, we will accept. If you refuse, we have another equally worthy to suggest."

"I do not need more time, mother," Joanna said. "I am willing, if—"

"If what, love?" Ian asked from the doorway.

"If Geoffrey is willing," Joanna said simply.

Color flooded into Ian's swarthy face, turning it dark red. "What do you mean, if Geoffrey is willing?" he roared. "We are offering him a pearl without price. Where could he find your match for beauty and virtue—"

"And lands," Alinor put in, but she was laughing merrily and Joanna was also. Ian always overreacted to the faintest slur cast upon his stepchildren.

"But Ian," Joanna protested, seeing he was still angry, "Geoffrey might think of me as a sister. That would be terrible." Then her eyes widened. "Oh, Ian, Lord Salisbury would not force Geoffrey, would he?"

"Do not be silly, Joanna," Alinor said sharply. That was one idea she wished to avoid above all. Joanna might well return love, but she would not proffer it. "You know William dotes upon Geoffrey, the more because he was born a bastard. You remember that, do you not? You have considered it?"

"What is there to consider in that?" Joanna asked.

"Geoffrey is dear to Salisbury and because of him is often at court. If you marry Geoffrey, you will spend much time there also. Jealousy is rife at court. More than one woman will taunt you that you had to marry a bastard, however near to the throne."

"Not more than one," Joanna said, and her eyes grew brighter and harder.

Alinor stared at her strong-willed daughter. A slow smile grew on her lips. Ian guffawed. Nonetheless, he said warningly, "You are not to raise your hand, your whip, or your knife to the queen's ladies, Joanna."

Joanna said nothing, but her eyes were light and shining and met Ian's challengingly.

He rubbed the back of his neck, as a man with a puzzle would, and then shook his head. "You must understand, my love, that much of the spite will come from places you cannot reach. It is no sense to punish the servants for the faults of the masters. The one man in the world the king loves is William of Salisbury, his half brother. Because of that, he hates Geoffrey."

"Is he mad?" Joanna asked amazedly.

"Oh no, merely greedy and jealous," Alinor remarked. "John must eat the world. He must have all, everything. Thus, it is hateful to him that William also has room in his heart to love his own son."

"But that *is* mad," Joanna insisted. "It is as if I should hate Adam or Simon because you love them."

"You have a sweet nature, heartling. You are willing to share what can be shared," Ian praised.

"Oh no," Joanna protested. "I will not share a jot of the love that is mine. For each of us, for Adam, for Simon, and for me, you have a different love, whole and complete, because we are different. When you look on Adam, you look on Adam and listen to Adam and think of Adam. You do not think with half your mind of me or of Simon. You did not love me more before Simon was born."

"Of course not!" Ian exclaimed.

"Nor will you love me less if another daughter is born."

"You are quite right, Joanna," Alinor assured her, "but jealousy is not reasonable—I know. You cannot argue about such matters. They simply are. The king hates Geoffrey—mad or not, he does—but he cannot do him any hurt because he is not really mad. John knows that to harm Geoffrey is to lose William. It came near to that once, and the matter was made clear. Nonetheless, the king cannot resist hurting Geoffrey in ways that do not show on the body and that Geoffrey dares not admit to his father."

"Because he fears the king?" Joanna's voice was neutral, but Alinor heard the danger signal. Joanna might talk of fearing pain because her husband would do his duty, but she would have nothing but contempt for a fearful man.

"No! Because Geoffrey is tender of his father. He knows William holds himself guilty for his son's bastardy. Can Geoffrey complain that he is insulted for bastardy without driving a knife into his father's heart? He must endure in silence or take such revenge as he can."

That made Ian laugh. "I assure you the *men* of the court watch their tongues. Geoffrey has taught lessons to a few for speaking too freely. One, at least, speaks no more at all. He is dead. There is nothing Geoffrey can do about the tongues of the women, however."

"He may leave that in my hands," Joanna said quietly and flatly.

Alinor drew breath at the threat communicated by the flat voice. She shook her head. "Well, Joanna, if you are sure that Geoffrey will suit you and you have no special conditions that you would like to make, the matter is settled."

"I am sure, at least, that I have no objection to Geoffrey," Joanna said tentatively. "As for conditions," she added far more certainly, "I know the disposition of the lands. They are yours, then mine and my sisters'—if I should be blessed with sisters—but what is given to me is mine, to be disposed of as I see fit."

Ian whistled softly between his teeth. There was plenty of Alinor under the outward resemblance of Joanna to her father. If Simon had had a good horse and good armor, he would have given away the bread out of his mouth without knowing or caring whether there was any more to be eaten. Alinor, much as Ian loved her, was a different kind. She was not ungenerous, but she had an inordinate sense of possession. She counted the grains in every head of every stalk of wheat that grew on her land and demanded an account if even one grain should be missing. She might easily give you a bushel or a wagonload, but no one could steal or take by force even a single grain. Under her stewardship, her estate had grown, but it was care and attention that increased it. She did not squeeze or oppress her people. She merely made it very clear that the best was expected of them and, with justice and often even kindness, she got the best from them. Joanna had been trained from the cradle, and it was apparent she would be a worthy successor to her mother.

"When the contract is written, you will see it. If you find fault, it will be amended," Alinor assured her daughter.

As soon as he was certain Joanna was out of hearing, Ian said to his wife, "I do not understand you, Alinor. You swore you would not press her into marriage until her own desire moved her, and you brought me to see that this was best. Now you have virtually ordered her to take Geoffrey. If you are doing this to Joanna to shield me—"

"No, I swear it. It has nothing to do with you." Alinor explained as best as she could the conversation she had had with her daughter and the reasons for her change in opinion. A few times Ian nodded in agreement, but mostly he looked puzzled and unhappy.

"I do not like it," he insisted when Alinor was finished.

"Have you come to distrust Geoffrey?" Alinor asked anxiously, "Or Salisbury?"

"No, not at all. To my mind Geoffrey is perfect for her. I have always thought so, but by now I have come to know Joanna. She is biddable—but only because she does not care about most things. When she does care—as she does about that accursed dog—she is neither to hold nor to bind."

"I know that."

"Yes, well, if the situation were as usual—if she could be betrothed and they could be together under our eyes or under Salisbury and Ela's eyes—we would see soon enough how the wind was blowing. But now all must be done in haste. And then we will leave them, newly married, Geoffrey to go to war carrying a burden for which he is not really ready, Joanna with the weight of the lands and the people and the fulfillment of Geoffrey's demands upon her. From some small thing that you or I could explain in two minutes a quarrel might arise between them, alone and young as they are, that could grow beyond mending."

"I know that too," Alinor said slowly. "Yet Joanna has good sense and Geoffrey is no fool—he has Salisbury behind him too, and Joanna can go to Ela for help."

"Not if they are married. I think she would be too proud. Listen, Alinor, if we betrothed them only it would serve our political purposes just as well and they would have time to grow accustomed. Geoffrey would have less real power, and Joanna would not feel that every order he gave was a personal affront."

Alinor raised her brows, but she did not permit the smile she felt to touch her lips. Poor Ian was very reluctant to give up "his" daughter. He would rather think the girl had no sense than to admit she was a woman grown. To Ian, Joanna would always remain a frail and helpless child—which she had never been once out of the cradle. Aside from reminding him of Joanna's age in years and reiterating that she was a most sensible girl, Alinor made no attempt to change Ian's attitude. It was a guarantee that Joanna would have a strong protector in any difference of opinion that might arise. Besides, just now, Ian's reluctance to see Joanna wedded and bedded seemed to have borne a most satisfactory fruit. Alinor's mild amusement faded as she considered from all angles what her husband had said.

"If Salisbury can be brought to agree," she said, "I believe you have the answer to even the few doubts and fears I felt."

CHAPTER TWO

William of Salisbury's hoarse roar brought a page, who had been half-dozing in a window seat, to his side in an instant. The earl had been dealing with estate matters and had come at last to a letter from Lord Ian that had arrived the previous day. The messenger from Roselynde had come upon Salisbury with one foot in the stirrup, preparing to ride out. Salisbury had paused just long enough to ask if there was anything urgent in the letter, and the messenger had replied doubtfully that he did not think so. He had not been urged to make haste, and the lord had been pleased and smiling when he handed the letter over. More he did not know.

After another moment's consideration, Salisbury had waved the messenger away toward the inner keep. Probably Ian was again doubting the wisdom of his departure for Ireland. Salisbury loved Ian dearly, but he often wished his friend's heart was harder and his aggressive courage a little less. In any case, Salisbury did not intend to give up a pleasant day's sport to pander to Ian's pride. Tomorrow would be soon enough, he thought, to rack his brains for more reasons why Ian should do what the smallest amount of common sense would have led him to propose himself.

"Good God!" Salisbury now exclaimed, when surprise receded enough for him to form words. "Summon Lord Geoffrey to me at once."

The page took off at a dead run, careened down the twisting stairs in imminent danger of breaking his neck, and, as soon as his eyes found their mark, bawled across the inner bailey, "Lord Geoffrey, your father orders your presence. Now! At once!"

The taller of two full-armed figures, who had been striking and thrusting at each other with swords, leapt back. "Why? What is wrong?" Geoffrey asked.

"I do not know." The page had come up to them, panting as he spoke. "But the lord was very angry."

Geoffrey shoved his shield off his arm and pushed back his helmet as he started toward the keep. His pace increased as he moved. Usually his father was of a very equable disposition. It would take something very serious to throw him into a rage. Geoffrey thought over his recent peccadillos, but he could not pick on anything that would overset his father. He had not challenged anyone or killed anyone recently—not very recently. Nonetheless, he was running himself by the time he reached Salisbury.

"What is wrong, papa?" he asked, slipping into the form he had used in childhood in his anxiety.

Salisbury raised his eyes from the letter he was rereading and beamed upon his son. "Wrong? Nothing!" he exclaimed. "I have an offer here I had almost given up hoping for."

Geoffrey heaved an enormous sigh and sheathed the sword he was carrying naked in his hand. "The page said you were in a rage. I could not imagine what had overset you."

"Oh, that. I was angry at myself because I thought it was only Ian worrying again because for once he is not trying to butt his way through a stone wall with his bare head. So I did not stop to read his letter when we went hunting yesterday, but it does not matter. A day's delay in answering—"

"You have an offer from Ian?" Geoffrey asked, plainly puzzled. Then his eyes lit. "For me? Does he want me to go with him?"

The eager expression made Salisbury laugh. "Fireeater," he said proudly and fondly. "There will be fighting enough here, and you will carry a heavier burden than you thought to bear, but leave that for later. Ian offers his daughter—I mean Lady Alinor's daughter—to you in marriage."

"Marriage! Joanna? In marriage?"

That made Salisbury laugh again. "Why are you surprised? I have had a score of offers for you. I had begun to doubt my wisdom in turning them away because Ian never seemed to want to come to the point about Joanna. But I have been hoping for this since he married Alinor. I wanted to contract you then—"

"I had no thought of marriage," Geoffrey remarked stiffly.

"No thought of marriage? Do not be a fool! If you do not marry, who is to inherit your lands?"

"I intended to leave them to William," Geoffrey said simply, "or perhaps to Isabella or Henry, if you thought that would be better."

Salisbury got up and gripped his son's shoulders. "Do not let me hear you speak like that again, Geoffrey. You should have been my eldest son by law as well as by birth. And you would have been, had not my father been eaten by greed and pride and ambition. Your mother was a good woman, and I loved her. What you have is your due. You are taking nothing from your brothers or your sister. God knows there is enough and more than enough for them."

"Perhaps, but for me there is too much. Ela says nothing, but she cannot like—"

"If there is something Ela does not like, she is the last one to say nothing," Salisbury laughed. Then he sobered and shook his head. "You are wrong, Geoffrey. Ela loves you very dearly. She grudges you nothing. Do you think I made the disposition of my property without consulting her?"

"She grudges *you* nothing," Geoffrey said. "No, I do not mean she is not fond of me. I know she is, but she desires above all that you should be happy."

There were other reasons too, Geoffrey guessed, for his stepmother to make no protest over the property assigned to him. She had not always been fond of him and had not been willing to take him into her home when he was a child. Now she was sorry and felt guilty about that refusal. Geoffrey could not mention that, partly because he did not want his father to think he held that long-past sorrow against Ela and partly because he never mentioned those bitter years.

"Whatever the reasons," Salisbury said dismissively, "the matter is settled. The lands are yours, or will be, and you must breed up sons to inherit them." He had dropped his hands from his son's shoulders, but now he took hold of his arms. "I want very much to see your children, Geoffrey. William is so young. I may never live to see his little ones." Then he dropped his hands and smiled. "In truth, had I not been waiting for this offer, you would have been married two or three years ago."

Geoffrey's expression had softened when his father spoke of grandchildren, but tensed again at his last sentence. "Why did you say nothing to me?"

"About what? That I intended you to marry? What was there to say? You showed no signs, ever, of wishing to become a monk. If you mean why I said nothing about Joanna, that was because Alinor would not agree to make a contract, and you know Ian would never press her. Joanna is not his daughter, when all is said, no matter how much he loves the girl."

"Lady Alinor does not desire me for a son?" The voice was flat, Geoffrey's face totally blank, yet his father sensed his enormous shock.

"Do not be a fool! Alinor has been trying to urge Joanna in your direction for years, but she had some crazy idea that the girl must choose for herself. Thank God Ian's political problems have brought her to a more reasonable way of thinking."

"Are you saying that Joanna does not wish to marry me?"

"I am saying no such thing!" Salisbury exclaimed. "I am only saying that a modest, well-brought up girl like Joanna—and do not forget that I know Joanna well because she spent considerable time in Ela's care when you and Alinor and Ian were in Ireland—would never demean herself by expressing an opinion on such a subject. I am sure she agreed to the marriage as soon as your name was suggested to her. I am sure because I know Ian and Alinor. If Joanna had any objections, they would never force her. I do not believe in that either. To force an unwilling maid to take a man she dislikes is only to lay a groundwork for future grief.''

"And if the man is unwilling?''

Salisbury's mouth dropped open in surprise, then concern filled his face. "Good God, Geoffrey, have you set your heart elsewhere? Why did you not speak to me? After what happened between your mother and me, did you think I would fail to sanction any marriage you desired? Say something, boy. Who is it?''

"No one. That—''

"You mean you cannot marry the woman? Oh well, then, that is no impediment. For a man—'' Salisbury shrugged. "So long as you are kind to Joanna and discreet, you may do as you choose. What your wife does not know cannot hurt her.''

"There is no other woman,'' Geoffrey said impatiently, "That is not what I meant.''

"You mean you do not wish to marry Joanna?'' Salisbury's voice rose in an incredulous howl. "Joanna? She is the most desirable thing I have seen in—in I cannot think how many years. She is beautiful enough to make me almost forget my age, her temper is sweet, her nature pliable, and she is rich—. She will have Roselynde and the bulk of Alinor's property even if another daughter is born. She will have it all if there are no more children. What can anyone possibly say about Joanna that is not good? What fault can you find in Joanna?''

"None. There is no fault to be found in her,'' Geoffrey agreed uncomfortably, although he well knew that the girl was neither so sweet nor so pliable as his father believed.

Salisbury sat down again heavily and stared wordlessly at his son. He discovered that Geoffrey's features were peculiarly unreadable. The young man had come so recently from his duties as squire that the training still sat heavily upon him. Thus, he had not yet developed the freedom to fidget. He stood very quietly, very erect under the weight of his armor, arms at his sides, hands relaxed and open.

"Geoffrey," Salisbury said, "I cannot understand you at all. You must tell me plainly what troubles you. If you cannot fault Joanna and you do not love another woman, what objection can you have to the marriage?"

"I do not know myself," Geoffrey muttered. "I am not very sure I do object. Only—only I have this feeling that—that it is too much. Joanna is too rich, too beautiful—"

"Hmmm," Salisbury mused, "you have more sense than I suspected—perhaps too much for a man your age, although that is likely to be just as well. It is true that a very beautiful and very rich wife can lead to trouble."

He fell silent again, studying Geoffrey, trying to look at him as a young woman might. His son was a little above middle height and still very slender. Not that the boy was not well made. His shoulders were broad enough and his hips narrow as a man's should be. The face was not out of the ordinary, rather long now that the roundness of childhood was gone, with a firm jaw, dented and ridged a little on the right where some chance blow had nicked the bone. There was another small scar high on the cheekbone under Geoffrey's left eye; it did not look like a battle scar, perhaps a branch had caught him while hunting. His nose was straight, undamaged as yet by war; his mouth long and very mobile, the lips thin but well shaped.

It was the eyes that were Geoffrey's most notable feature. Salisbury's heart checked for an instant as the dim memory of a woman long dead came suddenly, vividly alive. The same eyes had ensnared Salisbury into a forbidden love. They were of a peculiarly changeable hue, from a glittering golden yellow to a dull, mud brown, shaded by long lashes darker than the young man's hair. That was a good feature too, Salisbury thought, pulling his mind away from memories that held too much heat and not enough happiness. The style of the day, which allowed the hair to grow to just below the ears and to form a band across the forehead, was well suited to Geoffrey's very straight, fine, light brown hair.

All in all, there was nothing to displease a young woman in Geoffrey's appearance. Salisbury suffered another qualm of doubt. There was also nothing in particular to attract a girl who was accustomed to looking at Ian de Vipont. But that was ridiculous. There was not another man in the country with a face to match Ian's. Joanna must be well aware of that. Perhaps she would be glad of a more ordinary-looking husband. She could not have failed to notice how the ladies of the court clustered around her stepfather like ants around a honey pot.

For the first time, Salisbury himself wondered what Joanna felt about the proposed marriage. He had said he knew her well, and in one sense that was true; however, Joanna was a singularly reserved girl. She was not given to idle chatter and almost never spoke of her own feelings about any subject, even those in which she was obviously interested. Salisbury suppressed still another qualm. He *was* sure that Alinor and Ian would not force Joanna into anything. She must then at least be willing.

"There is sense in what you say," Salisbury repeated, "but I assure you a poor, ugly wife is no greater guarantee of happiness. Joanna is a good and dutiful girl. I do not believe she will play you false." He paused. "Geoffrey, what are we talking about? You know I desire this, yet I will not press you to do what you hate. Only let me say one thing more. You know the situation in which Ian finds himself?" Salisbury hardly waited for Geoffrey's nod before he continued. "The reason for offering Joanna to you at this time is partly so that she will be protected if the Welsh war should spread unrest in this country and partly so that a responsible man with a blood-bond to the family can lead Ian's and Alinor's and Adam's vassals."

"Lead—" Geoffrey's face paled a little. "Ian wants me to lead his men—all his men? Oh, papa, I am not sure—"

"I will help you, my son, in every way I can, yet the burden will be a heavy one. Still, what can he do? He must have someone he can trust, and you are dearest to him.''

Geoffrey swallowed. The pain in his father's voice dragged at him. King John was almost never mentioned between father and son. It was the one forbidden subject, the one thing they could never discuss. William of Salisbury loved his brother; Geoffrey hated his uncle. Each had what he felt were good and sufficient reasons. Geoffrey realized that his father had come as close to saying that John could not be trusted with Ian's vassals or with Ian's stepdaughter as it was possible for him. For Geoffrey to take Ian's men would save face all around. The king would have his due and, since one of the king's own kinsmen would be the man chosen to lead the men, Ian's distrust would not be obvious to anyone who did not already know how matters stood between King John and his vassal.

"Then there is no further question," Geoffrey replied. "I will marry Joanna and will do my uttermost to fulfill Ian's will.''

"It will not be so terribly hard," Salisbury encouraged. "The older vassals will advise you, and you would do well to listen to them. The main trouble lies in their rivalry among themselves when one of them is chosen to lead the others. Because you are outside the group and known to them as Ian's squire, you will have less trouble.''

"How will the men know I am chosen? Will they be bound to obey my summons?''

"I am not yet sure of the details. Ian has asked that we come to Roselynde to settle everything, and this seems reasonable to me. He says, of course, that he will come here if I cannot come to him, but he must be far busier than I. It will be pleasant for Ela to see Alinor again also—''

The son's eyes met the father's and gravity evaporated. Both began to laugh. Ela would certainly want to see Alinor and would surely accompany them, but the fuss and bother of getting Ela started on a journey could only be approximated by a major natural catastrophe.

"Well, I am glad to hear you both laughing." It was a faint, high-pitched feminine voice that somehow carried almost the full length of the great hall. "Otherwise I would suspect some dreadful event had taken place. What *are* you doing in full armor, Geoffrey?"

"I was practicing at sword play with William, my lady. These days I need my armor. He improves apace."

As he spoke, Geoffrey fetched a chair and set it near his father's. Lady Ela, who had traversed the great hall, sank into it as if she could barely keep to her feet. Then she waved a languid hand at Geoffrey. "Go and take it off, my love, do. You know it makes me short of breath to see you carrying all that steel."

"Let him be, Ela. It improves the strength to wear mail, and Geoffrey will need his strength."

There was no change in Ela's expression, but shockingly alert pale blue eyes flashed toward Salisbury and then dropped. "So you have pushed him into picking up Ian's burden," she sighed.

"How the devil do you know that?" Salisbury exclaimed.

"Do not shout at me, William. You make my head ache."

In fact, Salisbury had not been shouting. Now, however, he not only lowered his voice still further but used a less aggressive tone. "How did you know, Ela?" he repeated.

"Alinor wrote some weeks ago to ask certain questions about Geoffrey. It was not hard to put two and two together."

"But Lady Alinor knows me—" Geoffrey began.

His stepmother's tinkling laugh cut him off and made him flush. "Dear heart, she did not ask me about your honesty or your military qualifications—and she knows of your ability to sing and play the lute."

"Whatever you answered must have been what she wanted to hear," Salisbury said heartily. "I have an offer of Joanna from Ian."

Ela sighed.

"Do you not approve, my dear?" Salisbury asked.

"I cannot see the future, William." She raised her eyes

to Geoffrey. "I only know that Joanna is not what she seems."

"Good God, Ela, of what do you accuse the girl? I thought you liked her."

"Like her? I love her dearly, and I do not accuse her of anything. Oh, William, I am not impugning her virtue—how silly, and how unimportant. You knew Simon, William. Joanna is his daughter, and her mother has done nothing to tame her."

"Tame her! Why, I never came across a more obedient, meeker child. *I* could have wished for a little more spirit in her."

Ela shook her head gently, her eyes remaining fixed upon Geoffrey. "My love," she urged, "if you are determined on this course, think long and hard before you cross Joanna."

"Joanna is not— I mean, I have no choice, my lady. If Ian needs me, I must do whatever is in my power to help him."

"Mary have mercy!" Ela cried, sitting bolt upright and pressing a hand to her breast. "Bite your tongue! Never say that again nor allow the thought into your mind!"

Then, as she saw the jut of Geoffrey's jaw, Ela wished she had bitten her own tongue. She did not often set a foot amiss in dealing with people, but her guilt concerning her stepson made her overanxious for his happiness, and that occasionally made her clumsy.

"Geoffrey," she went on, more calmly, "you cannot desire to hurt Joanna, to make her cheap in her own eyes. How must a girl feel if she is told her husband accepted her only out of a sense of obligation to her stepfather?"

"There is no danger of Joanna thinking she is undesirable. Unless she is stone-blind, she must see all the men leer at her and follow her as if they were dogs and she a bitch in heat."

"Joanna thinks no such thing!" Salisbury bellowed. "She is a good, modest girl, as I have told you."

"William! My heart beats so! Do not shout at Geoffrey.

And you, Geoffrey, are quite wrong. I do not say that Joanna is not aware of her appearance. Ian is aware of his also. Does it give him much pleasure?''

That made Geoffrey's eyes flicker. In despair, Ian had more than once threatened to cut off his own nose. Ela watched Geoffrey in satisfaction. She knew quite well that a woman placed a great deal more store on her personal appearance than a man and that Joanna was not averse to using her beauty when necessary. Geoffrey, however, need not know that. Also, he feared and distrusted beautiful women. Ela wished to be sure that he would neither blame nor make disparaging remarks to so proud a girl as Joanna.

''Moreover,'' she continued, pointing out another problem, ''you must remember that Alinor has told that child since she was born that if she had been a cross-eyed hunchback with the legs of a goat she would have been equally desirable because of her dower and her inheritance.'' Ela shook her head again. ''You see my doubts. I tell you Joanna's nature is deep and strong, and, for her husband who must steer between jealousy and the need to prove she is not merely the means by which he intends to come at her lands—you will have a stony row to hoe, Geoffrey.''

''For God's sake Ela, shut your mouth!'' Salisbury hissed.

''It does not matter,'' Geoffrey said flatly. ''I will not change my mind. My lady has said nothing—nothing that I did not feel and could not find words for. When do you plan to be at Roselynde, my lord?''

Salisbury glanced at his wife. ''Let us say a fortnight from today. Why?''

''Because if you will give me leave, I would like to—to attend to some private matters. Unless you need me, I would prefer to meet you at Roselynde.''

''Private matters? Geoffrey, you have not lied to me? You—''

''No, my lord. I have been most honest—more honest, perhaps, than I should have been for I see I have made you unhappy. It has come to me that if I must deal with Ian's men I will have little time for my own. I wish to look in at my keeps.''

"Now that is a most excellent thought," Salisbury said approvingly. "Ian has chosen well—better than even he or I guessed, I believe. Go, by all means, but do not be late in coming to Roselynde.''

Geoffrey started to turn away. His father added, "Wait. Do you have enough money?''

"Sufficient to take me to Hemel, and there I have more than enough.''

Salisbury opened his mouth to say something more, but his voice was drowned in Ela's shriek. "Roselynde? In a fortnight? I can never be ready! Never!''

Geoffrey bit his lip. Salisbury raised his eyes to heaven and nodded and waved dismissal at his son, who bowed farewell to Lady Ela and moved away. The shrill, complaining tones followed him across the great hall, detailing all that must be done before she could be ready to travel, and her feebleness and inability to accomplish so much in so short a time.

Geoffrey, however, was already oblivious to Ela's complaints by the time he reached the stairs. Like any young man, he was taken up completely with his own affairs. This was the greatest, most important, most fearful thing that had ever happened to him. Ian's vassals, Alinor's and Adam's, that would make— Geoffrey's eyes widened. God help me, he thought, I will have near as many under my command as my father who leads the royal armies.

How did one manage such a force of men? How did one know where each vassal and castellan was camped, whether supplies were sufficient, whether assigned duties were being performed? The questions were merely a panic reaction. Geoffrey knew quite well how it was done; he had seen Ian at the work often enough. While others drank, gambled, whored, and slept, Ian rode through the camp, stopping to speak to each vassal and castellan, somehow finding time to look at the situation even of the least importance, speaking also, whenever he could, to the common men-at-arms. Not

all leaders bothered, of course. Many let the vassals manage
for themselves completely; some required the men to come
to them to report. Ian's method was not easy, but in a few
days he knew them all—at least as far as their spirit, cheerful or complaining, and their intention, to work or to shirk.
Thus he knew whether a complaint needed to be attended to
or sloughed off, and he knew also how much he could count
on each man when it came to fighting.

After all that, Ian spent half the night writing irate letters
to his wife, demanding more—more money, more supplies,
more arms—or complaining that what he had received was
bad quality or late in coming or should have been sent to
some other place. Geoffrey's thoughts checked at that point.
In his case, it would be Joanna who would receive those letters. This was the first time Joanna had come into his mind
as a serious consideration since his father had mentioned his
role as Ian's deputy. He had listened to and replied to what
Ela said about her with half his mind, the other half already
occupied with alternating dreams of glory and nightmares of
failure. Geoffrey thought of the wagon trains that had rolled
into camp bearing casks of salt meat, grain, fish, rounds of
cheese. Most of them, except what Ian purchased locally,
bore the stamp of Lady Alinor's seal, and the accounts were
in her own hand. Joanna was what—fourteen?—no, fifteen.
Could he depend upon her for equal efficiency?

Was it even safe for her to attempt the traveling from demesne to demesne to urge, gather, inspect? Lady Ela did not
perform those tasks, but Lady Ela had trained bailiffs and
stewards, and there were few or none such men in Lady
Alinor's household. Each farm had its bailiff, of course,
each household its steward, but it was Lady Alinor herself
who oversaw them all. Yet if Joanna failed, Geoffrey knew
he must fail also, no matter how hard he tried. Urgently, he
summoned up memories of Joanna, but none he had were at
all to the point. Mostly, he remembered her laughing, aid-
ing and abetting him in playing silly tricks on pompous
squires of his acquaintance, romping in wild games of
hoodman blind or hot cockles, and—the latest ones—

flirting with men who nearly drooled as she mocked them.

There were a few more serious memories: the tears pouring down Joanna's face as she substituted for her mother as chief mourner in the burial of an infant sister; the tenderness with which she received Brian—and an ugly sight he was, blind and half-dead from being taken too soon from his mother. But laughter and sorrow and tenderness could not point to the answer Geoffrey wanted. Could Joanna support him as he would need to be supported if he was to lead Ian's men successfully?

He told himself not to be a fool, that Ian and Alinor would never leave that responsibility on such young shoulders. But it was not possible to delude himself with that comfort for long. If Ian was willing to trust him with so much, it would not occur to him that Joanna might be unfit. Perhaps he should suggest that idea himself? Before he had finished formulating the notion, Geoffrey shuddered. To suggest to Ian that Joanna was not perfect, from the shortest hair of her flaming head to the tiniest nail on her smallest toe, could produce nothing but a burst of rage. Besides, Geoffrey was not sure Joanna was unfit. She had been left behind more than once to care for the lands while Alinor went abroad with her husband. Geoffrey had been with Ian and Alinor, of course, so he could not know how much management had been in Joanna's hands, how much in those of Sir Guy or others.

Obviously, what was necessary was to speak to Joanna himself—and it must be before the betrothal. Once that agreement was signed, he would be bound by it. Before the terms were agreed, however, he might make conditions, might ask that Joanna have some advisor accustomed to dealing with money and supplies in large quantities. Perhaps Ela would lend Joanna one of her men. What was more, he must speak to Joanna alone. For him to appear to test her in Ian's or Alinor's presence would serve no purpose. Ian would either get angry or would give her hints, and Joanna was always subdued in Alinor's presence and would wait for her mother to speak. However, to get Joanna alone would not be so easy. She would be very busy, especially if guests were to be invited. Besides, once he showed his face in Roselynde keep, Ian would probably have much to tell him and would expect to be accompanied by him if he rode out.

A week after Joanna had been informed that she was to marry Geoffrey, she came down the steps from the women's quarters wrapped in a cloak. She moved furtively, not because there was any reason to conceal what she was doing but because she was ashamed of herself. It had seemed to Joanna when she left her mother's bedchamber with Brian that day that nothing important had happened. After all, she had known Geoffrey almost all her life. He had often spent long periods at Roselynde. So he would return and they would share a bed instead of parting at night. The physical side of marriage was neither shocking nor frightening to Joanna.

Still, as the days passed, she had grown increasingly restless and uneasy. She took herself to task irritably, assuring herself that betrothal would make no difference in her life. She would not even leave Roselynde at first—at least, she would leave it only in the way she always had, to go on progress to the other estates that were her mother's. Even when Ian and her mother returned from Ireland and perhaps she would go to live most of the time on Geoffrey's lands, the change would hardly be noticeable. It was common for Joanna to remain for months in other keeps. She was fond of Roselynde, of course. It was hers! But marriage would not change that either. She would always spend part of her time on her mother's lands so that the people would be familiar with her. And in time she would return to her own.

Reason, however, had little effect on her emotions, Joanna found. She could not concentrate on her usual pursuits or common conversation. She had an irresistible urge to be alone, and to think the matter through. Only thinking did not seem to clarify anything. Often, Joanna found, she had sought quiet to think but thought of nothing. She simply sat or walked or rode with a mind completely blank. However, all efforts to resist the urge for seclusion failed. It made her so cross that maids and men alike had begun to shrink from her. Moreover, alternately, Joanna wished to kiss and kill her mother who remained obdurately "blind" to her daughter's distress.

The urge had again become overwhelming. Seizing upon the excuse that the light was failing, Joanna set aside her embroidery—upon which she had accomplished very little—and went for her cloak. The worst of February cold was over, but evenings in March were still very chilly even in the sheltered spice garden where Joanna intended to walk. It was a favorite spot and a place peculiarly her own. Alinor was too good a housewife to neglect the spice garden. It was very necessary to lend a few amenities to the harsh life of the keep, but Alinor tended it as a duty. Her nature was too impatient to appreciate plants fully. They answered so slowly to care. They did not wag their tails in happy greeting or nuzzle you with soft muzzles, or look at you with worshipping eyes and murmur thanks for kindness.

It was Joanna, as soon as she was old enough to understand, who had taken over the care of the garden. She loved everything about it, from the rich odor of earth and manure in the early spring to the sweet, heady scent of the flowers in summer. Even the bare stubble of winter was dear to her with its promise of new life. She never tired of walking through the garden, looking attentively for signs of trouble in the growing season, planning for the spring in winter, and choosing what must be harvested in the autumn.

At the gate, Joanna turned and said firmly, "Stay!" Brian whined, but he dropped obediently to the ground. Having fastened the gate carefully—Brian was not above testing it and "forgetting" he had been told to stay—Joanna walked slowly down the central path. Her eyes were bent upon the plant beds, but the light was going and she could see very little. A rustle off to the right drew her attention. Joanna uttered an exclamation of irritation and hurried down a side path in that direction. Inside the keep walls the number of pests a gardener had to contend with was limited. Hares, marmots, and moles were excluded, but cats and rats, too, liked to chew the tender, aromatic new growth. Joanna's step was soundless on the turf path. A cat could be driven away; if it was a rat, traps would have to be set. Her eyes swept the neatly dug rows seeking the telltale flattening or disruption of the earth that would mark the pest's presence. Nothing.

Just ahead were the rose trellises enclosing a bench on which one could sit. Joanna hesitated. There was nothing there to attract an animal. Still, it might have taken refuge among the canes or behind them. It was nearly full dark now and useless, really, to pursue the creature further, but Joanna circled, determined to stamp and shout and at least give the invader a fright.

She never had a chance to make a sound. Before she came quite around, a hard hand closed her mouth and a strong arm encircled her waist. "Hush, Joanna, do not cry out. It is I, Geoffrey." The body tensed to resist, relaxed. Geoffrey's grip loosened, a little reluctantly. It had been a very sweet-smelling, well-curved armful he had held. "I hope I did not frighten you."

"You startled me, certainly," she replied, but in a perfectly calm voice. "What are you doing here like a thief in the night, Geoffrey? How did you get in?"

His teeth flashed in the dusk, waking warm memories in Joanna of many mischievous pranks planned and executed. "Getting in was no trouble. The men all know me. I only had to say I wished to surprise you. They all know also—God knows how—of our proposed betrothal. Joanna— Joanna, I must— I had to speak to you."

For a moment she did not reply, straining her eyes in the very last of the light to see his face. The features were barely visible, but she could not determine his expression. "Speak to me about what?" she asked slowly.

All during his ride from Hemel, Geoffrey had been framing logical speeches and clever questions that would explain his presence and expose Joanna's knowledge—or lack of knowledge—of the gathering and dispatch of war supplies. What he said, however, was, "Are you willing? Really, Joanna?"

She gazed at him steadily, looking only slightly upward because they were much of a height. "I have no objection," she replied, a bit tentatively.

"Your mother did not overawe you?" Geoffrey asked.

Joanna blinked. "I am not afraid of my mother," she said, and Geoffrey stared at her at the tone of voice.

"But you are always so obedient," he protested.

Now she smiled. "Not *always*. But, Geoffrey, why should I not be obedient? My mother and I think alike on most everything. Do you suggest I should thwart her, against my own common sense and agreement, just for spite? Besides, I do not like to quarrel. There are very few things important enough to quarrel about."

For a moment, he was speechless with surprise. Then he said sharply, "Marriage is not important enough to quarrel about?"

"Be reasonable, Geoffrey," Joanna said patiently. "I must marry someone." Then it was her turn to stare, but she could see nothing except a pale blur where Geoffrey's face was; his features had become indistinguishable. "Oh, I see. It is you who are unwilling."

Her voice was neutral, as if the matter had no great significance for her. In fact, although Joanna's self-control was considerable, she would not have replied so indifferently had not so many violently opposed emotions caught at her simultaneously that she could express none. First came a strong and, to her, incomprehensible shock of disappointment. Her pride was hurt and to salve it, contempt came to her support. It was Geoffrey who was afraid of his father and who wished to place upon her the burden of repudiating the arrangement. That brought anger and, curiously, a sorrowful sense of relief, as if she was about to escape some great, unknown, but desirable, danger.

"You fool! No!" Geoffrey exclaimed violently, seizing her arms.

He looked down at his own hands, pale against the dull color of Joanna's everyday working garb, equally surprised at his words and his violence. He did not know what he had expected from Joanna, but it was neither the passionless rationality of her first statement nor the flat indifference of her second. She must marry someone, must she? And any turd on the ground was as good as any other. Doubtless there was no man she would consider her equal.

"Do you think I am an idiot?" he continued sarcastically. "Where could I find an equal offer? You are very beautiful and very rich—and very virtuous also, Joanna. I only wished to be sure I was not—not swallowing an unwilling sacrificial victim whole. But I see you know what you are about."

The sarcasm came a few heartbeats too late, fortunately. Joanna was aware of little beyond the passionate repudiation of her accusation. Pleasure flooded her, to be checked by the vague sense of some awful danger—a danger she knew she must flee and yet desired to examine more closely. Safety lay in immediate practicalities; perhaps from behind that bulwark, one could peer out and see the face of what really threatened.

"You mean you thought my mother would sacrifice me to Ian's need?" There was only the faintest quiver of uncertainty in Joanna's voice. "I do not think so," she went on hastily, not wishing to examine that subject. "And, in any case, the question did not arise—at least, not in connection with you. Really, Geoffrey, I was very well pleased when you were suggested to me. I know you long and well. It seemed to me most suitable."

"I am scarcely your match," he offered stiffly, infuriated by all this calm reasoning, wanting to strike some spark, any spark, from her.

"How can you say that?" Joanna urged, again missing the taunt and intent on practical, rather than emotional, things. You are of good blood on both sides. You are well endowed with lands—or will be—as I am. You are the son of an earl and close to the throne. And you must be of merit in battle or Ian would not trust our men in your hands."

For one instant, Geoffrey had a wild desire to push Joanna away, to shout that he was not willing, to ride back to Salisbury and tell his father the agreement must be withdrawn, that he could not bear to be married to Joanna. How could he endure to look upon that perfection, kiss it, caress it, bed it, as a—a what? A suitable stallion for breeding young? A suitable substitute war leader? A suitable political pawn? The memory of endless kindness, enormous obligation checked the impulse. Whatever his relationship with Joanna cost him, Geoffrey knew he could not disappoint Ian to whom he owed so much.

"If you are sure you are content, Joanna, then I am also content," he said softly. "Let us sit down, if you are not too cold. I have some other matters to discuss with you."

CHAPTER THREE

Even in the late afternoon, the great hall of Roselynde keep was rather dark. The light that flooded in through the western windows was lost in the great space, softening to a dim radiance. One could see well enough, but everything was soft, without hard edges or brilliance. Servants moved without hurry, clearing the remains of dinner from the tables. The best of the leftovers went into baskets to be handed out to beggars at the gates; the small or mangled scraps were scraped onto the floors where the cats and dogs and mice and rats would snatch them out of the rushes.

There was some noise as the trestle tables were lifted from their stands and piled against the walls, but not much. In fact, the servants were making an effort to be quiet because they wished to listen. Lord Geoffrey was playing and singing, and he was as skilled, many said more skilled, than any minstrel. The clear notes of voice and instrument, although they were not loud, seemed invested with a life of their own and traveled easily, filling the space.

Geoffrey FitzWilliam looked out into the hall as if he could follow the path of his notes with his eyes.

> Of one that is so fayr and bryght
> *velud maris stella*
> Bryghter than the dayis lyght
> *parens et puella*
> I crie to thee, thou saie to me
> Leuedy, preye thy sone for me
> *tam pia*
> That I mote come to thee
> *Maria*

The repetition of the first verse, having rounded off the song, the last note trembled into silence.

"I did not know you could sing in English."

Slowly, almost reluctantly, Geoffrey turned his eyes from the dim hall to the bright vignette of Joanna seated at the window. It was an exceptionally warm May. The shutters stood wide and the sun, blazing in at an angle, lit sparkles in the fine beading of perspiration on Joanna's upper lip and turned her thick braids into rivers of fire. Geoffrey should not be looking at those braids. They should have been decently coiled and concealed under a modest wimple, but Joanna had said flatly after they had returned from a session of sitting in justice that she was through with melting in the cause of propriety. Off had come the wimple; out had come the golden pins; down had tumbled the braids.

Geoffrey had watched at first with unabashed pleasure. Joanna was usually a pattern of propriety, but when she decided to act outside of the common norm, she did so with such assurance that the unusual seemed to become the only reasonable or rational thing possible. Certainly there was nothing at all provocative in her manner then. Geoffrey was wearing a good deal less than Joanna, having stripped right down to shirt and chausses as soon as he could rid himself of his armor. Cooled wine had slaked one thirst, but now it seemed to be raising another. All the time he was singing, Geoffrey was as aware of Joanna's presence as if she were pressing herself against him.

It was odd that this should come over him now. When he had arrived at Roselynde the previous day, he had been decidedly uneasy. He had not seen Joanna since their betrothal on the first of April. The ceremony over, the guests sped, he had done a grueling six weeks' round of the estates with Ian to summon the vassals and castellans to Whitechurch and to take oath of them that they would obey him. That had been easier than Geoffrey expected. The men all knew him, and they seemed flatteringly pleased at his advancement. Alinor and Joanna had been traveling also, although on a different route, but Joanna had returned directly to Roselynde when

Alinor turned to the west coast to meet her husband and take ship for Ireland.

After Geoffrey had news of their safe arrival from the returned ship, he had been at loose ends. He was not due to meet the king until the last week of May and, really, he had nothing to do until then. He could, of course, go to Hemel, but he knew his presence there would make his young castellan nervous during his preparation for war, making him feel his master did not trust him. If he went to Salisbury, his father might think it strange that he did not seek Joanna's company. Besides, there was a good deal of business to transact with her. That could be done by letter, but it would be an act of kindness to bring her the news in person of her family's safe arrival at their destination.

This excellent reasoning stood Geoffrey in good stead until he was within an hour's ride of Roselynde. At that point, he began to wonder what he would say to Joanna, how he would explain a two-hundred-mile ride out of the way of the place the army was to meet the king. In fact, he had begun to wonder why he had come.

However, his arrival was not in the least uncomfortable. Joanna was openly delighted to see him. She had run down into the bailey to greet him and had received his news of her family's safe arrival with thanks and pleasure. So strong had been her assumption that Roselynde was now Geoffrey's home, that it was the most natural thing in the world that he come there and that she serve him, that there had been no awkwardness at all. Even being undressed and bathed by Joanna instead of the maids had seemed perfectly natural; there was no sense of newness or strangeness, although it was the first time. No touch of heightened color in Joanna's cheek had given evidence of conquered embarrassment or of a thought beyond the words she spoke. Why then, sitting at ease five feet from her, was he suddenly as aware of her physical being as if she had been dancing naked?

It did not occur to Geoffrey that he was responding to Joanna's own awareness of him. When she had welcomed him so warmly the previous day, it had been as a well-known friend, a reliable partner in a difficult undertaking. Sitting in justice was a matter that troubled Joanna. Unlike her mother, she had a strong consciousness of right and wrong, not only as it affected her but in the abstract. In the past when Alinor left Joanna to manage the estates, there had been someone to help her—at first Lady Margaret and later Sir Guy. But Lady Margaret had returned to her son to help care for her grandchildren, and Sir Guy had gone with Ian to Ireland.

Within Roselynde, Joanna did not doubt her power to ascertain what was right. She knew the men and women and even the serfs on the demesne—if not as individuals at least as "good" or "troublesome" servants. What had been required of her this time, however, was the settlement of a dispute in the town of Roselynde. Here, she was far less secure. Ordinarily, the mayor and aldermen ruled the town with little interference from the lady of Roselynde, but a dispute had arisen among those worthies themselves, so an appeal had been made to the castle. The date had been set before Alinor's departure was decided upon and, in the hurry of other business, had been forgotten. Now Joanna found herself facing the unenviable task of taking her mother's place.

Under the circumstances, Geoffrey's arrival was like manna from heaven. The armed force he brought would be a strong inducement toward obedience to Joanna's decision if it was not popular, and his own presence was a guarantee of an intelligent opinion to support (or contradict, if necessary) her own. He had taken no part in the proceedings, as was proper, merely standing silent, full-armed, at the right hand of Joanna's chair, a visible symbol, no matter how young and slender the judge, that having been called in she was absolute.

In this event, the matter itself was unworthy either of Joanna's qualms or Geoffrey's stern presence. As she would have realized had she been a little older, it was not a weighty question of law that needed resolution or explication but a silly, spiteful nothing. This, once she had sat silent with downcast eyes, biting her lips to control the laughter that bubbled in her throat, Joanna was really better suited temperamentally to settle than Alinor. She had the patience to soothe the ruffled feathers of the contestants—instead of publicly calling them idiots—and satisfy one group's wounded pride without offending the other.

Courtesy demanded that gravity be maintained while the judge and her escort were refreshed in the mayor's house and received the ladies of the town worthies. Joanna and Geoffrey were both well and rigidly trained. There were many nobles who would have scorned an invitation from a common tradesman; there were many who would have laughed at the devouring interest in the eyes of the tradesmen's wives and daughters. Geoffrey patiently and softly answered questions about his accoutrements and ability that no noblewoman would have asked, and Joanna spoke freely on matters less romantic but of more immediate interest, like the problems of managing a household ten or twenty times larger than their own.

Training keeps the face grave and the voice steady, but it does not put old hearts into young bodies. Geoffrey and Joanna laughed all the way back to the keep, gasping out the naive remarks they had needed to endure and answer to each other until Geoffrey nearly dropped Joanna as he lifted her from her mare. She called him a clumsy lout; he slapped her on the buttock as freely as when they were children, and they staggered back into the keep together, to trip over Brian, laugh a little more, and finally rid themselves of armor and elaborate garments.

They were quieter at dinner. Joanna was a little tired with the heat and her past anxiety, and she listened quietly to Geoffrey's description of the arrangement Ian had made for mustering the troops. It dawned upon her while he spoke that the muster was for war, and that war in Wales was no tame matter. The thought brought Joanna's eyes from the clumsy behavior of a maidservant, which she had been watching with disapproval while Geoffrey spoke, to Geoffrey just beside her. The sweat-damp linen shirt he wore clung to his young body and Joanna suddenly felt a sharp pang of regret that they had been only betrothed instead of married. She had not objected when the idea was proposed to her, saying that she could not see that it mattered one way or the other.

Now, suddenly, it mattered. Joanna chewed a piece of meat and wondered how Geoffrey would taste when she kissed him or bit him. She could smell him as he sat beside her, and the salty, acrid odor was very exciting. The idea of coupling with Geoffrey, which she had considered obediently upon Alinor's order and had not found distasteful, now began to grow very attractive. She thought of Geoffrey's brief kiss at the betrothal ceremony and suffered a small sensation of disappointment. It had been no different from the many ''kisses of peace'' she had taken and received. All she remembered was that his breath was sweet and his mouth clean. A good digestion and good teeth, she had thought at the time.

That was not fair, Joanna realized, glancing sidelong at her betrothed again. A man would scarcely betray passion before a hundred or more noble witnesses, and she herself had been so preoccupied with other matters that she had considered Geoffrey no more than any other necessary furnishing to the ceremony, like fine clothing or rich plate. Altogether that entire episode had been unreal, a gay and gorgeous charade in which each participant had acted a proper role just as if they were players in a mystery pageant. This was real—the warmth that emanated from Geoffrey's body, the strong, biting odor of a healthy, active man.

''You never told me how long you would stay,'' Joanna said.

To her surprise, Geoffrey flushed a little. ''Three days more—unless you have need of me. It will take four or five days of riding to come to Whitechurch, and I would like to be there before the vassals arrive. Of course, it can be done in less time if there is something you wish me to do here.''

''No, nothing,'' Joanna murmured, but she understood Geoffrey's heightened color and she was oddly content.

He had been some seventy miles from Whitechurch when he saw Ian and Alinor to their ship and had ridden two hundred miles and more to see her, only to ride all the way back after four days. Joanna did not draw away as Geoffrey reached across to take a dish of sweet tarts that was set out to round off the meal, and his hand brushed her breast. Neither remarked on it, neither murmured an excuse, but Geoffrey's color remained high and Joanna pushed away what she had not yet eaten. They did not linger long at the table after that. Geoffrey made a half-hearted suggestion about riding out, but Joanna protested that it was too hot and proposed instead that Geoffrey play to her.

The lute was fetched, the embroidery frame set comfortably out of the direct glare but in the full light of the sun. Joanna bent to her work; Geoffrey plucked the strings idly. What sprang first to his mind were the sweet love laments of the troubadours, but the idea was faintly disgusting to him. He had sung those with considerable success to a number of ladies of light virtue at court. Somehow he could not present such tarnished things to Joanna. He did not worship her. One does not put a halo around the head of a girl who has boxed your ears soundly for dropping overripe fruit on her head. He knew her puckish humor and her earthy good sense too well to develop visions of heavenly purity. Nonetheless, Joanna was clean and good—solid gold compared with the tawdry tinsel of Queen Isabella's ladies. There would be love songs for Joanna too—but not those.

Almost afraid his tongue would trick him into the well-worn route, Geoffrey shifted languages altogether and sang the English lyric "Stella Maris." Joanna was a little surprised. She had expected a love song, but she was not really disappointed. As the song progressed, she felt rather pleased. It was, she agreed, not the time or place for sickly sweet sentiment. Yet the physical tension that had taken hold of her did not diminish much. It merely became mixed with an equally exciting sense of anticipation. The combination, however delicious, was unsettling. Joanna found she could not sit in silence and wait for Geoffrey to sing again, and she said what came first into her mind. As the words were spoken, Joanna blushed. She could not have said anything sillier even if she had tried. She knew quite well that Geoffrey sang English. He could speak it a little too, although not as well as she could.

However Geoffrey did not take her up on her idiocy or seem to notice her blush. ''The Church was on my mind,'' he said. It was absolutely necessary to say something, anything, except what was really on his mind. ''Some of the lands through which I rode were in a sad state. They were burying men by the side of the road. I have heard also that even the last rites were denied to those in Durham.''

''Some priests are fools,'' Joanna replied, lifting eyes that were clear and bright with anger. ''Why should the poor servant suffer because the master has committed a fault? Since King John has offended the pope—although I do not too well understand the ins and outs of that matter—it is reasonable that the pope punish the king. Why, however, should he place an interdict upon the people? *We* have not refused obedience.''

''I suppose the pope believes the king will take pity on his people.''

Joanna's burst of laughter was not, this time, a pleasant sound. ''Do not say so. Surely such a belief can only betoken a wanting mind either in the pope or in those who send him information.''

''Or perhaps it was to show the king his power, a warning of worse to follow.'' Geoffrey was far more interested in the play of emotion on Joanna's face than in the story of the pope and king.

''So the worse did follow. The king is excommunicated and has been for two years. I do not see that he is much affected by it, but my people. . . Do you remember Cedric Southfold? He served as messenger to my mother for years.''

''No, I— Yes, I do. What of him?''

''He died some weeks ago, but when he was very ill his old wife came weeping to me that the priest would not give him the viaticum. Poor old man to be burdened with such fear at the end of his life.''

"God have mercy on him," Geoffrey murmured. "That is a bitter death for a loyal servant and a good man."

"Oh, he died in peace," Joanna said, her full lips thinned to a hard line. "I sent Father Francis down to him and he gave him good comfort. I took my whip to that priest also, and I tied him to my mare's tail and dragged him off the demesne. There is a young priest now who sees his duty to me and to the pope more clearly."

Geoffrey sat upright and stared at his betrothed. "You took your whip to the priest and drove him off? But—"

"But what?" Joanna asked hotly. "Can he challenge *me* before the bishop of Winchester? Will Peter des Roches, who sits at supper with the excommunicated king, deny that there is a reasonable limit to obedience to the pope? I do not ask the priest to open the church or to say daily mass. What sins grow upon us for lack of such things we can atone for in the future. For the dying, there is no future. A man must not be damned for eternity by the failure of a rite because of a priest's whim. Cedric's sins were little sins—if he had any. Why should he be denied heaven and burn eternally in hell because of a quarrel between the king and the pope that had nothing to do with him?"

"I do not know," Geoffrey replied heavily. "Where is he buried?"

"Oh, mother settled that when the interdict was first announced. We gave a field right beside the churchyard to the church. All our people are buried there, and Father Francis assured them that as soon as the interdict was lifted he would consecrate the field."

"I hope he lives so long," Geoffrey remarked drily.

Joanna looked seriously at him. "Tell me what this quarrel is about, Geoffrey. Mother and Ian never speak of it. They never speak of the king at all, unless it is very necessary, and I do not like to ask because—because I can see the fear in mama's eyes when Ian talks of these matters. She fears for him."

"I, too. It is well he went to Pembroke in Ireland. The quarrel between the king and the pope is simple enough. There was a disputed election for archbishop of Canterbury. The monks desired the elevation of their subprior, Reginald; the king desired his friend John Grey, bishop of Norwich as archbishop."

"That toad? Peter of Winchester is loyal to the king, but Norwich is—"

"Your mother would say 'an ass licker,' " Geoffrey remarked innocently.

Joanna's eyes laughed at him while her face took on a look of great gravity. "A married dame's ways and language are not fitting for an innocent maiden," she cooed.

The expression was so enchanting that Geoffrey's hand tightened on his lute and the strings twanged. "There was also some meddling by the bishops suffragan to Canterbury," he went on hastily, "and the outcome was that the pope appointed as archbishop an Englishman, then in Rome, a man called Stephen Langton. He is, I understand, a wise, learned, and good man. The monks of Canterbury were pleased; the suffragan bishops were also pleased; the king, however, was furious."

"I do not much love the king," Joanna put in, "and certainly I would not wish to see John Grey as archbishop, but—but the king is not all wrong in this. It is his right to be consulted on so high an appointment, and his authority—"

Geoffrey shrugged. "That is true enough, but in a choice among evils I suppose I had rather have the pope's power a little strengthened and Langton as archbishop than have John's authority perfect and give control of the Church, through Grey, into the king's hands. I do not know. Ian says that Langton is a great man and will not be merely a creature of the papacy. In any case it is done. Langton has been consecrated. I will say that the pope tried to smooth matters over. He sent rich gifts at first and many sweet words. Even when John answered with contumacy, the pope wrote conciliatory letters admonishing the king most gently."

"Someone should have told him that was not the way to

go about things with King John,'' Joanna commented caustically.

''I suppose someone did, or perhaps Pope Innocent's temper is not quite so peaceable as a Holy Father's should be. When he saw John was stubborn in spite of his kindness, he threatened, but by then the king was in a fine Angevin rage. He sent de Cantelu and Cornhill to Canterbury and they drove out the monks and seized the Church property.''

''I see. Then came the interdict.''

''Naturally. By then John's rage was past and, I think, he would have come to an agreement readily. In fact, he tried. Langton's brother had a safe-conduct to come to England and discuss matters. I am not sure whether it was Langton or the pope who was at fault in that no agreement was reached. John professed himself willing to accept Langton but made a just condition that the king's authority be preserved. That was refused.''

''It is always thus,'' Joanna agreed, shaking her head. ''If you offer the Church a finger, you are like to find your whole hand has been eaten.''

''Is that the way for a modest maiden to speak?'' Geoffrey teased.

Large eyes filled with an entirely spurious innocence were raised to his. ''Did I use some word that was not proper, my lord?''

Geoffrey reddened again very slightly. It was the first time Joanna had ever called him ''my lord,'' and though it was said in jest it sounded very sweet to him.

''Each word by itself,'' he responded, ''was innocent enough. Added together—'' He shook his head at her and laughed. Then he grew more serious. ''But I do not see an end to it. At first, while the king hoped for a reconciliation, he held his hand. When he saw the pope adamant, he began to rob the churches—not only the revenues of the sees from which the bishops had fled, although that was bad enough—he confiscated the plate and chalices and sometimes even the crucifixes and melted them down for their gold and silver.''

"There are advantages to that," Joanna remarked callously. "At least it has saved us from paying the cost of the Scots and Irish wars. Even this Welsh campaign—you know, Geoffrey, that the king has not called a full levy. He is hiring mercenaries. In fact, his demands have been so light in the past two years that many of the vassals and castellans who were in debt to us are clearing their accounts."

"Do not be so pleased. Do you think we will come out of this scot-free? You know the Church. Sooner or later, the king will be driven to make peace—and there will be no peace until John agrees to repay what he has taken. Where do you think that repayment will come from?"

Coincidentally, Geoffrey was not the only one voicing doubts about the king's seizure of Church property. Peter des Roches, bishop of Winchester, was saying almost the same thing—except that he did not bother to comment on where the money for repayment would come from. The king, to whom he was speaking most earnestly, removed his eyes from the *tableau vivant* he was contemplating and looked toward Winchester. The two men were an almost laughable contrast, partly because they were much alike in coloring and wore their hair and beards cut in the same fashion. However, King John had become very heavy in the past few years, looking remarkably like a wine tun with a protruding head and limbs. Winchester, on the other hand, was thin as a whip and as supple.

"Perhaps," John agreed in his beautiful voice, "but by then I will have achieved my purpose. Ireland and Scotland already lie quiet under my yoke. When I have tamed the Welsh it will be time enough to make my peace. Then I will deal with the English barons." He smiled slowly. "And if I must repay, who will dare deny to give whatever I ask?"

"Indeed, my lord is wise." The voice was sweet and lilting.

Both men now looked back at the tableau John had been contemplating. Unlike its effect on her husband, time seemed to have passed without touching Isabella of Angoulême. She was as dark as John, her eyes huge pools of black shaded by long lashes and surmounted by thin, perfectly arched brows of hair so fine and glossy that they shone like silk. Her nose was small and straight; her lips deep red and formed into an exquisite, slightly pouting bow. Her skin was a marvel, a rich brunette delicately tinted with rose so that it seemed to have an inner glow. To look upon her was a pleasure almost physical; she was called the Helen of Europe—and with perfect justice.

At her knee, stood a boy of about four, tall for his age and a surprising contrast to both his parents, for his hair was fair and his eyes a clear blue. He was well formed, with a bright, intelligent expression, marred only slightly by one eyelid that drooped unnaturally. The only other oddity in the child was his stillness. Boys of four wriggle; this one did not, as though he knew he was part of a picture and, if he disturbed it, he would be sent away. On the floor at Isabella's feet another boy, a year younger, played with some bright objects and, in a bedecked cradle, an infant slept.

After seven years of barrenness, Isabella had done well by the Plantagenets. She had produced two sturdy sons and two attractive daughters, and there seemed no reason to believe she would not bring forth other children—all strong and lively and all delivered with little fuss and bother and not the slightest effect upon their mother's beautiful body. There were those who said that the children had not produced the slightest effect on their mother's icy heart either. This opinion was not universally held. Another party argued that Isabella *had* no heart and, therefore, it was unreasonable to expect her children to find a place there.

Both parties were wrong. Isabella had a perfectly normal heart. It beat steadily and strongly at the normal temperature of her body, keeping the roses in her lips and her cheeks abloom. Nor was it impervious to love, but its object had been chosen long, long before Isabella's children were born. In fact, the first time Isabella had looked in a polished metal mirror and been capable of understanding what she saw there, her heart had been so completely ravished that it became insensible to any feeling beyond what directly affected the object of its devotion. Wholly and completely, Isabella of Angoulême loved herself.

It was fortunate for Isabella that this was true. Otherwise her life would have been exceedingly unhappy. She had been betrothed from childhood to a young nobleman of power, wealth, and character—Hugh le Brun de Lusignan. Only weeks before her wedding, John met her, coveted her, and, in short order, married her. Isabella made no protest—and not because she was young and overawed. She had exchanged the count for the king, the vassal for the overlord, quite willingly. To her mind, being a queen could only set her beauty in a more appropriate frame.

Isabella was well satisfied with her bargain, even though it was clear within months of her wedding that her husband was a confirmed lecher. However, his open contempt for the women he bedded casually, coupled with the formality and respect he showed Isabella herself, prevented her pride from being hurt. Since no emotion other than pride had ever touched her relationship with her husband, she was content. She did not doubt that John loved her; he would never be long separated from her and spent much time in her company just looking at her—no matter whom he took to his bed.

With the coming of her children, Isabella's life was almost complete. Young Henry and Richard and the little girls had secured her position. She could never be put aside like John's previous wife for childlessness. There had been the danger, of course, that John would dote more upon the babes than upon herself, but that problem soon resolved itself. John no more than she wished to be bothered with squalling and puking infants and, by the time Henry was old enough to be amusing, his strong resemblance to John's hated older brother Richard was apparent. In fact, when Isabella saw how coldly her husband regarded the coloring and large stature of his son, she had feared John would accuse her of adultery. However, it soon became clear that his distrust was of the child, not of herself.

The other children meant even less to him. Perhaps he favored Richard, whose coloring resembled his own, a little, but in general John took no delight in childish babble. He enjoyed his family when it made a pretty picture —a beautiful wife surrounded by quiet, handsome babes—but he did not wish to be disturbed by any demands the picture made upon him. Once it was established that John's attention would not be drawn away from her by the children, Isabella dismissed them almost completely from her mind. They were well cared for she knew. They appeared on call, well dressed, healthy, and well mannered. When they became annoying, they were removed.

Thus there was only one blot on the bright surface of Isabella's life. There was only one person in the world who was her rival for influence upon John. Isabella did not understand the expression in her husband's eyes when they looked upon his half brother, William of Salisbury, but she knew he did not look on her that way. She knew too that in any contest of desire between her will and Salisbury's will, John would yield to his brother. The one quarrel she had ever had with her husband revolved around Salisbury. It was John who had insisted she take William's son —the bastard of a bastard—into her service. And then, when Salisbury had removed Geoffrey from her household because he said the boy was ill-treated, her husband had berated her like a madman; he had very nearly hit her. To this day, she was not sure what John had wanted her to do about Geoffrey FitzWilliam. He had seemed equally angry that the boy had survived and that he had been made unhappy.

The whole affair had annoyed Isabella very much. She could not help it if the bastard was the butt of her other pages, and if he was so careless and awkward that she frequently had to punish him. Surely John did not expect her to put herself out to smooth the sin-born child's path. And as for having him murdered—well, if that was what John wanted, he could do it himself. Isabella had no intention of endangering *her* salvation for her husband's convenience. If the boy would not sicken and die of himself or take his own life, it was his fault and not hers. She had certainly put no impediments in his path. Isabella came as close as it was possible for her passionless nature to hating William of Salisbury and Geoffrey FitzWilliam, but she did not dare attack either of them openly. They were never far from the surface of her thoughts, however, and if she could say a spiteful word or do them an ill turn, she did.

There had been a short pause after Isabella spoke while both John and the bishop of Winchester stared at her. They were not surprised at her remark. Isabella did not have much sense, but she had sense enough always to agree with and praise her husband. The pause was simply for a pleasurable contemplation of her loveliness. Isabella knew it and sat perfectly still for a time. When she felt she had conferred a sufficient favor by allowing their admiration, she spoke again.

"You know, my lord bishop, that every plan my husband has designed that rested upon the support of the barons has fallen apart through their cowardice and disloyalty. It is only when he is strong enough to act upon his own that they rush to take credit for his glory and act as if it were their doing alone."

"It is true enough," John sneered. "When I had none but my own household guard, they deserted me rather than sail for Normandy, but when I had a good mercenary army readied to subdue Ireland, then they rushed to my support." He laughed without mirth. "Many came who were not even summoned. And the same was true when I marched north to tame Scotland."

Peter des Roches did not contradict the king, although he was no fool. The barons had refused to sail for Normandy because an aroused Philip of France in control of every stronghold in the province was waiting to cut them to pieces. No one had refused the king's summons to Ireland because, by 1209, William, earl of Pembroke had been fighting there for two years already and the country was nearly beaten into submission. When King John arrived with his army, he had little to do beside march the massive force up and down and accept the Irish lords' capitulation.

The Scottish success was of a different order. William of Scotland was a tired man. Whether he had summoned one last spurt of energy in the hope of smoothing the path to the Scottish throne for his young son, Alexander, or whether he had been pushed into the war by his aggressive barons, Winchester could not guess. The end result had been that Salisbury had trapped the Scottish army and John had been able to impose humiliating terms of defeat—without ever coming to battle at all. The cooperation of the English barons in the Scottish war had nothing to do with the king's ability to buy mercenaries. It needed no effort to convince any English baron that subduing the Scots was to his benefit. Naturally, even the northerners, who were the most rebellious against John, would agree with him on that subject and would be most enthusiastic about such a campaign.

Essentially, the same was true of this coming Welsh campaign. Without making reference to the past, Winchester said, "I do not think you need to doubt the willingness of your barons to support you against the Welsh. I do not mean to speak against their loyalty, but, my lord, it is in their interest to serve you in this matter."

"Except those tied in love to the Welsh devil," the king snarled softly.

Winchester did not bother to remind John that only a year ago he had been calling Llewelyn his "dearest son" and the "Welsh devil" had been married to John's natural daughter Joan since 1204. Instead, he said, "Who—? Oh, you mean de Vipont. I know you do not love him, but—"

"He has fled away to Ireland so that he need not answer my summons."

"Now there, my lord, you are wrong. I have a great value for Ian de Vipont, and I know what he intends because I went to the betrothal of his daughter to your nephew. We spoke of the matter. His levy will be there—every man—and young Geoffrey will lead them." Winchester knew the king well, but he did not understand the expression that flicked across his face. Before he could ask a question that would clarify John's thoughts, however, there was an interruption from Isabella.

"That puling bastard," she exclaimed, "he—"

"No, no, my love," the king interrupted smoothly. "Geoffrey is a very brave and capable young man. I have told you many times that his birth is nothing against him. But he is young. It is a heavy responsibility for him."

"I suppose it is your brother Salisbury who will carry the load really," Winchester remarked neutrally.

"Oh no," the king said softly, smiling, "I am sure Geoffrey will lead his own men and de Vipont's too."

The discussion was making Winchester uneasy. The king had always seemed indifferent to or even slightly to favor his brother's bastard son, but there was nothing in his face or eyes now and, coupled with the caressing tone, that was a dangerous sign. Salisbury was dotingly fond of his bastard, and Salisbury was the mainstay of the kingdom. Winchester was not in the least sure that Salisbury would remain faithful if anything should happen to Geoffrey and any shadow of suspicion fall upon John. It seemed to the bishop that Salisbury's fixed, blind affection for his brother was neither so fixed nor so blind as it had been in the past. The earl had been badly shaken by the death of William Braose's wife and son.

Winchester shifted in his seat and dropped his eyes to the floor. He wished he had not thought of that. The truth was that even he had been shaken by that, and he was neither blind to the faults nor particularly fond of the king. John was growing either indifferent to or careless of showing the true depths of his degradation. He had made no secret of it when he locked Braose's lady and child into a tower and gave orders that neither food nor water be given to them. The man had committed treason, it was true, and the woman had aided and abetted him and had spoken foolishly and haughtily—but death by starvation was cruel beyond need or reason and the boy was scarce thirteen years old. What had he done? Salisbury had pleaded for Braose's son on his knees, offering his own legitimate heir as hostage. Winchester sighed. He had pleaded and reasoned also—hoping more that John would satisfy his brother than that any spirit of mercy would move the king—but he had been equally unsuccessful. The child had died with the mother after weeks of suffering.

That was not all. John had always played fast and loose with the wives and daughters of his nobility, but in the past he had confined himself either to willing women or to those who could be seduced or threatened into willingness. Of late, he did not even bother to put a gloss over what he was doing. He sent openly for any woman his fancy happened to light upon, and if she did not come, he sent men to seize her. Winchester had protested openly about this practice; he had called it a sin against God. John had laughed at him—publicly—saying he could not be more damned than he already was, excommunicated as he had been by the pope. And privately the king had sneered that he did not need to fear sin since, doubtless, he would be absolved for such trifles as rape and murder when he was absolved for the greater sins of flouting the Holy Father's will and—worse yet—laying hands upon Church property.

"So the bastard is betrothed," Isabella sneered, breaking into Winchester's thoughts. "You see, my lord, I said your brother would not care for your preferences. He has betrothed his son to the daughter of your enemy."

"You do not understand William," John replied, a little more sharply than he usually spoke to Isabella. "His purpose is to bind de Vipont to me more firmly by making a blood bond with him."

Although she did not answer in words, Isabella tossed her head. "Is the girl still as red as a fox? she asked. "I remember her when she came to court with Lady Ela."

"Yes," Winchester replied shortly. It was never wise to praise other women to Isabella.

"And a bitch like the mother, no doubt?" John asked.

"Oh no." Isabella answered before Winchester could speak. "Not at all. She is a pious prude and as meek as a nun's hen. What could she be else with such a mother.

Lady Alinor has trodden all the life out of her.''

Now Winchester was more than uneasy; he was actively frightened. It had not escaped his keen eye that despite her placid manners there was nothing at all downtrodden about Joanna and that Salisbury was almost as fond of her as he was of his own son. To meddle with Joanna was to court immediate disaster. Yet to say a word on the subject was to invite catastrophe by sparking the king's interest and the queen's spite. Fortunately at that moment the child in the cradle began to wail, Richard jumped up, scattering his toys, and young Henry went to see what had disturbed his sister. Winchester blessed all three with sincerity, even wishing he was a holier man so that his blessing would be more effective.

CHAPTER FOUR

On the evening before Geoffrey's departure, Joanna admitted to herself that she was sadly disappointed by the remainder of his stay at Roselynde. Her anticipation had come to nothing. After that hot afternoon they had spent talking of church and state affairs, no other tête-à-tête had occurred. Joanna could not say that Geoffrey was avoiding her deliberately; that would be ridiculous. Why should he? However, he certainly was keeping very busy.

First, he had wanted to hunt. Joanna had been surprised, but had obligingly sent out her huntsmen to mark game. The next day it was the fishing villages that drew his attention. He would ride the coast and check on the watchtowers and speak to the people. Joanna assured him that she was well accustomed to that duty.

"Yes, yes," Geoffrey had agreed hurriedly, bolting his breakfast, "but while Ian is away the people had better become accustomed to seeing me."

Joanna stared at him blankly. Every man on every demesne knew Geoffrey well. What kind of a lunatic reply was that? Joanna waited dinner an hour past its time and sat late in the hall, but Geoffrey did not return until long after she was abed. He had met young Bosham, he explained the next morning, and had gone home to dinner with him; then they had made a night of it.

"You look it," Joanna had said icily.

Geoffrey had the grace to blush, but he did not take the hint. Soon after he broke his fast, he was off again. Whether he came in to dinner, Joanna did not know. She had retreated to her own chamber in the women's quarters and informed her maids that she did not wish to be disturbed.

63

There she learned that cutting off one's nose to spite one's face is painful and unsatisfying. She was furious with Geoffrey, although she could not name a discourtesy or a fault to be furious about, and even more furious with herself for being furious. She did not understand *why* she should be angry.

Having spent the afternoon and evening enduring the battle between her pride, which refused to permit her to ask her maids whether Lord Geoffrey had come in, and her good sense, which told her it was ridiculous to torment herself only to appear indifferent, Joanna began reluctantly to prepare for bed. Tears came to her eyes, and she brushed them away impatiently, furious again because she was crying about nothing. Indeed, she did not even know *what* the nothing was she was crying about.

All she could think of as she removed her wimple and allowed her braids to fall was that Geoffrey had not sent to inquire about her. That was ridiculous! Probably he was not even in Roselynde and, even if he was, why should he send for her? The servants knew him long and would obey him in any household attention he might desire. Why should he wonder whether she was ill? She never was. Everyone knew she was as strong as a horse; all the Devauxs and Lemagnes were. Slowly Joanna's fingers undid her braids. She had not summoned her women. She would not permit them to see her senseless distress. Tears came again. Before Joanna could lift a hand to wipe them away, a large wet tongue squelched across her face.

"Brian, no!" Joanna exclaimed, pushing the dog away and wiping her face on her sleeve. The animal whined, and Joanna looked at him. Poor thing. Partly he was responding to her mood, she knew, but also the poor beast had been confined all day. Joanna felt terribly guilty. She had not thought to tell someone to take him out. "Come," she said, and rose hastily.

Either Geoffrey had not yet come in or he had already gone to bed, Joanna thought. The hall was lit only by a few torches; no candles burned in the family area, and the fire had been banked, only a few dull embers showing through the layer of ash. Joanna passed softly down the stairs after her glance through the doorway. There was no sense in waking the menservants who were already asleep on their pallets along the walls.

There was no challenge as Joanna passed out of the forebuilding into the inner bailey. The moon was well up and her hair was so red that it identified her even in that colorless light. Had she been in the shadow, it would have made no difference; the huge dog was a guarantee that the person accompanying him was a member of the household. Brian bounded into the open area joyfully. Joanna watched him for a few minutes and then walked around the corner and opened the gate to the garden.

The few night-blooming flowers spread their pale trumpets wide and Joanna touched first one and then another gently, soothed and comforted. Although she knew the garden as well as or better than she knew her own bedchamber, it was different at night. The scents were sweeter, she thought, and more exotic. A fitful breeze came in off the sea, salt and tangy yet mixed with the sweetness of the roses that grew on the cliffs. The scent drew her off to the right, down the path that led to the rose garden. She would sit there on the bench for a few minutes and breathe the sweetness until Brian signaled his desire to go in again.

The roses were thick on the trellises now, and the bench was shadowed from the moonlight. Nonetheless, there was something odd—"Who is there?" Joanna said imperiously.

"I—Geoffrey."

She hesitated. "Are you lying in wait for me again?"

He laughed. "No. I thought you were abed."

"What are you doing here?"

This time he hesitated, then instead of answering said provocatively, "I could ask the same question."

The provocative tone did not escape Joanna. Although she had already confessed by her second question that she remembered that they had met in secret—if so innocent a meeting could be said to be secret—in this spot before their betrothal, an imp of perversity seized Joanna. She would not give him the satisfaction of mentioning her memory again.

"I," she said haughtily, "had to take Brian out. Since I did not feel obliged to stand and watch him, I came here to sit a while." She did not wait for a comment, but asked, "Did you come in to dinner *today?*"

"You must know I did not."

"I did not know it—and it is just as well you did not, for there was no dinner fitting for you ordered."

A silence fell. Geoffrey did not say, as Joanna expected, that he had eaten worse fare than the servants had when on the march. He got slowly to his feet, almost as if he did not realize what he was doing. He came a step or two closer to Joanna and stretched a hand to touch her loose, flowing hair. Undone from its braids, it hung nearly to her knees, gleaming bright as red gold even in the moonlight, which bleached both their faces bone white.

"Where have you been all day?" Joanna asked breathlessly, less because she cared than because she had to say something quickly.

"Hiding from the devil," Geoffrey replied thickly.

He had a handful of her hair now, and he lifted it to his face. In spite of the roses that hung all around them, its scent was different, sharp and spicy-sweet, an odor to which Geoffrey could not put a name. He closed his hand on the hair and pulled gently. Perforce, Joanna came closer. She put up her own hand, ostensibly to make him let go, but when she touched him she made no effort to unwind his fingers from what they held.

"Whatever do you mean?" she asked, very nearly in a whisper and without any real knowledge of what she said. As that past day at dinner, she was quiveringly aware of Geoffrey's physical being, of his male odor, of the warmth of his body, of the strength of his hand under hers.

The answer she got was not in words. Geoffrey's free hand went round her and drew her tight against him. His mouth came down hard on her slightly parted lips. This was no kiss of peace. Joanna's first reaction was surprise at the pleasure the new kiss gave her. All at once the blood seemed to rush from her extremities to her body. Her arms and legs felt weak, her head too light. Only her lips, her breasts, and her loins seemed real to her, tingling and pulsing. The rest had become insubstantial. There could be no thought of pushing Geoffrey away. Her hand would not touch him at all; it would crumple, as a veil of silk blown outward by the wind crumples when it touches something hard.

Geoffrey released her lips; his eyes were black in the moonlight staring down. Joanna uttered a tremulous sigh; her eyes closed, her head dropped forward onto his shoulder, and she wavered where she stood. Geoffrey's grip on her waist tightened still more. He took a step backward and then another, almost carrying her. Her limpness frightened him a little.

"Joanna?" he whispered, "Joanna?"

She did not reply but, eyes still closed, raised her face in a mute invitation. It was so open an invitation that a man might have taken it as a practiced gesture. At the moment Geoffrey was in no condition for thinking at all. He sank backward onto the seat he had risen from, turning Joanna so that she came down into his lap. The movement roused her a little; her eyes fluttered open, but Geoffrey closed her mouth before she could speak and she sank back into her cocoon of pure sensation.

Although he was no very practiced lover, Geoffrey had some experience. He was a nice looking young man; he had challenged four men for insulting him and had beaten three and killed the fourth—which gave him a modest but firm reputation as a fighter. Also important, he was Salisbury's favorite, darling son and, as such, considered to have a direct line to the king's ear. The combination of attractions had brought him more frequent and more intimate attention from the ladies of the court than most young men of his age could boast, especially before they learned he never asked Salisbury for anything.

One lady, at least, had been of more use to Geoffrey than he had been to her—although she had desired least from him. She taught him a good deal about the physical side of women and about the techniques of sexual love. Techniques, of course, need considerable practice before they come to perfection and Geoffrey was not very old. However, Lady Elizabeth had been a determined teacher and Geoffrey had learned very thoroughly the two most important facts about lovemaking, facts few men learn from whores or serf girls hurriedly coupled in ditches. He had learned that a woman must be handled before coupling to make her ready and that a man must delay his own satisfaction until his partner has achieved hers. He had also learned that the torment of delay was a very sweet thing, that the longer the play, the more seemingly unendurable the waiting, the greater was the final joy, the richer its fulfillment.

Now, suppressing his instinctive desire to lay Joanna down on the soft, sweet-smelling turf, throw himself atop her, and take his pleasure, Geoffrey played with her lips, sucking and biting them gently. Joanna still made no move. If it had not been for her quick breath, fluttering against his cheek, Geoffrey could have believed her unconscious. One hand lay limp in her lap; the other still rested on his, for he retained his gentle grip on her hair, but did not hold him. Geoffrey shifted the arm around Joanna's waist, raising it so that his open hand could cup her breast. A little catch in her breathing betrayed her response and that she was not indifferent. Geoffrey opened his hand a trifle more, ran the thumb over the breast to touch the nipple. Under the caress it budded out hard against the confining layers of cloth.

Very soft, soft as a sigh, a tiny whimper of pleasure rose in Joanna's throat. Geoffrey felt her tense just a trifle, shift her body in his lap. Now was the moment for the next gentle assault, but to reach what he desired to touch, Geoffrey had to free his other hand. Gently he opened his fingers, releasing Joanna's hair. She did not stir and her hand slipped off his, sliding down his arm in what, surely, was a caress. Slowly Geoffrey began to move his hand downward.

Unfortunately—or fortunately—he had begun to tremble and sweat a little. The hand was damp; the long, strong hairs clung to it. Geoffrey, all unintentionally, pulled Joanna's hair.

The pain was not severe, but it was sharp and sudden. On the instant, she was out of his arms, off his lap, standing before him, panting like a hunted doe. That was a piece of good luck that Geoffrey did not appreciate at all at the moment. Had Joanna's move been less sudden, he would instinctively have tried to hold her; she would have struggled; irreparable damage might have been done. Now, although she had left him and her eyes were wide with shock, she did not run away.

"Joanna," Geoffrey whispered, realizing that if he moved a finger she *would* run, "beloved, I did not mean to hurt you. I will never hurt you if I can help it."

"So that is what you meant!" she exclaimed. Her breathing was slowing, but she licked her lips as if seeking the taste of his mouth.

"Come back, Joanna," Geoffrey pleaded softly.

"Oh no," she replied, gathering up her hair and throwing it behind her as if she was afraid he would seize it again. Then, blindingly, she smiled at him. "Oh no. You were quite right, Geoffrey. I think we had both better hide from the devil."

"Love is not of the devil," Geoffrey urged.

She laughed softly. "I do not think it is either—despite what the priests say. It is—it is a great pleasure."

"Then come back to me. I will do you no hurt. I will—I will let you go if you bid me."

That made her laugh again. "But I do not think I *could* bid you let me go if I came back. You know that!" She put out a hand to fend him off and backed away as he rose. "No, Geoffrey. It would be very wrong, I am sure."

"How can it be wrong? We are betrothed. We are man and wife except for the final blessing."

"There you have said it," Joanna replied seriously. "We are only betrothed. I know that Ian and my mother intended at first that we be married. I do not know why they changed their minds—'' Her voice faltered. It seemed to Joanna that they had told her something of their purpose, but she had been so disturbed in her mind—she knew not why—that she had not really listened or understood. "But it must have been for some good reason. I would not cause the failure of some plan of theirs—and of your father's too, for he agreed we should be betrothed instead of married—for a few minutes of pleasure. You know this is true, Geoffrey," she added pleadingly. "It was you who first said you were 'hiding from the devil.' ''

The conversation had cooled him. Geoffrey let the hand he had stretched toward Joanna drop. He knew quite well why Ian and Alinor had proposed a betrothal instead of a marriage and why his father had agreed. However, it was not a reason he could proffer at this moment because Joanna would never believe him. Besides, now that the urgent demands of his body were under control again, he realized that to mate with Joanna at this time would be a mistake. He felt that the decision Ian and Alinor had made was wrong; he and Joanna would have been better off abed together. Nonetheless, it was true that to bed her without the sanction of the Church would raise a guilt in her—a feeling of sin— that would end in unhappiness. That was indeed why he had spent three days riding aimlessly from place to place, until his troop thought he was crazed, and why he had taken to the whores in Bosham town the previous night with such energy that young Bosham thought he was an insatiable sexual giant.

"Very well," Geoffrey said, "I will not press you, but—"

Joanna giggled. "I was very angry because you would not stay at home. I thought—I do not know what I thought, but now I understand. Oh, Geoffrey, I am very sorry you are going tomorrow. Still—it is safer, much safer."

He did not answer that. His mind was back with the filthy, coarse whores of Bosham and the fine, high-bred whores of the court, and Joanna was so great a contrast to

them all that his bowels knotted. Meanwhile Joanna heard
her own words. Safer? Geoffrey was going to war. He
might be dead before she ever touched him again. Suddenly, a pain stabbed her breast and she was frightened,
more frightened than she had ever been in her life. Stop it!
her mind ordered. Geoffrey is a man—only a man. What
you felt was sweet, but *any* decent young man can rouse that
in you. If it is not Geoffrey, it will be another.

The pain and terror would subside. She would make them
subside, Joanna thought. She would not grow like her
mother, laughing with terror-haunted eyes that had lids
polished and heavy with much weeping. To be a good wife
to Geoffrey—that was right. To take pleasure in him
abed—that was right also. But all good men were alike good
men and equally suitable as partners. Nonetheless. . . .

"Geoffrey," she said urgently. "Be careful. Do not
permit yourself to be thrust into the forefront of the
fighting."

Those were the sweetest words Joanna had said to him
since they were betrothed. Geoffrey flushed a little with
pleasure. Perhaps she did not think so little of him. She had
been willing enough in his arms—but he had known she
would be willing, that was her duty. Duty? To say she *could*
not bid him let her be? Geoffrey let his eyes rest on her face,
colorless in the colorless moonlight, framed in the red-gold
of her hair almost like a picture an artist had forgotten to
color. Perhaps in spite of all the men that followed her
Joanna was innocent. Perhaps she believed her mother when
Alinor said they followed the gold in her purse rather than
her person. If so, his mother-by-marriage had done him an
immeasurable good. A little wooing, now that the gold was
already his, should convince her that he, at least, desired her
person and should win a priceless prize. Or was Joanna, like
Alinor, thinking of damage to her property right in her men?

"I will take every care that my men are as safe as may be
consistent with their duty and honor."

"I know that," Joanna responded, "but—but I do not
trust your uncle, Geoffrey. Mayhap I wrong him—"

"I do not trust him either," Geoffrey assured her, "but you need not worry about me. It is more likely I will be overprotected by my father than thrust forward by my uncle."

"I cannot be sorry for that," Joanna whispered.

It was true that Salisbury doted on his boy and would shield him if he could. Joanna's distress abated, leaving only a slight sensation of anxiety because there had been impatience mixed with the amused fondness in Geoffrey's reply. If he felt he was overwatched, he might do something foolish to prove his valor. Men were such idiots! Geoffrey had moved closer as Joanna spoke and she looked up at him.

"Do not quarrel with your father, Geoffrey, I pray you. Remember that however much he loves you he will do nothing that could bring shame upon you. And—and he is very wise in the making of war."

That grave judgment—about as valuable, in Geoffrey's opinion as a bird's comment on a treatise by Boethius— made him smile. He was about to assure Joanna—quite mendaciously—that he would be a meek and obedient son when a bark as loud as the bellow of an enraged bull tore the air. Joanna took to her heels with such swiftness that Geoffrey was left staring stupidly at the empty spot where she had been. He heard her order the dog to be quiet as he drew near the gate.

"Joanna," he remonstrated, "you treat that creature like a spoiled and ailing child. Nothing would have happened if you let him wait another few minutes."

"Nothing except that he would have wakened the whole keep," Joanna replied tartly. "If I do not tell him to 'stay' he expects to be able to come to me, and, if he cannot, first he begins to bark. Then, if that does not bring me to him, he runs to fetch someone he knows."

"That is ridiculous. You must break him of that habit, Joanna. Really—There are times when a little privacy is desirable." Joanna looked perfectly uncomprehending, and Geoffrey cleared his throat. "Sometimes in moments of— er—great pleasure, one—ah—cries out."

A brief stunned silence was followed by a burst of unmaidenly laughter. "I am sorry," Joanna choked, when she had mastered herself. She had had a vision of Brian's great bulk landing on them right in the middle of lovemaking. "I can see that something will have to be arranged. It is just as well you mentioned it." She began to giggle helplessly again. "He learns so slowly, and it would be a trifle distracting to have him howling outside the door or dragging half the castle folk to the door to open it for him."

"Joanna!" Geoffrey said repressively. He knew her puckish sense of humor and was well aware that her public modesty of speech and manner did not result from any prudery of mind. "If you teach that dog any silly tricks—"

"No, no, I will not," she assured him, laughing, and then more soberly. "It is very funny to think about, but I do not believe I would enjoy being interrupted any more than you would."

The sincerity in her voice gave Geoffrey enormous pleasure. He was proud of having awakened her enough so that she would look forward to their union with anticipation. It was also well done to let her go.

"I hope so," he replied, stroking her hair and her arm, "I will do my best to please you—always." Then, seeing she did not tense or flinch away, he took her gently into his arms to kiss again. This time, however, his embrace was planned, not a result of the desire that had seized him when he saw her unexpectedly in the moonlight, and his kiss had more tenderness than passion. "Do not rise to bid me farewell," he said softly when their lips parted. "I will leave before lauds, and it will be hard enough for me—do not come down, Joanna."

Joanna did not answer at first, merely bid Brian "stay" and opened the gate so they could come through. Finally she said, "If that is your desire, I will obey you, my lord, but—God go with you then, Geoffrey. God keep you."

In the shadow of the forebuilding he kissed her again, not quite so tenderly as before, but he broke the embrace quickly. "Farewell, then, beloved. God keep you also," he murmured. "Go up now, Joanna. Go up quickly."

Obediently, Joanna went in and up the stairs. She realized it was very late, but she pinched her maids awake and ordered them to ready her for bed. There was something very important she had to think about, and she did not wish to be distracted from her thoughts by the need to unbutton buttons and untie laces and fold her clothes and brush her hair. While she was being attended, however, she did not "think" at all. She drifted into a sea of sensation again, remembering acutely how she had felt in Geoffrey's arms. That was not the point, she told herself firmly, as the tugging of the brush in her hair ended her dreaming, just as Geoffrey's pull on her hair had ended her previous quiescence.

The point Joanna needed to think about was not how she felt about Geoffrey but how Geoffrey felt about her—and what to do about it. She had not been in the least troubled by Geoffrey's passion because she was prepared to render passion for passion and enjoy it. No priest would ever convince Joanna that the pleasures of the body were in themselves evil. The bull and the cow, the horse and mare, the dog and bitch all took pleasure in coupling. Those creatures could not sin because they had no souls. Thus, God had given that pleasure to all, and it was no sin in itself. Joanna was perfectly willing to acknowledge that the pleasure might lead one into sin or that it might be a higher good to mortify the body by denying it that pleasure and so obtain holiness of spirit, but that was not her role in life. Her role and her duty, for which she had been fitted since birth, was the care of her lands and her people, and part of that duty was the breeding up of sons and daughters to follow her.

That was all very well and good. That was Geoffrey's duty also, and it was right that they should both take pleasure in it—but there was that other thing, that one soft kiss that had nothing of the body in it. That kiss was a message from the soul, as was the soft and slightly broken voice that said, "Farewell, then, beloved." And, when he bid her not come down to say goodbye, he had said, "It will be hard enough for me.'' He did not speak of his body then because there would be women enough to fill that need. A smile flickered across her lips as she thought of Geoffrey's attempt to assuage his body on the whores of Bosham. It had not done much good. She had kindled him anew without even trying.

Joanna bit her lip. She knew she was allowing her mind to wander to avoid a painful thought. It appeared that Geoffrey loved her, or was coming to love her, as Ian loved her mother. Joanna had a sharp memory of Ian's agony when her mother had delivered Simon and the little sister who had lived only a few months. Joanna shook her head. Ian had suffered more than his wife. Alinor made nothing of childbearing, and Simon and his dead sister had been her fifth and sixth so there was much less chance she would die in childbed. Ian's fear had been foolish, but because he loved he suffered—foolishly.

Again Joanna shook her head, this time at herself. Her mother's life and Ian's were their own affair. Her business was with Geoffrey. She did not wish, would not allow herself, to love him. Yet if he loved her, was that fair? If it had been impossible for her to love him, that would be one thing. Unfortunately, it would be very possible, actually very easy, to love Geoffrey. It was another thing to deny love deliberately. Impatiently, Joanna dismissed her maids, slipped off her bed robe, and got into bed. The sheets were scented with spice and roses and brought another vivid memory of Geoffrey's caresses.

Certainly it would be wrong to hurt Geoffrey by coldness. That would be both a violation of her duty as a wife and an injustice to his love. But she dared not love him; she dared not. I am not as strong as mama, Joanna thought. If I suffer as she suffers, I will die; I cannot bear it. I do not know what is right. I only know that I cannot bear it. I will walk between the ways. I will be a good wife to Geoffrey, and I will keep my heart whole. Perhaps he will never know. Perhaps, she thought suddenly, he will forget this little tender love in the months he is away.

That should have been a comforting thought, but Joanna found it strangely distasteful. She turned uneasily, and the movement released another gust of scent from the portion of the sheets her body had warmed. The bench beneath the trellised roses came back to her mind. She wondered why betrothal had been chosen above marriage. I could write and ask, she thought. I could even ask for permission to marry. No, I cannot, Joanna corrected herself sharply. Mama and Ian would agree to it—or, at least, Ian would. He always gave Joanna anything she asked for, and he would make Alinor agree, even if it would be a bad thing for them. I must be patient, Joanna thought, sighing. I must endure.

CHAPTER FIVE

The week after Geoffrey left Roselynde was a sharp trial to Joanna. Everything seemed to be conspiring to increase Geoffrey's importance to her. The weather, which had been hot and fine, changed, and an alternation of heavy downpour and light drizzle had lasted for days. This had confined Joanna to the keep and to overseeing the spinning and weaving of the maids. The quality and quantity of the output increased somewhat, but the maids at Roselynde were always well trained and reasonably dutiful. The gown Joanna was making for Geoffrey also progressed. Joanna was an exquisite needlewoman and now, past the resentments of childhood, she enjoyed the work, particularly the delicate, elaborate embroidery. She took great pride in the pictures her fine needles and brilliant threads painted and was well pleased by the image she was creating in gold thread on the soft, golden green silk she had chosen.

This was part of her wedding present to her husband, and she had given considerable time and thought to what would become him. She had been pleased that Geoffrey's gold-brown hair and gold-brown eyes would be bleached into insignificance by the brilliant tints Ian wore. Frankly she was tired of sewing crimson and brilliant blues and greens. It was nice to love one's stepfather, but it was nicer to have a man of one's own to sew for, and it was nicer still to have them so different.

There was no need to remind oneself that this gown was for Geoffrey. Ian would have looked dreadful in it, his dark skin turned sallow by the soft color. Geoffrey, on the other hand, would glow more golden. At that point, Joanna checked her thoughts and sighed with exasperation. There was nothing golden about Geoffrey. He was a clean, nice-looking young man with very beautiful eyes—there she was, doing it again! She caught her needle in a safe spot in the fabric and pushed the frame away, searching in her mind for some active thing to do. If she sat pent up in the keep for much longer, Geoffrey would assume a halo.

That notion relieved Joanna's mood a little. When she thought of the scrapes Geoffrey had got her into, there was no chance of investing him with a halo of saintliness. Joanna jerked more upright in indignation suddenly. Why, it was Geoffrey who had dared her to climb that part of the cliff where she had fallen. How dare he scold her for something he had taught her to do. She burst out laughing. Just wait until she reminded him. The gloom descended again. That was all she could do—wait. Repressing an urge to scream, run around the hall, or beat her maids, Joanna slowly reached for her embroidery frame again. As if to prove that patience brings rewards, the movement was interrupted by the double tramp of heavy feet.

Joanna looked up eagerly. A messenger from Ireland, perhaps, or even word of a fight among the men-at-arms that she would have to settle. Anything would be welcome to break the tedium of the day. The first glance showed her that what came was no domestic crisis nor a letter from her mother. Beorn was leading a man she knew, and he was not a part of any household related to her. The second look tightened Joanna's throat and made her fold her hands together so that they should not twitch with nervousness. On his breast the man wore the royal arms of England. He was not merely a noble visitor passing through; he was acting as a messenger for the king. When the two men drew nearer, Joanna could only hope she did not look as pale as she felt.

Henry de Braybrook bowed gracefully before Joanna and proffered a scroll. "From the queen," he said.

"The queen?" Joanna echoed, at once relieved and puzzled.

Queen Isabella had never paid the slightest attention to her, except once to say—in her hearing—that it was a pity she was so red and fox-haired because one so red could never approach beauty. Caution, however, restrained Joanna from saying any more. She knew that Isabella hated Geoffrey and guessed the queen must know she was now betrothed to him. Her eyes were wary under their downcast lids as she reached for the message. It was very brief and in the beautiful, clear writing of a scribe. Joanna raised her eyes to Beorn. "Please see to Sir Henry's refreshment while I take this to Father Francis to read," she said. It was no business of anyone's that she could read and write—a most unwomanly ability and one that Braybrook might well not have himself.

When she returned, Sir Henry was seated with wine at hand, Beorn standing silently a slight distance away. Joanna looked at the old master-at-arms. "The queen invites me to come to her at Whitechurch," she said.

"*Leuedy,*" he burst out, "*thou sholdest nat faren.*"

Braybrook looked sharply from Beorn—who had spoken excellent French to him—to Joanna, but nothing showed in her face. After a moment of staring at Beorn, as if she did not understand what he said or was surprised by it, she smiled uncertainly at Sir Henry.

"This has thrown me all of a maze," she murmured. "I never dreamt to have so much honor done me as for the queen to call me to her. Thus, I am all unready for her gracious summons—"

"I would not deny her, Lady Joanna," Braybrook remarked. "She is—er—of high spirit and easily offended."

"Oh, I would not want to offend the queen," Joanna twittered in a high, unnatural voice, as if suddenly stricken by fear.

She unclasped her hands and allowed them to flutter apart, to her throat, to her lap when she had seated herself to play with her jeweled belt. Had Geoffrey been there he would have roared with laughter. Joanna was imitating Lady Ela with devastating effectiveness. Like a snake-charmed bird, Braybrook's eyes followed her hands, fixed on them when they nervously, seemingly unconsciously, smoothed the fabric of her gown so that her thighs were sharply outlined. Joanna, meanwhile, had raised her eyes to Beorn's, dropped them to Braybrook, and looked at Beorn significantly again. Infinitesimally the old man nodded. He would do nothing until he received orders.

"No, no, of course I cannot deny her, but I cannot go today, nor yet tomorrow—"

"Why not, Lady Joanna? I and my men will escort you safely. There is naught for you to do but bid your maids pack your garments. The queen will find all else for you."

Find all else, indeed, Joanna thought, rage at being considered such a ninny taking the place of fear, which had momentarily drained her face of color. Doubtless Isabella would find a locked room for her, bonds for her hands and a gag for her mouth. Yes, then Ian would come home. He would fight for the king; he would allow himself to be spitted like a pig to get her free. And her mother would come, weeping for her daughter's life. Oh yes, Isabella would certainly find all else.

"Oh yes, oh yes," Joanna twittered, picking at her skirt so that it rose and exposed her pretty slippers and ankles. "Of course. Then I can go tomorrow, but not today. See how it rains. Why my lord, how silly a thing I am. You are soaked through. You must have a hot bath and dry garments immediately.

Before he could protest, she had clapped her hands and a maid came running. "A bath for Sir Henry in the east wall chamber," Joanna gasped nervously. "You will pardon me," she cried, jumping to her feet. I must find you something suitable to wear. Oh, dear!" And she fled away, unheeding of Sir Henry's denials.

Upstairs, Joanna stood for a moment to catch her fluttering breath and rearrange her thoughts. Her first instinct, born of terror, was to order all of them killed. Reason corrected that notion at once. That would be open treason, an act of war. An accident might befall Sir Henry; that would solve the problem also because the men-at-arms were not dangerous without their master. Another moment's thought made Joanna dismiss that idea also. First of all, there was no reason to believe Braybrook was guilty of anything beyond carrying out his mistress's orders. He might be totally innocent of any evil intention and totally ignorant that treachery was intended—if it was intended. There was no proof yet that Isabella wished to do harm, except her known antipathy to Geoffrey. Perhaps there was some other reason for the invitation.

As practical thought supplanted fear, Joanna began to wonder if she had not leapt to a false conclusion. Geoffrey and Salisbury would be at Whitechurch also and in control of a great part of the army. How could the queen—or even the king, shielding himself behind the queen—plan to do her any harm then? Nonsense. In general, Salisbury might love his brother and look aside from the evil the king did, but Geoffrey would never allow Joanna to be a victim and neither would Salisbury allow the king's evil to touch *her*. Nonetheless, there was something rotten in Isabella's invitation. Obviously Braybrook had been told to bring her with him quickly and without opportunity to make provision for the protection of Roselynde and without her own troop of men.

Joanna stared blankly ahead of her for a few minutes. Then a smile began to pull the corners of her lips and she began to giggle delightedly. "Edwina," she called softly.

Edwina was the daughter of Beorn and Alinor's maid Ethelburga. She was plump, lively, flaxen-haired, and pretty, and had served Joanna all her life. Neither ever forgot her station or the difference between them, but Edwina would go a long way to serve Joanna and Joanna would stretch a good many points to protect Edwina.

The tale of the invitation and the danger that might be hidden in it was related in a minute. Then Joanna said, "Start the other girls packing. Then find Sir Henry some guesting clothes, the richer the better, even if you must raid Ian's chests, and go down and bathe him. In God's name, keep him busy."

"Is he handsome? Shall I bed him?"

"As for that, he is well-looking enough and I know no ill of him. Do as you like. Only keep him in that room for a hour or so. I must have time to speak to your father and to go to the garden and see the cooks." She began to laugh again. "His men are going to be afflicted with a most deplorable disturbance of the mind and a flux of the bowels."

"Oh my lady," Edwina gasped, giggling too, "but how can it be done? If all our people refuse to taste a certain dish—"

"Sacrifices by some must be made for the good of all," Joanna remarked. "It is not impossible that a troop of my men were out on some duty— Let us not waste time. I will tell you the whole later. Go now."

Edwina laughed and loosened the neck of her tunic so that when she leaned forward—as she must to wash Sir Henry—her full breasts would peep out. Joanna shook her head. Edwina was a dreadful slut. She had already had one bastard, but the little girl had died. When Joanna had warned her that her light ways would deprive her of a husband, Edwina merely shook her head and laughed. "You owe your lord a clean body and his own children," she had said, "so you must deny yourself the pleasures I take wherever I will. I am bound to you—so I may take pleasure where I find it. I need not fear for my children, no matter who the father. They will have a place as I have a place. I confess my sins; I do my penance; I receive absolution. What do I have to fear, either on earth or after?" A slut, Joanna thought, smiling, but it was a most useful trait at times.

She did not waste much time in contemplating Edwina, however. She had much to do. A light cloak covered her dress and headdress on the off chance that Sir Henry would look out the window. It was of no particular value in keeping her dry because, when she had culled the plants she desired from the sodden garden, she was soaking wet. Brian, waiting at the gate, moaned at her reproachfully and Joanna laughed at him. He hated the wet as much as any cat. She walked quickly around the west wall of the keep. Probably

Braybrook would be well occupied with Edwina by now, but she held her head down and concealed the fruits of her reaping as well as possible under her cloak.

In the cookhouse, she presented one sheaf of plants to the soup-maker. The man's eyes widened. "Lady," he pleaded, "do you wish that we all go mad?"

"Not all," Joanna replied, "and not mad. I desire that the men of the troop who came with Sir Henry see what is not there for a day or two. Some of our people must also be afflicted so that suspicion of foul play does not fall upon us, but you can warn about half the men-at-arms. Some of your helpers must also fall ill, or pretend illness—be sure of that! Keep some aside and steep it so that it can be used as a 'medicinal draught' tomorrow and the next day, but that should not be strong."

"Bitter," the cook was mumbling. "Wormwood is so bitter. What can I devise that will—ah, if I add—"

Joanna thrust the plants into his hands and moved along the bank of fires to where the vegetables and greens were being prepared. Since the other cooks had been listening, they knew what was coming and Joanna did not have to repeat herself. Nonetheless there were protests.

"If so much spurge is added," the cook moaned, "there will be a bloody flux all over the keep."

"A strong flux is what I desire," Joanna said firmly, "but not bloody, I hope."

"The castle folk will slay me," the man cried.

"Not if you are taken ill also," Joanna soothed, laughing in spite of herself.

The cook shuddered, but he took the plants Joanna held out to him with shrinking hands and summoned a scullion to wash them. Another boy was sent off to fetch Beorn to the stables. He was breathing heavily when he arrived, and Joanna shook her head at him.

"There is no need to run, Beorn," she remonstrated affectionately. "You are not so young as you once were."

The old man made an impatient gesture and passed his hand over his bald head. "Lady," he pleaded, "do not go with him. The king is no friend to us, and the queen, I fear, does his bidding. We can protect you. Do not be afraid. We are three to their one. We can fall upon them of a sudden and imprison them—''

"And be accused of treason? No, no, Beorn.'' Then she smiled. "Do you think my mother's daughter is a fool? I must go, since the queen summons me, but I will not go as Sir Henry's prize nor will I leave Roselynde open to any harm.'' Helplessly she began to giggle again. "Worse will befall Sir Henry's men than a drubbing. Never mind that. I have no time to explain. Rest assured that when we are ready to ride tomorrow, Braybrook's men will be unable to come.''

Beorn looked at his young mistress and sighed softly. He had been very surprised by the fear that seemed to grip her in Sir Henry's presence. Lady Joanna, even as a child, had not been one to show fear, although sometimes when the worst was over she had trembled like a leaf in his arms and whispered, "I was afraid, Beorn, I was afraid.'' It was a pretense then, to cover some plan. Well and good. He had only to listen and obey, and that he was well able to do.

"First, ready three messengers on fast horses—only Braybrook's men must not know of them. One must ride to Iford to summon Sir Giles. I know he did not go to Whitechurch; young Giles has gone in his stead. Sir Giles must come here to guard Roselynde while I am gone. I do not think the keep will be attacked, but if no one of authority is here, some dogsbody of the king might come and do evil from within.''

"That is wisely said, lady. Iford will be safe for Lady Giles is there.''

Joanna made no comment on that. Beorn tended to place far too much reliance on women because of his early training and his lifelong dependence on Alinor. Lady Giles, in Joanna's opinion, was about as much use as a damp cloth in place of a shield, but since she did not intend to spread the word of Sir Giles's residence in Roselynde, there was little reason to fear that any danger would threaten Iford. In any case, Lady Giles would probably have sense enough to send to her husband for help if she were threatened.

"The second messenger must go to Lady Ela at Salisbury. She did not intend to go to Whitechurch, I know. She will contrive a way to send me advice, I am sure."

This time it was Beorn who made no comment on his thoughts. He felt Lady Ela with her aches and her tremblings and her complainings was a frail reed to lean upon, but he knew his mistress often wrote and spoke to her. Perhaps she asked her lord for help. Beorn felt some reassurance. Lord Salisbury was a strong defending wall for anyone in trouble.

"The third must be a hard and trusty man. He will need to ride night and day, changing horses as needful, and he will need to be clever. He must find his way to Whitechurch and there, in secret, go to Lord Geoffrey or to the earl of Salisbury and carry news of this summoning. If it is thought that I should be taken by force on the way—it is a long road to Whitechurch—my lord and his father must know to seek me if I do not arrive."

"Seek you? But they are poised for war. Lady, it is better not to go."

"Do you doubt Lord Geoffrey will draw his men from the war to seek me? He will do it. And when he goes to tell the king what he does and why, whoever holds me will quickly give me up, for Geoffrey's withdrawal will mean the end of the Welsh campaign."

Probably she was right, Beorn thought. The young lord could not keep his eyes from her, and he had wakened Beorn not long after matins the morning he left to harangue him for an hour on the need to guard his mistress better. Beorn chuckled softly and then sighed. He did not need the warning, but there was little he could do. Lord Geoffrey was raving something about last year when Lady Joanna fell in climbing the cliff. How could I have prevented her? Beorn wondered. Quiet as she seems, she is as much a devil as Lady Alinor.

"Now for your part," Joanna continued, "choose out

fifty men, the best fighters and most loyal and send them out of the keep as quietly as may be. Let Knud the huntsman's son lead them.''

"What are they to do, lady? Should I not go also?''

"You cannot go because Sir Henry has seen you and I do not wish him to know that the men left after he arrived. They must seem to have been away, on patrol of the beacon towers, from dawn. As to what they are to do, I do not care, so long as they do not eat dinner in the keep. They *must not* eat here. They must return before dusk, however, and it may be necessary for them to fight, although I do not think it. Half the castle folk and all Sir Henry's men will be raving mad.''

"Is this a jest?'' Beorn asked uncertainly. Lady Joanna was a devil for buttering a path to see a man slide down it with his arms full of eggs.

"I told you worse would befall Braybrook's men than a drubbing. Do not eat of any potage or greens at this dinner. Cheese and roast meat must suffice you—or you can absent yourself from table on some pretense if that likes you better.''

"Lady Joanna—'' Beorn began.

"I do not do it for a jest—although how I will keep from laughing I do not know. Sir Henry's men will not be fit to ride—not tomorrow, nor the next day, nor the next. The only men fit will be my fifty who did not eat the bad—whatever it was—that struck down the castle folk. Sir Henry may do as he pleases—go or stay. Sir Giles will be here by tomorrow night to see that he does not make mischief. I will leave tomorrow with you and the fifty you have chosen, greatly fearing—as he warned me—to offend the queen.''

"It will not be safe, lady.'' Beorn was still worried. "You are letting madness loose in the keep. Madmen are not as others. They are stronger, and fear is gone out of them.''

"It will be safe enough,'' Joanna said with a nasty grin. "However mad they may become, they will be too weak and too racked with pain to do anything. Not only their heads but their bowels will be sore afflicted.''

"As you will, lady, but—Lady Joanna, you will not stay to watch or—or pretend to nurse them?"

"No," Joanna agreed. "I am sorry for it, but it would not befit a shy and timid maiden. You hear, Beorn? If you are asked what I am, you must say I am easily frightened and not overclever.''

"Lady—" Beorn protested.

"That is my order. That is how I wish to be known at court but I do not know whether I will be able to sustain it. No matter, for this time it must serve. I do not think the other men will be questioned, but pass the word. They can say I am much shielded by my mother and thus they have not come to know me. So help me, I will—I will put sand in their goose grease if they betray me! Now I must go in and change my gown, which is dripping wet, and write the messages I will send. Do not worry about me. Only do your best to see that no one is sore hurt if the wormwood should take hold before the spurge.''

Dinner was pleasant if a little dull. To Joanna's intense amusement, Braybrook seemed too weary to have much to say. That was a bonus Joanna had not planned, but it made her doubly pleased with Lidwina's efforts. Probably she could have avoided any probing questions Sir Henry might have asked; it was far better, however, that he should not ask. What was more, his langour prevented him from noticing that there were far fewer men-at-arms and servants eating dinner than was natural for a keep the size of Roselynde. Moreover, he said nothing further about the need to leave that day. Joanna had thought of several additional excellent reasons for delaying, but she did not need to use them. Braybrook seemed happily resigned to spending the night.

It was a little less than an hour after the tables had been cleared away that the first disturbance occurred. Two men-servants collided with each other right in the middle of the hall. Each had been walking quickly, looking nervously over his shoulder. The collision brought shrieks of terror instead of low oaths or angry mutters of ''Watch where you go.'' Two other servants, one a trusted older man, went over to calm them and were greeted with more terrified howls. Before the afflicted men were wrestled from the hall, a maidservant suddenly began to brush frantically at her gown and stamp her feet and cry aloud.

Joanna, who had been sitting in a window seat conversing idly with Sir Henry, leapt to her feet and clasped her hands nervously. "What is it? What is it?" she cried breathlessly.

The terrified effect of her shaken voice was so perfect that she choked altogether. In a last-ditch effort, she brought her hands to her face and clapped them over her mouth. Her shoulders trembled and, under her hands, her lips parted to gasp for air. A better portrait of a panic-stricken maiden would be hard to find. Very fortunately her back was now toward Braybrook, as she faced into the hall. He did not see the unquenchable laughter in her eyes.

"Snakes!" the maid shrieked, "Snakes! Snakes!"

At that point, Joanna yielded. She too shrieked, uttering one single muffled whoop as she fled the hall. Inside her own chamber, to which Edwina had tactfully closed the door, she laughed in peace. "God," she gasped to Edwina, "helps those who help themselves."

It was her mother's favorite dictum, repeated so often that Joanna frequently said it herself without really thinking about the words. The meaning was now abundantly clear, however. Joanna could arrange the poisoning of her guests, but it was God's hand that made the effects first apparent in her own servants in Sir Henry's presence. He would never, never doubt that the illness which afflicted his men was an accident. Even if he should realize some time in the future how convenient it was for Joanna that a debilitating disease should strike at that moment, he would never question the accidental nature of the disorder. First impressions are very lasting. Because he saw Joanna's servants stricken first, he would never wonder about the relative number who fell ill—all of his men and so few of Joanna's people.

For a little while, a wild disorder raged in Roselynde. The sane struggled and reasoned with the mad. Very soon, however, moans of a different tenor began to replace the shrieks of fear induced by hallucination. Men and women staggered from the castle into the bailey tearing at their clothes between spasms of vomiting. Unreal creatures and phantoms still crawled through the minds of the afflicted, but their bodies were too racked with discomfort for them to run or fight. They sobbed and whimpered, but they did neither themselves nor anyone else any harm.

Joanna closed the door to her women's quarters and would permit no one to enter or leave. When Braybrook came to remonstrate with her, she cried through the door that she feared contamination. Also through the door she gave direction that the afflicted should be removed from the keep and cared for in sheds in the bailey and that the keep should be most thoroughly cleaned by those servants who had not been stricken. At dusk, the troop of men who had been sent out returned to help carry the sick in out of the rain and to distribute cloaks and blankets to keep them warm.

By supper time, peace reigned in Roselynde again. One could not hear the moans and cries of the afflicted through the walls. Sir Henry again approached the women's quarters, and this time he was able to induce Joanna to come out. Over and over he assured her that what had stricken her people was no disease. It was the result of bad bread, he said. He had seen the like himself in France. In certain cases a red, rusty color came over stored grain and, if this grain were ground and used as bread, just such a madness and sickness as attacked Joanna's people would follow. If she ate no bread, he assured her, she would be safe.

Doubtfully, often shaken by tremblings during which she hid her face, Joanna came forth. She sat at the table upon which a supper of pasties, cheese, cold meat, and wine was ready, but she did not touch the food. All she did was plead with Braybrook to leave the castle with her at once. He remonstrated that it was already dark and, in any case, he could not go. He did not have a single man capable of sitting a horse or trustworthy not to attack his nearest companion when, suddenly, he saw an extra green eye appear on the man's forehead or horns sprout from his head.

"My men are fit. You have given order that no bread be eaten until new grain is brought in, have you not? Then, if what you say is true, they will not fall ill. I will not stay here. I am afraid." Joanna's voice rose to a thin cry of terror and her hands fluttered uncontrollably. "I am afraid," she repeated, panting in her effort to suppress another burst of untimely mirth. "I will not eat or drink anything at all tonight or tomorrow morn. Before the prime, I will go with my men. If you do not come with me, you are cruel. I am afraid."

With that, Joanna fled again to consume (in the privacy of her chamber) cold goose, roast pork, and large slabs of delicate manchet bread washed down by copious draughts of sweet wine. When, presumably, she had been soothed to sleep, Edwina stole down to Sir Henry's bed to gossip about the foolish timidity of her mistress and then to engage him in a far more interesting activity. Not long after this absorbing play began, the "sleeper" crept silently down the stairs and out into the bailey. Knud and Beorn, on the watch, came to her at once. She asked first how the sufferers were progressing. No one had died, she was told, nor was likely to. The visions were decreasing in intensity, but bowels were still gravely disordered.

"Good," Joanna replied unsympathetically, although she was relieved that there had been no deaths. Let the cooks prepare the 'medicinal' draught I ordered—but only Sir Henry's men are to be given that. Our people must have an infusion of chamomile and pennyroyal. It will be just as bitter but do more good. And if any think it strange that our people mend while the others do not, let the answer be that our people are better accustomed to the air and water here, which are tainted by the sea."

"How long are they to be kept disordered?" Beorn asked.

"Tomorrow and the day after. Then they are to be given the chamomile and pennyroyal. It will take them another day or two to recover enough to ride. By then I will be well out of their reach.''

"Who goes with you, lady?''

"The fifty chosen and, I think, both you and Knud, Beorn. Sir Giles will be here tomorrow by evensong, as I guess. Until then, Cedricsson may hold the keep. He need do no more than pull up the drawbridge and keep it up, allowing no man to enter for any reason until Sir Giles comes. That will be safe enough.''

CHAPTER SIX

When Lady Joanna left Roselynde the next morning, Brian ran beside her stirrup on one side and Braybrook rode beside her on the other and the troop that rode behind them was her own. After visiting his men, Sir Henry acknowledged they were in no condition to walk, much less to ride or guard anything. His mood was not of the best, but Lady Joanna was as sunny and good humored as could be in spite of a cold, persistent drizzle. She said again and again how happy she was to escape the keep where such a frightening sickness had come and how much she was looking forward to a gay time with the queen and her ladies.

Gradually, under the influence of Joanna's persistent cheerfulness and pleasant conversation, Braybrook grew pacified. Even when they had a difference of opinion about the route, he did not relapse into ill humor. He had wanted to ride north to Oxford and then northeast to Whitechurch. Joanna protested that, since they were riding generally northeast, she would like to visit Lady Ela at Salisbury. Sir Henry complained that the route through Salisbury was longer and less safe, but not with much conviction and he yielded readily when Joanna said that Lady Ela was her foster mother and she had not seen her for some time.

This easy compliance convinced Joanna that either Braybrook was indeed innocent of any plot against her, if there ever had been such a plot, or that the substitution of her troop for his had made whatever plan he had unworkable. She leaned toward the former notion more and more as they progressed because of the lightness of Sir Henry's spirit. He was, in her opinion, a silly man, but harmless. A long but uneventful ride broken by several pleasant, if damp, rest periods brought them to Salisbury to dry out and spend the night. Lady Ela was most suitably surprised by their arrival in public. She was also, when alone with Joanna in the women's quarters, quite reassuring. It did not seem possible, Lady Ela stated, that John should wish to harm Joanna or would choose this moment. She looked thoughtful when Joanna explained her reasoning, but still shook her head.

"I am quite sure he does *not* want Ian here, and nothing would bring Ian home faster than hearing you were missing." Ela smiled at Joanna's indignant expression. "John will never acknowledge Ian's abilities, but he does understand his care for his men. He thinks he will be able to use them as he likes because Geoffrey is leading. He underestimates Geoffrey."

"I hope so," Joanna said with sudden sharpness, her eyes clear and very bright. "That had not occurred to me," she murmured. "How fortunate that Isabella invited me."

Ela looked horrified. "Whatever do you mean?" she asked uneasily. "Surely you do not intend to interfere with the war plans. You do not intend to go to the camp! I am sure it would not be permitted."

"Who will stop me?" Joanna flushed, looking for that one instant so much like her mother despite the difference in coloring and feature that Ela gasped. In a moment, however, she had recovered the mask of a sweet maid. "No, I will not go to the field—not unless it becomes necessary— but I will pay close attention to the gentlemen who come from there and to what they say. Moreover, it will be fitting that I send Beorn to see and speak to his old companions."

"Do you not trust Geoffrey?" Ela asked a little stiffly.

Joanna's eyes flicked up at her once and were demurely lowered again. "As much as my mother trusts Ian," she replied.

With that, Lady Ela was at first content, but somewhere within her was a small core of uneasiness that grew and grew. After Joanna and her escort had left the next day, that sentence returned again and again to Ela's mind. Alinor trusted Ian—yes. If he told her to jump off a cliff or that he wished to open her veins with a knife and drink her blood, Alinor would jump at his word or docilely extend her arm to be cut. Her confidence that he would do nothing to hurt her personally was immeasurable and absolute. However, in the matter of the management of the estates—how much *did* Alinor trust Ian? She sat justice in all her own honors, and if she could not go—as when she was too near her time of delivery—she sent Joanna with Ian. She said it was so that the people would come to know her daughter, but was that all?

In war, Alinor was less self-assertive, but that depended upon circumstances. When Ian was leading the vassals in a private quarrel, Alinor paid no attention to what he did. She became alert only when Ian was part of a larger force, and she made no bones about saying to Ela that "his accursed lunatic honor would ruin them all some day." Ela sighed heavily. There could be no doubt that *that* was what Joanna meant. She was afraid that Geoffrey would be maneuvered by appeals to his honor into some situation that would hold more danger than was reasonable.

"But what can she do?" Ela asked herself pettishly. Then she sighed again. Only God knew what any of those Roselynde women would do when a stick or a stitch of theirs was threatened. Had not Alinor gathered an army to assault a castle when Ian was held prisoner in it some years ago? In the end she had not led the assault, but Ela did not doubt she would have done so if necessary. And Joanna, although no one would believe her when she warned them, was even worse. Joanna was much quieter, but much, much stubborner.

Ela sighed yet again and languidly lifted a hand to summon a maid. She did not want to go to Whitechurch. She never could bear to be near where William was fighting. That turned her mind to Alinor and Joanna again. Ela remembered how Alinor had sat, apparently unmoved, through two days of a tourney in which her husband had nearly been killed. Doubtless Joanna would do the same.

Ela had never seen Salisbury fight. That was true even though she had once attended a tourney in which he had participated. She had fainted before his first joust and then become so hysterical—the one and only real attack of hysteria she had ever had—that it was necessary to carry her from the field.

They will not really be fighting near, she comforted herself. Wales, specially Gwenydd, was many miles west of Whitechurch. And I am older now and not so silly, she murmured to herself. The assurances did little to ease her fear and distaste, but she could not allow a conflict to arise between Geoffrey and Joanna that would ruin their lives and, in spite of being convinced that nothing like abduction or imprisonment threatened Joanna, Ela did not understand the queen's invitation. Usually Isabella was harmless, but she could be spiteful. For everyone but herself, Ela knew, it was best that she be in Whitechurch. Resignedly, she gave instruction to the maid she had summoned.

Henry de Braybrook had never had so pleasant a journey in his life. He had been dreading it ever since the queen had sent for him and given him the task of escorting Lady Joanna. He had envisioned the multiple horrors of dealing with a frightened, uncertain girl who would constantly be too hot or too cold or too wet, a long train of baggage wains, which would constantly be mired on the muddy roads, and total boredom. Then, although it seemed at first as if even greater, unexpected horrors would afflict him, everything began to work out right. Edwina had been the first pleasant surprise. Then the sickness in the castle had convinced Lady Joanna to leave without the slightest protest or delay. Best of all, he had never met a hardier lady nor one more accustomed to travel. Although it rained every day, she never uttered a complaint. And she was a lively and interesting companion once she had gotten over her first timidity.

It was too bad, he thought, his eyes running over her once again, that she was already betrothed and he married. She was an exquisite piece and would be as rich as Croesus. Had

he known her before, he would have— Well, that was useless to think of; the property was certainly beyond his reach,
but the girl might not be. Just now no romance would advance very far. She was not yet bold enough or experienced
enough to think of abandoning her virginity before marriage. Afterwards, however, it might be another matter entirely. Some of the seemingly shrinking violets at court had
more than one lover on a string. Sir Henry sighed with pleasure. It was the best of all possible situations. He wooed the
lady during the day and worked off his frustrations on the
maid at night. And the maid was clearly a light-skirts. Edwina cared only for the futtering itself, not for him. Soon
her attention would wander and they would part on excellent
terms; then she might be a key to the mistress.

Joanna was as delighted with the journey as Sir Henry.
Although she retained a seed of suspicion, she was no
longer frightened. Lady Ela's reassurances and her own rea-
sonings indicated that there could be no overt threat. Like
Lady Ela, she did not understand the purpose of the queen's
invitation, unless—could Geoffrey have asked for her? That
was a delightful notion, but not to be dwelt upon. Caution,
great caution, was to be observed in dealing with Isabella.
Meanwhile, however, surrounded by her own men and
guarded by Brian, Joanna was enjoying herself. Braybrook
was a most pleasant companion and, best of all, not a very
astute one. Without realizing it, he was telling her a great
deal about the court and, equally without realizing it, he was
being hurried toward Whitechurch at a rate that few armed
troops could match.

Joanna's messenger had found the earl of Salisbury at the
abbey in Whitechurch and had delivered the message. From
there he had been sent out of the town, several miles away
to where the army was encamped. Geoffrey had chosen to
stay at the camp. This served a double purpose. It permitted
him to become better acquainted with his men and it kept
him clear of the king and queen. Salisbury approved the first
purpose heartily; he recognized the unspoken second and,

although he regretted the necessity, he acknowledged its wisdom.

Geoffrey, however, was not at the camp. The messenger missed him by only a few hours. He had ridden out with some of the vassals and a small troop to examine the terrain. The party was out four days and three nights and, altogether, it was a very successful trip. Geoffrey learned which men were flexible and intelligent, which stubborn with fixed ideas; he learned which men spoke glibly but did not see a problem, which grasped the significance of what they observed. As he listened and spoke to the men, Geoffrey vowed again and again that when Ian came back from Ireland, he would kneel down and kiss his mentor's feet. He remembered how often he had been impatient with his lord when Ian had lectured him on the meaning of this or that. Now, more and more often, Ian's voice would echo in his mind while a man spoke or after he spoke, and Geoffrey would see something significant behind the spoken words.

The men learned a great deal, too. The older vassals gained confidence in the foresight and earnest application to duty of their young leader. They were pleased by the attentiveness with which he listened to their advice and the politeness with which he reasoned against it when he did not accept it. The older men were less concerned with Geoffrey's absolute fighting skills than with his ability to see and avoid positions or assignments that were impossible. No one doubted Geoffrey's personal courage and, as for the rest, Sir Alfred of Ealand, Sir Walter of the Forstal, Sir Henry of Kingsclere were confident that they could support their battle leader so that, even if he were no Achilles or Ajax, he would do well enough.

The younger vassals were less interested in Geoffrey's administrative virtues. They knew him, until this meeting, exclusively as Lord Ian's squire. In battle they knew he supported his master bravely, although in battle Lord Ian did not need much in the way of support. Socially, they knew him not at all. The occasions when the vassals and castellans were called together were formal and Geoffrey had had rigid duties which kept him essentially apart from the knights. And, although they had all met on a more equal footing at Geoffrey's betrothal, he had spent most of his time closeted with Lord Ian and his father.

Now they discovered that Geoffrey was a very merry companion. He liked a sup of wine as well as the next man—and had a hard head for it; he liked a pretty girl as well as the next man—and did not worry overmuch about sin. Sir John of Mersea, Sir Robert de Remy, who held Telsey, and young Sir Giles of Iford decided they were going to enjoy this campaign.

All returned to camp in the best of good humors, the older men to eat and then stretch out on their camp beds which, if not equal to the soft feather beds of home, were a good deal better than the plain ground they had been sleeping on. The younger men were also thinking of bodily comforts, but not of sleep. Having picked out the cleanest of the camp whores, they had a rather loud party. Geoffrey's lute was tuned to a more raucous note and a livelier measure than "Stella Maris," and the women danced—with less and less clothing to obscure their movements as the late afternoon darkened into the long summer dusk.

Joanna's messenger had caught Geoffrey when he first rode into camp, but, having heard how quickly the man had come and that his father had already been informed, Geoffrey put the matter out of his mind temporarily. For one thing, he did not expect Joanna for at least another week; baggage carts moved slowly even when the roads were good and the rain of the past weeks would have turned them into a muddy mire. For another, Geoffrey was a little resentful. He knew it was not Joanna's fault, but her presence in Whitechurch would be a nuisance. It would oblige him to spend a good deal of his time at court. This would spoil his plans for completing his knowledge of the men he was leading and expose him to the constant pinpricks of Isabella's tongue.

Worst of all, it suddenly came to Geoffrey that Joanna would now be intimately associated with the ladies in his past. Although none of those was nursing a broken heart, several of them had loose tongues and at least one was a vicious bitch who would positively joy in betraying him to his betrothed. What the devil was he going to do about that? Of course, it was none of Joanna's business, and he could tell her that. He had not been betrothed to her then. Still, he would have preferred— He had been a fool. He should have stuck to the paid whores who did not rise up and intrude themselves into a man's life after he was through with them. That would teach him to be so fine and object to a little dirt. Better lice and stench than a mouth spitting venom. No more fine ladies, Geoffrey vowed. He would have Joanna soon enough, and until then he would take his amusement where it was safe to do so.

Under the circumstances, the lady of greensleeves Geoffrey had chosen was treated less casually than usual, and when the other young men were gone he told her to take off the rest of her clothes and began to divest himself of his own. The girl was a little surprised. High gentlemen usually did not bother with nakedness for her kind—the quicker the better for them, like taking a piss—but she was willing and unafraid. These four were gentlemen, only desiring a little natural fun. There were other ''gentlemen'' who used a girl of her profession for very queer pleasures they could not take with their wives or noble mistresses.

Just as Geoffrey was giving voice to a very bawdy tavern song, Joanna rode through the gates of Whitechurch. It took a little time to dispose of her men and arrange with Beorn that he or Knud should seek her out at irregular intervals on various specious excuses. Then she had to present herself to Isabella. The ladies looked very oddly at the huge dog that paced beside Joanna, but the beast was quiet and foolishly friendly and no one made any comment about it. Isabella only told Joanna, with a sly smile, that Geoffrey was not staying there; he had chosen the greater freedom of the camp. With an unmoved expression, Joanna asked for permission to inform Salisbury of her arrival. Obligingly, still smiling, Isabella gestured at a boy who was close by to carry the message. The boy, young and uncertain, had spilled the whole tale, and Salisbury, having bitten back the comment that sprang to his tongue concerning the queen's ancestry and character, then told the page to ride out to the camp and tell Geoffrey that his lady was come.

Half an hour later, the child was back in tears. He could not come near Lord Geoffrey, he explained. The lord and some friends were making merry, very merry. He had been afraid to intrude on their pleasure, and it did not sound to him as if the party would soon end. Salisbury looked with blank amazement at the trembling child, opening his mouth to blast him for such stupidity. Messages did not wait upon the end of pleasuring. Then he recalled to himself where the boy had been trained. Messages—and sometimes matters of far graver import than this boy carried—certainly did wait on the end of pleasuring in this court. With a resounding oath, Salisbury dismissed the frightened page, telling him to hold his tongue if he did not want it cut out, and strode off to the stables. So delicate and innocent a lady as Joanna must not be offended with such information nor must she be hurt by the absence of her betrothed husband at the dancing that evening.

Tostig of Hemel, Geoffrey's master-at-arms, caught the reins of Salisbury's horse as the earl swung off his mount a few yards from Geoffrey's tent. "My lord—" he cried urgently.

Salisbury thrust him aside ungently with an irritable grunt.

"But—" Tostig offered, following him a few steps.

Then he shrugged and fell back as Salisbury glared at him. He had tried. The father and son were on the best of terms and there was no serious wrong in what Lord Geoffrey was doing. It would not be the first time a father had learned his son was a man in all ways. He watched Salisbury duck under the tent flap, grinned and retreated.

"Get out of there and get dressed," the earl roared.

Geoffrey rose off the whore and onto his feet in as neat a

piece of levitation as Salisbury had seen in a long time. "What? What?" he gasped, groping for his sword before his eyes focused on the interruption.

As he looked at his son, Salisbury's irritation evaporated. Geoffrey was a most personable young man, even now with his eyes dazed, his hair lank, and sweat beading on his shoulders and trickling through the sparse hair on his chest and belly.

"Father!" Geoffrey exclaimed, "What it is? What is wrong?" And before the earl could answer, he shouted, "Tostig, my arms!"

"No," Salisbury said, "Court dress."

"Court—? Court dress?"

It was clear enough at this moment that Geoffrey's mind was still thrall to his thwarted body. Salisbury made an effort and did not laugh. He would not have been pleased, when he was Geoffrey's age, to be laughed at in a similar situation. In fact, he thought, he would not be overpleased if it happened right now. That notion was irresistible, and Salisbury did grin. It was a mistake. Geoffrey's face became suffused with color and his eyes lightened to gleam golden as a wolf's.

"No," he snarled. "I do not care to come to heel like a tame dog at the king's whim. If there is business, I will come at a reasonable hour tomorrow."

"It is nothing to do with John," Salisbury replied a little stiffly. "Joanna rode in just before vespers."

"Joanna!" Geoffrey exclaimed, his color diminishing, "It is impossible. Her messenger came only—"

"Impossible or not impossible, she is here."

A string of heartfelt obscenities trickled slowly out of Geoffrey's mouth, but when Tostig came in with his mail he said to his man, "Never mind my armor. Get me something decent to wear. I must ride to court."

The relief in the young master-at-arms's face was hidden as he bent over the chests of clothing. He knew just how much wine his lord had swallowed and he had been wondering what he would do if his master was so far gone that he wished to come to blows with his own father. Lord Geoffrey was not usually touchy, but the circumstances were not exactly an everyday occurrence.

Meanwhile, Geoffrey had looked vaguely at the whore, who had rolled hastily off the cot and was now crouched at the far side of the tent. He held out a hand toward his father. "Have you a purse? Give me some money. I—I do not know where—"

Salisbury fingered out the two smallest coins in his purse and pressed them into Geoffrey's palm. The young man walked across to the crouching woman, who, image of fear though she was, still held up a cupped hand. Geoffrey dropped the coins in and told her indifferently to get dressed and go, adding that there was nothing to fear. Then he swung his head back toward his father and blinked owlishly. "I am drunk," he announced.

"Then you will be no different than half the other men at court. Can you sit a horse?"

Geoffrey drew himself up with great dignity, which was a little marred by his nakedness and by an enormous hiccup. "That is a ridiculous question. I have never been so drunk that I could not sit a horse."

"May such abstemiousness long prevail," Salisbury replied drily and went to help Tostig dress him.

Now that the shock that had briefly sobered Geoffrey was receding, Salisbury could see that his son was, indeed, "well to live." He was not unduly worried. The ride in the cooling night air would doubtless sober him considerably, enough anyway to behave respectably. If not, he could take Geoffrey to his own chamber first and apply some rough and ready measures. It seemed, however, that Geoffrey had spoken the truth as far as his ability to ride—if not to mount. Tostig had to hold him upright, fit his foot into the stirrup, and hike him aloft while Salisbury grinned. But once in the saddle, Geoffrey was steady enough.

The father did not mind. He was rather pleased. Like most sons, Geoffrey kept his peccadillos within his own age group, presenting to his parent and his elders in general an appearance of good behavior. That was ordinary enough, but Geoffrey had had a mischievous, amused, and very experienced mentor in Lord Ian, who had preached to such an effect that Geoffrey was unusually discreet. This skill at concealment had made Salisbury worry a bit about the boy becoming a virtuous prig. It was plain, however, that there was no danger of that. What worried Salisbury at the moment was the frown that was growing between Geoffrey's brows.

"Your head aches, boy?" he remarked at last.

Geoffrey did not answer so obvious an invitation to say what was bothering him directly. Instead, he said, "You did say that Joanna was come, did you not?"

"Yes. I thought it unwise that you should not ride in to say a word of greeting when the distance is so short. Women take to weeping over very foolish things."

Again Geoffrey did not reply directly to what his father said. The frown grew deeper. "There were no pages in the court to carry this message? What of Peter or Gervase or Philip?"

The latter three were Salisbury's squires. When Geoffrey named them, Salisbury looked surprised. He could have sent one of them—Gervase or Philip who were older anyway—he simply had not thought of it. What was more important to him, however, was the trend of Geoffrey's thoughts. Some way, Geoffrey was accounting Salisbury's coming to poor John's discredit. Hastily, Salisbury told the story of the page who dared not interrupt the party. The frown smoothed out somewhat and Geoffrey smiled, but the curl of his lips showed contempt also. No one liked to be interrupted by business in the midst of pleasure—who should know better than himself at this moment—but the man or woman who would punish the message bringer for such an interruption was a churl. And the man or woman who would allow the delay in imparting information to become the custom of his servants was a fool as well.

That thought was nothing new in Geoffrey's mind. By habit, he pushed away the bitter knowledge that England was ruled by a man who was a churl and a fool. There was no one else, he reminded himself, repeating the litany that Ian had taught him. Many times that litany had saved him from irremediable words and acts. Now it permitted him to turn his mind to a different puzzle. After contemplating the dates dizzily for a few minutes, he unwisely shook his head, winced, and lifted a hand to his temple.

"Father, I make it four days—Joanna rode here from Roselynde in four days. Am I so drunk I cannot count, or is that true?"

"I did not speak to her," Salisbury replied, starting to frown himself, "but that does seem too short a time unless there was some reason for great haste and even then how could a woman endure such fatigue?"

Geoffrey paid no attention to that last question, which was rhetorical anyway. He had grown very fond of his stepmother over the past few years, and he did not make disparaging comparisons between her and Lady Alinor. Nonetheless, it never occurred to Geoffrey that women in general were frail. With Lady Alinor as the principal example in his life, he assumed that women who could not do anything a man could—save bear arms and set seed into a woman's belly—were either stupid or willfully weak. Now that he was sobering, he realized that Joanna must have moved without baggage, as Alinor often did. His concern was not for his betrothed's physical well-being but for the necessity that had driven her.

"I will not return to camp tonight," Geoffrey said. "Can I bed down with you, father?"

"You are very welcome, my son, but why?" Salisbury asked, grinning.

"I want to talk to Joanna—"

"Talk?" Salisbury teased more openly.

Geoffrey did not even seem aware of the obvious implication. "If she has some reason for flying at such speed from Roselynde, I want to hear it in private—and I do not wish to raise talk by dragging her off tonight."

Salisbury was silent. Geoffrey's businesslike tone was

bothering him. He had not been surprised when Geoffrey cursed at the news of Joanna's arrival. He assumed Geoffrey would have cursed at that moment at the information that he had been given a great fortune. Now that the shock was over, however, it seemed to him that Geoffrey should display more enthusiasm. Joanna was so lovely that she could raise enthusiasm—and something else—in a pillar of salt, yet Geoffrey seemed interested only in the practical aspects of her arrival.

In this, Salisbury did not take into consideration Geoffrey's relationship with the queen. Salisbury had never liked Isabella, not only because of her spite toward himself but more because he realized she would do nothing to help John. She did have some influence with her husband because he liked to please her and to make her smile, but Isabella would not even play the traditional role of a queen as a healer and peacemaker. Never once had she raised her voice or bent her knee to mitigate a punishment or soften an exaction. On the other hand, Salisbury neither hated nor feared Isabella. He knew she did not trouble herself with political affairs and, in general, she was too self-centered even to feel much personal spite. Her animosity toward himself he discounted completely, knowing quite well that John could not be influenced against him.

What Salisbury forgot was that Geoffrey, knowing the same things, did not react emotionally the same way. It was a boy of nine, already much disturbed by the death of his grandfather and the breakup of his home that Isabella had nearly destroyed. The scars remained. Despite the fact that Geoffrey now knew Isabella was vain, shallow, and stupid, that she was unable to do any real harm, he could not help crediting her with a sort of malign power. When the queen was involved in anything relating to him, it took on a black aspect and was bound, in his opinion, to come to a bad end. He could not, therefore, think of her invitation to Joanna in any way except that it would bring trouble that he must somehow circumvent.

This foreboding, added to a splitting headache, generated

by the injudicious imbibing of a considerable quantity of rather poor quality wine and a lack of opportunity to sleep off its effects, did not produce the best of humors. Geoffrey strode into the hall with two vertical creases in his brow between his eyes and a rather set mouth. As they entered, the music for a dance measure ended and the regimented lines of men and women broke into a chaotic mass, which immediately began to resort itself into groups. Geoffrey glanced slowly around and then made his way toward a rather large group that seemed to be composed exclusively of young men. Salisbury, about to protest that Geoffrey should seek out Joanna and not begin another convivial party, smiled instead. As one of the young men bent forward to kiss a hand, Salisbury caught a glimpse of a jeweled headdress and a bright flash of gray eyes. Geoffrey's instinct had been unerring. The center of the group of men was Joanna.

Preliminary pipings and lute notes indicated that a new dance was about to begin as Geoffrey reached the group. Henry de Braybrook, who had kissed Joanna's hand, was saying, "This dance is mine, Lady Joanna," with all the authority of a gentleman certain of his reception.

"No," Geoffrey growled, "it is mine and so is the woman."

Joanna cast Geoffrey one single flashing glance of affront, then curtsied low and bent her head.

"Your manners, sir, are of the gutter," Braybrook said stiffly.

"You are mistaken again," Geoffrey retorted, "they are of the camp—the same as yours should be but are not. And do not bother to try to insult me. The king will not permit any quarrel between us here and now. I have more serious business in a day or two. When I come back from Wales, try me again."

"Geoffrey—" Engelard d'Atie remonstrated.

Geoffrey glanced at him but said nothing. Instead, he turned to Joanna. "Do you really wish to dance, Joanna?" he asked, but not as if he wanted to know. The tone demanded a negative answer. "My head is splitting," he added.

"No, my lord. As you please, my lord," Joanna murmured softly.

"Come away from this noise then," Geoffrey said, and offered his hand formally.

Joanna curtsied generally to the group of young men and laid her fingers delicately on Geoffrey's wrist. He led her quickly toward an empty window-seat embrasure where, as soon as small movements and low speech could not be distinguished by anyone whose eyes had followed them, Joanna dug her long, well-sharpened nails viciously into the hand supporting hers. Geoffrey bit back an exclamation and snatched his hand away. A few drops of red showed on the skin. There was surprising strength in the long, slender, white fingers.

"Your manners are rather of the sty than of the gutter," Joanna hissed, smiling sweetly all the time. "Those of the gutter are at least human. Do not dare use me so in public when I cannot, for shame of my reputation, defend myself."

"How else was I to remove you from that crowd of rutting stags?" Geoffrey snarled, and then, before she could answer, "For God's sake, hold your tongue. My head is really splitting."

"And I can tell why. You stink of sour wine. Why did you not stay where you were and sleep it off?"

"Because my father came to drag me here, lest your ladyship be offended by my absence."

"I am more offended by your presence!"

"I will not long inflict it upon you. Is there some danger I must know of? What brought you flying here in four days?"

Joanna's anger was diminishing. In the balance between the indifference implied by Salisbury's need to "drag" Geoffrey to greet her and the naked jealousy of his action and his reference to "rutting stags," the jealousy was clearly dominant. The fixed smile on Joanna's lips became more natural, displaying a genuine and growing amusement. Geoffrey, after all, did not need to be jealous. Her lands and her person were already his. Since no action of hers could deprive him of the lands, it could only be her person of which he was jealous. Moreover, she approved heartily of the quick wit that suspected danger in Isabella's invitation. Her message had held no details, only the fact of the invitation and her intention to obey it. Although the messenger had been told to be secret, Joanna would not take the chance of writing either her fears or the truth. Messages could go mysteriously astray, especially at a royal court.

"Let us sit down," she said more pleasantly, and then, unable to resist teasing, "or should we move closer to the garderobe? You are growing quite green."

"Sit, by all means. You must be weary after so much dancing. And please leave me to the management of my own complexion. Joanna, I am not in the humor for jesting. If there is something you must tell me, then tell it to me quickly. I do not wish to give a reason for suspicion of our conferring together."

Joanna giggled. "You have given safe reason enough for that. Do but lean closer—only do not breathe on me or you will make me drunk too—and whatever suspicion wakes will be only of your jealousy. It was a wise thing to do, Geoffrey. I am sorry I scratched you."

Since Geoffrey's action had had no intentional wisdom in it, he was little enough pleased by Joanna's interpretation and merely grunted irritably at her. However, he did sit down beside her and lean close. Joanna turned her head away a trifle, as a young woman with hurt feelings and too much timidity to quarrel might do. It made an effective picture, shielded her from Geoffrey's breath, and permitted her to watch the room all at the same time.

"I do not know that there is any danger," Joanna said seriously, "but I do not understand why Isabella should send for me."

"Nor I, and I do not like it. I do not like it at all. Could you not have made some excuse for disobeying?"

"It was my first thought, but from Sir Henry's manner and answers to my protests, I saw that no excuse would be tolerated. It was better to make a virtue of necessity and hide my fears and suspicions."

"That is true. Sir Henry—which Sir Henry? There are twenty at least."

"Braybrook."

"Oh, that—" Geoffrey's eyes hardened. "Did he attempt you? Was that why you hurried? To be rid of him?"

"To be rid of him, yes, but not through any fault of his behavior to me."

Joanna paused a moment and struggled with herself. It was true there had not been any overt "fault" in Braybrook's behavior, but Joanna was not unaware that during the journey he had indeed been eating her with his eyes. The impulse to tease Geoffrey was enormous. After all, she was accustomed to teasing him; they had been children together. But she realized that there was no longer anything laughable in this form of teasing. Geoffrey was no longer her child-friend. He was a man, and the thought came suddenly to her that he was dangerous. She turned her head quickly to look at him. Perhaps his pallor came from too much wine, but his eyes were not those of a drunken man. They glowed a clear amber—hot.

"It had nothing to do with Sir Henry personally," Joanna repeated hastily, and embarked on the story of the escort Braybrook had brought for her and, in a low murmur, what had befallen them. She was relieved to see the set expression on Geoffrey's face relax and his lips begin to twitch with suppressed laughter.

"Joanna," he protested, "you might have killed them, and half the castle folk too."

"Oh no," she replied confidently. "You know my mother is a most excellent physician and I am also. I knew what I did. There was the reason for my haste. I was sure that they would ride hard to overtake us when they were recovered. I did not wish either to have the company of so strong a troop of men who would not obey me nor to need to find reasons to keep my own troop with us after they came up with us. Now I have my men here and Beorn and Knud seek me out in turns at this time and that time. Thus, a watch is kept upon me. And, of course, Brian is here. He is chained to my bed above with my clothes and jewels to guard since I did not want him cavorting about on the dance floor.

"I see you have taken all care that is needful."

Geoffrey's voice was surprisingly so discontented that Joanna glanced at him again. She had mostly been watching the room while she spoke, not wishing to make such a confession if anyone could overhear. His eyes were downcast this time, and his face told her nothing.

"I hope so," she answered. "Is there something in this that displeases you?"

"Yes! No, I mean, no, your care is well thought of and reasonable. It displeases me that you are here altogether. No, I do not mean that either, Joanna. I mean—Joanna, in heaven's name—"

She had covered her face, and her shoulders were heaving, but, before Geoffrey could offer comfort, her fingers parted enough so that he could see she was laughing. "Do you know what you mean?" she whispered.

"Yes, and so do you, you devil," Geoffrey growled. He bent his head closer. "You may laugh all you like, but it is true I am not glad to have you here. It will be expected that I dance attendance upon you, and I should be with my men."

"Of course you should be with the men." Joanna's eyes widened. "Do you think it was to draw you away from them that I was summoned here? Can there be some plan to cause disaffection—"

"No, that is too far-fetched, and I think all the men too firm in their loyalty." There was a pause. Geoffrey cleared his throat and sat up straighter. "Then you do not want me here?"

"Not at all," Joanna concurred heartily. "In fact, you will get dreadfully in my way."

"What?"

Momentarily, she lifted her eyes to his and her face was completely grave. "Oh Geoffrey, do not be a fool. I do not forget our parting in Roselynde garden, but since I was called here against my will, I would be an idiot to lose the opportunity to discover which way the winds of rumor blow at court. The king talks to Cantelu and to Braybrook—and I talk to the sons. But they will not talk to me if you come dragging me away by the arm or glowering at us across the room. No man will be able to talk to me in your presence. To look at the eyes you had in your head when you came for me could dry the spittle in any man's mouth."

"But not in yours, it seems." His eyes were golden with rage again, but Joanna met them fearlessly.

"No," she said drily, "not in mine." Then her expression softened. "If I have fears, they are for you, not of you, Geoffrey."

He did not appear to have heard that oblique confession of tenderness. "Do you expect me to agree to this?" he snarled.

Joanna blushed fiery red and her eyes shone palely. "I do not care whether you do or not. If the king intends more or less than he avows openly, I must know it so that I can shield my men. That is my first duty, and I will do it without regard to your liking or misliking."

Geoffrey's hands clenched into fists, and he became so pale that Joanna feared he would forget where he was and strike her. She swallowed her own chagrin and placed her hands over his.

"Do not be a fool," she urged. "I am betrothed to you. I swear I will bring you a clean body and a clean heart. Do not waste your time thinking of my doings. They will never be such as can bring shame upon you. I know my duty to you also, Geoffrey."

He stood up precipitately. "I hope you do," he said loudly, and walked away.

CHAPTER SEVEN

It was fortunate that in the next few minutes Geoffrey found his father and found him temporarily disengaged from company. Salisbury had watched his son at first, but when he saw him draw Joanna out of the crowd around her and hustle her away into privacy, he grinned. Apparently Geoffrey's businesslike attitude had lasted until the moment he laid eyes upon the beautiful girl. So much for his desire to avoid talk and not to drag her off. Satisfied, Salisbury sought out Aubery de Vere with whom he wanted to talk. Richard Marsh found them together a few minutes later and made an announcement that drew surprised protests from both. Richard shrugged his shoulders. He had already remonstrated with the king. Marsh then excused himself to Salisbury and asked de Vere a question about a private matter, which they turned aside to discuss, leaving Salisbury to think over Marsh's announcement.

"You were greatly mistaken in thinking Lady Joanna desired my company," Geoffrey said bitterly, breaking into his father's troubled thoughts. "She—"

"Lower your voice," Salisbury hissed. "Do you think the whole world except me is deaf?"

He was about to add a sharp remark to the effect that men whose judgment was addled by wine should stay clear of it, but the fault was his own. Geoffrey had been drunk, but he had chosen his time and place appropriately enough. If Salisbury had not dragged him off to court, no harm could have come of the indulgence. The trouble was, Salisbury thought, that he had been fooled. Geoffrey did not look drunk by the time they dismounted. Instead of being annoyed, he was aware of pride. The boy carried his wine

112

well. In fact, except for his pallor and the strident voice, he did not look or act drunk now. But he must be. He must have said something or done something to offend Joanna. Well, that could be mended easily enough, but not if Geoffrey went sulking back to camp.

"It is as well that you decided to stay," Salisbury began.

"There is no need for that now," Geoffrey interrupted. "I am going back to camp."

"Oh no, you are not, or—I do not care if you do, so long as you return here for lauds. There will be a war council as soon as we have heard mass."

"At sunrise?" Geoffrey protested, putting a hand to his throbbing head.

A shadow passed over his father's face, but all he said was, "Yes, the king is eager to be at the Welsh already."

"I know," Geoffrey replied drily.

The camp had sustained several visits from their royal leader. The last one had been the immediate motivation for Geoffrey's little jaunt into Wales. John had criticized the lack of oxen and carts in Geoffrey's preparations for the transport of supplies. To do the king justice, he had not argued when Geoffrey explained his reasons nor been unpleasant, but he had raised the question in public where the men Geoffrey would lead could hear. Ostensibly, John's visits had been to see for himself how well his vassals had responded to his summons, but Geoffrey thought privately that he did not really care. The number of mercenaries, under a skilled and ruthless but honest captain, Faulk de Bréauté, was greater than the levied troops.

Then another thought came to Geoffrey. "Did I miss that messenger too? How is it that no summons was left for me?" he bristled.

"There was no affront to you intended," Salisbury soothed, but his worried frown deepened. "No summons was sent to any of the men in the camp. Richard Marsh is just passing the word along now."

Geoffrey pressed the heels of his hands into his temples. "Do I hear you aright?" he asked uncertainly. "Did you say the king was calling a council of war and excluding all the vassals who have chosen to stay in camp with their men?''

"That was not the intention. I am sure it was not," Salisbury said, with just a shade too much emphasis.

Fire glowed in Geoffrey's eyes, and he opened his mouth—but he said nothing, merely clutched his father's forearm comfortingly. He could not add to the worry he saw on Salisbury's face. Then he glanced to the window seat where Joanna still sat quietly. Salisbury followed his eyes.

"Go back to her," he urged, "she is waiting for you."

Geoffrey uttered a bark of laughter. "You are wrong about that," he said caustically. "She is waiting for me to leave."

"For God's sake," Salisbury snapped impatiently, "go out to the garderobe and stick your finger down your throat. I will talk to Joanna. When you are sober, come back and tell the girl you are sorry for whatever you said to offend her."

"I am not drunk now," Geoffrey protested indignantly, "and I said nothing to offend Joanna."

"Then—"

"Nor did I do anything. I am greatly in her way, she tells me. She cannot talk freely to the gentlemen of the court while I 'glower' at her across the room."

"What? You are making that up, Geoffrey. Joanna would never—"

"Her motives are most pure," Geoffrey snarled. Then he realized he could not describe Joanna's motives to his father. "Oh, curse me that I ever agreed to have any part of her. All the women of that breed are devils. I am going to bed!"

Salisbury did not try to stop him. He had been a fool to interrupt Geoffrey in the middle of coupling and a worse fool to force him, drunk and unsatisfied, into the presence of a girl who would increase his frustration. Geoffrey must willfully have misunderstood something she said. He made his way toward Joanna purposefully, unaware that four other men were heading in the same direction. They hesitated, one cursing under his breath, when they saw him. To Salisbury's surprise Joanna greeted him with a broad smile.

"My lord," she murmured, "I hope you did not scold poor Geoffrey."

"Er—no. I——"

"He is full as a tick," Joanna giggled, "and he was very, very cross because I told him to go away and sleep it off."

"Is that what you said?"

"Well, I also agreed with him when he said he should be in camp with his men and not dancing with me."

Salisbury looked at his prospective daughter-by-marriage sharply. "If you knew he was drunk, why did you tease him?" he remonstrated, but he was more amused than angry.

"I did not mean it as teasing at first," she replied. "I meant only to assure him that I would not be offended by his doing his duty. In time of war, the men must come before dancing," she said seriously. Then she began to giggle again. "But when he called the gentlemen with me 'rutting stags,' I could not forbear roasting him a little." She sobered again, put a hand gently on Salisbury's. "I will make my peace with him when I next see him. Do not be angry with me."

"With you? Never, my child. It is my fault. I did not realize how drunk he was. I should have sobered him up before I brought him in here. I am glad you are so understanding about it."

"Yes. Do not trouble about me," Joanna agreed, "but—if I am not presuming, my lord—there is another who may be offended. Geoffrey was— He spoke quite rudely to Henry de Braybrook. I do not know what should be done, but—"

"Braybrook?" Salisbury's mouth tightened, but then he forced his lips into a smile. "Do not worry your head, my dear. I will make all smooth. Tell me what you have heard from Lord Ian and your mother."

"Nothing yet, my lord, except the word Geoffrey

brought me that they were safe arrived. I expect— My lord, I think Lord Oxford wants you.''

Salisbury saw that Aubery de Vere, who had freed himself from Marsh, was indeed signaling to him. He patted Joanna's shoulder and moved away quickly. The young men who had been hanging hesitantly at a distance promptly began to converge on the window seat again. Joanna smiled modestly, allowed her head to drop, but glanced up under the long, thick lashes whose dark red color gave her eyes so odd and yet so lustrous a gleam.

The young men who had been watching for their chance were not the only eyes bent upon Joanna. Queen Isabella did not like Joanna. She had decided that quite firmly soon after Joanna presented herself. It was not so much that the girl was beautiful that troubled Isabella, although she did not like rivals to her own dark perfection. Joanna was a prude and not at all amusing. Isabella rather liked Lady Alinor in spite of John's hatred of the woman. Lady Alinor said delightful things and was always most interested in Isabella's beautiful clothing and jewels. Joanna, on the other hand, was stupid and sullen. She was interested only in drawing the young men's attention to herself.

A slut, that was what Joanna was, Isabella thought, a slut who covered her nature by silence and pious mouthings. And that bastard of Salisbury's was as hot after her as all the other young fools even though he was betrothed to her. An enchanting smile touched Isabella's perfect lips. Proud as a fighting cock was Geoffrey the bastard. Well, she would abate his pride. He should have a whore for a wife. That would quench both his heat and his pride. Isabella's dark eyes shone with such beauty that her husband smiled at her. Automatically she preened, stretching her long neck and pulling in her chin to better display the exquisite line of cheek and jaw.

A delightful thought had come to Isabella. Joanna should be broached, if she still happened to be a virgin, and well used. Then if a court wedding could be arranged, the clean, dry sheets would blazon Geoffrey's shame to the whole world. A little care would be needed to make sure no trick was played, but doubtless by then rumors would be flying around the court and no one would believe the blood even if any showed.

John followed the direction of his wife's eyes and stared for a while, astounded. How had that piece of womanflesh escaped his notice? "Who is it at whom you stare?" he asked Isabella. One of the things he really appreciated about his wife was her total lack of jealousy in physical matters. So long as he did not honor the women he took to his bed, she did not care if he futtered the world.

"That is Lady Joanna—Salisbury's bastard's betrothed."

The king uttered a grunt of disappointment, and licked his lips regretfully. That was one he dared not meddle with—openly anyway. Perhaps after the Welsh campaign when the court was dispersed, something could be arranged. He would keep it in mind. It would be very amusing to take the daughter when he had once been thwarted by the mother. A quiet, meek girl, Isabella had said, with the life trampled out of her by her witch of a mother. Doubtless fear would make her hold her tongue if he could come upon her in secrecy, but if William ever found out—John would not think of that. He looked back at his wife and noted that her smile had disappeared and there was a spiteful droop to her lips. He was not sure whether for the first time a spark of jealousy had singed her or whether it was an especial spite against the girl. If the latter was true, Isabella might even be willing to help him use the daughter of the bitch as she deserved.

While she murmured demure replies to the gentlemen around her, Joanna considered the remark she had made to excuse Geoffrey's sudden departure and Salisbury's agreement with it. Although Joanna did not doubt that Geoffrey was carrying a full freight of wine, she did not think he was drunk in the sense of not knowing what he did. And he was dangerously jealous. The fool! Would she seek elsewhere when he provided safely and sinlessly everything she could want? Well, it was a nuisance, but she would have to be very, very careful that no breath of scandal should touch her name. Else it would mean dead men and danger to Geoffrey. Even if the challenges were fair, hatred would be engendered if Geoffrey went about killing men.

Having doused his head in cold water until the throbbing in it had diminished to a dull ache, Geoffrey dropped into his father's bed. He did not think he would sleep. He intended to devise a plan that would result in Joanna's immediate departure from the court. In fact, he underestimated the combined effects of a long ride, a lively party, an overindulgence in wine and underindulgence in women, and a rousing quarrel. When Salisbury came to bed several hours later, he was able to talk to his squires in perfectly ordinary tones and even to roll his son to one side without rousing him more than enough to grunt.

By morning, Geoffrey's head was back to normal. However, sober contemplation of Joanna's avowed intentions left him no more satisfied than when he had first heard them. He hated to appeal to his father for help, only there was no way to make Isabella send Joanna home but to get the king to tell her to do so. He could not say he distrusted Joanna, but he could say he feared Isabella would make her unhappy and that she would be disgusted by the loose behavior of the women in the court. Salisbury still thought of Joanna as a defenseless innocent, and he would believe that. Geoffrey grinned at the memory of how the "defenseless innocent" had got rid of her escort's troop and looked down at the gouge marks on his hand where her nails had bitten deep.

With that matter settled to his satisfaction, Geoffrey was able to give his full attention to the king when those who were bidden to the council convened in the refectory. What he heard drove Joanna completely out of his mind. John proposed that the quickest way to end the war was to pursue and take Llewelyn prisoner.

"When he is gone from them, the Welsh will fall upon each other and do our work for us," the king concluded. "Then we will appear in the light of saviors to them, protecting each from the other."

Geoffrey drew a deep breath and looked at the older men who surrounded him. There was nothing in their faces that aroused any hope that someone would protest this insanity. He realized with a sinking heart that no one thought ill of the king's plan. There had not been a war in Wales—not a real war of English against Welsh—since the time of old King Henry. There had been only that punitive expedition that Ian's lord, Sir Simon, had carried out nearly twenty years past. Few remembered that. If they remembered at all, it was that John had marched a large army into the country, and not far in, and Rhys apGruffydd had come and done homage.

For an ordinary campaign against a foe obviously much weaker than oneself, there was considerable merit in John's proposal. There was little sense in laying waste strongholds that did not threaten one's own forces. There was kindness and political good sense in not ravaging the land unnecessarily. Unfortunately, none of these reasonable notions appeared to apply to Wales. Of two things Geoffrey was sure. No army would ever catch Lord Llewelyn apIowerth among the forests and mountains of Wales; no challenge would ever tempt him into a pitched battle against a stronger enemy. But the men who had the experience and authority to raise these points were not present. Braose was in exile in France. Mortimer was sitting sullenly on his own land in the south with the excuse that a war in the north would start war in the south also. Actually, Mortimer would not take up arms against the king—not after what had happened to Braose for just speaking a little too freely—but if he had a preference it was that Llewelyn should rule Wales rather than John. Geoffrey FitzPeter, who had conducted a short campaign against Llewelyn's grandfather in 1198 was attending to his duties as justiciar in England. Pembroke and Ian were in Ireland.

Other voices besides John's had been raised, but these were largely in speculation as to where Llewelyn was most likely to make his stand. Geoffrey drew another deep breath. His age and lack of experience bade him stand still and listen to his elders and betters. That, however, was not the sum total of the situation. Perhaps Geoffrey FitzWilliam, a minor vassal of the king and a young man with no experience of leading men should be respectfully silent. However, the deputy of Ian de Vipont had a responsibility both to the king and to de Vipont's men. He listened for a few minutes more, considering the wisdom of what he should do. If he spoke, John would be angry. Moreover, his single voice in protest could accomplish nothing. Still, if Ian had been there, he would have spoken.

"Sire, you will not find Lord Llewelyn there." Geoffrey said clearly and loudly, stepping forward.

"There— What do you mean, 'there?' Four strongholds have been named. In which will we not find him?" the king asked testily. "And how do you know so much about the movements of our enemy? Are you in communication with him?" John added nastily.

"No, not with him, nor with Lord Ian's Welsh vassals, nor with my foster brother Owain apLlewelyn," Geoffrey answered firmly, hoping the naming of his Welsh connections would remind everyone that he was familiar with the country and the people. "But I have traveled often in Wales," he added to make his point, "and I have listened to their tales of war—"

"That is what you should be doing now—sitting at your nurse's knee and listening to tales, not interrupting a war council."

Geoffrey's eyes, which had been dull, lightened to bright amber as color strained his face. Salisbury put up a warning hand and took a step toward his son, but there was no way to reach Geoffrey before he spoke again.

"My lord, it is each vassal's duty to lay what knowledge he has before his liege lord. The Welsh have driven more than one English army from their lands. In their halls, they sing of how this was done. There is a kernel of meat under the shell of proud words."

"Rotten with worms," John sneered, and then, aware of Salisbury's eyes on him he said, "Well, what is this meat?"

"What I said already," Geoffrey got out with a

semblance of calm. "That you will not find Lord Llewelyn himself no matter where you seek. You would do better—"

"Oh, enough!" John exclaimed contemptuously. "When a boy-child, swollen with unmerited honor, begins to tell a war council what it had better do, it is time to cry enough. You are free to leave us, Lord Geoffrey, and to obey the orders we give you."

There was a moment of trembling silence while Geoffrey looked, not at the king but at his father. "Yes, my lord," he said softly, and bowed, and left the room.

A short walk brought him out into the cloister where he stopped to try to calm the rage that was threatening to send him back to speak his mind. Having swallowed that lunatic impulse, which left him feeling rather sick, Geoffrey wondered what next he should do. By choice he would go back to camp, but if he wished to speak to his father about Joanna it was necessary to wait until the council was over. As if his thinking had conjured her from thin air, a page tugged at his sleeve and told him that the lady awaited him in the garden.

Summoning to mind his own not-so-distant miseries when he had served in the same capacity, Geoffrey did not snap the child's head off, strike him, or refuse to accompany him. He closed his eyes, prayed for patience, and said, "Very well, lead on."

It would have been better if Joanna had been at a distance, but she had settled herself conveniently near the entrance to the pleasure grounds. Geoffrey had no time to cool and, when she rose to greet him, smiling pleasantly, snapped at her, "How can I serve you, madam?"

Long years of living with two volatile temperaments had made their mark on Joanna. Instead of shrieking, "Is that a proper way to greet me, whoreson?" as her mother might well have done, she said softly, "I have caught you at a bad time. I am sorry for it. I will not keep you. I promised your father I would make my peace with you before you returned to camp. Only let me say I am sorry I teased you last night, my lord."

Geoffrey rubbed at his forehead as if to scrub away the

lines between his brows. "I think it is more my place to say I am sorry. It seems to me I was not overcivil last night, nor yet just now."

"Last night you were drunk," Joanna said with a shrug. "I knew it. And today—" she raised her eyes to his, "today you are troubled with something of note."

"You may say that more than once," Geoffrey replied bitterly. "I have been listening to a pack of old fools—my father included—talking of how they will conquer Wales by bringing Lord Llewelyn to a pitched battle and capturing him."

"That is ridiculous," Joanna cried. "Even I know—"

"*You,*" Geoffrey snarled, "are a fool of a girl, and I am boy-child swollen with unmerited honor who needs still to be at my nurse's knee, according to the king. How can what we know be of merit?"

"But did you say nothing? Did you not point out that no one has *ever* brought the Welsh to a great battle?"

"I did not have time to point out anything. As soon as I raised my voice, I was scolded like a child and sent from the room. I—"

"Stop, Geoffrey," Joanna protested, quite alarmed at the color his face had turned. "There is no sense in raging against the king. You know him to be a churl and a fool. Let us rather consider what we can do to soften the ill that will fall upon us. Come, walk with me in the cool of the garden. Do not think upon that idiot's mouthings."

"There is nothing I *can* do! I am twenty. They have spent their lives making war."

The very truth of what he said was calming. He had known the council would not listen. It was sheer bad chance that not one lord of the Welsh Marches was present. Every man there had fought amost exclusively in France or in small private battles in England. None could really imagine what Wales was like, especially in the western parts. And as for the king—he never missed a chance to sneer at anyone if he could find it.

"It was partly my own fault," Geoffrey sighed. "Instead of only telling what I knew, I began to offer advice on what should be done. I am not used to holding so high a place that my words are directed to earls and bishops and kings."

"Never mind that now. I do not think they would have listened no matter how you spoke," Joanna soothed. "I did not mean what you could do to change the king's plans. I meant what we could do to save our men as much as possible. I remember Ian said how they nearly starved to death when he went with my father into Wales."

"Yes, that was how Ian came to meet Lord Llewelyn. Ian's troop was foraging for food and captured him. That was what I wished to tell them—that Wales is not full of farms that can be stripped for provender, nor are there wide roads to carry the ox carts."

"Then you will need asses and mules."

Geoffrey nodded. "For myself I have enough, and I think our own vassals are convinced and will buy where they can. But there are not sufficient animals in the country to carry provender for the entire army for the time needed. A few weeks while we assail a stronghold is no great difficulty, but to pursue Llewelyn—"

"So long as you and our men do not starve, I do not care," Joanna said callously. "I care for my own first."

"Then you had better care for all, unless you wish to see us engaged against our own comrades," Geoffrey remarked sharply.

Joanna's eyes misted with thought. "You are right. Whatever the leaders say, to the men an empty belly comes first. Geoffrey, if you know a better way to settle this matter, you had better convince your father and let him deal with the king."

"Of course. I said I was a fool to speak as I did, but I was surprised. It had not occurred to me that my father had never fought in Wales or that he and Ian should never have discussed the ways of war there."

"Ian would not!" Joanna exclaimed. "It would seem to

him an act of treachery against his clan brother.''

Geoffrey uttered an obscenity and then added, ''I had not thought of that! Where does this place me? In God's name, can I, in honor, use what Ian has taught me against his friends?''

''Do not begin to unravel a silk thread,'' Joanna said hastily, cursing herself for raising the question. ''If you can, in honor, bear arms, then you must bear them as wisely and as well as is in your power. That is like asking whether you should fight at half your strength because your enemy is the friend of a friend. Ian expects you to use whatever you know to the fullest—except—''

''Except what? Can there be an exception to honor?''

Joanna did not curse aloud nor raise her eyes to heaven nor sigh nor give any other sign of the exasperation that aroused in her an urgent desire to kick her betrothed in the shin. She realized she was meeting for the first time the bête noire that was her mother's nightmare. The conflict between honor and good sense had sparked more bitter quarrels in Joanna's home than any other problem.

''I do not know,'' she said quietly, ''but there must be sometimes a compromise with necessity. Do you think Ian should have cut off one of his arms and sent it to Llewelyn while the rest of his body went to the king?''

That produced a laugh, as she had intended, but Geoffrey did not, as she hoped, abandon the subject. He said, ''Do not talk like a fool of what you do not understand. Honor cannot be compromised, nor has Ian compromised it. He has fulfilled his obligations to each overlord completely.''

There was a brief silence while Joanna considered whether she should drop the problem she had meant to bring to Geoffrey's attention. The keeps her stepfather owned in Wales were neither large nor of great significance. In an ordinary way, unless the path of the army happened to cross them accidentally, they would be left in peace. It was not impossible, however, that John would deliberately go out of his way to attack them just to injure Ian. If John knew where they were, probably there was nothing Geoffrey could do to prevent that anyway. The question remained whether Geoffrey would feel obliged to lead the army to Ian's strongholds if asked to do so.

They were walking slowly side by side through the garden while the sun flicked in and out behind the hurrying clouds of early morning. The roses were still in full bloom. When their scent came to Geoffrey, memory came with it. He glanced around, drew Joanna into the shadow of the tall canes, and kissed her hungrily. She permitted the embrace passively, her mind still fixed on the problem of how to protect Ian's property from Geoffrey's honor.

After a few moments, Geoffrey released her lips. "Are you angry because I was not here to greet you?" he asked softly, "Or because of what I said last night?"

"I am not angry at all," Joanna assured him, a trifle absently.

"Then why—" he began, but before he could finish the question the explanation most obvious to a jealous mind overtook him. "I suppose you have already found someone more to your taste. I beg your pardon, I am sure, for forcing my attentions on you."

"What have I done?" Joanna gasped in the blankest surprise. "Why should you accuse me of such a thing? We are betrothed. How could anyone be more to my taste? What would it matter if anyone was?"

Naturally enough, Geoffrey did not answer any of her questions. He did not know how to describe the difference between her warm, eager passivity in the garden of Roselynde and the cold, indifferent passivity of this last kiss. As to the final two questions, they provided him equally with reassurance and with pain. Both betrayed that Joanna was completely innocent of and totally ignorant of love either for him or for anyone else.

"What is wrong?" Joanna repeated anxiously.

Even as she spoke, realization came to her. Somehow Geoffrey had felt that she was not paying attention to his kiss. It did not seem to Joanna that she had acted in any way differently from the previous time he had kissed her. Then too she had stood quietly and permitted him to do as he liked, but she had to accept what was obviously true. In Roselynde, she had felt his kiss—and somehow Geoffrey knew that this time she had not. In instant contrition, she put her arms around his neck.

"I am sorry," she whispered. Then curiously, "How did you know I was not paying attention? I am troubled because of Ian's Welsh lands. If the king wished to attack them but did not know where they were, would you have to lead him there?"

Instinctive reaction made Geoffrey fold his arms around Joanna when she embraced him, and he started to drop his head toward hers to renew their kiss. Now he pulled away, his lips tightening.

"Lead him to my father-by-marriage's property? Even the king could not ask that of me."

"Who knows what King John can ask?" Joanna insisted, intent upon wringing a promise from Geoffrey that he would not contribute in any way to the destruction of her step-father's lands.

"He cannot ask me the whereabouts of Ian's keeps unless his purpose is to make open bad feeling between us. He knows I will not lead the army there nor would my oath of loyalty to him demand that of me. The blood bond must come first. If we should come upon one of the keeps by accident, however, I am less sure of what I must do. I know their weak and strong points, of course, as I know the shape of my own fingers. Must I hold my peace and see some of the men I lead die? Or must I betray my lord to save the lives of his vassals? It is a sweet choice."

Since Geoffrey was already thinking along the lines she desired, Joanna did not press him further. If they came upon the keeps by accident, they would be taken whether Geoffrey gave aid or not. Satisfied, she raised her face a little more, to an angle that would better facilitate lip meeting lip. "I will pay attention now, if you kiss me again," she murmured invitingly.

CHAPTER EIGHT

Joanna paid attention to Geoffrey's kisses with such effect that Geoffrey found himself reluctant to raise the question of her departure. In fact, he did not have the chance because he did not see his father again until they were a week's march into Wales. Joanna was still at court, but Geoffrey had something more important on his mind. He did his best to follow Joanna's advice and convince Salisbury to wage a new kind of war. Salisbury listened politely, but he did not give much thought to what Geoffrey had said, putting down what seemed to him an exaggerated respect for a rather barbaric people to the influence of Owain apLlewelyn, who had been the senior squire when Geoffrey served under Ian. A few days later, however, the conversations he had had with his son were brought forcibly back to Salisbury's mind. A sneak raid in the night cost them some men and a large number of horses and oxen. During the next few days men were lost on the march also. In any heavily wooded area, a fusillade of arrows might suddenly fly out—or might not. To pursue was useless and dangerous, the leaders of the army found. The number of men hurt was actually insignificant. The damage done to their nerves and spirits was far more important.

By the end of the second week, Salisbury was recalling his talk with his son with a sinking heart. The guides sent by the prince of Powys were pointing out the area where they believed Lord Llewelyn and his army lay hidden. Salisbury had argued that no army could get up a trackless mountain—and the guides had laughed. They agreed that no army with carts of supplies and tents with furniture for its nobles and oxen to drag all could accomplish it. But an army could if its meat was still on the hoof, its grain in sacks to be carried by men and mules, its shelter and comfort the leaves of the trees and the open heavens. Salisbury thanked them and said he would consider; they laughed again. If he did not go now, they said, he would lose his prize—if it was not already gone. When he brought this news to John, Salisbury found that his feeling of hopeless frustration was not shared. John suggested that, since Geoffrey had been so foresighted as to be provided with the proper equipment for such a venture, that Geoffrey should go. If Salisbury thought Geoffrey unable, he could either appoint some other man to lead or ask Geoffrey to barter his supplies and animals for cars and oxen.

Salisbury stared stonily at the ground. Neither alternative John offered was worth considering for a moment. Geoffrey would never agree to either. He would sooner die or withdraw his force than yield their leadership to another man; he might yield his own small contingent to Salisbury himself, if urged, but he would never allow control of Ian's men to slip from his hands. That was his trust. As for the other—taking his pack animals and supplies—he would want to know why and, when he heard, would point out, quite correctly, that young or old, he had been more right than any other in his estimate of the Welsh and was thus best fitted for the mission. In fact, Salisbury knew John's idea was good and Geoffrey was able. Choking down his fear for his son, Salisbury agreed.

Lady Alinor had, of course, warned her daughter of the dangers inherent in court life and Joanna was not totally ignorant of it because she had spent time at court under Lady Ela's care. She discovered, however, that there are great differences between childhood at court and young maidenhood there. As a child, Joanna had enjoyed herself. It was the only time, aside from high festivals like her mother's second wedding, that she had had a wide variety of playmates of her own age and class. Some of those playmates were still there and they had greeted her kindly, but Joanna found that they had grown apart.

Under ordinary circumstances, such as the gathering of the court for Christmas or Easter or even a special convocation for political purposes, Joanna would have met a substantial group of women with tastes and interests much like her own. Not many would have been mistresses of their own property, like Joanna, but, as deputies for their husbands, they too would have sat in justice and overseen the workings of the keep and demesne. With such women, Joanna would have had much in common. Unfortunately, at a time when their husbands were summoned to war, those ladies were where Joanna had expected to be—at home, minding their lands. All that remained in Isabella's court were the permanent members of her suite, girls in training, women in various ways dependent upon the queen, or girls who were wards of the king awaiting his choice of husband. To "protect" them, certain gentlemen were excused from the war in Wales and left to attend upon the queen also.

For the women permanently attached to her, Isabella set the tone completely. Talk and interest centered solely upon appearance and the clothing and jewels that set off a woman's appearance or on scandal—who was linked to whom, for how long, and where they next would stay. Joanna was by no means uninterested in such subjects. If she was less vain than her beauty could have made her, she was nonetheless aware of it and took pleasure in increasing it in any way she could. Nor did she lack a lively interest in the intrigues of the court. The trouble was that these discussions soon grew too personal. Remarks that were at first incomprehensible were soon made all too clear by meaningful nods and titters. One of the men the women discussed frequently was Geoffrey.

Joanna was saved from making a fool of herself by three things. The first was simply that the man Isabella's ladies described was so totally different from the Geoffrey that Joanna knew that it took an abnormally long time for her to make the connection. In fact, in the beginning she was quite bewildered, believing that she was either being warned against some high-powered seducer or, more likely, being slyly induced to fall victim to him. When she understood at last, her immediate reaction was laughter. It was ridiculous that these bejeweled and scented and even painted ladies of wide experience should be sighing and spitting over Geoffrey in this way.

Fortunately, it was not until Joanna was alone and really had time to consider all the aspects of what she heard that a second wave of emotion rolled over her. It was only when she was lying in bed that she felt again the warmth of Geoffrey's mouth and the cravings awakened by the sure touch of his hands. Then it did not seem so funny that he should be able to arouse such feelings in others. Rage and spite roiled in her; tears rose in her eyes and hot words came to her lips. She hissed like an angry snake, so that Brian leapt to his feet from where he lay beside the bed and rumbled growls. Hushing him, Joanna had time to think of what she had muttered beneath her breath. The words were horribly familiar. More than once she had heard her mother fling them at her stepfather.

Whether or not Ian was guilty—and Joanna did not think he was, being better able than her jealous mother to judge the mingled bewilderment, exasperation, and amusement with which he defended himself—was not the point. The quarrels never reached into the past. Alinor did not blame Ian for love affairs engaged in before they were married. Calm returned to Joanna. It did not matter whose bed Geoffrey had warmed before they were betrothed; how could he be faithful to her when he never knew or expected to be her husband? Sure as fate, he had warmed no woman, except perhaps a casual whore, since then because Joanna knew where he had been and what he had been doing every day after the betrothal. The clincher made her smile. If Geoffrey were still involved with one of these court bitches, he would not have ridden two hundred miles to Roselynde when a letter could have given him ten more days in his mistress's bed.

Contentment restored, Joanna snuggled down into her bed and closed her eyes, which promptly opened again on a double thought. The first part of it smelled suspiciously like bad cheese set out to trap a rat. Mistresses eager to keep a man's devotion do not blazon his infidelity to his wife's face. Such stupidity breeds quarrels that make a man unhappy, and a wife has an edge in such a contest. Only a mistress very, very sure of her hold on her love might spitefully so bait a wife. But none of those women had fast hold on Geoffrey nor pretended to have. They talked of him as if he sprang from bed to bed with the agility of an acrobat and the slipperiness of an eel. Their purpose, then, could only be that she *should* know of his affairs—but why? A single jealous woman might wish to make her unhappy out of spite, but none of these women even pretended to be hearttouched, most of them obviously *liked* Geoffrey, and some of them even seemed to like *her*.

The answer had to be that they did Isabella's will. Only the queen had the power to produce such unanimity of action. Joanna turned flat on her back, staring upward into the gathering point of her bed curtains. After a moment she shook her head. She did not blame Isabella's ladies, not even those who were friendly to her. It was all a joke to them, they did not conceive that it was wrong. And Isabella was an idiot! For some reason, the woman had hated Geoffrey ever since he was a child and doubtless this was one more attempt to make him unhappy. *Isabella thinks to make me hate him for what he did before he was mine*, Joanna realized, *and perhaps she even hopes to turn me into a whore to spite him.*

That made Joanna grin—a smile that would have made her betrothed very uneasy if he had seen it. *Now he is mine*, Joanna thought, *I had sooner tame him, even if I must geld him to do it, than to spite him by soiling myself.* And then she laughed softly. Thinking back on her mother's furious accusations and Ian's anguished protests made Joanna very sure Geoffrey did not look elsewhere just now. Nonetheless, when Lady Ela arrived a week later, Joanna flew to her arms as to a haven.

"I see the long tongues have been wagging already," Lady Ela said as soon as they were able to find a corner in which to be private.

"I do not believe them," Joanna flashed passionately.

Eyes paler than her own but as bright as hers in a rage stared at Joanna. "What do you mean?" Ela asked sharply. "Do you mean you do not believe Geoffrey has ever mounted a mistress? I assure you he has before and may again."

"What he has done in the past is no business of mine," Joanna said softly, "and he may futter a whore in a ditch if I am not by and that is his need, but he will mount no mistress while I am his wife. He is mine!"

Lady Ela clapped her hands to her ears. "Is it Joanna I hear or Alinor?" she asked laughing. Then she said seriously, "I see what you mean, but you need not worry even about the past if what you fear is that Geoffrey's heart was touched. If you can win it, he will bring that to you as clean as your own."

To that, Joanna made no answer. Stricken by the knowledge that she did not wish to give her heart into Geoffrey's keeping, it did not seem right for her to demand his. Nor would she permit herself to examine why, if she did not want love, she was so set against Geoffrey's loving elsewhere. She could not say that to Ela, of course, and she shook her head.

"That is not really what troubles me," she said half truthfully. "What frets me beyond bearing is that I am helpless to stop their tongues. I could do it by changing the look of their faces with my hands, but Ian said I must not and, in truth, the blame is not all theirs. I believe the queen is behind it—"

"I believe it too, but do not say it aloud again," Ela interrupted. Then her lips twitched and her hands began to flutter. "It is so dark in here," she whined. "I am afflicted with a shadowing of the eyes from lack of light. It is damp. My chest feels a tightness."

"Dear madam," Joanna exclaimed immediately upon her cue, "lean here upon my arm. I will lead you into the garden where there is more light and the air is warm."

"I am not sure I can go so far," Ela whimpered.

A tiny hesitation was all the sign Joanna gave of her impulse to break into giggles. Obviously, Lady Ela had not really cared whether anyone heard what they said about Geoffrey. It was natural that Joanna should carry that trouble to her foster mother at once. Now, however, Ela wanted to impart information that needed secrecy.

"I am very strong," Joanna urged. "I will support you, and you may lean on the other side on Brian. Up, you fool," she said to the dog.

Thus, they tottered down the stairs and out into the open. Once outside, Lady Ela said with an air of pleased surprise that she could breathe more easily. Then she added, like a martyr who finds that the arrows piercing her do not hurt, that she believed she could walk a few steps. And between sighs of exhaustion and high-pitched exclamations on the fragility of her health, she imparted a few luscious pieces of scandal and a few comments that had been made about the queen by her ladies that should serve to silence certain tongues. Moreover, Lady Ela had her own methods of dealing with Isabella and she was able, temporarily at least, to divert the queen's shallow mind from Joanna.

As the queen lost interest and the ladies saw Ela's strong support backing Joanna—none could really doubt where the tidbits came from that Joanna smilingly related in private and wordlessly threatened to make public—most attempts to bait the girl died. Talk fell into a more impersonal vein in her presence. There was gossip of course, but most of the time it was the mechanics of entrapping male attention that absorbed the ladies.

In a relatively short time, such distractions began to pall on Joanna. There are only so many places to pin a brooch, only so many positions to place an armlet, only so many lengths to hang a necklet. Joanna was an exquisite needlewoman, but new stitches were not the be-all and end-all of her existence, no matter how beautiful the patterns they produced. She began to hunger after more solid substance for her days. She began to meet the enemy her mother had warned her against most specifically—ennui.

Joanna had mostly discounted those warnings. She suspected Lady Alinor's discontent was a result of her own impatient nature that must be up and doing at every moment. Joanna knew that she, herself—red hair or no red hair—was much slower in action, more content to watch and dream. In moments of total exasperation, her mother had occasionally called her a beautiful cow, but that was not true. Cows, as far as anyone can tell, can exist with perfectly blank minds, ruminating only on the contents of their several stomachs. Joanna, who was also willing to ruminate, needed something more interesting to contemplate.

The first path her thoughts found led, naturally enough, to Geoffrey. For some reason, a frequent mental repetition of the events of their parting did not bore Joanna at all. Unfortunately, the pattern of thought did not end there. After parting came the future, and, for Geoffrey, the future was war. Mostly, Joanna wondered how he was managing the men and how the supplies were holding out. Once in a while, however, she thought of battle, and then a panic seized upon her and shook her as a terrier shakes a rat. She fought off the fear, trying to smother it, trying to run away from it, trying to soothe herself with assurances that Geoffrey was only one young man out of many, many young men all equally personable.

That assurance, strangely enough, seemed to increase rather than subdue the fear. In desperation, Joanna did her best to put Geoffrey out of her mind entirely. There was no dearth of men at court, even though so many had ridden with the king. There were the older men, like Oxford, who wished to be near the scene of action although they were no longer physically involved. There were those who were charged with the routine of government, who remained in a safe place that was still conveniently close to transmit necessary information to the king, and there were the queen's gentlemen who were responsible for her safety and that of her children. Joanna flirted with them all.

In a sense, she was careful. She never moved far from Lady Ela, except to dance. She never danced more than once in an evening with any gentleman (except those old enough to be her grandfather), sitting out rather than seeming to show favor to anyone. Her conversation was absolutely unimpeachable; she spoke by preference of national affairs or trade, or, if that was impossible, of hunting or other sport. It was impossible, the gentlemen discovered, to sigh a love lyric to Joanna; it was also impossible to catch her alone to do so. Had that been the total sum of her behavior, Joanna would soon have found herself bereft of young male company in spite of the lure of her lovely features and ripe body. What kept Joanna's court around her was an indefinable hint of promise. Something in her eyes said, "I am not really good, I am only careful and fearful. Catch me at the right time, and I will yield."

In fact, Joanna would have been happy to dispense with the company of her young admirers if she could have obtained what she really wanted from the older men. She did glean some information from them by indirect routes, but they could not really be drawn into political indiscretions. Not only were they more experienced, but Joanna did not dare use the same techniques with them. Also, the older men could not believe that such a pretty little girl could be interested in such dry and difficult subjects.

It was from one of Richard Marsh's squires that Joanna learned that a legate of the pope had requested and received permission to come to England to try again to settle John's differences with the Church. A young knight in Oxford's service told her that matters were at the breaking point between Renaud of Dammartin, count of Boulogne, and the French king. That news sent Joanna to her writing desk to dispatch a warning to Sir Giles to transmit to the guildsmen of Roselynde town. The merchants would need to be prepared in case the French triumphed and wished to change trade arrangements.

Even so, time hung heavy on Joanna's hands. When, in the third week in June a battered troop came in bearing letters, Joanna nearly wept with frustration. In that delightful parting she had been paying so close attention, as she had promised, to Geoffrey's kisses that she had forgotten to tell her betrothed to write to her. And the news would take days to filter down to her, she knew. Then she called herself a fool three times over and set out with determination to find Richard Marsh. It was the most natural thing in the world that she should ask openly for news about the campaign in Wales when her betrothed husband was involved.

Before she found the chancellor, however, his page found her. Geoffrey had not needed a reminder. The page handed her a thick roll of parchment, closed with Geoffrey's seal, showing the rampant lioncel of Salisbury above the bend sinister, and the Danish axe of his mother's family below.

Somehow, Joanna felt that the only proper place to read it was the garden. She looked down at Brian, who looked up hopefully. "All right," Joanna said, "I will take you, but only if you are quiet." At the small cost of a few flower heads and a few sage and basil leaves, Brian was convinced to lie down at his mistress's feet while she read.

"To Lady Joanna, greetings. I hope this finds you as it leaves me, well. As we spoke of matters when I last had words with you, so has it fallen out. We came swiftly across into Gwynedd and pursued that will-o'-the-wisp Llewelyn until our supplies failed. I am almost sorry now for my foresight for it has brought much labor upon me and upon the poor men given into my care."

Joanna looked up from the letter momentarily. They must be in sore straits, she thought, to make Geoffrey sound so pettish, but so long as he was well and safe other matters could be mended.

"Because we were best fitted for that task, it has been our fate to bear the brunt of this pursuit. We are more weary and angry than hurt. Forewarned though I was by Lord Ian, still they tricked me finely—and not only me but Sir Peter and others better versed than I in war—leaving such signs as I could swear they were just ahead out of sight. We pursued the more eagerly until men and horses dropped from exhaustion. I must be grateful, I suppose, that the signs were false. Had the Welsh really been ahead, they could have returned and come upon us then and we could have protected ourselves no better than overtired babes.''

That made Joanna smile in spite of the bad news. It sounded much more like Geoffrey.

"In another way, it was as well that we were so assiduous at our hope'ess task and that there were men of credit with me to back my word. It seemed to me that my uncle's eyes held little warmth when I told him my tale, although his reaction was fair. In that, however, I might missay him. His anger might have another cause. I am again at fault in being too often right. Before I left to pursue Llewelyn, I warned him that, if the Welsh came down from the mountain before I and my men went up, they might raid in force. This they did with unusual stealth and made off with many horses and much-needed supplies.''

Blast and curse men and their sense of duty, Joanna thought. Geoffrey knew, after what he had already said, that there would be no gain in such warnings. Why did he not keep his mouth shut or speak only to his father? And I am as much a fool as he, Joanna decided, to desire what I know is impossible. Then she shrugged. The king was the king and talk or silence would make little difference.

"Then we followed again on what seemed a well-marked trail of many men and horses only to come to grief in a blind valley where not even a goat could climb out by any path save that we came in upon. All this while we were most bitterly harassed by their accursed bowmen. I would have liked to string my own bow and return their shots, and would have done it had I the least idea where or at what to shoot. The best I can say is that they did not fall upon us from ambush while we were trapped in the valley nor on our way out again. From this I conclude that Llewelyn is hard pressed for men. Even a quarter and perhaps a sixth of our force could have inflicted great loss upon us when we were so entrapped and entangled.''

Unconsciously, Joanna nodded in approval. Angry as he was, Geoffrey was still thinking.

"The men were so enraged that they near came to blows among themselves, but by God's help we held them back and escaped that trouble. It may be that was what Llewelyn hoped for. If so, he hoped in vain, but in another way his hopes were well fulfilled. We are now near to starving. I would have had enough for my own people, at least enough to stave off real hunger, if not what would either fill their bellies or please their taste, but I was constrained—not by any man but by good sense—to share out what we had."

Joanna knew the sharing had been necessary, but she resented it. It was plainly impossible considering the strained tempers of the men that Geoffrey had just described to let some go hungry while others fed full. But if all were near starving—were they returning? Joanna bent her eyes eagerly to the letter again.

"One good thing alone has come from this. My father looks and speaks to me as a man to a man. He knows I can be sore mistaken—I was as eager as any other on the trail that led us into entrapment—but he also knows that I do not speak to put myself forward but only when something *must* be said. I, too, have learned something. Whatever the king is, he is no longer a fool in matters of war. He was as quick as my father to see the worth of what I offered once he was convinced of the folly of his past decision. More, even, he has added to the plan several most excellent parts. For what he is, I cannot love him, but I am coming to see for myself the truth of what Ian has always told me. A great part of our trouble is that no man truly knows what is his right. But this letter grows so long it will fatigue the messenger to carry it. Of this matter I will speak more when I see you."

The words seemed to go from the parchment directly to Joanna's heart so that it fluttered as the letters rose and fell on the page. It may be long in the future, she reminded herself, and then mingled warnings quieted the stirring in her breast. The most direct fact was that obviously the campaign was not over if Geoffrey was writing of plans for war.

The most nebulous notion threatened that it was not safe to care whether she saw Geoffrey soon or not. Why not? She challenged herself. I have always been glad to see Geoffrey. He is my long-time friend. But she would not question why her heart should move now at the thought of his presence when it had never moved before, and she returned more eagerly to her perusal, skimming the words, seeking for the word "Whitechurch" or "Chester." It did not appear however, and Joanna was constrained to read more slowly.

"It has been decided that we can do no more in our present state and we will make the best speed we can to Oswestry, northwest of Shrewsbury. To that place, therefore, in so short a time as is possible, do you send all that can be gathered to feed our people fitting for a brief but strong attack. What we need, you know, but I beg you to add some cattle and sheep fit for slaughtering, enough for two sufficient meals for all my men. This I will pay for from my own purse, knowing it is no part of your duty to the king to provide such delicacies as fresh meat. The men, however, have been so good and uncomplaining, seeing how much they have suffered, that it is my earnest wish to pleasure them in some special way."

Joanna looked up again. Where was she to find cattle and sheep fit for slaughter? Whitechurch and its environs as far as even Chester were bare because the court and the gathering army had eaten all that was available. Shrewsbury itself was probably best, if she could get there before the king's procurers reached it. She fingered the keys that hung between her breasts, trying to remember how much money remained in her strongbox. Some of the other supplies might be obtainable there also. It annoyed Joanna to spend good gold for what, had there been more time, could have been culled from her own herds, but plainly her lands were too far to drive cattle in time. Even from Clyro, which was the closest, the beasts would arrive mere sacks of skin over bare bones—if they arrived in time. From Clyro, however, she could obtain much dry provender, grain and meat, and perhaps even salt meat and fish. Anxiously, she looked back at Geoffrey's letter. Time was of the essence.

"As soon as the men are a little rested and the supplies renewed, we will move upon Llewelyn's keeps and towns, as I first advised. I have high hopes of success because the king is sending Faulk de Bréaute south to take Cardigan and his place will be filled by the Welsh princes who are opposed to Llewelyn's usurpations. I have not always felt great trust in the promises of these men, as you know, but that they are coming in their own persons gives me greater confidence that they will truly do their best to forward our purpose. It is desired that we set forth again before the tenth day of July. I beg you, therefore, to make what haste you may. If it is not possible for you to serve me in this, I will buy what is needful, but the cost will be very high as many, including the king, will be forced to do the same and the prices will be driven up. Please be sure to write to me at Oswestry so that I will know whether to buy or to await what you send. This is all my news, so then, farewell—a sad, dry thing is a farewell thus written. I would rather, although it gave me much pain, to say farewell to you in my own person, as I did three weeks agone. I would still rather give you greeting. Written this twenty-second day of June, God knows where in Wales, by your loving husband Lord Geoffrey FitzWilliam.''

The summer breeze, soft and warm, stirred the leaves on the rose canes, speckling the parchment with dancing light and shadow. Joanna reread the last few lines and then read them still again. The words were flickering with the light, but she found no difficulty in making them out—nor would she have had any more difficulty had her eyes been closed. There was much to do—letters to be written, permission to leave, at least for a few days, to be obtained from the queen, her men to be warned and messengers readied—but Joanna reread very carefully the end of her letter, which told her nothing of any importance, nothing that she needed to know, until Brian got suddenly to his feet, tugging at the leash, and a shadow fell over the parchment.

"I do not believe my eyes," Henry de Braybrook said.

"In what do you fear they deceive you, my lord?" Joanna asked, rolling up her parchment and smiling up at him.

"I hardly know which of two marvels to name as more unlikely—your beautiful eyes fixed on a roll of writing or your beautiful person all alone—unless you have Lady Ela concealed under a rose bush."

Joanna laughed, although she was annoyed for she had gone to some trouble to conceal her abilities. "The one is the cause of the other—a little. Not wishing to be looked upon as out of the ordinary, I came here to read in private. You have found out my unmaidenly secret, but I hope you will not spread my disgrace about."

"Oh, no. I will keep it quiet," Braybrook assured her. He found it rather disgusting that Joanna should be literate. Such a woman was a freak, like a calf with two heads or a chicken with four legs. It was as unnatural for women to think as for men to produce children. Nonetheless, he would keep her secret because it would give him a little power over her. Also, it must be admitted that Joanna did not seem to have been much spoiled by her learning. She was always interested in everything he said and never contentious. What was more, she knew how to keep a confidence. He had tested her several times with juicy bits of gossip and, when he bid her be silent, she had not breathed a word. It was fun to tell Joanna things. She gazed at one with such wide, admiring eyes, with lips a little parted in wonder.

"If you believe it unmaidenly," he said gently, "why do you do it?"

"It is my mother's will," Joanna whispered, lowering her head and her eyes.

"Poor beautiful one," Braybrook murmured.

Joanna's hand tightened on the scroll of Geoffrey's writing as anger flashed through her. Amusement followed swiftly. The ass had not realized she was teasing. And what a cod's head to ask such a question! If she could not read, could Geoffrey write such a letter as he had written? Imagine allowing a clerk to read what he had said about the king.

How could a husband confide in a wife who would need a third party to communicate with him? But Braybrook, she thought, would never wish to confide in his wife. He would rather use what tidbits he knew to impress a whore—or a woman he wished to turn into a whore.

"I have comfort in that I am an obedient daughter," Joanna said in a rather choked voice.

"As dutiful as you are beautiful," he praised, crooking a finger under Joanna's chin and lifting her face. "I cannot tell you how it grieves me that you escaped my notice when I was seeking a wife."

Joanna's eyes widened and she bit her lip to restrain a mixture of mirth and irritation. Popinjay! As if he had ever entered anyone's mind as a suitable match for the future lady of Roselynde. That needed a *man*. Her struggle to find something to say that would not betray her true emotions kept her silent and gave Sir Henry a totally false notion of what she felt. He took the wide eyes as evidence of her amazement that he would have wished to marry her, the bitten lip as regret that it could not be.

"Oh, yes, my flower, I would have preferred you a million times over to the pale bud I now have, and I can hardly bear to think of you wasted on—"

"Please do not missay my husband to me," Joanna whispered, her voice so tight with fury that she could scarcely force out the words.

"Ah, my love, you are perfection. Such sweetness of temper! I can scarcely believe you will defend him who used you so coarsely."

Long red lashes veiled Joanna's eyes. Behind them she saw the gouges her nails had left in Geoffrey's hand, heard the snake's hiss of her own voice as she told him what she thought. Such sweetness of temper! A giggle shook her. She caught her breath.

"Do not weep," Braybrook whispered, leaning forward and sliding an arm around her.

A low growl rumbled in Brian's throat. Braybrook looked down at the dog who had always been so friendly as to be idiotic.

"He does not like people to touch me," Joanna gasped, lying fluently. Brian had reacted to her own stiffening of revulsion. He never growled when Geoffrey embraced her.

"Be still, Brian. Lie down."

The words seemed an open invitation, but Braybrook did not notice that Joanna had surreptitiously tugged the leash so that, when Brian obeyed, the dog collapsed directly between them. That was a nuisance, but he did not dare disrupt the mood still further by telling her to move the creature.

"My rose," he said softly, "you are such that a man must cherish you, not come drunken into your presence and refuse you your rightful pleasure in so small a thing as dancing."

By now the whole thing had become so ridiculous that Joanna felt a sense of unreality. Besides, he was such an ass, he deserved to wear long ears. It was as if she and Braybrook were players acting parts in one of those risible farces of stupid husband, sly lover, and unfaithful wife. Joanna fluttered her eyelashes.

"My pleasure must be what pleases my husband," she sighed.

"No, no," Oh Henry contradicted softly. "That is too much goodness. Then you are a slave. A woman has also a right to be happy, and it is her husband's duty to please her in such things as dancing and dress and using her with honor before others. When a husband fails in such matters, he has lost the right to his wife's loyalty."

"Oh, do you think so?" Joanna asked dulcetly, looking aside.

"Of a surety, my love. When such a prize as you, a very sun that lights the world with beauty is despised, the warm rays must be cast outward. They must illuminate a heart more ready to receive them."

Again Joanna choked. Sir Henry was much more romantic than Geoffrey. Geoffrey had called her torch-head a few times, but that was not meant as a compliment. That made the conversation between Braybrook and herself even more unreal to Joanna. She must tell Geoffrey, she thought, that she had been likened to the sun. He would probably inform her trenchantly that the reflection from the flames of hell on her head had been confused with a purer light.

"Oh, look at me," Braybrook cried softly, "see how my heart has taken fire from your loveliness. I cannot bear that you should know a moment's grief."

Exactly like the lines in a play, Joanna thought, her eyes stubbornly fixed on Brian's head lest the laughter in them give her away. No one really said such things. "I beg you, do not tempt me to sin," she got out in a quivering voice, sure that whoever had designed the play would approve of her rendering of his lines.

"I do not. I do not," Sir Henry assured her, seizing her hand. "It is your heart I desire. There can be no sin in a pure love."

The heart you desire is between my legs, Joanna thought crudely, but you are speaking the lines correctly. She looked up finally, so taken up with her amusing concept that they *both* knew they were involved in a farce of infidelity that her glance was replete with approval. It was on this note that this act of a farce must end. And right on cue, came the "interrupter."

"Say no more, my lord," Joanna murmured, withdrawing her hand gently. "The queen comes."

Braybrook was not surprised, but he was highly annoyed. It was Isabella who had sent him into the garden after Joanna, although he had not needed any urging. Sir Henry was reasonably sure that Isabella wanted to make trouble for the girl. He was perfectly willing to please her because it would permit him to take a most suitable revenge on Geoffrey. That Joanna should happen to be one of the most desirable pieces he had ever laid eyes upon was additional good luck. However, the queen was a fool. Joanna was no experienced court slut with whom a man could come to terms in five minutes. Doubtless she was heading speedily in that direction, but at present she was still green and needed elaborate coaxing. Isabella had not allowed sufficient time.

The queen herself, although not clever, had realized her mistake as soon as she saw Braybrook still standing formally before Joanna. She had not, of course, expected that Joanna would yield herself in the garden in the middle of the day, but she had hoped that she and her women would catch them in a more compromising situation. She did her best, turning aside with a shocked air to take another path, but Joanna frustrated that move. Leaping to her feet and tugging Brian, she called loudly, "Madam, pray wait, I beg you."

The sudden move his mistress made startled Brian, who also leapt to his feet. Meanwhile, Braybrook had stretched a hand toward Joanna to hold her back and half turned. Brian's shoulder caught the courtier on the hip, spun him round, and knocked him backward right into the prickly arms of the roses. He emitted a shriek, half-startled and half-pained. The dog, seeing a human on his own level and apparently troubled, lunged forward and swiped a large, moist tongue comfortingly across Braybrook's face, effectively pinning him into his ignominious position. Joanna stood quite paralyzed, choking, her only thought at the moment that this had happened at the wrong time. The oversetting of the sly lover did not come until the end of the play.

The laughter of the other women spurred Joanna into movement. She pulled Brian away with a breathless apology, curtsied, and ran toward the queen.

"Your —er—friend seems in need of help," Isabella remarked coldly.

The play was over as far as Joanna was concerned. It was necessary to return to serious matters. "Worse happens to men in war," she remarked humorously, not even glancing toward the thrashing sounds and low oaths that emanated from the roses. "I must beg a leave of you, madam, for a week or a fortnight."

"Do you beg leave for Braybrook also?" Isabella asked.

Joanna's eyes widened and an expression of total puzzlement covered her face. The jest was over and she had put it out of her mind. "What use could *he* be to me?" Joanna asked contemptuously. "I have serious business to do," she added. "I must away to Clyro and find more supplies for war by my lord's order. I have no time for play or foolishness at all."

"*You* must find supplies?" Isabella asked incredulously. "What have you to do with such? If supplies are needed, doubtless the bailiffs and stewards will be told."

"I am my mother's bailiff and steward," Joanna said, keeping the pride from her voice only with great effort, "and my lord's letter—" she showed Isabella Geoffrey's seal, "—bids me make the greatest haste I may to forward the king's desire. If it pleases you, madam, I will return as soon as my business is done, but I may not disobey the king's will, which is named in my lord's order."

However heedless Joanna might be in the pursuit of a jest, she was not at all foolish in the pursuit of a real purpose. The queen's appearance on the heels of Henry de Braybrook's silly attempt at lovemaking might be a coincidence—or it might not. Isabella's insistence on connecting her request to leave with Braybrook's presence might be a simple result of a love of scandal and having a dirty mind, which Joanna knew the queen to have, or it might be a deliberate attempt to smirch Joanna with the mud that so liberally bespattered the court. In any case, Joanna had realized that Isabella would not give her leave to go willingly. However, the queen never opposed the king's will, at least openly, and Joanna had invoked John's name to good purpose. Grudgingly, Isabella agreed. Joanna did not delay an instant but curtsied and went away.

Because she was annoyed with him, Braybrook stayed in Isabella's mind. Her thought processes were neither quick nor clear, but through repetition of the unsatisfactory scenes of the afternoon came the feeling that Joanna had escaped the punishment that she deserved and that Braybrook was responsible. The skewed logic of Isabella's brain then conceived what seemed a brilliant notion. She summoned a scribe and dictated an order that Braybrook accompany Joanna as escort to "perform all such services as will content that lady's heart and body."

Braybrook stared at the order, appalled. He had no intention of presenting himself to Joanna again as a suitor. The queen might be silly, but Braybrook was not. He had heard enough, even while struggling with the rose bushes, to understand that Joanna had been making fun of him all along—from the very first words about why she had come into the garden to read her letter. She was not at all ashamed of her skill; she had showed that letter to the queen as bold as brass. The little bitch had been toying with him, but he could see a way to turn that jest against her. Braybrook was now in complete sympathy with the queen's ultimate intention. He was now firmly determined to broach Joanna, cuckold Geoffrey, and thereby have his revenge on both. He, realized, however, if Isabella did not, that her order would not forward the purpose in any way.

It was useless, Braybrook knew, to try to reason with Isabella, and he was her gentleman, constrained to obey her orders. Reluctantly, he set out to find Joanna only to discover that she had left with her entire troop some hours earlier. At first Braybrook was relieved, but on second thought he realized that, far from being a lucky chance, Joanna's efficiency had landed him in real trouble. It would make no difference to Isabella that it was her order that came too late. She would blame him for not carrying out the order.

Suddenly, Braybrook stopped pacing the floor and snapped his fingers. Well, why not? If he stole away quietly, who would know he was not with Joanna? An unpleasant smile grew on his lips. If she denied his presence, he would shrug and smile and say he had the queen's order to attend her but—if the lady said he had not, then, since a gentleman did not contest a lady's word in *such* matters, he had not, of course. Meanwhile, he could have at least a week and probably two of the uninterrupted company of his present mistress. She would not betray him—well, she could not, since her husband was with the king in Wales.

CHAPTER NINE

Much as she had cause to dislike him, Joanna came near to blessing the king's name in the next three weeks. The feeling was purely personal. In financial terms, the war in Wales had cost double what it should have. From Joanna's point of view, this was not a disaster because Ian and Alinor had foreseen that no war ever costs what is estimated and had left careful instructions. Ian had told Geoffrey what men to hire, where to obtain them, and how much to pay if the terms of service of the vassals ran out. Alinor had told Joanna where to find the money for this and other things and where to *say* the money had come from—which were two different things.

Even for those who had not the resources that Geoffrey and Joanna commanded, the Welsh war was no great strain. King John himself paid the costs for any man who was pinched, and he did not oppress the people with taxation. He wrung the loins of the Church, exacting such heavy fines that it was rumored he had extracted one hundred thousand pounds from this source. Joanna heard much of this from the church in Roselynde town and the abbey some ten miles to the east, which cried to her for help she could not give, although she promised the priest and monks that they should not starve.

So much business was thrust upon her by the need to supply Geoffrey's troops, inform her mother and Ian of what was happening, and mitigate to some degree the terrors of the churchmen on her property that she had little time to fear for Geoffrey's safety and no opportunity to return to court. For this the king was responsible, and Joanna was duly grateful.

To feed the war party, Joanna had stripped Clyro naked of provender. Then it was necessary to draw supplies not only from Roselynde but Kingsclere and other keeps to replace Clyro's store and even to increase it in case this second assault on Llewelyn also failed and the king decided to try yet again. Unfortunately, Joanna had discovered that Sir Peter's lady was truly a weak reed. While Joanna purchased cattle and sheep at Shrewsbury and dispatched them to Oswestry in the care of Knud and part of her guard, she had sent Lady Mary a message to make ready for cartage to Oswestry sufficient grain and dried meat to feed the men for three weeks and such salt meat and fish as was available. To her horror when she arrived at Clyro she found total chaos.

The sacks were helter-skelter all unmarked with no way to tell what was meal for bread or unground kernel for other purposes. The maker's marks were on the casks of salt provision, but the stupid woman had not stopped to think that the men who dealt out the supplies came from all over the country and would not know which maker provided Clyro with salt fish and which prepared salt meat from the demesne cattle. It was all for Joanna to do: seeing that each cask was marked with the brand of a fish or an ox and each sack painted with a loaf of bread or an ear of corn. Also she had to attend to the purchase and borrowing of oxen and carts for transport. How Lady Mary thought the supplies would get from Clyro to Oswestry Joanna did not bother to ask.

In fact, unlike Lady Alinor who in her first rage might well have frightened Lady Mary out of what little wits she had, Joanna had merely cast her eyes up to heaven. Subsequently, she had patiently made what she wanted so clear, one word at a time, that Lady Mary was actually of some help. The usefulness, however, gave Joanna no mistaken notion that she had imbued the lady with either good sense or efficiency. It would be necessary for her to return to Clyro to oversee the replacement of the provisions she had commandeered and the stockpiling of the additional supplies. At least, Joanna thought, she was sure that she would be a welcome guest.

When the wains were loaded, Joanna engaged in a sharp struggle with herself. She had a violent desire to go with the supplies to Oswestry and found herself putting forward the most ridiculous reasons to do so. There was not the smallest purpose to going. A letter—short at that—could tell Geoffrey all he needed to know. Besides, Joanna realized she would be most horribly in the way in a town overrun with men, an additional burden on poor Geoffrey, who would have to find her lodging and would doubtless also try to find some hours to give to her in an already overfilled day. Joanna told herself she could not imagine why she wanted so desperately to go, and then blushed hotly in the privacy of her own chamber. It was a sad strait when a person began to lie to herself. What she wanted, Joanna acknowledged, was to taste Geoffrey's mouth again, to feel his hands on her body.

Recognized for what it was, the lust could be subdued. Joanna sighed and bent over her writing desk. She described succinctly the quantities of provisions she had sent and the markings used to distinguish them. Then went on, ''I must now betake myself to my mother's other keeps to gather up, a little here and a little there, what will replace the provision sent you. For now, Clyro is so empty that, if it were not summer and lambs and vegetables to be had, all here would starve. It is needful also to give comfort to the monks and priests on the Church lands adjoining ours. They have been stripped nakeder than Clyro and no restoration is promised them. I am the more earnest to keep their good will as I have heard a legate of the pope is on his way to England. When the king comes to terms with the Church, I wish it to be remembered that I was their faithful daughter even in their adversity.''

Joanna tickled her nose with the end of her quill as she reread what she had written and then ''tsked'' with irritation. She had forgotten something important.

''I will also gather over and above what is needed here so that you may draw upon the excess if the campaign should continue longer than is now planned. Send to me here at

Clyro, for I will return to this place as speedily as I can.''

That was really all Joanna had to say, but she sat with the quill in her hand, then dipped it and added, ''I was most desirous of coming to you myself, only for the pleasure of greeting and the pain of parting, but I knew there would be no place for me in Oswestry. I comfort myself for this loss in meeting with the thought that we may soon have the pleasure of greeting without the pain of parting. God keep you safe—and do you not be such a fool as to put Him to extra labor by exposing yourself more than is needful. Written this twenty-fifth day of June by Joanna of Roselynde, your loving and dutiful wife.''

When the letter was handed to Geoffrey by Knud, he barely glanced at it. Finding the information he needed written directly after the greeting, Geoffrey thrust the letter into a safe place with the intention of reading it more carefully when he was at leisure and could enjoy it. However, Geoffrey never was ''at leisure'' any more. The vassals who served under him had had time to take his full measure. They no longer cared that he was twenty years old, all they cared about was that Geoffrey seemed able, and willing, to solve their problems. Before he woke at dawn, those who had the night watches were waiting to speak to him. More often than not he was on horseback while the others ate their dinners, and, when he returned to snatch a dry, cold, unappetizing meal, still others were waiting with new troubles. Lacking Ian's experience, he allowed the men to take advantage of him. Where Ian would have answered with a brief sentence of advice, knowing that what was done was not of great importance, Geoffrey felt obliged to go and see for himself. Worse, where Ian would have told a man sharply that he should attend to such a thing himself, Geoffrey took the burden on his own shoulders.

Above and beyond the effort demanded by his own men, Salisbury and the king drew heavily on Geoffrey's time. There was no lack of advice on how best to conduct a campaign in Wales now. A number of Welsh princes, who hoped to see Lord Llewelyn's pride abated, were with the king and eager to show themselves earnest in his cause. They were not, however, in agreement about anything else very often, and the king insisted that Geoffrey attend the conferences so that he could watch them and listen to them in person, the better to judge the honesty of their advice as well as the practicality of it. Because he knew Owain well and Llewelyn, although less well, at least in a way that was free of envy, spite, and prejudice, Geoffrey was able to make a suggestion here and there.

The help he gave, increasing his father's pride in him, did Geoffrey no good with his uncle. John might hate his nephew and secretly hope he would catch his death in the coming action, but he was perfectly willing to use the young man as long as he was alive and found him useful enough not to plot his death actively. Thus, Geoffrey was indispensable at each war council. Salisbury did not realize how his son was driven. He saw Geoffrey only at council and they hardly exchanged a word that did not concern the subject immediately under discussion. The earl was also very busy and, if he gave Geoffrey a thought, it was of simple gratitude that his son did not run to him constantly for advice.

The army left Oswestry and as soon as they came to Llewelyn's land, the men were loosed. One village after another went up in flames. The pack animals fed on the unripe standing crops. The offal of meals and such beasts as died were thrown into the wells to foul the water. The main force was divided in two. One part clung to the coast road and the other followed the road through the river valleys. On both these paths the draft animals could draw the heavy wains of supplies. Strong parties ranged out a half day's ride northward and southward on every track they crossed, burning and pillaging whatever they found in their way. Some men were lost to the bowmen along the way who plagued them, but it did not hurt their spirit now. Their revenge was quick and sure. One small keep and then another and still another were taken in a matter of hours as the full force of England fell upon them.

Long marches were undertaken most willingly by the men who still seethed with anger and frustration at how they had been tricked and ambushed. Now they were getting their own back, and there was pleasure in it. At first, Geoffrey was at one with his men, but as his fatigue grew and he began to see familiar places raped and left broken he grew less glad. At the fortified village of Pen-y-Gaer, a flood of revulsion struck him. Geoffrey had stayed there with Ian and Llewelyn and Owain. They had hunted in the precipitous hills and sat by huge fires at night listening to their host, a man of exquisite manners and great learning, although he spoke no word of any language save Welsh, sing the history of his people. He had even taught Geoffrey a few hauntingly beautiful songs of enchantment and love and death.

The old hill fort, so old that no one knew when it had first been fortified, was a smoking ruin. The crops were ripped untimely from the earth for green fodder. The grazing fields were burnt over. Fire even flickered on the edges of the forest where an earnest attempt had been made to set the hills themselves ablaze. It was a poor return for the welcome Geoffrey had received. Guilt tore him. It was he who had suggested this. In pride and heedless haste he had urged this cruel path.

Yet it was the best way, the only way. They must walk this path or the path to ignominy, to being driven from the country like starved, whipped curs with their tails between their legs. Perhaps in the long view it would be worth while. If Wales lay at peace for many years with an impartial judge to settle the quarrels between the princes so that the land would not be torn and burnt, the good would outweigh the evil. The land would grow green again, Geoffrey told himself, and the old fortress would be rebuilt. He sighed and touched his horse, making his way toward Tostig and the men who were formed up to continue their march. Who knew how often the structures on this hill had been taken and burnt and rebuilt and taken and burnt and rebuilt yet again. Once more would not matter.

For all the burning, there had been little loss of life, so far. The people, as was their custom, had fled away to hide in the hills and forests, driving their cattle before them. The towns were another matter. At Bangor, the coast road and the inland route met and the full army reassembled. What would have happened had the town yielded was impossible to say. It seemed to Geoffrey that John was enjoying the devastation and might not be willing to accept an offer to yield. The question did not arise. The bishop of Bangor closed the gates and cursed the excommunicated king, crying anathema also on the army that was contaminated by his presence.

There was a brief council of war at which Geoffrey stood still and silent. He knew what must be done and his reason agreed heartily with the advice the king received and the orders he gave. Only his heart cried out that it was a fair town, with its river winding down to the sea. Why should it die? And when the men around the king spoke approval of the final plans, he said nothing, looking down at the hem of his surcoat which was blackened from brushing against the charred remains of the last village they had fired.

Salisbury caught up with his son before he reached his own men. "What is wrong, Geoffrey?" he asked. "Do you think we are mistaken in what we do?"

"No."

The blank monosyllable startled Salisbury into a closer examination of Geoffrey's face. "Child, what is it? Are you ill? Have you had bad news?"

Geoffrey pushed his stiff lips up into a smile. "No news at all, and I am quite well, father. I am only tired of seeing blackened earth where life once was."

"I think you could stop just after the word tired. You look tired to death! What *have* you been doing?"

The smile softened into greater naturalness. "Nothing of which you would disapprove. There has been no fresh womanflesh along the road, and what we carry with us is too rank for my taste. Nor have I been drunk since you saw me fuddled in the camp at Whitechurch. I have not had time."

"For that you should make time. What the devil makes you think I would disapprove of a healthful diversion?" Salisbury remonstrated. But there was no time now to get to the root of what was troubling Geoffrey. Horns were already sounding in parts of the temporary encampment. "I must go and you also," he went on, "but for God's sake, Geoffrey, have a care for yourself. When you are so tired, it is not well to trust overmuch to your own skill and judgment. Have some trusty men about you. Child, you have given me greater joy than anything else on this earth. Do not now make me curse the day I seeded you into your mother."

"I do not think either of us has much to fear," Geoffrey said bleakly, looking at the walls of Bangor.

In fact they were both right. The town was ill defended. In many places, the walls were scaled and the gates battered in with virtually no resistance. However, here and there, bands of determined men tried to stem the invasion. Having come over the wall with no more to contend against than a few arrows, which seemed to be aimed by a novice with the bow, Geoffrey ran headlong into a group of twenty. Their purpose obviously was to overturn the ill-constructed scaling ladders. Torn between the knowledge that he must protect his men and forward a purpose that was right but abhorrent to him and a feeling of sympathy for the desire of the men opposing him to preserve their city, Geoffrey fought with even more than his usual ferocity and less than his usual caution. Had not the older men under his command already decided among themselves to "keep one eye" on their excellent but inexperienced leader, Geoffrey might well have come to grief. As it was, he raged like a tempest through the quarter of the city assigned to him, steeping himself in the need to strike and parry so that his mind would not fix on what would come after.

They fought afoot. Horses would have been no advantage to them in the narrow twisting streets. To be mounted might have been an additional disadvantage in the face of the unusual perils they faced. Young Sir Giles, the heir of Iford, was felled by a large piece of masonry cast from a roof. As

Geoffrey bent to look at him, a band of men burst from surrounding doorways. Although their numbers were insignificant in comparison with Geoffrey's force, numbers meant little in the crowded space. It was a hard-fought twenty minutes, with Geoffrey standing over his fallen liege man as once, when he was a young squire, Ian had stood over him.

That time Geoffrey's force came near disaster. Most of the responsible vassals rushed to their lord's aid from side streets when they heard the sound of fighting, which concentrated the leadership into one small space. Then, from the rooftops, the archers began to fire. In the close packed mass of men, the arrows could scarcely miss, and in the heat of the fighting it was a little while before anyone even realized that death was raining down on them from above. Drawn from his concentration on the battle in which he was engaged, Geoffrey shouted to Sir Robert de Remy to set some men to bursting in the doors so that they could get above and wipe out the plague of archers.

When the furor died down, it was discovered that others were also hurt. Sir Alfred of Ealand had an arrow through the thigh and some men-at-arms whose armor was not as effective as the mail of the knights were dead or badly hurt. The wounded were sent back to camp with an escort and Geoffrey moved his men forward again. They went with more care now, clinging to the sides of the streets so that they would not be easy targets for stones from the roofs. With their backs to the wall and their shields before them, they were also less vulnerable to archers. The Welsh knew that, however. No attempt was made to shoot at them until they were once more engaged in combat.

The tactic could not work well a second time, of course. As soon as a group of men charged into the street to engage Geoffrey's troop, de Remy's men began to batter at all the doors along the street. That time only one of Geoffrey's men-at-arms was hit by an arrow and he sustained only a slight wound. Essentially that was the end of all resistance in Geoffrey's sector. The men who opposed him were not soldiers and had little experience of war. They were brave enough, but without a real leader to spur them on and provide a new plan of attack for them, they were soon discouraged.

Geoffrey led his men, unopposed now, through the town until his troops converged with Salisbury's, d'Albini's, William de Cantelu's, and Arundel's. Sure that Bangor was theirs, they then turned about and began a systematic looting from the center of the town outward, firing the houses when they had stripped them of everything desirable. They fanned out like the spokes of a wheel, robbing and burning until the men were sated with loot and set fire to places without even looking within. It was the most efficient destruction of a town Geoffrey had ever seen. "Take down the cities," he had advised and, of a truth, there was scarcely one stone standing upon another in Bangor when the flames died down.

Because all knew it would be impossible to move the men until they had tasted the women they had dragged from the burning town and examined the prizes they had taken, the king did not plan to move for the next few days. Discipline was relaxed to celebrate the victory—with the inevitable result. Quarrels broke out over women, over loot, from simple drunkenness. Geoffrey was not in the mood for celebration. He took his share of the valuable property, but he could not bring himself to take one of the weeping girls nor join one of the convivial parties. He would gladly have drunk himself into insensibility, but he did not get a chance. Before he had dipped very deep into the wine, he heard that the king's daughter Joan, who was Lord Llewelyn's wife, had ridden in and was pleading with her father to make peace with her husband. That lightened Geoffrey's spirit a little. The king was fond of Joan. There was some hope that Bangor would be the last holocaust Geoffrey would carry on his conscience.

He was waiting to hear what would come of Joan's visit when someone discovered he was sober. From then on,

Geoffrey was busier than ever, settling disputes, pacifying the combatants, and punishing those who transgressed too far. On the afternoon of the third day, one of the king's squires found him over in Wenneval's camp with a kneeling, weeping woman embracing his knees and two bloodied men, both nursing sore sword hands, shouting at him. To either side of the disarmed combatants, large groups of men were sheathing weapons.

It was clear enough what had happened without asking. Two battle captains had become embroiled over a woman and each had called upon his troop to support him. Then someone less drunk had realized where this was leading and had sought the nearest authority figure to settle the dispute before a minor war broke out in the camp. That was not the squire's business, however.

"Lord Geoffrey," he called over the voices of the angry men.

Geoffrey turned his head. "Be still!" he roared at the two he had just forcibly separated.

"Lord Llewelyn had just ridden in under safe conduct. The king desires that you come to him."

Although the men had fallen silent at Geoffrey's demand, the moment he turned his head to look at the squire they began to inch toward each other, growling. Hastily, Geoffrey turned back, lifting the sword he carried bared in his hand just a trifle. "Be still," he ordered again.

His voice was quieter, but the men not only shrank back from each other but away from him as well. There was a sudden deep blaze of rage in the young lord's eyes, which had turned a strange golden color, that boded no good for its object. The woman hamstringing Geoffrey by her embrace fell silent also, but she still clung to him, shuddering with dry sobs of fear.

"Tell my lord," Geoffrey said to the squire without turning his head, "that if I come to him now, Lord Llewelyn will be treated to the interesting sight of a full-scale war going on among our own men. Since I doubt this would induce him to make terms quickly, I must believe I will be of more use to my lord in the camp than at council.''

It was a reasonable enough excuse and Geoffrey did not believe that this particular squire had any animosity to him. Probably the message would be delivered as it had been given. Actually, he did not care how it was delivered. He had no intention of being present when Llewelyn made submission at any cost, even if he had to take to his bed and pretend he was dying. It was outrageous that the king had summoned him. John knew perfectly well that Geoffrey had often been Llewelyn's guest when he had served under Ian. He must have known also that Geoffrey had received many kindnesses from Llewelyn. Only John's warped mind, Geoffrey thought, could seek to increase the Welshman's misery and shame by summoning a man to whom he had been a gracious host, offering favors, to witness Llewelyn's humiliation.

Geoffrey was still furious when, late that night, Salisbury came to his tent. Geoffrey heard his father exchanging a low-voiced conversation with Tostig, who slept across the doorway of the tent, and got out of bed. "Come within. I am awake.''

"What ails you, child?'' Salisbury asked anxiously, peering at Geoffrey in the dim and uncertain light of an ill-shielded oil lamp.

"A sickness in the stomach and a sour taste in the mouth—and it is no sickness of the body, father, so do not ask what physician has seen to me.''

"What do you mean?''

"I was house guest to Lord Llewelyn, I cannot say how many times, a servant to his clan brother and vassal, a child he gave sweets, a young man to whom he pointed out with a wink the fairest and most available maidens. Lord Llewelyn himself taught me to use the long bow and praised my singing of Welsh songs. What kind of man, who had received so many kindnesses, would go to witness his humbling? What kind of a man would *bid* me witness it?''

Salisbury sat down on the stool and gestured Geoffrey to get back into bed. "You will take cold if you stand naked in the chill night air,'' he said absently, his mind obviously on his son's complaint. After a few minutes he shook his head. "I believe you are oversensitive my son. The Welsh princes, some of whom are tied to him in blood, made no objection."

"Oh, you do not understand!" Geoffrey cried. "It is different for them. They are changeable as the wind. This day they say they have a grudge against Llewelyn and would stamp on his head. Tomorrow they will run to him, crying that they are oppressed by others, and they will humble themselves and beg pardon and both will weep and, for a little while, all will be mended between them. Do you think Lord Llewelyn is a fool? He knows them and their ways. He knows Ian and me and our ways. Was not Owain there? Could I look my foster brother in the face at such a time? How *could* the king summon me for such a purpose? Rather he should have sent me to gather faggots for—"

"Geoffrey!"

The sharp, angry tone of authority cut off Geoffrey's voice. He clamped his teeth over the remainder of his furious words, but his eyes still smoldered. Salisbury sighed. Over the past few weeks he had forgotten how young Geoffrey was. To the boy it seemed as if a blow to the pride killed more surely than a blow to the body. Geoffrey had yet to learn that pride was like the fabled Hydra. If its head was cut off, two more heads grew in that place. Meanwhile, there was no use trying to force him to do something that would hurt him and embarrass him more than anyone else. John would simply have to get along without Geoffrey's advice.

"You have mistaken the king's intention," Salisbury went on, speaking more gently now. "You did not stop to think that John has many, many vassals. Do you believe he remembers the upbringing and friends of each of them? What was in his mind was that you had contributed much to this victory, and he wished to share it with you. If he ever knew you were beholden to Llewelyn—which I doubt—he had forgotten. He has very many things to think of and many troubles. Do not blame him for this small oversight. I will remind him tomorrow of your tie to Llewelyn. He will honor you the more that you served him so faithfully despite that tie and that you do not wish to bring more pain upon a defeated man.''

Geoffrey looked down at his hands, which were clenched so tight upon the bedclothes that his fingers ached. Deliberately, he loosened them and allowed his hands to lie open. He did not believe a word his father said. Perhaps Salisbury did not lie on purpose; he never could see his brother's real ugly nature. It was true that John had many vassals; however, Geoffrey was not only his nephew but was deputizing for Llewelyn's clan brother. The king could not have forgotten that nor that Geoffrey's knowledge of the Welsh, which John had found so useful, had come from his experiences in Llewelyn's court when he had been Ian's squire.

Perhaps, Geoffrey thought, trying to be fair, John could not know that there was real liking between myself and Llewelyn. John was not unreasonably harsh to the squires of his vassals, but he hardly knew they existed. *He* would never trouble to teach them new songs or show them how to track game, or tease them gently about their conquests in love. The effort to see the king's side of it was not much of a success. Geoffrey had scarcely gotten so far when the first thought recurred. It was not for himself that Geoffrey had been summoned, but as Ian's deputy. John neither knew nor cared about what, if any, relationship existed between Geoffrey and Llewelyn. It was to display Geoffrey as Ian's substitute, to point out that the horrible destruction in Wales was his idea, to make bad feeling between Ian and Llewelyn, if it was possible.

''I will be obliged to you if you can bring the king to excuse me from attendance upon him while Llewelyn is here,'' Geoffrey said. Then he lifted his eyes to his father's. ''I will not come in any case, unless I am bound hand and foot and dragged. I am sorry if I displease you, father, but I assure you that it is less out of disobedience to the king than out of fear of what I might be driven to do or say.'' Tears rose in his eyes. "I am none so proud of my share in this victory when I look on the blackened corpse of what once was a fair town. You warned me, and I did not listen. I am sorry now."

Salisbury rose and patted Geoffrey comfortingly on the shoulder. "Do not think you are the only one. No man likes to see such things. Do you believe it gives me joy? I can only tell myself that if a town must burn, why then, it is better that it be a Welsh town than an English one. And think instead that this may bring peace to Wales and then this one burning will save many, many others."

"Do you think so, papa?" Geoffrey asked with a spark of eagerness.

"I *hope* so," Salisbury replied, then smiled. "At my age, child, hope is all that is left." The smile died. He looked away, staring blindly at the blank side of the tent. "I am no longer sure enough of anything to believe."

Then reassured as to his son's physical health, Salisbury went out. He could do little for any other distress Geoffrey felt. Time and growing older would cure his qualms—if they ever would be cured. Geoffrey watched the tent flap settle behind his father and looked at the space for a while longer. Finally, he sighed and reached down beside the bed for the case that held a flagon of wine and goblets. He opened it, not really looking at what he did, and fumbled for a goblet, but he missed his aim and his fingers slid down behind the flagon where they encountered a small roll of parchment tucked in a corner. Startled, he withdrew it quickly and got out of bed to unroll it in the best light he could get from the lamp. He read the signature first, and his fixed expression gave way to a smile. It was Joanna's letter, which he had put away safely and then forgotten completely in the press of his responsibilities. He reached over for the blanket on the bed and drew it around him, his eyes on the letter. Joanna was certainly wise to remain on good terms with the Church, he thought. Only a fool would believe there would not soon be a settlement. She showed foresight also in collecting extra supplies although he knew now they would not be needed. His eyes traveled a little lower, checked, went back to reread.

She had wanted to come to Oswestry "only for the pleasure of greeting and the pain of parting!" Geoffrey sighed. Not half as much as he wished to go to her at Clyro this moment. He wished she had come, knowing quite well he would have been furious had she done so and that he could not have spared her a moment. But Clyro— Why should he not go to Clyro? He was doing no good here. He sighed again. That was not true, and he knew perfectly well he could not get leave to go even if he were to be so dead to his responsibilities as to abandon his men. Still he longed for Clyro, for the green hill, untouched by fire, and the dour gray keep lapped in peace—and for Joanna.

CHAPTER TEN

Joanna returned to Clyro from a whirlwind tour of her mother's property almost a week later than she expected. She found Sir Peter already at home and two letters waiting for her. One was a terse note from Geoffrey to tell her that Llewelyn had yielded and that he hoped she would remain, as she had said she would, at Clyro. He expected soon to be able to escort her back to Roselynde or wherever else she desired to go.

Sir Peter enlarged upon this, saying that he had been given leave to return home as soon as it was sure Llewelyn would make terms. Lord Geoffrey intended to see the other vassals out of Wales, however, to be sure they did not "forget" the war was over. Joanna was rather surprised that there was not a single personal word in the letter, not even a "loving husband" preceding the signature, but she assumed that Geoffrey was very busy and put the note aside with only a slight feeling of disappointment—until she opened the second missive.

This was from Lady Ela and was equally terse, bidding Joanna at all costs to rid herself of the company of Henry de Braybrook. In this matter, Lady Ela wrote, it was less dangerous to flout the order of the queen than to give substance to the rumors Isabella was spreading. It did not matter how innocent the relationship between Joanna and Braybrook was in truth. As Joanna well knew, Ela pointed out, no one wished to believe in innocence.

Dumbfounded, Joanna read and reread Lady Ela's letter. Then her eyes passed from it to Geoffrey's, which still lay on the table. Color flamed in her face, making her eyes as pale and bright as stars. She was far less infuriated by the slur cast by Geoffrey's jealousy on her purity than by the slur cast on her good taste. "Braybrook," she muttered furiously. "As if I would even spit on that mouther of empty phrases, that braying ass. Just because Geoffrey will roll in a bed with any piece of offal that offers itself, does he think I do not know the worth of what I give? Does he think me so much a fool as to take false coin—even in the name of love?"

Caution was innate in Joanna, however, and she did not spill her rage onto parchment, later to be regretted. First she asked Lady Mary whether any nobleman had come seeking her. Being assured that none had, she called Brian and went riding until time and physical fatigue cooled her temper. It then occurred to her that Geoffrey *might* be guiltless. It was not impossible that he had written before he heard any rumors, and his reserve might be owing to some cause at which she could not even guess. She had no intention either of answering his note or of waiting at Clyro longer than necessary to redistribute the extra provender she had assembled there. Geoffrey needed to learn that a polite request was more likely to win compliance to anything reasonable than a curt order.

Meanwhile, she addressed herself to writing to Lady Ela, stating flatly that she had left Whitechurch with *no* escort other than Beorn and Knud and the fighting troop. Moreover, she had not laid eyes on Sir Henry de Braybrook since her final morning at court when her last sight of him, struggling to disentangle himself from the rose bushes into which Brian had tipped him, was scarcely likely to engender romantic notions in her. Furthermore, she was shocked and hurt that Lady Ela could think her taste so vulgar and ill-formed as to take pleasure in Sir Henry's vapid mouthings.

"It is bad enough," she wrote, "that you should think so ill of my discretion and my powers of dispensing with unwanted attentions. It is far worse that you should believe I would permit that fewmet of a hare to come after me, join me secretly, and remain with me. Quite aside from ap-

pearances, I would have had to be rid of him—whatever
the queen's will—to save my sanity. Four days of Sir Henry
from Roselynde to Whitechurch was enough. Rather than
endure four weeks of him, I would have killed him with my
bare hands. I do not know what can be done to still the
queen's tongue—nothing, I suspect. As for my private
honor, except for one day at Shrewsbury, I can prove that
Sir Henry was not at any time next or nigh me. I have been
in company constantly with the wives and daughters of my
mother's vassals and castellans. Thus, I have no fear of
countering any tale told of me, but such things are never
brought into the open where they can be disproved.''

"All I can hope for," Joanna continued, "is that you can
by some means discover where Braybrook really was in this
time. I have a feeling that he was *not* innocently engaged
with his own wife and that discovery of his true whereabouts would provide me with a weapon. Unfortunately,
that weapon would be against him—and he is a poor frail
reed of a thing. Also, if he had allowed this rumor to be
spread out of spite against me, I do in some measure deserve
it. I was once again carried away by my delight in a jest—
but that is better told in your ear than in writing.''

By the time she had written so much, Joanna felt more
sorry for than angry with Braybrook. She had little doubt
that the queen was the impetus behind his actions. It seemed
to her that the poor man would be ground to dust between
the nether millstone of her own contempt for him and the
upper of the queen's conviction that he could win her if he
would only try hard enough. And, to make matters worse, if
Geoffrey's note had been cold out of jealousy, Braybrook
might well be chopped to pieces before he was ground to
dust. The turn of phrase made Joanna laugh, but she soon
sobered. It was not really funny at all. Sir Henry's father
was a favorite of the king's and a power in the court. For
Geoffrey to kill or even publicly to humiliate the son would
be dangerous, in spite of all Salisbury could do to protect
him.

Hastily, Joanna unrolled the letter she had just finished

and added a postscript. "If Geoffrey is at court and has heard of these matters, you may show him this letter if you think it wise. At all cost, however, do not permit him to attack Sir Henry who, I suspect, is more an unwilling tool than an intending seducer."

The new perspective in which she saw the situation made Joanna revise her intention of leaving for Roselynde at the earliest moment she could. Actually, the change of opinion did not matter, except as it marked the waning of her rage, because the day after Joanna had dispatched her messenger to Lady Ela, Geoffrey arrived. Joanna had been out with Sir Peter when he came into the keep, determining whether a particular stretch of hillside should be retained as common grazing field or returned to woodland, and they came back to find him still in full armor, sitting in a window seat and staring dully at the garden below.

Appalled, Sir Peter began to apologize for his wife's deficiencies, but in truth he did not know what to say. Mary was not the cleverest of women, but she did know what was owing in courtesy to a guest and, more particularly, to the betrothed husband of the next mistress of the estate.

Geoffrey looked blankly at the man for a moment, then sighed and smiled. "Rather it is I who should beg pardon," he soothed, realizing why Sir Peter was stumbling and stammering. "It was most discourteous of me to sit like this as if I expected ill in this place. I swear it is not so. Do you please tell your wife I am sorry if I was rude. I am sorely out of temper, but it is no fault of hers nor of yours."

The remark made Joanna lift her brows, but she did not reply to it directly. There was plenty of time for her to tell Geoffrey what she thought. The most essential thing, as far as Joanna was concerned was to obtain some privacy. Then if Geoffrey wished to quarrel, they could do so with decency.

"Since I must learn to put up with your tempers, my lord," Joanna said dulcetly, "do you come and let me unarm you so that your appearance will no longer be an offense to our host."

A slight flush rose into Geoffrey's cheeks. Sir Peter cleared his throat and shifted his feet uneasily. He was not too clever, but one thing he had learned from long association with the lady of Roselynde was to get out from under when she showed temper. He did not know Joanna as well as he knew Alinor, of course, but he greatly feared it was like mother like daughter.

"If you will give me leave," he said hastily, "I will go to my wife and tell her you are ready to bathe now, my lord."

"Yes, certainly," Geoffrey agreed, "and will you do me the favor of seeing that my men are disposed as is most convenient?"

Sir Peter nodded and moved away. Before he was quite out of earshot, however, he heard the young lord's voice change.

"That is no way to speak to me, Joanna. I am sorry to have alarmed Sir Peter, but that, as you saw, could be set right with a few words. There is much worse that I cannot set right at all."

All thought of unjust jealousy flew from Joanna's mind. It was clear enough that what Geoffrey said had no personal application to her. She dropped her hand to Brian's head, as if to steady herself and then said quietly. "How bad? How soon?"

"I do not know, and it is my own fault I do not know," Geoffrey replied bitterly.

That did not need to be explained to Joanna. Geoffrey had spoken out again when he should have been silent. "Only tell me, my lord," she said softly, "will I need to call up the vassals to our defense?"

Geoffrey had been looking at Joanna's hand on the dog's head. Now he looked up and smiled. "*Our* defense? Would you?" he asked, reaching out to draw Joanna closer.

"You are mine!" she exclaimed.

Torn between shock and laughter, Geoffrey dropped his hand. He did not confuse Joanna's flat statement with tenderness for him. He had heard her say the same thing often enough through the years concerning one thing or another, most of them inanimate. It was funny and painful at the same time to hear the words applied to himself.

"There is no need for that, and no danger to us more than to any other," he said, "but I am heartsick. It was I who urged the burning of Bangor, and it was done, and Llewelyn yielded. I hated it, but I thought it would be worth all if it brought a long peace between England and Wales and among the Welsh themselves. Instead, between all those wise men—the king, my father, FitzPeter, all of them— they are sowing the seeds of a worse hatred for England and a more violent rebellion in Wales than tore the land free after the first Henry had conquered it."

"When?" Joanna asked. "Should I leave the extra supplies stored here? Should I tell Sir Peter to hire more men?"

Then Geoffrey did laugh. Joanna's total preoccupation with the particular was refreshing, and her absolute reliance upon his knowledge and judgment was soothing "I might be mistaken," he warned.

Joanna shook her head. "I do not think it. You are clever, Geoffrey. You see, you remember, you learn, you add things together. Even if matters mend themselves so that what you foresee now does not come about, you will have been mistaken in the right way. There is no hurt in being prepared for trouble that does not come."

"Well, in any case it will not come until spring. The Welsh who fought against Llewelyn have not yet tasted John's justice to those he fears may do him hurt, and Llewelyn's rage against them is still too hot for them to run to him in the next few months. Then it will be winter. They will not fight while the snow lies in the mountains and closes their secret paths."

"Good. Then there is time to think and talk about what to do. Come now and let me unarm you." Joanna watched Geoffrey as he sighed and rose to follow her. She saw that he was very tired, but there was something else also. Her heart smote her. If he was grieving over a stupid piece of scandal, she could at least ease him of that. "I fear," she said softly, "that there is more burdening your heart than the troubles in Wales."

"You are so right," Geoffrey growled bitterly, "that lies heaviest on me because I am guilty of mixing myself into the matter, but, in truth, there is worse. I fear—" He stopped and looked at the maids who were laying out clothes for him to wear, cloths for drying, soap, herbs for scenting the hot water that the menservants were pouring into the large wooden tub.

"Let me unarm you while they finish," Joanna remarked, with a significant nod.

Servants were nothing, but they did have ears and they gossiped among themselves and to the servants of visitors. Thus, a few words, innocent or not so innocent, could be blown up into a whirlwind of rumor that could destroy the unwary. Joanna unbelted Geoffrey's sword and lifted off his hauberk with almost the quick efficiency of her mother. She wrinkled her nose over Geoffrey's tunic and shirt.

"From where did you come?"

"Northampton."

"Northampton! I thought you were in Wales."

"I was. The terms were made with Llewelyn on the twelfth. That same night, the king received a messenger saying that the emissaries from the pope had arrived and also Renaud Dammartin from Boulogne—"

"Then he has broken with Philip?"

"You had better say that the other way. Philip has broken with him. He has done more. He has disseised him. He has forced Lady Maude, Renaud's daughter, to marry his son out of Agnes of Meran."

"Philip Hurepel?" Joanna lifted her brows and bit her lip. "I am glad I warned the guildsmen in Roselynde town and sent word to Mersea. My people will be ready for any little game that lame one wishes to play."

"You warned them already? How did you know?"

"Cockerels crow at court when they strut before a hen— and there was only one kind of crowing to which this hen would listen."

The words, half-contemptuous, half self-satisfied were out before Joanna thought. Geoffrey's expression froze. Fool! I am a fool! Joanna thought. She snapped her fingers at the servants and they made haste to finish what they were doing and clear the room. Geoffrey had turned away, toward the tub, while Joanna sought wildly for something to say that would soothe him. Instead she pushed Geoffrey gently. "Go to. Get into the tub."

She poured water over Geoffrey's head and ran the soap over his fine hair. "Finish your tale. How came you to Northampton from Wales?"

"In the morning the king left for Whitechurch, where he had ordered Marsh and the rest of the court to meet him. I and some others remained with the army to be sure that the twenty-eight hostages would be given up to us as arranged. The Welsh allies were given leave to go. When the hostages came, we marched the men back to Whitechurch, but the king was gone from there. I had already sent a messenger craving leave to come here to you at Clyro, but I found waiting a command to bring the hostages with all haste to the king at Northampton."

Feeling Joanna toweling his hair dry, Geoffrey began to sit erect. "No, stay," she said. "It is easier for me to wash you. Wait, let me put a cloth behind you to ease your head."

What am I to her, Geoffrey wondered, as he watched Joanna fold the cloth she had used on his hair into a thick pad to protect his neck from the sharp edge of the tub. I am hers—like a farm or a serf or a horse, so she will care for me. She thanks God for me—on Sir Peter's word that I led and cared for the men well—because I am a careful steward of her property. But she did kiss me—of herself. . . .

"So then I know how you came to Northampton, but I do not see why you are so troubled," Joanna urged. "Come, tell me. It is like drawing teeth to get a tale from you. Was it something you saw on the march to Whitechurch?"

"Oh, no. I was content enough then, although to tell the truth I had my bellyful of John's company and I would have been better pleased— No matter. It was at Northampton that I saw shadows of things to come—evil shadows.''

The words were full of foreboding, but Geoffrey's voice was more relaxed, sad still, but not so desperate as he had sounded in the hall. Joanna had been badly frightened by the controlled hysteria under the words he had said then. It was that emotion to which she had responded by asking if she must call up her mother's vassals. Now she realized that it had been fatigue and the inability to talk to anyone that had come close to unbalancing Geoffrey. The warm water, the soothing attentions she gave him, the opportunity to say things aloud and hear a response to his ideas were permitting him to see the situation ahead in better perspective.

"You said the Welsh would break loose again. Why?"

"Because John now thinks to rule them with fear and power. When he first spoke of this campaign, he said he would keep England outside of Welsh affairs as the balancer and the settler of problems, thus also giving the princelings there no need to unite. I was well content with that. Nothing could be better. It was what Llewelyn was trying to do but with the advantage that John would be arbiter in Llewelyn's place and thus the Welsh would have no strong central leader who could weld them into one.''

"But if Llewelyn failed, why do you believe John could succeed?"

"Because John is *not* Welsh. Do you not see? Gwenwynwyn, Maelgwyn and his brother Rhys, and all the rest of the petty princes see Llewelyn as one of themselves, raising himself over their heads with no more right to lead than they have. That John is greater than any of them, they do not contest. Thus, had he kept himself apart from them, after proving he could overpower the greatest among them, they would have obeyed him gladly. They would even, I think, have paid a reasonable scutage to keep the king's favor, and they would certainly have been strong allies in any war against the French or the Scots or anyone.''

"Get out, Geoffrey, I am finished with you.''

Joanna stood back holding a large square of linen, which

she wrapped around her betrothed as he stepped from the tub. He shivered in the damp of the inner chamber, and she drew him toward the fire where she dropped the now-damp linen and began to dry him thoroughly with another cloth.

"Instead of keeping to this plan," Geoffrey continued, his voice sharpening, "John has decided to build strong places all through Wales from which he can rule directly and to build also a great keep at Aberystwyth. They will not endure this. I know they will not, and, fool that I am, I said so. That was when I was told that, since I had craved leave to come to you, I should go and meddle no more in matters of state that I was too young to understand."

Bitterness and hurt pride rang in Geoffrey's voice. Instinctively, Joanna responded with support. "The more the fools they to confuse youth with stupidity. I greatly fear you are right, Geoffrey, right in all ways. I do not think the Welsh princes will cry out against what they see and so give warning either. They will bide their time and then, when all have been lulled into thinking they are cowed, they will overrun the country and wrest it back into their own hands."

Although she did believe Geoffrey's analysis of the situation, Joanna spoke largely to assuage his hurt. Single minded, she was really concerned only about Clyro, and she thought that was probably far enough out of the strategic path to be safe. She would, of course, warn Sir Peter herself or ask Geoffrey to warn him, but she believed the attacks would be directed against the new royal strongholds, rather than at long-time residents known to be good neighbors. There was another aspect to the problem, however.

"Why does this trouble you so much, Geoffrey?" Joanna asked gently as she drew up and tied his chausses. "Do you fear they will flood over into England to take revenge?"

To her surprise his expression lightened. "No. No. That I had not thought about. Perhaps it was not all wasted. They have tasted England's might. They will try to throw off the yoke, but they will do nothing that can really arouse bitterness here. It lay on my heart that I urged the burning of

Wales, even some places where I was once a guest—and all for no purpose. But now you have said something of importance that I had missed. For Wales, and even for England, this may not fall out so ill. If they cast off John's influence, they will run back to Llewelyn. He may well gather all Wales under his power, but he will remember. He will do nothing that can arouse the English barons to fury. He will stay in Wales. Thus, if they fall only on the king's strongholds—''

''We cannot trust to that.''

''Certainly not. Sir Peter must be warned to prepare. I think it scarce likely any will attack Clyro, but when it is seen he is stuffed and garnished for war, it will be even more certain they will avoid this place.''

The last words were muffled as Joanna pulled a shirt over Geoffrey's head. When his face emerged it had darkened again.

''I am a fool,'' he continued. ''What will happen in Wales will happen and, as you have been too kind to say, it is of little importance to us except in the hurt to my pride. I should pay attention to my own affairs. Joanna—'' Geoffrey caught her hands just before she turned away to take the belt of his robe from the chest where it lay. ''Joanna, I am afraid.''

She looked up at him, her eyes widening. This was no fear for which one could feel contempt. Geoffrey's mind had looked upon Armageddon. ''What?'' she asked, her breath trembling through open mouth.

''The king will drive the barons to open rebellion, and it will be soon, and I—I hate him. My gorge rises in his presence when he speaks to me—lies, all lies—with that smooth voice, and yet I know I must stand with him. There is no one else strong enough and—and much as I hate to say it—he is not so bad a king to the realm at large. But the barons fear him. They *only* fear him. It is not as with Henry or Richard where the fear was much mixed with love. There is *no* love for John, except in my poor father, no love at all, even in those most loyal to him.''

"But this has been true for years, Geoffrey. What is new?"

"What is new is that the king's pride has grown all out of reason. In three years he has brought Scotland, Ireland, and Wales to an obedience no other king ever forced upon them. He does not see that Pembroke and Ian sit upon Ireland, that King William of the Scots is weak and his barons so taken with quarrels among themselves that they have no time to look toward England, that Wales—well, I need not speak of that again."

"I still do not understand." Joanna shook her head. "Come, sit down." She pressed him into a chair, shoved a footstool under his feet and then, instead of sitting in the chair opposite, brought another stool close beside him and sat down on that, taking his hand into hers. "Tell me what happened to make you feel this."

"The first thing was the king's answers to the emissaries from the pope. The legate is Pandulf, I believe a wise and worthy man. Durrand of the Knights Templars was with him, more, I would say to protect Pandulf than to negotiate. At first, I thought all would be well. John was polite and he said at once that he would welcome into England the new archbishop of Canterbury, Stephen Langton, and any or all of the exiled bishops. This greatly pleased Pandulf and I could see he was willing and empowered to bargain. That was where the sweet wine turned sour. Had John offered a mil on a pound for restitution and a few sweet words, all would have been well. Had he offered *nothing*, only said that the problem must be considered and worked out with the bishops and archbishop, it would have been enough. The Church would have made peace and set about wringing restitution from him penny by penny—which would have been good for us."

"I gather the king was adamant?"

"Adamant? He was worse! He laughed at the power of the pope openly, and said he had more kindness from God in his excommunicated state than he had ever had as a faithful son of the Church."

Joanna's breath hissed in. "So help me, John is inspired by the devil!" She shivered suddenly. "Geoffrey, can it be that all this good, all the victories, is a trap set by Satan?"

"I said I was afraid," Geoffrey muttered, "and I do not fear the works of man."

"What will the pope do? John is already excommunicated. What more can Innocent lay upon him?"

"There are two steps more he can take. I do not even remember a time when a pope was bold enough—but it is said Innocent is such a man. He can absolve all oaths of fealty to John."

"Absolve all oaths of fealty?" Joanna's voice was thin and she wet her lips nervously. "But Geoffrey, that will mean—"

"Chaos! Armageddon! There will be no law in the land."

"Geoffrey—" Joanna clutched the hand she held tighter. "I do not mean to hurt you, beloved, but—but—"

"But should we send for Ian? You do not hurt me. It was my first thought. I can hold the vassals to their duty in a war. Even if there should be rebellion, I think they would obey me—but this! I wrote a letter, but I held it open hoping that my father and the bishop of Winchester—who is at court although he has not shown himself to Pandulf—would bring John to his senses. Then—the news came that Braose had died in Corbeuil."

"Braose? What has he to do with us?"

"He himself? Nothing. What has to do with us—or rather with Ian—is John's reaction to the news. He gloated on it openly, openly reminded the court how Braose's wife had offended him and what had befallen her. His eyes rested on a few—not least on me!—and he smiled and said such a fate was prepared for *all* his enemies."

"My mother—" Joanna whispered.

Geoffrey put an arm around her and felt how she trembled. "I did not send the letter," he assured her.

"But they *must* know about the trouble with the pope. They will hear it from Pembroke even if we do not send word."

"Yes, yet I dare not send a warning of John's spite. You know what will happen if I do."

That brought a trembling smile to Joanna's lips, although she was still shuddering with fear. She blinked away tears. "As well warn Ian of danger as prod a bull with a sharp stick. He would come charging home— Geoffrey, Geoffrey, what will we do?"

"The first thing is that we must write a letter together. You will best know what to say to your mother so that she will try to keep Ian in Ireland. I will give the news so that Ian can see the danger is not immediate. And it is not, Joanna. It will take time for Pandulf to communicate with the pope. The next thing is that we must go to every vassal and castellan and sound them most carefully while we give them warning. I believe most will be loyal. They will see the benefit of our protection in a time of chaos."

The outline of positive action to be taken calmed Joanna. She drew a deep breath and nodded. "Will we have time enough?"

"If we go separately, yes. You must go to your mother's people. I will go north first because I wish to visit Ian's northern vassals twice. They are the most like to break away. That whole northern part is a hotbed of rebellion. Then I will go to my keeps, and, after that, I will go to Leicester to get Adam and take him with me over his own lands."

"Adam? Oh, Geoffrey, you will not let Adam come to any danger, will you? He is so heedless, so wild."

Geoffrey looked reprovingly at his betrothed. "Adam is thirteen, no longer a child. Of course I will guard him as needful, but no more than that. He must know his men and they him. And he is not so heedless as you think. There is a good mind under all that laughter."

"But he is as bad—or worse—than Ian in the face of danger—and you are no better!" Joanna cried. "Let me come with you. Adam listens to me sometimes."

By no means offended by Joanna's strictures on his reaction to danger, which he took as a compliment, Geoffrey smiled at her indulgently. "However I regard a danger to myself, I assure you I will not permit Adam to run headlong into trouble." Then his arm tightened around her. "I cannot have you with us, Joanna, and it is not because I would not wish it. There is something else the pope can do, something I pray he will not do, but we must be prepared—which is why Adam must be in Sussex with me and you must be at Roselynde with easy access to the other southern keeps."

"Roselynde? The southern keeps? On top of all else, do you fear trouble with France?"

"Of course, what is more likely? You know the French kings have always claimed overlordship of England. From William the Bastard on, every king of England has been a vassal of the king of France."

"For lands in France, but not in England!"

"That is true enough, but it is a matter that French kings have always been willing to forget without special encouragement. What if the pope should declare John not fit to be king? What if he should urge holy war against a man devil-inspired, who is leading his subjects down the path to hell?"

"King Philip will come upon us like a ravening wolf."

"Just so. You must warn the fishermen and the merchantmen to watch as they have never watched before and—if it comes about as I fear—you must be where they can come to you readily so that you may direct me to where I must go to defend the land."

"Geoffrey," Joanna was trembling again, but her voice was steady. "I cannot be in two places at once. If I must go on progress to the vassals, I cannot remain at Roselynde."

He bent and kissed her, then drew her up into his lap. "The French trouble cannot come upon us until the spring. Time is needed for the pope to have the news that John remains contumacious and for him to negotiate with Philip. It is not likely that Philip would miss an opportunity to be well paid for doing what he would be glad to do anyway."

Joanna closed her eyes and rested her head on Geoffrey's shoulder. She wished the earth would open and swallow King John and King Philip and the pope too, right into hell.

"There cannot be anything more," she sighed, "can there?"

"Nothing of real import, but straws that show the wind is blowing from a wicked direction. John has declared a scutage of two marks on all who did not ride with him into Wales."

"That is his right, surely, but two marks—that is a heavy fine."

"Yes. He means it as a warning, I think. He is talking already of sailing to France next year and winning back what was lost to Philip."

"Will he never learn?" Joanna sighed.

"You know," Geoffrey temporized, "I am not certain I think it so bad a thing. I said before in a fit of passion that I hated the king. I suppose I hate the man, but as a king, when dealing with matters he understands and where his wild fears of his own men do not lead him into error and where his pride does not push him into foolishness, he has gained wisdom. This business with France might do well. He does not intend to use the strength of England alone this time."

"I do not understand," Joanna complained.

"It is a long tale going back to King Richard who supported and made treaty with Otto of Germany to help him become emperor of the Holy Roman Empire. John did nothing to forward this after Richard died, but he bespoke Otto well and honored him when he came to visit. Now that Philip is grown so mighty, the other kings and great dukes in Europe are seeking a way to contain him."

"And they look to John?" Joanna said doubtfully.

"Not yet, perhaps, but they can be made to do so. The king has offered good comfort to Renaud Dammartin, together with lands worth three hundred pounds a year. Renaud will be John's emissary, and the more convincing from his own treatment at Philip's hands."

"You think this is wise?" her voice was neutral.

"Yes. Yes, I do. If an alliance can be forged so that the Flemish, the Germans, and those others that will be swayed by Dammartin attack from the east at the same time that the king attacks from the south and west of France, Philip will be caught between two fires.''

There was a short silence. Geoffrey's expression was abstracted but his mouth was slightly curved as if what he contemplated was rather pleasant. Joanna could not see his full face, but from the line of jaw and lip she knew he was no longer tense. A wave of resentment passed over her.

"You will go if the king summons you for a war with France?'' she asked quietly.

"Oh yes, most gladly. It would serve many purposes.''

"Even if it leaves England naked to whomever wishes to attack?''

Geoffrey bent his head to look down at her. "Who would be left to attack England? Philip will be busy enough. Boulogne will either be allied with us, if the men are faithful to Renaud, or under Philip's command. No one else has any claim on England. Besides, many will not go. There will be men enough to defend this land.''

The answer was logical and perfectly true, but it brought no comfort to Joanna. She had not been thinking of the danger to England. That was only an excuse to protest Geoffrey's eager acceptance of still another war.

"If your hopes are satisfied,'' she said tightly, "I am likely to be a widow before I am a wife.''

Instead of replying, Geoffrey bent his head still further and kissed her. He had meant to offer comfort and reassurance, but in a moment he was quite ready to put aside all matters of state. War and rebellion could wait a while; this was a more important matter to which he must attend. Remembering how he had sensed her indifference in the garden at Whitechurch, Joanna resolved not to respond to him. It was not, she discovered to her surprise, a thing one could decide with one's mind. Under the tender warmth of Geoffrey's mouth, her lips parted and grew fuller; her skin began to take on that tingling sensitivity which gave so much pleasure and was a precursor to a rush of warmth to the loins. Angrily, Joanna wrenched her head away and pulled herself free of Geoffrey's arms.

"You do not care what I suffer or what I fear so long as you can kill men," she spat.

The bitter, jealous words conceived in Geoffrey's heart by Joanna's action, died in his throat. He stared at her, his mouth open a little with surprise. Then he got slowly to his feet. "My love," he said very gently, "you never gave me any reason to think you would suffer for my hurt or fear for my loss."

Color mounted into Joanna's face. "Silent suffering is the natural state of a wife, is it not?" she asked defensively.

Geoffrey struggled against a desire to smile, which he knew would be disastrous. It was far from the natural state of most wives in King John's court. For the most part, they would have thought it a rare treat to see their husbands hung by the thumbs. But Joanna would know nothing of that. Geoffrey thought of the women she knew well—her own mother, who looked as if she would eat her husband every time she laid eyes upon him; Isobel, countess of Pembroke, who watched the breath in and out of her William's mouth lest he utter a sigh she might miss; Ela, his own stepmother who, for all her loud complaints and constant whining, would cut out her own heart and hand it to Salisbury if he wanted it.

"Do not blame me for what is doubly not my fault," he pleaded, when he saw her eyes still bright with anger. "I am a man, and I have been bred to war. Would you rather I sat cowering, fearing to live each day lest I be called to bear arms? Also, the wars are none of my making."

Joanna dropped her head and did not resist when Geoffrey drew her back into his arms. It was true. She would have hated him if he were a coward. It was unreasonable, then, to blame him for taking pleasure in what he had been trained for all his life. When he lifted her face to his, she yielded, meeting his lips willingly. After a moment her arms went up around his neck and her lips parted, opening the warm haven of her mouth to his questing tongue. Geoffrey's hands slipped down her back to her buttocks, pressed her against him, relaxed, pressed her close again. Unconsciously, Joanna's arms tightened and relaxed in the same rhythm so that her firm, high breasts, their nipples very protuberant now, were squeezed against his chest.

Very soon it was not enough. By mutual consent their mouths came apart. Geoffrey took a step toward the bed, turning Joanna in his arm so that she would not need to walk backward. She came with him, one step and then another, and then stopped.

"If my mother and Ian remain in Ireland," she whispered, "we cannot marry. Geoffrey—"

"Does it matter so much to you, Joanna?" he pleaded softly.

She looked at him, her eyes clouded with desire. "I do not know," she sighed. "Why could we not be married before they left? Why were we only betrothed?"

"It was to protect us—to protect you," Geoffrey assured her. "They had no other purpose than making it easier for you to repudiate me if, after we were together as we have been, you found me distasteful."

Wide-eyed, Joanna stared at him. She was by no means as innocent as she had been before this recent sojourn at court. She knew men in the throes of passion might say anything, tell any lie, to bring about the satisfaction of their desire. In general, Geoffrey was truthful, but he was no better than any other man with other women. With her? Joanna did not trust him in this, and she was even more distrustful of her own treacherous body, in which the fading thrills of pleasure only recalled and begged for a renewal of his caresses.

For Geoffrey the word "repudiation" had brought something to mind that cooled his ardor considerably. If he took Joanna now, she would not come as a maiden to her marriage bed. There would be only clean sheets to show in the marriage ceremony on the morning after their supposed first mating. That was the purpose of the ceremony, that a groom could repudiate his bride if she were not a virgin, and the proof of that virginity was bloodstained sheets. He would know, of course; there would be no question of repudiation, but it was not a good thing to smirch the reputation of one's own wife. All her life that piece of slander would stain her, and Geoffrey was not sure, even with his private knowledge of her virtue, that he could endure the sly looks and ugly hints that would follow. He sighed and loosened his grip on Joanna.

Equally desirous yet fearful of renewing their love play, they stared somberly at each other until, with a tiny shiver, Joanna slid out of Geoffrey's embrace entirely. For both there was the sense of something very sweet slipping away, and they swayed back toward each other.

"My lord, my lady," Lady Mary said softly from the doorway, "dinner is ready to be served. Will you come?"

CHAPTER ELEVEN

At first as September ended and October lay golden across the land, Joanna wondered whether Geoffrey had been right. A profound peace enwrapped England and the three countries John had conquered. In that peace a fine crop was harvested and pigs and cattle fattened on the gleanings among the stubble. Even the normal petty battles between one landowner and another seemed to have been suspended. Wherever Joanna traveled there was no sign of war, no burnt-over houses and fields, no dead men, no weeping women.

Only in the high halls of the nobility where Joanna was a guest was there the slightest hint that all was not perfect. No one grumbled aloud. No ill word was said of the king. Nonetheless, there was a sense of unease, of waiting, as if the men were perched on the edges of their chairs ready to seize a bared weapon and leap into action. Among her own people, Joanna spoke openly of the dangers Geoffrey had envisaged. And amid all that peace, to her surprise, she was not laughed at. From the older men in particular, she had sighs of relief and sage noddings of the head.

"The young lord is wiser than his years," Sir Giles of Iford said, "and you also, my lady, in that you see his wisdom. You need not fear me. I have reason, perhaps, not to love the king, but I will be loyal to your lady mother in any path she and Lord Ian choose. More especially if the worst befall us and men are absolved from their fealty, it will behoove us to cling together to preserve ourselves from a world run mad."

Sir Henry of Kingsclere did not understand nor pretend to

184

understand. "Your mother set me in this keep to guard it for her," he said simply. "I will obey her order and fight for the king—or against him—as she or you bid me."

Matters were not so straightforward on the great estates of Mersea. Joanna had gone there first because it was farthest away. Sir John did not laugh, but he was not convinced of the coming danger. Moreover, Mersea was powerful in herself, not so likely to be snapped up by a larger neighboring landowner and, thus, in less need of protection from the overlady. Perhaps it rankled Sir John, who was a young man, to have to bow down to a woman. Joanna did not press the point, merely asked how the merchants and fishing fleets were dealing with Philip Hurepel to remind Sir John of the warning she had sent him and that changes had already taken place. He was somewhat more thoughtful after that. He could hold his own on his lands, but he had no ear or eye at court and might be badly hurt without news from his overlady about what went on there and in the world at large.

Thus, when Joanna paid a second visit toward the end of November, Sir John made no bones about the fact he had changed his mind. He had scarcely lifted her from her mare when he drew her into an alcove in the great hall. "Have you had the news yet?" he asked, and, not waiting for her reply, "Lord Geoffrey was right. I did not think the pope would do it. He has absolved all men of their fealty to the king, all men from princes to serfs are bid to avoid John at table, in council, or in converse on pain of their own excommunication and are free of any allegiance to him."

It was no shock to Joanna. She had already heard of the sentence passed by the pope from the merchants of Roselynde town. Nonetheless, she felt an inner hollowness and she needed to fight back tears. She wanted Geoffrey or, lacking him, her mother and Ian. But she knew she could have no support from any of them. Owain had sent a secret message to Geoffrey warning him that Lord Ian must *not* return to England. He was not specific in his reasons, but there was no doubt in Geoffrey's mind or in Joanna's that the Welsh were making ready to cast the English out of Wales once again. And Geoffrey himself was frantically busy.

He had not had the largely enthusiastic response from Ian's vassals that Joanna had had from Alinor's. It was not that the men wished to be free of their overlord. Ian was deeply respected by his men and even loved. The trouble was that the king was so much hated that a strong conflict was aroused in them. They argued loud and long that, if Ian was absolved of his vows, he above all men should turn his back on the king. John had tried to have him killed more than once. John hated the lord and the lord's lady. It was mad, flying in the face of providence, to cling to one who was not only a bad king but a personal enemy.

"There is no one else," Geoffrey said wearily. "There is no one else. Would you rather have French Philip? Some man must be king or worse will befall us than John's hate."

"There is young Henry," one baron answered, "young Henry with a council to guide him—"

"Do not dream of it," Geoffrey snapped, maintaining his countenance with some effort. "You know as well as I what that would mean. Instead of the exactions of one man we would have a whole flock of crows plucking at us."

"Perhaps—perhaps not. But if it is God's will that the king not be king—"

Geoffrey had been in the south with Adam when Joanna sent him word that the sentence against John had been published on the Continent. It would not be officially published in England, of course; John could prevent that. However, he could not prevent the information from leaking out unofficially. Geoffrey made one swift round of Adam's southern keeps, then returned the boy to Leicester on his way north. He had a letter from Ian to show the vassals and he wanted the news and Ian's letter to reach them at the same time. If the news preceded him, there was more chance that the men would commit themselves to some lord opposed to the king before he could fix their interest and loyalty.

Thus, Joanna was on her own. Her fears did not show on

her placid face, and her hands and voice were steady when she said, "Well, my lord, then you are come to a point of decision. Will you stand with us, or must I tell my mother that the son of her dear friend and most trusted vassal, your father, has chosen to desert her?"

The situation was deliberately phrased in the ugliest possible way that still carried no threat. Shock and revelation showed in the young man's eyes.

"I never said that," Sir John replied indignantly. "I only said I did not believe the pope would go so far. My vow to your mother is nothing to do with hers to the king."

Since she had succeeded in making Sir John see where his thoughts were leading him and there could be no doubt that, having seen that path he had turned aside from it, Joanna put out her hands and took his. "Do not be angry with me. Forgive me that I misunderstood you. You know it is not out of great love for the king or blindness to his faults that we are determined to stand with him. Whatever offense the king has given the pope, the Holy Father is not considering us, also his children, I fear. He is ready to take away our king, but he has nothing to offer us in exchange. However much your head hurts you, it is better to keep it than to have it chopped off."

It was well worth a few days to confirm Sir John in his decision and Joanna spent them gladly, using the opportunity to warn her vassal about the possibility that Philip would invade England. She pointed out that this time the French king might have allies from the Low Countries, who would know well how to negotiate the bogs that protected Mersea from most invasions. However, she did not prolong her visit more than necessary. Partly this was because she did not wish to seem suspicious or to be watching Sir John, but mostly it was because Joanna was frightened and longed for the security of the great walls of Roselynde keep.

It was all very well to circumvent slyly the interdict by the pope. It was also all very well to drag a simple priest off her land at her horse's tail. Joanna was no credulous serf to be awed by the ability to read and write and chant in Latin into the belief that a priest was any more than a man. For that matter, she knew that bishops and popes were also men, and she had no hesitation in expressing her doubts of their good sense, not to mention their infallibility. But Joanna *did* believe in God and the Devil, *did* acknowledge the active participation of the Highest Good and the Greatest Evil in the affairs of men.

Somewhere deep in Joanna's mind there was an intimate connection between King John and the Father of Evil. The king had been the enemy in her home since the day she was born. Her memories of her father were now very dim, but one of them was of Simon in a real rage—to be clearly distinguished from the brief tempers Alinor drove him into—cursing the king as the misbegotten spawn of Satan. It was all becoming too real.

Geoffrey and Joanna had managed to avoid the court, but Lady Ela kept Joanna well supplied with news—and most of it was not good. Nothing of great importance had happened since the pope's emissaries and Renaud Dammartin had departed, but many minor incidents, far too many, showed the king's contempt for his nobles and his indifference to their opinion of him.

Joanna spent Christmas alone at Roselynde. She had not known whether she was pleased or disappointed when she returned there at the beginning of the second week in December and found Geoffrey's letter saying that he could not be with her. There was no doubt in her mind that she missed him, that she longed for his conversation, the sound of his sweet voice singing, his touch—but, since they had almost come to coupling in Clyro, there had been a marked constraint between them.

They had met twice for a few days and, while they discussed business and exchanged news, they were very happy together. The ease, however, did not persist. When they touched, even by accident, it was as if lightning passed between them. There was a shock, painful in intensity. Joanna could feel her heart check and then begin to hammer. Geoffrey would flush a little and withdraw stiffly. Joanna did not misread him. It was clear that he felt what she felt. His eyes burned yellow with desire. What she did misunderstand was the reason for his restraint. She was more convinced than ever that he had lied at Clyro, that there was some important purpose behind the choice of betrothal over marriage.

Thus, Joanna did not ask in any of the letters she wrote to Alinor for permission to marry. She was, in fact, careful not even to hint of her desire. Geoffrey came into her letters only as he served a political purpose. But her body was not docile to her will; reason meant nothing to her lips and her skin and her loins. Geoffrey had awakened her lust, and it would not be lulled back to sleep. When he was near, she found her nostrils spreading to catch his scent, her hand lifting, without volition to touch him, her knee moving to press his under the table.

It was some comfort to Joanna, for desire had not yet killed her sense of humor, that whatever Geoffrey did to assuage his lust while they were apart was of little help to him when they were together. She was both titillated and amused when he drew himself together so they should not brush in passing, when he tore his eyes from an absorbed contemplation of her face or throat or breast to fix them stubbornly on some less magnetic object. It was a comfort to know he suffered also, but a painful one when he would not even permit her to perform the common services of a hostess, such as bathing him and helping him dress. Joanna was not offended; she understood why. She had even laughed heartily at him when he roared at her to get out and let him be—but she wanted to touch him, she wanted to.

There was thus as much relief as sadness when Joanna read Geoffrey's letter and she sighed only a little when she packed the gifts she had made ready for her betrothed and sent them off with Knud to be delivered to him. Nonetheless, it was lonely in Roselynde, and Joanna set about arranging the twelve-day festivities very listlessly. It was going to be very odd to be sitting all alone in great state at the high table with no one to talk to or laugh with. Joanna was almost tempted to go to Iford or Kingsclere, just for the sake of company, but her sense of duty would not permit her to deprive the people of Roselynde of their celebrations for such a small thing as a little loneliness.

In the end, she had more pleasure from the holiday than she expected. On the morning of the first day, Sir Guy came riding in with a chest full of gifts from Alinor and Ian. He had come from Ireland and had concealed himself in Roselynde town just to give her a pleasant surprise. The afternoon of the same day brought two more welcome guests—the eldest son of one of Geoffrey's vassals and Salisbury's eldest squire, the former with Geoffrey's presents and the latter with those from Salisbury and Lady Ela. All her loved ones had remembered her, Joanna realized with warmth, and each intended to make every day of the holiday pleasant.

The first-day gifts were pretty trinkets. The second-day brought more valuable articles of clothing and jewelry. And so, in progression, culminating in a sapphire and gold necklet from Ian and Alinor, an exquisite gown and tunic, stiff with gold thread and gems from Salisbury and Ela, and, from Geoffrey, moonstones set in silver, glowing with the same misty light as Joanna's eyes. Next best to the joy she felt in being so thoughtfully remembered was that Joanna was not alone. The high table rang with laughter, for the young men were just about Joanna's own age and Sir Guy did nothing to damp their innocent merriment. For that time, womanly gifts and her sixteen years notwithstanding, Joanna was again a child intent only on ludicrous pranks and silly jests.

Even when the merriment was over and the two young guests had said their goodbyes, Sir Guy remained. It was very quiet in Ireland, he told Joanna, although neither Lord Pembroke nor Lord Ian believed the country could yet be left to itself. There was good hope, however, that ultimately the land would truly be content with England's rule. To Pembroke's and Ian's pleased surprise, John Grey, the bishop of Norwich, had turned into a fair and efficient administrator once out from under the king's influence. There was nothing wrong with Norwich's understanding, nor did he lack industry, imagination, and application. All he was missing was the courage to stand up against a man he feared. If John stayed out of Ireland, the country would do very well in Norwich's hands.

Sir Guy's continued presence had both advantages and disadvantages. Joanna was very glad of his support and his company. Also, when Geoffrey paid a flying visit in January, Sir Guy seemed to act as a buffer between them. Possibly because there was little occasion for them to be alone, unless they deliberately sought an opportunity, the violent sexual tension that had afflicted them did not arise. They were able to be friendly, to laugh and talk as they had in the past. Unfortunately, Sir Guy's presence also eliminated Joanna's best excuse for avoiding the court. Thus, in mid-February, when an invitation to attend the celebration of Easter and witness the knighting of Prince Alexander came from the king, Joanna had little choice but to obey. She sent a messenger off to tell Geoffrey she had been summoned and then, as slowly as possible, to give Geoffrey time to arrive before her, she made ready to go.

Geoffrey was more than a little puzzled by Joanna's message. Although he had not been back to court since he had been told to leave, he had all the news regularly from his father. He knew that Alexander was to be knighted but could understand neither why Joanna had been summoned so early nor, for that matter, why she had been summoned at all. To summon Ian, who had lands in the north, would be reasonable, but Joanna was not Ian's heir. He had a son of his own. Joanna was not even Ian's deputy; Geoffrey had that responsibility. In fact, Joanna had no business whatever with the prince of Scotland and no reason to witness his investiture.

Equally puzzling to Geoffrey was the fact that he had *not* been summoned. Perhaps that could be accounted for by the fact that the king was still annoyed with him, but he doubted it. He did not, in fact, think John was angry with him. The king had won the contest between them—if one could call a warning and the rejection of that warning a contest. Geoffrey had been scolded and sent away like a naughty child, and nothing at all had happened—yet—to show the king was wrong. Usually, that put John into a good humor. He would often recall the victim of such a humiliation and remind him, periodically and in public, of the incident. Geoffrey had assumed that his father had blocked such a recall. Salisbury understood the value of keeping his touchy son and his tactless brother apart.

Under the circumstances, Geoffrey said a hasty farewell to the vassal he was visiting and rode with all speed to London where the king was keeping Easter. He had no intention, however, of presenting himself to the king until he knew exactly what the situation was, and he rode directly from the Ludgate entrance in the city wall to his father's house just east of the Knights Templars' palace. He was not surprised to find his stepmother already in residence.

"Geoffrey, love," she twittered, "what do you here? And so dusty! And so tired! Come, sit. No, do not sit. Let the maids unarm you. You know I cannot bear to see you all in steel. How surprised your father will be."

Not unaccustomed to his stepmother's manner of speech, Geoffrey interpreted swiftly. His father would not be pleased to see him, and there was some reason why he should not appear to be either hurried or aggressive.

"The dust I cannot help, since the weather has been fine and I came by the road, and, as far as being tired, I cannot think why you should say so. I was only at Hemel and rode in from there. I did not bother to write to papa that I was coming because—because it was only to see Joanna."

The pale eyes, which had been casting him flickering glances of approval for answering so astutely, fixed for just a moment. "You clumsy things," Ela whined at her maids. "Will you never have done pulling him about. Finish! Give him that green gown. Yes, leave the wine. You are so slow I cannot bear to look at you. I will pour out myself rather than have you bumbling about. Begone!"

The maids retreated, so glad to get away without chastisement that they did not wonder too much about what made their mistress crosser than usual. In fact, it was not really unusual. Lady Ela had been in so terrible a humor the last few months that the subject was not really worth discussing any longer.

Inside the withdrawing chamber, Geoffrey had poured his own wine after Ela refused. "Did you come from Hemel?" she asked.

"I am not a liar," he said, smiling a little. "I was there last night, but I came from Ian's keeps in the north and, as you thought, in haste. Joanna wrote to me that she was summoned to court."

Lady Ela's lips tightened. "By the queen?"

"No, the king."

"I am surprised she did not send me word—no, of course she would not. She knows I am here in London."

Geoffrey watched his stepmother's face. She was not saying anything even vaguely relevant to what was going on in her mind, he thought. Suddenly she rose and walked away to a window that looked out into the long garden leading down to the river. After a moment, Geoffrey followed her. His father's boat was not at the steps, which meant that Salisbury had gone down river to the Tower or up to Westminster to be with the king. As he reached her, Lady Ela put out a hand and gripped her stepson's arm. It was so unusual a gesture that Geoffrey looked down at her hand.

"I am afraid," she whispered, her voice trembling. "I am afraid."

Lifting his eyes, Geoffrey caught his breath. She meant it this time. Ela was always saying she was afraid—afraid of heat, of cold, of exertion, of illness, of the sight of armor, of everything. But Geoffrey knew there was really very little that his stepmother feared. Only doubts of her husband's personal safety could really unnerve her. Instinctively, Geoffrey's hand reached for his sword hilt. The gesture was abortive both because the maids had removed his sword and because Ela clung to his arm, crying, "No! That cannot help. That is what I fear."

"You cannot mean that papa is in any danger here," Geoffrey said unbelievingly.

"None that a sword will deliver him from," Ela sighed. "Oh Geoffrey, I see ruin. I see ruin. And I cannot wean your father from his brother. I have tried—for years and years, I have tried. John is destroying himself, and we will all go down with him."

"What do you mean? What has happened?"

Lady Ela drew a long shuddering breath. "Nothing. Nothing has happened yet, but there are whispers and hints. More and more eyes turn to look at Prince Henry. He is a fine, sweet child, so different from both mother and father that— There is something else I have seen. FitzWalter spends much time with the queen, whispering in her ear."

Geoffrey raised his brows. "He is wasting his time."

"Is he?" Ela breathed fast and shallow. "Is he? Oh, she will not yield him her body, nor does he desire it I think, and he knows she has no power—now. However, he has made himself a prime favorite with her, her advisor on any little thing she desires done. What is more, Vesci and Fitz-Walter are of a sudden friends of the bosom."

"Vesci is nearly an open rebel. What has he to do with FitzWalter who owes the king much?"

"Is there any hatred like that of a mean man indebted?" Ela asked bitterly.

"What says my father?" Geoffrey asked. He was uneasy, remembering that the northern barons who were in contact with Vesci had spoken of making the child-prince, Henry, king to rule the nation through a council.

Ela uttered a sharp, mirthless laugh. "He says that the queen will do nothing against the king."

"He is not mistaken in that," Geoffrey agreed.

"Oh, you fool!" Ela cried. "Of course the queen will do nothing against the king, but look a little further. If the king should die, will not the queen fly to one she trusts for help? And will she not bring her children with her?"

Geoffrey's face blanched. There was no one Isabella hated as she hated Salisbury. She would not think twice about accepting FitzWalter's "protection" to avoid what she would think of as falling into Salisbury's power. The child-prince loved his uncle well, but the child would have nothing to say. There were doubtless many men who would prefer Salisbury to rule in the prince's name. However, if the queen held the prince's person, the honor of the loyal barons would drive them to obey whatever orders were issued in the child's name. The best that could come of such a situation was bloody civil war.

"Is there any present threat to the king?" Geoffrey asked tensely.

"I do not know," Ela sighed. "If there is, it is too secret as yet for rumors to have begun, but it cannot be long before some men's patience gives way." She stared out into the garden, then turned her eyes back to Geoffrey. "And you are one that is likely to be tried high. Geoffrey, go and sit down and promise me you will not fly into a rage. No!" she cried, high and sharp, seeing his eyes flame and his body tense, "Nothing has happened. Nothing! I only wish to warn you."

"An interesting warning it must be, if I must promise not to be angry beforehand," Geoffrey snarled, but, after staring at his stepmother for a little longer, he did go and sit in one of the cushioned chairs.

"You had better hear it from me," Ela said, following him. "Your late lights of love will make the matter sound worse."

The rage faded from Geoffrey's eyes. "Whores," he sighed. "I knew some of them would seek to make trouble. Do you think I would believe any filth they spewed?"

"Believe it? Not on consideration, perhaps, but— It is not only the ladies. Perhaps they are whores, Geoffrey, but none of them suffered any heartache over you as you suffered none over them. Most of them would have teased Joanna a little, but no more than that."

"She took it ill?" Geoffrey was surprised. He had seen Joanna several times after she had heard the gossip about him and she had made no reference to it nor had she seemed angry. "I meant to explain to her, but there were more important matters, and I—"

In the midst of her worry, Lady Ela had to smile. "I warned you that she was her mother's daughter. She said she would not blame you for what was past because you were not "hers" then, but that you would mount no mistress while she was your wife." She watched him keenly, but there was no expression on his face and his eyes were now fixed stubbornly on the tips of his shoes. "Geoffrey, do not be a fool! Do not ruin your life by setting out to spite Joanna."

"I have no intention of doing that," Geoffrey remarked neutrally.

"In any case, the fault is not Joanna's, nor yours either," Ela said hastily. "The trouble stems from Isabella."

Although no feature of Geoffrey's face moved, Ela could see his expression congeal as every tiny muscle beneath the skin tensed imperceptibly. Guilt lashed her. If she had done as Salisbury desired and had taken Geoffrey into her care, the hatred/fear/hatred that existed between the queen and her stepson would never have been born. Breathlessly, she told him of the rumors Isabella had spawned regarding Joanna and Braybrook and what Joanna had replied. Still there was no change in Geoffrey's expression and he did not interrupt her.

"You must not kill him, Geoffrey. Joanna says she believes he is as much a victim of Isabella's tongue as you or herself. You do not wish to set your father and Braybrook's into enmity, do you? Not now! In God's name, do you wish to be the cause of the rebellion that will destroy us all? We are poised on a knife edge."

"If you mean will I openly challenge Braybrook for dishonoring my wife—no. That would merely acknowledge that I believed it. It will depend upon Braybrook—"

Ela made a weary, defeated gesture. She could only hope that her words would have some effect. Geoffrey was not a fool and had been involved in court politics since he was a child. The danger was that he was young and very proud and, she thought, very much in love. His good sense would have formidable odds against it.

"In any case, Braybrook is naught," she went on flatly, "because there is real danger now of oversetting the realm more directly. Isabella must have brought this tale of Joanna's lack of virtue to John and he, being what he is, has decided to use her. It was *this* of which I wished to warn you. The Braybrook matter is nothing."

Geoffrey had lifted his eyes to her, but they held nothing. Dull, mud-colored, they did not even seem to reflect understanding of what she said. Then he shook his head. "Not his brother's daughter-by-marriage——"

"He would use his own daughter—if any had looks enough to attract him."

"Ela," Geoffrey said, almost smiling, his tension easing, "I do not love him, but you go too far. This must be nonsense."

"Is it? Is it? You have not been near him since last August. You do not know! Your father does not see—or will not let himself see. Since John has subdued Scotland, Ireland, and Wales he thinks himself invincible. Nothing is beyond him. You were there and saw how he treated the pope's envoys. When he heard the pope's sentence he laughed at that too—he almost dared the lords to rebel. He insults them to their faces, debauches their wives and daughters without even a pretense——"

"Ela, stop. You will make yourself ill," Geoffrey soothed, hearing the high, hysterical note growing in her voice. "You will warn Joanna. She will come to you, I am sure, as soon as she arrives in London. I will guard her. You will guard her. Among us all, I am sure we will keep her safe."

Dropping her head into her hands, Ela began to weep. Automatically, Geoffrey rose and went to comfort her, but he was thinking of his frantic efforts these past months to keep men loyal to John. Of course, the likelihood of those men coming to court and suffering the effects of the behavior Ela was describing was small, but they would not lack for news of it. Vesci would be quick enough to bear the ill tidings. Then it would be all to do over again. Geoffrey could have wept for weariness.

"There is no one else," he sighed softly, reminding himself. Then, patting Ela's shoulder, he said, "This trouble will soon be past. Papa wrote that the army John intends to take to France will be gathered as soon as the ceremonies of knighting are over. The king will be too busy then to be offensive, and after that—"

Ela's sobs had stopped and she was staring at Geoffrey with pale, angry eyes. "Do you offer that as comfort?" she asked in a strangled voice. "Do you promise me war to ease my heart?"

I have done it *again*, Geoffrey thought, exasperated with himself for forgetting Joanna's fury when he spoke well of the coming war with France. Never, never will I learn that whatever men love women hate—except one thing only. "Now Ela," he murmured, "you know it will be long before it comes to fighting, and it may never do so. I only meant that marshaling of the army and the business of its transportation will keep John too occupied to allow him time to think of petty slights."

Anger and fear gave way, reluctantly, to amusement in Lady Ela's face. She sighed but could not help smiling. "You meant no such thing. You are just like your father. No matter how little your looks accord, inside you are a mirror of him. For all these years that I have wept and pleaded and died with fear, he still comes to me anew each time, smiling, to tell me of battle." Ela's smile faded. "It is all you love, both of you, to kill and maim and burn."

"I do not love that," Geoffrey protested. "No man, unless he be mad, loves to hurt another, and certainly not my father who, if he has a fault, is too tenderhearted. I love the conflict, Ela, the striking at me that I must ward away and the skill of striking back and striking home." He shrugged. "I do not think of the blood and pain, neither of my opponent's nor of mine."

"That comes later, for wives to think of," Ela said drily, but in a moment she smiled again.

It was a useless discussion. Neither would ever convince the other. Perhaps it was for fear of the logic of women succeeding that boy children were removed from their mothers' influence so early. And Geoffrey had not had even those few years; his mother had died in bearing. There had been only his grandfather and Salisbury and then Ian who was, if anything, a worse fire-eater than the others. Yet there was no lack of softness in Geoffrey. She thought of how gentle his hard hands were when they stroked her shoulder, the tenderness of the way he bent his head over her. Once again she sighed. Men were men. Doubtless one of the reasons that women had been placed upon the earth was to keep them from all killing each other in a spirit of fun.

"What will you do now, love?" Ela asked in her normal voice. "Will you present yourself to the king?"

Geoffrey went back to his chair. "I was sent away and not recalled and, as for my own desire, I would not. I came because I could not understand why Joanna was summoned." His mouth twisted as over a foul taste. "If you are right about the reason for that, I must show myself. Even if John thinks he can frighten Joanna into silence, he must know he could not silence me."

"Oh yes," Ela said bitterly, "he knows that!"

There was the key to divide her husband and his brother. If John attacked Geoffrey openly, William would stand by his son. But the cost was too high. She listened with half an ear as Geoffrey said he would wait for Joanna to arrive and accompany her when she presented herself. Since this seemed as good an arrangement as any other, Ela turned the talk to that gossip which was necessary for Geoffrey to know to prevent him from making any faux pas.

Salisbury came in the late afternoon. He had dined with the king but was glad to have the excuse of Ela's frail health to escape the dancing, drinking, and wenching that formed the after-dinner entertainment of the court. He was, as Ela predicted, surprised and not too pleased to see his son, but, when he heard of the summons to Joanna, his eyes went blank with shock. He stared at Geoffrey and then at Ela, but neither said anything. There was nothing to be said. As disgusting as Ela's suggestion to Geoffrey had been, there was no need for her to repeat it to her husband. It came immediately to Salisbury's mind of itself. There did not seem to be any other explanation of the summons. Unless—Salisbury dropped his eyes. Was it better to believe that his sixteen-year-old daughter-by-marriage was so vicious and corrupt that she would pretend to have been summoned so that she could be with her lover?

Nonsense. Salisbury knew it was nonsense. If so, surely she would not have written to Geoffrey to come in haste. He knew his brother and he knew Joanna. Salisbury refilled the goblet he had just emptied and raised the flask suggestively toward his son. Geoffrey shook his head. There was still wine in his cup. Partly to avoid a topic that was obviously causing Salisbury pain, he reverted to his father's ill-concealed displeasure at his arrival and asked whether John was still angry at him. Salisbury's face lightened a little.

"No, of course not. He was never angry. The trouble is, Geoffrey, that you have acted so much the man that he forgets you are young and—and not always able to separate your heart from your politics. No," Salisbury held up a restraining hand and smiled. "Do not begin the argument again. It is too late. Most of the fortifications are already built and manned and no ill has come of it."

"The snows have not yet melted in the high places," Geoffrey said bleakly. But it was purposeless to argue over a fait accompli. What would happen, would happen. "Then if the king is not angry, why was I not summoned? Surely Ian's deputy should do honor to Prince Alexander. Ian and he will be not-so-distant neighbors some day and not too far in the future if what I hear of King William's health is true."

To Geoffrey's surprise, Salisbury looked over his head and then down into his wine. Ela laughed high and sharp. "Your father did not want you to hear the tales told of Joanna. He knows she is guiltless, but he does not trust you to keep your temper. Well, I agreed with him."

"What do you expect me to do?" Geoffrey grated.

"Shall I smile and thank the man who calls my wife a whore?"

"No man will say aught to you—and you know it," Salisbury muttered, his color high. "Do you think *I* would have endured such talk? It is the women."

"It is the queen!" Geoffrey exclaimed.

"I did not desire that you go about challenging husbands, sons, and brothers to silence tongues over which they have no control," Salisbury said, ignoring his son's passionate remark.

"But what am I to do?" Geoffrey cried.

Ela laughed again, a more natural giggle this time. "Nothing. Your father is quite right. The men will not say a word nor, for that matter, look a look. As for the women, I would leave them to Joanna."

Geoffrey sat silent, his nostrils pinched with fury and his mobile mouth set hard. Salisbury lifted and dropped his hands resignedly. If one's son were a spiritless clod, that would bring no joy. If he had spirit, it was natural that he would not accept an affront tamely. One must take the bitter with the better. There was one thing, however, that Salisbury had to make clear.

"It was not the king who objected to your summoning," Salisbury said. "I knew you would feel this way so I struck your name from the list of those to be called. I told the king I did so because I did not want you to take part in the tourney that will celebrate Alexander's knighting."

"What?" Geoffrey gasped. "Are you implying you think I cannot hold my own in a court tourney?"

"Do not be such a fool," Salisbury groaned, passing his hand over his face. "Your reputation is well enough established in war as well as in tourney. Besides, it is nothing to do with you. If anyone looked a coward, I did, acting like a hen with one chick."

"Do you expect me to refuse to fight?" Geoffrey asked coldly.

"Will you get down off that high horse," Salisbury snapped irritably. "Of course you will fight now that you are here. I will take part in it myself—''

"William!" Ela shrieked.

Geoffrey bit his lip and cast an apologetic glance at his father. In his effort to pacify his son, Salisbury had said what would make his home life hideous until the tourney was over. It was not that Lady Ela would deliberately whine and nag at her husband, as many thought she did—as she did do in public. After an initial outburst and after she realized that Salisbury's decision was irrevocable, Ela would seem to forget the matter and be very pleasant and cheerful. Only—Salisbury loved her. He would know her misery; he would see the marks of tears shed in his absence and carefully hidden; for her sake, he would be unhappy.

"Now, Ela," Salisbury soothed, "it will not even be a real tourney. A one-day affair. More a formal exercise than any real fighting."

"Then surely one of us will be enough," Geoffrey suggested. "Let me supply your place, papa. You owe it me," he added smiling, "for trying to deprive me of my sport."

"Well, well, we will see," Salisbury temporized, realizing that Geoffrey was attempting to offer a way to appease Ela. He did not believe she could be taken in, but he could see no reason to reject his son's peace offer. Nor did he see any reason to continue the subject. "When do you expect Joanna?" he asked.

"I have no idea," Geoffrey replied. "I was sure she would be here already. Even if I traveled quicker, she had far less distance to come and I must have started some days later because the messenger—" Geoffrey's voice faltered into silence and the color drained from his face.

Until he started to add up the days, he had not realized how long it was between the time Joanna had been summoned to court and this day. He knew that Joanna traveled no more slowly than any man.

"Taken?" he cried, leaping to his feet. "Could she have been taken?"

CHAPTER TWELVE

It was easy enough for Joanna to guess that the young jackanapes the king had sent with his summons was more spy than messenger. She did not fear violence for he brought no entourage, but unfortunately, however silly his looks, this creature would not be so easy to befool as that vain ass Henry de Braybrook. He was not at all interested in Edwina, and was mean enough to betray her (as he thought) to Joanna—who was heartily annoyed at having to pretend to punish her maid. Now, Edwina was pretty as a picture, as clean or cleaner than any gentlewoman, and if not as richly dressed, still very charmingly dressed. Few men would resist such an offer, and not one of John's gentlemen—not without a real reason. That fact alone would have set Joanna on guard, even if she had not been well enough versed in political realities to understand her summoning to Alexander's knighting was a complete non sequitur.

Thus, Joanna's message to Geoffrey had been sent off in complete secrecy and she sent no other. Moreover, she was careful not to betray the least reluctance or even surprise. Instead she dithered—if that word could be applied to such slow and placid indecision—until Sir Guy was forced to excuse himself and go away, knowing he would expose her either by laughing or by some exclamation of surprise. She packed and unpacked and repacked and then, when they were finally on the road, returned twice for forgotten objects. There was some chance that John's man would have heard of her efficiency during the Welsh war and become suspicious, but the delay was worth the risk. Joanna could only believe that this desire to get her early to court was an attempt to further smirch her reputation and she was determined that Geoffrey would arrive before her to give her countenance.

There was also a full baggage train this time. To questions about what she needed house furniture for, Joanna replied that her previous visit to court had proved to her that she could not sleep or be happy except with her own furniture around her. Since it was common enough for the great nobles to furnish their own chambers, the gentleman thought no more of the matter. Joanna was greatly relieved. She had neither had to lie nor to confess that she had no intention of staying with the queen's women as she had in the past. It was too vulnerable a position. Lady Alinor owned a house in London, and Joanna intended to establish herself there with fifty loyal men-at-arms to protect her and repel unwanted visitors.

The roads were miserable. The carts broke down. Even the weather cooperated. All in all, a journey that was an easy two-day ride stretched into near eight days and, with the two days Joanna had spent dithering over her packing, it was the evening of the first of March when the walls of Southwark came into view.

By now, Joanna's escort was thoroughly exasperated. He knew he would be in trouble with the king, but short of knocking the girl unconscious or binding and gagging her there was nothing he could have done to get her along faster. He might even have tried the latter expedients, except that her master-of-arms and a hard-eyed and tight-mouthed second-in-command never let her out of their sight for a moment until she was closed into her tent or safe in the women's quarters. To his request that they be dismissed, Joanna had replied that she had no power to do so. Their attendance, as that of the fifty men-at-arms who rode with them over the loud objections of the king's messenger, had been ordered by her mother and Lord Ian.

"They will obey neither you nor me, my lord," Joanna said placidly and mendaciously.

Thus, when they saw a large troop of men come thundering across London bridge, which they were headed toward, it really did not surprise John's man that Beorn should hail the leader with joy. It was all of a piece with the frustration, delay, and bad luck of this entire enterprise that the troop should be that of Lord Geoffrey FitzWilliam. It was fated, he knew. It must be that God's hand was raised to shield this woman. The depressed conviction left no room for suspicion. It seemed natural enough that Lord Geoffrey should be summoned to the knighting and should come to escort his betrothed into the city.

The same conviction did not touch the king. He knew Geoffrey was not supposed to receive a summons. He cursed his man soundly for a fool and a clod. Doubtless someone, perhaps even the messenger himself, had given information of John's summons to Salisbury and Salisbury had sent for Geoffrey as the easiest and most direct way to control the girl herself and suppress the tittle-tattle regarding her. John was annoyed, but not really angry. Obviously, his brother did not trust the little slut but, equally, he was not prepared to forgo her enormous dowry and inheritance. That was quite reasonable. The son, of course, was just the sort of hot-headed prig to repudiate the betrothal. John shook his head. William should have understood that he would be discreet with his brother's daughter-by-marriage.

The matter was of very little importance, however. John was not hungry at the moment. He was well employed trying to get Isabella with child again, and there were a few other tasty pieces around. Besides, it would be more amusing to tumble the girl after Geoffrey was irrevocably tied to her by marriage. He smiled a slow smile, put back into complete good humor by the thought of Geoffrey's torment. How his cockerel-proud nephew would squirm and rage. By then, even that loud-mouthed hothead would not be able to raise a protest. When Philip of France was humbled and Normandy was his own again, no man would dare complain even if the king should choose to spread-eagle that man's wife on the high table in the midst of dinner.

To add a note of comedy to the whole, it was Geoffrey who was furious when he saw his betrothed safe and sound and outwardly, at least, placid as a cow. There had been times in Geoffrey's life when he felt the cold hand of fear, but never had his gut been twisted with such agony as when he conceived of Joanna as a helpless prisoner. Both Salisbury and Ela had cried out that he was an idiot. Salisbury had gone so far in an effort to calm his son as to say in plain words that, whatever John's intentions, he would not use force at this stage. Ela had pleaded and reasoned that Joanna was not a fool. She would not ride out without adequate protection. Both had pointed out that it was quite mad to rush out seeking Joanna. He could not be sure which route she would take or whether or where she might have decided to visit someone on the way.

Nothing either said had the slightest effect on Geoffrey. He stormed out of the solar, shouting for his arms, his men, his horse. Salisbury started up as if to follow him, but Ela held him back, shaking her head at the fear bred by contagion in her husband's eyes.

"Let him go. He is tired and dreaming horrors. Often I do not agree with you as to what your brother will or will not do, William, but this time you are right. John believes the girl is a whore. He will not think of force until she denies him. Perhaps Geoffrey will find Joanna, perhaps not. Even if he does not, he is better off on the road than making mischief at court—which he would do in his present mood."

"If he does not find her, he will be a madman by the time he returns."

"Perhaps, but by then Joanna will certainly be here and she can deal with him."

"Joanna? God forbid. He will frighten her into refusing him."

Ela laughed. "Not Joanna. She has her fears, no doubt, but no raging man can make her turn a hair."

In that Ela was quite right. Joanna watched with mild amazement as Geoffrey faced down the king's messenger and sent him off like a cat with a burr under its tail. When he turned upon her eyes that leapt like flames with his rage, she made a sharp gesture that sent Beorn and Knud back from their positions just behind her to ride with the men.

"Where have you been?" Geoffrey asked, sounding as if someone had him by the throat.

Joanna blinked. "What do you mean, where have I been? Most lately I have been to Mersea, but you know that. I wrote—"

"Where have you been since you sent to me to tell me you had been summoned by the king?" Geoffrey asked, sounding, if possible, even worse.

"Are you mad?" Joanna rejoined calmly. "I have been at Roselynde and then on the road here. Where else—"

"Ten days? I make it ten days since you wrote to me. Do you expect me to believe it took you ten days to come some seventy miles?"

"Well, of course I expect you to believe it. Indeed, it was not at all easy to accomplish. If the weather had not helped me by turning wet, I should have had to feign illness, and I do not like to do that because it is too easy for the pretense to be discovered."

That silenced Geoffrey for a moment. He took a deep breath. "Are you telling me you deliberately spent ten days on the road in February? For what purpose?"

Joanna was not quite certain what had sent Geoffrey into such a fit of ill temper, but since she had nothing to hide and was absolutely sure Geoffrey would approve heartily of what she had done once he understood it, she could not forbear to have her fun. She lowered her eyes demurely.

"Oh, no, I have not been on the road for ten days," she replied, deliberately adding obscurity to confusion.

"You just said—"

"I agreed it was ten days since I wrote you, my lord."

Experience of Joanna's sense of humor should have taught Geoffrey better, but he was so completely taken up with the rage that comes with relief that knowledge lost its power. "Where have you been then?" he bellowed in a voice that made Joanna's mare shy across the road.

"I do not understand you, my lord," Joanna replied meekly, bringing her mount back into position. "I have told you already that I was on my way here.''

''Joanna!'' Geoffrey roared, but she had gone too far. Even rage could not obscure the deliberate idiocy of that answer. He stared at her balefully for a long moment, and then began to laugh. ''I will pay you back for that,'' he said, when he could speak, and then, seriously, ''I was frightened out of my wits when I realized it was ten days since you had been summoned and you still had not arrived.''

That was heartwarming, very flattering. Joanna could find no fault with that reason for bad temper. She smiled enchantingly. ''But you could not believe me such a fool as to arrive before you were at court to give me countenance. I will not live among Isabella's ladies again if I can by any means avoid it.''

The words touched a sore spot, and Geoffrey frowned. ''Why not?''

''Because I was near bored to death by them,'' Joanna replied tartly.

Again Geoffrey was silenced. He had a strong inclination to make a nasty remark concerning the gossip about Joanna and Braybrook, but he was aware that he was vulnerable on a similar score and, what was more, was guilty. Meanwhile, they had clattered across the bridge, Joanna exclaiming with wonder at the tight-packed shops and houses that lined it and at the rushing water. She had not had occasion to cross it before. When she came to London with Lady Ela, they had taken a more northern route from Salisbury and had forded the Thames many miles to the west where it was narrow and manageable.

Disarmed by her delight, Geoffrey dismounted and gained admittance to the back premises of one of the shops so that Joanna could watch the watermen shoot the arches. The tide was running in, and boats were coming up-river toward Westminster. Joanna laughed with excitement at the perilous undertaking, wanting to know how the boats came down again. Geoffrey explained that they came down when the tide turned, which Joanna understood very well except, she protested, that tides did not run in rivers. When Geof-

frey had explained about the estuary of the Thames and that
boats could go both ways, although with effort, in slack water, Joanna wanted to go on the river in a boat. She had
never done so because Lady Ela would not travel by boat,
claiming it made her sick. Geoffrey promised that his
father's waterman would take her very soon and extracted a
promise in return that she would go with no one else. It was
quite dangerous, he pointed out, and a number of people
had been drowned.

Then, since they were already dismounted, Joanna
wanted to visit the shops. Geoffrey agreed indulgently, but
he noted that the light of the short day was already fading. A
compromise was readily reached. Beorn and Joanna's troop
were sent to escort the servants and baggage to the house
while Geoffrey attended his betrothed in a tour. Actually,
Joanna found little that was better or more exotic than the
wares that came into Roselynde harbor, but Geoffrey did
purchase a short cloak of long, silvery fur, light and very
warm, that came from some barbaric land east of the Norse
countries and, from the same source, a large clear yellow
bead that held a beautiful winged insect imprisoned in its
depths.

They were both in the best of good humors by the time
Geoffrey lifted Joanna down from her horse in front of her
house. "I will not come in," he said. "I will ride up to my
father's house and tell him and Ela you are come."

Joanna nodded equably. "And tell Lady Ela that I will
wait upon her tomorrow. Will you return here to sleep,
Geoffrey?"

"Do you desire it?" he asked softly.

Instead of answering his question directly, Joanna said,
"When will it be safe for Ian to return to England?"

There was no chance that Geoffrey would misunderstand
her. The date of their wedding depended upon Ian's return.
Geoffrey's expression clouded and he shrugged. "The news
is so good from Ireland that my father—things are not easy
between us, Joanna. Although he does not accuse me he
suspects me of wishing to retain Ian's power and discourag-

ing his return for that reason. Papa still believes the Welsh are cowed and will not rise. As for Ian—if there is no trouble by summer, then Owain and I will both have been mistaken and Ian can come home—and no one will be more glad than I. I am bone weary and talked hoarse, and I am not sure I have accomplished my purpose.''

"You have done as well as any man could," Joanna soothed, "and I am sure you do your father an injustice in saying he believes any ill of you."

"Perhaps," he replied discontentedly, "but I am rubbed raw somewhere within, and I am ready to leap down any throat that offers."

"So I noticed," Joanna rejoined provocatively, controlling a quirk of the lips. Apparently, Geoffrey did not wish to be soothed so it was a good wife's duty to quarrel with him to his heart's content. Joanna had been told over and over that too great compliance was no virtue, and she had been told also how Queen Berengaria had lost her husband from a reluctance to give him a cause to rage at her.

If Geoffrey heard her invitation to begin to quarrel anew, he gave no sign of it. He continued speaking along a path already open in his mind. "And then my father, who can sometimes be as great a fool as any man alive, tells me he asked the king not to summon me to keep me from fighting in the—" Geoffrey stopped and uttered a bald obscenity. Only a few hours after Ela had skinned him for speaking of fighting with pleasure—and he knew Joanna felt the same—he had put his foot in his mouth again.

Joanna blinked at the word, not because she was shocked by it but because she could not understand what had set Geoffrey off. He had ignored her promising invitation to an argument, but then she noticed he was eyeing her with some trepidation. Apparently he expected *her* to be angry. She would have been happy to oblige him, but there was nothing at all in what he had been saying that could offend her.

"What is it?" she asked, willing to be cooperative, but puzzled.

"I was about to speak of something that gives me pleasure, but about which you and I think differently.''

That made Joanna blink again. There was only one thing at court that might give Geoffrey pleasure of which she would really disapprove. The expression on her face must have told its tale without words, because Geoffrey flushed deeply and then began to laugh.

"Joanna," he protested. Then, choosing the lesser of the evils said, "I was about to say that it will be a great relief to me to wag my sword in the tourney instead of my tongue. I am sorry if you do not like it, Joanna, but—"

"Why should I not like it?" Joanna asked in amazement.

She did not connect the discussion they had had at Clyro on the subject of war with fighting in a court tourney. Joanna knew that men were often injured in a tourney, but those injuries were not usually desperate and death was an even rarer occurrence. There was, unless some old, bitter grudge should have been saved for such an event, no intention to harm an opponent. Most times an injured man would be helped off the field, even tended by the man who had wounded him. Geoffrey did not realize that Joanna made a distinction between war and tourney. Ela did not seem to do so. An initial sense of relief gave way to the uneasy thought that Joanna was not angry because she did not care.

"You spoke ill enough of fighting some months ago," Geoffrey said.

"Did I? Oh, Geoffrey, if we are to stand here and talk, you might as well come in and be at ease."

He was not satisfied with her casual reply. "No. I want to tell my father you are here safe and I doubt whether I would be at ease with the servants sweeping and laying rushes and moving furniture around. You would soon enough wish me elsewhere."

Since that was the truth, Joanna only smiled, which did not give Geoffrey any satisfaction either. He kissed her hand formally and turned away, meaning the gesture as a reproach. It failed that purpose completely because Joanna accepted it as a reluctance to embrace her more intimately in front of the waiting men. She watched him ride off and went contentedly to do the household tasks which were, indeed, much easier to perform without an impatient man underfoot. Although she was a little surprised that he did not return to sleep in the bed she had made ready for him, Joanna did not take offense or regard it as a punishment. As yet, she was less "in love" than of a loving nature; thus, she was not yet sensitive to each word and expression as Geoffrey was. She did not read obscure meanings into gestures or smiles. Had Joanna seen or heard of any action that overtly displayed Geoffrey's love for another, she would have been hurt and furious. However, she did not yet seek for assurance of love in every glance and suffer disappointment when she did not find it.

Thus, Joanna met Geoffrey with smiles when he came to escort her first to his father's house and then to court. Having spent the night brooding over imagined coldness, Geoffrey was not pleased with his betrothed's mild manner. It was unfortunate that the distance between Salisbury's house and her own was so short. Had it been longer, Joanna would have realized that something personal was troubling Geoffrey. As it was she assumed he was still brooding over his political differences with his father, and once they were in company with others the distractions of greetings and exchanging news fixed Joanna's attention elsewhere.

The meeting with the king went very well. John was at his best, kind and jocular, laughing openly because Salisbury had frustrated his attempts to please his nephew and niece-by-marriage by providing them both with a surprise meeting.

"Here am I, having gone to the trouble to send Lady Joanna a private summons, just so that Geoffrey would find her here—and my own dear brother casts a stick between my legs by begging me *not* to summon his son. But you see that good intentions are rewarded. Geoffrey came of himself, so I have done well and pleased everyone."

Certainly that speech had pleased. Salisbury beamed and even Geoffrey smiled. It was a logical and most innocent explanation of John's action, and not out of character. The king could be very kind and thoughtful for those of whom he was fond, especially when the gesture cost him nothing. His lechery had made him suspect, but Salisbury and Geoffrey were willing to believe that his depravity did not go so far as desiring to soil his own family. Joanna was more wary because she had been raised on tales of how tenacious John was of a grudge, but she was perfectly willing to act as if the king had bestowed a favor on her. Certainly, she would not permit an apparent ingratitude on her part to increase John's animosity toward her mother and stepfather. She would simply do her best to avoid his notice, after giving pretty thanks for his kind thought, but that could easily be disguised as the modesty of a young maiden, not an affront.

In fact, John's actions seemed to confirm what he had said. He nodded to Joanna's curtsy and made no objection when she retreated, beckoning Geoffrey forward to ask him very quietly whether he intended to take part in the tourney. "Your father will not like it, and I can arrange—"

"If you please, my lord, I have already discussed the matter with my father. He has withdrawn his objections."

The king seemed gratified and began to talk about the details of the event with his nephew, remarking that he was most anxious to give the affair a grand air even though it was to be brief. He would not wish that there be any shade of contempt as a victor might show for a vanquished enemy. That was all to be forgotten now; Scotland and England were to be friends. Geoffrey privately wished that John would show equally good sense with regard to the Welsh or even to his own noblemen, but he agreed with his uncle readily and as readily agreed to be introduced to Alexander and to show the young man suitable attentions. Geoffrey was very happy to oblige his uncle since he was even more directly obliging Ian. A solid friendship with the prince of Scotland might well close the northern door to any of Ian's vassals who thought to disobey him and take refuge in the Scots court.

Geoffrey found Alexander to be a very pleasant young man with tastes and interests that fitted most excellently with his own. They were fast in talk ten minutes after John brought them together and still talking an hour later. Engelard d'Atie and William de Cantelu had joined them and they were making a good deal of cheerful noise arguing about the relative merits of various hunting hawks. Obviously, words would change no one's opinions, so Geoffrey suggested they go out to try the birds the next day, offering to get his uncle's permission to use a royal hunting preserve in easy distance. This offer was greeted with enthusiasm and soon the plans were widened to spend a night or two in the royal hunting lodge and see what other game they could come upon.

Very faintly as they made final plans amid a good deal of laughter, Geoffrey's conscience pricked him. Joanna had sent for him so that his company would shield her from unwanted attentions, but then Geoffrey reminded himself that she did not seem to want his attention either. He certainly no longer suspected the king of offering any threat to her and told himself that Ela could manage anyone else. He was annoyed too by the fact that, as usual, a group of young men had collected around Joanna like ants around a honey pot. At least Braybrook was not there. The relief was short-lived as Geoffrey's quick glance around the room soon fell upon that gentleman. He was not, as he should have been, paying assiduous attention to another woman to indicate he had no interest in Joanna. Instead he stood by himself, ostentatiously trying to appear to avoid her while now and again making a gesture or casting a glance from her to Geoffrey that showed where his attention was truly fixed.

Geoffrey was not the only one who noticed Braybrook. Joanna was also horribly aware of what he was doing. What she could not decide was why. Had the queen ordered him to continue to make advances? If so, he was both ways a sniveling coward—too afraid to deny Isabella and too afraid to obey her and face Geoffrey. There was also the possibility that the idiot was truly attracted to her and thought he was concealing the fact by the way he was behaving. Within minutes Joanna did not care why. All she wanted to know was what to do herself. It was not lost upon her that Geoffrey had grown silent and Engelard d'Atie, a long-time friend had read the signs aright and had drawn Alexander and William de Cantelu aside. Worse, among the courtiers and ladies who stood between and around herself, Braybrook, and Geoffrey, conversation ran in fits and starts while sly glances were cast at them.

A few more minutes made it absolutely necessary to do something. Joanna excused herself courteously to the gentlemen around her but with her mind very clearly elsewhere. Actually, she was fighting to control her temper and the strong impulse to walk over and spit in Braybrook's face. No consideration of good manners or modesty withheld her. She had, in fact, taken a step in that direction before the realization came to her that such an act might do more to confirm the sickening rumors than to eliminate them. So violent a reaction on her part must betoken strong feeling, the rumor mongers would gleefully relate. Having moved, however, it was absolutely necessary to continue moving. To hesitate was again to underline Braybrook's importance to her.

Urgent need is a good teacher to the quick in mind Joanna stepped forward without any apparent hesitation. Her eyes were now fixed upon her too-quiet betrothed. Less than halfway to Geoffrey, her route crossed Braybrook's position. She nodded her head, smiled pleasantly, sketched a curtsy as one does for an old acquaintance, and continued with unbroken purpose to Geoffrey's side.

"My lord," she said softly, looking without flinching into flaming yellow eyes above a hard mouth and pinched nostrils, "I forgot to ask you whether I should make ready a bed for you this night."

Geoffrey was furious. It was very clear to him that Braybrook was no victim of the queen's tongue; in some way, although it was not yet certain what way, he was an active participant. However, Geoffrey was not drunk now and was well aware that any move he made against Braybrook would not only be a political mistake but would smirch Joanna's name. At the moment he could have cheerfully murdered Joanna for placing him in this position, yet he knew she had done nothing to deserve anger; it was not her fault she had been born beautiful. He licked his lips, trying to ease the stiffness of clenched teeth and set jaw.

"You had better, I suppose, but why do you come now to ask?"

"Because I intend to leave very soon. Ela is not here, and you are well occupied. I have excuse enough in that my house is not yet in order and Lady Ela is not well. As soon as the queen comes and I have spoken to her, I will go."

Mollified by Joanna's obvious disinterest in the attention she had been receiving, Geoffrey tipped his head very slightly in Braybrook's direction. "And what about that half-baked preening cock?"

Joanna curled her lip. "I do not know whether he is an idiot or a craven. If it were not that there could be no worse time to start a feud between his father and yours, I would bid you crack him like a louse. Short of that, I do not know what to do. To spit in his face, which I would like to do myself, would only draw attention."

The contempt in her voice could not be feigned. Further mollified, Geoffrey smiled at her. "Let us go together and bid him good day. I am not known for a patient nature. If it is seen that I scorn him, some tongues may be stilled."

Generally speaking that would have been an excellent idea; however, Joanna wished Geoffrey had not been so near the truth when he said he had not a patient nature. Usually he was very sweet tempered, but in anything that touched his pride he was even too quick to react. Also, between political pressures and jealousy he was, as he admitted himself, rubbed raw and oversensitive. Nonetheless, it would be far worse to seem reluctant to face Braybrook in his presence. Besides, for all that Ian said and Geoffrey said, for all that her mind accepted the political necessity, Joanna did not really care if Geoffrey offended Braybrook and thereby made more trouble for the king.

"Good day to you, Sir Henry," Geoffrey said, having

led Joanna to Braybrook's side before that gentleman could retreat without making a fool of himself. Geoffrey's voice was pleasant, his smile was not. "You seem to be in some way made uneasy by Lady Joanna and myself. Can I offer you some assistance?"

It was patently evident that Braybrook had not expected this open, frontal attack. His confused consternation was so obvious that it surprised Joanna into laughter, and Geoffrey's smile broadened into a grin. Eyes from all over the room flashed toward them and away again. Everyone was fascinated by the confrontation, but no one wished to be dragged in between such powerful forces as the elder Braybrook and the earl of Salisbury. Sir Henry was well aware of that; he knew that, although no one was watching openly, all ears were cocked and all eyes alert. Until that moment he had been so well satisfied with his attempt to discomfit and shame Joanna that he had almost felt repaid for the rosebush incident. Now, however, spite and rage were renewed tenfold and mingled to deprive him of caution momentarily.

"I was uneasy indeed seeing that there have been those who said the lady favored my company."

Joanna did not have time to be shocked or appalled by this foolhardy counterattack because Geoffrey began to laugh aloud.

"But we both know that Lady Joanna has far too much sense for that," he said provocatively, "so you have no need to be shy of me. I will not eat you for what others say."

For one instant, Joanna feared that Braybrook would forget his knowledge of Geoffrey's murderous abilities. He turned a most unhealthy color, which made Geoffrey laugh again.

"We both know, at least, that Lady Joanna denies she was in my company," Braybrook spat, "and I would never contest a lady's word."

"You—" Joanna began, but Geoffrey's hand closed over her wrist so that her voice cut off on a gasp of pain.

"How wise you are," Geoffrey said, sneering openly

now, and before Braybrook could react, he bowed, very deeply—a further insult, considering what had passed between them—and drew Joanna away.

"That worm!" Joanna exclaimed. "That—"

"Now, now," Geoffrey chortled softly, "do not forget you are a lady, even though he is certainly no gentleman."

There could be no doubt, even in so jealous a heart as Geoffrey's, what Joanna felt for Braybrook. That knowledge, the public victory he had won over the man, and the reasonable explanation of the king's invitation combined to put Geoffrey in a better mood than he had been in for a long time. The only cloud in his sky was the arrangement he had made with Prince Alexander. Hastily he confessed it to Joanna, who gave him more satisfaction by seeming disappointed at first and then saying with resignation, "Well, it will make things dull for me, but perhaps it is better. I can avoid coming to court altogether. Ela will be perfectly willing to continue 'sick' while you are away, and I will attend upon her."

Although she made no mention of the king, Joanna was well pleased to have an excuse that would keep her out of his sight. She also had the satisfaction before she left of hearing a few snide comments about the set-down Geoffrey had given Braybrook, which gave her the opportunity to remark in the queen's hearing that she could not understand men. They were silly beyond measure to think that their sweet words were of any value beyond a good reason for laughter. "My lands and my honor have worth," she said proudly, "all else is dross."

Shortly afterward Joanna took her leave. She had meant her words for Isabella, hoping to make clear that it was useless to try to tempt her. In that, she was completely unsuccessful. Once Isabella's shallow mind had conceived an idea it was virtually impossible to unseat it. Worse yet, the words were maliciously reported to Braybrook and added considerable fuel to the fire that was already burning in him. Before long, several hangers-on had attached themselves to Joanna's servants and several of her men-at-arms who were off duty found that London was a very friendly place where you might be accosted on the street, plied with drink, and returned quite safely, even though nearly insensible, to your quarters.

The third and fourth of March passed quietly. The weather was unsettled, nasty damp and quite cold, so that Joanna was happy enough to sit by Lady Ela's fire or her own, gossiping and embroidering. She did not feel any lack of stimulation because Salisbury brought Ela all the news, and Ela and Joanna discussed it thoroughly from a different point of view than his while he was away. Geoffrey too was enjoying himself, although not as cozily as Joanna. The king had been delighted to give permission to hunt and had made the young men free of his hawks, his hounds, and his horses as well. Wine and women they bought and brought from town. If they were cold and wet during the day, they had excellent sport and could look forward to being well-warmed at night.

During the night of the fourth, the clouds blew away so that the fifth of March dawned bright and mild. The young men had been hawking from the earliest dawn. At sunrise, the few clouds low on the horizon flamed pink and orange. Watching, ravished by the loveliness around him, Geoffrey was suddenly smitten by his conscience. He remembered how Joanna had said it would be dull for her and how resignedly, but without whining, she had put her pleasure aside. The bag of birds that morning was excellent and they breakfasted well on the fresh-roasted bodies, but the sunlight had driven the other game into cover early. Idleness renewed Geoffrey's pangs of conscience. A twig cast into a stream they passed reminded him of his promise to take Joanna on the river.

For Henry de Braybrook, it was not the weather of the third and fourth alone that made the world look gray. His sensitized nerves saw mocking laughter in every pair of eyes and heard a sneer in every voice that addressed him. Worse, his father was surprisingly unsympathetic. Usually, the elder Braybrook was happy to have a cause for complaint against Geoffrey, but this time he merely growled at his son to be patient and above all to do nothing that might drive Lord Geoffrey into antagonistic action. This effectively deprived Sir Henry even of the outlet of preparing barbed phrases with which to lacerate Geoffrey's tender pride.

Only FitzWalter did not sneer. He spoke bitterly of Geoffrey and of Ian from whom, he complained, Geoffrey had learned his haughty manners. They needed humbling, both of them, FitzWalter hissed. Personally Ian was out of reach, but he and Geoffrey could both be brought down through the no less haughty bitch that would be wife to one and was daughter to the other. What was more, FitzWalter whispered, there was a path to this desirable goal that would, at one and the same time, provide safety and might make Salisbury turn on the king—which would leave the field of influence that much clearer for Braybrook's father. Sir Henry, with a clear mental vision of the bloodless corpse of one man who had pushed Geoffrey too far, had been shaking his head. At the word "safety" however, he paused and listened more intently.

When FitzWalter was finished, Braybrook's eyes were gleaming. "But if the king denies it—" he hesitated.

"How will he deny it? Will any dare accuse him to his face? And if the cub does yowl his protest, it will serve our purpose even better. Think of John's rage at being so accused when he is innocent. As for the king's denials," FitzWalter laughed coarsely, "everyone knows what the king is. Everyone will know also, because I will see that it is known, that he summoned the bitch from Roselynde secretly—and she came. You need not fear. No one will seek further for any explanation."

"But the king will know," Braybrook breathed, tempted but still fearful.

"Will know what? Unless he is openly accused, who would carry such a tale to his ears? And if he is accused, his rage will fall upon those who tell such lies about him. If we are fortunate, it will fall upon that loud-mouthed cock-o'-the-walk Geoffrey FitzWilliam. The stupid father will defend his befouled cub and further anger the king. Then your father will have a free path to the king's ear. And the queen will give us all the aid in her power. You know that.''

Braybrook bit his lip. It did seem an almost perfect plan and it would benefit everyone except those two he hated. Tentatively he agreed and confessed that he had had a similar idea. He already had in mind the men he would hire. Moreover he was well aware of Joanna's movements from the spies he had set upon her household. He was also aware of where the guardsmen were and what they did. The only way to seize the girl for the short time necessary was from the river. FitzWalter encouraged him; the plans were finalized. When the sun came out on the fifth of March, Braybrook felt that fate was favoring him and he summoned his hirelings and planned to move as soon as the tide was right.

The mild morning of the fifth of March changed Joanna's plans for the day also. It drew her out into the rather neglected garden, where a brief survey set her to clicking her tongue against her teeth. There was no hope that such a small patch of land could provide food, but there was no reason why it should not provide pleasure. Joanna summoned the caretaker and spoke sharply and to the point. Perennial beds were to be weeded—at once. Beds for annuals were to be dug—at once. And the little hut that had sheltered a boat and boatmen in her great-grandfather's time was to be cleared and patched—at once.

The remainder of the morning passed pleasantly in wandering around the markets of Chepeside to buy seed. She then returned home to see how the work she had ordered was progressing and to set the hardy, slow-germinating seed herself. She became so involved in this task and so very dirty that she had a bath when she returned to the house and then a leisurely dinner.

In the early afternoon Joanna received a message from Geoffrey that put her into the best of humor. He would come, he said, at the end of slack water to take her downriver when the tide should turn. At once she took pity on the men who had done very well in clearing and furbishing and dismissed them to lighter work. This also permitted her to examine what had been done and what was yet to be done without the distraction of excuses and arguments and suggestions while she waited for Geoffrey to arrive. This time when she entered the garden it was necessary to lock Brian out. The fresh-dug earth would be too much for his self-control. Joanna bid him stay and wandered to and fro, marking a branch here and there for pruning and bending to examine the woody stems of the perennials for signs of new shoots. The sound of a boat grating against the stone steps that went down to the river made her lift her head and smile radiantly.

CHAPTER THIRTEEN

Because it was controlled by the tide, passage upriver for those who intended to come down again was taken at a particular time. One calculated how long one's business would take, rowed upriver with the tide, allowed that length of time, and then came downriver with the outgoing current. Therefore, Geoffrey ordered his father's boatman to row up toward the end of slack water so that Joanna could have the pleasure of shooting the arches of London Bridge when there was some current, but not enough to make the passage dangerous. He had not left much time between the moment of their arrival and the turning of the tide because he knew Joanna would be ready. Her pleasure would be greatest if they moved off at once, before waiting could dull the edge of anticipation.

Braybrook's boat had come upriver much earlier, on the full swing of the tide. Then it had pulled out of the current and moored to wait the turn. When his purpose was accomplished, Braybrook intended to be able to retreat in haste. He did not fear recognition; he and his men would be masked. In addition, the men were wearing the king's livery. Hopefully, Joanna would be so terrified that she would not notice that Braybrook's bulk did not match John's. Even if she did, what could she say? Perhaps she would say nothing, thinking to conceal her shame. That would be best of all, for it would be manifest sooner or later when it came to bedding that she was no maid.

Several devices had been planned to draw Joanna out of the house alone, but a little while before Braybrook intended to act he found no trick would be necessary. Of herself, Joanna came from the house, closed the gate on that monster of a dog, and began to look about her garden. The time was not perfect. The river would not be running down as strongly as Braybrook desired, but the opportunity was too good to miss. As soon as it was certain that Joanna did not intend to return immediately to the house, Braybrook gave his order and his men unmoored the craft and brought it down to the river steps of Joanna's garden. Two men were ready to leap out and pursue the girl if she became nervous and retreated toward the house, but Braybrook swelled with anticipated victory when instead Joanna came eagerly forward.

A little way downriver, Geoffrey's much smaller boat was making its way to the same goal. In fact, Geoffrey watched idly as the other craft moved into its new position. He did not think it particularly odd because it was often necessary for a boat to land a man in order to determine the correct place to dock. He would have needed to do the same, except that his father's boatman was familiar with Alinor's house from taking Salisbury to visit Ian when they were both at court. The boatman and his son did not see the maneuver of the other craft. They were both at the oars. The tide had just begun to turn and, although the current against them was not yet strong, it was necessary to put forth some effort to drive the boat upriver.

It was when Geoffrey heard a dog's bellowing that seemed loud enough to raise ripples on the river that he felt the first stirring of uneasiness. This had no immediate connection with the boat he was watching. He merely wondered whether Joanna was going to be weak-minded enough to wish to take Brian with them. He hated to spoil her fun, but he could not permit it. The boat was too small for a beast that size, which might be panicked by the erratic movement. However much he protested, Brian would have to stay chained up at home.

The grating of a boat against the steps had brought Joanna eagerly down the garden. She was a little surprised because Geoffrey was earlier than she expected and, when she saw the size of the boat, with its six oars and a canopy covering a sheltered area, she was a little disappointed too. She had wanted the real thrill of shooting the arches at the full running of the tide in a small craft, close to the water. A flash of impatience at the idea that Geoffrey might become an overanxious husband was firmly repressed. His care showed his affection, and it might be no fault of his. Perhaps Salisbury, too accustomed to Ela's megrims, had insisted on the precautions of a sturdier boat and a slower current.

She did not intend to get aboard, merely to greet Geoffrey and tell him to wait while she took Brian back to the house and tied him up. Then Joanna thought she might induce Geoffrey to come in for a few minutes. If she could give him a cup of wine and keep him talking about the sport he had had for half an hour or so, she would at least be able to go downriver in a stronger current. Because her mind was busy with this little device, Joanna did not take in two significant facts. One was that Geoffrey did not come out of the boat to meet her; the other was that the men all seemed to be looking back into the boat, their faces turned away from her—which was unnatural.

Two steps down, Joanna paused, struck by a sudden suspicion. Instantly, two men leapt from the boat. For three heartbeats, Joanna was frozen with shock at the black, blank area where their faces should have been. Short as the delay was, it was too long. As she turned to run, she was seized. One single muffled cry escaped her before a hard hand was jammed against her lips. The sound was not nearly loud enough and far too brief to reach the house. Brian, waiting at the fence, leapt to his feet and let loose an experimental fusillade of barks. No sharp order to "be still" followed. Brian barked again, louder, longer. Still there was no response. Brian rose to his hind legs, placed his forepaws on the fence that separated him from the beloved smell, which to him meant all food, all comfort, all love, and bellowed loud and long.

During the second spate of barking, Geoffrey's boatman passed the dock and swung around to come in. Briefly as they went by, they were facing Braybrook's boat. Both exclaimed with surprise at the same moment that Geoffrey issued a sharp order to hurry. The violence and urgency of the dog had finally made him uneasy. Surely by now Joanna would have quieted the beast if she had just gone down into the boat to answer a question. For the first time it occurred to him that the boat he had been watching had docked at Joanna's house and that, if it had been a casual visitor, she should be visible somewhere.

"There is no room—" the boatman began.

"Pull alongside," Geoffrey snapped, drawing his sword.

He was not, of course, armed for fighting. No one in his right mind went on the river in full mail. On the other hand, there were cutpurses and thieves everywhere in the city, even on the river, and a man who had a good sword wore it as much as a warning as for a weapon. The boatmen's eyes widened as they saw Geoffrey's sword come out, but the younger of the two rose and gripped an oar as a man would hold a quarterstaff while he made ready a grappling hook with the other hand. However, it was less easily done than said to bring the boats alongside. The larger of the two craft was rocking so violently that the men trying to cast off from the dock were having trouble with the ropes and the others, still at the oars, were watching them.

Within the vessel, Braybrook had received almost as violent a surprise as Joanna. She had been so stunned by the assault upon her that, aside from the brief cry and attempt to run, she had allowed herself to be passively dragged aboard and behind the shielding canopy in the stern. The men, expecting rather that she would faint than fight, were supporting her more than holding her, although one kept a firm grip on her mouth to prevent screaming. By the time she was concealed from view, however, Joanna's shock had yielded to outrage. She promptly kicked one of the men holding her in the shin and, when pain made him relax his grip a trifle, she twisted half-free and kicked the other in the groin. That man released her completely to grab for his maltreated private parts. Seeing Joanna almost free, Braybrook sprang forward and met the fist blow she had intended for the one man who still held her.

Joanna was no frail flower, and her arm had been strengthened over the years by the chastisement of erring servants. Braybrook staggered back, blood spurting from his nose under the mask. Joanna brought her foot down with explosive force on that of her captor. He let out a howl that drew the attention of everyone on the boat. Unfortunately, his voice drowned Joanna's when his hand fell away from her mouth and she shrieked for Brian.

Good and bad are often intermingled. Although the dog did not hear his mistress, the cry fixed the attention of Braybrook's hirelings just long enough for Geoffrey's man to hook the vessels together. As the large boat tipped down toward the smaller craft, Geoffrey sprang aboard with the younger boatman just behind him. He had time to disable one of the men still seated at the oars, but the other three turned almost simultaneously toward him, drawing their weapons. The boatman made a swipe at one with the oar he carried. It was an awkward weapon, however, and the swordsman avoided it easily, thrusting dangerously in riposte. Geoffrey parried a stroke by one of the others and slashed at the third with the backstroke. Aside from the brief clash of metal on metal, no one made a sound. Braybrook's men were too surprised, Geoffrey too choked with rage and fear.

Inside the cabin the tables had turned. Fury and energy notwithstanding, three men were more than a match for one girl. Joanna was again a prisoner, far more firmly and cautiously held than before. Unable to strike her across the face because of his man's gagging hand, Braybrook seized her tunic and tore downward. The cloth was well woven, but Braybrook's strength was increased by fury and the seams gave way at the shoulder and sleeve, baring Joanna nearly to the waist and leaving red wheals on her white skin where the pressure had been greatest. If Braybrook had assumed that pain and shame would cow Joanna, he was wrong. Twisting and struggling even more violently, she managed at last to fasten her teeth in the hand that gagged her. With an oath, the man let go.

"Brian!" Joanna shrieked, "Brian! Come!"

As if her voice had broken an enchantment, sound erupted all over the embattled craft. Geoffrey connected with one of the men opposing him, who screamed. The other shouted a warning and a call for help to those behind the canopy and thrust at Geoffrey whose sword was still engaged. Geoffrey's boatman cried out as his opponent's sword chopped through his oar near the blade, but the blow had done him more good than harm, reducing the unwieldiness of the weapon. Swinging it swiftly while Braybrook's man was recovering his stance, the boatman cracked his opponent across the temple and tumbled him into the water.

Meanwhile the odor of fear and fury had been drifting up toward Brian on the soft breeze of the river. His hysterical barking finally drew eyes from the women's quarters of the house while his increasingly frantic lunges made the fence shake and bend. There were, of course, no windows on the ground floor and the doors faced the street so that the men-at-arms had heard nothing of what was going on in the garden behind them. Edwina cursed Brian impatiently as she unhooked the hides that sealed the windows. When her peremptory order for him to be still had no effect, she looked beyond him to see what was causing his excitement. The swift movement of figures on the boat did not connect in Edwina's mind with violence until, all at once, very faintly, she thought she heard Joanna call to Brian and almost immediately saw one of the men topple off the boat into the river. Then the sun flashed on lifted swords. Edwina screamed and flew toward the stairs that led to the men-at-arms' quarters on the floor below.

Geoffrey gasped and threw himself backward, unable to free his sword to parry the blow launched at him by the second man. Unfortunately, there was little room for maneuvering in the boat. The sword point sliced across his chest, tearing fabric and flesh for an inch or two before he fell backward over a rower's bench. The impact knocked the breath from Geoffrey so completely that he could not cry out for help from his boatman who had turned momentarily to follow the fate of the man he had knocked into the water.

The thin cry that alerted Edwina combined with the smell of blood and fear turned Brian into a feral beast. Free of inhibition, he laid the fence flat in a single lunge and covered the length of the garden in a few bounds. The last leap carried the now-silent dog from the top of the steps into the boat where, turning midair toward the beloved scent, he struck full on the chest of the man whose return stroke would have decapitated Geoffrey. Dog and man tumbled in a heap onto the deck. Only the dog rose from that impact and the slaver on his jaws was dyed red.

Now the two men who had been holding Joanna burst out from behind the canopy. Their rush checked suddenly as they confronted what looked, in that moment, like a gray lion with a blood-dripping mouth. Before either could move again, silent as a wraith, the dog leapt between them. Since they had each been braced for a direct attack, both were taken unawares when Brian passed through and staggered sideways. Geoffrey's boatman spun away from the river and shouted a challenge; Geoffrey caught his breath, freed his legs from the rower's bench, and came upright. Within the cabin, a man screamed and Joanna shrieked "No! No!" From the house came a roar of angry voices and men began to pour around the side of the building in various stages of undress but all with weapons in their hands and shields on their arms.

Braybrook's two remaining men dropped their weapons and held up empty hands, crying quarter. Blind to all but Joanna's voice, Geoffrey burst by them and in through the canopy. He was just in time to see a side wall of the shelter torn loose and a man with blood streaming from his back and buttocks throw himself through and into the river. Joanna, clinging desperately to Brian's collar and crying so hard that she could no longer command her voice, was almost dragged out in pursuit of Brian's prey.

"Brian! Down!" Geoffrey roared. "Down!"

The dog dropped, belly flat, tail and ears down, cowering to the authority of that voice. Joanna let go of his collar and swung around, clutching her torn dress to her breasts. Still unable to speak, she cast herself into Geoffrey's arms. He nearly thrust her away in his fury, desiring, like the dog, to follow the escaper. The fighter's sense of timing, recognizing that his prey was beyond reach saved him from that idiocy. With only one regretful glance at the spot where what he wanted to tear apart had disappeared, Geoffrey turned his attention to Joanna.

"Hush," he soothed, "hush. It is all over now, all over. I am here. No one can hurt you."

The boat heaved anew as Joanna's men poured aboard. Geoffrey cursed under his breath. Those idiots would sink the craft. Fortunately before they had quite accomplished that, Geoffrey heard Beorn shouting instructions that the living men should be taken off at once and held prisoner. In the same breath, the old man called, "Lady, lady, where are you?"

"I have her safe," Geoffrey shouted, just as Beorn burst in the door.

"Lord Geoffrey," he gasped.

"The banks," Geoffrey snarled. "Search the banks. Whoever did this went out through the side."

Beorn charged out again and there was a new eruption of shouting. Geoffrey drew a deep, steadying breath and moved a step or two sideways so that he could drop his sword onto the narrow bed affixed to one side of the ship. Then he put both arms around Joanna and lowered his head so he could kiss her hair from which the wimple had been torn. She was silent now, not sobbing, but shaking so hard that her body beat against his like a fluttering bird. Geoffrey swallowed, trying to loosen the knot rage had tied in his throat. It was inconceivable to him that his placid, fearless Joanna could be so terrified.

"Hush, beloved," he murmured. "Beorn will find him and you will be avenged. If you desire, we will have him apart finger by finger, muscle by muscle, and bone by bone." The tear in Geoffrey's chest began to hurt as his own shock and rage diminished, and he started to feel a little light-headed. Beorn burst through the curtains again and whispered urgently in Geoffrey's ear. The young man's expression froze, and he swallowed sickly. No wonder Joanna had been terrified. "Oh my God," he whispered, "strip them and hold them secret and safe."

"What of the searchers?" Beorn asked anxiously.

An agonized indecision distorted Geoffrey's face for a moment. Then he drew a deep breath. "Whatever he is, he is all we have," he snarled. "Call off your men."

Beorn seemed to be torn between rage and relief, but he said no more, merely nodded and went out again. Geoffrey looked down at his betrothed. He closed his eyes and tightened his grip upon her. It was not her fault she had been born beautiful. This was his fault, all his. She had written to ask for his protection and he had gone off like an idiot to hunt, virtually issuing a public invitation to his uncle to take her by force by asking permission to hunt the royal forest.

"Joanna," he said softly, "beloved, come sit here with me." He loosened her grip on him and turned her away to lead her to the bed, only to gasp and cry out, "What did he do? Where are you hurt?"

The anguish in Geoffrey's voice steadied Joanna. "Nothing," she forced out. "Only tore my dress." Then her eyes, which had flown to Geoffrey's face followed his and fell upon the blood-stained cloth she still clutched to her bosom with one hand and the blood-smeared flesh beneath it. "It is not my blood," she gasped, and then, "Geoffrey, you are hurt!"

Breath trickled out of him in relief. The shock of seeing blood on Joanna made him forget he had been holding her against his bleeding chest. "Not much," he assured her.

"Let me see," she cried.

"In a moment. Joanna, who was the man?" He saw her eyes widen and stroked her hair and cheek. "Do not be afeared love. It is ended. Over. I will not leave you alone again, I swear it. Not for an hour, not for a minute, until you are safe behind Roselynde's walls. Do not be frightened, but tell me who it was."

"I do not know," she whispered.

"Whatever threats were made I swear no harm will come to you or yours or to me either. I know the men wear the king's livery. Who was the man, Joanna?"

"The king's livery? Oh, no!" Joanna took a deep breath and tried to control her shuddering. "I do not hide knowledge out of fear, Geoffrey. I really do not know. They were all masked."

There had been no masks when Geoffrey came aboard, but that was so odd a thing for Joanna to say that it must be true. It was reasonable that as soon as danger threatened the masks would be torn away. One needed to see and breathe without obstruction in a fight. Still, Geoffrey had to voice his worst fear. He had to know.

"Joanna, look at me. Was it the king?"

Her eyes met his, still dilated with fright but concealing nothing. Her surprise at the question was genuine. "No. I know it was not he."

"How do you know if he was masked? Did he speak?"

"Not a word. No one made a sound." Joanna began to tremble again, and Geoffrey put an arm around her and drew her close. "That made it worse—so awful! No one said a word, but I could feel the hate. Hate!" Her eyes closed and tears squeezed out under the lids. "Why should anyone hate me, Geoffrey? I have never willingly done any man or woman ill. It was terrible! Terrible!"

"Hush, love, no one hates you. No one could." Geoffrey tightened his grip and wiped the tears from her cheeks with the heel of his hand. "But there are some who hate me— accursed that I am to have left you alone to face their spite—and, beloved, the king hates your mother. Are you sure—"

"That it was not the king, I am sure," Joanna replied steadily. "He was the wrong shape for John. Who could mistake the king? He is a tub upon legs. And, whatever he feels about my mother, John does not hate *me*. He looks at me as if I were a particularly tasty tidbit on his plate—with no more emotion than that—and sometimes with a flicker of malicious humor, but not hate."

There was one more possibility. "Could this filth's intention have been to bring you to the king by force?"

"No," Joanna said, drawing in on herself in revulsion. "He intended to have me here or somewhere downriver and to leave me naked and bleeding on the bank for all to see. Look at my gown! Would any man with orders from the king dare despoil me?"

Geoffrey made a strangled sound and Joanna began to sob again.

"He hated me," she wept. "Me! What have I done that anyone should hate me?"

"There are men with rotten souls, my love," Geoffrey comforted. "They do not need a real reason to hate. It might be that you did not smile upon him in passing, or that you did smile and he took it for a mockery—"

Only a small portion of Geoffrey's mind was on what he was saying, but it made dreadful sense to Joanna and she stopped weeping and caught her breath. Geoffrey did not notice. He was thinking of his uncle. He was ashamed again at having thought the worst of John without real reason. John was a fool in many ways, but not, Geoffrey knew, in the practices of deceit. If John had intended to take Joanna by force or guile, he was not such an idiot as to send his men decked out in his own colors. Perhaps he was mad-proud enough to do that to another woman, but not to Joanna, not to his brother's daughter-by-marriage.

"I do not think the king had any part in this," Joanna said more calmly, echoing Geoffrey's thoughts. "I think it was intended that I should blame John and either keep silence out of fear or tell you so that you would act against your uncle and fall out of favor."

"It may be worse than that," Geoffrey said slowly. "It might be that this was a device intended to break my father away from his brother. It needs only that, I fear, to begin a dissension that would topple the king from the throne altogether."

Joanna did not contest that statement. To the world at large and to John himself it might seem that the king was never more powerful, but Joanna knew how worried Salisbury was, knew that he believed it needed only one spark to set the tinder of the barons' dissatisfaction afire and blaze up into a civil war. Usually she would have thought to herself that it might well be worth civil war to be rid of John, but now she was outraged. She was not less sure of the hatred her attacker felt for her—and she was ashamed, realizing that she had done something, although not a thing to deserve this—but she could not deny that there might have been purpose layered on purpose in the attack. Joanna had a strong sense of fair play. If Braybrook hated her, and she was almost sure it had been he, that was one thing. But to use that hate to bring trouble upon an innocent bystander was outrageous.

The impersonal sense of injustice permitted Joanna to conquer the remainder of her fear and revulsion. She could not imagine her innocent jest having engendered such hatred in anyone. However, if dislike for her were mixed with another, deeper purpose, the attack became more rational and less fearful. It became reasonable that the man would not speak if he believed she would recognize his voice and know he had nothing to do with the king. Joanna sat more upright, her eyes clearing.

"Geoffrey, I think—good heavens, why are we sitting here talking while you drip blood. Shall I see to you here, or will you come up to the house?"

"You are quickly recovered, are you not?" Geoffrey asked suspiciously.

"Yes, because it comes to me that you are right. It was the hate that frightened me; that anyone could hate me so deeply was insane. But someone could dislike me, and dislike you too, and see that discomfiting us could harm the king also. That is not mad. It is wicked, and I am very, very angry—but not frightened. I know how to guard myself against those with real purposes. Never mind me. Let me see your hurt Geoffrey."

A brief examination made Joanna insist that Geoffrey

come back to the house so she could sew the tear. He did not argue, merely telling her to go ahead and he would follow. He then rescued his boatmen, who had been taken prisoner along with the others and told them to secure both crafts until he was sure what to do about the larger one. Finally, he told Beorn to take the prisoners where their screams would not disturb him and Joanna and find out what they knew. When Joanna was finished with him, he sent off a message to his father, which naturally brought Salisbury and Ela up to Joanna's house in anxious haste. They found one victim calmly embroidering, the other lounging in a cushioned chair with an angry frown on his face and a number of pieces of black cloth in his hands.

"You are hurt, boy," Salisbury said, judging correctly Geoffrey's posture.

"A slit in my hide—nothing," Geoffrey replied, holding out the crude masks. "Look here."

Salisbury instead looked at Joanna, who nodded and smiled, confirming that Geoffrey's hurt was slight. A faint expression of satisfaction appeared in Salisbury's eyes as he looked back at his son. "You will not be able to take part in the tourney then," he said.

To his surprise, Geoffrey cocked a brow at him, but did not offer any argument. Instead he said, "You need not fear that Braybrook and I will come to blows. It is he—I would almost wager my life upon it—who will not take part."

"Was it he?" Salisbury asked anxiously, referring to the attack on Joanna. "What have you done to him? With him?"

"I have done nothing." Geoffrey grinned nastily. "But I believe Brian has had a mouthful out of his ass—a big enough mouthful that Braybrook will not sit a horse for some time to come."

"Brian?" Salisbury looked at the dog who, hearing his name, lolled out his tongue with an idiotic expression of good nature and began to thump the ground with his tail. "Does it have courage and sense enough to bite its own fleas?'' he asked contemptuously, careful not to use the dog's name again for fear he would rush over and make love to him.

"Do not underestimate Brian," Joanna said with a slight reminiscent shudder. "I had all I could do to keep him from tearing out Braybrook's throat—if it was he."

"The dog killed one of the guardsmen that way," Geoffrey added soberly. I have never seen it done so fast. Never mind that, but look here at these garments."

His gesture indicated an untidy heap of clothing on the floor beside his chair. Salisbury walked over, bent, and then rose without touching them, his face gray.

"I do not believe it," he breathed.

"Neither do we," Geoffrey assured him at once. "A man does not come to commit an abomination with his guardsmen decked out in his own colors and then cover their faces and his with these." He held out the masks again.

"Too late," Ela whispered, her eyes blank and blinded by tears. "It is too late."

Salisbury paid no attention to her, but his expression was just as set. "What will you do?" he asked his son.

"You tell me," Geoffrey said. "When Beorn told me the men were wearing John's colors, naturally I bid him call off the searching parties. The last thing I desired was to find the king or even one of his acknowledged henchmen. Later, when Joanna told me they wore masks, I began to realize that the king could have no part in this. Then Beorn put the question to the two men we captured. They did not know the man who had hired them; he was not the same as the man on the boat and they had never seen that man's face. They had been told they were on the king's business and would be protected; that was all they knew. This convinced me more than all that John is innocent. What idiot would hire strangers for a dirty deed and then dress them in his own colors?''

"But why?"

Geoffrey looked at his father for a long moment, then dropped his eyes. If Salisbury could ask such a question, there was no sense in answering it other than on a purely practical level. "Since John is guiltless, then dressing the men in his livery could only be a deliberate attempt to blacken him, possibly if Joanna cried aloud of—of what had befallen her, to make you bitter against him. What I do not know is whether it is better to spread the story of the fruitless attack and Brian's part in checking it—which will soon make the guilty man known to all. How many men in the court will have dog bites on back and buttock? Or whether we should act as if it never happened."

"Can it be kept secret?" Salisbury asked uneasily.

"Why not? Whoever did it will never talk, even if it was not that lily-livered cur Braybrook. The men are dead—all except the one who fell into the river. If he is not drowned, he will still hold his tongue."

"Joanna," Salisbury said gently, "do you agree to this? It is you who have been offended."

"For the little hurt done me, I have been well avenged between Brian's work and Geoffrey's. And I do not like to see any man unjustly used—even the king. I will agree to whatever you and Geoffrey think is best."

"Then secrecy is best," Salisbury sighed. "I do not like it, but to speak the truth, if a whisper of these garments comes to the court, nothing anyone said could keep the king's name clean."

"No, for good reason," Ela remarked bitterly. "William, do you not see what this means? If Braybrook's son was party to this scheme—"

"The boy is a fool," Salisbury growled. "I swear the father knows nothing of this. And there is no proof it was Henry. Why do you think it?"

"Whom else have Joanna and I both offended?" Geoffrey asked. He shrugged, then winced. "It will be put to the proof soon enough. If he is missing from the court tomorrow— Which reminds me that if this matter is to be kept secret, I *must* fight in the tourney. I cannot confess to being hurt, and I have no other reason to avoid it."

Salisbury nodded without concern. "We will see how you

feel. Some excuse can be found at the last hour if the wound troubles you. This will be nothing. Everyone likes Alexander and all wish to avoid marring his knighting with death or sadness.''

Concealment having been decided upon, there were ends to tie up. Salisbury's boatman was summoned and told to discover the owner of the craft Braybrook had used and return it so that there would be no outcry over its loss. The bodies of the hirelings were cast into a cart and sent out with a detail of men to be buried in secret. There was no need for Geoffrey to show himself in court that evening. It was reasonable that, having taken his betrothed on the river after a hard morning's hunting, he would wish to spend a quiet few hours by the fireside.

The next day, Braybrook was indeed missing from court. When Geoffrey arrived, some wondered aloud whether Braybrook's absence was a response to Geoffrey's reappearance. To such hints, Geoffrey returned no answer beside a smile, and he took up his usual pursuits except that he was never out of eyeshot of Joanna. Fortunately, only a few days remained before the culmination of the festivities. On the night of March 7, Alexander stood his vigil. The knighting and feast took place on March 8. Had Joanna been able to get any sense out of her betrothed, she might have demurred at his fighting in the tourney the next day. Geoffrey, however, was too drunk by the end of the feast to do anything but giggle when she protested that his wound, although not serious, was still unhealed and would make him awkward.

She did not argue long, discovering that Geoffrey was no safe company for her that night. Hardly were they alone, when he embraced her far too fervently. In fact, had he not been too inebriated to balance himself properly or to be effective as a lover, he would have accomplished what Braybrook failed to do. Joanna was far more amused than shocked. Ian had a tendency to become amorous when he was drunk also, and Joanna had watched Alinor's technique for handling him when it was impossible to yield to his desire. She escaped without difficulty. Then, having tempted him down the stairs with offers of unspecified delights—including more wine—she bid Knud and Beorn put him to bed.

There would be no sense in arguing the subject the next morning, Joanna decided. She was not really fearful for Geoffrey. She had felt out the temper of the court in the past three days. It was very clear that what Salisbury had said was true. Everyone intended that the tourney should be a set piece of chivalry and excitement without death or serious injury to becloud the pleasure. What was less clear to Joanna was the reason behind the intention. Salisbury said it was because everyone liked Alexander. That the young man was a general favorite was true, but Ela said—and Joanna reluctantly agreed—that it was not for his sake that every face was wreathed in smiles.

Those smiles made Joanna's throat tighten with fear. They curved the lips of men who had very little reason to smile in John's presence. The king, knowing this, preened himself all the more, believing that all feared him so greatly that they dared do nothing beyond grovel, no matter what insult he put upon them. But it was not fear that Joanna saw in the eyes that were kept lowered when they fronted the king.

"They wish to smooth over all quarrels so that no questions need be raised on any subject," Joanna told Geoffrey before they left for the tourney. "Something is being planned. I know it."

"I know it too," Geoffrey snarled, holding a hand to his throbbing head. "What do you want me to do? I have told my father and seen him look near to weeping while he shrugged my warning away. He knows also. Do you think he has not tried to make John moderate his ways? At least whatever will happen will not happen today. I will think about it tomorrow."

CHAPTER FOURTEEN

There seemed to be little need for unpleasant thoughts on any subject on the day after the tourney. The event went off exactly as expected. A good time was had by all and no permanent harm was done to anyone. Geoffrey won no prizes. He was far too slight to be a dangerous jouster, but long practice against Ian had taught him to hold his own defensively so that, although he could not unseat any of his three opponents, they could not unseat him either. He was no more successful in the melee. The wild ferocity of Geoffrey's attack, which made him so dangerous an opponent in war and had already defeated four opponents in trial by combat, was obviously out of place in so good-natured an event. Besides, everyone was holding back a little. It was agreed without spoken words that Alexander must take the prize.

That agreement, Joanna thought, covered what might have been obvious otherwise. Suddenly, it seemed to her that few men wished to combat seriously against Eustace de Vesci and Robert FitzWalter. This was less obvious than it should have been because Vesci had married Alexander's bastard half sister Margaret. It was thus natural for him to fight in Alexander's party, and resistance against that party was not very strong. The increase of status that came with Vesci's marriage also served to obscure how many men sought his attention.

"And why," Ela hissed in Joanna's ear, "does that dolt John think William of Scotland gave his daughter to Vesci? Does not William hope that this son-by-marriage will root out the incubus that oppresses him?"

However, in spite of Ela's dire predictions and Joanna's

fears, nothing happened. John continued to flaunt his power in the faces of his subjects. Joanna had a taste of it herself after she returned to Roselynde when she learned that the sheriff of Southampton had instructions to enclose the dock at Portsmouth with a strong wall. This in itself was not bad, but if fortifications were to be added to the wall, those fortifications would command the entrance to Roselynde harbor. It was a first step in a direction Joanna did not like at all. There was nothing she could do, except protest, and she was too wise to do that. The king had a right to build upon his own property, and it was most reasonable to build a structure that would be a protection to any ship that docked at Portsmouth. It would also be a protection against reavers or invaders from France. The only bad part was that the king could not be trusted. John's character was such that, instead of being glad that the country would be protected from attack, Joanna felt the structure to be a threat against the king's own subjects.

The news of the construction at Portsmouth arrived during the last week of May. Joanna sent a messenger posthaste to Alinor in Ireland and herself rode south to see what was being done. The visit and various conversations with the builder overseeing the work told her little. Nothing obviously threatening was being built, but she remained uneasy. Her feeling was shared completely by her mother, who replied by a letter that arrived in the third week of June. Alinor suggested that, if John was not in London, Joanna should betake herself there and use her feminine wiles on the officer of the royal Exchequer who was responsible for the purchase of materials and payments for the construction.

"From him, if you are sufficiently clever," Alinor wrote, "you will be able to determine what is truly intended. He will not tell you in words, but if more stone is ordered or more workmen than are reasonable for a wall, you will know that more than a wall will be built. Also ropes and timber fittings for trenchbuts and mangonels will point in which direction the wind blows. I do not need to explain these matters to you more fully, I am sure, but send to me whatever information you uncover of any kind, more especially whatever might seem to you trivial or funny or unfitting. Also be sure you send to me by separate messenger, a trusty man instructed to put the letter into my hand secretly when my lord is not by, and who knows how to hold his tongue. If Ian hears of the task I have set you to, he will beat me witless for corrupting your purity of mind. For the same cause keep the matter close hid from Geoffrey, who is one ilk with my beloved fool on this subject.''

The last two sentences gave Joanna the giggles. It was perfectly true that both Ian and Geoffrey would be horrified by Alinor's suggestion. They would approve neither of Joanna's attempt to discover what the king wished to keep hidden nor of the method suggested for uncovering the truth. Although Joanna was not nearly as amoral as her mother, having absorbed a great deal of Simon's uprightness and love of justice, neither was she in the least bound by the codes of honor hammered into the brains of men. What she would do would harm no one and might be of infinite benefit to herself and her family.

Fortunately, there would be no problem in keeping the matter secret from Geoffrey. He was at present in the north with the king who was assisting King William of Scotland to capture Cuthred MacWilliam, the Celtic pretender to the throne. Joanna merely omitted to send Geoffrey word that she was going to London. Instead, she instructed Sir Guy to send on any messengers who might come as fast as relays of horseflesh could carry them. If the men rode day and night, changing horses as necessary when the animals tired, it would mean barely twenty-four hours' delay in her reply.

All went smoothly enough at first. Joanna presented herself with a muddled and incoherent complaint about a demand (which, in fact, had never been made) from the Exchequer for timber for the works at Portsmouth. Before the matter was explained to her satisfaction, she was very nearly a favorite daughter of the man involved. The information she obtained from him was both good and bad. It was clear that John did intend further fortifications at

Portsmouth, but, at present, at least, these were not pro-posed for the purpose of threatening Roselynde. Summons had already gone out, Joanna was told, for an army to be as-sembled and sent into Poitiers. From there, John intended to attack Philip and win back Normandy. The works at Portsmouth had the double purpose of protecting the fleet that was to be assembled there and to guard against reprisals from Philip.

Although Joanna's immediate questions were answered, she did not leave London at once. She wanted to discover, in addition, who would command the establishment at Portsmouth. As soon as that was known, friendly relations had to be established with the man. In this Joanna was less successful, not because her influence was failing but be-cause the answer was as yet unknown.

There was no particular reason for Joanna to be at Roselynde or anywhere else, so she decided to remain in London a week or two longer on the chance that the ap-pointment to governorship of Portsmouth would be made. This would also give her the opportunity to watch over the newly established garden of the London house at a critical time and ensure that it would have a firm foundation that would need only minimal care for the remainder of the summer. Besides, Joanna was developing a taste for Lon-don itself. Roselynde town was a fine port that commanded all the luxuries, but the variety of London was infinite.

It was not destined to absorb her for long, however. On the fifth of July, Joanna received a message sent on from Sir Peter at Clyro Hill. He did not know the truth of the matter, the scribe wrote at Sir Peter's dictation, but he wished his lady to be warned even if the rumors turned out to be false later. He had heard that the king's strongholds in Wales were under attack. He was seeking more definite informa-tion while he stuffed and garnished his keep for war. This was a mere precaution, Sir Peter said, and should not alarm Lady Joanna. He did not think they were in any danger, since he had taken Lord Geoffrey's warning the previous au-tumn to heart. All the walls were strong and the machines of war were new and ready. Moreover, he had taken good care that word of his readiness should be spread abroad. If she wished to come to oversee what was done, Lady Joanna would be most welcome, Sir Peter concluded, but if she could not come she could rest assured that he would send her news as soon as he heard it himself and he would defend the castle and the lands faithfully.

There was no need for Joanna to wait for more uncertain rumors to be passed on by Sir Peter. Geoffrey came storming into her London house five days later. He had ridden down from the north at breakneck speed only to find Joanna missing from Roselynde. None of the servants could tell him where she had gone (a precaution she had taken to prevent Geoffrey from learning of her trip that backfired badly) but all knew that a messenger from Wales had come. Unfortunately, Geoffrey did not ask whether the messenger had come before or after Joanna had left the keep and no one thought to pass along that piece of information. Sir Guy returned from hunting barely in time to prevent Geoffrey from setting out to follow Joanna to Wales. Having first convinced Geoffrey not to murder him for allowing Joanna to go off alone on such a venture, he then assured the young lord that Joanna was safe in London. Sir Guy expected that Geoffrey would rest there that night and was resolving in his mind some tactful, if untruthful, explanations for Joanna's trip. He then realized that Geoffrey did not intend to demand any further explanations from him; he was bent upon obtaining the rest of his information direct.

Reasonably enough, Geoffrey was gaunt and hollow-eyed and somewhat out of temper when he arrived in London long after compline. Joanna was not exactly pleased to see him either, but she got up from her bed, put on a night robe, greeted him with composure, and invited him upstairs.

"What the devil are you doing in London? What the devil was in that message from Clyro?" Geoffrey snarled as soon as they were in the relative privacy of the solar. "Have you not heard that Wales is risen?"

"Sir Peter sent me word there were rumors of it, but Clyro is quiet, and he had, when he wrote, no certain news." Since Joanna had no intention of telling Geoffrey what she was doing in London, she was relieved that his main interest seemed to be Wales.

"It is certain," he snapped. "I had a letter from Owain. Llewelyn has not yet joined the other princes, but it is his intention to do so soon. I near killed myself riding south."

"But why?" Joanna asked in amazement. "You could have sent me a letter to say what had happened. What was the need that you come yourself and wake me in the middle of the night?"

For some incomprehensible reason, Geoffrey looked mortally offended at her innocent questions. Then he laughed harshly. "Knowing you, Owain bid me restrain you from rushing off to Wales to oversee the preparations at Clyro Hill yourself."

"Is there need?" Joanna asked urgently, her hands already moving toward the belt of her robe as if she would undo it and begin to dress in that moment. "Do you think they will attack Clyro?"

"No, no, Clyro is quite safe. Owain assures me that those who rebelled against Llewelyn are now most humble, pleading that he lead them and promising submission and obedience. You know that Llewelyn will not trouble your mother's lands. His intention is only to root out all of the king's strongholds."

Joanna looked alertly at Geoffrey. It grew more puzzling by the moment why he had ridden in from the north. "Is that why you came in such haste? To muster men for the king?"

Geoffrey's tired face became even more haggard, but he only said, "You know the summons are gone out already to arm and gather for war—"

"But that was against France."

"Yes, and when I left the king that was how matters remained." Geoffrey's voice was constricted. "John was speaking of a small punitive expedition to go into Wales."

"Did you not—" Joanna began and then bit her tongue on the rest of the sentence as she saw Geoffrey wince.

"Am I a traitor to my oath of fealty?" he muttered. "I spoke out and said I thought the matter was more serious, but I would not say why I believed it. I could not betray Owain, could I?" He put a hand to his face. "I will go mad, Joanna. I am being torn in two."

Not for men, nor yet to keep her from riding into Wales—which he must have known she was too sensible to do—Geoffrey had come to her for comfort, to have a hurt healed. Joanna went to him at once to offer the insidious solace of loving attention. "Sit down," she murmured, avoiding the topic, and began to unlace his mail hood. She went for a cloth while he pushed the hood back and when she handed it to him wiped the streaming sweat from his face and rubbed at his hair.

"What am I to do?" He looked at the cloth in his hands as if he had never seen such a thing before and had no idea of what he was doing with it. "I cannot go into Wales and burn it again. I cannot, Joanna. When my father and the king said I always saw black in Wales, I held my tongue and told myself it was out of loyalty to Owain, but I fear—"

"Let me take off that hauberk," Joanna urged.

"Do you understand what I am saying to you?" Geoffrey asked sharply.

"Enough to know you are worried about nothing," Joanna remarked calmly. "It does not matter a hair or a pin what you told or did not tell the king. Since the army is summoned anyway, it cannot do any harm that you did not insist upon the danger in Wales. When the men are assembled, John has only to order them to march into Wales instead of taking ship for Poitiers."

Geoffrey looked blankly at his betrothed. "It is not a question of what harm might come," he said, his voice rising. "It is a question of my duty and honor. If John orders us into Wales, will I be able to do my duty, knowing it to be hopeless, knowing that the death and the burning will go on and on endlessly?"

Helplessly, Joanna shook her head. What ailed Geoffrey to talk such nonsense? What was really troubling him? Moreover, it was usless to say what a woman thought of a man's duty and honor. Besides, she was a lady and did not use such language—at least, not often.

"Let me unarm you," she insisted, not knowing in what other way to help him.

She bent forward to grasp the hauberk so that Geoffrey need only lift himself a few inches for her to draw it over his hips. The scent of spice and roses was very strong on her night-warm body. Geoffrey's arms went around her and pulled her down onto his lap. He kissed her hungrily, her lips and throat.

"God knows when we can marry," he groaned. "Do you understand that this time the Welsh will not yield? They have had a taste of John and do not want another. They will empty their citics and let us burn them. The war may continue for years."

Pleasure rushed through Joanna. It was not politics but passion that was unsettling Geoffrey. She pulled her face away enough to take in Geoffrey's hungry eyes, his usually flexible, thin lips full and rigid now with desire. The thin silk night robe was little protection against the rings of steel that bruised her arms and back. She did not know what to say and her treacherous body was urging her to yield, desire already overriding discomfort, dulling the pain his fierce embrace gave her. Indeed, his grip was little less brutal than Braybrook's when he seized her in the boat, but Joanna did not shrivel with fear and revulsion.

"Geoffrey—" she whispered, having not the faintest idea of what she would say next.

"Nothing I can do will content me," he muttered, pulling her close again to nuzzle under her hair and kiss her throat. "I want *you*, Joanna. The desire for you grows and grows. You hang before my eyes when I lie alone at night and even—oh, God—"

Joanna neither laughed nor became angry, although she knew quite well what Geoffrey had almost confessed. Even when he had another woman, he had been about to say, he still desired her. Joanna knew there must be others, but just now she was growing too excited to care. As soon as he stopped speaking, Geoffrey had employed his mouth to a better purpose, forcing his head under her chin, brushing aside her robe with his cheek, and kissing her chest lower and lower until his lips found the curve of a breast rising from the cleavage. He was following that now and shifting his grip on her so that his fingers could catch the robe and draw it aside. Before she realized what he had accomplished, Geoffrey dropped his head still lower and took her nipple in his mouth.

A cry in response to a pleasure nearly as agonizing as pain rose in Joanna's throat. To silence it, although she had no idea why silence was imperative, Joanna bent her head forward and buried her face in the back of Geoffrey's neck. The mail hood scratched her cheek and he stank of stale sweat and tired horse. That made no difference; if anything, the pain and odor excited her still more. She pulled free the arm that was clamped between her side and Geoffrey's. He tightened his grip, fearing she would try to fight free, but that had not even occurrred to her. All Joanna wanted was to find Geoffrey's flesh. She slid her arm up his back and pulled the hood away, exposing Geoffrey's nape so that she could fasten her lips to that.

A muffled moan came up from the area of Joanna's breast. The feel of her lips on the back of his neck was obliterating what little sanity Geoffrey had left. No one had ever kissed that spot within his memory. He moaned again, spread his legs, and tried futilely to shift Joanna so that the pressure of her body would come where he needed it. Hauberks, however, are designed to ward off far greater pressures than the weight of a slender girl, and the chausses, shirt and tunic under it provide little freedom. Geoffrey was on the horns of a dilemma. He could not bear to release the sweet flesh he was tasting; he could not move more than his lower body lest he interrupt the work of those warm lips that were sending chills down his backbone, which somehow turned to a raging fire across his loins. Nonetheless, he had to move or he could not satisfy the need that was now so strong he ached from the thighs to the belly.

The sounds Geoffrey was making were almost as stimulating to Joanna as what he was doing. Utterly beside herself, she cried, "Ah! Ah!" aloud and clutched at her lover's head.

Outside the door, Edwina sighed with relief. She had been listening at the door intently for a long time; she was tired and wanted to go back to sleep herself. For a time it had seemed as if the lord and Joanna would talk all night, but at last they had fallen silent. Now Edwina was sure, with the certainty that fatigue and wanting something very much brings, that she had heard her mistress call out her name. Very quickly, before they could begin to talk again, she opened the door.

"All is ready, my lady," she called cheerfully, her eyes directed toward the spot she had decided was the best to set up the bed.

As she spoke, Edwina turned to look at Joanna. At the sound of her voice, Geoffrey's head had come up and what he had been doing was all too apparent. Edwina uttered a half gasp, half giggle and backed out more precipitately than she had entered. The door was closing before Geoffrey could draw breath to roar, "Out!"

For one moment both he and Joanna were frozen, Geoffrey's arms tense with indecision. If she sought to flee him, he did not know whether he would strive to hold her. The paralysis was broken when, with a soft sob, Joanna allowed her head to drop forward onto his shoulder. She would not resist him. Where force might have turned Geoffrey into a lunatic, the yielding restored reason. However, reason could not conquer a need that a year's waiting and musing upon his prize had honed to a razor sharpness.

"I will not despoil you," Geoffrey whispered, "I swear it. Let me ease myself, Joanna."

She raised her eyes and they were like the soft mist of dawn over a clear spring sky. Geoffrey shifted his hold upon

Joanna and stood up with her in his arms. He carried her through the solar and laid her softly on the bed. Dire need lends strength and agility. It was no easy thing for a man to shed a hauberk unaided, but Geoffey had it off in one swift pull, indifferent to the way the steel rings scoured his face and tore an earlobe. The precious garment, ordinarily so carefully examined and folded was tossed aside without a glance. Tunic, shirt, and chausses followed, one cross garter untied, the other torn loose. All the time, Geoffrey stared at Joanna, fearing that the enchantment that held her would break.

The trance of desire was deep, and his frantic haste to remove his clothing cried aloud of the need that was as exciting to Joanna as a caress. Wh. n he was naked, Geoffrey's fearful urgency diminished. He did not fling himself upon her. He came to the bed slowly, slowly leaned forward to touch his mouth to hers. Joanna's eyelids quivered and slowly, as the kiss grew more insistent, closed. Gently and carefully, kissing her still, Geoffrey unknotted Joanna's belt and drew her robe aside. Then he released her lips and looked at what he had.

Her flesh was white, whiter than he had ever seen, and fair women were no novelty in this northern land. The raised nipples were like pink roses at the summit of her firm breasts, and brilliant, even in the dim light of the night candle, the red-gold curls drew the eye to the mount of Venus. Breathing as if he had run a mile in full armor, Geoffrey placed a knee beside Joanna's thigh and mounted her. Under him, her body jerked, her eyes flew open. He let himself down hastily, damming her mouth with his lips and cupping her breasts with thumbs raised to rub the nipples. She whimpered again and, involuntarily, her thighs parted. There was still one thin thread of sanity in Geoffrey and, for all the raging and plunging of lust, it held firm. Sobbing, he thrust himself between Joanna's thighs and closed her legs with pressure from his own.

When he was done, he lay quiet above her, less with exhaustion than for fear of Joanna's reaction. If he had frightened her or angered her enough, she could withdraw from the marriage. He would have lost fulfillment for a simulacrum. Geoffrey bit his lips. For a little while, he had better speak softly and sweetly, more as if he were pleading for a mistress's favor than ordering a wife. Now she was still, although she had struggled fiercely under him while he moved. Very gently, he turned his head and kissed her—and tasted blood. Geoffrey's eyes snapped open and he lifted himself to see.

"Beloved, beloved," he whispered, stroking the tumbled, fiery hair, "did I bite you? I am sorry, sorry, beloved. I would not hurt you on purpose for the surety of heaven. Joanna, Joanna, do not weep. I did you no hurt. You are a maid still. I swear it."

Joanna knew that all too well. The tears that were leaking out of her eyes were drawn there by frustration, not by grief. The bitten lip was no fault of Geoffrey's either. It was her own teeth that had drawn the blood. He was content, but her body still raged, deprived by Geoffrey's restraint of what it craved. It was as well he had held her still with his weight for a little time or she would have clawed him and cursed him for his care of her virtue. Now, although she still quivered and ached and throbbed, her mind was master again, and she was grateful.

Since it was obvious that Joanna intended no immediate violence, Geoffrey came off her completely. He drew her robe together tenderly, having nothing with which to wipe her thighs and hesitating to touch her so intimately just now, and retied the belt. She lay still with closed eyes, her face unreadable to him.

"Sweet love, forgive me," he pleaded. "You are as you were, and none will know of this. I will go out and bid that maid be silent in such a way that torture will not wring a hint from her."

At that, a faint, quivering smile touched Joanna's lips. She opened her eyes and shook her head. "You need not fear Edwina's indiscretion. She is close bound to me and will do or say nothing that could hurt me."

"Then I am forgiven? When I heard that Wales had flown to arms, instead of thinking of our dead men-at-arms and the destruction of our plans against France, all I could think was that Ian would be bound to Ireland for God knows how long and for that long we could not marry."

"But you can think more clearly now?" Joanna asked, her voice trembling between indignation and amusement.

"No!" Geoffrey exploded. "That is not the same as—" He caught her expression, and shed the false humility he had assumed. "I tell you, it is time we were married. You must be sure by now whether you can make a life with me. You must write to your mother and tell her we wish to be wed."

Slowly, reluctantly, Joanna shook her head. "You say it was only to protect me that we were betrothed instead of married, but that cannot be. I told my mother and Ian, as soon as they named you to me, that I was content and ready. I never had a doubt. After all, Geoffrey, you were not unknown to me. There must be some other cause."

"I tell you, there is not. Ian made it plain to me and to my father that—"

"Your father," Joanna murmured. "Do not be angry, but is it not possible that Ian had something in his mind he could not tell your father? I do not mean for lack of trust, but for fear of hurting him?"

"It is possible," he answered unwillingly, "but— Damn you, Joanna, do you not care? Do you feel nothing for me?"

"How ridiculous! You must know my body answers yours. What did you think I was trying to do before?"

"You might have been trying to free yourself," Geoffrey answered doubtfully, and then, when Joanna laughed, he was flattered and smiled back. "I was too busy with my own concerns," he admitted, "to think much about anything."

The confession that Joanna desired him soothed Geoffrey. At the time, he did not think of the careful distinction she had made. He was currently so much absorbed by the body's need that he did not consider what more would be necessary after that was fulfilled. He touched Joanna's cheek and then kissed her gently on the forehead. She sighed a little but did not stir and Geoffrey turned away to gather up his scattered clothing, surprised at how he had flung it about. One shoe was gone completely, and he hunted further and further from the bed until he found it near the seat that was built across the window. The shutters were fastened back because the day had been blazingly hot. Now, however, a wind was rising. The night candle flickered and, when a stronger gust blew in, went out.

Geoffrey leaned out to unhook the thong which held the shutter fast. As he drew one side toward him, his eyes traveled idly first up toward the sky and then out across the river. The sky above was dark. The moon and stars were hidden by a heavy veil of cloud, which was not unexpected. When a wind came after so hot a day, it was almost surely because a storm was brewing. Turning toward the other shutter, Geoffrey froze. South, across the river, the sky had an ugly red glow. Dawn? Geoffrey wondered. Even as the thought crossed his mind he knew it was not possible.

"Joanna," he called sharply, "come here."

He heard the bed creak in instant response and spared a thought to thank God for his betrothed's good sense and good nature. One time a silly bitch he had tumbled had simpered, when he called her to warn of danger, that if he wanted what she had he could come to her.

"What is it?" Joanna asked.

The soft breath on his cheek and the scent of her, woman and spice, nearly distracted him from what he had to say. However, in the few seconds that he had taken to call and she to come, the glare south of the river had deepened.

"Look there." Geoffrey pointed. "Is it my eyes? Can there be a false dawn that color?"

"It is not near time for dawn," Joanna replied, her voice thinner than usual, "and the sun does not rise in that place. It is fire, Geoffrey."

"Holy God," he breathed, "merciful Mother, have pity!"

CHAPTER FIFTEEN

For a few heavy heartbeats Geoffrey and Joanna leaned at the window. Then, softly, Geoffrey asked, "When did it last rain here, Joanna? How long has it been hot?"

"It was hot when I came. At Roselynde we were giving thanks that the harvest was so well advanced. You remember, after it turned so mild in March, it stayed warm. But there has been rain in plenty, Geoffrey, only—only not very recently. Two days after I came it rained."

"All day?"

"No, it was short, but very hard."

She could not see his face in the dark, but there was no mistaking the anxiety in his voice. "You think of crops, Joanna. For the broken earth of a tilled field, rain is rain. It soaks into the earth and that is good. For the hard-packed ways of a town and the old walls of houses, it is different. If the rain is not slow and easy, falling for many hours, it only runs away to the river. It does not wet the wood. When did it rain as I said?"

Joanna shook her head, then realized he could not see her. "Not since I have come, that is nigh two weeks." She drew a deep breath as if to steady herself. "But it is on the other side of the river, Geoffrey. It will do us no harm."

"Likely true," Geoffrey agreed. He looked up at the sky but could see nothing. "Still, I do not like that wind. I will ride out, I think, and see where the fire is."

Fear leapt up and fastened teeth in Joanna's throat. Fire was always a fearful thing, but in London where the houses were all built of wood and all packed close together so that sparks could leap from one to the other, it was a ravening beast to be fled in haste. There was little chance of fighting it even here, where large gardens separated the houses of noblemen from each other; there was no chance at all further downriver where the poorer tradesmen's dwellings clustered close.

"Ride out to see where the fire is?" Joanna scolded. "What are you, a child that needs to watch things burn?"

The tremor in her voice gave her away. Instead of losing his temper and telling her to go back to bed or mind her needle if she could not sleep, Geoffrey took Joanna in his arms. "I must see if I and my men can be of help. Also, Engelard has a house on that side of the river, and I know he is with the king."

There was a short, tense silence. Joanna knew that if Engelard d'Atie had a house in Southwark, it was tenanted by a mistress. A single wave of fury swept Joanna at the notion that Geoffrey should endanger himself for some common doxy. Shame followed. She knew nothing about the woman who might be as well born and as innocent as Geoffrey's mother. In any case, it would be impossible for Geoffrey to face himself or his friend, knowing he had been at hand and had not tried to help.

"Go then," she said, keeping her voice steady with an effort, "but have a care. Unless the rain comes soon, the fire will run fast before this wind."

They both glanced out the window again and drew breath. The red glow seemed to be spreading and brighter. Geoffrey dragged his tunic over his unlaced shirt while Joanna found a pair of cross garters to replace the pair he had torn.

"I will be lighter without mail," he said, paused, and added, "Set someone to watch, beloved. If by some hard chance it should leap the river, gather your things and go. I will not be long behind you, but do not wait for me."

Geoffrey did not wait for a reply, afraid Joanna would begin to cry. The temptation to comfort her would be near irresistible but merely a self-indulgence. There was no real danger here. He hurried down the stairs, shouting for his men to dress and take weapons but not armor, then out to the stable area to kick the grooms awake and get the horses saddled.

It was quiet enough on this shore of the river, the horses' hooves thudding dully on the wide dirt road that led toward the Chepeside. Alert to what he would not have noticed at another time, Geoffrey cursed the dust that rose and tickled his nose. That it should rise at all at this hour of the night was a bad sign. In spite of the heavy clouds and the wind that flapped his destrier's mane and bellied out his tunic, there was too little dew in the air to wet down the dust. That meant that the wind did not yet carry rain with it.

At first, they went very slowly because it was a black night without moon or stars. As they drew eastward, however, a brighter glare lit the sky and began to reflect on their path so that they were able to spur their horses into a trot. Geoffrey passed his father's house and glanced back at his men. Should he leave a group in case the fire leapt the river? He looked up at the sky. If that came across, ten men could do no more to save the place than none. Still, there was no need to leave those within unaware. He called to the youngest of his men-at-arms to go wake the caretaker and his few servants and warn them to watch the fire.

They continued, quickening their pace. Now the gusts of wind brought a smell of burning and even a sense of heat. Geoffrey no longer needed to wonder whether he should slow his pace to warn each house he passed. Most showed lights already, the inhabitants awakened by the sounds of the people streaming westward on the road. Thus far, there was no problem in moving in the opposite direction, but Geoffrey feared things would soon get worse. He cocked an ear to the murmur rising from the group of men following him. It was a deep litany of blasphemy. So far so good; there was no sign of panic. In a battle, Geoffrey would never have listened or doubted his men for a minute. They were brave and well trained, but a fire was different.

A few minutes more brought them to the road that led across the bridge. Here they found the trouble Geoffrey had foreseen. The road was choked with people, most with laden carts. Although he stopped several and questioned them, Geoffrey could not get a clear picture of the situation. Indeed, it seemed as if it might be less serious than he had thought. Everyone he questioned had fled without seeing the fire itself. All were tenants who, having removed their own furniture and possessions, cared little whether or not the house that sheltered them burned to the ground. For them the light in the sky and the odor of smoke had been reason enough to fly.

Drawing their swords and applying the flats liberally to heads, shoulders, and the flanks of the beasts of burden, Geoffrey and his men struggled across the bridge. For a little way, matters on the opposite side were just as bad, but as they worked their way west along the river, the crowd thinned. Although the fire was clearly further south, Geoffrey took little comfort from that. The glare from the sky now lit the road as bright as a sunset and the gusts of wind that came from the south were almost too hot to breathe.

"Lord," Tostig muttered, leaning from his horse toward Geoffrey, "what do we here?"

The fact that his master-at-arms asked such a question was a mark of the man's fear. "We do not have far to go," Geoffrey replied, raising his voice against a growing dull roar. "I must be sure Lady Maud is out and away."

A few loud obscenities rose from the tail of men following, but Geoffrey was relieved. They were of a general nature concerning the trouble caused by women and marked a renewal in the heart of his men rather than any increased fearfulness. Most knew Lady Maud's house, having accompanied their lord there to revelries given by Sir Engelard. The way was not far.

When they reached Lady Maud's, it was Geoffrey who voiced obscenities. The house was awake all right, but the frightened servants were running about without sense or direction. Some were weeping, some praying, a few were carrying buckets of water from the river and throwing them on the house. He swung off his horse and ran past the outbuildings and stable yards where frightened horses and mules stamped and whinnied. Halfway up the stairs he could hear the screams and sobs of terrified women. Cursing louder, he pushed open the door. Lady Maud knelt before a crucifix, wailing for help, for mercy, for forgiveness of her sins.

Geoffrey did not try to reason with her or even, beyond a word or two, try to calm her fear. Fighting loose of the avalanche of maids who fell upon him, screaming for succor, he dragged the hysterical woman to her feet. With Maud gripped firmly in one hand, he slapped two of the nearest maids hard enough to make immediate pain and fear more imperative than their terror of the nearing flames. As those women dressed their mistress, Geoffrey cowed the others into obedience. They were to dress themselves and take whatever was most precious that they could carry. His authority and the realization that they would soon leave brought order.

Lady Maud was now rational again—at least as rational as she ever was for she was as thoroughly silly as she was beautiful. Geoffrey shepherded her down the stairs, not because he wanted her out of the house yet but because he knew if he left her she would relapse into hysteria and infect the other women whom she was supposed to control. As he bade her for the tenth time to be still or he would slap her silent, he made a mental apology for each time he cursed Joanna for too strong a will.

The moment Geoffrey reached the garden, however, it was apparent that he had been none too soon in removing Lady Maud from the house. Tostig had organized the servants into a bucket chain and part of the outbuildings were well doused, as was the front of the house. Ladders were being set up to soak the roof. Meanwhile, the men-at-arms were leading out the horses and dragging Lady Maud's traveling cart from its shed. But then the wind came in a blast from behind the cluster of buildings across the road. Geoffrey slapped a hand to his face as something flew against him and burned his cheek. And a sheet of flame, hundreds of feet long and God alone knew how high, swept up, just as great breakers in a storm rose and swept over the beach near Roselynde, and fell across the houses opposite.

For a single shocked moment, paralysis held them all. Then chaos broke out. The horses reared and tried to bolt; men and women screamed; Lady Maud flung herself upon Geoffrey, enveloping his head in her flowing sleeves so that for a moment he could not see or breathe. Mercifully, the gust of wind died and the wave of flame fell. There was no apparent result beyond a slight increase in the dull roar they had been hearing for some time. Fortunately, only Geoffrey and the experienced men-at-arms knew what that was. They had heard it often enough in Wales. Geoffrey bellowed at the men to leave the traveling cart, to saddle every horse there was, with blankets and cord if nothing else were available. The maids were to be mounted behind any man who could ride.

In the midst of these arrangements an altercation broke out at the foot of the garden. Tostig and some men ran down while Geoffrey struggled to free himself from Lady Maud's clinging arms. Finally in desperation, he lifted her like a sack over his shoulder. Relief blossomed as does a flower when he found that the fight had been between some panicked servants who wanted to steal the boat tied at the stairs and flee and others who were more fearful of what would happen to them if Engelard ever discovered what they had done than of the fire. Geoffrey had not known that Engelard's boat was left with Lady Maud, and everyone had been too excited and busy to remind him. Breathing prayers of thanksgiving, Geoffrey dumped his burden unceremoniously into the boat, detailed two steady men-at-arms to keep her there, by force if need be. Back at the house he found four men who assured him they could handle the craft and seemed to be calm and knowledgeable enough about it to be telling the truth. He sent them with two older, more stable maids carrying the money and jewels to take Lady Maud across the river. If possible, they were to put her into Joanna's care, he ordered.

The furniture was being dismantled and the clothes packed with sufficient speed so Geoffrey went down again to help with the horses. He glanced anxiously at the buildings across the road and growled curses again at the flickers of light behind the windows. They were burning from the back already. He raised a shout to abandon whatever was not yet packed and get to horse. Then, just as his voice died, as if it had been playing with him, giving the illusion of a chance of safety, the wind rose again. In minutes, the buildings were gutted and in front of the appalled eyes of the men and women rushing out of the house, a sheet of flame burst out through the roofs with a roar that drowned even the shriek of terror that rose with the fire.

Geoffrey could never remember what had happened in the next few minutes. The milling horses and shrieking people, the wall of fire that roared and leapt, sticking out long tongues of flame toward them as if in derision of their puny efforts to save themselves, the wild physical effort of forcing struggling, hysterical women into the arms of men nearly as helpless with fear and onto the backs of fighting, rearing horses all blended inextricably into a mad nightmare of futility. Yet it was not futile. Somehow everyone was cleared out of the house, mounted, and driven out past the worst of the burning.

In the relative quiet of a churchyard in an area from which everyone seemed to have fled, reason and order were restored. Geoffrey and Tostig took hasty council together, examining the sky because they were out of sight of any flames, and trying to judge in which direction the fire was spreading. They agreed that it was moving north and east toward them but that it was hopeless to try to go west because the flames had reached the river on that side.

"I am afraid we will never get to the bridge before the fire does," Geoffrey said. "The roads will be choked a mile back, and with this bunch of fools that will begin to scream and weep and frighten the horses, I dare not take a chance on being caught. Let us try to ride south and see if we cannot come around behind the flames to a safe place."

The cavalcade got under way again but did not advance far. Soon their way was blocked by men and horses retreating from a spot where the flames were spreading too fast to fight. This news produced a new outburst of terror that was quelled by a stronger outburst from Geoffrey, who could not help wondering as he shouted down the cries of fear how long his voice would hold out.

"My lord, my lord," someone shouted into the relative quiet that followed Geoffrey's command.

"Yes?" Geoffrey responded instinctively.

A tall, powerful man in the blackened robes of an alderman pushed through the crowd. "Will you help us, my lord?" he cried.

"In what way?" Geoffrey asked cautiously. "I have these people that I must see to safety."

"My lord, the fire must be stopped from running north here. If it reaches to the river—" His voice shook.

Probably he has warehouses by the river, Geoffrey thought sardonically. Nonetheless, he was in complete agreement with the idea voiced. If the fire reached the river in this area, there was the chance that the flaming debris would be blown onto the structures lining the bridge and would run across to ignite the other bank also.

"There are few houses here," the alderman continued. "If we can tear them down, my lord, and wet the others, perhaps we can check it."

"I will help if I can," Geoffrey agreed, thinking the plan most sensible, "but I must be rid of these women who are near mad with fear. And most of the horses too are more a danger than a help."

"I can send a guide who knows the streets to see them safe out into the country."

"Good. Then what do you want of me?"

"Authority to empty and pull down the houses, my lord. Those in them will not listen to me. They do not understand that the fire will take all anyway."

Geoffrey understood. The owners of the houses wanted promise of compensation before they would give permission for demolition. This, of course, the alderman would not offer. The apprentices and journeymen with the alderman were useful enough to pull down houses and fetch water, but they had no weapons and were useless for enforcing his will. He needed Geoffrey, or any other nobleman, because the commons would think many times before bringing a suit for recompense against a nobleman's order and the men-at-arms could enforce the order without argument.

"Very well," Geoffrey agreed.

Instructions were given. Several of Lady Maud's men-servants volunteered to stay with the fire fighters. The rest of the group was entrusted to a sensible-looking, middle-aged man who seemed to know what he was doing. All the horses except Geoffrey's Orage, Tostig's mount, and two more for running errands were also dispatched with four men-at-arms to be sure that the animals were not "adopted" by strangers on the way. Free of the helpless who could only distract them, they turned to their work.

The men-at-arms drove the occupants out of the house and helped to drag out what could be carried away. The alderman's men swarmed up the walls to knock holes in the roof so that grappling hooks could be fixed into the rooftree. Many willing hands pulled the ropes attached to the hooks. The building groaned. More men came to lend their weight to the ropes, but suddenly a cry went up.

At the bottom of the garden was a row of trees that moaned and struggled in the wind. Behind them a thin line of light began to crawl through the dry grass, a little evil stream spawned out of the red inferno that lit the sky in the distance. Geoffrey shouted to the men to bring wet blankets, to wet their feet. He slid down from Orage, looping his rein over a gatepost, snatched up the first soaked cloth, and ran toward the crawling line of light, but a wind roared out of the mouth of that distant red hell sending him reeling back. Suddenly the stream widened into a river and light leapt into the trees. The branches writhed and fire danced from leaf to leaf. Geoffrey stood transfixed, unaware that the fine hair on his brow was shriveling in the heat, astonished at the weird, terrifying beauty of trees of living flame.

* * *

For a little while after Geoffrey had left her, Joanna watched the glow in the sky across the river. Fear for him made her heart flutter and bred a sickness in her bowels. Finally, she fastened the shutters and, feeling her way, found flint and tinder and lit the night candle again. When she removed her night robe and went to lay it upon a chest, she passed the burnished metal mirror. The eyes that looked back at her out of it made her catch her breath. There was no color to them in the dim light, but they were her mother's eyes—wells of fear.

"I do not love him," she whispered. "I do not. Any man can wake in me the same pleasure and desire."

The thin whisper faded and Joanna tore her eyes from the telltale mirror image. Braybrook's hands had held her breasts; his mouth had come upon hers. Her gorge had risen at his kiss, bringing the bitter bile of vomit to her throat and her flesh had seemed to shrivel under his hands. Not *any* man, she acknowledged, and then insisted, "It was because he tried to force me." That was poor comfort. She had not really been afraid, only disgusted. Her mind turned to other young men in the court, but the first when compared to Geoffrey was a gross clod and the second a weak reed and the third a babbling fool, Joanna threw herself on her bed. Perhaps Geoffrey was the most desirable of the young men she knew. It made no difference. She *would* not love him, *would* not worry about him. She would sleep.

It was not so hard to do as Joanna expected. A hot day, an equally warm bout of unfulfilled sexual excitement, and the wrenchings of anxiety added up to fatigue in a young, healthy body. It was fortunate that the respite Joanna had was deep, for it was not long. First light had not yet pierced the heavy clouds when Edwina shook her mistress firmly.

"There is a Lady Maud here with two maidservants and two of Lord Geoffrey's men-at-arms. They have brought her to seek shelter with you on Lord Geoffrey's order."

"Engelard's mistress?" Joanna muttered crossly, but she rose nonetheless and drew on a clean night robe.

In the solar she found a fair, pretty woman, much

smirched with soot and tears. Her initial coolness was soon warmed. Lady Maud was not common dross and, although silly, she was sweet-natured, more distressed for her lover's losses than for her own suffering. Joanna listened to her tale with growing horror and, when she was done, rushed to the bedroom to throw open the shutters and stare across the river. What she saw only increased her horror. Although there was no fire on the bank directly opposite her own house, further east the whole of Southwark seemed to be hidden in a heavy pall of smoke that was lit by a color no dawn could bring. And Geoffrey, that madman, had not taken ship with Lady Maud like any sensible being.

Even as she muttered those words to herself, Joanna knew he was right. He could not abandon his men or the horses or servants. There was nothing to fear, Joanna assured herself. Geoffrey was not really a fool. Doubtless he was leading the group around the fire. If they crossed by the bridge, he would be home very soon.

Meanwhile, there were things to do. The bed Geoffrey would have slept in was brought and set up in Joanna's bedchamber, a bath was prepared and clean clothing made ready to comfort Lady Maud. Joanna tried to draw the lady's mind to other subjects, but she could talk only of the fire and how good Geoffrey had been. It was a relief to get her into bed, and Joanna was glad that morning had come and she could use that as an excuse to leave Lady Maud alone in the bedchamber. It was much harder not to worry about Geoffrey when a chattering fool continued to laud his bravery. Joanna would rather have heard his good sense praised.

After breaking her fast with apparent calm to soothe the servants, Joanna went down to the bottom of the garden. She could see less from there than from her bedchamber window and she returned to the house where in her well-run household there was nothing for her to do but work on her embroidery. Soon it seemed to Joanna that hours and hours had passed, although judging from the tasks upon which the servants were engaged it was still morning. There was little satisfaction in that knowledge, only a vista of tense, endless waiting.

A notion crept into Joanna's head, a wild, foolish notion far more fitting for Alinor, who was incapable of waiting for good or evil, than for Joanna the sensible. Geoffrey will kill me if he ever finds out, she thought, more especially after what I said to him about the childishness of going to watch things burn. Joanna erased the idea from the surface of her mind, but it continued to work busily from below until, at last, what seemed like a good reason for activity took fast hold upon her. Salisbury's house was much nearer the pall of smoke than hers, and there were only servants there. Surely it was her duty to make certain all was safe there, if not from the fire then from the thieves and looters any disaster let loose from their normal haunts.

She did not get her way completely without argument. Beorn expostulated that it would be sufficient to send some men to Salisbury's house, but Joanna was able to counter that because Salisbury's servants would have no reason to trust a band of men-at-arms who arrived from nowhere and began to give orders. If Joanna was present, there could be no doubt as to the legitimacy of her authority In a crisis. Next Beorn objected that she would thus leave her own house unprotected. That provided Joanna with just the opening she wanted. Beorn with fifteen men should stay. Knud and the remainder of the men, the older, more experienced ones, would go with her.

In the long run, whatever objections Beorn had would need to give way before Joanna's orders, but he did not even argue very hard. Unless caught up in a jest, the young mistress usually had more sense than her mother. She was most unlikely to run into danger in a fit of temper or just to amuse herself.

Before very long, clothed in her oldest and darkest garments, Joanna set off. She did not take Brian. Something was making the dog very uneasy and hard to manage. It seemed safer to leave him tied in the stable. At first there was little to mark the trouble except the dearth of wagons drawing produce into the Chepeside. The wind had nearly died away just after dawn. Now and again there was a fitful gust, but this still blew from the southwest, as it had since it rose the night before. In the slack periods, it seemed to Joanna that a scent of burning tinged the air, but the westerlies soon replaced that with the odor of dry, dusty earth mingled with the common odor of the river.

At Salisbury's house all was quiet. There was no sign of fire and they had heard nothing since Geoffrey's man woke them in the night. She had been foolish, Joanna acknowledged to herself. Doubtless now that the wind was down, there would be little more danger. It would be wise for her to return home before Geoffrey arrived there. Likely he would be tired and want attention. Nonetheless, since she had come, Joanna took the time to go up and inspect Lady Ela's quarters. Salisbury and his wife were so often in London that Lady Ela might have left some clothing and some small pieces of furniture. Joanna's memory had not played her false. There were, indeed, chests of clothing, chairs and tables, and a store of expensive, scented wax candles. After a moment's thought, Joanna gave orders that everything should be packed and moved downstairs ready to be carted away if the need arose.

Once, while she was giving detailed instructions, there was a terrible odor of burning. With one accord, Joanna and the caretaker rushed to the window to fling open the shutters. There was nothing new to see. The wind was still and no fire or smoke showed anywhere nearer than before. Glancing at the sky, Joanna wondered if the pall of smoke had drifted closer, but it was certainly not close enough to indicate any danger. The shutters were drawn closed. Joanna finished what she was saying and assured the caretaker that she would send a cart and horses to move the goods if there should be any real threat. She was on her way to her horse when a small party at the gate demanded admittance. Joanna nodded permission and Knud opened up, calling to his men to be alert.

There was no danger from the entering group, however,

which was led by a harassed alderman who was seeking Geoffrey. He had been told, he said, that Lord Geoffrey had been seen in Southwark with the men who were trying unsuccessfully to keep the fire from the bridge.

"Unsuccessfully?" Joanna asked tensely. "Has it come across the river then?"

"I fear so, my lady, but there is no present danger to you here. Since the wind has died we have the fire well under control."

Joanna had a flash of memory of that odor of burning, but there was something far more important to her. "You expected to find Lord Geoffrey here? You are sure he came across before the bridge took fire?"

"Not sure, no, my lady, but I hoped to find him here. Our trouble now that the fire is less is that many merchants fled their shops when they saw the bridge aflame. Now that danger is past, the looters are out. Most of the lord mayor's men are on the eastern edge of the fire, watching lest it begin anew. I hoped Lord Geoffrey would keep the peace in the Chepeside."

"You have no idea where else Lord Geoffrey might be? Are you sure he was in Southwark before the bridge took fire?"

"Of the latter, yes. One of the aldermen from Southwark begged the help of his men to make a firebreak, but they were too late and near overtaken by the flames."

"Since the alderman came safe away, I assume Lord Geoffrey did also?"

"I—I believe so. That is why I sought him here—"

"He did not come away *with* the Southwark alderman?" The day was not cool, but Joanna suddenly shivered. Her hands felt like ice.

"No, my lady. It was still thought the houses on the bridge and the watchtowers might be saved. Lord Geoffrey and his men remained."

Madman! Joanna thought, and briefly closed her eyes.

"Do you know whether any other noblemen are in residence, my lady?" the alderman asked anxiously, too taken up with his own problems to absorb Joanna's blanched complexion and frightened eyes.

"I know only of some gentlemen of the Exchequer," she replied vaguely, and then, "Oh, no, they are churchmen, of course— I do not know—perhaps you can send a man to the Knights Templars. Usually there are a few men at the Temple. They will help." The need to seem calm and to think of something real steadied her a little. "I have a troop here," she said more firmly. "We can do something until you find more suitable help."

Relief brightened the alderman's eyes. "My thanks, my lady, my thanks. You will save us God knows how much loss. If you will tell the men to make ready—"

There was a short, sharp gust of wind that tore at Joanna's wimple and fluttered her skirt. With it came the smell of fire. The alderman's voice faltered and his head snapped around to the east. Before he or Joanna could speak, the wind had died away. The scent of burning lingered on the air for a few moments, but there was neither smoke nor smuts. A long rumble of thunder followed.

"Pray God it will rain," the alderman whispered, his voice shaking. "Pray God it will rain."

There was silence for a few tense moments, but neither the wind nor the thunder returned. Joanna faced around and gave Knud brisk orders.

"Lady—" he protested.

"There is no danger," Joanna assured him firmly. "We will not go near the fire. It is only to be sure that looters do not break into the merchants' quarter."

At that point Beorn would have presumed upon his long service with the mother and carried the daughter away to safety by force. Knud was a young man, however, and, because Alinor traveled with her husband much of the time, was accustomed to obeying Joanna. He lifted her to her horse, therefore, with only faint misgivings and went away to order one man to ride back and send a cart for Salisbury's goods. After the alderman had dispatched two men to the Temple to seek more help, the troop moved out eastward toward the Chepe. Had Knud heard the horror with which the alderman received Joanna's statement that she would accompany them, he might have been more cautious. By the time Knud drew his horse up behind his mistress, however, the question was settled. The alderman understood that he could have Joanna with her men or not have the men.

When they arrived, it seemed the fears had been unnecessary. Although the odor of burning was much stronger, that was to be expected since they were almost directly across from Southwark now. Nothing could be seen of the ruins of that place because the Chepe was well inland from the river bank. The lord mayor's plan, which the alderman was trying to implement, was to scour the lanes and houses throughout the commercial district and confine everyone discovered, who was not a resident of the area, in the great open square of the Chepe. Then, at leisure, each person could be interrogated and, if he had a good character and a purpose for being where he was, he would be permitted to go his way. This work was already well under way, some fifty or sixty ragged, grimy, disgruntled men and women squatting or standing under the watchful eyes of the lord mayor's men. More were being herded into the Chepeside continuously as groups of armed men scoured the lanes.

It was reasonable that Joanna's men should take over the duty of controlling the temporary prisoners. The lord mayor's men were more familiar with the area and could search it more effectively and they were more likely to recognize those who had legitimate business there. For a time, Joanna questioned those who were confined, trying to discover someone who had seen Geoffrey, but even the few who thought they recognized her description were very uncertain. Yet she could not stop asking; someone must have seen Geoffrey.

One description of horrors after another was poured into Joanna's ears, regardless of her attempts to stem the flow. It was as if the images were fixed in the minds of those who had seen them and they could do nothing except describe them. A woman, blank-faced, dead-eyed, related how the whole front of their shop on the bridge had fallen on her husband and two older sons, exposing a cavern of flame that had not been there when they fled the house only a few minutes before. She did not know how she had come off the bridge. A man, hearing Joanna's voice, had turned the wild eyes of a madman upon her. "The mouth of hell," he screamed. "I have looked into the mouth of hell. The whole world will burn. I have seen it, a wall of flame flying forward to engulf us all."

His screeching made the whole crowd uneasy, and the people looked fearfully to the east and surged forward so that Joanna's men needed to draw their swords and apply the flat of them to heads and shoulders to keep order. Obviously it was dangerous to question these people. Another madman or hysteric might create so great a panic that the armed troop could not control them. Joanna's eyes were drawn to a wailing babe and she winced, seeing the raw and blackened flesh on a tiny arm and leg. If only she had her unguents and medicinal creams . . .

The tired wailing tore her mind from its fixed image of Geoffrey surrounded by flames. Unguents— Unguents— How stupid I am, Joanna thought. There are apothecary shops right here near the Chepe. She had even been in some of them, seeking rare simples that would not grow in the cool climate of England. Purposefully she looked about, trying to remember exactly where the shops were. Without thinking, she lifted a hand to hold down the edge of her wimple which had flown up into her face. Her mare danced uncertainly and blew heavily through her nostrils. Joanna coughed as hot, smoke-tinged air caught her lungs.

Joanna glanced uncertainly toward the east. Surely the cloud of smoke that hung over the city was lower and heavier? Still, there were no shouts of alarm from the lord mayor's men who were to the east of the Chepe in the Poulterer's Lane and up toward Cornhill. Poulterer's Lane and Cornhill reminded her. The apothecaries were hard by the spice merchants, and some dealt in both spices and medicinals. They were to the south of the Chepeside, east of where she was but not so far east as the poulterers. That should be safe enough.

Joanna called to Knud and explained her purpose. Cautiously, he suggested they should take some of the men in case they should meet looters, but Joanna said it was not necessary. The crowd was so restless that every man was necessary and the shop she had in mind was not far down the lane. They would hardly be out of sight of the men. Joanna touched her mare with her heel and loosened her rein. The animal balked a bit, but when her rider insisted went delicately forward.

As she had remembered, the shop was only a short distance south of the market place. It was, as might be expected, tightly shut, but Joanna was determined to have what she needed. She bade Knud dismount and knock on the door. Perhaps someone was within. If not—Joanna paused to cough again—Knud should try a few of the shops farther down the street. Knud looked around. Certainly the street was quiet enough. There was no sign of thieves and, besides, this was a less likely target for looters than the goldsmiths or butchers or mercers. Little could be realized from jars of unguents or a few handfuls of spice, and the lord mayor's men had been through this area already. It seemed safe enough to Knud to leave his mistress for a few minutes if she remained mounted. He voiced this idea and Joanna agreed readily, coughing again. The air in the narrow lane hardly stirred, but it seemed full of smoke and the horses were moving so restlessly that when Knud dismounted Joanna held out her hand for the rein of his mount.

Knocking loud and long had no effect, and Knud moved down the street, peering up at chimneys and through the shutters to determine, if he could, whether anyone was inside. He had found a likely shop quite a way down the street on the other side of the lane when Joanna heard a confused noise swelling slowly behind her. She turned anxiously, but a curve in the lane hid the open area of the Chepe. The noise swelled again. It sounded frantic and ugly. Joanna drew breath to shout for Knud to come back but began to cough so violently that she could not utter a sound.

Suddenly, the street was full of a cloud of ash so thick that Joanna could barely see and some of it was so hot that she felt as if her hands and face were being stung by a myriad of tiny bees. Dimly, she heard Knud shout in alarm, but a roar—the mindless malevolent bellow of a crowd gone mad—drowned his voice. Then Knud's horse reared and screamed. Instinctively, Joanna's hand tightened on the lead rein. It would have been wiser to release the animal, but she had no time to think of that. Her own mare reared also, and as Joanna curbed her sharply, she lashed out and struck Knud's horse slantwise on the shoulder. That blow, added to the pain of a burning smut which had landed on his rump panicked the horse completely. With a second scream of terror, the animal pulled away to obey instinct and flee from pain and fear, wrenching the rein from Joanna's hand with such force that she was nearly torn from the saddle.

Knud had run back up the street when the first gust of hot ash had been sucked into the lane by an errant downdraft. He was just in time to see his horse tear free and gallop off toward the Chepe. His eyes were on his mount; he did not realize that Joanna's own rein had also been wrenched from her hand and that she had lost a stirrup. In fact, his mistress rode as well as he did, and it never occurred to him that she could be in trouble. His one thought was to recapture his horse before it hurt itself. He did not hear Joanna's startled cry as her mare bolted, terrified by a suddenly loose rein, a smell of fresh fire, and the odor of panic that rose from hundreds of people.

The animal knew only one thing—the scents that generated fear came from behind. Without her mistress's guidance, Joanna's mare flew before her terror, away from the smell of fire and fear and toward the smell of water. She ran straight for the water, indifferent to the bends of the lane except to avoid running headlong into a solid object. At the second bend, Joanna's frail hold upon her saddle was lost, and she was flung against the corner of a building and thence to the ground to lie still like a broken doll.

CHAPTER SIXTEEN

While Joanna and the alderman had been discussing his whereabouts in the courtyard of Salisbury's house, Geoffrey was taking leave of the mayor of London. Their courtesies were grave and formal, but there was real warmth beneath the stilted phrases. The lord mayor regretted that he could offer no reward to Geoffrey's men who had labored like heroes, but said frankly that all his resources and those of his fellow guildsmen must be husbanded to restore what had been destroyed. Geoffrey looked at his men, most of whom were sitting limply on the ground with their heads on their knees.

He smiled tiredly. "If you would reward them, Lord Mayor, lend me a boat or a barge that will carry them up-river. They are fordone, poor devils, and I sent the horses back from Southwark. Truly, they are in no case to walk even the few miles home to rest."

The lord mayor was too weary and too worried to smile back, but his eyes lighted. He really was glad to be able to do something for these men who had worked beyond exhaustion to save his city. The arrangements were quickly made. Geoffrey saw his men safely onto the boats. He was so tired himself that he was briefly tempted to join them, but that would mean leaving Tostig, who was no less tired, to lead his destrier home. Sighing, he remounted. A roll of thunder made him look up hopefully. The fire seemed safely contained now, but the remains of many buildings still glowed and crackled and a good flood of rain would make all really safe.

Unfortunately, there was no more sign of rain than there had been. The clouds were low and heavy, seeming to reach down and mingle with the pall of smoke, but there was no coolness in them. They were lit from time to time with evil flashes of lightning, which seemed to be generated by the heat that rose up from the baked earth and the smoldering ruins. The wind was down, thank God. Now and then a fitful gust blew from the east. It did not concern Geoffrey, who was aware of the wide band of burnt-out land between the remains of the fire and the western part of the city.

What Geoffrey did not know, because he and his men had retreated across the bridge fighting the holocaust every step and had then been laboring to warn people and contain the eastern edge of the fire, was that a band of buildings on the western side of the bridge had been fired. These warehouses and dwellings did not burn violently but sullenly smoldered. There was little draft to fan the flames and the buildings had been well wetted in the early attempts to prevent the fire from spreading to the north bank of the Thames. Little by little, the heat of the day plus the heat of a city in flames had dried out the damp.

With the first gusts of hot wind from the east, here and there a wicked little yellow tongue licked out to taste the unburned structure. No one was there to see, to cry a warning. Those who feared had fled much farther from the fire. Those who had courage were on the eastern end of the fire where, until the wind died, it had threatened to swallow all in its path. The little yellow tongues licked more quickly, more fiercely, spawned many others. Because it was the outside of the buildings and the roofs that had been wetted, the sharp red teeth of fire that gnawed what the yellow tongues first licked ate away the vitals of the homes and warehouses. Soon, mad orange eyes that flickered and leapt looked out of the windows that were open or glared behind closed shutters.

Geoffrey's body was inured to hard labor. He was accustomed to days in the saddle topped by days of fighting and more days in the saddle. He was accustomed to doing without sleep or with very little sleep for long periods. Nonetheless, this bout of activity had brought him near the end of his ability to endure. He had ridden down to

Roselynde from the Scottish border driven by an emotional desire he did not understand with only such rest as could be snatched when the horses could go no farther. There, fury had given him strength to continue to London where he had been physically drained even further by his interlude with Joanna. After that, first a sense of duty and then real terror had driven him on and on. Now, swaying in the saddle, he was only conscious enough to keep his seat.

Orage, the destrier, was as tired as his master. He plodded numbly along, head down, keeping to the smoothest, widest path. Behind Geoffrey, Tostig was a little more awake. Therefore, he noticed they were on the road to the Chepe, not the track that ran north of the town and would surely be clear of the burnt areas. Tostig sighed. He had had enough of this fire and the city, but obviously his master was bent upon making sure everything was safe.

When the first blasts of the changing wind struck them from behind, carrying the smell of burning and a blast of hot ash, Tostig feared Geoffrey would turn back. His master said nothing, however, and Tostig was certainly not about to bring trouble upon himself by making suggestions he did not want to carry out. He was relieved when they passed Cornhill, came through the Poulterer's Lane and reached the Chepeside. It was obvious to him that there were men enough here and everything was well under control. Their help would not be needed. It was at that happy thought that his mind stuck until the colors worn by some of the men-at-arms drew an oath of recognition from him.

South of where Cornhill ran into Poulterer's Lane, the evil orange eyes grew bolder. They looked right through the sealed shutters, which first blackened and then fell away to ash. Soon the yellow tongues were lapping around the flaming eyes, tasting the frames of the windows and the now totally dry beams in the walls. In a little time, a very little time, the roofs would catch, fall in, and the flame would again run free, ready to leap across to new roofs, to fly on the wings of the wind to new walls.

Simultaneous with Tostig's exclamation of surprise, one

of the men-at-arms cried, "Halt!" and then, when he recognized Geoffrey, "Oh, my lord, pardon. I did not see who it was at first." Prodded awake by both voices, Geoffrey stared dazedly at Joanna's man. The face was vaguely familiar. His eyes slid down and fixed on the well-known colors of Roselynde.

"Good God, what do you here?" Geoffrey cried, adding anxiously, "Did the fire leap the river to the west?"

"No, my lord. There was no fire. We came first to your father's house, then here, where we were told to hold these people."

"Why—" Geoffrey began, and then swallowed the remainder of the question. It was useless to ask these men why anything was done. That was none of their business. They were required only to follow orders. "Who led you here?" he asked instead.

"The lady and Knud, my lord."

"Lady Jo—" Geoffrey began, and choked as a blast of hot air filled with burning ash enveloped them.

Then, instantly, he was wide awake, awake to the fact that the wind came from the east, to the fact that some of the smuts that were flying about were still glowing red, to the fact that the crowd, now several hundred strong, was moaning and screaming in terror and would soon become too much for the men-at-arms to control. Joanna's man knew it, too. He cast a frightened glance at the milling men and women. One more fire-hot blast and they would break loose, their terror of being caught by the flames outweighing the lesser fear of the punishment the guards would inflict.

"Where are Knud and the lady?" Geoffrey demanded.

"I saw them there," the man replied, pointing, "but—"

There was a shrill, mindless shriek from the crowd, then a man's voice, high with hysteria, shouting, "Fire! Fire!" Tostig cried, "God! No!" and Geoffrey's head snapped around. Paler than at night, but no less evil-looking, there was again a red glare reflected from the low-hanging clouds. A roar burst from the confined people, a wailing of insane terror mingled with rage against those who had confined them so that now they would die in agony. The roar died down as the madness took firm hold. In that half silence came another roar, that of devouring flames mixed with a few screams of fear as the men scouring the lanes saw that the fire had spread west. Then sound burst out anew, and with the second wave of sound the whole mass of people began to move.

Geoffrey had no need to pause to think. "Let them go," he bellowed, gesturing to Tostig and the man near him to spread the order.

No force of men could hold them quiet or force them to leave the Chepeside in a safe and orderly manner. The crowd was now a ravening beast and would tear apart anyone or anything that stood in its way. Geoffrey saw a man-at-arms go down, saw his horse seized, saw the man who seized it torn away from his prize, thrown down, and another grasp at the horse—all in a matter of seconds. Joanna was on horseback! If these mad creatures laid eyes upon her they would— With a gasp of fear, he roweled his tired stallion into a trot toward the south end of the Chepe.

Just as he turned west, a riderless horse charged out of the lane mouth ahead of him and, encountering the edges of the mob before it, a wall of humanity to the left, and fire to the right, it reared and screamed with terror, lashing out with its hooves so that those who had thought to seize it shrank away, preferring their own feet. Hard on the heels of the animal, Knud burst forth from the alley.

"Where is Lady Joanna?" cried Geoffrey.

"In the lane, my lord," Knud gasped, gesturing with his head at the opening from which he had run.

Relief made Geoffrey sway in the saddle. Joanna was not part of the seething caldron of death. The relief was short lived. From the corner of his eye, Geoffrey had seen men and women darting into the mouth of that lane. Worse, the crackle and roar of the fire was nearer. It was moving fast, very fast.

"Go get your men out of this—those that still live," Geoffrey ordered. Take them north till you find the ways free and then to my father's house. Wait there for us. I will see to Lady Joanna myself."

He spurred into the lane, not waiting for a reply. Knud stared after him for a moment appalled. Beorn would kill him if anything happened to the lady. It was his duty to keep her safe. It was also his duty to save his men. His eye caught a knot of three men-at-arms struggling against the crowd. He began to force his way forward to them. Lord Geoffrey would take care of Lady Joanna. He had said so, and Knud believed the young lord was well able to fulfill what he promised.

In fact, that confidence was very nearly misplaced. Geoffrey, like most of the people fleeing the fire, would have paid scant attention to the huddle of dark clothes at the bend in the lane. Fortunately, greed overpowered fear in the mind of one of the men who fled the fire. His eye was caught by the metallic glitter of an ornament on the purse fastened to Joanna's belt, and he turned aside to snatch at what he saw. That twisted Joanna's body and her wimple, already unseated by her fall, came away completely, revealing the full glory of her hair.

"Joanna!" Geoffrey bellowed.

He struck the thief dead and came off his horse to snatch Joanna up in his free arm. There was something in the feel of her body that stilled the agony which had gripped his breast and begun to climb into his throat. There was warmth and resilience to it. Geoffrey had lifted enough dead men to recognize the total flaccidity of lifelessness. He clutched her closer and she sighed, "Oh," and then, more strongly with a shade of indignation, "You hurt me."

Relief and rage welled up in Geoffrey simultaneously. He did not know whether he wished to hug Joanna tight and weep with joy or strangle her and scream with rage. More frustrating still, he did not have time for either emotion. A fresh wave of people could be heard pouring into the lane. Geoffrey shook Joanna roughly.

"Stand," he ordered. "Stand until I can mount and pull you up."

He pressed her against the building, put one of her hands on a jutting beam, and turned toward his horse. The poor beast was so tired that it had not moved a step from the spot at which Geoffrey had dismounted. Even the waves of sparks and smoke no longer woke much response in Orage. War-horses were far more accustomed to being close to flames than an ordinary animal, and the past twelve hours had further numbed the stallion's fear mechanism. Geoffrey sheathed his sword, grasped his rein, and swung into the saddle, cursing the fact that he did not have another usable arm. Two were simply not enough. He needed to guide the horse, hold Joanna, and fight. The refugees pouring around the bend in the lane had sent up a shout at the sight of the mounted figure. They were mad with terror and resentment. Any person on horseback was their enemy at this moment.

Instinct saved Joanna, who was still only semiconscious, from endangering them both still further. When Geoffrey left her, she started to topple forward. The fear of falling is deep, deep in the phylogenetic memory of man, however, and Joanna's hand closed on the beam upon which Geoffrey had pressed it. She held to it so tight that, although her knees had started to buckle, she remained upright long enough for Geoffrey to wrench Orage sideways and seize her. He could feel the muscles and tendons in his shoulder scream in protest. Joanna was a slender girl, but she was almost as tall and almost as hard-muscled as Geoffrey himself. She was no feather to lift in one arm.

The stress did not last long. Before Geoffrey needed to do more than raise her from the ground, Joanna's head had cleared enough so that she lifted her foot to set it on Geoffrey's in the stirrup. With that help, it was short work to set her firmly in the saddle in front of him. Now, desperately, Geoffrey roweled his horse into faster motion. The dull plodding quickened for a few steps into a trot and then stopped. Geoffrey applied the spur again, but it was too late to avoid the oncoming mob. He could do no more than back his horse into a break between two buildings, pass his reins into the hand that was holding Joanna, and unsheathe his sword again.

In an ordinary way such a mob, armed only with knives and snatched-up makeshift clubs, was no danger to a mounted man with a real weapon in hand. Usually the destrier would fight too, with death-dealing hooves and snapping teeth, but Orage was too tired to lift and slash with his front hooves. Indeed, Geoffrey expected the poor creature would drop dead of a burst heart at any moment. Worse, Geoffrey could not swing his sword freely because of Joanna. Had he known they would need to stand and fight, he would have seated her pillion behind him. While he still thought they could escape in front of the mob, of course, he wished to hold her before him so he could protect her with his body. Also he feared she would not be able to hold on alone.

Howls of glee greeted Geoffrey's defensive move. He ground his teeth and then tightened his arm as he felt Joanna shift in the saddle. "Loose me." Her voice was thin, but clear. "Loose me, I wish to take hold of your ax. Defend your right. I will defend your left."

Geoffrey's mouth opened, but nothing came out. He knew in extremity a woman might try to defend herself with her knife, but the perfectly collected manner in which Joanna reached down, looped the leather thong of the ax over one wrist, and hefted it in both hands left him voiceless. She was worse than her mother! Even in Ian's worst tirades about his headstrong wife he had never accused Alinor of seizing his weapons.

The sword on one side, the ax on the other, made the leaders of the mob hesitate. In that one quiet instant, Joanna's eyes took in the markings on the weapon she had lifted.

"Geoffrey!" she cried, "Beloved! You are safe!"

No single remark could have been further from the truth or more ridiculous. As if to underscore the wild inaccuracy, before Joanna's last word was quite out of her mouth, the entire mass of houses just beyond those opposite them fell in.

The crash, the roar, the sheet of flame that leapt heavenward, the blast of air straight out of the mouth of a burning hell had one beneficial effect. No thought remained in any man's head beyond self-preservation. The yells of terror were louder than the shout of expectation had been and, as one man, the entire mob turned to run. Some started blindly southward; others turned hysterically back in the direction from which they had come. At once, all were locked into a madly struggling mass. Joanna, who had faced their animosity boldly whimpered with pity. She could hardly feel fear of the leaping flames that could be seen through the alleys between the houses so great was her horror. Geoffrey was also horrified, but he knew there was no way to save these people from themselves. What worried him was that there was no way to get past them either. For an icy moment, panic gripped him. Geoffrey was no coward, but he did not wish to burn to death trapped in that alley. It was not a clean or easy way to die.

A swift glance over his shoulder showed him that the alley under the overhang of the houses at least went all the way back. There was no wall immediately behind them, but he could not turn the horse; the opening was too narrow for that. A quick question brought Geoffrey the assurance that Joanna could walk. He let her down from the saddle and she sidled past Orage. Then he dismounted himself. He knew quite well that if he had good sense he would go at once and just leave the tired stallion. Probably there would be fences, perhaps gates that would be wide enough for men, or capable of being climbed but impossible for horses to pass. Joanna was his first and foremost responsibility. Nonetheless, it was impossible to allow a dear and trusted servant to die in pain and terror. With tears in his eyes, Geoffrey came around and lifted his sword to swing at the trusting stallion's throat.

"It is wide enough here to turn Orage. Back him through, Geoffrey."

The voice, which had been thread-thin with shock and

fear, was fuller although still high-pitched with excitement. There must be a way out, Geoffrey thought, sparing time to rub his cheek gratefully along the horse's soft muzzle as he dropped his sword. A single glance behind wiped all thoughts from his mind beyond the need to escape immediately. The mob was still struggling in the lane, the battle intensified by those who continued to pour into it from the Chepe, but now the roofs of the houses on that very street were already aflame. Geoffrey began to press backward, and Orage moved sluggishly to his urging.

When he came into the yard behind the house, Geoffrey was horrified to see that it was just that—a yard. On all sides they were blocked off by a tall fence. Before he could berate Joanna for the false hope she had raised in him, she was proffering the ax and pointing to a locked gate. Geoffrey stared for a moment, sick with disappointment. Then, doggedly, he took the ax and struck.

"I'll have to kill Orage," he said with the second blow. "I cannot leave him here to die in the fire."

"Kill him? Leave him here? Certainly not!" Outrage brought Joanna's voice to its usual full timbre.

A knight's destrier was a valuable piece of property. It was not unknown for a man to pledge a small estate to buy a really good horse. Joanna had been strongly oriented to the preservation of property by her mother; in fact, she would struggle to that end nearly to the last breath in her body. The thought of voluntarily destroying or abandoning so valuable an animal was an abomination to her. She was not surprised at what she considered Geoffrey's casual attitude toward his possession. Her mother had explained that men were idiots about such things. From her own experience, Joanna knew that her father had been most careless about his personal possessions and Ian was just as bad, giving away farms and other things (if Alinor did not stop him) as if they could be replaced by wishing. It was a wife's duty to curb such extravagance as best she could.

Geoffrey cast a glance at her over his shoulder. She was standing very near, just out of range of the swinging ax, straight and tall, apparently quite calm, and firmly gripping the stallion's rein. The glance also took in the bright peaks of fire now rising from the roofs across the street. An untimely convulsion of mirth seized Geoffrey. Everything since he had lifted Joanna from the filthy lane was upside down and completely mad—the way she had taken his ax; the pleased voice in which she had announced that he was safe; the calm with which she directed him to use a war ax to hew wood; the indignation with which, in the face of almost certain death, she insisted on dragging along a tired horse. His next stroke went awry, but it did not matter. The wood around the lock splintered, and he threw himself against the gate.

It seemed that laughter bred miracles. Instead of a narrow gateway through which only a man could pass, a double closure swung open onto a passage that skirted another fence and then turned sharply to the right. Holding his weapon in readiness, Geoffrey plunged forward. There was so much noise, between the sounds of the fire and the shrieks of the mob that he did not know what he would find around the corner. One thing was sure, however, that it was necessary to get out of the trap they were in. The heat was such that, although he could not see the flames yet, Geoffrey was sure the buildings alongside were burning. It was all the more dangerous for not being visible. Geoffrey expected that the whole mass would explode into flames at any moment.

The miracle held. Around the corner was another alley that plainly opened into the lane beyond. With Joanna at his heels, Geoffrey ran forward. The situation was so desperate that he did not care what was in the lane. Somehow he would force a passage. That, fortunately, was not necessary because there was no tangled mob. Those people who appeared flashed by, running as fast as they could. In the mouth of the alley, Geoffrey paused, intending to mount Joanna. When he turned, his mouth dried with fear. The houses they had just passed were alight. He threw Joanna into the saddle, seized the rein, and began to run himself, tugging at the horse. Perhaps his panic and that of the others in the lane communicated itself to the animal, or perhaps the few minutes of rest acted as a slight restorative. Whatever the reason, the destrier managed to work up a sodden trot that did not slow Geoffrey. Nor did anyone try to attack them. For the few who glanced their way, the bared ax was warning enough. Most did not even look; they only ran, blind with terror.

It was the wailing ahead that warned Geoffrey that the miracle was over. There was no panic or rage in that sound, only ultimate despair. Those who uttered that cry had given up hope. They would struggle no more. They would drop where they stood and let the fire swallow them. It was horrible and it was contagious, but Geoffrey was immune. He had heard that cry from the throats of the defeated often enough. The wailing grew stronger as others took it up and as they neared the cause.

"Geoffrey," Joanna whimpered.

For the first time there was fear in her voice. Geoffrey did not reply. He had no comfort to offer her. Across the foot of the lane, a wall of fire blocked their path. To their left, the houses were already burning and from that inferno great flaming smuts flew across the lane to smolder on the roofs and window ledges of the houses to the right. In minutes they, too, would be in flames. Both his and Joanna's fair skins were reddened and blistering. It was an agony to breathe.

A few of the people milling about ahead of them broke away and rushed back the way they had come. Geoffrey did not even turn his head. They would never reach the square. In only a few minutes, the whole lane in which they now stood would be another solid bed of fire. The fronts of the buildings that overhung the lane would crash down into it. There was no escape in that direction. Instinctively, Geoffrey pressed back out of the path of the fleeing few. He would not delay them, would not add to their agony of mind in the little while they had left. His heel caught on something that emitted a wooden thump and, when he pulled his spur loose, there was a sloshing sound.

Water! A wash of shame passed through Geoffrey. He

was almost as bad as those for whom he felt such contempt for wailing in despair. Fear was paralyzing him too, and it was little to his credit that he did not wail aloud but stood still and let disaster overtake him.

"Come down," he said to Joanna, "take off your clothes, everything except your shift. Soak them in the rain barrel. Quick."

As he spoke he unbelted his sword and fastened it to the saddle, pulled off his tunic and shirt and threw them into the barrel. Then he laid his ax between his feet and turned to pull Joanna from the horse and undress her by force if she were too frightened to move. She was frightened; her eyes were staring so wide that whites showed all around the iris and she was trembling. Nonetheless her training held good. When there was something to do, she could do it no matter what her fear. She had slid down herself and her cotte was already in the barrel. Geoffrey fished out his shirt. She was just dropping her tunic in after it when she saw him binding the sopping shirt over the horse's head so that the animal could not see and would draw in air through the cooling medium of the wet cloth. Joanna did not need to be told further. She pulled on her soaking wet tunic as Geoffrey drew on his own.

"Tear it in half," she gasped, offering the cotte.

"You will need it," he protested.

"If you die, I will die also," Joanna sobbed.

That, of course, was true, Geoffrey realized. He tore the cotte in half down the seams and wrapped it around his head and face while Joanna adjusted her share. Then, with a desperate effort, he raised the barrel and tipped a generous portion of its contents over Joanna so that she was soaked anew. After that, she helping, they raised it further and soaked the horse as well as they could. The remaining little, Geoffrey tipped over himself. Together they turned to face the wall of flame.

"Take me in your arms, Geoffrey," Joanna whispered, "I am afraid."

He could not do that because it would place her where she

would be most exposed to the fire. What he did was to push her between himself and the horse, give her the rein, and pass his left arm around her waist so that she was a little shielded by their bodies. Then he picked up the ax and shoved Joanna forward toward the fire. It almost seemed as if she would resist, but in that instant the gable of the house from which they had taken the water barrel burst into flame. With a gasping sob, Joanna turned her face into Geoffrey's shoulder and let him lead her.

It was an act of faith without foundation. Geoffrey knew no better than the girl he led where they could go. All he knew was that they had to be free of the narrow lane before the burning houses fell in upon them and that the way forward was shorter than the way behind. Ahead the cries had diminished. Some huddled forms showed dark on the ground against the red glare which had, for all its violence, a sickly hue against the gray daylight. Those were dead already or good as dead from hearts that had burst with fear or lungs seared by the heat. There was here and there still movement. Geoffrey drew breath sharply as he saw a man off to his right run suddenly straight into the fire.

His first thought was that so great a madness of terror had gripped the man that he could no longer wait for death. Geoffrey had seen that before, had seen men throw themselves onto his sword. But that was to find an easier death than what they faced. Death by fire was another matter. Before he could follow that thought through to its conclusion, however, another darted into the same place, and this man drew a woman with him. Geoffrey uttered a short exclamation of hope and turned sharply right, tugging Joanna with him. What he saw stopped him in his tracks. There was a long building ahead of them, completely enveloped in flames. Beyond it another very similar structure burned just as fiercely. Between the two was an opening, the black mouth of a tunnel arched over with fire.

Impossible. He could not lead Joanna into that. Desperately, he looked behind—and the buildings virtually blew up in his face. Joanna's shriek of terror was drowned by the roar and crash. Flames exploded skyward and in all directions. Geoffrey cried out himself as one of the projected spheres struck his head covering and, running down, seared his cheek before he doused it with a trailing end of wet cloth. The stallion suddenly screamed aloud as another of the flaming gobs landed on him. Head outstretched, the horse bolted forward. Joanna was dragged with him, her hand frozen to the rein, and Geoffrey, holding fast to her, followed, will he nill he, directly into the black mouth he feared.

The heat that struck them made the air they had breathed so painfully before seem cool. If they had breathed, doubtless they would have died, their lungs burnt and useless. But to breathe was not possible. The smoke was like a solid thing and closed their throats. Nor was it possible to see. For all the red flame above and to each side, the black, acrid fumes closed the eyes against the will. Dragged by the blinded stallion who could not gallop because of Joanna's pull on the reins, they stumbled through hell until the ground gave way before their feet and they plunged downward—into black wetness.

CHAPTER SEVENTEEN

Geoffrey and Joanna were nearer dying in the moments after they escaped the fire that destroyed London in 1212 than when they had been trapped by the flames. Tangled in sodden garments, blinded and gagged by the cloth shielding their heads, they were very nearly drowned when Geoffrey's destrier dragged them into the Thames. It was only the terror that kept Joanna's hand clenched upon the horse's rein that saved them. When they fell, she had indeed let go in the instinct of thrusting her hands out to protect herself from falling, but she was so close to Orage that, clutching anything in the cold shock of the river, her hand came upon the saddlebow and she held fast.

Because there is nothing worse than being blind in the face of the unknown, Joanna tore at what covered her head with her free hand. Because she was frightened, she cried out for Geoffrey with her first free breath. He heard, reached toward the sound, and caught the stallion's neck strap. In a moment his head was free also. Borne up by the struggling horse, both coughed and gasped but neither was stunned any longer. They knew they were in the river, that somehow the horse had sensed water and run toward it.

Once the shock was over there was little more danger. Geoffrey freed the stallion's head so that the animal was less encumbered and shifted his grip from neck strap to cheek strap so that he could direct the horse's movement. Both he and Joanna were excellent swimmers, the inconvenience of their clothing compensated by the support they received from Orage. In addition, the tide was running strongly up-river and in only a few minutes they were past the burning area. Nonetheless, they did not leave the river, merely seeking a shallow place where they could rest and then continuing until the close-packed houses of the merchants were behind them. In a quiet garden where only the gusts of smoke-laden wind told of the holocaust they had escaped, Geoffrey and Joanna finally clambered ashore.

There was another short period of tension when the caretaker of the house took exception to two bedraggled scarecrows invading his master's sacred precincts. In the caution-engendered silence, Joanna's sweet, cultured voice explained what had happened and reoriented the caretaker's opinion. He hastened to offer what comforts were available in the empty house. There was little enough—goose grease for the worst of their burns, backless stools to rest upon, coarse food and wine, rough garments. However, the caretaker's son was dispatched with a message to Beorn and Edwina so that the deficiencies of their temporary haven would soon be amended.

Before nightfall, they were at home, abed, and so sound asleep that neither stirred at all when the thunder and lightning, which had increased throughout the afternoon, finally gave birth to rain. A violent downpour followed, which checked the fire. Even after the first fury of the storm abated, rain continued to fall, quenching the last of the embers. This good news Joanna and Geoffrey heard when they woke and by dinner time they were sufficiently recovered from their shock and exertion to have quarreled sharply.

Each expressed no very favorable opinion of the other's intelligence, for allowing himself (or herself) to have become embroiled in so desperate a situation. Words nearly as hot as the flames they had escaped were exchanged until Lady Maud finally gave up pretending that she did not hear from the window seat where she had taken refuge and stared from one to the other in astonishment. It was incredible to her that Joanna should dare blame and contradict her lord with eyes that glowed like pale stars. It was equally inconceivable that Geoffrey's fury, shown more clearly by his pinched, white nostrils, thinned lips, and the leaping light in his golden eyes than by his words, should not erupt into blows. Most ridiculous of all, the great dog, Brian, ran from one to the other howling his dismay that his god and goddess should emit waves of rage. Both ignored the dog, merely raising their voices to overpower his bellowing. Lady Maud put her hands to her ears.

"You idiot!" Geoffrey snarled, "I tell you I did not come there apurpose—however fortunate it was for you that I did come there. I fell asleep on my horse, which took the widest, easiest road. I would have been safe home, without half these burns, if you had not thrust yourself where no sane woman should be."

Having already explained several times that she had been assured that all danger from the fire was over, Joanna did not bother to offer that palliative. Unlike Alinor, Joanna was not quarrelsome for the fun of it nor because fighting lent a real spice to a reconciliation abed, nor did she become so angry that she no longer heard what was said. In addition, she had become aware of Lady Maud's desperate attempt to shut them out of her hearing. It was ridiculous to continue an argument in which neither was right or wrong and upon a subject that, almost certainly, would never arise again.

"Very well," Joanna said, dropping her voice, "indeed, it must be true that I am an idiot. No one *but* an idiot would be so concerned about you as to seek news of you when you plunge into trouble. I promise you, I shall not do it again."

Upon the words, she walked out of the solar and into the bedchamber behind it. Bereft of a target, Geoffrey closed his teeth over what more he had to say. In the silence, Joanna's last speech seemed to echo in his ears and finally penetrated to his brain. The flush died from his face, leaving the marks of the burns raw-red on the fair skin. He looked speculatively at the door through which Joanna had gone, a pleased smile replacing his previous hard expression. She was still an idiot, but that was forgivable, anything was forgivable when he considered what she had said. Only now he had to make his peace with her. Geoffrey's smile faded. Joanna was not quick to anger, but she was also not easy to appease.

Geoffrey put a hand to his face in a characteristic gesture

of puzzlement, and winced. Lady Maud, seeing, offered to obtain some salve to soothe the burn he had touched. After a blank look of incomprehension, for his mind was miles away from the physical discomfort, Geoffrey smiled at her broadly even while he shook his head. Joanna might be an idiot; Lady Maud certainly was—but he was not. He knew the perfect excuse for affecting a reconciliation with his betrothed when it was offered to him on a golden platter. Without further hesitation, Geoffrey opened the door into the bedchamber and went through.

"Joanna—" She was standing by the window and did not turn. "The burns begin to hurt again, Joanna," he said softly. "Will you tend to them?"

He came further forward so that, when she moved from the window, they were standing side by side with the light full on her face. At first Geoffrey was relieved. The brilliance of anger had left her eyes and her expression was placid.

"Of course," she answered quietly. "Sit down."

It was not until Joanna returned with her salves that Geoffrey began to feel uneasy. She tended him deftly and gently, but she did not speak and there was a withdrawn look about her, as if she was treating someone she hardly knew and did not wish to become better acquainted with. Geoffrey found himself at a loss. With him, Joanna had never been subtle. If she was still angry, he would have expected her to apply the necessary remedies and say, "Do not speak to me. I am angry," or, "Go away. I am angry." Instead, as the silence lengthened and threatened to become awkward, Joanna made a polite comment about how fortunate it was that the rain continued.

"Rain?" Geoffrey stared at her blankly. "The rain has long since quenched the fire. There are more important things to talk about than the weather."

"Yes, my lord," Joanna agreed. She hesitated a moment as if seeking for something suitable to say and then, just before Geoffrey could swallow his chagrin and ask what was wrong, she said, "I must return to Roselynde. There will be nothing but rebuilding here now. Do you desire that I take Lady Maud with me?''

Lady Maud was the last thing in Geoffrey's mind at the moment, but he was so nonplussed by Joanna's manner and selection of subject that he replied automatically to what she said. "No. Not that there is anything wrong with Lady Maud. She suits Engelard, and he would be glad to have her to wife, but his father desires a more profitable marriage. She is not a bad woman." He looked attentively at Joanna, suddenly wondering if that was the source of her coldness. "I would not have sent her to you, Joanna, if I knew her to be of loose character."

"What would you have done? Thrown her into the street?"

"I would have sent Tostig to take her to a suitable inn," Geoffrey said sharply. "In any case, I did not mean you to house her for more than one night. She would drive you insane. She is the silliest woman I have ever known."

A slight smile touched Joanna's lips, as if a stranger had said something with which she agreed but was too polite to acknowledge openly. "She is good natured and kind hearted. She can remain here until you find a suitable place," Joanna suggested pleasantly.

Geoffrey was appalled. He had assumed that he would accompany Joanna back to Roselynde, but it was quite clear that she not only did not expect that but did not desire it. "For God's sake," he burst out, "you did not use to hold a grudge when I told you a home truth. If you wished me to use a gentler word than 'idiot' when I corrected you—"

"Oh no," Joanna interrupted tonelessly, "you were quite right. It was an idiotic thing to do. Indeed, I am not angry."

It was true, she was no longer angry. She had been, and in the heat of the moment, had spoken aloud the truth she had seen in her own eyes in the mirror the previous morning. She had said then she *would not* love Geoffrey, yet only a few hours later she had found specious excuses to go seeking him where—as he had said—no sane woman would have gone. Joanna was not hypocrite enough to tell herself she had gone to help the alderman. He had wanted her men, not her; in fact, he had done his best to convince her not to come. Another fact was also clear. Had she not been separated from them by accident, she would have been a useless burden and a grave danger to her men-at-arms when the mob broke loose. As it was, two men were dead and a dozen injured. Had they needed to protect her, more would have been hurt and dead.

Worse than all, Joanna had known she was acting foolishly, had known that Geoffrey would be furious when he discovered what she had done. Still, the impulse to seek him had been irresistible. Joanna did not remember suffering much from fear for him, except very briefly when she heard that Geoffrey had stayed to fight the fire. There had simply been this overpowering need to find him and be with him. It was a subject that needed to be examined very carefully. If this was love, then it was too late to say she *would not* love Geoffrey.

There was then something else to be decided. She still had the option to annul the betrothal. That was not a thing to decide in a moment or even in an hour. It would require serious consideration. Such an annulment would cost much money and much pain to others beside herself. Joanna knew she would need the peace and security of Roselynde around her before she could make so serious a decision.

Geoffrey stared at his betrothed's withdrawn face. He had to accept the fact that she was not angry. Joanna did not chew the cud of bitterness. She expressed her feelings with openness within the circle of her family, never having been given any reason to conceal them. The warmth with which she responded to his lovemaking was a simple proof. Then what was troubling her? Geoffrey could see nothing at all in her face and eyes now. He took a step closer, about to chance his luck on sweet words and a warm embrace when Edwina entered to announce that an alderman of London was below seeking Lord Geoffrey.

Although Joanna gave no sign, she could have sighed with relief. It was easy enough to guess Geoffrey's intention, and she had not known what to do. To resist him would be unkind. Moreover, Joanna was not sure how effective resistance would be. Not that Geoffrey would force her; he was, she suspected, too knowing for that. Anyway the question probably would not arise. What Joanna feared was that she would yield at his first touch, conquered before she began to fight by her growing lust for Geoffrey's body. She seized upon the temporary respite eagerly, pretending somewhat more concern about the city of London than she truly felt, and bid Edwina bring the visitor to the solar before Geoffrey could protest. Thrown off balance again, Geoffrey stood silent. He knew the violence that any interference with "business" could generate in the women of Roselynde and his divided mind overlooked the fact that the alderman had asked for him.

It seemed at first that the request for Geoffrey was merely the normal reaction to the presence of a male in the household. The alderman's remarks, after civil greetings and assurances that the fire was truly quenched were addressed to Joanna. He had the happiness, he said, to report that Joanna's mare had been found unharmed and was now safe in her own stable. However, after profuse thanks and the promise of a reward to the honest finder had been made, the man did not rise to take his leave. Neither Joanna nor Geoffrey was surprised. They had thought it odd for a person of such importance to take upon himself the return of a horse.

The alderman had been shaking his head, brushing away thanks. "It is a poor recompense," he said to Geoffrey, "for the great help you and your lady extended to us in our hour of need."

"I am only sorry that what help we were able to give had so small or ill an effect," Geoffrey replied, polite but puzzled.

"That is of no account. The willingness is all, and the love for us that willingness displayed emboldens me to beg further favors."

Now they came to the meat of the matter, Joanna thought, knitting her brows. But what favor could they extend to the city of London? A few pounds which they would willingly contribute to help rebuilding would certainly not be essential enough to call an alderman away from more important duties. Joanna braced herself to curb Geoffrey's instinctive generosity, fearing that these blandishments would preface an inordinate demand. In a way they did, but not in the way Joanna feared.

"My lord," the alderman continued, his voice breaking and tears rising in his eyes, "we are ruined. The city is destroyed, the workmen injured and scattered. The very tools of our rebuilding are left from us."

"I believe you," Geoffrey replied. "I would weep for and with you in good faith, but I do not see what I can do to help. I am not rich enough to raise the city from its ashes."

"Nor is any man," the alderman agreed, to Joanna's relief, "any man except the king. My lord," he went on hastily, as if he feared Geoffrey would interrupt him, "the marks of the fire are on your face and hands. The king is your uncle. He knows you would not lie to him. I beg you, plead with him for us. Tell him how we are bereft. Tell him we cannot give the men and money we agreed to contribute to the war."

"Good God, I had forgotten that," Geoffrey exclaimed.

"My lord, we promised in good faith," the man continued desperately, "but God has seen fit to lay this curse upon us at precisely this hour. You know our state. If the king were here he would understand, but words upon paper are poor, pale things and . . . and the king has been so . . . so exigent of late—"

A faint chill washed over Joanna. As little as she liked John, she knew that normally he would have been sympathetic to London's troubles. Disasters usually brought out the best in the king and woke in him a fierce energy for setting things aright. She remembered that even her mother had words of praise for him after the great storm that had devastated England when Joanna was ten. John had been generous with both his strength and his money, rushing about the kingdom to be sure that the laws were enforced and that no one took advantage of those who had been ruined by the snow and wind. He had forgiven debts and taxes so that the money could be applied to rebuilding and restocking. But the six years that had passed had not improved John's character. Joanna glanced anxiously at Geoffrey. Her sense of right and justice would not permit her to argue against his going to his uncle, but she feared that the king's rage and spite would be turned upon the bearer of the message as well as upon the senders.

"I will plead for you, of course," Geoffrey was saying soberly. "But you are right to call the fire at this time a curse. So many matters press so weightily on the king in this hour that— I do not know—any other time I need only have begged him to come in person. When he saw what was here, you would have had great help of him. Just now when the Welsh are rising and the king's whole heart is set upon recovering our losses in France—" Geoffrey sighed and stood up, the alderman rising with him. "I will ask him to come, but I think you cannot hope for that. I can only promise to do my best, and I will endeavor also to interest my father in your losses."

The alderman knelt and kissed Geoffrey's hand. "God is merciful even to the blackest of sinners. We are punished for the evils that lived in this place, like Sodom and Gomorrah, but you are our hope, my lord."

"Do not hope too much," Geoffrey said sadly, and sighed again. "Let me have letters setting out your loss, your troubles, and your needs. I will add in words what I saw with my own eyes."

"So much did we trust in your goodness," the alderman said, reaching inside his robe, "that I was emboldened to bring such letters with me."

He drew out three rolls of parchment with the great seal of London dangling from them. Geoffrey was not surprised. Obviously, the letters would have had to be written and sent whether or not he agreed to carry them. He was a little disappointed only because their ready appearance deprived him of another day in Joanna's presence. The extra time would have given him an excuse to probe more deeply into her peculiar behavior, but perhaps it was best to leave well enough alone. The experience in the fire had shocked her. It was not really surprising that she should be uncertain in her mood. Likely, she was far more overset than either of them realized. Time was a great healer and it would work far better, Geoffrey knew, if he did not by accident and ignorance mishandle and inflame the troubled spot.

That thought was comfortable enough to permit Geoffrey to make ready and leave without delay although he was not perfectly easy in his mind about Joanna. She retained that air of withdrawal and polite helpfulness that a well-bred woman presents to a guest of importance who is a complete stranger. On two occasions there was a difference. Twice Geoffrey caught Joanna looking at him with the eyes of a woman who gazes at a dead lover. The desolation of her loss brought him to her, but she did not accept his comfort or his embrace.

Once she simply evaded him, hurrying into the bed-chamber. When Geoffrey would have followed, hoping to apply better comfort in private than he could with the servants all about, he found that she had not paused to weep alone. She met him in the doorway, all business. A new and very handsome gown hung over her arm. With all the traveling about, Joanna said placidly, Geoffrey would not have a robe suitable for the king's presence. He must take this new one she had made along with him

The second time she had put out a hand to ward him off and turned her head away, saying sharply that if he began to kiss her there would not be enough of the day left to make his leaving worthwhile. When he smiled and assured her he would be glad to stay and to make up the time by riding through the night, she had looked first more desolate and then very angry, although she made it plain that her anger was not with him.

Such a contradiction of signs and hints, showing no clear

path to follow, reinforced Geoffrey's decision to leave
Joanna's pacification to time, but made him very discontented. He found himself on the long ride north going over
and over in his mind all their meetings and conversations.
Thus, for the first time, he became aware that, for all her
lively response to his passion, Joanna had never said she
loved him. Indeed, she had never used an endearment,
never called him dear heart, or love, or beloved—yes, she
had said that, once. In the madness of the time in the fire,
she had said, "Beloved, you are safe."

I am splitting straws, Geoffrey thought, but the uneasiness persisted. Geoffrey did not confuse passion with love.
Even discounting the probably feigned responses of paid
whores, he had example enough in the women he had had at
court. He knew quite well that although most of them had
responded to his lovemaking as warmly as Joanna, not one
had loved him. That had never troubled him at all; in fact,
he would have been horrified and bitterly remorseful if any
deep emotion had touched one of those ladies. Until now,
however, he had never paralleled their actions and Joanna's.
Not that Geoffrey thought Joanna light of virtue. No, he did
not! Would not! Nonsense! Her response was as innocent
and unknowing as a young heifer or an unbred mare.

That was true. Jealousy repressed, Geoffrey faced up to
what he knew was a more essential problem. Did Joanna
love him? Another review and still another of their meetings
and partings left him totally unsatisfied. He simply could
not determine from Joanna's very self-contradictory behavior what she felt. *Peste*! Geoffrey thought, what does it
matter? Whatever she felt, Geoffrey knew Joanna would
never betray him with her body. No man would have more
of her than a kiss on hand or cheek or the cold kiss of peace.

That was true also, but it gave him very little comfort.
With a desperate, desolate sinking at heart, Geoffrey
realized that he loved Joanna utterly and completely. He did
not love her as the friend and companion of many years nor
tenderly and dutifully as a good man loves his wife—as his
own father loved Lady Ela. He loved Joanna with the hot

desire that kept Lord Ian awake and twisting in his bed when he was parted from Lady Alinor and with the despairing agony that, even twenty years after his loss, showed in his father's eyes when—so rarely—he spoke of Geoffrey's mother.

This was no passion of the body. That Ian enjoyed coupling with his wife Geoffrey knew, but Ian did not suffer that restless hunger when Lady Alinor was with him, even when he could not lie with her. When she was heavy with child, for example, Ian would joke of his frustration, blaming his wife's jealous nature for prohibiting him from easing himself on a whore. It was only a jest. Lady Alinor was not jealous in that silly way. Ian did not desire any other woman, and, so long as he could look at his wife, talk to her, touch her, he was quite content to endure the lack of a purely physical pleasure because he got no satisfaction from taking it elsewhere.

Geoffrey bit his lip and cursed softly. He knew that bitter truth from his own recent experiences. Since he had been betrothed to Joanna, it seemed to him he was always hungry and that the hunger grew worse the more it was fed. Hardly a night passed that his bed was empty, and he was as eager for another each new night as if he had been celibate for a year. Yet he had no contentment. He could scarce look at the women when he flung them their coins and cast them out. He had wondered vaguely from time to time what ailed him, blaming the whores' lack of beauty or lack of cleanliness for the images of Joanna that rose constantly to his mind. Now he knew.

It was not so dreadful a thing to love one's wife, Geoffrey thought. Certainly Ian was happy. Yes, he was, even when on occasion he quarreled bitterly with Lady Alinor and raved that he would kill her or mutilate himself in some dreadful way so that she would cease from tormenting him. That too was half in jest. Whatever his momentary rage or pain, Ian was sure of his wife's deep love. She glowed only in his presence, and her heart looked out of her eyes when she gazed upon him. Geoffrey shifted uneasily in his saddle.

It was not so dreadful a thing to love one's wife when that wife loved in return. What was in Joanna's eyes when she looked at *him*?

He had come full round to the beginning and he had even less comfort for it. Now he understood his own trouble, but he was no closer to Joanna's. She sought me in the teeth of the fire, he told himself. If that was not love—no matter how idiotic—what was? Then why did she turn cold as ice the next day, acting as politely indifferent as if he were a casual guest passing through her house that she never expected to see again? No matter how he turned that question he could find no answer to it. In disgust, he swore he would think no more of it nor of Joanna, and set about planning in his mind what he would tell the king. When he thought of the fire, of the scenes of devastation and leaping flames, these were swiftly overlaid by the fiery tones of Joanna's hair spread on the pillows. Geoffrey groaned and cursed at himself to no avail. Before he knew it, he was treading the same round track of questions that had no answers.

The painful cycle was broken at last when Geoffrey finally found the king. It had not been quick or easy. When he liked, John could move about his kingdom with disconcerting swiftness and the destination he stated to his hosts in the morning upon leaving was not always the resting place he stopped in the evening. Early in his reign, such deviations from plan had usually been the innocent result of a message that summoned the king from his path or an unexpected diversion to take advantage of a hunt for a great boar or a great stag that had been noted nearby. At this time, however, the detours were more frequent and more often the result of a sudden suspicion that rose in John's mind or an ugly desire to catch a subject unaware so that he could be fined or punished for some failure of duty.

No fewer than four times had Geoffrey gone off on the wrong track and needed to retrace his steps and start anew. It was nearly the end of July before he was able to give John

the sad news and present the pleas of the Londoners for re-
mission and assistance. The king was in a vile mood. He
glared at Geoffrey and consulted the date on the letters.

"Did you crawl from London on your hands and knees
that you have taken so long in coming to me?" John
snarled.

"No, my lord," Geoffrey replied drily, "but I believe I
have ridden thrice around England in doing so. So quickly
did you ride that I could not catch you."

"Who set the fire?"

That time Geoffrey did not have to try to control his
voice. He could not find one at first. If the king was implying that London had been burnt down just to avoid his levy,
he was quite mad. Then Geoffrey caught the malicious
gleam in the dark eyes fixed upon his. No, the king was not
mad—at least, no madder than he had ever been. He is
merely trying to bait me into anger, Geoffrey thought. Although the burns had begun to heal in the time he had been
on the road, Geoffrey knew the scars were still plain on his
face and hands. Thus John knew his nephew had been engaged in fighting the fire and that his sympathy would be
with the city. It was either a cruel type of fun of the king
hoped that Geoffrey could be driven into rudeness or defiance. But why?

Then it came to him. If Geoffrey's manner was offensive,
John might use that as an excuse to deny the petition of the
Londoners. Geoffrey liked neither the king's humor nor his
deviousness. Either way, he determined, John would not
have the satisfaction of winning this battle of wits and self-
control. Geoffrey lowered his eyes demurely, the very picture of a modest young man, and told the tale he had learned
from the alderman of Southwark of the candle that fell into
the straw in St. Mary's Church. He added, before John
could comment on the fact that a wide river separated
Southwark from London, a description of the wind that
blew the conflagration across the bridge to destroy London.

By the time Geoffrey emerged from the king's chamber,

he was all but laughing. He had bested John at every point by the simple expedient of keeping his own temper. His lips grew a little rigid as some of the provocations offered him returned to his mind, but the memory of John nearly foaming at the mouth when he was dismissed relaxed him again. His amusement faded before long. There really was nothing funny in a king who found his pleasure in enraging his nobles.

Over the next few days, Geoffrey found less and less to amuse him. The Welsh matter seemed well in hand, although the news from Wales was not good. John had obviously realized that this was more than petty restlessness. The army summoned to attack France had been redirected to assemble at Chester. Geoffrey was not looking forward to another campaign in Wales, but far worse than that was the ugly feeling in the court. FitzWalter and de Vesci strutted and were continually surrounded by knots of men who spoke in too-soft voices—unless the king was present. Then they avoided each other and made loud, senseless jokes about destroying the Welsh and driving the French from Normandy. That the king seemed unconscious of this behavior did not trouble Geoffrey. He was sure that John's suspicious mind had noted it well. He regretted only that the king should choose the sly path of entrapment rather than open rebuke, and he hated the tension which grew and grew, noting that even the most loyal had drawn faces and eyes heavy with lack of sleep.

The latter might have been owing to the restless peregrinations of the king. The court was moving toward Chester, but not directly. They rode this way and that, more as if John were seeking something than with any intention of overseeing the muster. Geoffrey asked twice for leave to go to his men and was refused without reason but with looks that insinuated much. Those times, had it not been for his father's presence, Geoffrey would have lost his temper despite his resolution. Perhaps, he thought later, it was because what the king hinted this time really was a temptation deep in his heart. He had sworn his oath to uphold John, and he would do it, but, had honor not bound him, he would have been gladder to go down to defeat in Llewelyn's service than grasp victory in John's.

The only good thing that could be said for Geoffrey's situation was that more pressing troubles left him little time to worry about Joanna. In that he was better off than his betrothed, who was no nearer a decision on which path would subject her to less misery. If she repudiated the contract with Geoffrey, would that diminish her love? Certainly his absences in the past year had not diminished it. She would have another husband to occupy her mind, of course. Joanna shuddered with distaste. It seemed more likely to her that a different husband would fix her attention more firmly on Geoffrey because of the constant, unfavorable comparisons she would be forced to make.

It did not occur to Joanna that it was odd that Geoffrey should have become handsomer, braver, and more perfect—not that any man did not require careful watching and management—than Ian or even her rosy and marvelous memory of her father. She did not question the logic of whether Ian and Simon had diminished in stature or Geoffrey had unaccountably increased. All that was clear to her was that there was no man to match him in all England, and probably in all the world. Thus, to marry anyone else would subject her to lifelong sorrow and regret. Joanna was not of the kind who would knowingly choose second best and take pleasure in it.

Then, obviously, the answer was to go ahead with the marriage. This conviction always produced an immediate lightening of Joanna's spirit. She was not unaware of how disappointed Ian and her mother would be and how hurt William of Salisbury and Ela would be if she said she wished to break the marriage contract. The pleasure she felt would last for a little while, during which time she would dwell happily on the memory of Geoffrey's caresses, Geoffrey's sweet voice and skilled fingers lending life and joy to long evenings, Geoffrey's sturdy strength backing her as she sat to give justice or faced any other problem. Hard on the heels of those memories would come others—the courage and sense of duty that sent Geoffrey out not only to protect his friend Engelard's mistress but to fight the fire to save others with whom he had no connection. Of course, she admired the courage and sense of duty, but such attributes would always thrust Geoffrey forward into any danger that threatened.

Again her heart died at the thought. Again she saw the terror-haunted eyes that had looked for so many years out of her mother's face. The pang that would rend her when she thought of Geoffrey dead would nearly draw a cry of agony from her. She could not face a lifetime of such pain; she could not. Better the dull misery, the sullen ache of a longing for what she could not have. It was true any husband her mother chose would be a courageous and most honorable man and, thus, would also be exposed to danger, but Joanna would not care. She only cared about Geoffrey.

Would she care less about Geoffrey if he was not her husband? Geoffrey and Ian were close tied in love. She would still know when Geoffrey went into danger. She would still see him very often, still fear for him. Then why not marry him and make everyone happy? Except herself . . . And so the thoughts went round and round.

One aspect of the problem Joanna did her best to avoid. It was one thing to consider a different husband for herself, quite another to consider a different wife for Geoffrey. The stab of jealousy induced by that idea was no less painful than the agony fear induced. It was not possible to avoid the idea completely. A letter of thanks from Lady Maud, written in the most graceful terms by a skilled scribe, brought the painful question vividly to Joanna's mind. Somehow, the letter seemed fuller of Geoffrey than of thanks. In the midst of all his pleasures and duties at court, Lady Maud informed Joanna, Geoffrey had not forgotten so poor a creature as herself. He had explained her fate and her troubles to Engelard so well that all had been solved.

It seemed to Joanna that the compliments should have been showered on Engelard, who had been to the trouble of finding a new dwelling and the money with which to rent and furnish it. Joanna did not blame Geoffrey for Lady Maud's admiration—no, not at all! Merely it showed that any woman, even one whose heart should have been given elsewhere, would be glad to have him. There was little chance, Joanna thought, of a marriage of convenience where an indifferent wife would not strive to win Geoffrey's affection. And even if he loved Joanna now, would not that in time wean him to a new love? It must, and Joanna knew she would be a monster to wish it would not.

Jealousy could be repressed but not quenched entirely. Joanna could not resist writing a note to Geoffrey to warn him—jestingly, of course—that he had better be careful lest he make a conquest which would turn a friend into an enemy. She enclosed Lady Maud's letter, which she felt would be self-explanatory.

At the time when Geoffrey received Joanna's packet, it would not have mattered if Lady Maud had said baldly that she was madly in love with him. He would have made no better sense of that than he did of Joanna's more subtle hints about a letter of thanks that contained one graceful reference to his services. Geoffrey might well have been amused if he had comprehended his betrothed's jealous misreading of a most innocent missive, but he was beyond amusement by anything at all. In the early morning of the fourteenth of August, the sky had fallen in.

The court had been near Derby in a keep so small that Geoffrey was sharing his father's bed. Thus, he had been among the very first to hear of the message John received to the effect that Llewelyn had openly joined the rebels at last, that Aberystwyth had fallen and been razed, and that the Welsh princes boasted openly that not a single king's man would remain on Welsh soil. Although he must have known that these events were very likely, John seemed stung into madness by the news. The court was roused and a council held. There was no holding back. All were agreed that the Welsh must be punished.

Such was the unanimity of opinion, that Geoffrey did not

note it as odd that FitzWalter and de Vesci were among the most vociferous in urging the king to immediate action. Even if he had noticed, he would have thought little of it, assuming that their enthusiasm was another ploy to divert John's suspicion from them. When he had the council's agreement, however, John did not ride for Chester.

Geoffrey stared at Joanna's letter. The words she had written made little sense to him. Only her name and the seal of Roselynde and the dear, familiar slant of the hand she wrote had meaning. They were a haven against horror; they brought an image of peace and reason to his shuddering soul. Yet he could not ride to her and find that peace and reason. The sky had fallen in.

CHAPTER EIGHTEEN

"Geoffrey FitzWilliam to his dearest wife Joanna," Geoffrey wrote slowly on the evening of the seventeenth of August. He was not yet sure what he would write. He was not sure he should write at all, but he longed so for the rose-covered hills, for the fresh salt air, for the strong stone walls, for the security and stability that was Roselynde. He could not go. Honor bound him to what he had disliked in the morning, loathed and been sickened by in the afternoon, and pitied in the evening.

Yet something of him had to go to Roselynde. He needed to look into Joanna's soft gray eyes where reason dwelt. He needed to hear her voice, which did not rave but spoke grave good sense even when fear pressed upon her. He had hidden himself in this small chamber. Perhaps that was wrong. Perhaps he should be out and doing instead of preparing a letter to be sent instead of himself to the place he wished to be. But doing what? He could not endure to join the scrabbling men who were trying to shore up the crumbling monarchy. Certainly, he would not join those who were rushing about snatching at pieces of that monarchy to aggrandize themselves. Nor was he inclined to take advantage of the panic-stricken king who had cried out, "Save yourselves!" at one moment. Some had chosen to assume those words were permission to flee the court and association with the doomed monarch.

"I am in receipt of your letter," Geoffrey wrote, "but I fear many of those I thought to be my friends are already become my enemies without any doing of any kind on my part."

At that point he hesitated, but he could not leave so ambiguous and frightening a statement to stand alone. Geoffrey went on then to describe the news from Wales. There he stopped again; however that gave the impression that his next move would be to join the army at Chester and march against the Welsh—a most false impression. By tomorrow or the next day, there would be no army at Chester. Suddenly a weight of bitterness overcame him. It was true that he had not wanted to fight another war in Wales, but this ending to the project was even less to be desired. It was the king—all the king. If any man other than John had been on the throne—Geoffrey was racked alternately by hate and pity until he could no longer act as a silent vessel for the emotions.

"You might think," he wrote, "that such news would bring us to arms on the moment, but it did not. I do not know even now, nor will I ever know, whether some knowledge of what was to come was already in the king's mind or whether it was an accident of spite, but John, after sending some of the men off, turned about and, instead of riding to Chester, came to Nottingham. I was much puzzled, having forgotten that the Welsh hostages were held at Nottingham, but I was soon reminded. Before he even sat down to meat, which was ready prepared, the king ordered the hanging of those who were given to us to secure the good behavior of the Welsh princes."

Geoffrey closed his eyes and bowed his head, swallowing and swallowing again. Among those hostages had been little boys and girls, five, six, and seven years of age. He dropped the quill and pressed the heels of his hands into his eyes, trying to blot out the image of the terrified children, trying to blot out the image of his father, with tears streaming down his face, pleading on his knees for the lives of the littlest. Geoffrey shuddered. The king had wept also, but he had answered—reasonably—that if they preserved the lives of the little ones, only babes would be given as hostage in the future and they would be worthless because it would be known that no punishment would be wreaked upon them. The reason was good, but what had reason to do with the life of a tiny, dark-haired fairy of a girl, just five years old, who now swung from a gibbet in the castle bailey.

There was no need to tell Joanna that. Geoffrey took his hands from his face, wiping the wet from his cheeks so that no drop would mark the page. He hoped Joanna would not remember that there were such little ones among the hostages.

"The king then summoned us to meat. I would not go, being somewhat heavy of heart through friendship with the kin of some of those newly dead. Thus I do not know the truth of what next befell, but I have been told it was like unto a play. Hardly were the diners seated when a messenger from William of Scotland craved leave to bring the king letters, these being of so urgent import, he claimed, that they could not wait the ending of the meal. Hard upon his heels, when the king had scarce read what was in that letter, came another messenger, crying the same urgency, this time from the king's daughter Joan."

Geoffrey was sorry he had missed the event. Perhaps if he had seen it with his own eyes, he could have guessed whether the messengers were genuine and the time of their arrival a coincidence or whether the letters had come earlier and the scene had been contrived by the king. In fact, each description he had heard had been so colored by the prejudice of the teller that he could not even guess at the truth. One had said that the king was dumbfounded, white, and stricken by shock and fear. A less sympathetic observer commented wryly upon John's histrionic gestures but remarked that his eyes, rather than perusing the written words, slid slyly from face to face while he held the letters before him.

"What I *do* know," Geoffrey continued more slowly now that—from his point of view—the worst poison was expelled, "is that the tale told in each letter was the same. Both wrote to warn John that a plot was afoot to destroy him, either by taking him prisoner or by killing him outright and that the army assembled in Chester was to be used for this purpose. I wish I could believe that this was only a device forced by Llewelyn on his wife and told apurpose to William of Scotland so that John would not go into Wales, but from my previous talking with Ian's vassals I fear, indeed, there is truth in it. Moreover, FitzWalter and de Vesci are fled from court. Some say that they were innocent, as Braose and Pembroke were innocent, but feared the king's suspicion, though of a truth, from what I have myself seen, I believe they were guilty. Thus, the king wrote on the sixteenth day of this month to dismiss the army. I do not know what will be done in Wales, likely nothing. Certainly we will not go into France this year because—''

''What do you here? To whom do you write?''

Geoffrey looked up sharply, startled by the hard, suspicious note in his father's voice. Another time, perhaps, he would have taken offense that Salisbury would suspect him of dishonorable intent. The times were so mad, however, that no one could be expected to act in a normal way. Besides, he did not doubt that most of his father's distrust rose from his own sense of horror and revulsion at his brother's doings. Salisbury was being pushed to the very edge. Perhaps when he heard of the plot he, like Geoffrey, had suffered a momentary flash of disappointment because it had not succeeded. Geoffrey accepted that disappointment as a natural result of his dislike of the king. He suffered no guilt over it, merely needing to remind himself anew that, whatever John was, they would be far worse off without him. Salisbury, however, would be shattered by such a reaction. Aside from his personal feeling that he had betrayed his brother, he would reason that, if he felt that way, doubtless everyone else would feel even more strongly the same.

Therefore, Geoffrey answered his father without heat. ''I came here to be quiet. I write to Joanna.'' He pushed the parchment towards Salisbury. ''Read it if you will.''

''I beg your pardon, child,'' Salisbury sighed, coming forward, but only to drop heavily into a chair. He did not glance at the letter on the table.

''Has worse befallen us?'' Geoffrey asked quietly.

''No.'' Salisbury stared past his son. ''The disclosure of their purposes and means has thrown the rebels into disor-

der. The two worst are fled. The others will, I think, try
only to hide their taint—at least for now. We are strong
enough while they are shaken with doubt.''

"How long will that last?" Geoffrey asked, "And what
can be done to prolong their doubt and improve our
position?"

Pleasure in Geoffrey's loyalty and in the unshaken practicality of his attitude eased the white, strained look of Salisbury's face. "The king has taken action," he said eagerly.
"You must not think him a coward for seeming so overset
by the news. No, nor was it a device," he added hastily
after a glance at Geoffrey's face where the mobile lips had
thinned with distaste. "John was truly overset, but not by
fear. He did not believe that any man hated him so much. It
is a shock to discover that men who have eaten at your table
and drunk your wine can have carried so much treachery in
their hearts."

Geoffrey rose and walked to the hearth where a small fire
burned. Surely his father could no longer believe what he
had said. Even he should not be able to hide from himself
what his brother was. Geoffrey could not understand it, but
it seemed beyond doubt that John took a perverse enjoyment
in the hate of his barons. He insulted and taunted them
gratuitously, as he had done when Geoffrey came with news
of the fire from London. In a kingdom full of willing
women and indifferent, complaisant husbands, the king
seemed to seek out and soil those women who would have
resisted if they could and whose husbands and fathers prized
the honor and virtue of their females. When he was offended, the king used the vilest means of punishment, like
starving Braose's wife and child to death.

"What action has the king taken?" Geoffrey asked, more
anxious to avoid thinking further along the path his mind
had taken than really interested.

"To those whom he thinks least attached to the rebel's
cause or most wavering, he wrote demanding hostages and
requiring that they yield to more loyal men the keeps they
hold for him."

Geoffrey was silent. After what had happened to the

Welsh hostages, it would certainly be a sign of good faith or of total indifference to his children in any man who would send a son or a daughter to John. It was sickening to Geoffrey that a king should demand hostages from his own noblemen. From a conquered enemy, it was necessary, of course. Sworn treaties should be sufficient to bind men, but the bitterness of defeat and hatred was not really conducive to the keeping of treaties. A king's man, on the other hand, should obey his lord from love and respect, knowing he would be punished if he did wrong but not fearing his master beyond reason. Thus, if the king summoned a subject to him owing to doubts of his loyalty, any man who had not actively wronged his lord should be glad to come and explain himself and feel free to complain of his injuries. Geoffrey shrugged. It was far too late for that now. The sad fact was that most of John's "enemies" hated him far less than his own barons.

"The problem," Salisbury went on slowly, "is not with them nor with the outright rebels. In the west, the lesser barons will be too busy watching what Llewelyn does to think of challenging the king. In the east, the south, and the midlands, we are strong enough so that none will move unless there is already an active and unified rebellion. That can come only from the north where Vesci holds much power and, I fear, has influenced even those who are not his own men."

Salisbury paused and Geoffrey turned toward him, his color high and his eyes dangerously bright. Did his father think he would betray Ian's men to the king's tender mercies? Geoffrey had little doubt that the northern vassals would have joined with Vesci's rebellion had it come to fruition, but he certainly would not admit that and give John an excuse to act against them. As yet they had done nothing. They were torn between hatred of the king and loyalty to Ian, whom they knew would uphold John for honor's sake in spite of his own dislike for his master. To threaten those men now would merely push them into the rebel's camp, making them feel they had nothing to lose. Before Geoffrey could decide how to say this without implying that Ian's men already had one foot in that camp, Salisbury spoke again.

"I hope you will not take it amiss, Geoffrey, if I should write to Ian and beg him to come home. It is not that I doubt your loyalty nor your ability, my son. I know the men would follow you in war without a hesitation or a second thought. It is only that you are young, and more weight in a matter of politics is given to the words of a man of wider experience. Moreover, it would be thought that your close tie to me and to your uncle would somewhat obscure—"

He stopped because it was obviously needless to continue. The careful blankness of Geoffrey's expression, which had briefly given way to a flash of rage and resentment, had changed completely. His son was smiling, his eyes sparkling as bright with relief and pleasure as they had previously shone with anger. Salisbury blamed himself again for believing Geoffrey to be enamored of the power of leading Ian's vassals. On the contrary, it appeared that the task was a burden he would fain to be rid of.

In fact, neither consideration had brought the delight Salisbury saw to Geoffrey's face. It was, in fact, a purely personal joy that lighted Geoffrey from within. To him Ian's return meant the termination of his penance with regard to Joanna. With Ian came Lady Alinor and, hard on Lady Alinor's heels, his wedding. All other considerations, up to and including civil war, were of no account at all to Geoffrey in comparison with that. He was sure that, once married, he could sort out his wife's emotions. Perhaps—oh, joyful thought—she flashed hot and cold because she was afraid to love him, afraid that her mother and stepfather were using the betrothal as some political ploy and never intended the marriage to take place.

It would be reasonable for her to withhold her love in that case. Joanna might have this quirk and that, but to the uttermost that she could command herself her husband would always hold her loyalty and devotion. It would be a hard and bitter thing to give that to one man while love for another tore her heart.

She should have known Ian better than that, Geoffrey

thought, and then wondered with a slight tightening of the breast whether Joanna might know more than Ian. Lady Alinor was certainly *not* above such a ploy. It was true that Lady Alinor would never hurt her daughter deliberately, but that only increased the possibility of Joanna's knowing better than anyone else why betrothal rather than marriage had been settled upon. Had Joanna been trying to warn him that her mother had secret plans when she insisted she could not consummate their relationship before they were actually married? Certainly Lady Alinor would lay no plans that could affect Joanna's happiness without consulting her. If the betrothal was a ploy, Geoffrey realized, they were both in it together, mother and daughter. There was no sense in trying to convince himself that Joanna obeyed her mother out of fear. He might have deluded himself in that way in the past, but no longer. He knew Joanna a lot better now. There were many facets of her character that he had not understood when they were playmates together, and Joanna's relationship with Alinor was one.

Geoffrey was fond of Lady Alinor. She had always been kind, even loving, to him, but there was no avoiding the fact that the word "honor" did not exist in her vocabulary and "right" when Lady Alinor said it meant what was of benefit to her and hers. Even Ian did not trust her in political matters. But would Lady Alinor, who had always been so good to him, use him in this heartless way? Not if she knew it was heartless—but how could she know it? He had not been in love with Joanna when the marriage was proposed to him. He would never have dared look at his lord's daughter— even if she was only a stepdaughter—with such an idea. Lady Alinor had every reason to believe he regarded Joanna as a sister. Perhaps she even believed he did not particularly desire the marriage. It seemed to him in retrospect that he had not acted very enthusiastic or even paid much attention to Joanna while Lady Alinor and Ian were still in England.

Would Joanna lend herself to such a deception? She had far more sense of "right" and "wrong" than her mother. Nonetheless, she was a woman, and women's concepts of honor were *most* peculiar. Geoffrey was sure Joanna would never intend to hurt him. Only she had no more reason in the beginning to believe she would be hurting him than Lady Alinor did. He had hardly spoken to her before her mother left the country—only that one time in the garden. Geoffrey thought back on the occasion. He did not remember exactly what had been said, but certainly there had been no question of love. They had spoken of the suitability of the match and then about Joanna's duties in managing the estate.

"You need not fear that Ian will be placed in a difficult position by this recall," Salisbury said, misreading the troubled expression that had followed the joy on Geoffrey's face. "I think we must—for some years in any case—accept Wales as being lost to us."

Geoffrey blinked. He had completely forgotten his father and the troubles of the country, even though he was looking directly at him. Having been brought up with a strong sense of responsibility, he was ashamed of his inattention and indifference.

"I am sure you would not set any trap for Lord Ian," Geoffrey said, "and it is true that he will find it easier than I to hold the north steady. I do not speak of his vassals, but Ian's influence with the other men of the area is considerable—of course, you know that." Try as he would, Geoffrey's mind would not stay fixed on the king's troubles. He saw Salisbury shift his weight preparatory to rising. "Father," he said hastily, "I know your hands are full enough and I know also that I should be thinking of greater matters, but my own affairs are dear to me even in times like these. I do not wish that this trouble should be allowed to interfere with my marriage. I would wish to take Joanna to wife as soon as possible."

A broad smile illuminated Salisbury's face, momentarily wiping away the lines of strain and trouble. "Indeed you shall," he replied heartily. "You have waited long enough. Far too long, in my belief. I never could understand why Lady Alinor insisted on betrothal instead of marriage. If

Joanna had been a child, there would have been some reason in it. Most girls of twelve or thirteen are too young to bear children, I think, but Joanna was past fifteen and a woman grown. You may be sure I will see to it. I will speak to John of the matter straight away. He will be glad to hear of it. It will give him something pleasant to think about for a change, and it will be a strong mark of support for him that Ian's stepdaughter should marry his nephew. Hmmm. Yes.''

Salisbury gave his son another broad smile and left the room with more spring to his step than he had when he entered. It was just as well because Geoffrey could have found nothing to say. He was appalled at the thought of his wedding being used as a political lever, and Joanna would be fit to tear his eyes out with her nails when she heard. The labor and expense of preparing for hundreds of guests, most of whom she did not know or did not like, would fall upon her. Nonetheless, it was the best thing for his purpose—which was to have Joanna to wife.

Even if she was unwilling? The question could not be avoided. Geoffrey contemplated it with deep furrows between his brows. Then slowly his forehead smoothed and his mouth softened. No, Joanna was not unwilling. She might have agreed to a false betrothal at first believing he would care no more than she when the time came to break the pact, but never, never would she have pretended love or passion. She wanted him near as much as he wanted her. She had said so that night, just before he had seen the start of the fire in Southwark. Perhaps she did not yet love him, but surely she wanted him. It was the best, in fact the only, reason for her alternating warmth and withdrawal. When her own desires conquered her, she was all his; when she remembered her mother's purpose, she turned, or tried to turn, cold.

Geoffrey proceeded to rack his brains for any reason Lady Alinor could have for arranging a false betrothal. The obvious one was that she did not wish to leave Joanna unprotected and the prey of any man yet wanted the girl to be free to make a different choice if she desired. But that was no secret; Lord Ian had avowed as much, although he had phrased it so that breaking the betrothal would only follow if Joanna discovered she *could* not love Geoffrey. The only other thing Geoffrey could think of was that Lady Alinor had foreseen the conspiracy against John and expected it to be successful. If John fell, Salisbury would fall with him and doubtless Geoffrey with his father. Naturally, Lady Alinor would not wish to be tied in blood to him in that situation.

Geoffrey took his upper lip between his teeth and chewed it gently. He would not blame Lady Alinor for that; in fact, he would not wish to drag Joanna down with him. Then he shook his head. No harm could come of what he had done. Long before Lord Ian could return to England the immediate crisis would be over. If the majority of the army disbanded as the king ordered, there would be no chance of taking John by force and killing or deposing him. In that case, even if the worst should befall and an active rebellion should begin, there could be no question of a sudden fall from power to a state of outlawry for the king's adherents. There might be a long and bitter civil war, but the end of that was certainly no foregone conclusion.

Nor was there any doubt that Lady Alinor would be ranged with the king's adherents in such a war. It would not be by her choice. She would do her uttermost to remain neutral and separate from both king and rebels, but she would not succeed. Lady Alinor was a strong woman and in many things she had her way. In this matter, however, Lord Ian would be adamant. He had sworn to uphold the king. More than that, Ian truly believed that, however bad John was, he was better than the chaos that would follow any attempt to overturn him. Lady Alinor could only abandon the king's party by abandoning her husband, and, life or death, win or lose, she would never leave or hurt Lord Ian.

Thus, Lady Alinor could be no more involved in the king's fate if Joanna was married to the king's nephew than if she were not. The marriage could harm no one and, if his father was correct, might do much good. Not only was Ian a man of great influence in the north, but he had become a close friend of the earl of Pembroke. If Ian came from Ireland where he had been close with Pembroke and he permitted his stepdaughter to marry the king's nephew, it would be assumed that Pembroke also favored the marriage. This would be doubly a warning to those of rebellious tendency. Pembroke also held Joanna very dear because she was the daughter of his closest friend, now six years dead, and Pembroke was the greatest military leader England had since the death of King Richard.

My father was right, Geoffrey thought. This marriage will be a very good thing in all ways. He returned to the table, sat down, and drew the parchment toward him again. By the time he had dipped his quill, a rather mischievous smile was lifting his lips. He read what he had written and then continued, ''. . . it would not be safe for John to leave the country. It is most truly said, however, that it is an ill wind that blows no one some good. All this evil is likely to bring me my heart's desire at last. My father was just with me and tells me that he writes this very evening to bring Lord Ian and your mother home.''

At this point Geoffrey paused and brushed his nose absently with the feather of the quill. Should he be an arrant coward and cast the blame for the gigantic and hurried wedding they would probably have onto his father? He grinned at the idea but dismissed it. This was too good an opportunity to make it irrevocably clear to Joanna that he expected and intended to marry her and would not agree to breaking their marriage contract.

''As soon as I heard this, I told him it was my dearest wish that we should be married at once, as soon as was possible after your mother arrived. What followed you will not like as well, but I believe you will see the necessity and will curb your wrath.''

Geoffrey was not so sure Joanna would curb her wrath,

but so long as she agreed he did not really care if she were angry. He went on to explain the political situation and the effect that their marriage would have.

"So you see," he wrote finally, "there can be no question of delay. Each day that the wedding is not announced will harden the conviction that Lord Ian (and because of his intimacy with him, the earl of Pembroke) is seeking to sever his bonds to the king. I cannot deny that this gives me the greatest pleasure—not for the reasons it should, that our marriage may save this realm a bloody war where brother might be pitted against brother, but out of pure selfishness. Joanna, my Joanna, anything that will bring you into my arms would be welcome to me. I am glad that our wedding may do much good, but were it otherwise, were it even that every good I have named would be an evil instead, I would still insist that we be married forthwith. Make ready then, dear heart, for I hope in only a few weeks you will be really, completely, and entirely mine."

After an initial thrill of pleasure which his handwriting always gave her and which Joanna firmly repressed, she read Geoffrey's letter with relative calm until she came to the final part. It was no surprise to her that John's subjects had been driven to conspire against him. The possibility of conspiracy and rebellion had seemed very strong to her the last time she had been at court. She was grateful to Geoffrey for his quick warning. There would be time enough to inform her mother's vassals and castellans to prepare to defend themselves, to avoid all contact with those suspected of rebel sympathies, and to offer no aid or comfort to the king's men either. They should arm well and keep to themselves, using the good excuse that their lord and lady were out of the country and they had no orders as to what next to do.

As for Clyro, Joanna thought, it would be safe enough. Sir Peter need only be told not to house nor defend the king's men and to send a discreet messenger to Lord Llewelyn with news of John's order to disband the army. Llewelyn would, of course, already have heard of so important a move on the borders of Wales, but it would be a strong symbol of good will to send the information. In any case, Joanna was not concerned for Clyro as long as Llewelyn could control the other Welsh princes. His bond with Ian was strong, far too strong to risk over a small, unimportant piece of property like Clyro.

When she came to the news of Salisbury's sending for Ian, she drew breath sharply and her eyes flew so quickly over the remaining words that she got little sense from them. All that came clear, terribly clear, were Geoffrey's final words. His, she would be his, completely and entirely his. A huge upwelling of joy drowned in a tide of fear. Was it not likely that Geoffrey would go straight from his marriage bed to fight the king's enemies? She could not bear it. She could not. Her eyes slid back a few lines and guilt mingled with fear. Geoffrey loved her. He was so eager. She had been greatly at fault to yield to his lovemaking. She had given him good cause to believe that she was as eager as he to be wed. What should she do? What could she do?

Perhaps her mother could help. Joanna sought further back in the letter, hoping for information as to when Ian and Alinor might be expected to arrive. If she sent a messenger at once, could he arrive in Ireland before her mother and Ian left? What Joanna found instead of the information she sought was Geoffrey's explanation of the political situation and the significance her marriage to him would have. She read and reread the lines and found herself utterly convinced by his reasoning.

Joanna knew that the political situation would make no difference to Ian or Alinor. If she said she was unwilling to marry Geoffrey, they would break the contract and face the consequences without the slightest hesitation. Joanna shuddered. It might have been possible to sacrifice Geoffrey. She could have told herself that he would soon console himself with a new love. It simply was not possible, however, to contemplate the real danger and trouble her refusal would bring to every person in the world she loved. No longer was it merely a matter of their disappointment at the failure of a match they thought would be a source of happiness and benefit to all. Now her refusal would result in disaster.

CHAPTER NINETEEN

Lady Alinor allowed her maid to brush her hair the full number of strokes and determinedly kept her eyes away from Ian's squire, who seemed to be taking ten times as long as usual to disrobe his lord. She did not clench her teeth nor her fists, and she even made shift to smile at Gertrude and thank her in the usual way. Ian said nothing to his squire, staring absently over the boy's head at a handsome tapestry that adorned the wall and somewhat moderated the chill damp which oozed through the stones. However, that was usual. Lord Ian was not a great babbler of idle nothings.

When he was naked and ready for bed, Ian tousled the squire's hair and said, "Court dress for tomorrow, Stephen." The boy groaned and Ian laughed and slapped him lightly on the shoulder as a dismissal.

He followed Gertrude out of the room, closing the door behind him. Almost instantly Lady Alinor leapt to her feet, but Ian shook his head and she sat down again abruptly and began buffing her nails with a chamois fastened to an oval piece of wood. In a few minutes there was a scratch at the door. Ian, who had climbed into bed and propped himself against the pillows, flashed a smile at his wife and called, "Come." One of Isabella's ladies entered promptly. She asked most solicitously whether Lady Alinor had everything she needed, whether the queen could provide any comfort, any article that might have been sent on ahead to Roselynde because Alinor had not known that her journey would be interrupted.

"I am not so improvident a traveler," Lady Alinor replied, smiling. She noted how the lady's eyes scanned her face, Ian's, and the room. "But thank the queen and tell her I am most sensible of her kindness.''

The lady turned to go and Ian made an idle comment to his wife about the subject matter of the tapestry, which drew a laugh from her and a light riposte about the uncleanness of his mind. The door, she noted, without turning her head, did not quite close. The click of the latch, quite apparent when Stephen left, did not occur. Lady Alinor smiled at her husband and continued to talk, mentioning after a few minutes that their son had been a little less active than usual on the last lap of their journey.

"You mean he sat quiet for more than five breaths?" Ian asked sardonically. "Have you not offered up thanks for the small mercies granted by heaven?"

Lady Alinor laughed. Simon was a devil incarnate. She had thought Adam an active, mischievous child, but Simon outdid him by far. He was not so large or strong as Adam at the same age, but he was more lithe, climbed like an ape, and was at least as curious.

"Well, it was restful," she agreed, "but I will offer no thanks if it is a sign of illness. I think I had better go and take a look at him."

She rose without haste, for she did not wish to catch the queen's lady or perhaps one of the king's servants listening at the door. The antechamber was empty when she crossed it. Nonetheless, she went into the small wall chamber opposite and looked carefully at her youngest son. There was no anxiety in her glance. Simon had been a little quieter than usual—for a short time—because she had threatened to lift his hide with his father's belt if he did not cease from tormenting everyone. He was the image of Ian with his eyes closed, for he had his father's silky black curls and sensuous, sensitive mouth. He had inherited his mother's eyes, however, and the bright hazel, with its glints of green and gold, gave a markedly devilish aspect to the dark beauty he had taken from Ian.

Forgetting for a moment why she had come, Alinor cast her eyes up to heaven. Adam was already in trouble with women. Robert of Leicester had written of his progress and jestingly included a description of the determined pursuit of Alinor's son by every nubile female in his household from maidservants to his wife's gently born wards. "And he does not run away very fast either," Leicester complained. "In fact, I am quite sure he has been caught several times." Adam, Alinor thought, although a well set up young man, was not a patch on what Simon would be at his age. She could only thank God it would be his wife's problem rather than hers and make a mental note to herself that they would need to look for a particularly gentle and complaisant girl. Even if Simon should happen to be of a faithful temperament—and Alinor doubted he would be because of his avid passion for new experiences—his wife would be sorely tried.

That was in the far future. Simon was, after all, only three years old. There were more immediate problems. After another affectionate glance at her son, Alinor re-crossed the antechamber and closed the door to her bedchamber behind her firmly, but as softly as possible. She came directly to the bed after that, shed her bedgown, and got in beside her husband. Alinor hoped that they had disarmed whatever suspicion was felt about them. It was surprising to her that the queen rather than the king had set a spy, but unless someone was hidden under the bed, no one could now hear what was said. They looked at each other, both mouths opening at once. Alinor smiled.

"Tell me," she urged, "it is the king who calls the tune."

"Yes, but I wish I knew what tune it was. I have known him long, almost thirty years now, and I do not know *this* mood. Salisbury says John did not realize how much displeasure his behavior was causing—that what he did was meaningless to him and he did not believe, no matter how often he was told, that it had meaning to others. The news of the conspiracy shocked him into a recognition that he must change his ways."

"Salisbury would say that."

There was a short pause and then Ian said, "This time he may be right."

"Are you asking me to believe that John's character is altered?"

"No, but John is not stupid and never was. From the time he took the throne from Richard, one threat after another haunted him, and the loss of Normandy shook his power so that, had Arthur still lived, John believes—and I do too—that he would no longer hold the throne. Then things began to mend. Scotland bowed to him, then Ireland, and then Wales. He had even, or so he believes, defied the Church successfully. With each increase of power, his arrogance also grew. None defied him, some because of fear; others, like Pembroke, because, although the king was morally wrong to suspect and punish an innocent man, he was nonetheless within his right in what he demanded."

"I know all this," Alinor suggested tartly.

"But you have not added the events together. With the gathering of the army to invade Normandy, John seemed to reach a new peak in power. He was poised on the point of eating first Normandy and then France also. At this, so near the summit of his desires, he has been struck down—not completely, not deposed or killed or defeated utterly, but firmly smitten as by the chiding hand of the greatest Father of all."

"Do *you* believe this is God's work?" Alinor asked in a tentative, slightly awed voice.

"I do not set myself up as one who knows the unknowable," Ian said slowly. "From what Salisbury has been able to determine, the rebellion was well knit, well planned, and kept remarkably secret for so wide-spread a conspiracy. He is not a religious man, not out of the ordinary, yet he credits the revelation of the conspiracy as miraculous."

"Geoffrey thinks John knew before—or rather that the way and time of arrival of the messengers was the king's doing," Alinor protested.

Ian smiled. "Geoffrey has keen eyes and keen ears for one so young and may well be right. I said John was not stupid. What could better convince his barons of his change of heart than to make them believe that God has warned him of the evil of his ways and he has accepted that angry warning with a whole heart?''

Alinor sighed with relief. ''That sounds more reasonable to me. It is like John to wriggle his way out of a mess of his making by claiming that God helps him.''

''I am not sure God did not,'' Ian said soberly. He shrugged at his wife's startled expression. ''My love, I have told you over and over what our state should be if John would be deposed or be killed. I do not love the king. I doubt that even the infinite love and compassion of Jesus and Mary would be sufficient to embrace John as he is. However, I do believe that the people of this land are beloved of God, the Son, and the Mother. Would the Holy Ones abandon us all to chaos, to unending war and blood and death, only because they disapproved the actions of one man? I know the priests tell us it is not for us to question or understand the ways of God, why, for instance, pure babes die and evil men live and flourish—but this matter is so very—''

''Yet the people have been sore punished by the interdict for the king's fault,'' Alinor interrupted rebelliously.

Ian touched her hair gently. ''No man or woman is sinless,'' he said softly. ''God knows we all deserve a whipping, and the interdict is a light lash—but that is no matter. I do not ask you to believe in a miracle if you do not wish. What is important is that I think *John* believes it. Setting aside the time of arrival of the messengers, which John may well have arranged, he is convinced that God intervened to protect him.''

''He would be.'' Alinor snorted lightly with contempt. ''And doubtless next he will convince himself that God's help was owing to the modesty and perfection of his past behavior.''

Ian grinned at her, but shook his head. ''There you are wrong. I think John has learned a sharp lesson. Unfortunately, I do not know whether it is the right lesson—time alone will tell that—but there are already some excellent results. John has sent a message inviting Stephen Langton and all the exiled bishops to return. He will restore their property and promises restitution of what was confiscated as soon as he can find the means.''

''What?'' Alinor exclaimed, with widening eyes and rising color. ''You call that an excellent result? You know the king will bleed us to make peace with the Church.''

''Not so,'' Ian said firmly. ''Langton and the pope's emissary Pandulf are not such great fools as to expect John to squeeze his barons when they are already threatening revolt.''

''I do not know what Langton and Pandulf are,'' Alinor snapped, ''but *you* are a fool if you believe the Church will take less than its due—even if we all starve. God may love us. I will believe you if you say it, but the Church loves its gold.''

''The Church is governed by men, some wise and some foolish. I tell you that Langton and Pandulf are wise men. I do not deny they will, in the end, see that everything taken from the Church is restored. I believe, however, that they will do it in such a way that the country is not overturned.''

Alinor did not look much better pleased. ''Fast or slow,'' she muttered, ''the blood will be drawn from us. The king took it and the king spent it, but we will repay it.''

''Be reasonable, Alinor,'' Ian responded sharply, ''in an ordinary way we would have paid double what the wars in Ireland and Wales cost. You know the purpose to which John put what he extracted from the Church. He is many things, but no spendthrift.''

Alinor tossed her head irritably. She hated to concede anything at all in the king's favor, but she could not argue against what Ian said and so held her tongue. Ian smiled at her affectionately.

''What you will be glad to hear,'' he continued, ''is that what will eventually be squeezed from us to pay the Church will not be without any return. John has agreed—no, I say that as if he was unwilling, and I do not think he is. John has urged, even eagerly, that the bishops, headed by the archbishop of Canterbury, mediate between him and the rebels, discover what has caused so great a discontent in them, and suggest a peace agreement."

"I do not believe it," Alinor said flatly. After as minute an examination of her husband's face as she could make in the dim light of the night candle, she sighed. "I see that you believe it. Ian, Ian, your soft heart will be our destruction. Such a yielding is against the king's whole nature. I do not mean that I disbelieve he urged this mediation. He can *say* anything—"

"It is more than saying, Alinor. John has already sent out letters proposing this." Then Ian shrugged. "I am not so soft-headed as you think. What the end of this will be I cannot guess. I do not believe the king has changed his nature, but he has certainly changed his methods, and that is a good thing in itself. It means that for this time—the autumn and winter anyway—there will be no war, at least not among the barons of England."

Stubbornly, Alinor shook her head. "He lies."

"Perhaps about his purpose, not about what he will do at this time," Ian insisted. "His long purpose may still be to reduce all of us in the realm to a condition in which we can do nothing but obey. I believe, however, that he now knows his end cannot be achieved by his single power and the fear this induces. He needs allies, strong allies, and he believes God Himself has pointed out the ally he must choose."

Now Alinor nodded vigorously in agreement. "Of course. Now I see. Submission—for which *we* will pay— will bring a multitude of goods. Rebellion will again become an offense against the Church as well as against the king. Philip of France will no longer have an excuse to launch a 'holy war,' which he has been threatening to do for—" Her voice checked. "I wonder if that could be the reason," she murmured.

"The reason for what?"

"For a most curious proposal—well, more than a proposal. It was near a command. Isabella insists that Joanna and Geoffrey be married at court and proposes to supply the wedding feast and all other matters for the celebration."

Ian did not look surprised, which rather confirmed Alinor's notion that the queen was motivated by more than a sudden and abnormal spurt of generosity, although Alinor knew Isabella liked her.

"The king mentioned the wedding also," Ian said. "He repeated what Salisbury had written—and what Geoffrey confirmed, scarcely waiting to greet me—that Geoffrey was most eager to marry as quickly as possible." Ian looked consideringly at Alinor. "He also suggested that the wedding be at court, but there was no command about it. His manner was so fair that I scarcely knew the man. He said frankly and openly that politically the marriage would do him much good, that it would serve the double purpose of reaffirming my bond to him and displaying his reconciliation with the Church. Still, he said he would not press me to it, that he knew it would give little pleasure to us and to the children to be put upon show at such a time. He hoped—"

"Geoffrey, Salisbury, Isabella, the king—" Alinor interrupted, "but I have not heard one word from Joanna. In fact, I have not had a letter from her in longer than usual."

"That is not unreasonable," Ian soothed. "Geoffrey said he wrote that we were being summoned home. There would be little sense in sending messengers to follow us when she expected we would soon be at Roselynde."

"But we are not at Roselynde," Alinor pointed out with a worried frown. "We were near as nothing waylaid as we came off ship and summoned here with the greatest urgency—for what? What has happened to Joanna that everyone except she is clamoring for an immediate wedding? Ian—"

The muscles of her husband's body tensed, as if he would leap out of bed, but then he relaxed. "Alinor, for God's sake, think whom you are including together! Could Geoffrey and Isabella possibly have the same reason for desiring an immediate marriage? You spoke to Geoffrey as well as I. Can you believe Geoffrey would be party to anything that would hurt Joanna?"

For a few minutes, Alinor continued to look worried, and

then began to sputter. "I can think of something which, from the same cause but for different reasons, would make both urge a hasty marriage."

"What cause?"

"If Joanna is with child and Isabella came to know of it, she would enjoy the shame that came upon Geoffrey when Joanna proved no maid."

"Joanna would never—" Ian began, but his wife's hearty laughter interrupted him and his common sense told him such a remark was nonsense. However much his heart said that Joanna was a sweet little girl, he really knew she was a woman ripe, even overripe, for marriage. His frown did not clear, though. "But Geoffrey," Ian protested, "he has made no argument about this court wedding. Surely he would be no party to shaming his own wife."

"Either he is far less innocent about such matters than he should be," Alinor said with twinkling eyes. "or else he underestimates the effect of lack of proof of maidenhead. After all, he may feel that if he does not repudiate Joanna there can be no other effect. But it seems odd to me that Geoffrey, who has suffered so much from court gossip, would underestimate it."

"It is more likely that Joanna is still a virgin," Ian insisted.

Suddenly Alinor's eyes widened. Could Joanna, awakened by the thought of being a wife, have fallen in love with someone other than Geoffrey while Geoffrey was away at the war or on other business? But if she had, why not say so? The answer to that was obvious enough. Joanna knew the political situation as well as anyone else. She was far too dutiful a girl to bring on a state crisis because of a personal preference. In addition, Joanna might know Geoffrey was in love with her. She must know it. Geoffrey made no attempt to hide it.

Out of kindness, Joanna might well force herself to marry Geoffrey when she loved another to spare Geoffrey hurt. How she could be stupid enough to think such an act a kindness, Alinor could not understand, but tender hearts were often misled into great cruelty through lack of resolution to administer one sharp wound. They never thought that a lifetime of constant pain was far worse than a few months of agony.

"What is it, Alinor?" Ian asked as he watched her expression change.

"I must speak to Joanna," Alinor said urgently, and told him why. "I hope it is not so," she concluded, "but it is one answer, the least pleasant, to all the odd things. Geoffrey might believe that if he married her at once and publicly he will wean her from this other love. Isabella, like the fool she is, may believe that my daughter would hop into any bed that tempted her and thus is happy to pay for the wedding to blazon out Geoffrey's shame. John's motives and Salisbury's are what they said. It all fits, Ian."

Her husband closed his eyes. "God help us all if you are right," he sighed, "it is a disaster." Then he shrugged his hard-muscled shoulders. "It does not matter. Joanna cannot be sold into slavery for a political cause." Actually, Ian did not really believe what he said. Had it been any other woman in the world, he would have applauded the forced marriage, but Joanna— Joanna was different. "I will think of something," he went on. "Shall I—"

"Do nothing." Now Alinor was reconsidering. "We are building a castle of dry sand. Tomorrow I will go to fetch Joanna. I will leave Simon here with you. Even John can have no suspicion of my actions while you and the babe are hostage for me. Isabella will put the worst interpretation on my going, I do not doubt. Do not be surprised if you begin to hear rumors of how old whores are turned into fresh virgins with bladders of chickens' blood."

Less than a week later, a tired, mud-spattered Alinor confronted her daughter in the privacy of her bedchamber. "Open your mouth and speak the truth only," Alinor ordered. "This is too important a matter to allow kindness or duty or politics to cloud honesty. Do you love any man other than Geoffrey FitzWilliam?"

To Alinor's consternation, Joanna's face flamed and her

eyes grew brilliant with anger. "You should be ashamed to ask such a question of me,' she cried. "You bore me! You raised me! Do you not know me better than to listen to court gossip about me?''

Alinor clamped her jaw tight over hot words that could only hurt them both. "Do not be a fool, Joanna," she said when she had mastered her voice. "I do not accuse you of anything. My only interest is in your happiness. I told you before that you must only marry where you love.''

"And I told you that I was well content with Geoffrey.''

"Well content is not enough. Who is the other man?''

"I tell you it is rumor only, disgusting rumors spread about to smirch me.''

"And I tell you I have heard no rumors." As the words came out of her mouth, Alinor realized that was suspicious in itself. If Isabella knew, then her ladies knew. It was very odd that none of those malicious tongues had wagged—unless the queen had forbidden it. "Since I have heard nothing," Alinor went on, "you had better tell me the whole. Who is the man?''

For a moment Joanna looked rebellious; then her color faded and the brilliance died from her eyes. Reason always had a strong hold upon her, and it was necessary that Alinor know what had happened. "Henry de Braybrook," she replied.

An expression of revolted horror distorted Alinor's face. "Braybrook?" she whispered. How could her daughter, who had Simon and Ian for examples of what a man should be, prefer a popinjay like Braybrook to Geoffrey?

"Well, it is not my fault," Joanna cried furiously, and then she sighed. Honesty forced her to admit that it was, to some degree, her fault. Haltingly, she began the tale of the queen's summons and her defense against it, the ridiculous wooing in the garden at Whitechurch. By the time she was halfway through, the loathing was gone from Alinor's face and she was laughing uproariously.

"I have told you and told you," she gasped when she

stopped whooping with laughter, "that your love of a jest would ruin us all."

The reprimand was not given nor meant seriously, and Joanna began to giggle also. "It was not so funny later," she said, sobering, and went on to describe Braybrook's absence from court during her absence, the rumors that followed, and his attempt to rape her in London.

To her surprise, Alinor merely looked thoughtful. "The attempt on you is of no account since he did not succeed except that it is of interest that he was so desperate about it. The rumors are more important. Had Braybrook told Isabella that he had despoiled you? But I am wandering from the most important matter of all. Obviously Braybrook holds no place in your affections. Joanna, answer me plain. Does Geoffrey?"

A mulish expression flitted across Joanna's face, but then she sighed "Yes."

"Thank God for that!" Alinor exclaimed. To clear all doubt once and for all, she asked, "Will you swear to me that you love Geoffrey and no other man?"

Joanna met her mother's eyes. "Yes, I swear it. I wish it were not so. I wish I loved no man. To love is to die a thousand times a day."

Alinor took her daughter into her arms in a rare embrace. "It is so," she agreed with sympathy, "but it is also the only way to taste life. Child, you cannot avoid that kind of death, except by being dead yourself. If it is not your husband you fear for, it will be your brother or your father or your sons—or your daughters when they marry and bear children. Since a woman must die of fear as long as she lives, she might as well have the joy of tasting love."

"It is not the same," Joanna said bleakly. "I fear for Ian and for Adam in a different way. For Geoffrey there is a tearing of my very vitals. I cannot bear it."

Perfectly content, for she had at last heard what she wanted to hear, Alinor soothed Joanna as best she could. Her mind, however, had leapt well ahead and was actually busy with the projected marriage. Isabella apparently was pressing for a court affair under a misapprehension, and her insistence could be cured by a few clear words from Alinor. However, the political reasons for a court wedding still held good, and a court wedding it would be. That, however, meant the presence of every enemy she and Ian had, and a few more who did not love her quick-tempered son-by-marriage or her daughter's odd humors—as well as their friends. The presence of enemies meant the sheets must be stained and Joanna must be prepared to use trickery if nature should betray her.

Alinor patted Joanna briskly on the shoulder. "That pain will be in the future, I hope, unless you allow yourself to become as silly as Ela and turn faint at the thought of a tourney or a practice passage of arms."

"I am not so bad as that," Joanna said with a faint smile. "Does it indeed appear that this trouble will pass without war?"

"There is good hope of it, at least at present. I will tell you the whole later, but for now what will help best to keep the peace is that you and Geoffrey marry at once and at court."

"Geoffrey wrote of a great marriage, but at court? Oh, very well," Joanna agreed.

"You do not object?"

"Why should I?"

Apparently, Joanna did not see the implication or else was confident, because she was a virgin, that all would be well. If so, matters must be explained to her clearly. Of course, there was always the chance that she and Geoffrey were lovers already and had arranged for proof. Alinor wanted to know what they intended to do, in that case. Considering the queen's suspicions, there would be some effort made to catch them. A clumsy trick would not serve. Alinor tried to recall how hairy Geoffrey was, but she could only remember his body as it had been when he was a boy. She had had occasion to see him naked when he was a man, but politeness and an automatic self-defense mechanism prevented her from "noticing" him.

"You have spent a good deal of time alone with Geoffrey," Alinor began.

"Not really," Joanna replied, rather puzzled.

Alinor laughed. "Twenty minutes are enough if both be willing. My love, are you still a maiden?"

"Of course," Joanna assured her. "I knew there was some reason that you and Ian wished me to be betrothed rather than married. I would not permit—" Joanna blushed. She had come near doing more than permitting Geoffrey to couple with her. She had nearly urged him to do so the night of the fire.

The blush was a delightful sign. Alinor knew she had been right about her daughter, that hidden behind that placid exterior was a healthy lust—and apparently Geoffrey had awakened it finely. Good for him! But what in the world was the girl talking about?

"Reason?" Alinor repeated "Our only reason was to protect you. We feared that you and Geoffrey, young as you were and burdened with more than you should carry, would rub each other wrongly and, instead of love, would grow into hate."

"Oh!" Joanna's blush deepened. "That was what Geoffrey said, but I thought he was just urging me because—"

Alinor laughed heartily. "You guessed well. Geoffrey may be truthful enough in a general way, but in such a cause all men develop tongues as quick and agile as snakes. But you look quite regretful Joanna," Alinor went on mischievously. "Would you have yielded?"

"Yes," Joanna replied simply.

The dutiful self-sacrifice of her daughter always surprised and faintly annoyed Alinor. "What in the world held you back? What reason could we have had that I would have concealed from you?"

"I thought it might be something to do with the king that you did not wish to come to Salisbury's ears. It does not matter now. Since there is to be this public celebration, it is just as well that I am a maiden. Geoffrey thought of that.''

"Then he has more brains than most men," Alinor remarked tartly, "but it is not sufficient to *be* a maiden. You must prove you are one. Your father had my maidenhead, but not one drop of blood did he have to show for it. I was fortunate that he was not a young man and knew the difference, blood or no blood, between a maid and a woman."

"How could that be?" Joanna asked, appalled at the idea that Alinor's failing might be a family characteristic and be passed on to her. Geoffrey, who burned when another man only looked at her—what would he think?

"Who knows?" Alinor replied. "Some women are lightly deflowered, others only with much pain and effort. For those with a delicate maidenhead, riding a horse or a hard fall will tear it. If it is stronger, it will withstand much harsher measures. I knew a woman who needed to be cut with a knife before her husband could mount her properly. Poor man, the jests he endured; the offers he was forced to listen to."

"But mother," Joanna put in, not much interested at this moment in the trials of some unknown man. "If I am like you, what will I do? I do not understand. Once Gertrude told me you bled like a wounded man. Yet you said—''

"Gertrude was exactly right," Alinor interrupted, giggling, "for it was your father who bled for me. Do you remember how hairy he was, Joanna? Perhaps not. Well, he was like a bear—only red and gray, of course. He cut himself just beside his shaft, where the hair was thickest. We thought it just a scratch, only enough to set a few drops on the sheet and on my thighs, but he must have nicked a small vein. When we coupled again, later, the wound opened and near flooded us out of the bed." Alinor laughed and laughed, remembering Berengaria's innocent horror and the knowing eyes and raised brows of Richard's sister Joanna, who was her daughter's godmother. Then she sobered. "Would Geoffrey do as much for you? Could he? I mean, has he a thick enough bush?"

"I do not know," Joanna murmured, "I do not know the answer to either question. As to hair, he is not like father. What he has is soft and fine, and he is so fair—it is pale gold on his body. A cut would show, I fear. As to his willingness—if he believed me, of course he would, but he is so jealous—"

"And he is so young," Alinor added somewhat troubled. "There are other ways, but they are easier of detection, and if *Geoffrey* should discover the trick you will never convince him of your innocence."

"Can you explain to him, mother, that you had this trouble?" Joanna asked anxiously.

"Not I, nor Ian either. For us to speak of such matters would only increase Geoffrey's suspicions. After all, Joanna," Alinor pointed out, smiling faintly, "we might be a little prejudiced in your favor. No, I will speak to Ela. I told her the story long ago. I need only remind her now. If she will explain to Geoffrey, it will be best."

"Will he believe her?" Joanna whispered. "Will he believe anyone?"

CHAPTER TWENTY

At any time, a court wedding would create a slight pleasurable stir. It would be an occasion for even grander gowns and more elaborate jewelry than an ordinary wedding. The fact that the guest list would be much longer meant that supplies would be ordered in greater quantity and come from farther afield. The fact that the guest list would be much grander meant that more elaborate and more costly dishes would be prepared and that the entertainment would be of higher quality and greater sophistication. In November of 1212, Geoffrey's and Joanna's wedding was a focus of attention to an extraordinary degree. It was also the only pleasant thing the courtiers had to think about and called forth nearly hysterical gaiety.

The sanguine hopes of October had gradually faded. Although there was still no active rebellion, John's confident supposition that Pandulf and Stephen Langton would arrive in England within weeks of his invitation turned out to be false. The situation with respect to the Church had actually deteriorated. Langton and Pandulf, finally impatient after years of fruitless negotiations, had set out for Rome. John's messenger, hastening after them, had caught them on the road but received a very cold welcome. This was not the first time that John had called them to England with fair promises to settle their differences, and each previous invitation—in their opinions—had been a mockery. They would come, they told the messenger orally, after the pope had heard their pleas and he and the council of bishops and cardinals had decided what to do.

John had sent new envoys out directly to the pope when he had that answer, but that the pope would continue indulgent was not to be expected. News of the successful rebellion in Wales, where Llewelyn was behaving with startling wisdom and modesty—proof that he had learned a lesson—which promised a long period of peace and independence for that country, would surely have come to Innocent's ears. Nor could it be hoped that Innocent would be ignorant of the conspiracy to overthrow the king. The time was ripe to draw the teeth of the viper that had stung the Church again and again.

For those faithful to the king, the times were gray and forbidding as the November weather. The one bright spot was the union of Ian's strength in the north with Salisbury's in the midlands and south. Lending an additional glow of hope was the faithful support of the earl of Pembroke who had sent to John with Lord Ian a testament of loyalty, signed by himself and twenty-six barons renewing their oaths of fealty and offering to do whatever service the king required of them. Nonetheless, there was little expectation that the king could retain his power without a bitter struggle and many, although they did not speak of it aloud, did not believe John could retain his throne at all.

News trickled back to England from across the narrow sea. Alinor had it from the merchants in Roselynde town and from the fisherfolk who met and talked with fisherfolk from the continental shore. All said the same. Boats were abuilding, men were being gathered, and weapons of war were being stocked. Philip of France was no sluggard. He hated the Angevins, root, stock, and branch. In addition, England would make a very nice storehouse from which he could draw men and supplies for the conflicts in Europe. Louis, his son, could rule there. It would give Louis good practice in controlling a rebellious populace.

All John's supporters believed that the moment Philip struck, perhaps a third of the barons would rise and join him. Another third would sit still, too unsure to take sides with Philip but too distrustful of the king to come to his aid. Struck by invasion from without and rebellion from within, what chance did they have?

It was no wonder that all eyes were fixed on Geoffrey and Joanna. Everywhere else disaster threatened. It was far better to talk and think and jest about the marriage of the king's bastard nephew and the daughter of the lady who had sent John scurrying with his tail between his legs. That old story, which Alinor had believed known only to her present husband, her dead first husband, and one other faithful vassal, had suddenly become current.

Furious but helpless, Alinor could only deny with spurious amazement that she had ever resisted the king's attentions—or had any reason to resist them. All that denial accomplished was to make some scandal-loving fools look significantly from the king's eldest son, who was as fair as his grandfather and his Uncle Richard, to Joanna's red head. If the queen and the king were both dark and their son golden fair, was it impossible that John had succeeded with Lady Alinor, and Joanna also took after old King Henry? The old king had had red hair some said. Like mother, like daughter said others, reviving with pleasure the scandalous rumors of the preceding spring about Joanna and young Braybrook.

Two bastards and consanguineous too, the rumors ran, and both lecherous from both sides. Had the times been less precarious, there would have been dead men in the court. Salisbury, Engelard d'Atie, and William de Cantelu had to remove Geoffrey by force from the great hall one day, and it had not been easy to revive the young fool whom Geoffrey had near choked to death. Another time only the king's personal intervention had saved the elder Braybrook from being torn apart by Ian. Shorter than his tall vassal by more than a head, John was nonetheless as strong as a bull. Perhaps he could not have bested Ian in a fight, but by interposing his own body between the men and wrapping Ian in his powerful arms the king had provided the few minutes needed for Braybrook's escape.

"I beg you to let him be," John pleaded, when he had finally quieted Ian enough to lead him into a private wall chamber. "Doubtless you know the truth of that tale. Lady

Alinor did resist me—quite successfully—and in any case it was years after that when Lady Joanna was born. God knows, I am not innocent with regard to women, but—'' a faint smile bent John's lips, ''I would not touch that viper of yours for anything—except perhaps if it would bring peace to my kingdom.''

''I will not challenge him,'' Ian agreed, passing his hand over his face. ''He meant what he said for a jest, but—''

''We are all raw and sore,'' John sighed. ''It is very hard to wait. In the uneasiness of our hearts, each man pricks his neighbor to ease his own pain.''

The voice that said those words knew the truth of them. Something inside Ian shuddered, and he was deflected from his own rage as he wondered what gargantuan pain had eaten the king all the years of his life that made him take joy in hurting others. Whatever it had been, it was temporarily stilled, or John had better control of himself than any Angevin before him. For this past month, John had been the perfect king—attentive to business and gentle, although by no means cringing, to his vassals. The king had done much good. He had eased the severity of those who enforced the Forest laws, given strict orders to his officers to cease molesting pilgrims and merchants and given justice without fear or favor to those who appealed to him.

It was too late, of course, but in this time, when he could with perfect right have been distrustful of almost every man he ruled, John seemed to have shed suspicion. He displayed no foolish confidence. He was well aware of the disaffection around him and he took sensible precautions to protect himself and his children and to check the spread of panic. Nonetheless, he showed no fear of the future. Quietly, he took counsel with those he did trust and mapped out plans for the defense of his kingdom against enemies from both within and without.

If John had not learned how to control himself in times of success, he had certainly learned how to behave in times of adversity, Ian thought. It was some comfort to know that the king would go down to defeat like a man. Ian only wished he was equally confident that—if they should somehow triumph against all the odds—John would not revert or even degenerate into a worse tyrant.

The worst sufferers, of course, were Joanna and Geoffrey. Their condition was pitiable. Pursued by whispers, which hissed behind her back and dissolved into false smiles when she turned to confront them, Joanna took refuge in an apparent bovine placidity. Because she dared not permit any crack in her protective shield that might allow her fear and incipient hysteria to break out, she treated Geoffrey with the same dull acceptance that she presented to malicious ill-wishers and genuine sympathizers alike.

Joanna's first private meeting with her betrothed had been uncomfortable. She had stiffened like a spear shaft when he tried to take her in his arms, and when he begged her to tell him why she was so cold, she had torn loose altogether and run away. Poor Joanna dared not answer for she knew she would burst into tears and beg Geoffrey to believe in her, not to repudiate her if her body betrayed her and refused to give proof that she truly was a virgin. It was the worst thing she could do, she thought. It would increase his suspicion and jealousy to show that she was conscious there could be a doubt of her purity.

Night and day, awake and asleep, she thought and dreamed about Geoffrey's reaction. Had Ela told him? Ordinarily, Joanna would not have doubted her foster mother, but Ela was not normal these days. Her world was dissolving around her, and she often spent days at a time in bed, just staring. If Ela had told him, had he accepted his step-mother's information as true? Ela would do anything to save Salisbury and, thus, much against her will, to save the king. Geoffrey might think the tale just a device to make him keep an unchaste wife for political reasons. Even if he believed Ela, would he help Joanna if she needed help? Would he think he could overawe the court into silence? If he believed Ela, why did he not tell Joanna all would be well? Why did he not assure her he would love her and protect her no matter what happened?

The second private meeting between Joanna and Geoffrey had been a disaster. This time, knowing the filthy tales that were abroad, Geoffrey made no physical approach to Joanna, hoping that his restraint would communicate his respect for her. Naturally enough, considering her private fears, Joanna saw what was meant to be a tender consideration as a cold rejection. In desperation, Geoffrey faltered out some platitudes on his happiness at the nearness of their proposed union, looking so miserable all the while that his hesitant advances seemed like calculated insults.

"For God's sake," he had blazed at last, "if you want none of me, say so. Doubtless it will bring the kingdom down around our ears, but—"

"You know and I know that it is absolutely imperative that we marry," Joanna replied stonily. "You can—"

She was about to say that he could repudiate her later, if he could not trust her honesty, but fortunately she did not get that far. Geoffrey had flung the table near him right across the room, badly denting two gold goblets and shattering to pieces a priceless glass decanter. Then he had rushed out, slamming the door, before he flung Joanna after the other objects. Joanna knelt on the wine-soaked floor picking up the pieces of glass and sobbing softly.

"Broken, it is all broken," she wept when Edwina flew into the room five minutes later.

"Hush, dearling, hush," the maid comforted, holding Joanna against her warm, full bosom. "Life does not break like glass, love. Life mends itself."

It gave no appearance of mending over the last week before the wedding. Joanna and Geoffrey were not speaking to each other at all, except for icily polite salutations at greeting and parting. Strangely enough, the one emotion that did not wound Geoffrey was jealousy. He never doubted Lady Alinor's faithfulness to her first husband and, even if he had, did not care who Joanna's father was. The rumors about Braybrook, when he realized they were rife again, only pained him for Joanna's sake. His whole attention was concentrated on the agonizing fact that, apparently, Joanna did not wish to marry him. It would not have been so bad if he could have believed she did not understand her own heart. Then he could have hoped to win it. She had still been unsure before the fire, yet she had been fond enough to seek him amidst the holocaust. They had quarreled and, somehow, that had set her to examining her own feelings more closely. Plainly what she discovered had not been in his favor.

Her feelings did not matter, of course—except to him. Joanna would marry him because she was a dutiful girl with a clear vision of the catastrophe that would follow her refusal. She would be a good wife too, Geoffrey thought, grinding his teeth and barely restraining himself from tearing his hair or beating his head on the wall because his father would rush over and stop him and begin to ask questions again. Joanna was resigned to her fate. She had made her decision. Calmly and placidly she would couple with him, bear his children, help him to keep his lands and hers in perfect order, nurse him when he was sick or wounded—and all the time, deep, deep in a buried corner of her heart she would wish she was free of him.

Lady Alinor was not blind to the trouble of the young people as Lady Ela was. There was, however, nothing Alinor could do for them. If she spoke to Joanna to try to comfort her, the girl might break down completely. She could not speak to Geoffrey because she did not know the basis of his obvious distress. To reassure him of the wrong thing might cause greater difficulties. All she could do was hope that Joanna's control would hold and that Salisbury could keep Geoffrey from killing someone important.

From her heart Lady Alinor cursed the necessity of this court marriage. Not only had it laid two young people, already under a severe strain, open to the vicious tongues of a fearful and disappointed crowd but it had removed all possibility of keeping Geoffrey and Joanna employed. In an ordinary way, both of them would have been kept so busy making ready to entertain their guests, that they would have had no time to quarrel with each other or even to think much about each other. Alinor would have seen to it that the full weight of ordering supplies and overseeing their use fell upon her daughter. Geoffrey would have been sent out to hunt, not for pleasure but like a butcher for meat for the table. And she would have harried both with constant complaints until every spark of fear or uncertainty would have been channeled into anger at her unreasonable demands. Lady Alinor's one comfort was the memory of how miserable her first wedding had been and how happy the marriage that followed it.

At last, however, the first day of December dawned. Joanna, both out of fondness and superstition, had chosen her mother's wedding day to be her own. She lay in her bed, watching the cold light of winter grow slowly stronger, remembering her mother's glowing beauty and sparkling happiness on that day six years ago. She hoped her long sleepless night would not be too apparent in shadowing her eyes and draining the color from her cheeks. She wished the queen had not been so generous in providing a magnificent wedding gown. It was true that Isabella's choice was tasteful and appropriate for Joanna's coloring and normal complexion, but the rich blue tunic and cloth-of-gold cotte would make her look like a corpse if she was as pale as she felt.

The morning was not nearly as bad as Joanna feared, however. For one thing, the ladies were much better humored than usual, given over as they were to the intense pleasure of dressing in their best. For another, Joanna was cheered by the obvious pleasure that her mother and Lady Ela showed in the event. If Geoffrey had taken ill the information Lady Ela was supposed to have given him, surely Lady Ela would not be so easy. Geoffrey's wedding gift also aroused hope. A cascade of shimmering gray water spilled from the box he sent when it was opened. Moonstones! He must have spent the whole year collecting them, Joanna thought, for the stone was not common. Most people preferred the brilliant colors of emerald, ruby, or sapphire. But moonstones were the color of Joanna's eyes and they became her excellently well. Joanna looked at the beautifully set necklace, armlets, and bands to hold the wimple, and a faint smile touched her lips. Her jewels would not be duplicated by anyone. Here must be every moonstone in England, and perhaps in all Europe.

The king could not attend the wedding because he was excommunicate, and his presence would have invalidated the ceremony. Peter des Roches, bishop of Winchester, performed it, and it was fortunate that he was a strong man with a good voice. No frail prelate could have bellowed the service loud enough to be heard by the huge crowd of courtiers that pressed into the church porch, spilled down the steps, and flowed out over the square. God knows, Joanna thought, with a little flicker of her normal, easily roused sense of humor, this wedding, which may be repudiated tomorrow, is doubtless the best-witnessed marriage that has ever taken place.

Geoffrey caught the little smile and his heart leapt. Perhaps she is glad, he thought, or, at least, only doubtful. Perhaps her sadness has only been born of the filth we are drowned in and her fear of what will befall us all. Perhaps it is only a maid's unwillingness to change her state. No one could have a more indulgent father than Ian or a happier home than that provided by Lady Alinor. It cannot be easy to leave that, to trust herself to a stranger.

They were all shivering by the time the bishop finished the benediction and told Geoffrey to kiss his wife. He would have liked really to kiss her and see what response he would obtain, but he feared both Joanna's reaction and that of the watching crowd. Better to cling to his hope rather than put it to the proof here where it might become a standing jest against him in the future. Geoffrey barely touched Joanna's lips, and she accepted the kiss as placidly as he appeared to give it. The cold touch again sank poor Joanna's heart, which had been beating harder with hope when Geoffrey took her hand. She would not weep! She would not!

The resolution held even when her mother clutched her tight, whispering, "Child, child, you will always be my child.'' Joanna had no time to read fearful implications into that simple cry of love because Lady Ela seized upon her. She was sobbing, her pretty fair face blotched with tears and her eyes reddened. "Be good to him," she cried softly. "As you are a little my daughter, Joanna, make up to him the ill I have done him."

It was Ian who broke her determined calm, for he too was weeping. He said nothing, only held Joanna tight to him, as he had held her so many times when she was a little girl and had fled to him for solace from some grief or punishment. She clung to him, who had so ably replaced her father, and burst into a storm of tears. "Do not weep, love," Ian soothed. "He is a good man, and I love him, but there is nothing for you to fear. If he hurts you—I will kill him!''

That checked Joanna's tears as swiftly as they had come. "No, no," she whispered, terrified, already seeing her husband dead by her stepfather's mighty hand because she knew Geoffrey would never defend himself against Ian. "My God, do not lay that burden of fear upon me. Whatever is between Geoffrey and me, he loves you and you love him—"

Before she could finish, Alinor pulled Ian away with some force, hissing, "You idiot! Do you not see she is overset already? Do you want more scandal? With a little more 'kindness' she will be screaming for release from a marriage she greatly desires. I tell you she loves him and he her. Let them only be alone and away from this madhouse, and all will be well."

There were others, many others, who proffered good wishes, some sincerely and some with ill-concealed hopes that were contrary to their words. Both groups could see signs that their expectations for the marriage would be fulfilled. Bride and groom were both abstracted, and both stole quick glances at the other when they thought it would not be noticed. Those who wished it so read eagerness and love into what they saw. Those who wished ill to the pair, saw fear and suspicion in the behavior. And both groups were at least a little right in their reading of the signs.

The one good thing about the turmoil in Joanna's mind was that the disconcerting fact that John would be her next neighbor and table companion did not dawn upon her until Geoffrey led her to her seat and pulled out the bench so she could slip in beside the king's chair. Joanna bent her knees in automatic curtsy and dropped her eyes modestly to the floor. This day, she was now sure, was accursed. On one side was John, whom she feared and disliked, on the other side Geoffrey, whom at this moment she feared almost more than his uncle. She had not a word to say to either one upon any subject and in any case she could neither speak nor eat because her throat was shut tight with nervousness.

"Hey, Jo, look at me!" It was a merry whisper just behind.

"Adam," Joanna breathed, feeling that salvation had come to her.

"Ain't I grand?" Adam teased, in the coarsest vernacular, preening himself with deliberate vulgarity. Then he hit his sister an encouraging blow on the back that nearly knocked her flat on the table, exclaiming, "Lucky girl!"

"Adam!" Joanna protested, clutching at the nearest available support, which happened to be Geoffrey.

"Gently," Geoffrey whispered, "that is my property you are mauling about."

"Sorry," Adam offered contritely. "I forget I keep growing up and you stay little. I only seem to remember that you could belt me across the room once." He dismissed that past with a careless wave of the hand and reverted to his present proud moment. "Am I ever glad you decided on a court wedding! It got me a whole chestful of new clothes and—look at me—serving the high table at a royal castle."

"You will not be doing so for long if you do not shut up and serve instead of talking," Geoffrey hissed, half laughing nonetheless.

A warm, rich chortle came from Joanna's left. She and Geoffrey froze, but Adam bowed deeply and gracefully and grinned irrepressibly.

"Your brother is a fine figure of a man, and not much

overawed by royalty,'' John said to Joanna.

The eyes that Joanna had until now kept lowered were suddenly raised to the king's. They glittered with a pale, hard light. The full lips were thinned, the fine nostrils flared. No wild vixen could have looked fiercer in the defense of her cubs. Inadvertently, the king drew a sharp breath. He had just seen again the face of Simon Lemagne as he had seen it so often before battle. But Joanna had already realized that she had prepared to defend Adam without cause. There had been no sly threat in John's comment, nor was there anything but good humor and then, for a moment, surprise on his face. Her expression softened. Little as she had been aware of anything beyond her own troubles, still she had heard many, even Ian, praising the king's change of heart and manner. Good terms coupled with wariness were always better than open enmity.

''Oh, my lord,'' she said softly, ''I think he is possessed of devils. If there is mischief afoot, you may be sure that he is either in it or—and more specially if he be apart from it and with a most innocent expression—that he began it.''

She then told an anecdote or two about Adam as a little boy. She blessed her brother's intervention from the bottom of her heart, finding herself able to talk lightly and easily to the king. She heard Adam make a remark to Geoffrey that she could not quite catch and heard Geoffrey agree but say that he had better bear himself more seemly. The king had taken as a jest what was meant as a jest. Nonetheless, to continue acting the fool would be disrespectful to John, who had been kind, and force the king either to be severe, which he did not wish to be, or to look a fool himself. There was so much good sense in what Geoffrey said and so much kindness in the way he said it that Joanna began to wonder whether she was building into Geoffrey monstrous intentions that were foreign to his nature.

It was fortunate that Joanna had brought a little inner calm to herself, for she was to share her conversation with John and Geoffrey for nearly six hours. Isabella's servants had done her proud. The feast was of four courses, with ten dishes in each course. First came a jellied dish of minnows, followed by a baked salmon belly. Stewed eels were next and then a dish of boiled porpoise with peas. Sweet followed spicy in the form of a herring rolled and baked in dark sugar, which was accompanied by a relish of greens. When the palate had been refreshed by this change of pace, broiled pike, roast lamprey, roast sole, and roast porpoise were presented. The course was completed by a magnificent subtlety, a towering sculpture of cake and jelly, representing a young maid and young man, handfast.

The musicians had, of course, been playing throughout the meal, but when the subtlety was set upon the high table, and lesser sweets upon the other tables in order of their importance, they struck up a livelier measure. Well aware of his duty, Geoffrey stepped over the bench, assisted Joanna to rise, and led her to the clear space on the floor. A column of willing dancers followed swiftly and for the next half hour they worked off the intake of food and wine with lively exercise. By the time they were blown and panting, the servingmen were waiting impatiently at the doors. Laughing and chattering, the dancers returned to their places. Joanna's eyes were alight with pleasure and Geoffrey's hair was curling a little on his damp forehead.

Now the tumblers came on to the floor to entertain. They were quick, the jesters lewd and rude. Joanna had almost forgotten by now that this was *her* wedding and that the pleasant young man on one side of her was her husband and the heavy man on the other the king. She was animated and merry, her eyes glowing as softly lucent as the great moonstones that decked her bosom, arms, and wimple. No matter how wonderful the feat performed by the entertainers, Geoffrey's eyes often strayed from them to his prize. The king's eyes did not do so, but his thoughts were not really much different. He regretted that he could not sup from Joanna's cup right after her husband had filled it. He had seen old Sir Simon in her and knew that fear would not shut her mouth. Nonetheless, all the smoke that beclouded her virtue had to come from some fire. Let him only hold his land until he could cozen the pope to support him, John thought. Then he would buy her—such women were always for sale—right under his brother's nose.

There was time for a short dance to stretch the legs before the next dinner course was brought forward. John led Joanna to the floor this time, Geoffrey, as required, squiring Isabella. Joanna was much surprised at how light John was on his feet and spoke of it, and the king was flattered and assured of his eventual satisfaction. There would be no need to force this one he thought, a little regretfully. There would have been much joy in taming the vixen. Geoffrey was less pleased by his partner even though she was a most graceful dancer and said nothing that could offend him. In fact, she was so pleasant that Geoffrey grew a little cold inside. How he hated Isabella!

Although it was still daylight outside, the light was failing in the hall where the windows were covered by scraped hides. Torches were carried in and the great candelabras that hung from the rafters were lowered so that their candles could be lit. As those servingmen scurried out, the third course began to arrive. This was the game course and boar and venison followed each other in a profusion of sauces and methods of preparation. Everyone was eating a little more slowly now.

The second dance with Geoffrey was more dignified and slower paced than the first. It was the custom to have the slow dance measures after the third course because by then a good many of the dancers were not only stuffed with food but slightly drunk as well.

During the serving of the fourth course—sweets—there was an eruption of loud, angry voices that rose even above the deafening noise produced by several hundred people eating, drinking, and talking. The king, who had been greedily examining a dish of comfits to choose out the largest and sweetest, threw up his head. To her right, Joanna could feel Geoffrey freeze, an apple halfway to his mouth. Ian and Salisbury were already half across the benches, but the bawling died down as those more sober enforced peace upon their drunken companions. An ever-present danger of any large feast was that men, made too truthful by wine, would speak their minds too plainly and come to knives or swords. What was odd was not the outbreak of brawling but the rapidity with which it was silenced.

With a chill that brought back all her anxieties, Joanna noticed that surprisingly few of the men were drunk. Certainly John, Ian, Salisbury, and Geoffrey, who all enjoyed a good pull at the wineskin on suitable occasions, were stone-cold sober. Obviously, Geoffrey might have a personal reason not to drink; he did not wish to be incapable of performing his marital duty. A deeper cold washed over Joanna and she thrust that from her mind. But the fact that the others were not allowing themselves to celebrate as they normally would was a bad sign, a very bad sign. Clearly, very few of the guests dared get into a condition in which their tongues might run away with them.

Joanna's eyes ran up and down the table and her fears were confirmed by what she saw on her mother's and Lady Ela's faces. They were characteristically different, of course. Lady Alinor looked wary and dangerous, her hazel eyes bright, her body tense with impatience. Joanna almost smiled. Her mother could never bear to wait for trouble. These days she was, perhaps, less eager to stir it up, but if she knew trouble was inevitable, she wished to face it at once. Lady Ela looked near to weeping with anxiety. Her hands clutched the table to hide their shaking, but she talked whiningly and continuously of how dreadful it was to be married, how harsh and inconsiderate husbands were, and did much to distract everyone's mind from real fears. For all her trembling and weeping, Ela would be a staunch support to her husband, and she would go down with him with no regret except that she could not save him.

Isabella, on the other hand, seemed hardly aware of the disturbance, how quickly it was quelled, or what that signified. She looked rather like an exquisite, self-satisfied cat that had got successfully into—and out of—the family cream pitcher. Joanna wondered a little at the queen's indifference to her husband's problems. There was not now and, as Joanna thought of it she realized there never had been, a shadow of anxiety on that beautiful face. The question brought its own answer. Isabella did not care what happened to John. She was sure nothing would happen to her, and that was all that mattered. Joanna remembered the talk about FitzWalter and the queen. Very probably FitzWalter promised Isabella that her son Henry would rule in her husband's stead, and her state would be unchanged. That would account for the calm. Joanna was shaken with revulsion. Was that what she had desired for herself, that complacency of indifference?

She glanced at Geoffrey, who had bitten into an apple and was chewing with enjoyment, his head a little bent to hear better something Lady Alinor was saying to him. There had been a few moments of strained quiet after the brawlers were subdued, but the noise was now rising to normal levels. Ian was relaxed again, also listening to Alinor. Dutifully, Joanna turned toward the king. He was engaged with the master of the revels, urging that the players be brought on to occupy the feasters' attentions more completely than jugglers could. However, in turning Joanna caught Isabella's eyes upon her. The cat-in-the-cream-pot expression was even more intense, and a slow smile parted the exquisite lips to show the pearly teeth. Although Joanna could school her expression into perfectly uncomprehending placidity, she could not control the blood in her body. She felt the color drain from her cheeks and knew Isabella had seen the change in her complexion. The queen laughed, very softly, very sweetly, very happily. The vixen was trapped and knew it.

What merit is innocence, Joanna wondered, turning her eyes to a marvelous jelly that had been set before her. It was well worth looking at, a towering structure, quivering and quaking yet somehow supporting itself and remaining intact. She and the jelly had much in common. As long as no one touched them, they would present an appearance of firmness; as soon as either was broached, the formless stuff each was made up of would be exposed. Isabella was sure of her coming shame. Isabella did not care that the kingdom might be broken apart; she was too stupid to understand that neither John nor FitzWalter could guarantee anyone's safety in the upheaval of a civil war. Somehow, Isabella knew that Geoffrey would not protect her, or had even convinced him not to do so, Joanna thought.

Because fear is irrational, it never occurred to Joanna that there could be no less likely alliance than one between her husband and the queen. In fact, Geoffrey hated the queen so thoroughly that to know Isabella desired something was enough to make him go to considerable lengths to prevent that thing from happening. If Joanna's brain had been operating on any level at all, she would have realized that the queen's confidence must be based upon false premises. Isabella could not know that Alinor had had no maidenhead to yield up and that her daughter might be similarly afflicted. All Joanna knew was that Isabella intended to bring about her ruin and there was nothing she could do about it.

The players who appeared must have been skilled. Joanna had the impression of roars of laughter, stamping feet, whistles and shouts of appreciation. She had not the vaguest notion of what was presented. She laughed when the others laughed, drank a little more than she usually did, and endured with outward calm a hell unparalleled in all her happy young life. An enduring courage that would not break under any pressure supported her. When the first play was over, there was more dancing. Joanna was aware of being passed from one man's arm to that of another. There was a good deal of laughter which she shared, having not the slightest notion of its cause. From time to time, she heard Geoffrey's voice, protesting amid bursts of laughter, but he never danced with her and that frightened her still more.

There came a time when Joanna could scarcely breathe between terror and pretense and exertion. Before she could collapse into most welcome unconsciousness, however, she was back in her seat and another play, even more incomprehensible to her, was being received with equal or greater acclamation. Perhaps they danced again. By that time Joanna was so dazed that she had no idea at all of what her body did or her lips said. Suddenly, however, she wakened to find herself stark naked, shivering with cold, the focus of what seemed like hundreds of staring eyes. She nearly screamed aloud, thinking she had already been proven unchaste and was about to be punished for it. But her mother was there, her own dear mother and dear Lady Ela, and both were smiling.

A woman's hand gripped her hair and lifted even that curtain of modesty from her body and a warm hand on her shoulder propelled her around. "Is she not perfect?" Isabella cooed in her sweet, lilting voice. "Look at that skin, like milk, how immaculate—not a single scratch or scar upon it."

Not punishment, Joanna realized sickly, her trial had not yet begun. She tried to whip herself into some action, into shrinking coyly from the gazes fastened upon her as a shy maiden might, into listening to the flying jests and sallies, but she could do nothing more. She stood like a statue, literally white as milk, even her lips pale, only colored by her flaming hair and the red-gold curls peeping from beneath her arms and glowing on her mount of Venus.

How long the torment lasted, Joanna could not guess. Not long, she supposed, for she did hear comments upon her shivering and Lady Ela's shrill voice bewailing the fact that if they did not soon warm her she would be dead of the cold before she was a wife. Soon after she was thrust into the bed with a goblet of warm wine between her hands. The crowd remained a while longer, teasing Geoffrey, but he drove them from the room at last with a laughing pretense of anger. Geoffrey was, in fact, truly amused. The blatant envy of every man and Joanna's apparent lightness of spirit since the feast had started had done much to cheer him.

Joanna looked down into the goblet of wine. It was too late—too late to withdraw, too late to plead, too late to do anything beyond endure what fate had in store for her. The wine cup was removed gently from her hands. Warm lips touched her cheek; warm fingers lifted her hair, and the lips moved to nibble, to suck gently at her ear. Nothing happened. For the first time, Geoffrey's caress did not arouse her. He slid into bed beside her, found her lips, slid down, shoving the pillows away, pulling her flat beside him. His free hand wandered over her shoulder, cupped her breast. Nothing. She felt nothing.

"Take me, Geoffrey. In mercy, take me. Do not make me wait," she whispered.

CHAPTER TWENTY-ONE

It had not been easy. It had been terrible. Joanna did not cry out, but tears oozed between her tight-shut lids and her breathing was racked with sobs. She dared not look at her husband. From the evidence of her ears, he had been little better pleased than she with their first union. His breath hissed between his teeth with effort or displeasure. The latter, Joanna feared, because twice she heard quite distinguishable, if muffled, oaths. Even after he became silent and then, finally sighed with pleasure, he had remained astride her for a time, as if he was too tired to move.

At last he rolled away. Joanna waited, as still as she could be, trying to control her sobbing, hoping he would fall asleep so that she could look for the proof of her suffering on the sheets. Instead of turning away, however, Geoffrey turned toward her.

"I am sorry I hurt you, Joanna," he said softly, and then, rather irritably, "Why did you urge me? I thought you were ready."

When she did not reply, Geoffrey wiped the tears from her cheeks and thought to himself he was a fool. How would she know anything about that? "Come," he said in a gentler tone, "open your eyes and look at me. I will not trouble you again if you are not willing. I am not changed into a monster. It will grow easier."

Still Joanna did not speak. Geoffrey propped himself on an elbow and looked at his wife. She was no longer crying and she had obediently opened her eyes, but her face was closed, her thoughts withdrawn, fixed upon something totally unrelated to him. Perhaps Joanna had not been weeping with pain but with regret or, possibly, with disgust. Had

357

she urged him to remove from herself the last hope of being saved from a hateful marriage? She had been so gay, so happy, so lightly teasing all during the feast and celebration that Geoffrey had put aside his doubts as figments of his own imagination. Now they rushed back. He had an impulse to strike her, to cry aloud that she was a fool to condemn them both to hell. But he knew why she had done it; he would have done the same, for he knew his duty. If only he did not love her, he would be praising her virtue. Well, it was too late. They were bound together and had better find a way to live together.

"I will tell you one thing, Joanna," Geoffrey said with a strained smile. "If I ever stray from your bed, it will not be to take another maidenhead. I have heard men speak of the pleasure of deflowering a maid. They are mad. It is no pleasure. You were not the only sufferer. I assure you that by my will, I will have no more ado with virgins."

"Oh, Geoffrey, is it so? Are you sure?"

Blank surprise overspread Geoffrey's face. "What do you mean, am I sure? Did you think this was going to give me a taste for raping little girls?"

Joanna did not laugh. She was too intent on her own problem to catch the joke. However, she did look bright and eager. "Do you think I have given proof?"

"Proof!" Geoffrey groaned. "I near killed myself making you into a woman. What more proof do I need? I know I have been where no man has been before."

"I am glad," Joanna breathed, "so glad. I thought—I feared you might doubt me."

"Doubt you? You mean because of Braybrook? You are an idiot Joanna. I have said it before and I say it again."

But Geoffrey grinned at his wife and stretched luxuriously. He was more a fool than she to have tormented himself, worrying that he was repugnant to her. All her oddities were only nervousness. Doubted her? Why? Oh, the tale Ela had told him. He would have thought that Lady Alinor had more sense than to tell an innocent like Joanna the story of her bloodless defloration. Why did she not come directly to him? Did Lady Alinor think he knew Joanna so little that he would suspect she told him such a tale to hide her daughter's depravity? Women were all idiots, even the clever ones. No, especially the clever ones. They were so intent on out-maneuvering their men that they caused themselves—and everyone else—endless trouble. His tension past, Geoffrey yawned widely and let his eyes close. Joanna stirred uneasily beside him.

"You do not doubt me," she said in a small voice, "but what of others? I wish to be sure that—"

"Look then," Geoffrey muttered sleepily, "but I know the signs are there. I could feel when you yielded and the blood came."

Joanna lifted the covers and, sure enough, Geoffrey and she and the sheets too were well bedaubed with red. She sighed contentedly and lay back but, although the worst of her pain was gone, she was still a little uncomfortable and keyed up and sleep did not come. Instead a nasty, cold notion slid into her tired mind. Geoffrey did trust her, that was plain; he trusted her enough to be sure she had bled. But what if she had not? Would he have done for her what her father did for her mother? Of course he would, Joanna assured herself. It was ridiculous to think otherwise. Knowing her pure, would he hesitate to prove her so?

Restlessly, Joanna turned to one side and then to the other. In his sleep, Geoffrey growled impatiently. Joanna lay still again. It was unfair to bother him with such an idiocy. Eventually, Joanna also slept, but not soundly. For many years she had not shared her bed, and the presence of another body made her uneasy. She turned in her sleep, made contact with Geoffrey's sinewy back, and woke with a shock of alarm. Fortunately, memory of where she was and who was beside her came before she cried out for help—a fine joke that would have been—but her troubled wondering returned with the awareness of Geoffrey's presence.

The bed made an odd sound. He would have saved her honor, Joanna insisted to herself, and, ridiculously, a lump rose in her throat. Now she would never know. She would never know whether her husband loved her enough to lie for her. It seemed to Joanna's still overexcited, overtired mind that that would have been the ultimate proof of devotion. Geoffrey was trained to the notion that to lie was dishonor; if he would lie for her, she was more important to him than honor. The bed made an odd noise again. But it could not, Joanna thought. She had not moved, and Geoffrey lay like a log. There it was again! Joanna stiffened, listening. Surely that could not be the leather straps creaking.

"Geoffrey," she said, shaking him, "there is a rat under the bed."

"What?" he groaned.

"A rat. There is a rat under the bed," she insisted. This had never happened to her before. Brian slept in her chamber and where the dog was rats did not come.

"No," Geoffrey mumbled, "go to sleep. It will do you no hurt. It is a kitten."

"A what? A kitten? Why is there a kitten under the bed? Geoffrey!"

Reluctantly, Geoffrey opened his eyes. "Kitten?" he said vaguely, "oh, yes." He yawned hugely and closed his eyes again.

"You lazy thing," Joanna cried, "get up and kill that rat or drive it away. I will never sleep with it squeaking and scratching under there."

"Oh God," Geoffrey groaned, rolling out and getting down on the floor.

"You fool, you are naked. It will bite you. Take a knife or something."

However, Geoffrey ignored her warning and wormed himself half under the bed, cursing vilely. Joanna glanced around for something to strike the rat with if it ran out on her side. Nothing emerged, but she heard the creak of leather, as if some strain had been applied to the bed straps and then Geoffrey began to inch his way out again. He rose to his knees and tossed a cloth bag, which heaved and squeaked protestingly, to Joanna.

"I told you it was a kitten," he said irritably. "Your fool

of a maid was supposed to drug it so it would sleep, but I suppose she did not give it enough."

While he spoke and got back into bed, Joanna undid the cord that fastened the small sack. Immediately, a tortoise-shell kitten popped out. It was pretty and in high dudgeon at the indignity just visited upon it, but as Joanna bemusedly stroked it and tickled it under the chin it regained its equanimity and began to purr.

"But Geoffrey," Joanna protested, "why is it here? I mean, it is a very odd thing to find a kitten tied to the bed straps. It—"

"What the devil is wrong with you?" Geoffrey snarled. "If you had not bled, what did you think I would do? Isabella has been taunting me for days. Did you not see her look me over, hair by hair, and cry out to all that there was not so much as an unhealed scratch on me. Where could I draw blood that she would not have marked it? She looked you over too. I would have bled the cat while it slept and—"

He never got to finish the story and explain how he proposed to get rid of the evidence. Joanna flung her arms around his neck. "Oh Geoffrey, Geoffrey, I will be a good wife to you. I will be good and obedient and faithful until the day I die, I swear it. You are so kind—"

"What a fool you are, Joanna," he said softly, holding her tight against him and pulling her down. "You are truly mine now. Did you think I would let anyone hurt you in any way for any reason?"

The last words were muffled against her throat. A brief panic combined of memory of pain and of her previous inability to respond to Geoffrey's caress was routed immediately by the warmth that spread from the touch of his lips. Joanna sighed and the tenseness went out of her muscles. Gently, Geoffrey pulled his arms from under her limp body to give him freedom of movement. He continued to kiss her for a while, then lifted his head to look at her. She made a tiny, complaining murmur when the caress stopped, and her eyes opened slowly.

"Are you willing?" Geoffrey whispered.

It seemed to Joanna a very strange question to ask. She had forgotten he had promised not to take her again if she did not wish to risk a second hurt. In any case, she had no desire to speak and merely lifted a hand to pull Geoffrey's head toward her.

Geoffrey accepted the gesture as it was meant, but this time he took no chances. He kissed her and fondled her; he sucked her lips, her breasts, the little tongue between her nether lips. Joanna's passive pleasure changed to active desire. She whimpered and wriggled and uttered little cries. Twice she tried to slip her body under his, but Geoffrey was enjoying the drawn-out titillation of his senses which was impossible with the whores he had been using. With them he lacked the inclination for foreplay beyond the necessary stimulation of his own desire; he was too aware that the response was merely a bored simulation to encourage his generosity in payment.

Joanna was real. Every sigh and cry she uttered sent a pulse of pleasure through him. The salt taste of blood and woman made his shaft move as if it had a life of its own. Joanna was nearly weeping with frustration and excitement. She clutched at Geoffrey frantically, unaware that her long nails were scoring his body. She kissed every part of him she could reach until, when he twisted completely around to give his mouth a better purchase, his shaft touched her cheek. Beside herself with passion, Joanna kissed that too, sought to swallow it whole. Geoffrey stiffened and groaned, then hurriedly reversed his position.

The second time was easy. Whatever pain of unaccustomed stretching Joanna endured merely added to the exquisite pleasure. Fortunately, she took no long time to come to climax. With her first cry, in which surprise mingled with thrilled release, Geoffrey yielded to his own need. They subsided together, gasping and sighing.

"My, my," Joanna murmured, "oh, my, that was delightful."

The naiveté of the remark and the voice, expressing the kind of pleasure one obtains from receiving a totally unexpected and totally welcome gift, set Geoffrey to laughing. "What did you expect?" he asked.

"How should I know what to expect?" Joanna responded reasonably. "To be told a thing is pleasant is a far cry from experiencing it oneself. Besides, pleasant is not the right word."

"No? What would you say?" Geoffrey teased.

"I would say— No, I will say nothing. You are already too puffed up with pride," Joanna laughed. "If I praise you, you will become overweening and unbearable."

Geoffrey at once adopted a most false, crestfallen expression. "But if you do not praise me, likely I will think I have failed in my duty as a husband and fall into a melancholy. Then—"

Joanna made a swift movement, as if to box Geoffrey's ear, and he caught her hand. In the playful wrestling, the covers were completely dislodged. Geoffrey grew still suddenly.

"How beautiful you are, Joanna," he breathed.

She was looking at him also, but with more consternation than pleasure "Oh, Geoffrey," she cried, "look how I scratched you. I am so sorry." And the word "scratched" connected with its usual companion phrase "like a cat" in her mind. "The kitten!" she exclaimed, "Have we killed it?"

They searched the bed and then under it only to find the little creature curled comfortably in a cushioned chair. When the violent movements of the larger inhabitants had made the bed uncomfortable, the kitten had removed itself, with all the self-possession of its older relatives, to a situation less subject to earthquakes. Joanna tickled its head and then turned to stroke Geoffrey's scratches, again murmuring her contrition.

He laughed ruefully. "Had I known you were going to claw the skin from my flesh I would not have bothered about the kitten. Even Isabella would not have noticed a deeper slash or two among what I have. And what she will say about this, I can imagine.''

Joanna lifted a shoulder contemptuously. ''Let her say what she likes. You think she would not have discovered your stratagem? Or imagined one to describe even if none had been planned?''

''How would she discover it? Through your maid?''

''Edwina? No. She is utterly mine and her tongue does not wag unless I bid it wag, but I would imagine that others have sought through the room. Even if they did not find the kitten— Oh, let her spew out her venom. Those who will credit what Isabella says *wish* to believe ill of us. Those who love us know what we are. Come back to bed, Geoffrey, I am cold.''

The casual attitude puzzled Geoffrey. He could not understand the apparent contradiction between Joanna's premarital concern for the opinion of others and her postmarital indifference. It did not occur to him that the only opinion she really cared about was his own because it seemed so obvious to him that he would know the truth. He was too sleepy to worry about it and when Joanna had replaced the covers climbed gratefully into the bed only hoping that his wife would not be taken with a desire to talk. One of the court ladies had been so afflicted. Geoffrey had dispensed with her favors as soon as he discovered the condition was chronic, but one could not dispense with one's wife.

However, Joanna had no particular inclination to talk. She was discovering another joy of married life. Previously, when she left her warm bed in the night it took some time on her return for her shivering body to warm the sheets and covers enough to provide comfort. Now she had to do no more than press herself against her husband and there was warmth. Geoffrey murmured a sleepy complaint about her icy hands and feet; he did not thrust her away, however, but drew her even closer, which added content to comfort. Joanna sighed and snuggled her head into the hollow of Geoffrey's shoulder. For what remained of this blessed night she would be perfectly happy. She would not allow herself to fall into the fault her mother complained she shared with her father. She would not look into the future and frighten herself with the dangers and sorrows to come.

In the normal course of events, Joanna would have had a long morning to clutch her joy to her. The custom was that, when the married pair woke and called for their servants, the noble lords and ladies would be summoned to inspect the sheets. Isabella, however, had no intention of allowing Edwina or Tostig to precede her into the bridal chamber. Both slept far more soundly than their master or mistress, well drugged. It was a lady of Isabella's who entered, exclaimed a loud apology, saying that she thought she heard a call, and retreated so clumsily that somehow she bumped the table upon which were set wine and a few tasty tidbits for those who might be wakeful in the night.

Geoffrey was wide awake at once. He had snapped to alertness when the door opened, but had moved nothing except his eyes, assuming it was Edwina come to remove the kitten. The loud apology and jostling of the table brought both Joanna and him upright. They exchanged a single glance, and then Joanna called, "Edwina?"

"No, my lady. Your maid seems to have tasted a little too deeply of the wine."

Behind the concealment of the bed curtains Geoffrey and Joanna exchanged another glance. Joanna had been right. Isabella either had known exactly what was planned or had simply been on guard against any assistance from Joanna's maid. Probably one of the queen's ladies had been on guard in the antechamber all night long. Geoffrey flushed briefly with rage, but Joanna was more amused than angered. What was important now was to smooth things over.

"Wicked girl!" Joanna exclaimed and then laughed indulgently. "Ah, well, on such a day one must be a little forgiving."

On the words, Geoffrey pulled back the bed curtains on his side.

"I am sorry to have wakened you, my lord," the lady

said, but she was not sorry. Their sleep was a guarantee that they had not altered anything in the room this morning.

As soon as she left, Joanna popped out of bed to use the chamber pot, pointing significantly to the door, which had not closed completely. Geoffrey nodded, anger again darkening his expression, but he climbed out as she rose to relieve his bladder also. He opened his mouth to say something, not wishing the silence between them to seem unnatural but instead gestured with his head to the sound of voices in the antechamber. Joanna threw his bed robe to him and got back into the bed just as Isabella swept without warning into the room.

The indecent haste and improper purpose for which the queen had come was underlined by those who attended her. Without exception they were her own creatures or the wives of those who had reason to hate or envy the houses of Salisbury and Roselynde. It also underlined her stupidity. Ordinarily, there would have been jesting and conversation until the full group of witnesses assembled. Then the covers would have been drawn off Joanna, she would have been helped from the bed, reexamined to be sure she had not cut herself to supply the blood—all amid good-natured teasing—and the sheets would have been removed by her maids to be retained as evidence of her purity. Instead, before Geoffrey could even shove the chamber pot out of the way, one of Isabella's ladies was looking under the bed.

"It is gone, madam," she announced with satisfaction. "There was a cloth bag with an animal inside it when I looked at the room last night."

"Yes—" Joanna began, but her voice was cut off by a snarl of rage from Geoffrey.

"How is that your business, madam?"

Isabella did not seem to hear the question. She produced the speech she had planned to answer the question Geoffrey should have asked. "I say that the blood on the sheets is not Lady Joanna's but some other creature's. My woman saw the maid, Edwina, conceal something, and I—"

Geoffrey made an inarticulate noise and started around the bed toward the queen. The ladies drew together and began to back away, all except Isabella who could not conceive of anyone offering violence to her sacred person. Joanna sprang from the bed and clasped Geoffrey in her arms so that he would have to knock her down and walk on her before he could get at the queen.

"Geoffrey," she cried, "the queen means no harm. She only wishes to protect you. She could not know of our private jest. Think! Think!"

The desperate urgency of the last two words penetrated the surge of anger. To attack the queen would be to undo all the good his marriage to Joanna had accomplished. Geoffrey's flush receded, leaving him with burning yellow eyes in a face the color of well-bleached linen.

"I assure you, madam, that the blood is my wife's," he said icily. "I had sufficient pain and trouble in taking her maidenhead to assure me ten times over of her innocence."

"And the kitten is here," Joanna added hastily, hearing Geoffrey's voice begin to tremble. She gestured toward the chair. "Here also is the bag in which Edwina kept it. You can see that the fur inside the bag is the same as the kitten's. I am sorry to have given you a fright upon your nephew's behalf, madam."

Isabella was not a clever woman, but she had told a convincing enough tale so that the women who had accompanied her had high expectations of a bitter confrontation between the houses of Salisbury and Roselynde that would end in further riving the kingdom. Great surprise and dissatisfaction was generated by Geoffrey's guarantee of Joanna's virginity and Joanna's open avowal of her maid's part in concealing the obviously healthy and content little kitten. This was written so openly on the faces of most of the witnesses that Joanna, rather than being angry, found great difficulty in stifling the impulse to laugh. She was enjoying the queen's discomfiture intensely. A joke that backfired was often the best joke of all.

"You may examine the kitten," she said gravely, although her voice was a little tremulous with inner mirth. "You will find it whole, without a scratch. I assure you, madam, it was brought to satisfy a private jest between my husband and myself—something I would prefer not to repeat that he said concerning the nature of—of women. It had nothing to do with the blood on the sheets.''

''Well, whoever said it did?''

The king's rich and mellow voice came from the doorway, where he blocked entrance for the remainder of the witnesses. His smile was pleasant, but there was an odd note in his voice and an odd expression in the eyes he turned on Isabella. It almost frightened her. She had hardly ever seen John look at her with anything but admiration. Stupid, ungrateful man, she thought. John hated Geoffrey as much as she did, yet when she had taken this marvelous opportunity to shame Geoffrey before all, John was angry. And it was all Geoffrey's fault—lying for that vixen. Isabella was sure that Geoffrey was lying, either to save his own pride or, more likely, out of desire to make trouble. Shame was not sufficient; Geoffrey FitzWilliam would have to die.

''A slight misunderstanding, my lord,'' Geoffrey said, lowering his eyes.

Much as he detested his brother's son, John had to give Geoffrey credit for good behavior. It was fortunate that he was such a dutiful idiot. Isabella was such a fool that— Was she only a fool? Could she have taken some contagion from FitzWalter? Until that moment John could have sworn that FitzWalter was too clever to do more than flatter Isabella so that she would run to him in case of trouble, but—Isabella would have to be watched, closely watched. Meanwhile, it would be necessary to be very careful with regard to Geoffrey. He must not be teased or twitted. From his face, and the expressions of the other women, he had come very near to forgetting his duty this time.

''I hope the misunderstanding is amended?'' John asked smoothly.

Geoffrey said nothing, the muscles in his jaws bunching.

''Oh yes,'' Joanna cried eagerly. ''It was only a mistake. We understand.''

So she is a slut, John thought. Does my nephew know and protects her to save himself shame, or is it only a vague suspicion that makes him all the hotter in her defense and will drive him mad? The thought amused John and put him into an excellent humor. He stepped aside from the doorway, allowing the remaining witnesses to pour into the room. In the hurly-burly of jest and counterjest, of exclamations both sympathetic and envious, over the condition of Geoffrey's skin, Lady Alinor found a moment to tell Joanna urgently to be quiet and look sad. The morning then ran its normal course until they breakfasted and prepared to ride out to hunt.

Joanna had scarce said a word and had kept her eyes fixed upon her food. Geoffrey was not surprised. He was still furious himself and thought Joanna shared that emotion. It was thus with considerable relief that he rose to join the hunt, knowing that the exercise would permit him to calm himself. He saw Joanna begin to rise also and walked out toward the door. Joanna's movement, however, was never completed. Passing behind her, Alinor held her daughter firmly in her place.

"You are no doubt too sore to ride, Joanna," Alinor said kindly. Color flooded Joanna's face. Alinor patted her consolingly on the shoulder. "You are a good girl to try to put a brave face on, but there is no need. I will stay also. I will comfort you and explain to you that marriage is a good thing despite this trial that women must bear."

Joanna uttered a muffled sound that could have been a sob and her body was seen to heave once convulsively. Then she raised a crimson face and tear-filled eyes to her mother. "Oh, thank you," she murmured softly.

By the door Geoffrey realized he had lost his wife. He stopped but was shoved forward by his father-by-marriage. "Joanna does not ride with us," Ian said. "She has been used too hardily to sit on a saddle today." Geoffrey opened his mouth on an indignant protest, but Ian gave him no time to voice it. "Lady Alinor will explain to her again that such things are necessary and lead to great pleasures," Ian went on pointedly. "And I think I should explain to you how to be more gentle."

"I do not need such advice before all men," Geoffrey said angrily, and when he came to the stables mounted quickly and rode away, keeping well apart from Ian.

An hour later when the chase had spread the huntsmen well over the forest, Ian's gray destrier shied a little as Geoffrey's Orage breasted a thicket just ahead and stopped, blocking his path. "What is wrong?" Geoffrey asked anxiously, and then when Ian did not answer immediately, he frowned. "Did I read you amiss? As soon as my head cooled, I was sure you meant us to talk in private. Surely you cannot really think I used Joanna harshly."

Ian gestured sharply for him to be still, listened a moment, then shrugged and indicated that they should ride back through the thicket and out into a little clearing where no one could come upon them by surprise or overhear if they talked softly. Then he smiled.

"I did want private speech with you. Joanna would have clawed you elsewhere for defense rather than pleasure." Ian laughed, but blushed darkly. It was still very hard for him to accept the idea of his little Joanna writhing with pleasure under the servicing of a man. It was best not to think of that at all. "There is nothing wrong," he went on, "but I have interesting news from a source John would not approve. I have been in treasonous communication with Llewelyn."

Geoffrey smiled at that. However much Ian loved his clan brother, he was not the man to commit treason—except in John's warped imagination. Then he looked puzzled. "It must be very interesting news for Llewelyn to risk your neck to send it. Good God, surely he does not intend to come against England!"

"No, no. Llewelyn is most content with what he has. In fact, he is rather well disposed toward John just now. After all, it was John's mismanagement that dropped all of Wales into Llewelyn's hand with little effort or loss on his part. No, the news concerns Philip."

For a moment, the memory of twenty-eight bodies, some of them very small, on gibbets darkened Geoffrey's eyes. Did the Welsh forget so easily? Or was their pain less because ten or a hundred English had died for each of those who hung? He shook the memory off.

"Philip? What the devil does Llewelyn know of Philip?"

"More than you would suppose. Each time Llewelyn comes at odds with John, he flirts with Philip, and Philip knows even less about the Welsh than we do. He believes, I think, that with the proper cozening the 'stupid' barbarians will give him free port of entry to this island. So Philip welcomes Llewelyn's emissaries into France and shows them often how powerful he is, believing they will wish to ally themselves with the strong."

"Llewelyn may not love John, but he would not be such a fool as to open his land to a strong army over which he could have no control," Geoffrey said with a gentle hoot of laughter.

"There are those who think that if a man wears simple clothing and speaks a foreign tongue simply that his brains must also be simple. In truth, I think Llewelyn may have been offended by Philip's assumption that, because he would fight to free his own lands from his father-by-marriage, that he would also stab John in the back. When all is said, Llewelyn is married to John's daughter. However they may fight between themselves, Llewelyn, at least, would not welcome an outsider into a family quarrel. I think the news he sends is true. He says that Count Ferrand is no longer so enamored of his overlord as he once was. Ferrand has learned that Philip encouraged Louis to attempt seizure of two of Ferrand's towns—St. Omer and Aire. Now, the towns are most like to fall to Louis because the people have little love for Ferrand and thus little heart to defend themselves. If the towns fall, Llewelyn thinks that Ferrand will be ripe for Renaud of Dammartin's handling and that John should bid Renaud to make haste to Flanders and promise Ferrand John's help."

As Ian spoke, the slight suspicion that had appeared on Geoffrey's face faded. Ian was as prone to see good in his "brother" as Salisbury was to see good in the king. However, Geoffrey also believed the news Llewelyn sent was true, not out of fondness for Llewelyn or out of believing in Llewelyn's fondness for John. Simply, it would be greatly to Llewelyn's advantage if John's attention was fixed upon Europe until he was firm in the saddle of Wales.

"This is good news," Geoffrey said. "Why must we sit here and speak of it in secrecy?"

Ian laughed briefly. "Llewelyn may be in good humor with John, but I doubt that the reverse is true. Do you suggest I tell John my news and where I had it? Besides, I wish to bear myself as lowly as possible. It is needful for me to ride north again. If I seem anxious to direct John's attention to Flanders, will he wonder whether I ride to join the rebels? Geoffrey, even among those who came to this wedding, there is a carelessness in their manner toward the king that bodes ill. If anything oversets John so that he breaks out into anger or any other ill behavior, that will be the end. Men will run to arms."

Geoffrey nodded. "I understand. How do you desire that I—"

There was a crashing in the brush. Without another word, both lifted their reins and touched spurred heels to their horses' sides, moving off in opposite directions. Later, when they came together at the killing of a stag, they greeted each other somewhat stiffly. It could be seen, however, that Lord Ian was making an effort to be conciliatory and, eventually, they rode off side by side, talking as easily as usual.

Within the keep, Alinor and Joanna were also sitting amicably together and discussing what might be done to ease the merchants if, as they expected, their ships were to be confiscated for war service against France. The discussion had not begun quite so amicably. Soon after the hunters had left the hall, Alinor had led her daughter away to a quiet window seat.

"You did not have to make me laugh and then pinch me so hard," Joanna protested in an undervoice. "I understood what you desired."

Alinor uttered a mischievous chuckle. "I wished you to

look thoroughly distressed, and so you did—blushing and weeping. Never mind, it will never show amid the other bruises.''

"I have no other bruises," Joanna said indignantly. "Geoffrey is not a wild beast."

The smile grew broader on Alinor's lips. She had indeed guessed right about her daughter's capacity for passion. If Joanna had not felt what made the marks on her body, she had been deep in ecstasy. "I am glad you were enjoying yourself so thoroughly," she said softly, "but I did not draw you here to talk of Geoffrey—at least, I have one question to ask about him. What do you think, Joanna, can you draw him away from the king's cause?"

Joanna looked down as if her mother was explaining something she understood but did not wish to accept. "You know the king is nothing to Geoffrey," she muttered. "It is Salisbury he clings to. Are you asking me to tear Geoffrey free of his father?" She paused, thinking, then said, "Perhaps I could—" Joanna no longer underestimated her power over her husband, "but what would remain would not be a man. Is our state so dire?" she asked anxiously, but before Alinor could answer, she lifted her eyes "No! I do not care, I will not destroy Geoffrey for any reason."

"No," Alinor agreed, patting her daughter's hand. "I chose him because of what he is. I would not desire him other than loyal and honorable. Ela is making me nervous. She foresees doom, and I—I am not easy either. It would be better for us if we had a foot in each camp, but I know it cannot be done—I just thought. Oh, well, we must sink or swim with John, so he had better be supported so that he does swim."

"Ela always foresees doom," Joanna offered.

"It is true. She is growing more and more fearful. Ian thinks we may still scrape through without war and he wishes to do all he can. That is what I drew you apart to tell you. You must find some excuse not to go to Hemel with Geoffrey."

"Oh mother—" Joanna whispered, appalled.

Alinor laughed. "No, I said that wrong. I meant you and Geoffrey between you must find some reason for Geoffrey to accompany you south to my lands rather than, as would be natural, to go to his. Ian must go north again to sit on the hotheads there and I do not wish to leave the coastlands without a leader who can rally the men. There is a real danger Philip will invade—"

"In midwinter?" Joanna protested.

"Word is spread that Philip is expending much gold to buy cardinals who will urge Innocent to declare John deposed and name Philip God's instrument for this purpose. If what he desires happens, Philip will not dare wait because the order could be countermanded and Philip knows as well as anyone else that John has envoys in Rome. If they can convince the pope that John is in earnest, Innocent will be only too willing to change his mind about deposition. It is a bad precedent."

"John must know all this. Why is it necessary to whisper in secret that Geoffrey and I will go to Roselynde?"

"That need not be secret, only the reason for it—that Ian rides north. He goes to save the king, but will John believe that? So far his behavior is perfect, but who knows what little thing will overset him?"

Anger thinned Joanna's generous mouth. "We will do it, of course," she said, "but I tell you plain I think it hard that Geoffrey and I must first be put on show like wares at a fair, and insulted by the queen, all for the sake of— And poor Geoffrey must be set to hard labor so soon. Even a serf is granted holiday after his wedding."

"As your state is higher than that of a serf, so must your burdens be greater," Alinor reminded her.

"And if Philip should come," Joanna murmured, more to herself than to her mother, "instead of being at Hemel and coming to battle as one of a great army, Geoffrey must bear the first brunt of the attack."

CHAPTER TWENTY-TWO

It was a quiet, anxious Christmas at Roselynde. The news Geoffrey had from his father at court was very bad. Most of the barons John invited to join him did not come nor even bother to send excuses. It began to be a real question which way the nobles would jump when Philip invaded, and there was little doubt there would be an invasion. Ships, men, and supplies were ready in France. Philip seemed to be waiting only for the pope's blessing on his project, and that might come at any time. Geoffrey, charged not only with the defense of Alinor's lands but with Adam's property in Sussex, was deeply concerned because it seemed as if he would need to be in three places at once when the attack came.

Ian could be of no help at all. In an effort to give a sharp lesson to rebel agitators and also to occupy the minds and bodies of his own warlike vassals, he had initiated a series of small actions against the strongholds of those most bitterly opposed to the king. He was neck-deep in war, made more dangerous and difficult by the winter weather. Geoffrey wrote for advice late in January and after considerable discussion with Alinor and serious thought about the various chances involved, Ian suggested that Adam leave Leicester temporarily and go to Kemp with Sir Guy as a stabilizing influence. Adam was young, but Leicester had trained him very well. In any case, Adam's purpose would not be to wage war but to ensure that his castellans would not yield to Philip without resistance if invasion should come while Geoffrey was elsewhere.

"It is not at all likely that the French will come ashore near Kemp apurpose. There is no good, large harbor there," Ian explained. "But, should a storm rise in the narrow sea, as is so common in winter and early spring, it is not impossible that some stray bands will be blown to land there. If Adam is in the keep, there can be neither panic nor treachery. He is wild, but not so much a fool as to chance battle against high odds. And even if Sir Guy cannot stop him, he can send to you for help whether Adam approves or not.''

This advice caused the first really bitter disagreement between Geoffrey and Joanna. Partly it was Geoffrey's fault for phrasing the idea carelessly. He told Joanna, quite casually, that he was sending for Adam to defend his own lands.

"Adam!'' Joanna cried, her heart turning over with fear for her baby brother, "Adam is a child! What madness is this?''

"Adam is not a child,'' Geoffrey retorted, all the more hotly because he was trying to convince himself of what he was saying. "He is nearly sixteen years of age. In a year or two he would be knighted and defending his own lands in any case.''

"He might be managing them, with Ian standing by his shoulder,'' Joanna said passionately. "He would not be expected to defend them alone against the might of Philip of France.''

At that point Geoffrey made another mistake. He should have shown her Ian's letter, but in a foolish fit of loyalty he did not want to make Joanna angry with Ian. That would not have been the result. Joanna knew that Ian doted upon Adam; the fact that he had advised the move would have convinced her that there was little danger for her brother. Instead, Geoffrey tried to reason with his wife.

"Nor is Adam expected to do that. Sir Guy will go with him to be sure he does nothing foolish.''

Unfortunately, although Joanna was fond of Sir Guy and perfectly sure of his loyalty and good intentions, she was by no means in the least sure that he could control Adam. "Sir Guy!'' she exclaimed. "And how firm do you believe he will be in opposing Adam's will?''

Touched painfully upon his own fears, for Geoffrey knew

that if harm came to Adam not only would Joanna never forgive him but he would never forgive himself, he turned on her. "What do you desire that I do?" he roared, and then, more quietly, "I must go to Mersea to see to Sir John's defenses. Do not forget that if Dammartin cannot part Ferrand from Philip, the men of the Low Countries who know well how to deal with Mersea's marshes will be part of Philip's force. In that case, Mersea might bear the brunt of a heavy attack. So might Roselynde, which has a good harbor. Kemp is the least likely of all our lands to be struck in force."

"I see," Joanna breathed, but there was no change in the set, white misery of her expression.

"I will talk to him," Geoffrey assured her. I will explain what ruin he will bring upon us if he engages with inadequate forces and fails. Adam is wild, but not stupid and, whether from Mersea or from Roselynde, I am sure I will be able to come to his help before any harm befalls him."

"I see," Joanna repeated, and walked away without further argument.

Geoffrey felt uneasily that he had failed her. She counted upon him to protect her and hers from harm and, instead, he was drawing her brother out of safety into the conflict. It was, Geoffrey acknowledged, his duty to protect his wife and her relatives from harm if he could, but he could not repress a flicker of resentment at the fact that Joanna seemed to fear hurt and danger to any one of them more than for him. Geoffrey no longer worried about being distasteful to his wife. It was obvious he was not. She was openly fond of him, but he could see little difference between her fondness for him and her fondness for Brian. She played with them both—throwing sticks for Brian and tumbling in bed with him—with equal good humor and pleasure.

It seemed to Geoffrey that this uncomfortable notion was rather confirmed when, in spite of the depression that held her pale and silent most of the day and evening, Joanna came to him with even more passion than usual that night. Evidently, she accepted his reasoning and was making her apology in the way she thought would please him best. However, even while Geoffrey writhed and moaned softly as Joanna worked him deeper into the red well of pleasure, some small part of him wished that she would *talk* to him— say she was sorry, say that she loved him, say that she feared for him also as well as for the others she loved— instead of paying him with physical gestures. It smacked too much of fondling a domestic animal to show you were pleased with it.

This was completely unfair, a not uncommon situation to a young man very deeply in love. Geoffrey knew Joanna was a reserved person who rarely voiced her feelings. But in this case it was fortunate that he kept his longing to himself. Her silence and misery was far more a result of guilt than of fear. As soon as Geoffrey said he would come to Adam's rescue, Joanna fully realized that to protect Adam would be to expose Geoffrey to greater danger. Her immediate impulse was to cry out that Geoffrey should leave Adam to his own devices. This disgusting notion, of throwing her little brother to the wolves to preserve her husband, so horrified Joanna as to inhibit her from voicing any further opinion on the subject. All Joanna could do was clutch Geoffrey to her while she had him, trying twice and thrice in the night to unite herself with him completely. This unusual behavior made Geoffrey even more uneasy so that he put off leaving for Mersea from day to day, Joanna eagerly helping him to find excuses to stay.

On March 5, action was forced upon them. An official order, which Joanna opened as Alinor's deputy, came from John. The lady of Roselynde was the king's bailiff for Roselynde town and in this capacity she was ordered "to go in person, together with the bailiffs of the port, to the harbor in your bailiwick and make a careful list of all the ships there found capable of carrying six horses or more; and that, in our name, you order the masters as well as the owners of those ships, as they regard themselves, their ships, and all their property, to have them at Portsmouth at mid-Lent, well equipped with stores, tried seamen, and good soldiers, to enter our service for our deliverance."

Cursing himself, Geoffrey dispatched Sir Guy to Kemp, wrote to Leicester and to Adam, and left at once for Mersea, knowing that orders must also have gone out to the sheriffs at about the same time to summon the barons to war. Invasion was then imminent. While he lingered in Roselynde, Geoffrey had hoped that danger was passing. It seemed to him that if the pope had intended to order John deposed, the order should have been already published. But there was no news of it from the Roselynde fishermen or merchants. It was in Mersea, where Geoffrey found Sir John deeply involved in preparations for defense of his own lands and for answering the king's summons, that Geoffrey finally learned the current rumors. These came not from France but from the court of Ferrand of Flanders, who was suddenly most genial toward English merchants whom, in the past, he had burdened with punitive taxes or forbidden trade altogether.

Stephen Langton had obtained letters of deposition from the pope, but John's emissaries were already in Rome and had so well impressed Pandulf that he had lingered behind while they presented their case to Innocent. They had convinced the pope of John's sincerity, also, describing how, at the peak of his power, the king had felt the hand of God and had repented of all spites done the Holy Church. Pandulf had then asked and received permission to bid Langton hold back the letters of deposition while John's sincerity was tested one last time. The legate Pandulf was no frail priest. He had taken horse, forced a passage across the Alps, and ridden night and day until he overtook Langton. Unless John again refused the pope's terms, there would be no order to depose him.

That was a considerable relief, but the remainder of the news was not so good. Philip, it appeared, had no intentions of allowing his preparations to go to waste. Counting on the disaffection of the nobility of England, Philip planned to invade anyway. But, Sir John continued, Philip was having his own troubles with disaffection. As evidenced by the sudden cosseting of English merchants, Dammartin was influencing Ferrand. Philip's son Louis had taken St. Omer and Aire, and Ferrand, emboldened by Dammartin's offers of help from John, had demanded the return of those towns to him before he would lend his aid in an invasion of England.

Geoffrey was most grateful for the news and said so. His usual source, his father, had been silent for some weeks because he was not at court. The strain of the past year had been too much for Lady Ela. Shortly after Christmas she had really fallen ill, and Salisbury had taken her home where she would be at peace. She was improving, but was not yet strong enough for her husband to leave her.

So far, Geoffrey's visit had been a miracle of smooth agreement, considering the times. He had been welcomed into the keep with cries of joy, hustled out of his wet, muddy clothing, bathed and warmed by the fire, pressed to drink hot spiced wine to ward off a chill, and generally cosseted as if he were a prodigal son. Now that the most urgent items of news had been exchanged and the women and children retired to their quarters, Sir John and he lounged alone by the fire. There was wine in goblets at each man's elbow, but neither was drinking much. Geoffrey was faced with the unpleasant need to assure himself that Sir John's warm welcome was not a blind; that his talk of preparation for war was more than just talk. He was puzzling over how to introduce this delicate topic without implying any distrust of Sir John when the problem solved itself.

"If Dammartin should fail," Geoffrey said, "the Flemmands will come with Philip. You are somewhat north of where they might be expected to make first landfall, but winds are variable and Mersea does lie in a direct line from the ports of Flanders. Moreover, the Flemmands, as you know, will be familiar with the ways of overpassing your marshes."

"I thought that was what brought you here," Sir John said. "Thank you for waiting until my wife left us. She does not like to hear of such things—and you are quite right. That is what I have been busy about. Will you do me the honor, my lord, to look over what I have devised to defend us and speak to those I have appointed to rule while I answer the king's summons?''

"I will gladly look," Geoffrey agreed, masking his relief. He was, after all, younger than Sir John and was always a bit surprised at the deference shown him in military matters because he did not realize the impression he had made on the men who accompanied him through the Welsh campaign. "But I doubt I will have any advice to offer you. You know these lands and the men too, far better than I.''

To that Sir John smiled approval. Geoffrey's open acknowledgement of such truths and his own willingness to take advice were two good reasons why Sir John was so willing to ask. He knew the young lord would not meddle just for the sake of meddling or to show his power.

"That may be true," he replied, "but it is the strange eye that sees small things familiarity overlooks. I may also hope," he added anxiously, "that you or Lord Ian will bring me aid if I find myself overmatched?''

"Unless we are utterly overpowered ourselves, I can promise you that," Geoffrey assured him. "The inland keeps will be safe if we hold firm, and the forces of Ealand or Kingsclere can be dispatched to you. I have sent them notice already that more men must be readied than what will fulfill the king's summons, and I am buying mercenaries as I see those worthwhile.''

Geoffrey hesitated. Sir John had implied that he intended to answer John's summons and had made that decision before Geoffrey arrived. Considering how ambivalent Sir John had been toward the king when Joanna visited him last autumn, the change in attitude was interesting. Again Geoffrey was saved from the need to ask delicate questions by Sir John's trust and respect.

"I suppose Lady Joanna told you that I was not much displeased when there was some hope of absolving the lords from their vows of obedience to the king," he remarked.

"She told me," Geoffrey replied with a shrug. "You were not alone in the way you felt, but there is no one else. I will say again what I have said to others—it is not reasonable to cut off one's head because it aches. No more is it reasonable to destroy a king because he is not perfect. The body will not survive the first; the realm will not survive the second.''

Sir John did not look convinced. ''Well,'' he temporized, ''heads cannot be replaced, kings can.'' Then his jaw set. ''However that may be, I do not intend that French Philip shall have the ordering of who shall or shall not sit upon the throne of England.''

· Soon it was apparent that Sir John's sentiments were held by the majority of the country. They might overturn the king themselves, but they wanted no outside interference in what they regarded as a private struggle. The response to the king's summons was overwhelming. Men poured out of great keeps and small holdings, and they came prepared to fight. For a wonder, John's mood held steady. He greeted his vassals cordially, thanked them for their loyalty, and listened to their advice without any sign of either cringing or pride. His disposition of his forces was sensible. Groups large enough to withstand a first assault were dispatched to Ipswich, Dover, Faversham and other threatened ports. The groups were made up largely of men whose lands were in the area and who would have good reason to fight hard, guided by a leader with his own troops whose loyalty John trusted. The main body, sixty thousand strong, was encamped on Barham Down, closest to the easiest landfall from France but yet clear to move if the attack should come elsewhere.

Geoffrey himself was not kept long with the main forces. He was directed to leave his own troops from Hemel and the other inland estates in Ian's hands and himself take the men from Roselynde, Iford, Kemp, and the other seaside villages to Portsmouth. Their familiarity with the sea and ships, would make them more useful there in the armada gathered to stop Philip at sea and inflict damage upon the ships and ports of France before or after the invasion was launched.

Although Geoffrey saw the logic in the king's order, he

cursed it vilely. Portsmouth was far too close to Roselynde. Joanna would expect him, and Geoffrey feared he would be unable to resist riding home. He wanted to be there, but if he was at Roselynde he could not properly do his duty. In his efforts to explain to Joanna why he would come the few miles between Portsmouth and Roselynde so seldom, Geoffrey inadvertently painted a picture of his central importance to the enterprise.

To Joanna this was instantly equated with a spearhead position in the fighting. Her one desire was to embrace her husband's knees and weep and plead until he promised to withdraw from the action. Since Joanna knew quite well that such behavior could only add an enormous burden of worry to what Geoffrey would be carrying and would not turn him from his purpose, she could only listen to him in silence. Eventually, she gained sufficient control of herself to reply with outward placidity that Geoffrey must, of course, do his duty as he thought best. In one way this calm acceptance of his absence was a relief to Geoffrey, but it also increased his conviction that he meant little more to Joanna than her favorite dog.

At Portsmouth Geoffrey found Salisbury in charge. This was not surprising in spite of the fact that Salisbury knew very little about the sea or seamen. The armada which was devised to stop Philip at sea was easily as important to the defense of the country as the army assembled on Barham Down. To whom else would John entrust it? Salisbury was intelligent and adaptable. Perhaps he could not learn to steer or sail a ship in a few days or weeks, but he could certainly learn the principles of fighting afloat.

Geoffrey did know a good deal about the sea and seamen. He had sailed with the merchants and fishermen from Roselynde, had fought pirates and sea reavers all along Lady Alinor's coastal possessions when he was Ian's squire. Salisbury seized upon him with bellows of delight, and Geoffrey was soon as busy and burdened as he had been at any time during the Welsh campaign. He did not have time to think about Joanna and whom she loved best. All but the faintest trace of dissatisfaction was pushed out of his mind when John ordered his well-prepared navy into action.

They were to try out their power in raids against Fécamp, Dieppe, and the French shipping in the river Seine. On April 8, Philip convened his council at Soissons and announced publicly his intention of invading England. As soon as the news came across the channel, which Philip took good care it should do, hoping to strike terror into John, Salisbury began his strikes. At Fécamp and on the Seine they were successful. The raid on Dieppe was also damaging to the French, but there Geoffrey was wounded and very nearly drowned. To save his son the pain of being jolted over miles of bad road in a springless cart, Salisbury ordered that the ship that carried him should leave the main force and sail on to make port in Roselynde rather than Portsmouth.

Joanna had immediate news of her husband's arrival and condition. While Geoffrey was being tenderly carried from the ship, a servant from the harbor master's household was sent galloping up the hill to the keep. By the time Geoffrey had been moved up the road, all was ready for him. The tears had been dashed from Joanna's eyes, the terror had been firmly repressed into a little cold knot in the pit of her stomach. One did not add to the torment of a wounded man by weeping and wailing over him. Joanna greeted Geoffrey with calm assurances that he would soon be well, dressed his hurts anew, fed him, and smiled upon him.

Geoffrey could not complain of any lack in his wife's tenderness and care. She watched him every moment, even foresaw his needs before he was completely aware himself that he wanted a drink or to shift his position or some other easing. She talked to him gently and cheerfully on any topic she thought would interest him and divert his mind, was always ready to read to him or gamble with him as he grew better.

Nonetheless there was a small, empty hollow deep inside Geoffrey. His examples of loving wives were Lady Alinor and Lady Ela. Neither by the remotest stretch of the truth could be said to have a calm disposition. Both tended to show affection and relief by scolding. If Ian was hurt, Alinor alternately called him a jackass for not being more careful and embraced and kissed him fiercely. If Salisbury should be wounded, Lady Ela berated her husband for being inconsiderate and taking chances that might lead to her widowhood, interspersing her scolding liberally with caresses. In fact, Geoffrey did not want Joanna to act in a like manner. He had often wondered how Ian and his father bore so patiently with their wives. He did not know what he wanted. Had he been sure that the attention Joanna gave him was proof of love, he would have regarded himself as the happiest man alive—but he was not sure and the attention was so dear to him that he was afraid to ask lest even that be taken away.

Aside from her natural fears for Geoffrey's physical safety, Joanna had been very happy in her marriage. She was quite sure Geoffrey loved her. He was nothing loath to speak his mind on that subject and endearments followed each thanks for her service to him. She was now as much in love as he and, thus, was more sensitive to each glance and gesture. As he grew better, she grew more uneasy. Something in the way his eyes followed her told her all was not well, and, for all the "thanks" and "beloveds" that his lips spoke, she was aware that Geoffrey was dissatisfied. She racked her brains for a hint of how she had failed him without discovering any answer. She even asked, "What lacks you?" far too often, for Joanna knew it was very wrong to tease a sick man with questions.

As it was, she was so eager to please Geoffrey that she did things she knew were foolish, like returning to his bed long before he was really strong enough. Not that it did him any harm; Joanna took good care that Geoffrey lay still and did not risk reopening his wound. Her compliance soothed him, but only for a while. All too soon the trouble returned to shadow his eyes even while his lips smiled. Joanna could only conclude that the dissatisfaction was not with her, that Geoffrey was already fretting because he was not with the fighting force. Fear for him lay heavy on her, poisoning her pleasure in his presence and making her behavior unnatural.

Young and strong as he was, cared for with infinite gentleness and attention, Geoffrey healed swiftly. He noted that as he grew stronger, began to ride and exercise in arms with Tostig, Joanna grew more remote. It occurred to him that the only subject Joanna was reluctant to discuss was the coming war. Unfortunately, that was no clear signpost to where her strongest affections lay. Everyone Joanna loved was involved in some way—Adam guarding Kemp and that part of the southern coast, Ian with John at Barham Downs, Alinor, relying on her daughter's ability to hold Roselynde, settled into Mersea while Sir John was with the king's forces at Ipswich. He could not bring himself to ask for whom Joanna feared most deeply, and Joanna increased his doubt by refusing to speak at all when Geoffrey speculated about whether it would be better to meet Philip on land or by sea. Guilt held her silent. She could not wish to endanger Ian and perhaps even Adam in a land battle, but in her heart she knew what choice she would make if choice was forced upon her.

Before his growing need could push Geoffrey into demanding an avowal from Joanna, Salisbury rode into Roselynde as dusk was falling on May 26. Ostensibly, he came to visit his son, but he was plainly overjoyed to see how near Geoffrey was to total recovery. He had news of the greatest importance, and it was just as well that Salisbury's attention was fixed upon that or he would have noticed the coldness with which his daughter-by-marriage greeted him. Geoffrey saw and his heart was gladdened. He guessed that his wife knew Salisbury had come to recall him to his duty if he was able for it, and she was very angry. Softly, he warned Joanna to hold her tongue and, with a warm glow of satisfaction within, turned his mind to what his father was saying.

"I am not so sure I like that," Salisbury was grumbling.

"That the king made submission to the pope?" Geoffrey

asked uncertainly, aware that he had missed something while his attention was occupied with Joanna.

Salisbury gave his son an indulgent glance. He had seen where Geoffrey's eyes were fixed as he related his news. Patiently, he started again. "Not that. You know I have always advised John to make peace with the Church, although I could have wished—never mind, it is done, and Pandulf is a most sensible person. He recognizes that restitution must be made slowly, and he is to be the judge in disputed cases. There will be no trouble there. My doubts lie in the scheme John has concocted to put a spoke in Philip's wheel. He has resigned the kingdom utterly into the pope's hands, and has done fealty to Innocent—or, rather, to Pandulf as Innocent's legate—as vassal ruler of England."

Geoffrey whistled softly through his teeth. That would certainly put a spoke in Philip's wheel. If Philip invaded England now, he would be committing an act of deep sacrilege by attacking the pope's own domain. The move was as clever a piece of chicanery as John had ever planned—except for one thing.

"What will this cost?" Geoffrey asked suspiciously.

"A thousand marks a year."

"That is a tidy sum but perhaps not too high a price to pay for the benefits it will buy," Geoffrey said slowly.

"For now, I agree, but for the long future I have my doubts. What if the pope should be offended by some prince in Italy? Rightfully, he could call upon John as a vassal to come to his aid."

"I should hope Innocent would have more sense," Joanna remarked tartly. "He must know that John's barons are not docile and would not leave their land to fight Innocent's wars. What could such an order bring about except to induce the barons to rebel against the king?"

"It is not likely Innocent would call John to Italy to solve a secular problem," Geoffrey agreed, but absently. "He might call another crusade—" His voice trailed away and a frown grew between his brows. Suddenly he said, "But we do not credit my uncle with the right motives or enough cleverness." His voice was flat, betraying no bitterness in deference to his father. "I do not believe John fears Philip enough to yield his absolute right. Do you not see what a weapon this will be in the king's hands in any conflict with his noblemen? To oppose him in anything, will be to defy the pope."

The sound of Joanna's little indrawn breath was masked by Salisbury's hearty and cheerful acknowledgement. Whether he had not previously thought of this result or had wanted Geoffrey to draw the conclusion for himself was not clear. In any case, he abandoned the subject to go on to the next piece of news, which had more immediate implications. Pandulf had left England on May 22 to induce Philip to abandon his plan of invasion. To the papal legate's urging, Count Ferrand of Flanders had added his own, at last declaring openly that he would not go against the pope's will and, thus, if Philip persisted would withdraw himself from his alliance with France. Instead of inducing caution, which would be a normal reaction for the king of France, this declaration threw Philip into a violent rage. In turn, he declared Ferrand his enemy. The count of Flanders had barely time to flee Philip's court and save himself from imprisonment. He had no time to gather forces to resist his erstwhile overlord, and Philip had promptly invaded Flanders, using the army mustered to attack England. On May 25, a messenger had arrived from Ferrand begging John for the help Renaud Dammartin had promised him in the king's name.

Geoffrey smiled on his father, his eyes lighting. "When do we go?"' he asked.

"Are you ready?" Salisbury counter-questioned.

Joanna thrust the needle she had been using to embroider a glove cuff into the cloth as if it were a dagger aimed at Salisbury's heart.

"Oh yes," Geoffrey assured his father. "I am a little stiff still, but I have been riding out and fencing with Tostig this week past."

Joanna slammed the small embroidery frame down onto the table that held her silks with such force that half the skeins flew into the air and then down onto the floor. Salisbury looked away. Geoffrey smiled at his wife. Joanna bit her lips and walked stiffly out of the hall and up to her own chamber.

"I fear Joanna does not agree with you, my boy," Salisbury said anxiously. "I do not deny I need you sorely. I have been as a man bereft of his right arm since you were hurt. However, it would be far better for me to continue thus than to have you hurt again or have your wound reopened. I am not sure I trust your word on this. Perhaps I will ask Joanna outright—"

"No!" Geoffrey interrupted. "I swear to you I am not misjudging my state. You may look me over yourself and you will see I am well healed. If I had been still unready, Joanna would have spoken out quickly enough. When do we go?"

"Tomorrow morning to make ready and sail with the morning tide the next day," Salisbury replied still doubtful.

"Good," Geoffrey exclaimed. "There will be less time for Joanna to fret. Tell me, now she is gone, what is afoot?"

Salisbury began to describe the situation as related to him by William, count of Holland and Renaud Dammartin, who were both already in Portsmouth and would accompany them. While he spoke his worry lessened. Geoffrey would not be leading any battles in this enterprise because Holland and Dammartin would serve in that capacity. Salisbury could keep Geoffrey beside him and be sure that he was well guarded and did not overstrain himself. When their plans were laid, Geoffrey having accepted his father's suggestion about his battle station without argument because he acknowledged that the other men were more experienced and of higher station, Geoffrey saw Salisbury to bed and went up to join his wife.

Joanna rose from beside the fire where she had been sitting and staring into the flames and began to help him undress without a word.

"I must go," Geoffrey said softly, "you know I must."

"I know you are willing, even desirous of going," Joanna replied coldly. "If we were threatened, I would agree you must go. As we are attacking, I can only believe you wish to go."

Geoffrey thought that over. There was a good deal of truth in it, of course. He controlled an impulse to grin and said, "When a friend cries for help, it is as necessary to reply as it is to defend oneself."

"A 'dear' friend, indeed, who until a few months ago was our avowed enemy," Joanna snapped.

"Do not be a fool," Geoffrey snapped back. "New or old, his trouble came out of defending us. That is an act of true friendship and to it we must respond."

What Geoffrey said was true, but it did nothing to improve Joanna's mood. She flopped ill-temperedly down to yank at his cross garters and shoelaces. Since her head was bent, Geoffrey permitted himself to smile. He untied the string of his chausses and Joanna tugged them down, nearly oversetting him as she pulled shoe, loosened cross garter, and chausses leg off his foot all at once without warning. Geoffrey grasped at her to steady himself, but Joanna was also off balance and tipped sideways. By a miracle of contortion, Geoffrey caught the seat of the chair and prevented himself from falling heavily on his wife. The chair slid away; Joanna cried out with fear that he would hurt himself; they found themselves entangled on the rug before the hearth with fifteen stone of dog astride them anxiously licking first one face and then the other.

"Off!" they roared in unison. "Out!" and then subsided into laughter.

"Are you hurt, Geoffrey?" Joanna asked, not knowing whether she wished for it or feared it. Her husband had made no motion to rise, and she could not move without jostling him, being pinned half under his body.

"Only in my heart," he replied, and nibbled at her chin. "You are so beautiful, Joanna," he murmured, continuing to nibble down her throat between the words.

Joanna had been made so furious by the eagerness with

which Geoffrey welcomed his father's suggestion that he return to action, that she had intended to give him a cold farewell. He might love her better than other women, but it was sure he did not love her better than killing other men. Nonetheless, it was impossible after their mutual laughter to draw on a cloak of wounded pride. Besides, she was by no means immune to her husband's flattery or to what he was doing, and the idea of coupling on the carpet before the fire lent an odd spice also.

"Geoffrey," she sighed, her hands wandering down his body, "do you *wish* to leave me?"

"Are you mad?" he sighed, but he had better uses for his mouth than answering silly questions, and soon Joanna was too far gone to ask any others.

By hooking the toes of his free leg into them, Geoffrey had rid himself of the remaining leg of his chausses and shoe without breaking Joanna's concentration. It was easier to untie her belt and open her robe, but when he turned her on her back he could feel her shiver. The floor struck cold even through the carpet. Geoffrey pulled Joanna back against his naked warmth and lay flat himself, lifting her atop him so that her open robe flowed over both like a coverlet.

"Come," he whispered, "mount astride me as you did when I was still too sore to play the man. Pleasure me thus."

Had Joanna been able to think, the reminder of the danger Geoffrey so eagerly sought might have turned her to ice. It did not work that way. Pain wrung her but the pang seemed to intensify the pleasure in her loins as when Geoffrey sucked her breasts hard enough to bruise them the pain heightened her passion. Tears came to her eyes, and the feeling of them running down her face also added a weird excitement to the love play.

For Geoffrey too there was a stimulating oddity in this mating. The notion that his wife wept while her body moved sinuously upon his, the chill of the floor at his back and the warmth of Joanna's breasts against his chest, even the knowledge that he dare not cry out or groan with pleasure for fear of bringing Brian upon them again made the waves of sensation radiating from his shaft more piercing. Twice he needed to seize Joanna's hips and hold her still lest he come to a premature climax. The third time he tried to quiet her she struggled against him, too near her own orgasm to care or understand, and that set them both off.

Later, when Geoffrey regained enough strength, he carried Joanna to bed. "You need not fear for me this time," he comforted, drawing her to lie against him. "My father is more tender of me than you wish to believe." Joanna stiffened and began to pull away, but Geoffrey laughed and held her tight. "I tell you, he desires me as a scribe and to do the accounts and suchlike. He has battle leaders enough. Dammartin and the count of Holland are with him."

Joanna sighed and relaxed. She really knew that Salisbury would not endanger Geoffrey needlessly, and it was useless to be angry and weep because men were men. "Will you truly have a care for yourself? Truly?"

"Am I of such great value to you then?" Geoffrey asked lightly, warm with pleasure, sure this time she would say outright that she loved him.

"Better the devil I know than one unknown, who might be worse," Joanna replied matching his tone.

Shock kept him still. Nothing seemed able to wring an avowal of love from Joanna. In the past when he sighed that he loved her, Geoffrey thought bitterly, she replied with kisses. Now that he asked openly for an answer, she jested—or did she? Had she spoken the truth? Was he only the "devil" she knew, dear because he was safe and familiar? If he had not won her to love in near half a year of marriage, could he hope he ever would win her? Geoffrey's lips parted to ask plainly, to demand an answer, but Joanna had slipped into sleep.

Grateful for the reprieve, he murmured softly, "I am a fool. I know she loves me. I know it." But there was no assurance in his voice and, if he hoped to win a half-conscious response from Joanna, he failed in that too.

CHAPTER TWENTY-THREE

Geoffrey and Salisbury left before the first light the next morning. Geoffrey was still somewhat stiff of movement, favoring his right side where a sword stroke under his guard had sliced him open from breastbone to waist. Seeing this, Salisbury spoke privately to Tostig and to his own senior squire, who was near ripe for knighting. Even if they had to knock him down and sit on him, Salisbury instructed, Geoffrey was not to become involved in any heavy fighting.

Tostig shook his head. "If there is fighting, my lord," he growled, "I will need to catch him before I can knock him down. How do you think he was so hurt? It was because he had run ahead of us all and was surrounded."

Salisbury laughed, not displeased. "Well, guard him close as you can. I will speak to him myself."

He found Geoffrey out on one of the docks, shouting directions about warping in a boat. When the nervous, blindfolded horses were starting over the gangplank, Salisbury drew his son aside and told him plainly that he was not satisfied with the completeness of his recovery and if Geoffrey would not pass his word to do no more than defend himself when necessary, he would leave him behind. Geoffrey opened his mouth indignantly but then shut it.

"Very well," he said, "for one week from this day, I will abide by your condition, but then we must come to new terms." Then he busied himself with loading and organizing the five hundred ships, seven hundred knights, and thousands of foot soldiers and archers that made up their force. When he fell onto his pallet in the bow of his father's ship that night, he slept far more soundly than he had for some time past in his own soft bed.

They sailed with the morning tide, beating east and then a little north through the strait of Dover. There, a small boat came out with the news that many ships had passed through two days ago. Such a large fleet could only be Philip's navy. A discussion ensued as to whether they should try to engage at sea or hold to their original plan of joining forces with Ferrand. On Dammartin's advice, they pursued their course toward the mouth of the Zwyn in spite of awkward offshore winds. It would be unwise, Dammartin suggested significantly, to raise any doubts in Ferrand's mind, even briefly. The count's own men were not too firm in their loyalty, and if John seemed slow to send the aid upon which they counted, they might panic and yield.

The decision proved fortunate in an unexpected way. Upon turning into the estuary, lookouts were sent up to report on the condition of the port. Suddenly, as the port of Damme came into view, all voices sang out with astonishment. The port was one solid mass of ships. Salisbury's force had accomplished both purposes at once. Stealthily, the ships in the lead backed water, signaling warnings to those that followed. Three small boats manned by Flemish sailors were sent out to scout the defenses.

Before Salisbury's armada had even completed their preparations for fighting, the scouts were back, almost overwhelmed with the good news they carried. The fleet was naked to their will, being guarded by no more than a few sword-armed sailors. Evidently, Philip had believed that John was shivering with fear of his invasion and would not spare a man or a ship to fulfill his promise to Ferrand. The French knights were either at the siege of Ghent or were scattered far and wide over the countryside plundering the rich Flemish towns.

Every man for whom there was place leapt eagerly to the oars. Salisbury's ships poured into the harbor as fast as they could. Brass-lunged heralds called for immediate surrender. By and large the order received quick compliance since it was clear that the French position was indefensible. Twice a better manned ship approached by Salisbury's vessel showed signs of fight, hoping to escape with the help of the offshore wind. In these cases, Geoffrey joyfully unlimbered the great Welsh longbow he carried and picked off any exposed member of the crew while small boats ran up alongside and sent English knights and men-at-arms aboard.

The second ship put up a fierce resistance. The surprise caused by this fiery defense nearly accomplished its purpose. The ship had been cut free from its anchor line and turned to catch the wind by the sailors while the men-at-arms fought off those attempting to board before Geoffrey at last spotted the guiding spirit—a man in the mail of a belted knight—and pinned him to the deck with a well-placed arrow. Even wounded, the knight called on his men to keep fighting, but a rain of crossbow bolts drove the sailors from their tasks and the havoc wrought by the superior accuracy of the unfamiliar weapon Geoffrey wielded soon doused the remaining flickers of resistance. Geoffrey called out to spare the life of the ardent fighter and see to his hurts and then turned his attention to more important matters.

Having slaughtered and thrown into the sea the crews of the ships that were afloat, the English sent strong landing parties to take the ships that had been beached. The ferocity with which the mariners had been treated had its effect. Those set to guard the beached ships and supplies fled in haste, as did most of the residents of the town, leaving the conquerors a clear field. The remainder of the men-at-arms and the horses were taken ashore to be organized into guard parties. Some would be sent out to be sure the French did not return and attack them by surprise; the others were set to stripping the beached ships of everything of value they had carried.

By virtue of the agreement he had made with his father, Geoffrey was condemned to be in charge of collecting and transporting the booty. To his utter delight, it soon became apparent that most of Philip's upper nobility had come with the fleet, carrying the elegant clothing and jewels that were necessary to a King's entourage even when on active service. There would be many a new ring and necklet to bedeck his beautiful Joanna. In fact, every man who had taken part in this expedition would be a great deal richer when he returned home than he had been when it started.

More important in the long run was the enormous tonnage of supplies, the meat, corn, wine, flour, and arms that were still in the bellies of the ships. It was incredible, but nonetheless true, that Philip had not waited to unload the supplies for his campaign before he sent his army out to plunder the land. He had been too sure of his supremacy, too contemptuous of his enemies. Doubtless, he would not make that mistake again, but the lesson would come too late for the Flemish campaign. Without food for his army, the siege of Ghent could not be prosecuted. Without ships, the army would have to retreat overland. Without the extra arms and armor, the French would take heavy losses as they fought their way back through a hostile countryside.

When it grew too dark to continue loading, the parties ranging out from the town were thinned into a line of guards. More guards were set on the beached ships, and the captured vessels that were already fully laden were dispatched back to England with prize crews aboard. With the return of Salisbury and his party, Geoffrey found that he had been the only really hard pressed member of the army. The others had a calm, pleasant ride through the countryside, although they were loud in complaint over the damage the French had done. By the time they got onto that subject, Geoffrey had imbibed rather freely of the excellent wine the French had brought along for their own pleasure. It struck him very funny that his father and such other notable war lords as Dammartin and William of Holland should deplore in Flanders what they themselves would do in France if they had half a chance.

This line of thought led to a slightly maudlin decision that he was no better than they. Had he not bid the men spare the life of that knight and not even remembered to ask his name or whether he had survived? Thought and action being one when the passage between them was lubricated with wine, Geoffrey lunged to his feet and began to stagger out to make inquiries.

"Where do you go?" Salisbury called as his eye was caught by his son's unsteady gait. They were too near the docks to make drunken wandering safe.

Geoffrey explained, and his father snorted derisively. "You are full as an untapped wineskin. Where will you look in the dark? Like enough, if he is alive, he is on his way to England. Tomorrow, if you still want to know, I will inquire."

It was highly unlikely that either would have remembered in the morning, but a middle-aged knight further down the room called out to say that if Lord Geoffrey meant the man wounded by the longbow arrow, he had taken him prisoner. The man's name was Léon de Baisieux and he was not like to die unless the stiffening sickness took him. For some reason, more associated with a newly filled goblet than anything else, Geoffrey now felt he had vindicated himself and settled back to enjoy the party.

Later he was called upon to sing. A handsome lute, also part of the plunder, was thrust into his hands By then most of the rowdier drunks were either under the tables or had left the hall to settle elsewhere the quarrels they had started A gentle melancholy pervaded the remaining celebrants. It seemed appropriate to sing laments, and the only one Geoffrey could call to mind at the moment was King Richard's song, written when he was a prisoner in Germany. The fine logic of drunkenness immediately connected Coeur de Lion, who had been a prisoner, with Léon de Baisieux, who was now a prisoner, and fixed the name in Geoffrey's memory.

Perhaps Geoffrey would have done something about the man once his interest and sense of responsibility had been awakened, but the next day was even busier than the one before. Count Ferrand arrived to ratify the alliance with King John—and to receive his share of the booty. Salisbury, Dammartin, and Holland were fully occupied with their noble guest. Geoffrey was completely immersed in his duty as temporary quartermaster. Meanwhile, most of the knights, afflicted with high spirits or bad tempers owing to overindulgence, decided to work off their energies. They ranged further afield than they should have and ran directly into the main body of Philip's forces. For their carelessness, they were punished by being badly beaten and taking heavy losses. Finally, those remaining disengaged and retreated in decent order.

The news carried by the bloody survivors stimulated even more frantic activity. Ferrand said hasty goodbyes and rode off to rejoin his own army, taking with him Dammartin, William of Holland and those knights who had come to join his service, and most of the mercenary troops. Geoffrey completed the loading of the English ships and captured French vessels with all haste and then ordered that the beached vessels be set afire; there was no longer time to refloat them. Even when they were back in England, Geoffrey had his hands full. Salisbury rode at once to bring his brother the good news. Unloading, storage, division of the spoils, and discharge of some of the ships pressed into service, which would be replaced by the captured French vessels, were left in Geoffrey's hands. Then Geoffrey was summoned to court to give an accounting of what he had done.

The problems of one minor French prisoner were pushed out of Geoffrey's mind by the new storm gathering in England. When John had the news of the brilliant success of Salisbury's expedition, he dismissed the army gathered to resist invasion. This was now completely out of the question since Philip's ships and supplies were either in his enemy's hands or burnt to cinders. The news from Flanders in the next weeks remained excellent. Philip withdrew under severe pressure from the coalition of Lowlanders and German duchies under the Emperor Otto that Dammartin had been working for years to establish. There was no doubt that the French king had suffered a heavy reversal, Geoffrey told Joanna when he was finally given permission to return home. Not only was Philip short of men and money, but the confidence of his allies was shaken. It was the perfect time to recapture Normandy and to make good the other losses on the Continent in John's opinion.

"And he is perfectly right," Geoffrey said heavily to Joanna in the privacy of their bedchamber.

The joy with which Joanna had received him back from his foray into Flanders had done something to mitigate Geoffrey's doubts about her feelings. When he now said to himself, "I know she loves me" there was somewhat more certainty in him—but there was still something missing.

Joanna touched Edwina, who was brushing her hair, and gestured for the maid to leave. When the door closed behind her, she said, "Your words are very fair, my lord, but your looks are sad. A year ago you seemed eager enough to go to France, and only last month, you could hardly wait to go aboard ship for Flanders. Since I cannot believe that you have so soon had your fill of fighting, I cannot understand what troubles you."

He raised his eyes from the dregs of the wine in the goblet he was turning round and round in his hands. "It is nothing to do with *me*. You may laugh at me, Joanna, but I am sorry for my uncle."

"You too?" Joanna exclaimed with disgust. "My mother writes that she believes Ian's softness of heart has gone to his head. Like you, he is overwhelmed with pity for the king. I do not know what ails you both. John has surely given you sufficient proof of his peculiar love—he would love to have both your heads delivered to him on a silver salver."

"That is past—"

"Past? Do you too suffer from softening of the head? Have you ever known John to forgive or forget a grudge?"

Geoffrey laughed wryly. "At least you know whereof you speak. I have never come across any person, man or woman, more tenacious of a purpose than you."

"You are not just," Joanna protested. "I may be tenacious of purpose, but not of hate—"

"Not of hate? What do you call your feeling for my uncle?"

"I do not hate the king," Joanna said indignantly. "Why should I? He has never done me or mine the least harm. Nonetheless, I do not forget—not ever, not for a moment—that he *wishes* us harm. We are only safe from him so long as we watch to see that we fall into no traps he has laid. Do not you be a fool, Geoffrey. Your uncle has tried more than once to end your life, and he will never give over trying."

"Perhaps—" Geoffrey shrugged. "But he seems much changed and chastened. Mayhap this reconciliation to the Church has gone deeper than we first thought. Ian says—"

"I know what Ian says," Joanna interrupted impatiently. "I love Ian dearly. He has been a father to me, true and tender, but you know what he is. If the devil himself came to Ian with a sad story, Ian would soon be dropping tears over him and trying to help."

Geoffrey could not help laughing, but his frown returned. "In any case, this is naught to do with Ian or myself. It is true that if John attacked Philip now he would have a fair chance to win back Normandy and strengthen his position in the south. It is the best chance there has been or is like to be, yet the barons will not agree. They excuse themselves by saying that John is still excommunicate, but it is only an excuse. They do not wish to go to France."

"And why should they?" Joanna rejoined. "Perhaps a few who lost lands there might desire the return of their holdings, but most have no interest. Moreover, you should ask yourself whether Normandy will welcome King John. It has been told to me that when the Norman barons begged for the king's help in 1204 he could not be bothered to come to them. Another thing, to speak the truth, is that Philip is a better overlord than John. He is greedy, desiring to swallow all, but once the lands are his he is not unjust or unreasonable. It is my belief that the Norman barons would fight hard to repel John."

That was the truth. Geoffrey rose restlessly and paced the room, fingering the gold-embroidered curtains of the bed and adding a little more wine to his goblet. "All this is nothing to the point," he said irritably. "I said I was sorry for my uncle, and I am. This time he is right in the sense that it is the most favorable time to make war. If we went now, we might succeed; if we go later, when Philip has had time to regather his strength, we may not. Yet John will never give up the hope of retaking Normandy. That means that sooner or later we *will* go, and if we lose John will be bitterly blamed—and it will not be his fault.''

For the next few months, however, it did not look as if there would be much chance for John to achieve his purpose. The king took the first rebuff of his barons with amazing calm. Instead of thundering threats and denunciations, he did all in his power to remove their objections. He urgently summoned the archbishop of Canterbury and the exiled bishops to come home and absolve him of excommunication, sending assurances that they would be safe and restitution would be made. On July 16, Stephen Langton landed at Dover. The king met him and fell prostrate at his feet. The archbishop lifted him and kissed him. Within a few days the formalities were completed. John was absolved of all sin and renewed his coronation oath. All was sweetness and light.

Again John called a great council to be held at St. Albans on August 4. Between July 21 when the summons went out and the actual convening of the council, John made all the arrangements for governing England while he was absent in France and recalled his barons to war service. They came, but they had conceived a new device for frustrating the king's purpose. They complained that the long period they had spent guarding against invasion had impoverished them. They would go to France with the king, but only if he paid their expenses.

Now the velvet glove slipped a little. His differences with the Church settled, John felt he had a strong ally. Nonetheless, he was reasonable. He said that he was more impoverished than his nobles. He had contributed to their expenses while they waited for Philip on Barham Down; he was strained to the uttermost paying restitution to the Church while they had benefited from the Church funds he had taken to spare them the expense of the Welsh war. Most important, they *owed* him service by the law and custom of feudal tenure, and he would not yield to their extortion.

At this point, Ian sent Alinor and little Simon home to Roselynde. It was not easily accomplished. Alinor was ready to send Simon home to be cared for by Joanna, but she wished to stay. She feared that John would see her departure as a first step on Ian's part toward treason. Ian acknowledged that it might arouse the king's suspicions but he would not take the chance that Alinor might be seized and used as a hostage. Geoffrey, who had answered the king's summons, would not take Joanna to court for exactly the same reason. Throughout the hot days of early August, the two women busied themselves as well as they could with the daily duties of the keep and lands—and kept one ear constantly cocked for the hasty tread of a messenger.

In a few days they knew the worst had befallen. John ordered the men to set sail, and they refused. In an attempt to shame them all, John himself, with his closest companions and his household, took ship. Salisbury was among those who followed and Geoffrey went with his father, unwilling and heavy-hearted at taking part in a fiasco that might turn into a real disaster, but incapable of adding to Salisbury's misery.

On shore, the unifying determination not to be dragged into a foreign venture when they were already drained did not last. Two parties formed, those who wished to defy the king utterly and force him to acknowledge that he could call upon the lords only when they wished to be called and those who did not wish to serve abroad but wanted to show that they were willing to obey the king in other things.

The more rebellious of the two groups was largely composed of northern lords who had no interest in France at all. These struck their tents and promptly left for home as soon as the king departed. With them went Ian, still hoping against hope that he could bring them to reason and prevent armed rebellion. He left messages for the king to this effect with Peter des Roches and Aubery de Vere, but there was little hope in any of them that John would believe him or, rather, there was little hope John would not seize the opportunity to declare Ian an outlaw.

The next news came in an agonized letter from Geoffrey. Seeing that his device had failed, the king returned to England. When he realized what had happened, he flew into a rage that drew force from every humiliation he had swallowed with seeming patience since the Welsh rebellion. Abandoning all pretense at legal procedures, John ordered those men who remained in camp to march on and attack those who had left.

"God help me," Geoffrey wrote bitterly, "which shall I betray—my father or my dear father-by-marriage, my loving begetter or my kind lord? We have reasoned and wept and prayed upon our knees. My father has been struck across the face by the king for only begging that those who left be sent warning and ordered to return and explain themselves. We are all mad here and far too close to you for my liking. Close your gates, my love, and do not open them even if Ian or I should come begging shelter."

Joanna's voice faltered and her lips trembled so that she had to stop reading aloud for a moment. The two women clung together, shivering with horror. This was the ultimate disaster, worse than either had feared. Whatever terrors they had conjured up, it had never occurred to them that their husbands could be pitted against each other.

In the end the inconceivable did not happen. John had trusted too much to the pope's acceptance of the idea that any act against the king was an act against the Church. The pope was far away, and Stephen Langton was by no means of the same persuasion as his master on this subject. He was a northerner himself and, in spite of being a long-time resident in France and Italy, he was well aware of the notions current in the north. Langton hurried to intercept the king at Northampton and warned him that the arbitrary punishment of the barons without due process of law would violate the oath he had taken when he was absolved. He had sworn then "to judge his subjects according to the just decrees of his courts" and not according to his own whim or temper.

This interference was not well received. The king turned angrily on the man he had humbly called "father" only a month earlier and told him he had no business to meddle in the secular affairs of the country, that the king's authority over his barons was not subject to the Church. With renewed fury—although it did not seem to those with him that the fury needed renewal—John left Northampton and set out for Nottingham. Grimly, Langton pursued him and, openly defiant, told the full court that the violation of an oath sworn on holy relics was the business of the Church whether the oath concerned secular or religious matters. Furthermore, said Langton, he would excommunicate every single man in the entire army if they moved one step farther with the intention of illegally punishing men who had not been tried or given an opportunity to explain or defend themselves.

At this point John realized what kind of man he was dealing with. This was no mere mouthpiece of the pope. The king's most faithful supporters, the Cantelus, de Bréaute, even Salisbury, had backed away. They would not have done so in the face of a full army, John knew. Yet before a single man, unarmed, gaunt and tired, dressed in a simple priest's robe covered with dust, they quailed like children about to be beaten. John looked at his archbishop, at the firm mouth, the hard jaw, the burning dark eyes and conceived a hatred that put all his other animosities into the class of love.

For one long moment John was tempted to cry out, "Kill him! Kill him!" as his father had cried out in rage when Becket spited him, but the king's voice was frozen in his throat by Langton's glance. Then the insane impulse passed. John remembered what it had cost Henry to make peace with the Church after Becket's murder and the difficulties he had himself undergone to bring himself into the pope's good graces. There were other, far more effective ways to deal with Langton. Slowly, the king swallowed the hot bile of his rage until it coiled, cold and purposeful, under his heart.

Softly and reasonably, he spoke to the archbishop about the rights of a king in the face of overt rebellion. Langton replied more gently but no less firmly that there was no rebellion. No man had raised a weapon or uttered a threat. The king had left the men, and they had taken that as dismissal and had gone home. Put it aside, for now, John said and invited Langton to wash and eat and rest so that the matter could be discussed more fully and more calmly.

John had no real expectation that Langton would change his mind, but what the archbishop had said opened a door. If the barons of the north could be prodded into threat or attack, the king would have won his case out of Langton's own mouth. But the court was not deaf. As soon as John had retired, Geoffrey and Tostig with only three men-at-arms were riding hell-bent for the lands of Ian's chief vassal. That Geoffrey was welcomed in, despite his relationship to the king, was a mark of the respect and affection Ian's men had developed for him over the period of Ian's absence. The vassal listened to what he had to say and, somewhat reluctantly, agreed to send for Ian. The next day he came, hollow-eyed with worry and fruitless effort.

"Do you mean," Ian cried joyfully after hearing Geoffrey's news, "that the king will turn back and bring the action to be judged by a court of peers?"

"That is what the archbishop intends, but I am sure it will not be so easy. The outcome will depend upon the behavior of the men here in the north, I think."

"What do you mean?"

Geoffrey repeated with emphasis Langton's argument that since no man had threatened or attacked the king there had been no rebellion. "Those of us who wish for peace believe that John will do all in his power, short of using arms, to tempt an attack upon him. Then he will be able to use Langton's own words to gag him and take what revenge he likes."

"I do not know. I do not know," Ian muttered. "You think he will come here—and then what?"

"He will camp, march about, perhaps even demand quartering for his men," Geoffrey said slowly. "I do not believe he will raid or do any damage more than can be blamed upon a few undisciplined men. Certainly, he will not threaten battle or demand yielding of any keep. Well, I know he cannot do that. Even as I rode out, I saw priests and monks going among the men of the army and telling them that if they fight, except to defend themselves against attack, the archbishop of Canterbury in his own person would excommunicate them and condemn them to hell.''

Ian rubbed his hands together nervously. ''Then all that is required is that the king's presence should be ignored. If no one attacks him, he will not attack. Perhaps—just perhaps—I can bring it off! They may arm and close themselves into their keeps. So long as they do not speak at all or speak sweet words, they need do no more. Very well. I must go at once—'' He stared past Geoffrey. ''I must go in two directions at the same time. God! I am so tired.''

Geoffrey looked at his father-by-marriage and was suddenly aware that Ian was not an invincible and tireless god. He was a man, and no longer a young man. Here and there were threads of silver that gleamed among the black curls. There were ugly gray patches under his dark eyes, and his cheeks seemed to have fallen in.

''Can I go either way for you, my lord?'' Geoffrey asked.

''How long can you be absent from court without danger?'' Ian wanted to know.

''I doubt time will make much difference,'' Geoffrey replied drily. ''If John wishes to take offense, he will be no angrier for a week than for a day. And my father knows where I am and what my purpose is.''

Ian was not sure himself whether the sigh he uttered was of relief or regret. He was sorry that Geoffrey's very necessary action would probably reawaken John's hatred, but since it was already so he might as well make sure that the hatred had not been stirred in vain. The next day Ian rode off to try to bring Vesci's men to see reason and Geoffrey went to propose the same things to the remainder of Ian's vassals.

To the great benefit of the nation, they were successful. John spent the next two weeks vainly marching his army up and down the hills of Lancashire and Yorkshire without gaining so much as an angry look or word. Again crisis was averted, but the breach between king and nobles grew wider and deeper. Well aware that his intervention had merely placed a plaster over a festering sore without cleaning it, Langton made a strong effort at the council called to meet at London on August 25 to provide a basis for a more stable, more permanent relationship between the king and his barons.

He invited a number of the most influential lords to come to him so that he might better understand and perhaps help solve their differences with the king. Every man invited came, and came promptly. There was nothing secret in the meetings. Openly avowed king's men were invited as well as those who complained against John. Naturally, the most eager were men like Ian and Geoffrey, who could neither bear the king's ways nor bear to violate their oaths of fealty to him.

Three main results came out of the meetings. The first was a clear statement of how the barons wanted a king to act. The second was to give the archbishop a most accurate and rather unpleasant picture of the king he felt it his duty to guide. Among the points made in the statement, the first mentioned and the unanimous support given to the desire for assurances against imprisonment and injustice did not trouble Langton much. Every king, even the Holy Father, was accused of those faults because the guilty cried that they were put upon unfairly even more loudly than the innocent.

What surprised Langton was the prominence given to protection of daughters and widows and the passion with which the incorporation of separate mention of women, as distinct from other heirs, was urged. Generally, females were not worth mentioning in a state document, yet John's men devoted two separate, special articles to them and grew pale or red with passion in pressing their point when the archbishop questioned the need. That special protection for women should be mentioned and defined even before the question of service overseas and scutage, which had been the overt causes of a near rebellion, had an unpleasant significance.

The third result was one unknown to the participants in the archbishop's conferences. John promptly dispatched an emissary to the pope complaining that Langton was plotting against him with his nobles. A substantial sum of money went with the messengers together with the reminder that the attempt to curb the king's power was directed as much against Innocent as against himself. If his knights could not be ordered to fight overseas, he pointed out, it would be impossible for him to go on crusade or to support the pope in any struggle that should arise on the Continent. Consoled by the expectation that he would soon wield a whip that would tame Langton, John maintained his outward calm and even seemed to consider the proposals the archbishop made as a basis for a permanent peace with the barons.

A golden autumn followed. Harvests were plentiful and cattle grew fat in the fields where sun and rain succeeded each other in perfect proportion. The boughs of the trees hung low with the heavy burden of ripe fruit and nuts carpeted the ground below the hazel hedges and walnut trees. Gazing upon their full granaries, their bulging cellars, their enormous hay ricks, and their fat food animals, the barons began to think less harshly of a little martial exercise well away from their own rich lands. Perhaps it would not be so bad an idea to fight Philip in Poitiers. It would not be impossible to win back Normandy and, in any case, France was rich. There should be handsome booty to be had.

While the smaller landlords' attitude thus softened toward the king's desire, the great barons also came around to believing that a war in France might not be worth opposing. The king's absolute fixity of purpose over so many years discouraged opposition. Sooner or later the attempt would have to be made, and this time truly seemed the best. Although Philip's forces were no longer in such disarray as they had been in the spring, the coalition that Renaud Dammartin had worked so long to form was now well-wielded together, and the leaders were ready to press their advantage by attacking Philip from the northeast. If John attacked from Poitiers and the Emperor Otto from Flanders, Philip would be torn in two and likely to be beaten on both fronts.

Moreover, the matter of the withdrawal of the northern barons without permission and the charter hung, as it were, suspended. It was understood without words that if the king got his way in the matter of the war with France, he would forget the controversy over the withdrawal. His attitude toward the charter was more ambivalent, but not unreasonable. It contained nothing, except for the provision about serving overseas, that he had not promised many times before. However, these things had never before been written down and sealed so that the words might be read aloud at some other time. In the past, knowledge of the promises had rested on the memories of witnesses, some of whom could always be counted upon to contradict the others. A written charter could not have doubts cast upon it and might be inconvenient.

Geoffrey and Joanna had been summoned from Hemel, where they had finally taken up residence once the most immediate threat of rebellion was past, to a family conference at Salisbury. Ian and Alinor were also there so that they could decide upon a unified stand to take on these questions. On the subject of the charter, there was no difference of opinion; all approved the idea heartily, even Salisbury. On the question of the war with France, the men were all on one side, the women all on the other.

"Of course, it is possible that we will lose more than we will gain—when was it ever otherwise with war?" Ian retorted angrily to a piece of reasoned pleading by Alinor, "but it does not matter. If John summons me, I will go. I came near to personal treason last spring to avert a civil war. Certainly, I will not violate my oath, or even seem to do so, for a lesser cause. I tell you, it is my duty, and I will go."

"But you yourself helped write the charter which says that it is *not* your duty to go," Lady Ela pointed out, her voice trembling.

"The king has not acknowledged the charter," Ian reminded her grimly.

"And you know that does not matter to me," Salisbury put in gently, patting his wife's shoulder. "Charter or no charter, if John asks something of me that I can with honor perform, I must do it. Nay, Ela, do not weep. He has given me everything—even you, my dear. How can I deny him what is so near his heart and a thing that is no way wrong or unwise?''

Eyes turned to Geoffrey, who was leaning back in a chair fondling Brian's head, which rested in his lap. He flushed slightly when he realized both older men were waiting for him to speak, according him full rights as an adult member of the group. He was quick enough to take command on his own, but in the presence of his father and his lord was content to obey. Apparently, however, he must pull his own weight—or, he thought sardonically, glancing at the faces of the women, share the blame—in this decision.

"Oh, I will go," he said indifferently. "I never thought so ill of a war against Philip in France, and now that we have strong allies, plenty of ships and supplies, it is a good time."

The decisions and reasoning of the men were as characteristic as the reactions of the women. Ela sobbed disconsolately. She did not argue or plead. Occasionally, if his purpose was not really fixed, Ela could change Salisbury's mind, but she did not hope for that in this case. Once he had brought out the argument of his debt to his brother, nothing would move him. She wept because she was afraid and because it was a relief to her.

"Then I go also," Alinor said.

"Alinor—" Ian protested despairingly.

Since Joanna was old enough to be a really satisfactory deputy, Alinor had accompanied her husband everywhere, but not actually to war. In Ireland, she stayed either with her vassal or with Pembroke's wife, Isobel, who was her oldest and dearest friend. This was the most unreasonable stand Alinor had ever taken, yet Ian knew no way of stopping her from doing what she said. If he refused to take her, she would follow on her own, which was far more dangerous. Seeing the horror in her husband's eyes and in Salisbury's, Alinor began to laugh.

"Not to the battlefield, my love," she explained. "Isabella has suggested that I make one of her party. She likes me because I know how to amuse her and do not sleep with John—not that she would much object to the latter, but it makes for ease of speech between us. I will go with the queen."

"Who said Isabella would go?"

"She does go," Salisbury confirmed. "Prince Henry will remain in the care of Peter of Winchester, Pembroke, and the legate, but John takes Isabella, Richard, his daughters, and Alinor of Brittany. Henry will be here as a symbol of the king, and he will be safe because there would be no purpose in seizing him while Richard and the others are safe with John."

There was a momentary silence while this remark was digested. Everyone knew the truth. John was not at all fond of his eldest son, so holding him to ransom or as hostage could have little effect in controlling the king so long as his second heir was safe in his own hands. It was a pity. There was much good in young Henry, but he was learning deceit and how to shift blame to others from the unfortunate relationship he had with his father. The fact that the boy had a quick mind and a pliable nature only made matters worse. He half understood far too much of what went on around him while he was yet too young to see the deeper significance of the conflicts.

"But is it wise to bring Isabella into France where Hugh de Lusignan—" Ian began.

Salisbury shrugged. "I raised the point that Lusignan might regard that as an insult, seeing that John married the girl only a week or so before she was supposed to marry Hugh, but it is so many years. And John—" Salisbury shrugged again. "He watches her. I do not know why, she is so stupid—"

Joanna could have solved that puzzle, but she did not really hear what Salisbury said. She sat and plied her needle in silence, as was fitting. Her expression was placid, her hand steady, and her eyes, which might have told a different story, were fixed upon her work. She had hoped that Salisbury and Ian would order Geoffrey to stay to deputize for them in case an emergency should arise here in England. The hope had flamed high when, after Salisbury had described the king's arrangements about troops, he had raised this point.

"No," Geoffrey protested. "While Pembroke, Winchester, and Langton hold the reins of government, there can be no great upheaval. In all small matters Joanna can manage very well if she has Sir Guy to lead the men in actual fighting. If she should need more daring advice, she can call upon Adam. He is near seventeen now and I warrant he is sound for the task of defending a keep or driving away attackers even if he be not ripe for leading a great battle. I measured him last winter when we feared invasion. So well had he dealt with Kemp and the men on his other lands that I had naught to say to him."

It was not unexpected that Salisbury would accept this view eagerly. He was near fifty and beginning to feel the weight of his years, and he had become very dependent upon Geoffrey as an aide. Joanna glanced despairingly at Ian, but he only smiled reassuringly at her.

"You do not need to worry, my love," he comforted. "I dare swear Geoffrey has judged the matter correctly to a hairsbreadth. Winchester is John's man, but he is wise also. He will squeeze those who remain until they cry out, but not so hard they will dare take up arms against William of Pembroke. Moreover, Langton will watch over all. I know John has not invested him with any of the power that rightfully goes to the archbishop and that the legate has appointed priests on John's recommendation in spite of Langton's will. Nonetheless, both Winchester and the legate understand that Langton has the trust of the barons, even those most bitterly opposed to John who will not come with him. If Langton speaks out against something, the king's deputies will listen. You need not fear that there will be any serious disorder in England."

Since this was exactly the opposite of what Joanna

wanted to hear, Ian's kind speech served no particular purpose beyond exasperating his wife. Alinor understood that Joanna, although she might not admit it, would cheerfully have precipitated a cataclysm in England if that would keep Geoffrey at home. She inspected her daughter's figure carefully, but there was no sign in the narrow waist and small, high breasts that Joanna had conceived. Apparently, the girl took after her in being relatively unfertile. That was unfortunate. A full nursery and carrying a young one beneath one's heart was a great comforter of the spirit.

"But you must not feel that you will suffer from ennui just because Ian says the land will lie quiet," Alinor suggested with a lift of one brow. That was obviously a jest. With the responsibility for Alinor's and Geoffrey's lands, even if Adam were given the responsibility for Ian's vassals, Joanna would have more than enough to keep her busy. "I will leave Simon with you," Alinor continued, laughing. "He will as easily keep you from dullness as any war."

Joanna's face lit with pleasure. In fact, her mind and her mother's had been very close. She also had been regretting bitterly that she was not with child. Geoffrey did not seem to care. A few times, believing that her barrenness might be the cause of Geoffrey's half-concealed dissatisfaction, Joanna had mentioned her regret at being unable to provide him with an heir. Instead of showing any sensitivity on the subject, he only laughed, asked if she were taking this subtle way to complain of his efforts in that direction, and promised to try harder. When he saw she was really troubled, he had comforted her more seriously, pointing out her mother's case and that of the queen, who had not conceived for seven years and then, in a shorter span, had had five healthy young ones.

It was not the fear of being permanently barren that bothered Joanna. She was only afraid that Geoffrey would get himself killed before she had something of him to keep. Simon was no substitute for a child of Geoffrey's of course, but Joanna knew he would certainly keep her busy and amused. Watching her, Geoffrey was again stabbed by jealousy. It was not that he resented her love for Simon—no one could help loving Simon, engaging devil that he was. Only, whatever distress Joanna had seemed to feel over his departure, which was not much judging from her silence and tranquility, appeared to be completely assuaged by Ian's assurance there would be no danger and by the offer of Simon as an object of attention.

Geoffrey told himself that it was normal and natural for Joanna to think of him as a protector; that was, after all, his first duty toward her. It was also true that Joanna needed an object to work for and care for. Would it ever matter to her who that object was? Geoffrey knew he was an idiot to fret over such a stupidity. He had the most beautiful and most dutiful wife a man could hope for. She was buxom in bed and at board, merry and affectionate. What did it matter that she offered the same heart to all those she loved, since he was one of them?

It was selfish to wish to be first with her. It was insane to be hurt because she did not weep and try to hold him back from going to France. Since he must go, it would be dreadful to endure the pain of such a parting. He did not really want a weeping wife. Nonetheless he wanted something!

CHAPTER TWENTY-FOUR

On February 6, 1214, John sailed for La Rochelle. With him went Ian and Alinor but not Salisbury and Geoffrey. The only man in the world John trusted as he trusted himself would go to join his allies in Flanders to be sure their purpose did not waver. It was necessary for John to begin operations early because the men of Poitou and La Manche liked him even less than the English. He had not oppressed them personally much, but memories are long in the country of the *langue d'oc*. There Richard was still adored, his faults now forgotten, and John was not only compared unfavorably to him in military matters but also accounted somewhat guilty of his death, even though John and Richard were not at war at that time. They knew that John had dealt treacherously with Richard, and that rankled in memory.

Thus, John needed to make sure Aquitaine would be a firm base, a sound anvil upon which the hammer of the attack from Flanders could smash Philip of France. To do this it was first necessary to show enough force to bring the doubtful Poitevin lords to heel. Second, there was the problem of the Lusignans. Since John had stolen Isabella, virtually on the eve of her wedding, the family had been his inveterate enemies, and they were very powerful.

Through February and March the news Joanna received was all excellent. The fortress of Milecu fell almost at once, and this brought in a number of barons who realized John was not only serious in his intentions but had power enough to enforce them. In March, John took his army down the Charente through Angoulême to the Limousin. Those nobles who did not come voluntarily to do fealty and to swell his forces, he reduced with an efficient ferocity that served as an object lesson to others. In April, he marched into Gascony, repeating his tactics and making all secure in the south at his back. Men did fealty and came themselves or gave John hostages. The king made certain that the tale of the hanging of the Welsh hostages was told and retold, both of the kind care they had had while their kin were faithful and of the ruthless execution when those who gave them as pledges rebelled.

By the end of April, John was ready to turn his attention to Lusignan. First, he let it be known that he was prepared to be conciliatory. He offered his eldest legitimate daughter, also called Joan, to the son of that Hugh who had been betrothed to Isabella as a reasonable palliation of the offense he had given. However, he made it plain that he was not sorry when the offer was ignored. Ian wrote to Alinor and she to Joanna that the king, "felt the hand of God upon him. Since he has settled his differences with the Church and the pope makes everything easy for him—even robbing churchmen and the Church itself so that John's burden should be less—a cloud is lifted from his mind. Never has the king been so sure in war and so surely right. All that he lays his hand to turns to our good."

Although they were ready, John waited a few weeks until the truce he had made with the counts of La Manche and Eu came to an end. Not even in so small a matter would he violate his word, given with holy relics to witness, at this time. Then he marched on Mervant and took it—though it was said to be impregnable—by assault. From there they moved to Voucant, but that was a harder nut to crack because Lusignan's brother Geoffrey and two of his sons were in the keep. The defense might be expected to be more determined, and they brought up their siege engines. In three days it could be seen that an assault would soon be possible.

Early in June, Joanna had news of what seemed to be the final outcome of the quarrel with the Lusignans. Alinor wrote, "Ian is here for a few days rest. He had an arrow in the thigh when they took Mervant, but naturally did not regard that as any reason not to go with the king to Voucant.

Fortunately, an assault was not necessary there. Just as they were making ready to storm the walls, Hugh Lusignan himself rode in and made his homage to John. Better yet, he persuaded his brother Geoffrey and the cubs to throw themselves upon the king's mercy. Then— I am almost growing to believe Ian's notion that God's hand is in this matter— word came to them that Louis, Philip's son, was besieging Geoffrey Lusignan's castle of Montcontour. Truce was declared between the king and Lusignan and they all rode off together to attack a common enemy. Louis promptly lifted the siege and withdrew so that Hugh and Geoffrey saw the benefit of being at peace with their overlord.''

''Ian is in the best of spirits,'' Alinor continued, ''even though he is hobbling about like a cripple. He thinks the contract made to marry Joan to Hugh's son will heal the hurt to Hugh's pride that was done when Isabella was reft from him. I, however, fear that it was not only Hugh's pride that was hurt. I think he desired, and still desires, Isabella herself. Ian says I am mad and that no man as sensible as Hugh could want a movable statue like Isabella, but he forgets that Isabella was fourteen when John took her and Hugh was, himself, very young. Since then Hugh has not seen her, and I believe her image has grown more perfect in his mind. He cannot, after all, know what she really is. To me, this bodes ill. Hugh is said to be an honorable man. I doubt that he will attack John treacherously, but I fear that he will find some 'honorable' stratagem to do the king hurt.''

Alinor ran the feather of the quill back and forth against her cheek. She did not wish to add to her daughter's unhappiness, but there was a warning she must transmit. ''Having mentioned Isabella, I must tell you that although she is not, in general, ill natured, being too much enamored of herself to feel much about anyone else, she has conceived for you and for Geoffrey a hatred that is deep and lasting. I am very, very glad, my love, that Geoffrey will be with his father in Flanders rather than here. You must do whatever is in your power to prevent Geoffrey from coming here. The queen's gentlemen are often at the front with the king and all of them know that Isabella would grant *any* favor to the man who accomplished Geoffrey's death. What makes this worse is that they are aware this would please John almost as much as Isabella, so long as Salisbury does not come to know his approval. Ordinarily this would not matter, Geoffrey being well able to take care of himself, but it is altogether too easy for a stray arrow or blow to be launched from behind in a battle.''

Rather than alarming Joanna, the warning served to reconcile her a little to the situation that existed. Geoffrey had already left for Flanders with his father. Perhaps he would be better off there, even when it came to war, than at home. Had Geoffrey remained in England, John or Isabella could have found some cause to summon him to France. As it was, the king would let well enough alone, knowing that his brother's suspicions would be aroused by a singling out of Geoffrey. All in all, the letter left Joanna in a strange, uneasy mood. Her pride in the prowess of the English fighting men was flattered by John's successes; yet, had the king's attempt to bring his French barons to obedience failed, likely the attack in Flanders would not have been carried through. Joanna could only pray that Ian was wrong, that God was not directing John's moves, and that the Lusignans would somehow bring about John's defeat without involving Ian in the disaster.

Certainly, there seemed to be no immediate answer to Joanna's prayer. In the English camp in Flanders there was great rejoicing at the smoothness with which the plans to crush France were proceeding. Every move John made was successful. A feint toward the French army drove them to retreat again and permitted him to seize Ancennis. Then he marched upon Angers as if to encircle it and, when the defenders drew in upon the city, he struck west across the border of Brittany and attacked and took the seaport of Nantes. This contained a very rich prize, the person of Philip's cousin, Peter of Dreux, who ruled Brittany in the right of his wife, Alice.

Having thus secured a seaport closer and more convenient

to his operations, John turned his attention again toward Angers. The citizens and garrison of that city had seen enough. They opened the gates and welcomed the king into the principal seat of his father's holdings, long lost to him. However, a few miles outside of Angers stood the fortress of Roche-au-Maine, and there Philip's seneschal held firm. In the middle of June, John settled his forces around this stronghold intending to reduce it and remove the most important focus of resistance to his power in Anjou.

Philip's son Louis, however, also believed that Roche-au-Maine was essential. Gathering his forces, the French prince began to move upon the king. During the last week in June, John's spies reported this and the king wrote to Salisbury, Ferrand of Flanders, and the Emperor Otto. He urged them to attack Philip, who was on the Flemish border, as soon and as strongly as possible. It was, John said, the best opportunity they would have as his forces were far stronger than Louis's, yet Louis would not dare leave Roche-au-Maine to be taken. If Philip could not come to help Louis, John expected to beat the prince easily and the whole south of France would be open to him. Moreover, Louis would be unable to come to his father's support; therefore, the task of the allies in Flanders would also be much easier.

Unfortunately, when John's letters arrived, his allies were not ready to do his bidding. It was through no fault of their own. Ferrand was under arms and, of course, Salisbury had been in Flanders for some weeks, cleaning out small detachments of French and French sympathizers in a keep here and there. Otto, however, was having trouble gathering his Rhineland princes and dukes. Although all were willing to fight Philip, they were so busy bickering among themselves that it was difficult to drag them away from their private feuds. At last they mustered and began to march northwest.

Before Otto had reached the border, John's fortunes had taken a drastic and desperate turn for the worse. Hurried messengers carried the news that the newly cowed nobles of Poitou had played the king false. When he summoned a council to decide the order of battle against Louis, they said with one voice that they would not fight. Treachery, John thundered. Lusignan denied the charge. He had done his lord's bidding in taking Ancennis and Nantes; he had come here to the siege and had done good service. However, he pointed out, Philip was *also* his overlord; he held lands in France as well as in John's territories. Thus he could not attack his overlord's son.

At this point, John lost his hard-won veneer of a rational and moderate king. Instead of discussing reasonably the number of men owed him against the number owed Philip and demanding in a rational way that the men owed to him be left, either with a leader of their master's choice or a leader to be supplied by John, the king said what could not be endured. Ian nearly wept aloud, but he was powerless to interfere in any way, and Salisbury, who might have been able to curb his brother, was hundreds of miles away.

Naturally, having been insulted in their own persons, the Poitevin lords gathered up their men, every last one, and deserted. But in their eyes was satisfaction and laughter, not anger. They had counted upon the Angevin temper to extricate them, without violation of their oaths, from a position they were unwilling to hold. John was between two very hot fires. He could not punish them, because Louis would fall upon him from the rear. He no longer had strength enough to fight Louis; if he stayed in Anjou he would be defeated. If Louis pursued him, he would be defeated anyway.

Whether John sensed the malicious delight of the Poitevins or his own loss of control affected him, Ian could not decide. All he saw was the effect. Suddenly John was shaken to the core. His absolute belief that God was his supporter had been destroyed. Ian could not understand it. The king had had setbacks before and had not doubted. Agreed, they could not continue the siege or fight Louis, but all was not lost. If Philip was defeated or taken prisoner by the army in Flanders, all might yet be well. The changeable Poitevins would come crawling back, and Louis could be broken—that is, if they were not first broken themselves.

Ian was in a dreadful position. He knew John's hatred for him had been viciously reinforced by his part in the quarrel with the northern nobles. For everyone's sake, he avoided contact with the king as much as possible and now, in this bitter moment, he dared not offer either comfort or advice or even inquire as to John's plans. He did not know whether John would send news of the situation to Flanders. Doubt held him inactive for a few days, but he dared wait no longer and wrote to Salisbury describing what had happened.

"All is not completely black," he concluded. "It seems that when Louis had news that we had lifted the siege of Roche-au-Maine he believed that we were moving to attack him and, instead of coming to battle, he retreated in haste. This gave us good time to regroup and to move in good order and without loss to La Rochelle. I believe that Louis will remain on guard in this part of the country for a time, but it cannot be long before he understands the blow we have sustained. When he is sure the king is powerless, doubtless he will move the larger part of his army to his father's support. Thus I urge you, if you intend to attack Philip at all that you do so very soon. If you defeat the French king, all may yet be saved and your chance of winning over him will be far greater before Louis's forces are added to his own."

The news from Aquitaine distressed Salisbury, but he agreed wholeheartedly with Ian, and his determination and that of the others to come to grips with Philip did not change. He, Ferrand, and Renaud Dammartin all wrote urging Otto to make haste. By the third week in July Otto had arrived at Vivelles, where he declared himself equally unshaken, and the combined forces moved on to Valenciennes immediately.

They were just in time to avert complete disaster. The delay caused by Otto's vassals had given Philip the time to summon the full strength of his levies. The French king was already moving into Flanders with the intention of cutting Otto off from his English and Flemish allies. The meeting at

Valenciennes eliminated that hope. Philip turned back from Tournai and settled himself into an open plain near the village of Bouvines.

On the twenty-fourth of July, Salisbury, Dammartin, Ferrand, Otto and the chief men of each group met in person to discuss their next move. As his father's right hand, Geoffrey was present. He knew he would have nothing to say about what was decided, but he had no quarrel with that. He had no special knowledge or skill that could excuse the intrusion of his opinion into this high-level council of war, and these men—at least Dammartin and his father—were experts. Geoffrey's business was to listen and to learn.

The first need was to arrange the men, and one of Ferrand's people described to them the countryside, in particular naming the strongholds in the area and indicating their sympathies. At one point Geoffrey was startled by the familiarity of a name.

"Baisieux?" he interrupted. "Is the lord there called Léon?"

"He was, but he is prisoner in England, my lord. The keep is held by two ladies, his mother and his wife. They will offer neither harm nor help because they will not open their gates at all, except to a force too strong for them to resist."

Geoffrey nodded and made a mental note to go and pay his respects to the ladies when the battle was over. He felt slightly guilty about Sir Léon, as if the fact that he had wounded him left a responsibility for his welfare. He had heard nothing about the man after he returned to England, but that v as not surprising. The fact that, a full year later, he was still a prisoner meant that his womenfolk could not scrape together the ransom and that his overlord, Philip or whoever, would not pay for him—or that the women did not want him back, of course. Whatever the cause, Geoffrey was curious about Sir Léon's fate and stopped Ferrand's man to get directions to Baisieux.

It did not take long to make the physical arrangements. The terrain was easy, flat and open, with a river behind the

French forces. Ferrand would hold the left flank; Otto, as fitted his rank and position as titular leader, would hold the center. Salisbury, with the English forces, and Dammartin, who had no real army but was followed by a group of devoted knights, would hold the right. That left only the time of battle to be decided.

"At once," Hugh of Boves said. He quoted the proverb, "Delay is dangerous when things are ready." With that, all agreed and the matter was settled.

Afterward, however, there was far too little planning for Geoffrey's taste. He was accustomed to Ian's relatively elaborate outlines for action and reaction in taking or defending a keep, and he had always given his own men detailed instructions for the attacks made in Wales. When he presented this notion privately to his father, Salisbury smiled at him.

"It is different," he remarked. "A keep, even a large one, is small compared to what we have here. A plan can be settled because word can come from all parts of the battle in only a few minutes. Thus, orders may be changed or canceled. Here, we may be spread over a considerable distance and any messenger is more like to be killed or so delayed in fighting to protect himself that communication is almost impossible. Also, we do not know each other's men very well."

"You fear treachery?" Geoffrey asked, appalled.

"Not from Ferrand or Otto, but if one of their men should be in Philip's pay, which is not at all impossible, and came to me saying I should change my plan, might not Otto or Ferrand think *I* was treacherous? It is better to act as the situation demands. Besides," Salisbury added drily, "I do not think at my time of life I would like to be told how to arrange my battle or where or when to attack. And I do not believe Otto or Ferrand would like it either."

It was all reasonable, but still Geoffrey was disturbed. He would have preferred to have one acknowledged leader to whom all could apply for help or direction. Of course, if the leader was a coward or a fool, that was disastrous, but at least the disaster would be apparent early and enable the battle to break up with little loss. Geoffrey chided himself for carping. On his part of the field there was one leader, and a good one. If the other battles failed, they might still turn the tide or they would be able to hold together and withdraw with honor.

The last idea brought a pang of anxiety, restating a question that had come to his mind earlier in the day. Geoffrey was not a vainglorious fool in military matters. He understood the value of strategic withdrawal from a lost battle, and he knew his father did also, but he wondered if that knowledge could have any influence on Salisbury's behavior in this particular case. His father had been greatly distressed by the tone of John's last letter. Would Salisbury fight on in the face of certain defeat, hoping for a miracle with which to restore John's faith?

Eventually, Geoffrey slipped from his bed, lit a candle, drew on his surcoat in lieu of a bed robe, and sat down to soothe himself by writing to Joanna. He did not, of course, mention any of his doubts nor even much about the battle except to say it was useless to worry because it would be long over before she received the letter. Mostly it was a letter of love, of praise of her beauty and laments of how he missed her and desired her, of assurances of his fidelity, of comparison of her perfections to the failings of the women with whom he had been in company.

"I could almost hate you," he wrote, "for you have destroyed any hope of joy for me outside of yourself. You are like to the sun and have so dazzled and blinded my eyes that I can see nothing else even when I can no longer see you. You will not believe me, I suppose, or will laugh at me, but I have not even taken a whore in all these weeks of weary nights. Beloved, I am sick for you. My loins ache for you. Yet I cannot ease myself elsewhere. You blame me, I know, for love of war, but believe that I do not love it for parting us. Indeed, so does the need for you grow upon me that I fear it will unman me in the end and make me hate war only because it parts us."

The funny—or not so funny—part, Geoffrey thought, was that the whole thing was true, not merely the ordinary lies one wrote to a woman. He smiled wryly and wondered whether Joanna would believe him—and then whether she would care. Then, abruptly, he signed and sealed his letter and laid it aside to be put in with the other dispatches for England. Although he had been glad enough of it at the time, he remembered with pain now that Joanna had never given the smallest sign of jealousy. She had never even mentioned the liaisons he had had with the ladies of the court of which she must have been informed. That notion was no more comfortable than the uneasy thoughts of the battle the next day. Nonetheless, the two discomforts edging each other in and out of his mind made for a kind of confusion that grew into a dazed weariness and slid away into sleep.

Having taken so long to find rest, Geoffrey overslept the next morning. By the time Tostig felt it was necessary to wake him, he had missed mass and needed to rush himself into his armor and then out to organize the men and perform the duties imposed by being his father's aide, while bolting down some bread, cheese, and wine. At the last moment he remembered his letter, seized it, and thrust it up his mailed sleeve. Here it would not interfere with his movement and would be held in place by his gauntlet but could be withdrawn quickly as soon as he found the messenger who was to carry the dispatches.

Geoffrey's first sight of the battlefield, gained from the top of the little rise that had screened the English camp from the French, drove all thoughts of letters or any extraneous matters from his mind. The French were already under arms but Philip had apparently elected not to attack. However, that was not what startled Geoffrey. Philip had ordered that the bridge that spanned the river Marcq be destroyed. It was plain that the French king did not regard this as any ordinary battle. By destroying the bridge, he had eliminated any chance of easy retreat for his men and himself. He planned to fight until he won or was killed or taken prisoner. Geoffrey rode back to tell Salisbury, but his father did not seem surprised. He merely nodded and agreed that this battle would, indeed, break France.

The reply woke a surge of enthusiasm in Geoffrey. If they won, if Philip was forced to disgorge the Angevin territories he had swallowed, perhaps John would be eased in his heart and be willing to live at peace with his barons. Geoffrey thought of the few peaceful months he had had at Hemel with Joanna. Even those had been strained by tension and anxiety, but if that were gone? It would be a sweet life—a sweet life. Only this battle, this one battle in which Philip could be taken, and then home, and Joanna.

Certainly it was a fine day for fighting, clear and bright. The odd stretching of time before a battle was already in effect. It seemed to take terribly long for the men to form, for the knights and mounted men-at-arms to get into the saddle. Geoffrey's own movements seemed to him to be weirdly slow and dreamlike. Yet, when he glanced at the sun, what he believed to have taken hours had occupied no more than minutes.

Knowing that his time sense was unreliable was no real help. Geoffrey found that he was biting his lips, clenching and unclenching his hands, and breathing faster. Orage danced and bucked as the rider's growing tension communicated itself. Geoffrey cursed and curbed the stallion, then patted and praised it, knowing the fault was his own. Although Geoffrey now led his own contingent of knights and men-at-arms, his place was not far from Salisbury. It was arranged that if Salisbury should fall, Renaud Dammartin should command the battle, and if he should be killed or taken prisoner that the responsibility should devolve upon Geoffrey.

Soon, Geoffrey thought, curbing himself as he had curbed his destrier, soon. He could see his father rising in the stirrups to look up and down the field. A squire was sent off. Under his breath, Geoffrey groaned and cursed again. Someone was late or out of position or something else was wrong. More delay. Geoffrey's head lifted sharply. Off to the left there was a confused murmur of sound. Ferrand was engaged! It must be Ferrand because the noise would be louder, the individual cries and clangs cleaner, if it were Otto's force.

"Let us go," Geoffrey hissed. "Let us go so that both edges will pinch Philip and drive him forward into Otto's arms."

That Salisbury's thought was similar was apparent because he was straining upright, almost seeming ready to climb to his feet on top of his horse the better to hurry his squire. Geoffrey ground his teeth with impatience, his eyes set fixedly on Salisbury. He was almost afraid to blink lest he be a part of a second late in driving forward once Salisbury gave the signal to move. At last—hours, weeks, months later—possibly in real time four or five minutes, the young man could be seen returning. Geoffrey lowered his lance into position, tensing all his muscles as he did so to control the trembling of his body.

It did not help, of course. Possibly the tenseness increased the shaking, but Geoffrey did not know how to subdue his characteristic reaction and he was ashamed of it. He was always afraid those near him would believe he shook with fear. In fact, he was not sure that was untrue. Mostly he felt excited and eager, but there was, somewhere inside him, a sense of chill, a dread of being no more or of being so maimed that he would no longer be a man. Had he been capable of attending to what went on around him, beyond his fixed concentration on Salisbury, he would have been relieved of the worry about being thought a coward.

Tostig, just behind and to the left of his master, lowered his own lance and turned his head toward Roger, the castellan of Hemel who was beside him, to Geoffrey's right. "I hope your spurs are well sharpened," he said wryly. "Do you see our lord straining at the leash? Be ready. As soon as Salisbury moves, he will charge. If you are not quick, you will be left behind."

"I have—" the castellan began, but in that moment the squire reached Salisbury and the earl fewtered his own lance and called aloud.

On the sound, Geoffrey clapped spurs to Orage, eased his

hold on the slack of the reins, which were tied to the saddle pommel, and bellowed, "Forward!"

The horse, fretting as it was under the tight rein while it sensed the excitement of its rider, leapt forward eagerly. The French seeing them come up over the little rise, also kicked their horses into action. Geoffrey had no idea of whom, among Philip's noblemen, he would face, and he did not care. He had had little contact with the French court beyond being polite to an envoy now and again and had no friends among Philip's men. In any case, the violence that invariably seized him when combat was offered had a firm grip on him. Somewhere deep inside, old wounds opened, spilling out the encysted bitterness of a rather frail, proud boy who had perforce swallowed the taunts and insults he could not silence.

Geoffrey was light for a full-armed man. His destrier, interbred with the mighty grays of the Roselynde line, was strong and swift. In ten strides Orage had outdistanced Geoffrey's group, although Tostig and Roger of Hemel, roweling their horses like mad, were not far behind. Still, Geoffrey had room to maneuver, which was greatly limited for the more solid line of men opposing him. He did not seem to notice this at first, riding straight as a well-launched arrow toward the man exactly opposite. This was a deception. Whatever the old rage that sprang up in him, lending strength to his arms and ferocity to his movements, Geoffrey was no berserker. He had been well schooled, even overelaborately, because Ian knew Geoffrey's slender body did not have the brute force to batter a path without skill and subtlety.

At the last moment possible, Geoffrey jammed his knee into the destrier's shoulder, sending the well-trained animal off at an angle. In the same instant, he threw himself forward into the lance thrust, taking the man to his right by surprise. Geoffrey's spear slid in under the Frenchman's, and, even though the man turned his own lance when he realized what had happened, there was little force in it because he had not been quite ready. Until Geoffrey's swift maneuver startled him, the Frenchman's attention had been fixed on the castellan of Hemel, whom he had expected to encounter.

The shock of the blow, the Frenchman's shriek as the point penetrated his armor, only whetted Geoffrey's appetite. So many times had the boy Geoffrey struck back when he was physically assaulted and heard laughter from his larger, older tormentors that he still dreamed of pain-filled cries in response to his blows. He wrenched the lance back brutally as his opponent fell and was rewarded with another shriek. That man would fight no more this day, and likely not on any other either. But Geoffrey did not think of that, nor would it have gladdened him if he had. He was far too busy slatting off the lance of the man he had initially been riding toward, pulling his own into position again, and roweling his horse to make it regain the speed the encounter had slowed.

To his left, a little behind the first wave, Geoffrey found another opponent. That one, either inexperienced or a fool, had lifted his head a trifle too far over his shield's edge. Geoffrey caught him in the face. Whether the lance point tore through the metal visor, Geoffrey did not know. His opponent this time did not cry out, but Geoffrey heard, even over the shouts of the men engaging behind him, the sharp crack—like a dry branch snapping beneath the heel—of a broken neck. The lance point was caught in the visor and the man was a total dead weight. Geoffrey pulled and lifted, but the weapon did not come free. The shaft snapped, some two or three feet from the head.

Again, Geoffrey set spurs to Orage, turning him right once more and using the broken shaft to strike aside a lance aimed at him. In the same motion, he released the useless shaft and drew his sword. He was in time for a single blow at the man whose lance he had avoided, but it fell on the shield and did no harm, and the impetus of both destriers carried the combatants past each other. However, there was no lack of opponents; Geoffrey was engaged before he could turn his horse to finish with the man at whom he had struck.

By now the charge was over. The French line was broken, but the knights, led by the warlike bishop of Beauvais, who had fought beside King Richard on the Crusade and against him in the French wars with equal joy and ferocity, were by no means beaten. French and English spread over the field in small groups, each fighting its own battle, each victorious group leaving its dead and wounded where they fell, mingled with the dead and wounded of their enemies, to take on another group. There was little difference in numbers on this wing of the battle, none at all in skill, courage, or determination. Within the first half hour, Geoffrey knew that there would be no quick conclusion. The French would not panic and run, and neither would the English. Both sides would fight until exhaustion or night ended the battle unless one was truly overwhelmed.

Once his initial impetus was halted, Geoffrey's men had a chance to catch up with him. Richard of Elsfield's left side was red with blood, and Tostig had lost his sword because his right arm was broken and cut to the bone. In addition, two English men-at-arms were dead or out of action when that little fracas was over. Geoffrey drew enormous breaths and eased his aching sword arm. Miraculously, he was as yet untouched. His eyes checked his men as his ears checked the battle in general. From the latter source he could not gain much information beyond the fact that both armies were completely engaged. The roar made up of shouts of encouragement, cries of pain and surprise, and battle calls combined with the clang of metal upon metal and the thud of weapons upon wood and leather seemed general.

"Tostig, go back to camp," Geoffrey ordered. "No, do not argue. You are useless to me, with your arm broken and so cut, and you will be a danger to me because I will forever be trying to protect you. Go! Now! While we have time to breathe."

Geoffrey's voice checked. Far away, very faintly through the other sounds of battle, there was a howling. No matter how dim or distant, the sound was unmistakable in its slow swelling. It was the wail of panic, the lament of men broken—not one man or a few, whose voices would be lost—thousands of them. Geoffrey's eyes blazed golden. He could not yet know which side was fleeing away, but from the distance of the sound it was Ferrand's Belgians or the army of the counts of Champagne, Perche, and St. Paul, who were opposed to him. No matter who had failed, however, it would mean even more intense action either in pursuit or defense.

"Now!" Geoffrey ordered more sharply, "Go now!"

He was eager for action again and wished to be rid of his liabilities. Tostig, grimacing with pain, turned away as he was bidden, but his heart was lighter. While Geoffrey had been speaking to Richard of Elsfield, he had time for a few words with Roger of Hemel, who had promised to guard his master without permitting any other concern to distract him. The diminished group drew together. The little time of peace they had, which perhaps had been lengthened by the carnage surrounding them, making others somewhat chary of attack, was over. Even if he could have stretched the time, Geoffrey had no inclination to do so. Nonetheless, his exertions had taken the edge off his first wild fury. A sense of responsibility as well as eagerness now moved him. He scanned the field, spotted his father's battle banner, and pointed at it with his sword.

"Forward!"

At first, there seemed little effect from whatever had occurred on the left flank of the battle. They were engaged with two more groups before they came much nearer Salisbury's standard. After they had beaten off the second group and found another moment to breathe, it seemed that the noise of fighting in the center was more intense. Geoffrey said nothing, merely pointing the direction in which they were to make their next attack.

Through the haze that fatigue was building up in his mind, it began to dawn upon Geoffrey that it was a bad sign. If Ferrand had broken the French, Otto's army would have spread out, filling the ground where Ferrand's people had left a vacuum as they pursued their fleeing enemies. Thus, the battle noise should have diminished. The increase in intensity must mean that the French had broken through the left wing and were pressing in on Otto from that side as well as from the front.

All too soon the vague concern grew to a troubled conviction. The numbers of those opposing them were decidedly augmented. Nonetheless, there was no cause for real worry, Geoffrey told himself. The English wing was still advancing. The driving spearhead of their attack was Salisbury. The earl was fighting like a demon, as if he had cast off twenty or thirty years. He struck and slashed, seemingly tireless, and his blows were so powerful that no man could withstand him. Behind and around him, his vassals kept pace, completely caught up in the heat of what seemed a tide running strongly toward the haven of victory. All they saw was that the men facing them were fewer, that they moved forward slowly but surely and the French fell back before them.

Geoffrey's party was still separated from his father's, but not by much. So intense was his intention of combining their groups that he gave no mind to the general situation. It was, after all, his father's responsibility to consider the army as a whole; Geoffrey's duty was only to follow where Salisbury led. In the heat of the fighting, Geoffrey had forgotten that he was more than twenty years younger than his father, that if his body ached with effort Salisbury's condition must be worse. The glimpses Geoffrey caught of his father between blows given and received were so heroic that he slipped back to boyhood when Salisbury was a kind and invincible giant a thousand feet tall, never weak, worried, or tired.

Roger of Hemel was not so caught up in the fever of advancing. However, he needed to give all his attention to the immediate situation. As Lord Geoffrey grew fatigued, he tended to guard himself less efficiently, although he did not abate a whit of his ferocity. The castellan of Hemel had all he could do to protect his lord and himself without concerning himself with what others were doing.

What he saw when he did look gave Sir Roger very serious concern. The battle still was being fought in separate little groups, which was natural enough, but instead of being evenly distributed over a roughly rectangular or spherical area or even spread out in a long line, the groups were drawn into what approximated a broad arrowhead. This in itself was not an emergency. It often happened when a strong and eager leader drove forward, pulling his whole army behind him, as it were. What alarmed Roger of Hemel was that each time he found time to glance around, the point of the arrowhead seemed sharper. Salisbury, with Geoffrey's group to the left and one or two others was outpacing the rest of the force. Another glance around, as Geoffrey struck down the man who was opposing him and gave Sir Roger time to breathe, confirmed this fear and added another. There seemed to be more French coming from the left. If they continued as they were, it was entirely possible that the spearhead would be cut off.

"My lord," the castellan gasped, "my lord, look what we are about."

Whether Geoffrey heard was impossible for Roger of Hemel to know because in that moment a group of men charged them with set lances. They were far too busy to be in the least concerned with anything other than the preservation of their own lives. Sir Roger warded off one spear with his shield and beat another down with his sword blade. That maneuver was not completely successful, for the point, passing over his thigh, ran into his horse's back. The animal reared and screamed, plunging sideways away from the source of the hurt. As he went down, Sir Roger had one last glimpse of Geoffrey, still horsed, beating one lance blade aside and twisting desperately to avoid another which he could not reach with sword or shield.

If it had not been for that charge, Geoffrey might not have permitted Roger of Hemel's words to make any impression upon him. The coincidence of his castellan's warning and the onset of what must be men who were either fresh or had had time to rest and return to the sidelines for new arms fixed the warning in his mind. One did not carry extra lances onto a battlefield. Therefore, men with lances meant that Philip was doing well enough elsewhere to commit reserves to the right wing. Originally, the numbers of English and French had been roughly equal. That would no longer be true.

For a few minutes, Geoffrey was not aware that he had lost Sir Roger. He managed not only to cast aside the spear of one opponent but to carry the upward blow forward in a thrust that pierced the hood of the man and cut the big vessels in the neck under the ear. Bright red spurted far and ran down his sword blade before he could withdraw it. It added nothing to the color of the weapon, which was already so dyed with blood that, in the bright light of midday, it seemed as if Geoffrey was fighting with a long, perfect ruby.

The successful move was not without cost. Although the forward lunge and twist saved Geoffrey from being spitted through the belly by the second Frenchman's spear, it also precluded him from drawing his shield far enough forward to slat off the lance. The weapon caught in his mail, just where it folded in at the meeting of leg and body. Before the point tore open his groin, Geoffrey twisted further in his saddle and slashed so violently at the lance-wielder that he jerked back. To reach his opponent over the length of the lance, Geoffrey had to lean sharply forward. He connected, heard a cry as the well-sharpened point drove into the exposed right shoulder of his opponent.

The Frenchman's hand lost its grip on his lance, but it was a trifle too late to save Geoffrey completely. In his heedless violence, he had driven the point of the weapon into the flesh of his hip. Regardless of the fact that the weight of the shaft was twisting the lance point upward, tearing his body further, Geoffrey struck again and again, finally wounding his now-weaponless opponent severely enough so that he slid from his horse. Releasing the hand grip of his shield and letting it hang from the arm strap, Geoffrey grabbed the haft of the lance just above the head and tore it free. It was then that he became aware that Roger of Hemel was gone. He was struck from behind, which could never have happened if Sir Roger had been with him.

Geoffrey and the men still with him had been fighting steadily, with only intervals of a few minutes, for nearly four hours now. He had a dozen minor cuts, innumerable bruises, and two fairly bad wounds from which he was now losing blood in serious quantity. None of that even crossed his mind. What did worry him was that he had seen that Roger of Hemel's warning concerned a real danger. In all the twisting and turning, Geoffrey's eyes had swept nearly the whole field of battle. Although his attention was really on his opponents, he was war-wise enough for impressions of what he saw to remain in his brain.

He had to warn his father. He had to. They must retreat and consolidate their forces or all would be lost. Even as Geoffrey thought that, icy fear washed over him. The noise of battle was both louder and more muted than it should have been. In the fury of thrust and parry it took some time for the significance of that evidence of his ears to make sense and to explain his instinctive fright. Simply, it meant that there was no other battle. The dull roar that testified to screams, shouts, and blows at a distance was absent. What remained were the shrill cries, the sharp clang of weapons being employed near at hand.

Desperation was a fire in Geoffrey's weakening body. He struck and thrust like a madman, nearly heedless of blows launched at him. The ferocity of his attack saved him something, but more than one new cut and bruise were added to the many he bore. The wild activity also tore his two bad wounds wider and the blood ran quicker and thicker. Through all, however, his eyes constantly flicked to Salisbury, now only some five yards away from him. At last the earl struck down the man he was fighting.

"Papa!" Geoffrey screamed, "Papa, look! We are near surrounded. "Go back! Go back!"

Perhaps Geoffrey was not the first to cry that warning. Many shouts had been directed at Salisbury in the last half hour, but the pain- and fear-filled voice of his child pierced through the fighting fog as nothing else could. He turned his head toward the sound, saw the blood-covered form. "Geoffrey!" he cried, and wrenched his horse toward his son.

In that moment, a man who had been to his right and was now directly in front of him slashed at him. Salisbury blocked the blow automatically, but his eyes and mind were still fixed upon his child. He did not see another man who had been striving toward him almost as single-mindedly as Geoffrey, come up slightly behind him. He raised the formidable war club he carried. With a joyful hosanna to God, he brought the full force of the club, unimpeded by any need to ward off a counterblow at the same time, down on the top of Salisbury's head.

Like a stricken ox, the earl fell from his saddle all of a piece, making no effort to save himself. In the single instant before another opponent rode between him and his father, Geoffrey saw Salisbury topple, totally limp under the horses' hooves.

"Papa!" he shrieked, spurring Orage forward like a maniac, hardly realizing it was a man with a raised sword that was blocking his view, "Papa!"

CHAPTER TWENTY-FIVE

As the days of a sweet, rich summer passed, Joanna found to her discomfort that fear was not the worst enemy with which she had to contend. Although she had more than enough to do in the overt management of her mother's and Geoffrey's lands and in the more tactful, and thus more time-consuming, inspection of Ian's property, she was very far from content. She could not blame her restlessness on boredom. Between the antics of Simon, whom she took with her to the keeps of Ian's vassals, and the stupidity (or too-great shrewdness) of the wives of the vassals and castellans who were serving with Ian, she had plenty to occupy her.

Not to put a fine shroud on a stinking corpse, Joanna had to admit that what she craved was Geoffrey's body. She was not, as she had feared, racked with constant pangs of fear. Occasionally, it was true that a huge hand seemed to grip her entrails and wrench at them until she could have screamed. Most of the time, however, her thoughts were far more pleasant although almost as unsettling. What her mind dwelt upon was Geoffrey's caresses, his hands and lips on her body, and the sweet culmination of that eagerly sought torment. She found herself sitting with eyes closed over her embroidery murmuring, "Beloved, beloved, come home to me," which surprised her. Joanna was not given to the use of endearments, except to small children like Simon.

Once, to occupy her mind, she had tried to determine why that was so. It was true her mother did not very often call her by sweet names, but she was free enough with "dear hearts" and "beloveds" to Ian. And Ian had always used love words to his stepdaughter. Yet, Joanna thought, I

437

have never returned them, never called him anything but "Ian," even though I do love him. Suddenly a bright light in her brain clarified that line of thought.

In the past Joanna had been afraid to permit the smallest tinge of similarity to her mother's love for Ian to color their relationship. Ian could call her "love" lightly because she was his daughter and *only* his daughter in his heart. As a man loves a woman, there had never been anyone but Alinor for Ian. For herself, Joanna realized, it would have been all too easy to love Ian as a man.

And now? Joanna smiled with satisfaction. No, there was only Geoffrey. In spite of Ian's overwhelming beauty, it was Geoffrey's fair, slender body she desired, not her stepfather's swarthy strength.

A frown creased Joanna's forehead. Had Geoffrey been aware of her failure to use to him the terms a loving wife gives a husband? He had never said anything—but, of course, he would not. Unless he believes the lack to be a result of fear or shyness, a man does not ask his wife to call him "beloved," not a man with Geoffrey's tender pride. How could he know the lack was merely long habit?

Could this be the cause of the little strain, the slight disappointment or dissatisfaction she had felt in Geoffrey? Many times she had worried about that faint shadow that stained the perfection of their marriage, but she had never been able to find the slightest cause for it. Joanna laid down her needle and bit her lip. It was not a thing that could be mended in a minute. If she suddenly changed her pattern and began to call Geoffrey her love, the beat of her heart, would he not wonder why? Nor did she think it wise or safe to explain what she had discovered about herself. To plant in Geoffrey's jealous heart the thought that she might once have feared her own emotions for Ian might only make him more uneasy.

Then the worry cleared from her face. It was not a matter that needed instant mending, now that she knew. Little by little, she could speak her heart aloud more often. It would not matter if Geoffrey thought he had won her to love slowly. Perhaps it would be better that way. Let him believe her heart was slow and considerate in its submission. Possibly that would give him assurance that it would not lightly change.

These concerns were largely obliterated, however, when Joanna had news of the treachery of the Poitevin lords that had ended John's hopes for reconquering Anjou. The request that John sent for more support, Joanna could rightfully ignore. Ian had brought with him every man required by his feudal obligations. However, the request worried her. Had John been successful and called for more men to consolidate his gains or take over the strongholds previously controlled by Philip, all would have been well. Even disaffected vassals would think seriously before challenging a victorious king. The news that he had lost all he had gained and perhaps even more in that some previously loyal barons had defected cast an ugly light over the expedition. Joanna waited for two weeks, sounding out visitors to Roselynde keep and town, and then wrote to Alinor.

"I understand from your letter," Joanna began after the salutation, "that the fault for what took place was nowise the king's, that he acted in all ways as was right and proper, but I fear those facts will be lost upon the men who remained here. As you well know, none of them have any love for the king, and all will ignore—or, for the worst-disposed—will even lie about these matters. Already rumors fly about and all of them are unfavorable. The kindest say the king fell into a lethargy and would not act and the men, in despair, went home. Some say the king insulted the wives and daughters of the vassals and that was why they withdrew; others are even worse and say the king fled first, leaving the barons without a leader. I do not *know* where these ill winds blow from, but I can guess and Lady Ela agrees that most likely their sources are where you would expect—Vesci in the north and FitzWalter in the east."

"This I know you will have expected, but what makes me particularly uneasy is that Oxford happened to be here on his way to Portsmouth when the copy of the king's letter was given to me. He has always been moderate in his dealings with the king, yet he spoke very bitterly about Peter of Winchester's rule. It has been, as I wrote you before, harsher than it should, but, as you know, there is so much resistance to whatever is asked that I fear harshness has become a habit. Oxford grew quite heated when he saw John's letter, saying that anyone who answered the summons was a fool, merely throwing good money after bad and, moreover, that he would pay no scutage for withholding his men from a mad venture that could benefit no one in this land. I am sorry to add to your troubles. I know it cannot be easy for you or for Ian, situated as you are, but I felt you must be warned that things do not go well here and that the king is like to have a cold welcome when he returns."

"I have some good news to temper the ill. Geoffrey writes that all goes very well in Flanders. Salisbury has virtually cleared the country of all French troops and sympathizers, and they only await the Emperor Otto's arrival before they engage King Philip himself. If they win a great victory, it may help for a short time, but I must add that Oxford was talking again about the charter. I know Ian also believes that peace will be restored if the king can be brought to sign this. I thought I should mention it, especially considering the source from where I heard it. I do not suppose Ian can broach the subject himself because whatever he thinks good the king hates, but perhaps d'Atie or Cantelu could hint to the king that he should not condemn the idea of a charter out of hand."

Joanna then turned to personal news. Fortunately, that was all good. Simon was still a devil, but a charming one and his health was excellent. Adam was growing up by leaps and bounds. He spent most of his time in his own keeps now, Leicester having given him leave to oversee his lands more closely because the castellans were mostly with Ian in France. He had ridden over to Roselynde to spend a week with his sister.

It was a very good thing that Joanna had spent some space on Adam. That was the one spark of light, the one cheerful subject Alinor and Ian had as a relief, for Joanna's letter had arrived at the end of the second week of August, a week after the news of the disaster at Bouvines. The personal effects of this catastrophe, which made anything Joanna wrote about the reception the king would have irrelevant, had stunned Alinor into numbness and disbelief.

The first communication direct from France, from Philip himself, which arrived two days after the initial news, had lit a spark of hope. Salisbury was not dead. Hoping and praying, Alinor had waited for further news. This day it had come. Now she had a thing to tell Joanna that tore her heart violently so that a pain made her press her arms across her breast and rock to and fro moaning. When the spasm passed, Alinor wiped the tears that ran down her face and obscured her vision and picked up her pen.

"My dearest, my most sweet and beloved daughter, I pray that the Mother of mercy will give you strength to bear the news I write. I pray also that you will not in your bitterness despise me for being the sender of these tidings or for exposing you to this sorrow by urging your marriage. Geoffrey is lost. Beloved, beloved, have courage. I do not know what else to say. I cannot even comfort you by bringing you his dear body to lay to rest nor even by telling you where to go to weep over his grave. Heart of my heart, my pain is nothing to yours, yet it racks me apart so I can hardly write."

The evidence of that was plain. Alinor's usually firm and flowing hand was tremulous and the ink was splotched and smeared with the tears she could not catch, which had fallen on the parchment and had been blotted away. For a while she stopped writing again. The new messenger who had arrived was a nobleman close to Philip. Ian had gone to speak to him personally. Perhaps they had found Geoffrey's body after all. The only thing they knew for certain was that he was not among the prisoners taken. Alinor sobbed disconsolately, crying so hard that she could not see. Her maid Gertrude crept to her side and patted her hand.

"Madam," she whispered, "your lord comes. You bade me warn you."

Desperately, Alinor wiped her eyes and face and struggled to control her sobbing. Ian was distraught enough. She did not wish to burden him with her grief as well as his own. She did choke herself into quiet before he entered the room—he walked so slowly—and she was glad of it. Ian looked worse than when he had gone out. His face was gray and his luminous eyes dull and fixed. Nervously, Alinor rose and went round the table to meet him.

"What is it Ian? Is the news worse?"

"The terms are unbelievable. I will tell you of that later. What is worse is Geoffrey—" his voice cracked and he took a deep breath. "Geoffrey was definitely not among the prisoners nor among those who were sore wounded and died. It cannot be an oversight that he is not mentioned—I mean, he is mentioned, and by name. It seems that Salisbury begged Philip to inquire specially and Philip was so good as to do so. Geoffrey is not among the live or the dead that they have identified."

Alinor's tears broke out afresh and her husband took her into his arms. "I begged you not to hope," he whispered.

"I did not," she sobbed, "not really. See," she gestured toward the parchment on the table, "I have begun my letter to Joanna." She paused and struggled with herself but without success. Clinging to her husband she wailed aloud. "I cannot bear it. I cannot bear that Joanna should suffer—"

She choked the rest of it off. Even in the midst of her grief it was impossible to mention to her second husband what she had endured in the loss of her first man. Ian knew, of course. He had loved Simon himself enough to give that name to his own firstborn son. Still, it was not a thing to be said aloud between them. Alinor dashed the tears from her face.

"What a stupid thing to say. I must bear it, so I can. Come, beloved, sit down." She pressed him into a chair and brought him a goblet of wine. "Why cannot his body be found?" she whispered. "Others have been named as dead, even many of the lesser men, have they not? How could he be overlooked? Oh, Ian, is there no hope?"

He could not let her cling to hope and transmit that hope

to Joanna. That would mean months, perhaps even years of agony—waiting, fearing, begging and praying for news that could never come. Tears oozed out under his closed lids.

"They did not look for him at once," he said, very softly, his voice breaking. "Salisbury did not regain his senses until late in the night and even after that he was wandering in his wits for most of the next day. After the battle, after Philip's men had withdrawn with their own dead and wounded—Alinor, believe me, just believe me. There is no hope. Do not make me say more."

He did not need to say more. Indeed, he had to leap to his feet to catch his wife whose eyes had rolled up in her head at the unbearable idea he had conveyed to her. Alinor knew of the scavengers who crept out onto a battlefield to rob the dead—and to kill those who clung to a thread of life so that they could also be robbed. Geoffrey had not been found because his armor and shield were rich. The carrion pickers had doubtless stripped him naked. Perhaps his face had even been battered in so that it was unrecognizable.

Alinor did not actually faint. Ian carried her to the bed and made her sip some of the wine she had brought to him. Then he sat down beside her and took her hand in his. They did not speak. There was nothing to say. One thing Ian had not told his wife, one little thing, that made his agony more intense because it would not allow his hope to die. Geoffrey's shield had not been found either. It puzzled him. Even if the shield had been torn away to make it easy to strip the body, it should have been there, close to the naked corpse. The vultures who scavenged battlefields were often embittered enough to mutilate the bodies, but they had no use for shields. Mail and weapons could be sold or even melted down for their metal, but a shield was too large and heavy to make the small amount of metal on it worth the effort of carrying it away. Many poor despoiled corpses were identified by the shields left beside them.

It was not a thing he would mention to Alinor. If that little, wounding, stinging hope, which would not allow him to grieve in peace and accept his grief, ever should bring on a fever of joy, Alinor would not blame him for keeping his secret. Joy heals all. Dinner hour passed, but neither of them moved. Hunger did not touch them. Slowly, the long evening of late August darkened into twilight.

Just before full dark, the latch on the door made a little sound. Ian's head snapped around; he got to his feet with his hand on his sword hilt. The form that crept fearfully in at the door was no threat, at least no physical threat.

"Lady Alinor?"

"I am here," Alinor replied. "Who is it?"

"Lady Elizabeth."

Alinor sat up. Lady Elizabeth was one of the queen's attendant women. She had been a minor heiress, and John had given her in marriage to his stupid, gross bastard son, partly because it was a cheap way to provide for the boy and partly because he wanted to enjoy the girl himself. The virtual loss of her property and the total loss of her virtue had in no way embittered Lady Elizabeth, who took the king between her legs as merrily as she took any other man who offered. She was not particularly attractive, except for her unfailing good nature and, according to repute, her equally unfailing lust and inventiveness in sex play. It was said, laughingly, that she even serviced her husband with perfect good humor, although she was not quite sure which one he was.

Lady Elizabeth's morality was her own affair, and Alinor had nothing against her. She was no cause for jealousy. Elizabeth might cast longing glances at Ian, but certainly she was no temptation to him. Alinor had very little contact with her. Because she had no regular duties about the queen, Alinor came only when she was specifically summoned, on those occasions when Isabella felt in the mood for Alinor's wit and tales of traveling in strange lands.

"I am very sorry," Alinor said unsteadily, "I cannot go to the queen now. I— Please tell her I am ill."

There could be no other reason for Lady Elizabeth to seek her out, Alinor thought, but the young woman shook her head. Alinor could barely make out the gesture.

"I do not come from the queen—oh, yes, I do, but I mean I do not come to summon you to her. I—I must speak to you, Lady Alinor."

The voice was trembling. Could Lady Elizabeth have lost someone also? From what was said about her she could not differentiate one man from another, but what was said in Isabella's court was not always true. Alinor got off the bed and fumbled on the table for flint and tinder.

"Of course," she said. Perhaps the little whore had a heart; perhaps she only thought she had a heart. In any case, at this moment Alinor could not have been unkind to the devil himself if he were grieving. "Let me light the candles. Do not be alarmed. Ian is here, but he will go if—"

"No—Oh, I do not know. I have something to tell you, but I think it is very dangerous—very—oh. I know you will not betray me Lady Alinor, but—but Lord Ian—"

"To whom is this dangerous, Lady Elizabeth?" Ian asked softly.

"To me. Oh, dear, I should hold my tongue. I know I should. It cannot matter now, and yet— What if it did? He was so kind, you see. He never— And he was so respectful of me, even after—"

"I assure you if the danger is to you I will not betray you," Ian said. If he could have laughed at anything, he would have laughed at this silly little hen, thinking she was important enough for him to tell tales of her.

"Oh, I know you would not do so on purpose, but you will be so angry, you see, and you will show it—because gentlemen are not very good—most gentlemen —at hiding such things, and then she will want to know how you found out. She is *very* stupid, far stupider than I, but I was the only one there because she had sent the maids away. She thought I would be glad of it. She thought I was angry because he stopped— But I understood that. It was only in fun. We never cared for each other—only *liking*. And I showed him things—what to touch and how—"

"Forgive me, Lady Elizabeth," Alinor said gently, "but

you have begun in the middle. We do not know who 'he' is or who 'she' is. Will you not sit down? If you think Ian should not stay, he will not.''

''But Lord Ian must know. He is the one who will have to— That is, if—''

This might go on all night, Ian thought. He glanced at Alinor and saw that, although she was still dreadfully pale, the worst of this spate of grief was over. It might recur, probably it would, but not for a little while, not while Lady Elizabeth held her attention. ''I will go,'' Ian said firmly, walking toward the door. ''If there is something I must do, Lady Elizabeth, my wife will tell me. That way I can truthfully say you told me nothing and all will be well.''

It was the best thing he could have done. Clear of the distraction of Ian's too-handsome person, for it was that as much as fear that had been unsettling Lady Elizabeth, she came to the point.

''It is about Lord Geoffrey,'' she whispered.

''Geoffrey?'' Alinor quavered, her eyes filling.

''I am sure it is too late, but—but if there is any chance I—I want him to have it.''

The tears did not fall. They seemed to be sucked back to their source as Alinor's every sense came alert. Plainly, Lady Elizabeth knew of Geoffrey's death, yet she hinted that, had he been alive, there was some danger to him from—well, it could only be from the queen. Alinor urged her visitor into a chair and sat down close beside her. She wondered briefly whether this was some device of the king's, but no one had ever accused Lady Elizabeth of anything beyond an overgreat willingness to couple. Her good intentions and good nature were proverbial.

As if she had seen Alinor's doubts, the young woman said, ''Please understand, Geoffrey and I *liked* each other. To me he was—what?—a child to be taught and led—a star pupil? I took him to my bed because,'' she lifted her head defiantly, ''you may laugh at me if you like, but it was because he was sweet and good and I did not wish him to be embittered. The ladies of the court all made up to him and then asked for favors from Salisbury. I wanted him to know that a woman can be with a man for pure pleasure—asking nothing but the exchange of joy.''

"That is a good thing to teach a young man," Alinor murmured. "Perhaps my daughter has much for which to thank you." There was a silence as both women realized that now Geoffrey no longer was at all.

"Is it true that his body has not been found?" Lady Elizabeth asked.

Alinor sobbed, choked it back. "Yes, it is true."

"Then I must speak," Lady Elizabeth sighed. "I know it is very likely he is dead, but if there is the smallest chance— You see, he was the only one who—who remembered. I taught others also, but—but after they found a—a better partner—"

"I am sure they could not find a better," Alinor said impulsively. "No one could be kinder."

Lady Elizabeth cast Alinor a grateful glance but was not deflected from what she had been saying. "The others did not think me good enough to spit on when I had no more to offer. Geoffrey was different. He was never ashamed to talk to me, no, nor 'too busy' to come to me when I wanted him, even when he had another mistress—until he married. Then he came no more, but I understood that. We were *friends* you see. He still—" She broke off again.

"He was of very sweet and tender heart," Alinor sighed, tiredly wiping away tears, "always kind."

"I did not come to increase your grief or to ease my own heart by talking of him," Lady Elizabeth said apologetically. "I am Isabella's lady, and I really like her. She is stupid, many say, but I suppose so am I. We suit each other, and usually she is very good to me. You know this. That is why I spoke of Geoffrey and me. I wanted you to understand why I seemed to be betraying the queen. To speak the truth, I do not know why she had this hatred for Geoffrey. She is a *good* woman. I have never known her to hate anyone before."

Because she is so selfish she cannot be bothered to feel

much about anyone, Alinor thought, but she said nothing. If Lady Elizabeth was happy with her mistress and had seen no deeper into Isabella's nature after all the years she had served her, there was no need to try to change her mind or teach her better.

Lady Elizabeth drew a deep breath, as if bracing herself, and said, "The queen told me that it was very fortunate Geoffrey was killed and his body lost at Bouvines because that saved her a great sum of money. When the news of Salisbury's capture came, she secretly sent a message back to Philip with the herald offering double Geoffrey's ransom for his *dead* body if he had been taken prisoner."

"What?" Alinor gasped, frozen into her seat.

"Isabella said she wished to make the same offer for Salisbury's corpse, but that the king would never help her to pay *that* bribe—so I must assume that John knows of what she has done and—and approves it. You can look for no help from the king."

The paralyzing horror that had gripped Alinor when she heard what the queen had done receded slowly. The blaze of hope that sprang up in its place also receded, but it did not disappear completely. If so great a sum to be paid for Geoffrey's corpse had not been claimed, it could not be for lack of searching. Probably that only increased the possibility that Geoffrey's stripped body had been cast into a common grave at Bouvines, but perhaps there was some chance—

"Thank you, Lady Elizabeth, thank you," Alinor stammered.

The young woman shrugged. "I do not suppose it matters. He must have died on the field and been lost among the other bodies. Nonetheless, if he is lying sore hurt in some serf's hut or by some miracle is somewhere in France or Flanders still alive, I thought that his friends should know the threat that still hangs over him. I will go now. Above all, I do not wish to be discovered here."

At the door Alinor thanked her again, but when she had closed it she wondered whether the thanks were merited. Hope warred with desolation in her, making it impossible even to sit still. Above and beyond her own unease was the problem of what to say to Joanna. Dared she even offer a hint of the hope that tormented her? Such a hope would be ten times worse for Joanna. Then her pacing stopped short. What an idiot I am, Alinor thought, wondering what to tell Joanna. I must tell her. She must be prepared to pay. First, however, we must counter the queen's offer. Ian must somehow get a message into France that Geoffrey's wife will pay three times, five times, ten times his ransom to have him returned safe and well.

Lady Alinor need not have feared the effect of her letter upon her daughter. Joanna was already aware of everything Alinor wrote except for Isabella's offer. That added a trifle to her cup of bitterness, but not much. Anyone who would murder a helpless prisoner out of greed would be just as willing to keep him alive when a greater bribe was offered, and Joanna was aware that the news of the greater bribe was already abroad in France.

Joanna had been apprised of her husband's almost certain death at nearly the same time her mother's messenger had taken ship for England. King Philip of France was not, generally speaking, a cruel man. He could be immoderately vengeful when he believed himself to have been slighted or injured, but he was not baselessly vicious. Thus, he was not unkind to Salisbury, whom he knew well from John's sojourns in the French court in the past. When the distraught father pleaded with tears for news of his son, Philip had commanded that an earnest search be made for Geoffrey. He had even permitted Salisbury to write to his bereaved daughter-by-marriage the sad news that Geoffrey had not been taken prisoner and must be presumed dead, although his body could not be found. Perhaps if Philip had not been so sure the young man was already dead, he would have prevented the circulation of Isabella's double ransom offer, but under the circumstances he did not see why he should not oblige John's wife. He might want a small favor from her some day.

Salisbury's letter could not be transmitted direct because

of the state of war, but it wound its way through the proper intermediaries and came, at last, to Roselynde. For three days after that, Joanna had done nothing but read and reread that letter. She did not eat nor really sleep. She did not weep. Edwina watched her mistress with growing anxiety.

On the third day, Edwina tore Salisbury's letter from Joanna's hands. That gained no more response than anything else. Joanna knew the words by heart and sat murmuring them over and over to herself. By the evening, Edwina was certain that Joanna would die if she was not immediately drawn back to the real world. She called Brian and went with the dog to Alinor's chief huntsman.

"Can you hurt the dog so that he seems near to death but will not really die?" Edwina asked the old man.

"Brian? You want me to hurt Brian? You are mad. The young mistress will kill me by cutting me apart an inch at a time, and the lady, when she hears, will roast the pieces over a slow fire."

"It is the young mistress who will die if you do not," Edwina said and burst into tears, dropping to her knees and throwing her arms around Brian's neck to weep into his rough coat. "I cannot rouse her nor make her eat or sleep. If I thought she would care, I would tell you to hurt *me*. I can think of nothing else. Brian was his—the young lord's. He gave her the dog."

"I know that," the huntsman said, his broad face twisted with pain. All knew of Geoffrey's death and all grieved. "But Brian—" He put a hand on the great dog's head, and the amiable animal beat himself with the wagging of his tail.

"She will die," Edwina moaned, rocking to and fro. "She will die. I have done everything, everything. If the dog cries, perhaps she will hear."

The huntsman looked at Edwina. He did not doubt her distress either for her mistress or for the dog, nor did he doubt her knowledge. He gripped Brian's collar and drew him out of Edwina's grasp. She knelt where she was for a few moments, sobbing, and then leapt to her feet to pursue the huntsman.

"Be careful," she cried. "Do not let him fear or be much hurt. Oh, poor Brian. He will not understand. If only I could make him understand."

"It is as well he does not. He would do himself a far greater hurt to serve Lady Joanna than I will do him." The huntsman was much more cheerful. He had thought of an expedient that would work very well and do Brian very little harm.

Edwina waited, her knuckles pressed nervously to her lips. In a few minutes there was a single loud yelp. Another few minutes passed and the huntsman came back, staggering under the dog's great weight. Edwina gasped. Brian's neck, ribs, and haunch were soaked with blood and his head hung limply.

"You have killed him," she cried.

"Fool!" the huntsman grunted. "I have stunned him, made three thin slits in his hide, and near drowned him in the blood of three hares. Quick before he rouses. This ox will not even realize he is hurt and will lick off all the blood with high pleasure."

They went into the keep and up to Joanna's chamber, the huntsman lagging behind and breathing in gasps from lugging Brian up the stairs.

"Madam," Edwina cried, "oh, madam, Brian is hurt. He is near dead, I think. My lady, look to Brian."

Joanna did not even turn her head.

"Brian is dying, my lady," Edwina shrieked.

The terror in her voice, which came from the apparent failure of this last hope, penetrated slowly Joanna's head lifted, and the huntsman staggered in, dropping the dog, who was already regaining consciousness and was whimpering a little with fear at the unusual sensation of being carried. As he struck the ground at Joanna's feet, Brian uttered a piteous yelp. Joanna's eyes fixed on the bloodied body, took in the dog's pathetic, ineffectual efforts to rise— ineffectual owing to the fact that the huntsman had his foot firmly planted on the overlap of Brian's collar.

"No! No!" Joanna whimpered. "He is all I have left of

my lord. Brian! Brian!'' The last words came out in a full-throated wail.

Edwina wanted to dance and sing. Instead she urged, "Let us wash him and tend him, my lady. Perhaps we can save him. Do you go for your salves. I will run to bring water.''

Dazedly, uncertainly, Joanna got to her feet. Brian uttered a howl of agony—the huntsman had surreptitiously applied his other foot to the dog's ear. Galvanized by pity and horror, Joanna sprang toward the chest where the medicinals were kept. Now the huntsman knelt beside the dog as if to hold him steady while Joanna treated him, although actually he was exerting all his strength to keep the creature from leaping gaily to his feet. Poor Brian, utterly confused and with a dull ache in his thick head, whimpered and whined.

It took a long time to sponge off enough of the blood so that Joanna could see the actual wounds. Even dazed as she was, she did wonder how three shallow cuts, although they were quite long, could produce so much gore, but it did not seem important enough to speak about. While Joanna stitched up the cuts, Edwina made certain other preparations which resulted—after she had fed Brian some bread sopped in milk "to comfort him"—in the dog falling into a heavy sleep. A sleep deep enough that Brian would not rouse to her voice was so unusual that anxiety nagged at Joanna and would not permit her to slip back into shocked numbness. She sat on the floor with the dog's heavy head in her lap and cried over him, and, the floodgates being opened, cried over Geoffrey, and cried, and cried, and cried herself to sleep.

The next morning, there was no longer any way to conceal the fact that Brian was in his usual most excellent health. Edwina's fears that her mistress would slide into blankness were lightened, however, when Joanna came quietly to table at breakfast time and ate, even if only a little.

She was no longer beyond attention. She saw at last Edwina's drawn, unhappy face, Sir Guy's heavy red-rimmed eyes, the anxious glances of the servants. Years of training then asserted themselves. Well or ill, Joanna knew the responsibility of the keep, of all her mother's lands and, now, all of Geoffrey's lands lay upon her. If the head is lost, the body dies; that precept had been pounded into her since she could first understand words. Dutifully, she tried to go about her normal business.

When the weary day ended, Joanna cried herself to sleep in the empty bed, only to wake to begin another hopeless struggle. In the morning her mother's letter came. The tenderness that was so seldom displayed in times of ease was a little comfort. Edwina watched fearfully, but Joanna's grief did not seem to be much increased by Alinor's confirmation of Salisbury's news or the ugly tale of the doubled ransom. However, by midafternoon Joanna began to think she could endure no more. She withdrew to her chamber, with a sharp order to be left in peace for a few hours, to escape from the tender concern that bound her to her pain.

By habit she sat down before her embroidery frame and lifted the needle. She had just begun work when Edwina came rushing into the room, wide-eyed and trembling. "Madam, madam," she cried, "Tostig is here! Tostig and Roger of Hemel! Come! Oh, come quickly!"

For one long moment Joanna remained frozen. Then she raised her eyes to her maid. "How do they look?" she whispered.

"Much hurt, both, and sad, but not—not—oh, I fear to give you hope, but my lady, my dear, they do not look so—so fearful sad as they should. Come! Come quickly!"

Then Joanna leapt to her feet, sending the embroidery frame, the table with her silks, her chair, all flying. She flew herself, across the women's quarters and down the twisting stairs, stumbling and catching at the wall.

"Is he dead? Is he really dead?" she cried aloud across the hall, afraid to ask the question she really wanted answered.

Tostig looked toward her and staggered forward. He had lost two stone of weight and was gray-faced, his eyes burning with fever. "I do not know," he croaked. "Not dead on the field."

"What do you mean?" Joanna shrieked.

"I mean that I looked at every body—every single body on that field—and my lord was not among them."

Joanna swayed on her feet and Edwina put an arm around her to support her. "Are you sure?" Joanna quavered. "Are you very, very sure?"

Tostig began to look frightened. "I do not understand you, my lady. Of course I am sure. I would not let the carrion that scavenges the field touch my lord."

"Sit down my love, come sit down," Edwina crooned, drawing Joanna toward a chair. "I will set a stool for Tostig. You see he can barely stand, and Sir Roger too must rest."

Sir Guy was supporting Roger of Hemel, and he helped him forward. "Madam," Sir Roger said wearily, "it is true. Lord Geoffrey was not among the slain on the field." He looked into the pale flame of Joanna's eyes, and tears came to his own. "Madam," he whispered reluctantly, "it was a very bitter battle. I pray you to set a curb on your hope. He might have been taken prisoner sore wounded, and—and—"

But Joanna knew Geoffrey could not have died after being taken prisoner because Isabella had offered a fortune for his corpse. Even if he had been buried before the news came of the price the English queen would pay for the dead body, it would have been dug up and delivered. Thus, if he was not a nameless, naked body buried in a mass grave at Bouvines, he was alive! Joanna fought down gladness. Only a great fool desires to be deluded in such matters. She licked her lips fearfully.

"You must tell me exactly what happened," she said, trying to force firmness into her voice."

Geoffrey's master-at-arms did not look at his mistress but into his bitter memories. "I was wounded and my lord sent me from the field," he began. "Because he said I would be a danger to him, I went. I waited by my lord's tent for when he should return. Not long after noon, I knew the battle went ill, and I gathered together my lord's possessions. His jewels and the gold I hid upon my person. I have them here.''

He began to fumble at his tunic with his left hand, but Joanna waved at him to desist and continue.

"Then," Tostig went on, "between one hour and two hours later, men began to flee into the camp. One told me that Lord Salisbury was dead and that Dammartin was surrounded and sure to die or be made prisoner. I asked for my own lord, but the man did not know of him.''

"Salisbury is not dead," Joanna informed them. "He was taken prisoner, mostly unhurt. I have had a letter from him. Wait, now," she said as Tostig swallowed painfully and took a deep breath. "In my own need I have overlooked yours.'' She snapped a finger at a maid, ordering, "Bring wine, and—do you wish to eat? No? Bring wine.''

But Tostig did not wait for the wine. The bitter memories filled him. Despite his illness and pain, he needed to spew them out. "When I heard that," he continued, "I went to where I could see, and to my sorrow I saw it was the truth. I —'' his voice shook with remembered fear and grief. "But I could not see my lord although I went from place to place. Then, when Dammartin fell and was taken with his men, the whole battle was broken and all who remained fled away, the French pursuing. I could do no more than hide myself, but I lay where I could watch.''

A maid brought a small table to Tostig's left. Another placed a goblet of wine on it. A second pair served Sir Roger.

"The French came after that and took their own dead and wounded and those wounded of ours who would be worth a ransom. Then others began to creep toward the field—you know what they are. One came near to me, and I killed him with my knife in my left hand and cast off my clothes, which would mark me as an English soldier, and put on his rags. Then I ran down to the battlefield with the others. I was quicker than they because I looked only at the men in mail and did not pause to take anything. I looked close. My lord was not there.''

"You could not have looked over the whole field before—before those others had a chance to despoil—'' Joanna's voice broke.

"That is true, but I found my lord's sword and shield.''

"What?''

"They are below, my lady,'' Sir Guy said softly. "I did not wish—''

Joanna understood. No one had questioned Tostig or Sir Roger before calling her. As soon as they saw the sword and shield, they were certain of Geoffrey's death. Sir Guy had wanted to keep the painful mementoes out of her sight until she was more resigned. Tostig had put his good hand over his face and begun to sob. Sir Guy patted his back and pushed the wine into his hand. The master-at-arms took a deep trembling breath and drank. He knew and Joanna knew as well, that Geoffrey would never drop his sword while he was conscious. Therefore, it was impossible that he had re-treated after his father was taken and had gone to join Otto.

If he had been taken prisoner, the sword and shield would have been taken also as trophies. Certainly the scavengers would have taken the sword, which was a very fine one, a gift from Salisbury on his son's knighting. Even if by some chance they had overlooked it when they despoiled Geoffrey's body, they would not have moved the body far from where the sword and shield lay. Tostig should then have found him.

"I—I could not believe it. I went round and round look-ing again and again,'' Tostig said piteously. "Each time I went a little further. It is true the vultures had been in that place. The sword was half-buried in the dust and hidden under the shield, which was why it was not taken. Then I thought that for some reason they might have—might have moved him. His armor was rich and several might have quarreled—''

"Oh no,'' Joanna breathed, closing her eyes, although that could not block out a picture of Geoffrey's body being dragged about first by a leg, then by an arm, as several dogs will fight, pulling a chicken or a hare from each other.''

"That was how he found me," Roger of Hemel put in a little more loudly than necessary to draw Joanna's mind from the ugly image he guessed she had created. "Both the French and the corpse pickers had left me for dead. I do not know how I come to be alive, in truth. The last I remember was my horse being struck and going down with him. The next was of Tostig dragging me to shelter. He returned to the field again. It was a little time before I was clear in my head, but when night fell I was better and Tostig came back and told me what he had done and found. I decided to wait there until the next day when I hoped to be able to walk. My lady, I swear we looked on the face of every dead man on that field—every man. Lord Geoffrey was not there. He must have been taken prisoner and for some reason the sword and shield were forgotten.''

"He was not taken prisoner," Joanna said, "that was what Lord Salisbury wrote to say—that Geoffrey was not a prisoner.''

The men looked at her, stunned, then horror began to grow in their eyes. Tostig's head dropped forward and he began to cry in long, racking sobs.

"No, do not weep," Joanna soothed, "at least, not yet. He is not dead. He cannot be.''

She told them then of the offer to pay ransom to obtain Geoffrey's body, except that to keep from enraging them in their weakness she did not admit the ransom would be doubled for a corpse or that the offer was made by the queen. Instead she pretended it was done by the king out of love for Salisbury, so that he might not need to grieve over a son buried in an unmarked and untended grave. When she was finished there was total silence in the place where they sat. Sir Roger and Tostig just stared, unbelievingly.

"Where is he?" Tostig cried at last, levering himself painfully to his feet as if, in spite of his illness, he would run and look. "If he was not dead on the field, and not escaped, and not a prisoner—dead or alive—where is he?''

CHAPTER TWENTY-SIX

That was a question that Geoffrey himself would have liked to have answered at about the time Tostig was asking it. He had a dim awareness that time had passed, a good deal of time. He had vague memories of screaming with pain and babbling with fever, and it seemed that the torment had lasted forever and ever. To compound the horror, there had been a woman mixed up in it, a woman who changed inexplicably from an old crone to a much younger creature. Somehow, also, the woman had gotten mixed up with his old fear of the queen—only this time it was the ugly crone who had tormented him and the beautiful—no, Geoffrey thought, she was not beautiful nor even very young, only soft-voiced and she had been kind.

The woman must be real—only it was two different women, of course, who had spoken to him at different times. Then he had fainted or slept between visits so that it seemed to him it was one woman, changing magically from age to youth. That piece of clear deduction made Geoffrey feel much better. It gave him something to work with, but as he considered further he realized it was no help. He had no idea, really, how often either woman had come or whether they had come together or how long a time had passed between their visits. He must have been very close to death, he realized.

He slept then, as suddenly as light is extinguished by snuffing out a candle, and woke as suddenly when he was firmly gripped by two pairs of strong hands. Instinctively, he struggled against the restraint without much effect because of his weakness, until a renewal of heightened pain in his left hip brought the realization that he was being held so

458

that his wounds could be dressed. Doubtless when he was fevered he fought against the pain, being unable to realize it was for his own good. To the best of his ability then, he relaxed his body and lay still, merely turning his head to look curiously at his attendant. It must have been the older woman who had treated him at first and thus he had associated her with torture. It was not she, but the younger one who salved his wounds now.

Although she must have realized he was conscious from the change in his behavior, she finished what she was doing before she lifted her head to speak to him. When she did so, her face was hard, her eyes cold. Geoffrey never learned what an effort that had been, which was just as well.

"So you have your senses again," she said. "Now, who are you?"

Shocked, Geoffrey hesitated a moment. He had associated this woman with gentleness, but her voice and manner showed nothing of that. Tears of weakness rose in his eyes; he swallowed them back and replied, "I am Geoffrey FitzWilliam."

The woman cast her eyes up to heaven with impatience. "There cannot be more than ten hundred Geoffrey FitzWilliams in England, France, Brittany, Normandy—say true, what are you to William, earl of Salisbury?"

"Say true!" Geoffrey exclaimed indignantly. "I do not lie on greater matters nor on those for which I feel shame. Why should I lie when I am proud. William, earl of Salisbury is my father."

"Salisbury's heir," the woman breathed like a prayer.

If Geoffrey had blood enough, it would have risen into his face. Nonetheless he replied steadily, "I am his son but not his heir. I am a bastard, out of Lady Margaret of Hemel."

That pleased her less. She looked at Geoffrey sharply. "Upon what terms do you stand with your father?"

All at once Geoffrey remembered the last time he had seen Salisbury, falling from his horse limp as a dead man. He himself had been the cause. He had called out a warning and his father, perhaps not hearing properly, doubtless thought he called for help and had tried to come to him, neglecting his own safety.

"I have killed him," Geoffrey breathed, tears coming into his eyes again. "God curse me, I have killed him." His voice rose to an agonized wail, but the woman cut him off impatiently.

"You have done no such thing. Salisbury is alive and well—better than you by far from what I have heard. He is prisoner in Paris."

"Alive? He is alive?"

"Yes."

The woman did not repeat her question. There was no need for it. Bastard or not, it was clear that the father and son were close-knit, which meant that Geoffrey could probably draw on Salisbury's purse for more than a plain knight's ransom. She had thought so from the beginning, for her uncle-by-marriage, who had brought Geoffrey to the keep, had told her how Salisbury reacted when Geoffrey called to him. That was why Louis of Baisieux did not kill the young man, who had not even guarded himself against the blow. Instead, at the last minute, he had turned his sword so that only the flat of it crashed against Geoffrey's temple.

Loss of blood and exhaustion had done the rest. As Geoffrey toppled, unconscious, from his saddle, he had been seized. His sword had already fallen; his captor stripped away his shield and cast that down, both because it was in the way and because he wished to keep secret the identity of the man he carried across his saddlebow. He had no intention of permitting Geoffrey to be added to the general pool of prisoners and have his ransom go mostly or completely into King Philip's purse.

In the rolls of the Exchequer, Louis of Baisieux owed an enormous debt to the king of France. This debt he did not acknowledge as just, although he paid a little on it year by year to keep his land. He served Philip grudgingly, always ready to avoid an obligation if he could.

When he took Geoffrey, Louis was not sure whom he had captured. Only from the fine horse, rich armor, surcoat, and shield, he believed the man was wealthy. From Salisbury's reaction, he believed his captive was important to the brother of the king of England. If so, this was a prize Philip of France would want to have in his hands—and if Philip wanted it, Louis was determined he would not get it. He dared not bring Geoffrey to his own small keep. If Geoffrey was important, a search might be made for him. Louis was known to have taken part in the battle (most unwillingly), and might be asked to show his prisoners. Thus, he had brought Geoffrey to the keep of his nephew, his sister's son. Léon of Baisieux was a prisoner in England and had not been at Bouvines so it was unlikely Geoffrey would be sought in his keep.

In fact, the search for Geoffrey was more intense than Louis expected. Nonetheless, he clung to his decision, more stubborn the more desirable Geoffrey seemed—besides, he was not certain he had the right Geoffrey; Geoffrey was a very common name. Then, when Isabella's offer trickled down through the secret vines that such rumors travel, Louis was trapped in his denial. At first he wished to take the chance of handing Geoffrey over. The sum named would virtually clear his debt. It would not even be necessary to kill Geoffrey. He was already so near death that moving him to Paris would kill him.

To Louis's intense surprise, for she was ordinarily as meek as a lamb, Léon's wife, Gilliane, opposed this idea. She had pointed out that Louis paid very little on his debt; therefore, to clear it would not be nearly as profitable as having the whole ransom in his own purse. There was sense in that. Moreover, they might gain even more than mere money, Gilliane said. It might well be possible to exchange Geoffrey's person for that of her husband and, since Geoffrey was rich, get the ransom too. Louis had his doubts, but Gilliane added a clincher in that, if Geoffrey died, they could always say they had found him in a serf's hut and collect the reward anyway. Between his reluctance to benefit

Philip in any way and his fear of explaining why he had not admitted having Geoffrey as a prisoner sooner, Louis yielded to Gilliane's reasoning.

In fact Louis's doubts had a sound foundation. Gilliane usually knew nothing and cared less about money and the running of estates, but he told himself that Gilliane wanted Léon back. This was true, but there were other reasons for Gilliane's sudden quickness of mind that Louis would not have approved. Yes, she wanted Léon back. It was dangerous to be without a man; her sons needed their father. Louis did what he could, but he had his own property and children to consider also. Moreover, Gilliane hated and feared the duties of the estate that devolved upon her and she knew she did not perform them competently. She loved Léon too—he was kind; he never beat her without good reason. Of course, she loved him, as much as one could love a man who never seemed to notice one was alive, except for the few minutes spent in coupling. Even then Gilliane often wondered whether he knew or cared whose body received him.

Apparently, Geoffrey was of a different kind. When Gilliane had first undressed him, the letter he had written to Joanna fell from his sleeve. Curious, Gilliane had called a clerk and had it read to her. She had not known that real men wrote such words to their wives. Only in the romances that the minstrels sang had she ever heard such tenderness. She did not really think of Geoffrey as a lover. He was too young for her, and it would be a sin, and, anyway, if he could look upon her in that way the letter would be a monstrous lie—but her heart softened toward him. Then, as the days passed and she fought for his life with every bit of skill and knowledge she had, he became dear to her as a child that one tends and protects is dear. Now as she looked at him, she was glad. The Geoffrey who cared so much for his father was very likely to have written the truth of his heart in that letter.

"I assure you that Lord Salisbury is not only alive but little hurt, if at all," Gilliane said, unable to resist soothing the anxiety she saw still in Geoffrey's eyes. "He rode upon his own horse into Paris, I heard."

"Thank God for that," Geoffrey sighed. Then, glancing around, "Where am I, my lady? Who are you?"

"I am Lady Gilliane, and you are in the keep of Léon de Baisieux."

"What!" Geoffrey exclaimed, and, weakly, began to laugh.

A look of distress crossed Gilliane's face, but she shrugged her shoulders and started to rise.

"Do not go," Geoffrey begged. "I am not wandering in my wits again, I swear. It is only that before the battle, the very day before when I heard how near Baisieux was, I said to myself that I must come and pay my respects to you and to Sir Léon's mother—if the older lady who lives here is his mother."

Gilliane plumped down upon her seat again, staring with surprise. "It is his mother indeed. How do you know Léon? Is he your prisoner? Have you seen him? How is he?"

"He is not my prisoner, nor have I seen him since a year ago, nor do I know aught of his present state," Geoffrey began. But suddenly a cold sweat bathed his body and beaded on his face, and the words slurred and run into each other.

A strange conflict rose in Gilliane's breast. Propriety bade her prod Geoffrey further. After all, she should more ardently desire news of her husband than the welfare of this stranger—this evil stranger, her mother-by-marriage would say. In truth, however, she was far more anxious to prevent Geoffrey from overtiring himself than to learn more about Léon. Practicality came to her rescue. Geoffrey had already said he had no recent news of Léon. It was therefore unreasonable to fatigue her patient merely to satisfy her own curiosity as to how Geoffrey knew Léon and what he thought of him.

"Sleep," she said, getting up again. "You will tell me when you are stronger."

* * *

For a week and a half, Joanna suffered a torment that, she thought, would make hell restful. There was, there could be, no comfort of any kind. Had she known Geoffrey to be dead, however dreadful the pain, she would have endured, absorbed it into her soul, and eventually taken up her life again. This she had begun to do, and then. . . . Now things were worse. She could not settle to making herself believe she would never see him, never touch, kiss, love him, again. Every time she told herself that, had he been still alive, news of his whereabouts must have already reached them, contrary notions, each more horrible than the last, presented themselves. Perhaps he was mad, or alive but completely senseless. Perhaps he had fallen into the hands of some madman who took pleasure in torturing captives. Perhaps someone was starving him to death slowly for Isabella's double ransom.

If Tostig and Roger of Hemel had not been so desperately ill, Joanna knew she would have lost her mind. They had made their way to Roselynde because their wills and desperation drove them beyond the real capacity of their bodies. Within the safety of its walls, with the added shock of learning their lord had mysteriously disappeared, both collapsed. Joanna had much to do simply to keep breath in their bodies at first and then to turn them toward life. As each made the turn, however, he unmeaningly tortured his poor benefactress by asking constantly if she had news of Geoffrey and when she told him "no," discussing over and over how the lord could have been lost.

She came away from the chamber in which they lay early one evening almost wishing they had died, and before she could reach the safe sanctuary of her own chamber she was waylaid by Sir Guy who told her a priest wished to speak to her. Joanna walked to the hearth with lagging steps, trying to firm her spirit.

"Are you the Lady Joanna of Roselynde, daughter of Lady Alinor?"

Joanna's attention fixed; her heart began to pound. "Yes, I am."

"I have a message for you if you will let me see your hair."

Any other time, Joanna would have been furious. Now, trembling with eagerness, she undid her wimple and exposed the bright braids beneath her headdress. The only reason for such great need to be sure of her identity must be to avoid any chance of news of this message coming to the wrong ears. Then the message must be from Geoffrey or—or about him."

"The message," she urged with burning eyes, "what is your message?"

Instead of replying, the priest drew a roll of parchment from the bosom of his gown and handed it to her. Joanna broke the seal without even looking. It was too easy to take the ring from a dead man's hand, and if the seal was someone else's the priest would tell her. What she saw within the roll in a single glance made her clutch the senseless skin to her breast and cry aloud.

"He is alive! Thanks be to God, he is alive!" and then, tremblingly to the priest, "Thank you, oh thank you, Father, thank you."

"Perhaps you had better read what is written before you are so full of thanks."

The color that had rushed to Joanna's face drained away again. "But it is in his hand," she stammered, "in his own hand! Is he not alive?"

"Yes, yes. I did not mean to frighten you. Lord Geoffrey is alive and well cared for and whole of limb and wit," the priest assured her kindly, "but—"

Back came Joanna's color and she laughed aloud. "Then I care for nothing else. All else I can contrive for, even if it be to move the earth, so long as he lives and is safe." She seized the priest and kissed him and then she kissed Sir Guy. But when Joanna tried to question the priest about Geoffrey, she received little satisfaction. He had seen her husband only twice—once, when Geoffrey was first brought to the keep and Lady Gilliane thought he would die, the priest had been called to administer the viaticum. But Geoffrey had recovered, the priest said hastily, and this last time, when the letter was handed to him, Geoffrey was sitting up in a chair.

"He has not been to mass?" Joanna asked. She was really inquiring about whether he was too weak to walk to the chapel, but she saw the priest's eyes shift uneasily and fear touched her again. "What, is he imprisoned?" she cried. "He is an honorable man. It is not needful to lock him in like a wild beast."

"It is for his own good," the priest replied severely. "If the king's agents had found him, he would *not* be alive and well now."

It might be true, Joanna knew, but there was something else that was not being told her. She turned anxiously to the precious letter she held in her hand.

"Considering the disaster that has overtaken us," Geoffrey wrote after a tender salutation, "my situation is none so ill, but I am afraid that it will cost you high to have me back. Isabella has offered twice my ransom to obtain my dead body, and I have promised that Sir Louis of Baisieux, who took me prisoner, will lose nothing by his kindness in preserving my life. This I hope will not be difficult."

There followed a long passage describing what might be expected from the strongboxes of Geoffrey's various keeps. Joanna scarcely glanced through this. She had no intention of wasting time going from one place to another all over England to collect jewels and money when she could take what she needed from Roselynde. The sum could be restored to her mother from Geoffrey's coffers when he was home safe.

That came to an end and the next line caught and held Joanna's attention. "There is another matter, however, that may give you some trouble. Lady Gilliane's husband, that Léon of Baisieux whom I wounded and ordered spared because of his great spirit on the ships in Damme, is held for ransom by Sir Walter of Halfand in East Sussex. It is neces-

sary that you ransom him and send him with my ransom to
Baisieux keep. Sir Léon's mother has, for some reason unknown to me, a great distrust of us. She seems to believe
that harm has befallen her son and no news of this has been
sent here because Sir Walter hopes to collect the ransom
even though his prisoner is dead. There is some slight reason to fear this because no word has been received here
from Sir Léon since news of his capture and ransom was
sent. I think, myself, that Sir Walter may be with the king or
that it was considered unwise to send a letter to France in
view of the animosity that existed between John and Philip.
I hope this is so.''

Joanna reread the last few lines several times. She was
mistress of herself again, and little sign of the new fear that
racked her showed, except that her color faded and her
hands began to tremble. Geoffrey had been very careful, but
it seemed to Joanna that he was implying a frightful threat.
If Sir Léon was not brought home, Geoffrey would be killed
and the double ransom collected from Isabella.

There was little more to read— Geoffrey's love, but
somewhat strained and stiff as if, Joanna thought, he expected that the letter might be read by others. That was almost certainly so, but it was of little importance. This was
no time for words of love. That would come when they were
together. Now was time to act. She turned to Sir Guy.

''From where did Adam write that note of sympathy?''
she asked.

''He was up by Hansey, but I believe he must be back in
Kemp by now.''

''Bid a messenger to make ready, I will write to Sir Walter, but my man is to ride to Adam, who knows Sussex and
will send on someone who knows where this Halfand is.
There is no sense in my man wandering around seeking an
unknown place. Tell the messenger that I will ride forth tomorrow at my best speed, and if he is not well ahead of me,
he will ride nowhere ever again.''

''But where do you go, my lady? And why?''

Joanna looked surprised and then realized Sir Guy did not

know the contents of the letter. She informed him briefly of her purpose. The priest gaped, both at the manner and the intention. He was even more surprised when, to Sir Guy's protests that there was no need for her to go, she replied sharply, "Do not be a fool. Why should Sir Léon be brought back here? I will take ship with him as far east as possible. The less time we are in the narrow sea, the less chance a French ship will come upon us. I will take as little risk as I can. And for that same reason, I wish to land in Flanders rather than a French port."

"Lady Joanna," Sir Guy groaned, "you are not going to France. I beg you to think again. We are still at war with Philip. There is no treaty, not even a truce as yet. If you are taken—"

"I do not intend to be taken. Do not waste my time. I have much to do before I leave with the sun tomorrow."

"My child," the priest expostulated, "whence is this haste? And, indeed, it is not safe—" His voice cut off. If Satan had been female, just so must have the AntiChrist looked when thrust out of heaven. A face of blazing beauty, surrounded by the red flames of her hair, but every feature marked with such pride! Such fury!

"He is mine!"

Sir Guy shuddered. How had he ever deluded himself there was a hair of difference between the mother and the daughter? He had heard that cry before. Well, he would argue no more. If she said she would go to hell, he would do his best to get her there safely.

"He is mine," Joanna repeated more softly, looking significantly at the priest, "and I do not choose that my lord should be in the power of any other person for one day, one hour, one minute longer than is absolutely needful."

The priest said nothing; Joanna's jaw set hard. Lady Gilliane wanted her husband, did she? Well, Geoffrey would come safe away first or Sir Léon would return to his wife in a set of baskets—fingers and toes in one, arms and legs in another, and so forth. She turned away and gestured servants to her and the orders flew like hail. The maids ran to pack clothing; the men to make ready the mistress's tent and arrange the little furniture necessary; the cooking pots and bedding, to go into packs that could be fitted on horses and mules. Sir Guy raised his eyes to God for a moment, but he started away to call a messenger and choose the men-at-arms that would ride with them.

Well before dawn the next day they were on the road, and by midafternoon were approaching Kemp. Before they reached the castle, where the men hoped to at least dismount and stretch their legs, Adam met them in the road. Joanna's messenger, spurred by his mistress's threat, had arrived with the dawn. Then Adam, no more dilatory than his sister and galvanized by the news of Geoffrey's safety, sprang into action. He had ridden to Halfand himself, astride one of the great, swift gray stallions. It was no more than twenty miles, and he was back at Kemp in time to meet Joanna with disappointing news.

"He is not there," Adam called as soon as he identified Joanna surely.

She laid her whip on her mare so violently that the tired beast closed the gap between herself and her brother in a few strides. "Dead? Oh, my God, do not say he is dead!"

"No, but Sir Walter gave him as a surety for a debt to FitzWalter—of all people."

Joanna closed her eyes for a moment, but when she opened them her jaw was set hard. "Do you know where FitzWalter bides?"

"I have done better than just find that out," Adam assured her. "I know where Sir Léon himself is, and Sir Walter has already written to the man who holds him that you come to redeem his debt and that Sir Léon is to be given into your hands. If you have the money, we can go at once."

"I have the money," Joanna said, "but what do you mean 'we' can go at once?"

Adam's bright hazel eyes darkened. "You know how mama can sometimes 'smell' trouble coming? Well, this time I smell it."

"Sir Walter?"

"I think not. He seems a simple, honest man. I do not know what troubles me, only, I will not let you go alone onto the land of one of FitzWalter's vassals. You know FitzWalter has long coddled the Braybrooks, father and son, and young Henry loves you not—or too much, whichever you prefer. The father is with John, but Henry and FitzWalter were both in London when I was there scarce a week ago."

"What were you doing in London?"

"Do not be such a ninny," Adam replied, laughing. "Do you think I am a fool like John to meddle with my vassals' wives and daughters? Nor do I have a taste for serf girls, at least, not as a steady diet."

"Oh," Joanna said faintly, and looked at her "baby" brother with clearer eyes.

Even in the saddle he towered over her, head and shoulders. He had gained considerably in height and bulk since Joanna had seen him, and he had been large even then. In the last six months, it seemed he had changed completely from a boy to a man. Not that his sexual activities made him a man. Joanna was aware that Adam was very attractive and had been sexually active since he was about fourteen. The mention of his attitude had merely made the difference in him visible to her. Adam was unconcerned with her revelation and had reverted to the main problem.

"I do not see why FitzWalter's castellan should even apprise him of the matter," Adam grumbled. "After all, Sir Léon is of no personal importance as a prisoner. He is only surety for a debt. Nonetheless, Horndon on the Hill is only a little more than twenty miles from London. I think it better to take no chance. If we change horses and go at once, we can take Sir Léon and be well away before FitzWalter even hears he is to be ransomed and by whom."

"I agree with all my heart," Joanna responded, "but FitzWalter is a hard master and his castellan might not wish to do anything, even so reasonable as this, without his yea-say."

"I realize that now," Adam said furiously, "but I did not

think of it when I should have. Instead of letting Sir Walter's messenger go, I should have taken the letter myself. But let us start. We can decide what is best to do on the way.''

"It cannot matter," Joanna soothed as they rode toward Kemp to change horses. "If he will not release Sir Léon without FitzWalter's permission, it would not matter whether he knew ahead of time or we brought the letter ourselves.''

"Except then we would have been within—and he would have found it very difficult to deny us anything," Adam remarked grimly.

"That might still be arranged," Joanna said suddenly, and smiled nastily. "Sir Guy," she called over her shoulder, "ride forward here with us." When his horse had been prodded level with theirs, she went on, "I have fifty men. How many can you bring from Kemp, Adam?''

"If I strip the keep, a hundred and fifty or so, I suppose. That is not enough to—''

"We do not even need so many," Joanna interrupted. I will go forward alone, with only ten or fifteen. You know since Winchester and Pembroke have ruled here that most lawlessness has been put down. It is not unreasonable that I should take only a few men as escort on a journey. Even if he does not intend to give me Sir Léon, the man can scarcely refuse me a night's lodging, so I will be taken within. You will stay hid with the rest of the men near as possible. If he gives us Sir Léon, I will make some excuse to leave at once. If he refuses, Sir Guy will make shift to open the gates for you and the men. Well, Sir Guy, can this be done?''

"Now my lady, my lord, you know this is not wise. What can a few days' delay while FitzWalter's permission—'' His voice faded. FitzWalter had an old spite against Joanna's stepfather. Moreover, it might seem to him that Lady Joanna was completely without protectors—her husband was thought to be dead; her father-by-marriage was known to be a prisoner; her stepfather was in France. FitzWalter would not count Adam as a danger—the more fool he, Sir Guy thought, glancing at that redoubtable young man. It might seem the ideal time to grab a prize.

"Yes," he said, nodding firmly, "it can be done easily enough."

Expecting approval, Joanna looked at Adam and was surprised to see a worried frown still fixed on his face. She felt a twinge of exasperation. Could Adam have become so manlike that he was going to say it was too dangerous for a woman? Ian was always trying to keep her padded with feathers and Geoffrey was getting that way too since they were married.

"It is a most excellent plan," Adam said slowly and then, almost absently, "be sure if you are denied Sir Léon to take a real knife to bed with you, Joanna, not that jeweled toy you eat with—and do not like an idiot fall asleep." He looked around suddenly. "Why in hell did you not bring Brian with you?"

"He was hurt, and I did not wish him to run so far. Also, he is too bold a mark. If I wish to change my identity in France, he would give me away. But although you say excellent, Adam, you look black as thunder."

Joanna was divided between amusement at the thought of what Ian and Geoffrey would say if they heard Adam's precautions for her safety and concern about what was worrying him.

"Curse me," he exclaimed irritably, "I do not know why. I do not see how we can fail. Even if Sir Guy should be suspected and the keep cannot be opened, I can have a full army at the gate in a week. Still, something lies heavy on my heart, Jo. I smell trouble. In my nostrils something—I do not know what—stinks to high heaven."

CHAPTER TWENTY-SEVEN

At first Adam's ability to sense danger seemed greatly at fault. Nothing occurred on the road to Horndon on the Hill, but that was not surprising because, with the men Adam brought, they were over a hundred strong. Their numbers created one difficulty in that they were delayed by the small capacity of the boats that ferried across the Thames. Once the entire party was assembled on the north shore, however, it was only little more than an hour before Adam was disposing of his men in a small woodland they believed to be about five miles from Horndon keep. Since it was still before dawn and Joanna and her men had been in the saddle for twenty-four hours, except for brief rests and the time on the ferry, Adam insisted that they take time to sleep.

"No," he said to Joanna before she could protest. "You cannot arrive at dawn looking like death. You might just as well scream in the man's ear that this matter is of overgreat importance. Do you want to make him suspicious?"

"No," she agreed meekly, knowing he was right and again aware that Adam was a man, not a boy.

In the end, the caution seemed unnecessary. When Joanna arrived at Horndon with Sir Guy, Knud, and eight men-at-arms, she was greeted pleasantly but completely casually. Sir Léon had been warned and was ready and, although the castellan counted every coin to be certain every penny was paid, he made no more than a polite demur when Joanna said she would leave after dinner. He asked, of course, what she wanted with Sir Léon and she promptly told him a farradiddle about Salisbury requesting that the man be freed because his wife had appealed to him before the battle. He then proffered condolences on the loss of her husband. Joanna swiftly turned her face away, a gesture that might mean anything at all—a desire to conceal grief or joy or any other emotion anyone wished to read into it. Tonelessly, she said only that it was not certain yet. Her reluctance to talk on the subject, for whatever reason, was plain. Politely, the castellan forbore to say more.

It seemed to Joanna that she did not breathe from the moment she entered the keep until she left it, but there had been no hostile move, not even a suggestion of one. She was not sure whether it was her fatigue, Adam's premonition, or something within herself, but even now, when they were clear of arrow shot, she remained uneasy.

The road wound down from the hill upon which the keep sat. The land was flatter as it ran south toward the Thames some ten miles away. To the west another road branched off in the direction of London. Along this, some distance away, Joanna spied a troop of men riding. They were moving quickly but not in great haste. This was reasonable because the afternoon was drawing on and they might have far to go. There was no reason at all to believe they were headed for Horndon. This was a well-settled district and there were good-sized towns and ports and other keeps east along the road. Nonetheless, the breath caught in Joanna's throat.

Just as fear touched her, Sir Guy spurred forward, saying urgently, "My lady—"

"Yes, I see," she replied, "can we beat them to the crossroads?"

"We have no choice. Knud, ride forward with four men, four behind Lady Joanna. Sir Léon, I must lash you to your saddle. Keep your place in front of me or I will stun you and carry you like a sack of grain. I have no time now for talk of honor. My lady, ride fast. Even if they be innocent, I have no taste to meet fifty or sixty men when I have ten."

From then on Joanna had to give her full attention to her unfamiliar mount and her riding. She had no time to watch the oncoming troop. The few glances she was able to spare gave her little comfort. It seemed to her that they, too, had increased their speed. If that was real and not merely a vision generated by her fear, it was a very bad sign. The leader of the troop could see her party as clearly as she saw his. She tried to tell herself that the spurt of speed they had put on would attract even a perfectly indifferent person and arouse curiosity. They might be outlaws fleeing. There was no conviction in the thought. Upon the hill with the afternoon light on them, it must have been apparent that they were a respectable party led by a woman and a knight.

Now they could hear shouts from the oncoming troop. Joanna and her men laid on frantically with whips and heels, and they careened past the worst danger point with what seemed only bare yards to spare. Fortunately, the horses were relatively fresh. They had been well rested during the time Joanna slept in the camp in the woods and again while the ransom was paid and amenities exchanged in Horndon. Thus they were able to sustain the same wild pace down the road, narrowly clearing another party, which had separated from the rear of the main body and cut across some fields to try to head them off.

Although threats and promises were shouted after them, Joanna realized that no arrows had been released. That almost certainly identified their pursuers as FitzWalter's people. Only his men would be aware of the value of the prize and thus reluctant to take any chance of harming Joanna. Most of the shouts were now directed to pointing out that Joanna's party could not possibly escape. No one would shelter them, and the river would soon bring a stop to their flight. Obviously, they did not know of Adam waiting less than three miles ahead.

That knowledge and the fact that their horses were slightly outdistancing their pursuers gave Joanna some confidence. Her mind was able to free itself from the immediate danger and wonder how FitzWalter knew so quickly of her offer to ransom the Frenchman. Had the casual attitude of the castellan been a trap? Surely not. There were all sorts of perfectly reasonable devices he could have used to delay her so that she would be kept in the keep. Most probably the castellan had sent word of the transaction immediately, not because he was suspicious but because he did not want FitzWalter to become suspicious of him.

Soon Joanna became aware that the noise behind them

was diminishing. She cast a hopeful glance over her shoulder. The troop was still hard on their heels, although a little farther back; they had merely become tired of shouting. That was too bad. Adam would be warned by the pounding hooves and probably he had scouts out, but the warning would come late. The sound of voices would carry much farther and communicate far more urgency. Joanna herself could not cry a warning to her brother because that would betray his presence to the pursuers. However, there was more than one way to skin a hare.

"Leave us be!" she screamed at the men who followed. "We have done no one any harm. We are peaceful travelers only."

Naturally, that brought a spate of new threats of what would befall them if they did not stop and assurances of safety and freedom if they did. Joanna was staring anxiously ahead, looking for a familiar sign along the wooded area of the road they were passing. Fear almost dominated her again. This was the place, yet the woods seemed empty. In the moment she thought that, she was nearly startled into losing her reins and her seat by a roar of voices which burst out alongside and just behind her small party. Surprised into irrationality, she cried her brother's name aloud before she realized that it must be he and his men who had charged out of the wood, lances set.

The unexpected ambush was a complete success. The pursuers had not even drawn their weapons, so little did they expect danger or resistance from Joanna's few men. Adam's lance spitted three before it broke and he cast it down. The first wave of his men were nearly as successful as their powerful leader, most of them taking two victims before they needed to draw swords. Of course the advantage lasted only for the first half minute of contact. The screams of the wounded and the cries of warning of those who managed to avoid injury alerted the men who followed.

Adam's force was by far the larger, but that was of no immediate advantage because the narrow road was the only space clear enough to fight in. It was necessary for his men to make their way through the wood to come upon the tail of erstwhile pursuers, which stretched out to the rear. This did not bother Adam in the least. Bellowing joyously, he laid out three more men at what had been the head of the column and began to work his way systematically back to the end of the troop. He did not seem to be paying any attention to what his men did, but Joanna could tell that they had been well instructed beforehand.

With the realization that it was her brother who had come to her rescue, Joanna had pulled her lathered mare to a halt and turned about. Her first reaction, after relief, was a renewal of fear. If Adam should come to harm, she would never forgive herself for allowing him to come along. However, it was impossible after a few minutes either to continue to feel much fear or to delude herself that she still had any control over her brother's actions. If Adam was hurt, it would be by an act of God. Joanna knew a good deal about fighting. She had watched her stepfather train his squires and seen their mock combat since she was a child. It was perfectly clear to her that her brother outclassed every other man there both in strength and skill. In addition, there was his obvious delight in what he was doing; nothing, it was plain, could give him greater pleasure.

Then a burst of concerted movement toward the center of the group drew Joanna's attention. A hiss of combined anger and concern was drawn from her. In the center of a knot of men who were clearly more desirous of escaping than of continuing the battle, Joanna saw Henry de Braybrook's shield. Politically speaking, it would be as great a disaster to harm or kill him as to become his prisoner. Her eyes flashed toward Adam, but it seemed to her there was no chance of stopping that magnificent machine of destruction.

"Sir Guy," she cried desperately, "go around the battle. Bid the men to let Braybrook go."

The knight spat an agonized oath. His duty was first to protect Joanna, but he was aware of the danger involved. With their most powerful protector a prisoner, any accusation brought against Adam by Braybrook's father might result in dangerous penalties being levied by the king, who did not love Alinor or her family. If Braybrook escaped unharmed, he might be ashamed to admit the conflict and anyway Adam could lodge a complaint for abduction with Peter of Winchester to counter any complaint Braybrook would make. As long as Sir Henry was not hurt, there would be little need to take a complaint from him seriously.

In a few quick words, Sir Guy instructed Knud who, in any case, knew what he was supposed to do, and rode off into the wood. Joanna watched in a fever of indecision. She would have loved to have seen Adam squash Braybrook like a worm, but she knew there would be no way to keep secret what had happened. Perhaps if they could have killed every man of Braybrook's troop—but Joanna could see that some had already taken to their heels and were fleeing back the way they had come.

That made her aware of a new danger. If Sir Guy got Braybrook loose, the whole troop would retreat. Would Adam be so caught up in the fighting that he would pursue them? If he did, they would soon be under the walls of Horndon and, almost certainly, that would bring the men of the castle out on them. Then they would be outnumbered. What should she do? Follow Adam to almost certain capture? That would mean a long delay in freeing Geoffrey, at best. Would Lady Gilliane and Sir Léon's mother lose patience and decide to take Isabella's offer? Should she recall her own men and fly with Sir Léon to the coast? But that would reduce Adam's force dangerously and might mean her brother's death.

With dilated eyes, Joanna watched the fighting, horrified to see it grow even more intense as Adam drove in toward Braybrook's group. Then, just as it seemed Adam's next stroke would break through the band of men protecting Sir Henry, the men behind Braybrook began to give way. In another heartbeat, a path was opened and the popinjay turned and fled into the wood. His guards followed promptly. Joanna held her breath, used the breath to shriek her brother's name as she saw his sword coming down toward Sir Guy's head.

Whether Adam heard her or recognized the raised shield, he aborted the blow. Joanna had closed her eyes, terrified

that her brother's temper, aroused by the fighting, might be
vented on Sir Guy when frustrated of more legitimate prey.
Impotent to do anything else, she breathed hasty prayers,
which were promptly answered. The sounds of fighting died
down with almost as great rapidity as they had begun. Inspired by success, Joanna added a few more Aves for good
luck.

"For Jesus' sake, Jo, do not be such a goose," Adam's
laughing voice said. "Why are you sitting there with your
eyes shut muttering Hail Marys? It was the greatest fun, and
we were never in the slightest danger."

"You may not have been," Joanna said indignantly,
"but I was. And if you want the truth, I was not praying for
you. I was afraid you would murder poor Sir Guy for letting
Braybrook escape." While she spoke, she looked him over
carefully. It was a waste of time. Adam was not even breathing hard.

"Oh, I am not such a fool as to have done Braybrook any
real harm. I was hoping to make a hole in his other buttock
to match the one Brian made."

"Who told you about that?" Joanna asked, thanking God
she had not known Adam was aware of Braybrook's attempt
on her. She would have been ten times as frightened

"Geoffrey told me. He warned me to watch dear Henry
close. He was afraid the spiteful worm would do me a hurt
to hurt you. Never mind that now. We must go and go
quickly, before they come out of the keep after us. I am not
sure they will. FitzWalter may not want to be mixed into
this—at least, he must have told Braybrook that you would
be here and may have guessed what would follow, but he
may not wish to be openly involved. I hope so, but I dare
not trust in it."

"So you did think of that. I was afraid that in the heat of
the fighting you would forget and be tempted to pursue
them."

"Will you stop thinking of me as an idiot babe! It is one
thing to play at games with you. It is quite another to play
the fool in battle. I am too well taught to be carried away by
the 'heat of fighting' or any other kind of heat either."

It was the truth. Adam was a man, completely a man. Joanna saw that he had even given orders to the men before coming to her. The whole were already binding up the wounds of the injured and getting them on horses, those sorely hurt—of whom there were very few—tied pillion behind others lightly hurt but not sound enough to fight. These Adam then ordered to ride ahead with Joanna, Sir Guy, Sir Léon, and about twenty unhurt men. The remainder would stay behind with him to guard the rear.

"It remains only to decide where you want to go," Adam said.

"I had thought to go to Dover and take ship there for Flanders with a Lowlander who does not love the French and would agree to some tale concerning whence I came, but now— Dover is too far, I think, and my last wish is to need to wait for the ferry to cross the Thames while those from the keep ride down upon us."

"If that is best for you, I will make shift to hold them off," Adam assured her.

"No," Joanna replied. "I think now I will ride for Mersea. The distance is not much farther and I can be sure of a safe haven from FitzWalter or anyone else if there is no ship to take me at once."

The first hour of their journey was tense because it was necessary to ride back almost under the very gates of Horndon to strike the road for Mersea. They drove their horses as hard as they could, considering the work the beasts had already had. When all except Adam's great gray destrier were stumbling and plodding with hanging heads, Adam at last called a rest. Joanna went at once to see to the wounded men as well as she could with only the few salves she carried for a chance hurt on a journey. She had a full stock of medicine packed away, but that was for Geoffrey if he needed it and she would not use a fingerful for any other purpose.

Adam had had no rest at all since dawn the preceding day. Even the tameless energy of his big body and his youth must be a little worn down by thirty-six hours of responsibility and violent activity. When Joanna was finished doing what she could for the men, she found her brother asleep. She moved away knowing she would disturb his rest if she sat and stared at him. Probably she should follow his example, Joanna thought, but she was too keyed up to rest and, after a moment's consideration, sought out the prize that all this effort had won.

Sir Léon was sitting with his back against a tree with Knud's eye upon him. When Joanna approached, obviously about to speak to him, Knud prodded the prisoner roughly to his feet, hissing, "You stand and bow when the lady comes near, hear!"

"That is not necessary, Knud," Joanna said caustically, "Sir Léon is not my man, after all. If his manners are of the gutter, it is no affair of yours or mine." She waited a moment, but the man simply gaped at her, and she shrugged scornfully. "Ah, well, I see the 'gentleman' is too proud—in spite of the fact that I have just bought him free. I will accept your courtesy, Knud."

Having been his mistress's escort many times, Knud knew what was expected of him during a rest period too short to bother unpacking. He whipped off his cloak and laid it doubled on the ground for Joanna to sit upon. "Shall I make a 'rest' for you, lady?" he asked.

Joanna smiled. "No, move the cloak to the tree. Go and lie down. I will give warning if our 'guest' should take any odd notions."

Obediently, Knud moved a little distance away, too far to hear low voices but near enough to get at Sir Léon should he try to run or make a threatening gesture toward Joanna.

"Madam," Sir Léon said at last in a voice made thin by bewilderment, "what do you mean 'you have bought me free?' Who are you? What is going on? Was that fight over me? If so, someone is badly mistaken. I am a simple knight, of no value to anyone except my own family."

Joanna's cold expression softened somewhat. Perhaps the man was not deliberately rude but simply bemused. It was true that she had not told him anything, but she assumed he would have been told by the castellan that his ransom was being paid. She gestured to him to be seated.

"I am the Lady Joanna of Roselynde and I have paid your ransom. The fight had nothing to do with you. That was a private matter and need be no concern of yours."

Sir Léon plumped down on the ground as if the strength had gone out of his legs. "Paid my ranson," he breathed, "Why?"

"Because your wife holds my husband and she would not agree to free him unless I brought you as well as the money."

"My wife? Gilliane?" There was blank incredulity in Sir Léon's face.

Astonished at his surprise, Joanna raised her brows. "Is there some reason why your wife should not desire to have you back?"

Before he could reply to the provocative question, Sir Guy came to ask Joanna if she wished to eat or drink. His deferential manner and the fact that he served Joanna himself and then discreetly withdrew out of earshot, made Sir Léon's eyes open.

"The lord of Roselynde must be a great man," he said.

"There is no lord of Roselynde," Joanna snapped. "My mother is the lady of Roselynde. I will be the lady after her, and my daughter—God grant me one—will be lady after me. My husband is Lord Geoffrey FitzWilliam. His sons may have his lands."

For a minute that proud speech held Sir Léon mute. He blinked, cleared his throat, and recalled his mind with some effort to what was more essential to him than the inconceivable fact of a woman with power and the will to use it.

"Then I am free? But—"

"You will be free when Lord Geoffrey is by my side."

"But how is that to be managed? I will give parole gladly, of course, but it will be difficult for me—"

"You have nothing to say or to do except by my order," Joanna remarked succinctly, "until, as I said, Lord Geoffrey is at liberty. I will take you to France and to your keep, and I will hold you straitly until my husband is released."

"*You* will take me to France? But—but—a woman— I

have heard little news, it is true. Is the war over? Is a treaty signed?''

"What are wars to me?" Joanna snapped. "I go to free my husband, and with God's help—which I do not doubt to have because God helps those who help themselves—I will accomplish my purpose. Until then, I will take your parole not to try to escape, but there will be sharp eyes and strong arms to see that you do not. If you do not wish to be trussed like a fowl and carried like a sack of oats, you would do well to keep your word. If you are honest, you will have as easy a journey as I. If you are not—I will give you reason to be sorry for it.''

Joanna pulled back her skirt a little and curled her legs under her preparatory to rising. She looked at Sir Léon, even extended a hand toward him, but he merely stared at it uncomprehendingly. Before the hand was withdrawn, both Sir Guy and Knud were beside her. Rank has its privileges. Joanna placed her hand in Sir Guy's and he lifted her to her feet. She looked down at Sir Léon, shook her head, and laughed.

"I hope, Sir Léon, that your neglect was owing to resentment. If it was not, I understand well why you were surprised that your wife should want you back. Certainly I would not. I imagine any woman could do very well without the company of so coarse a lout. My common servant is more 'gentle' in his manners.''

Until that moment resentment was very far from Sir Léon's mind. His emotions were compounded equally of amazement at Joanna's personality, puzzlement at how his wife had come to hold so important a prisoner, and gratitude to everyone and anyone for having brought about a thing he had almost ceased to hope for. The contempt with which Joanna regarded him stung, however, specially as he did not see how he had deserved it. He had been taken prisoner, but certainly not through tame yielding, and that could happen to any man overwhelmed by superior force. Besides, her own husband had been taken prisoner. That Joanna felt no contempt for Lord Geoffrey—in spite of the queer things she said about his property—was clear enough.

Each time she sneered at him Sir Léon thought, she had demeaned his manners. Wherein had they failed? He had not spit nor stuck his fingers in his nose nor passed wind. And what had manners to do with whether Gilliane wanted him back? Of course she wanted him back. She was a woman, capable only of sewing and overseeing the duties of the house. He watched, bemused, as a dozen men hastily shed their cloaks so that some could be spread on the ground, the knight's folded and used for a pillow for Joanna to lie down upon. Ridiculous! If they had to fight again the men would be stiff and cold. Voices then were hushed; if a man wished to speak, he plucked his partner by the sleeve and drew well away. One would think the creature was made of glass, and yet Sir Léon himself had seen her ride as hard as any man and watch a battle from scarce a spear's length away without blanching.

From the time of that rest, from which all rose greatly refreshed, everything went right. The weather was good; they were not pursued; and when they came to Mersea there was a ship in harbor that would admirably serve their purpose. The merchant had cargo for Bruges. He would deliver that, then sail to Dunkerque, where Joanna and her party would debark. If they were questioned at the port, the master would agree to a simple tale. Sir Léon had gone to Bruges to bring home a recently widowed, childless sister. There he had fallen ill and was still too weak to bear arms. Thus, he had hired Sir Guy and five other men to protect him, his sister, and her dower (the excuse for the baggage carrying Geoffrey's ranson) which was, of course, being returned with her.

Sir John had gasped with shock and then argued violently against Joanna's trip to France. He had offered himself as her deputy. He had reasoned, appealed to Adam for support—and failed. Adam was aware that most women were not capable of such things, but that had nothing to do with his mother and his sister. Most women were good only for futtering; one could not talk to them nor depend upon them for anything. Barring going into battle, however,

Alinor and Joanna could do anything—and they were the only women *worth* anything.

Even Adam had protested at the small force Joanna planned to take, but she had pointed out that Philip's France was a quieter and more orderly place than John's England. Moreover, a large force of any kind traveling near the Flemish border would be greatly suspect and sure to be stopped.

"And can you imagine what would happen if the men were overheard speaking English?" Joanna said, exasperated with their silliness. "Where will I find a larger force of men that speaks French? As it is, Knud and the other four will have to mind their tongues."

It was an unanswerable argument. Sir John gave up and switched to another problem. "Do you trust Sir Léon? With so few men, once he is in his own country, what is to stop him from betraying you or simply riding off and abandoning you?"

Joanna smiled. "I think he is an honorable man, even if he is a clod, but I will be safe rather than sorry, I assure you. Sir Léon will neither speak a false word nor escape because 'his sister,' as is fitting, will ride pillion behind him and that 'dear sister' will carry in her hand a long, very sharp knife, which will be hidden by her cloak and pressed into Sir Léon's back."

Sir John cleared his throat and closed his eyes; Adam began to laugh.

"That sounds all right," Adam agreed, "but do not poke him for fun, Joanna. His wife probably wants him with a whole skin."

"I," Joanna said indignantly, "do not consider sticking people with knives funny."

How sweet and soft she looks, Sir John thought, but even if she did not think it funny, there was no doubt that she would stab the man without the slightest hesitation.

"That will be safe enough while riding," he pointed out, "but it is too far from Dunkerque to Baisieux to go without a stop."

"For that there is also an easy answer," Joanna replied.

"Remember that Sir Léon has been ill. Whenever he dismounts, Knud and Sir Guy will help him down and 'support' his faltering footsteps. And should he say anything—er—out of the ordinary, his poor 'sister' will burst into tears and beg him to recognize her and cease from raving."

Adam began to laugh again. "Oh, Jo, let me come. I will be far better than Sir Guy at comforting Sir Léon's poor distracted sister."

Joanna giggled but shook her head at him. "No, someone from Roselynde with authority must be in England to watch over the lands. Besides, you would only make me laugh and spoil everything."

The planning had been done in private, but at dinner that day Sir Léon was informed of the excuse that would be used to cover Joanna's trip to France. He acceded with great willingness to all except the need for the precautions against his escape.

"I may be only a simple knight," he protested, "but I am a man of honor. In any case, why should I wish to escape? You are taking me where I wish to go and you are also paying ransom for my wife's prisoner."

The men looked rather self-conscious. All were in sympathy with his feeling. Even Adam rubbed his nose in embarrassment. "You know, Joanna," he said softly, "I would not like it if my word was not good enough. Perhaps—"

"I," Joanna pointed out icily, "am not a man and have no honor. Poor weak woman that I am, I must protect myself. If Sir Léon breaks his word, can I go and demand that he meet me body to body to make good his promise? Either he goes as I say or he goes bound hand and foot and loaded with chains in England and drugged into sleep, a sick man, in a horse litter in France." She stared at Sir Léon, her eyes pale, brilliant stars in her angry face.

"Say yes," Sir Guy, next to Sir Léon, whispered urgently. "She will do it—or worse."

Thus urged, Sir Léon agreed quickly. Actually, he did not much care and had protested for form's sake. What he had said was perfectly true. He had no intention of escap-

ing. Joanna was fulfilling his sweetest dreams; why should
he try to run away from her?

What was more singular and therefore more absorbing to
him was the deferential attention paid Joanna by *all* the
men, not only her own servants. Sir John, the master of this
great keep and wide estates, bowed to her, kissed her hand,
assisted her every step, although he must have known she
was strong as a dray horse. Even the big, magnificent
fighter that Sir Léon now knew was Lady Joanna's brother
bowed and scraped, pulling the bench out for her to sit upon
and serving her attentively, cutting all the best pieces from
the haunch for her trencher.

Inside, Sir Léon grew a little cold, wondering what awful
power the woman wielded. Perhaps she was a witch. He
turned to Sir Guy, planning a question that might clarify the
matter, and noticed that the knight was paying very similar
attentions to the young girl, Sir John's daughter, who sat
beside him. The sneers at his manners began to make
sense—at least, not sense. To Sir Léon it did not seem to be
at all sensible to waste such attentions on a woman, but, if
that was the way the great ones lived, why should he mark
himself as a lesser being by omitting what cost nothing to
perform.

Attentive watching taught much—that "manners" were
ingrained and rather meaningless habit among these people.
Young Adam certainly stood in no awe of his sister, Sir
Léon soon realized. He spoke to her with great familiarity
and, from time to time, they squabbled like children, breaking into laughter moments later. Sir John's wife bore bruises
that surely spoke of a beating administered by her husband,
yet he used the same forms of courtesy to her. Carefully, Sir
Léon began aping the ways of his betters and Sir Guy, anxious for a pleasant journey that would irritate his mistress as
little as possible, helped with hints and advice.

There was plenty of time to practice. Although only a few
days were spent at Mersea waiting for the ship to load, during which time Lady Joanna's maid arrived from Kemp
where she had been left, the weather was so good after they
set sail that the passage was made at a snail's pace. Often

the sailors were set to pulling at the oars because the ship was completely becalmed. Even when there was a breeze, it was so light that the ship moved hardly faster than when rowed. Joanna's outward manner remained placid, but inside she fretted and fumed and feared and her tongue grew sharper and sharper. Sir Léon found the company of a sharp-tongued woman, who could not be beaten, could be very painful. He found himself leaping to his feet and bowing at the flicker of a woman's skirt—twice to his embarrassment to Edwina the maid.

That, however, brought him a whole new set of lessons. From that merry-hearted slut he learned what Lady Elizabeth had taught Geoffrey, that a man's pleasure could be immeasurably heightened by restraint and the cooperation of his partner. Edwina was, after all, no common, paid whore, no terrified serf girl. When she said do thus and so and I will show you a new delight, he did—and was delighted. The only trouble in his mind was that, now and again, he heard an echo of Joanna saying, "I understand well why you are surprised that your wife should want you back." At the time he had thought her mad. Now he began to wonder uneasily what Gilliane was learning from some months of Lord Geoffrey's company.

The morals of these high folks, he thought, were as coarse as their manners were fine. Did not Lady Joanna turn a blind eye to her maid's doings? Did she not spend many hours in the alcove curtained off for her all alone with Sir Guy? Would Lord Geoffrey respect the wife of a simple knight or would he use Gilliane as Léon himself used the wives and daughters of his serfs? He began to curse the calm winds as heartily as Joanna did, fret as uneasily at the slow unloading and reloading of cargo in Bruges.

At last they came ashore at Dunkerque and were mounted. After that they proceeded at the rate Joanna wished to set. Still, they covered near ninety miles from Dunkerque to Baisieux in remarkably short time. Joanna knew from Sir Léon's rising excitement when they were coming near. When he breathed, "My land, my own land," with tears in his eyes, Joanna made a sharp gesture behind her and Sir Guy was suddenly athwart them, drawn sword presented to Sir Léon's unarmored breast. He gasped with surprise and horror, too stunned by this sudden, completely unexpected threat to struggle as he was bound hand and foot to the mare. Now Joanna took the reins, sheathing the knife at her belt. Knud rode on one side, Sir Guy on the other with the three men-at-arms grouping and guarding the baggage animals.

To Sir Léon's startled protests, Joanna replied, "Did you think I intended to ride into your keep, thus yielding myself, my money, and my husband *all* into your power? I am a woman, but, as you should know by now, not a fool."

"I am an honorable man," he exclaimed. "I swear, I never had such a thought! Never!"

"Perhaps," Joanna agreed, "perhaps, but there are more things than you know involved here."

It had occurred to Joanna on the ship that two dangers still threatened. Although she and her party had been careful not to mention Isabella's offer to Sir Léon, it was not impossible that FitzWalter knew of it. If so, his castellan might know also and, on orders, might have explained to the "simple knight" that, having collected Geoffrey's double ransom, the amount could be doubled yet again by killing the entire party, burying Joanna and her men quietly, and sending Geoffrey's body to Isabella. What could be safer or simpler? It was certainly the kind of treachery FitzWalter would think of and enjoy.

After these weeks of Sir Léon's company, Joanna did not think this first threat a very strong probability. There was, however, also the chance that Sir Léon's wife had thought that matter out for herself. Lady Gilliane could not know Joanna would bring the ransom herself, but whoever brought it could be eliminated. Joanna's breath grew shorter. Perhaps Geoffrey was already dead. Perhaps the woman had kept him alive only long enough to write that letter. If a hair on his head had been harmed, Joanna thought, she would send Sir Léon back to his wife all right—in very small pieces.

When they came in sight of the keep, Sir Guy moved forward to implement the next step of the plan he and Joanna had worked out in the hours he had spent shut into her stuffy quarters aboard ship. The gates had been closed when their party came into view. Although Sir Guy had no intention of entering anyway, his heart sank. To close the gates against so small a party was a very bad sign. Usually travelers were welcomed into any keep with open arms for the sake of the variety and news they brought. Nonetheless, he called out, identifying them and demanding that Lord Geoffrey be sent out, either alone or with no more than five men to guard him.

The guard in the small tower shouted down excitedly. In a few minutes, a woman appeared in the tower. "Is it really you, Léon?" she called. "It is a bare three weeks since I sent the priest off, and he has not even returned with an answer."

"Speak to her," Joanna ordered. "Tell her something only you could know so that she may be sure it is truly you, in case she cannot see you clear enough."

"Gilliane, it is I. I—"

But there was no need for him to continue. Obviously his wife recognized his voice. She uttered a cry and turned to run down the steps. In the same instant the bars of the gates could be heard shifting and, as soon as possible, they opened wide. The woman appeared.

"Come in," she called, "come in and be welcome." Her voice shook.

"We will not enter," Sir Guy replied. "Send Lord Geoffrey out."

"But he is still very weak," Lady Gilliane protested. "Come in, I beg you."

Weak? Maybe dead? Joanna's heart fluttered in her breast. Uncaring of arrows that might be launched from the keep or any other danger, she rode forward—the reins in her left hand, the knife in her right flashing as it came across Sir Léon's throat.

"Send him out!" she screamed. "Carry him out if must be, but if he is not out before the sun touches that treetop it is nearing, I will kill your husband here before your eyes."

"In God's name, Gilliane," Sir Léon shouted, "she will do it. She will! Send out her man!"

CHAPTER TWENTY-EIGHT

Even in her short life, Joanna had suffered many sorrows and anxieties. She had watched beside her father and her infant sister as they died. She had suffered agonies in the last few weeks over Geoffrey. Nonetheless, the ten minutes between the time Lady Gilliane ran from the gates of Baisieux keep and the time a frail and haggard Geoffrey, supported by two servants, appeared in Lady Gilliane's place were the longest in her whole life.

"Geoffrey!" she shrieked.

Her impulse was to fling herself from the saddle and run to him. With an effort that was near physical pain, she suppressed it. Instead, she turned her mare and whipped it back out of arrow range.

"Here," she cried, "come to me here, where they cannot kill you."

"You fool!" Geoffrey roared, producing a remarkable volume of sound for one who, a moment ago, appeared half-fainting. Invigorated by a burst of rage, he cast off the supporting arms of the servants and limped forward. "What do you here in an enemy land? With only five men to guard you? Put down that knife! Get off that horse! What do you mean by offering such an insult to people who have shown me so much kindness!"

Ordinarily, Joanna did not have the quick temper of Lady Alinor, but in the last weeks she had endured too much. All at once it seemed as if all her torments were her husband's fault—the weeks of fear, the stunned frozen horror, the nights and days of weeping. Her immediate reaction was a rage that rendered her speechless and drove from her mind completely the fact that the object of all her misery was before her eyes. She did, indeed, throw down the knife. She threw it at Geoffrey! Fortunately, her aim was erratic because Sir Léon's body prevented her from a straight cast. She missed, which was just as well because Geoffrey was still much too feeble and sore to dodge.

"Am I a fool?" she gasped, tumbling from the horse and fronting her husband furiously. "You know what Isabella's offer was. Did you think I would ride right into the lion's mouth so that I and you and the money I brought could be swallowed and then you could be disgorged, dead, and another double ransom collected?"

"I would not!" Sir Léon gasped. "Nor any of mine. Why should you think me so treacherous a cur?"

"Joanna!" Geoffrey exclaimed, appalled. "Enough! Whatever you feared, it must now be plain to you that no treachery is intended. Was it needful to say aloud such thoughts?" He turned his head to Sir Guy, who had ridden back as soon as he saw Joanna move and had dismounted when he saw Geoffrey's face in case he should need support. "Sir Guy, please unbind Sir Léon and take my wife up before you into the keep."

Sir Guy turned pale. He was not Geoffrey's man but Alinor's and thus Joanna's. Perhaps in most other families that would be a technicality not worth considering; the husband would be the master. This was not true for the ladies of Roselynde. Ian and Alinor were most scrupulous not to give conflicting orders, even when they were quarreling, nor had the situation ever arisen between Joanna and Geoffrey previously.

"My lord," he pleaded, "I—"

In the few moments that had passed, Joanna had really taken in Geoffrey's appearance. Moreover, no one had ridden out of the keep to overwhelm them when she dismounted and removed all threat from Sir Léon. What was more, the man himself had not made any attempt to find safety behind his own walls. Even bound as he was, he could have kicked the mare into motion. He seemed far more interested in refuting Joanna's accusation than in taking advantage of a situation in which he plainly held the upper hand.

"Yes, free him," Joanna concurred, thus lifting Sir Guy from the horns of the dilemma upon which he had been painfully perched. "I beg your pardon, Sir Leon," she continued, "I hope you understand that a woman must take precautions a man might scorn to take."

Joanna did not, however, turn her head toward him. Her eyes remained fixed upon Geoffrey, and she moved forward slowly, as if a sudden gesture on her part might topple him from his feet. Her soft gray eyes were misty with concern.

"How badly were you hurt?" she breathed.

Geoffrey's lips twitched with suppressed laughter even as tears of joy rose into his eyes. "Since I am now near well, it does not matter," he said to reassure her. "I have been well cared for."

"Will you mount my horse, my lord?" Sir Guy asked, having finished with Sir Léon's bonds and feeling that Geoffrey should not be on his feet any longer than necessary.

"No," Geoffrey protested, "that will hurt worse than walking back."

"There is no need," Sir Léon said, having also dismounted. "Gilliane will send out a litter and some men to carry it. Sit down here, Lord Geoffrey, and rest."

"It is not necessary," Geoffrey insisted.

"Please, Geoffrey," Joanna begged.

He turned on her, laughing. "That is a fine turnabout. A minute since, you threw your knife at my head. It was you and your crazy suspicions that dragged me out here. Now, of a sudden, you fear for my welfare."

Geoffrey teased and laughed because if he did not laugh and tease he would fall into Joanna's arms, weeping. His surprise past, there was such joy in him, such relief, that he did not know how to contain it. Yet it was too great a thing to display before others. Geoffrey denied his need for help only because his need to be alone with Joanna made nothing of his pain and weakness. All he could think was that it would take too long for a litter to be brought; that if he walked at once he would be sooner safe in her arms.

"If you will each give me an arm," he said, glancing at

Sir Léon and Sir Guy, ''I will be at rest quicker and easier than any other way. Joanna, do not fret me further by arguing. Mount up and lead in the men.''

Geoffrey did not look at Joanna. His eyes were blurring anyway. The excitement, which had given him that abnormal burst of strength had also drained him abnormally. Joanna stared after her husband. Was that all the greeting she was to have—first insults and then laughter? Rage and relief, joy and anxiety, were suddenly roiled together even more confusingly than before by another emotion which had touched Joanna only once previously and then very briefly. When she asked of his health he had said, very quickly—too quickly?—that he had been well cared for. Just how well had he been cared for by Lady Gilliane? Well enough so that his wife's arrival was no pleasant surprise? Joanna gestured sharply and Knud came down from his mount to lift her to the mare's saddle.

As she rode past, Geoffrey did not even glance up at her. Joanna burned, too caught up in her own imaginings to think he might be too tired to lift his head or so near fainting he did not hear the horses. She entered the keep, slid down from the mare into Knud's hands, and turned to look more closely at Sir Léon's wife. Lady Gilliane had not a glance for her either. She was staring outward with tear-filled eyes toward the three oncoming men. It never occurred to Joanna that the tears might have been to welcome her own husband. She weeps to lose a lover, Joanna thought, and tossed her head.

In fact, Lady Gilliane was not perfectly clear why her eyes were full of tears. The relief she felt at seeing Léon was enormous. No longer would she need to worry about whether the servants were doing their duty or how she could discover if they were not doing it. But the thought of losing Lord Geoffrey, of being bereft of the interest and courtesy that made her a person in her own eyes as well as his, of never again having a man look at her and *see* her, kiss her hand, pour wine and hand it first to her—there was pain in that.

''Will you count the gold now, or may that matter wait

until I have settled my husband in his bed?''

The voice was low, but hard and cold as ice. Gilliane turned and gasped. No wonder Geoffrey had written that his wife was like the sun and dazzled his eyes so that he could see no other. Truly she was, but— Joanna returned the other woman's stare with a slight sense of satisfaction. In looks there could be no contest between them and, in addition, Lady Gilliane was some years older. Jealousy faded to a small core of irritation. For Geoffrey to turn, even temporarily, to such a substitute was demeaning. The silence was extending uncomfortably.

Joanna raised her voice. ''Shall I bid my men carry the chests of gold to your hall, or may I bring Geoffrey's clothing and my medicines to his chamber so that I can settle him into bed first?'' she repeated.

''The gold—'' Gilliane faltered, ''oh, I do not know. Léon will tell you what next to do.'' What a relief to be able to say that.

A blistering retort to such silliness rose to Joanna's lips, but she set her teeth over it. It would be unwise to come to open insult. She bid Knud, who was standing by, to unpack what would be needed for Geoffrey and take Edwina down from her pillion seat behind one of the men-at-arms. She told Edwina to find a servant who could show her Geoffrey's chamber and see that all was ready there. Knud was then to pile the ransom together and set the men to guard it. If Sir Léon was anxious to begin counting it, Sir Guy must stand in for her as she wished first to attend Geoffrey. As she said it, she looked toward him again. It seemed they were coming ever more slowly. Joanna was about to ask Gilliane for a litter, whatever Geoffrey said, when the men stopped altogether and Sir Guy lifted Geoffrey into his arms. Joanna caught her breath. Geoffrey was slender, but Sir Guy could not have lifted him without great effort before he was hurt.

''I said that he was too weak,'' Lady Gilliane cried out accusingly.

Inwardly, Joanna winced, but her quiet face gave no sign of her remorse and, as Sir Guy came through the gates with

Sir Léon at his heels, she said only, "Will you show us the way to his chamber or tell a servant to show us?"

They crossed the small bailey; it was a very small keep and had no moat, drawbridge, or portcullis, only a gate and simple wall. Automatically, Gilliane turned down the steps to the cells. There was no longer any reason to keep Geoffrey there, and she could have gone to a wall chamber. Gilliane was so used to thinking of Geoffrey down there that she led Joanna in that direction without considering the impression it would make. In truth, at the time it made no impression on Joanna who was in no condition to consider whether she was going up or down a flight of stairs.

There was a bed; she flung off the coverlets, ran her hand over the sheet, winced at its roughness, thinking how that would feel on a fevered body. Then Sir Guy was there. It was too late now to change the sheets for her own. He knelt so that he could place his burden on the bed with the least jostling although Geoffrey was obviously beyond feeling anything just then. Joanna reached for the tie of the tunic; another hand followed hers.

"I will care for him now," Joanna said quietly, but if a look could kill, Gilliane would have fallen to the floor, stone dead. "Do not waste your time on *my* husband. Go to greet your own."

Gilliane withdrew her hand and went to the door, but no farther. It seemed to her that Joanna was too young and too highbred to do what was necessary. She expected her to offer Geoffrey a drink or, if she went so far as undressing him, to turn away shuddering from his torn body. Almost smiling, Gilliane waited to be recalled. Instead, she saw a masterly operation, the end result of many years of Lady Alinor's careful instruction.

Geoffrey was stripped naked in two minutes. Joanna did shudder when she saw his wounds, but it did not impair her efficiency. She muttered imprecations when she saw how ill they were sewn, pulled together any which way. A small sharp knife opened the stitches and Joanna blasphemed a little more when she saw there were pus pockets. No wonder the wounds were still suppurating after all these weeks. She began to clean them deep inside with "water of life," in which was steeped a powdered seaweed that made the liquor a dark brown. King John's inept rule had the effect of making Joanna, despite her youth, far better acquainted with war wounds than Gilliane.

Sometime during the operation Geoffrey regained consciousness. Before he opened his eyes, he winced away from pain more severe than he was accustomed to, but Sir Guy was ready and held him firm. "Quiet," a soft voice urged, "be quiet. Tomorrow you will be better." His eyes opened. "Joanna," he breathed, "thank God."

Lady Gilliane slipped quietly away, swallowing a resigned bitterness mixed with a queer relief. She had struggled hard to save Geoffrey, subduing her revulsion to attend him, and he had not a single thought for her. It was better so. Better that he should thank God for his wife who would doubtless be credited with his healing. Nonetheless, there was a sad gladness in her. No longer would an ugly little desire, bred out of Geoffrey's gentle courtesy and his willingness to help with advice and explanations about matters of estate, grow in her and need to be rooted out.

When Joanna was finished with Geoffrey and he had caught his breath, he asked anxiously, "Is it well, Joanna? I knew I was not healing right, but I did not know what to tell the lady, and it seemed churlish to complain when I could not say what was wrong."

"It will be well now," Joanna assured him. "It is a good thing you did not heal," she added with a flicker of malice, which Geoffrey fortunately did not notice. "I had to open you in two places and fit the flesh better, but you will heal now so that you can move easily. Sleep," she soothed, "I swear to you, you will be whole."

He sighed with relief. Joanna was not such a fool as to lie about that. If he was to be crippled, he would need time to settle his mind to it and begin to plan a new fighting style or whatever other compensation would be necessary. His eyes began to close but he pushed up the heavy lids.

"Is all well at home?"

"Of course. How should it not be? I have seen to everything. What else had I to do with you gone? Oh, there are one or two matters of justice that I laid over for you to settle because they regard points of honor, but they are small things. Even the country is quiet. Winchester holds the reins and Pembroke the whip. The steed knows better than to prance under such management.''

That was not an outright lie. It merely concealed so much of the truth that it might as well have been. Joanna was not nearly so scrupulous about misleading her husband for his own good on political matters as about his body. It was true England was quiet under the control of Winchester and Pembroke, but it was the quiet of a seething pot which, growing hotter and hotter under a tight lid, erupts at last, throwing off the cover and spewing its contents all around.

Geoffrey was not unaware that Joanna's veracity on this subject was not to be compared with her veracity about his physical condition. He felt nothing beyond a profound gratitude about that. His question had been dutiful, a result of a strong sense of responsibility; however, he was very grateful that it had not called forth a stream of anxious worries. Far too often when he politely asked Lady Gilliane if he could do something for her, she had taken advantage of the formal question. He had found it very exhausting to try to explain what he felt any sensible woman should know, but it was not in his nature to spare himself. Nor could he stop asking; courtesy had been pounded into him until the formal words came out before he thought. He smiled, warmed and comforted by Joanna's presence, knowing nothing would be required of him until he felt able for it.

Joanna sat quietly by his side until she was sure he was deeply asleep, then she turned to Sir Guy, stiffening as she saw him standing in the doorway, naked sword in hand. He gestured her toward him.

"Do you realize we are in a cell that can be locked?" he whispered.

Joanna had not realized. Fear rose in her. There was danger here! There was! She knew it. She had felt it all along. Nonetheless, as she glanced around good sense warred with that "smell" of danger.

"I do not think there is any danger it will be locked to keep us in," she said slowly. "If that had been intended, it would have been done while we were all busy about my lord. Also, he has been here long. See the chair and table and rug. It must have been to keep Lord Geoffrey safe, rather than to keep him inside. Indeed, where could he go, what could he do, in the state he is?"

Whatever Sir Guy would have answered was cut off by the arrival of Sir Léon, rather red and short of breath. "I would like to speak to Lord Geoffrey," he said somewhat stiffly.

"He is alseep," Joanna objected impatiently. "What is it you desire of him? I am able for more than he just now. Speak to me."

Sir Léon did not want to speak to Joanna. He did not like her. She might be beautiful, but she was hard, unwomanly, proud, overbearing; in fact, she had every fault a woman could have. Still, from Sir Guy's naked sword and wary expression, it was obvious they were aware of where they were. In the face of Joanna's long suspicion, some explanation must be offered.

"I only wished to beg his pardon for locking him in this place," Sir Léon grated out. "No insult to Lord Geoffrey's honor was intended. It was only to ensure his safety against search and seizure by King Philip's men. As soon as he wakes, you will move to more suitable quarters."

It was a reasonable explanation, but the "smell" of danger lingered in Joanna's mind. After a while, as she sat beside Geoffrey, she began to wonder if it was idleness rather than any real thing that was making her uneasy. She had brought no work along on this hurried journey and now she regretted it because it was an effort not to stare at Geoffrey. That would disturb him but, worse, his nearness was waking a most untimely hunger in her, a hunger that must remain unsatisfied for some considerable time owing to Geoffrey's condition. The combined discomforts of anxiety, idleness, and frustration served to unsettle Joanna and make her unreasonable. Staring at the blank walls, she became infuriated because Geoffrey had welcomed her as a nurse rather than as a woman. If that was what he wanted, she told herself spitefully, that was what he would have. Call him her love, her heart—not she!

Meanwhile, Sir Léon was discovering that Geoffrey's capture was having enormous and unexpected benefits quite aside from the wealth that would accrue to his uncle. At first, that did not seem likely. The initial meeting between Sir Léon and his wife had not been easy. His jealousy had been sharply reawakened when he had seen the expression on Gilliane's face as Geoffrey was carried in and had been further exacerbated when she disappeared below before greeting him rather than sending a servant. In addition, he had been infuriated to find Geoffrey imprisoned in a cell rather than treated as a guest. Because he was fearful of what he might learn from investigation of the first two problems, he had attacked the last matter first. The shock the explanation gave him, sent him down to apologize to Geoffrey before he did anything else. His brief contact with Joanna had sent him back up the stairs with a sudden, overwhelming gratitude for his own wife.

Having seen Geoffrey's condition, Sir Léon no longer suspected Gilliane of any physical infidelity. What had appeared on her face, however, was a warning that his wife was a woman of strong feelings—a thing he would never have noticed before the need to read Joanna's expression had made him aware that women had feelings. To his surprise, he found that he was as possessive of Gilliane's feelings as of her body.

Truthfully, he had never thought about her much. Gilliane had been chosen for him by his parents, as was proper, and he had found her pleasant enough—obedient, hardworking, and a good breeder. What more did he need? Long absence and a crush of new experience had jolted him from his rut, however. After many years of marriage, Sir Léon suddenly saw his wife as woman. She was looking back at him, her hands held forward placatingly, obviously nervous and distressed more than joyous. She was not beautiful, but she was no haughty bitch either. Sir Léon came across the hall and took Gilliane's hands. She looked down at them, up at him, and surged forward against him, crying aloud how glad she was to have him back, how much she had missed him, all mixed together with apologies for her inability to keep the men to their work and lesson the boys.

It was a rich reward, Sir Léon thought, for so simple a gesture as taking Gilliane's hands. It inspired him to use upon his wife the techniques he had learned while traveling with Joanna. So well did the small courtesies of holding a bench for her and choosing tidbits to put upon her trencher serve, that, when they went to bed he eagerly displayed the more intimate lessons he had learned from Edwina. Gilliane was not made jealous in the least by this expansion in her husband's sexual repertoire. It never occurred to her for a moment that Léon would, or even should, be faithful to her. She considered herself fortunate that he had never set up a mistress in the keep as some men did. Gilliane thanked God in full and overflowing measure for the joy she received and did not question its source.

Whatever little flicker of longing Gilliane had felt for Geoffrey was expunged as completely and finally as a mark on soft sand is erased by the flow of the tide. Any resentment she had felt toward Joanna was also washed away. Somehow she credited them with bringing her this new joy, and she went about her duties the next day with a heart that sang, with footsteps as light as a girl's and a face that had shed twenty years, and with a determination to do her guests a good turn if it was in any way possible.

Later in the afternoon, Léon's uncle, Louis, arrived, having been summoned by messenger the previous day. The ransom was counted and delivered. Geoffrey and Joanna were now truly guests, housed in the best guest room and free to leave whenever they desired. Unfortunately, that was more theory than fact because Geoffrey was still in too much pain and too weak to ride, and to carry him in a horse litter away from France would cry aloud to the world the strong possibility that he had been wounded at Bouvines. This would be an open invitation to be made prisoner again.

It was known that no ransoms had yet been paid to Philip. Thus, any wounded knight who could not identify himself as Philip's man was fair game.

With herculean effort, Joanna maintained a placid demeanor during the next week. Geoffrey was winning his battle for health. His appetite was greatly improved. All the small cuts were clean and closed, and the large ones were less red and swollen and much drier. His bones were not so prominent, no longer threatening to pierce through his ·tight-drawn skin, and he did not tire quite so easily. If they had been at home, the satisfaction Joanna felt in this improvement together with the demands made upon her time and energy by her mother's estate would have kept Joanna relatively content. At Baisieux, however, there was nothing for her to do but attend Geoffrey. They talked together, ate together, played together—everything except slept together. And it seemed to Joanna that every accidental touch of Geoffrey's hand, every word out of his mouth, stoked her fire higher.

Her manner grew daily more strained. By the end of the week, Geoffrey's health had improved considerably and he was very aware that something was wrong with Joanna. He was horrified at the way she winced aside from his outstretched hand when he prepared to lead her from the dinner table, at the way she seemed anxious to look anywhere, at anything, except him. He made a few tentative efforts to discover what was wrong, only to be rebuffed more and more coldly and finally lost his own temper.

"Since I seem to be unwelcome to you," he snapped, "I will go back to my bed."

"Yes, yes, do," Joanna responded.

Geoffrey nearly slapped her. He would have done so had they not been in a stranger's hall. The worst of it was that she did not seem aware of what she had said. His judgment was quite right. Almost weeping with frustration, Joanna fled to find Gilliane as soon as Geoffrey was gone. She knew she had given Gilliane no reason to like or wish to help her, but she was desperate.

"At home I am busy all day," Joanna explained

breathlessly. "I am not used to idleness. I have not even my embroidery."

Gilliane was very much surprised. She had not thought such a grand lady did anything, but she took in the feverish spots in Joanna's cheeks, the tenseness, and understood the girl needed help. Comfortingly, she slipped an arm around Joanna.

"Do not fret, child. Soon he will be well, but come, you can help me in the dairy. I must look to the cheeses today, and it will do you good to walk outside for a time. You are too much within."

At first Joanna thought she would scream with impatience as Gilliane talked to her about cheeses, but little by little she grew interested. Roselynde made cheese too, of course, but this was of a different taste and texture. They sampled and discussed mixtures of cow and goat milk, length of hanging and smoking times, and Joanna felt her innards stop shaking. She was frankly regretful when Gilliane turned back toward the keep, but felt better again when the older woman suggested that she embroider a tunic for the elder of the two sons, who was to be presented for fostering and needed some handsome clothes. It would at least be a place to rest her eyes so that she would not need constantly to struggle not to stare at Geoffrey.

As they entered the hall, Joanna looked down. She did not know whether Geoffrey was up and about again and she did not wish to lose her newfound calm. Thus, she was very startled to hear Gilliane cry, "Mother! What are you doing?"

Joanna's eyes came up just in time to see an elderly woman step away from the entrance to the wall chamber in which Geoffrey lay. Something shone briefly in the old woman's hand as she turned toward them but was concealed by her skirt before Joanna could see what it was.

"I suppose I can walk about my own home," the old woman said.

"But mother," Gilliane protested breathlessly, hurrying forward, "you know you have been ill. You know Léon said you must stay above in the women's chambers. Come with me now. Come, before he returns and is angry!''

"You and Léon are fools!'' the old woman spat, "and Louis is so lily-livered he will take the chance of the prize slipping through his fingers so as to be clear of any suspicion. They are devils, I tell you. There is no honor when one deals with the devil.''

Gilliane had now seized the woman, turned her about, and was drawing her forcibly toward the stairs leading to the women's quarters. Joanna stood transfixed. She was not sure why, but a terrible chill passed over her. The woman's words were incomprehensible. Nonetheless, there was hate and an enormous threat in them. Fear grew and movement came back to Joanna. That was a knife in the old woman's hand! She ran headlong into Geoffrey's chamber and, throwing back the bed curtains, began to examine him feverishly.

Startled awake, he seized her hands. "Joanna! What are you doing?''

"Are you hurt?'' she whispered tensely, "Are you hurt?''

"Hurt? Are you mad? You have been tending my hurts for a week.'' He saw she was trembling. "What ails you, Joanna?''

"I fear—I fear!''

"Do not begin that again!'' Geoffrey snapped, irritable from being wakened too suddenly and remembering how furious he had been when they parted. "I tell you, we are safe here. Sir Léon and Lady Gilliane wish us no harm.''

"Yes, that is true, but the old woman—''

"Sir Léon's mother? I have never seen her, except—'' Geoffrey's voice grew uncertain as he remembered the vague dreams of delirium, of being tortured by an old woman. He pulled Joanna closer. "Why do you fear her?''

"She had a knife. I did not see it clear, but I am sure it was a knife, and she was coming in here. Gilliane was frightened too. She almost dragged her back to the women's quarters. Gilliane said the old woman was sick—but, Geoffrey, she was not, not weak or pale. I fear— She said—she said one did not need to be honorable in dealing with devils—''

"How sad," Geoffrey interrupted, looking concerned but not in the least alarmed. "The poor woman must be disordered in her wits. That is why they keep her above. Probably she believes any stranger is a devil. I suppose she would give Gilliane no peace until she promised that Sir Léon must come home before I was freed."

"But she had a knife. Geoffrey, she had—''

"No, my love, no," he soothed, smiling. "More like she had a crucifix—and was about to exorcise me. One does not leave knives where madwomen can get at them."

It was possible. Joanna drew a shuddering breath. Geoffrey pulled her still closer, his bad humor greatly assuaged by her fear for him, but she stiffened and resisted.

"Let me go," Joanna whispered, beginning to tremble again but unwilling to pull away forcibly lest she hurt him. "Do not touch me, Geoffrey, please do not."

"What have I done?" Geoffrey asked, unsure of whether he was more hurt or angry. "Why do you shrink from me? Why will you not look in my face? Have the few marks upon me made me loathesome to you? Have you cast your eyes elsewhere, thinking me dead?"

The last question made it clear to Geoffrey himself that he was furious rather than hurt. He tightened his grip upon Joanna brutally. Utterly unstrung by her frustration and a horrible chill of fear that Geoffrey's reasoning had not really removed, Joanna began to sob. It seemed to confirm Geoffrey's worst fears. He released one of her hands and slapped her face, then began to struggle to lift himself upright without letting her go completely.

"No, no," Joanna cried, choking, "no, Geoffrey. You will hurt yourself. Indeed, indeed, there is no one but you. Let me go, oh, please let me go. I want what you cannot give me now. My love, let me go. I cannot bear my need for you."

Geoffrey stopped moving instantly, but he did not let Joanna go. There was a short silence. Joanna wept afresh and slowly subsided onto the bed, her face buried in the pillow beside Geoffrey's head. She heard him chuckle softly.

"Little fool," he whispered into her ear, "no damage was done to that part of me. Call me 'love' again, and you will see how able I am."

"No, Geoffrey, no."

"What a wife you are," he laughed. "I swear you are the most disagreeable woman in the world. All you say is 'no.' Do you wish me to repudiate our marriage on the grounds that you will not perform your marital duty? For shame!"

"Oh, Geoffrey, do not tease me," Joanna sighed, turning on her side to face him and sniffing, a tremulous smile beginning to show on her lips. "I am so miserable."

"You mean uncomfortable," he corrected, grinning. "I know. If you will but bestir yourself to look, you will see that I am just as uncomfortable myself. A delicious discomfort—is it not?"

"You are mad," Joanna faltered. "You will open your wounds again. Let me go. I am over it now. It was only my fright. Let me go."

"Ah, but I am not over it. Not in the least. And I assure you it will do me more harm to be left in this state than to have my urgent need satisfied."

"Geoffrey, no. I am afraid—"

Her voice trembled into silence. He held her firmly with one hand, but the other was very active. Joanna's eyes closed and she shivered, her body moving uncontrollably under his touch, her breath coming in irregular gasps. With a last flicker of sense, she tried to pull away, sighing, "Someone will come. It is midafternoon. Geoffrey, stop."

"Close the bed curtains," he replied thickly, "and take off that gown. Do not deny me! In the name of God, it is more than three months since I have touched a woman. Now that you have roused me, you must content me. You will not hurt me. I will show you how. Only take off your clothes."

"Are you sure?" she asked, but her hands were already tearing off her garments, throwing them helter-skelter away. "Are you sure, Geoffrey?"

He did not answer, only laughed, his eyes shining and

golden. Such a sweet answer as this was to the ugly questions he had asked. He untied his chausses and pulled them down, wincing as he lifted his buttocks and dislodged the pad that covered his hip. Joanna winced too and drew back as her eyes fell upon the raw flesh, but Geoffrey seized her before she could move far. His arm went high around her back and fastened on her breast. Both nipples hardened and swelled even more, although they were already firm and protuberant. Joanna's eyes slid from the sore to Geoffrey's upstanding shaft. He laughed again and spread his legs wide.

"Mount astride me sidelong," he urged eagerly, "so you rest on my good hip. So! Ah! Just so!"

To say more was not necessary. As Joanna slid down upon him, up and then down again, Geoffrey moaned softly, but she did not fear the sound was drawn from him by pain. The position was odd only at first. Joanna found she could support herself on a bent elbow just high enough to put hardly any pressure on her husband's body. This was convenient because if Geoffrey bent his head sideways, it brought the breast he was not fingering just athwart his lips. He accepted the invitation eagerly and soon Joanna heard herself crying softly, "Hurry, oh hurry, please hurry."

It was a most unnecessary plea. As the climax she could not resist convulsed her, Geoffrey was jerking beneath her in his own. Somehow, in spite of the violence of her release, Joanna managed to twist backward and turn so that she fell beside Geoffrey rather than atop him. For a time there was no sound but the mutual rasp of labored breathing. Then Geoffrey began to chuckle again.

"You are filled with endless delights and surprises," he murmured. "You gave me a most pretty answer to a base fool's question and then, when I was wild with fear I would die away too soon, there you are squeaking at me 'hurry, hurry.' Never have I heard such sweet words."

"I did not squeak," Joanna protested, her eyes laughing, while she pretended indignation. "I only—"

"You are sought, my lady." Edwina's voice was neutral and came tactfully from outside the door.

"Oh dear," Joanna exclaimed, blushing up to her hair and right down to her breasts.

That set Geoffrey off again. "We are man and wife," he chortled. "You are not caught in sin."

"No," Joanna hissed, half-amused and half-annoyed, scrambling into her clothing as quickly as she could, "but what must be thought of me to permit or, worse, to press a man in your condition to such an act?"

"Do not you dare ever say such a thing," Geoffrey expostulated, laughing harder. "What must be thought of *me* to need such urging?"

In the hall, Gilliane waited in a fever of impatience and anxiety. Edwina had known what her lady was doing; she had heard the opening moves and had just settled down to listen with enjoyment when Lady Gilliane had entered the antechamber. Most firmly, Edwina closed the door and resisted interruption. Even if the castle had been attacked at that moment, for no reason except threat of immediate death would Edwina have called her mistress. She, after all, bore the brunt of Joanna's bad temper. She was not going to allow anything to interfere with the relief of Joanna's frustration. Lady Joanna was attending her husband, Edwina said stubbornly; she would come in a few minutes, when she was finished.

Gilliane was too distressed to judge correctly Joanna's heavy eyes and flushed face when she came from the inner chamber. "Is Lord Geoffrey worse?" she asked anxiously.

Joanna was surprised. From the day after their arrival, Gilliane had shown only a polite interest in Geoffrey. Now her question had an intensity that was far beyond politeness. "No," Joanna replied, and then thinking of what they had been doing, "I hope not, but he is asleep now, I think."

Gilliane hesitated. It was against her training to wake a man except for an immediate emergency, but what she had to say seemed to need a man's decisiveness. On the other hand, it would be far easier to say what she must to Joanna. God knew what a man would do when he heard it.

"I will faithfully recount to him anything you wish him to hear," Joanna promised, more concerned with letting Geoffrey rest than with what she might be getting into.

That decided Gilliane. Besides, what Léon had said about Joanna, although not complimentary, infused Gilliane with the hope that Joanna might know what to do.

"You must tell him what you think best," Gilliane began. "My mother-by-marriage is a good woman," she said next, "but—but she has had a hard life. Her husband was killed in the wars between Richard and Philip and she had a desperate struggle to hold these lands. Then Léon was taken—"

"It is the English she thinks of as devils," Joanna said with sudden revelation. "She is not mad; she just hates the English."

"Of course she is not mad." Gilliane looked surprised. "Well, perhaps a little on that subject, but why should you— Oh, I see, because she has remained in the women's chambers. Yes. Well, that was because Léon knew she would not be civil to Geoffrey and he is most strict on polite behavior to a guest. He said she must pretend to be ill. But—"

"That was why you locked Geoffrey up."

Gilliane nodded. "Yes, she was willing to keep him because Louis said there would be a great ransom, but when she heard of the English queen's offer. . . . The idea grew in her mind, and it seems that she has been thinking more and more of it since you brought the gold—thinking to double it again. I am sorry. It is dreadful, but she is growing old and—and the past is more real to her than the present."

Joanna was not much afraid of the old woman. Having been warned, the danger was gone. The chill she had felt, the "smell" of fear did not rise up. It would only mean that Geoffrey must be guarded while he slept. Even she or Edwina could overpower Sir Léon's mother. "I will take care," she assured Gilliane, "that my husband is never alone. I—" She stopped speaking abruptly as Gilliane shook her head.

"That is not important except to explain what is worse. Louis is not like Léon, although he used to be. He is not a bad man, but he is bitter? Ambitious? His ties are to his family and very strongly to his older sister whom he supported in her worst troubles. It seems that she has infected him with her hate and,'' Gilliane swallowed and her next words came out in a rush, ''—and Louis plans to set upon your husband when he leaves and—''

''How can you know this?'' Joanna breathed. She was more than chilled with apprehension now; she was icy with terror.

''When I stopped her from—from what she intended, she was so angry that she—'' Gilliane flushed unbecomingly. ''She believes I—I betrayed Léon with your husband. She said I could not save my lover thus, and she told me—''

''How will Sir Louis know when Geoffrey leaves?'' Joanna asked, pressing terror down, fixing on practicalities.

''We are near neighbors, as you know. The serfs, the servants, they are all bound together. Louis has been substitute master here so often that if he bid them send him word they would do so, any or all of them.''

Joanna knew that the male servants paid little attention to Gilliane. She did not ask for her help. ''Cannot Sir Léon—'' she began and, seeing the terror in Gilliane's eyes realized what she was asking.

If Sir Léon was apprised of his uncle's plans, either that would start a quarrel between them, or, what Joanna feared much worse, being intent on Geoffrey's welfare rather than that of her host, he might be convinced to join the plot. It would be madness to hint such a thing to Gilliane. Joanna stared sightlessly at the floor, driving her mind to stop squirreling around and fix on some plan that would save them.

''We must not begin any quarrel between your husband and his uncle,'' Joanna began again, her voice only slightly tremulous. ''We must arrange somehow that both of them be gone, best together so that neither can blame the other. Only for a day or two. Think, Gilliane, what do Léon and Louis customarily do together that takes them from their keeps for a few days at a time?''

The first response to that, to Joanna's surprise, was an angry flush. Then she understood. Louis and Léon went whoring together. Gilliane herself was surprised by her reaction. She had never minded in the past, yet now the thought that Léon would seek his pleasure elsewhere angered her. In any case, that was not a pastime any modest, pious wife would urge upon her husband. She racked her brains for a moment, then nodded.

"They have a hunting place in a wood, I am not sure where, but I know it is at some distance and that when they go it is for a few days—but how can I suggest— It is not my business to tell Léon what he should do."

A brief effort subdued Joanna's impatience with that sentiment. Naturally, a wife did not tell a husband what to do. Even such indulgent husbands as Ian and Geoffrey would respond to such temerity with a box on the ear. Nonetheless, there were many, many ways to make a man do something you desired without *telling* him.

"There is no need to tell him, but you could say that you have not had fresh venison for a long time. And you could say also that Louis has been so busy between caring for his lands and trying to help you that it is long and long since he had a time free to hunt. And you could say that you thought venison was a more strengthening meat than beef or mutton, and boar still more strengthening, hinting that such meats would be of benefit to Geoffrey and a politeness due a guest in ill health —"

"He would know I was pushing him if I said all that."

Joanna bit her lip, but her voice did not betray her irritation. "You must not say it all at once, of course. You must say one thing now, another at another time, always waiting until your husband starts the matter."

"But Léon must know nothing—"

No wonder most wives bore black and blue marks, Joanna thought, if they were so clumsy in handling their men. "Listen to me," she urged. "If Sir Léon should mention his uncle—which I have heard him do a dozen times a day—then you might say first how helpful Louis was to you. That is true, is it not? Then you can say that he had no time for recreation. Then you could mention hunting and then Geoffrey's health and—"

Gilliane stared at Joanna wide-eyed, and then a slow

smile began to grow on her face. "So I could," she murmured thoughtfully. "Yes, I believe I could." The smile disappeared and she looked anxiously at Joanna. "The bad thing is that it will have to be done soon. I am afraid Louis will refuse to go if we wait until Geoffrey has most of his strength back. Léon's mother is not mad. When her rage cools, she will begin to think of what she told me. She will suspect I am trying to save Lord Geoffrey by this ruse, even if Léon does not believe it is a ruse, and she will tell Louis. Even then, I do not know how much time you would have. I fear that when you leave she will find a way to send a messenger to Léon and Louis. I would not dare stop her openly. I am sorry—"

"Dear Gilliane," Joanna said, "do not apologize. You have done more for Geoffrey and for me than we had any right to expect. And I never even thanked you, never even said how grateful I was that you preserved him for me. You could well have hated me for my unmannerly bearing—"

"Oh, no." Gilliane smiled with singular sweetness. "You do not know it, but you have done as much for me—more perhaps than I for you."

CHAPTER TWENTY-NINE

The plan that Joanna and Gilliane devised worked well, but unfortunately it worked too soon. Both women had expected that it would take a week or two to implant the idea of a hunt into Sir Léon's head. What happened was that no sooner had Gilliane mentioned the word venison than Sir Léon was off. At least, that was how it appeared to the startled plotters. Actually, Sir Leon took the time to apologize to Geoffrey for leaving, giving him the excellent excuse his wife had provided—that boar and venison were strengthening to an invalid. He also sent a messenger to his uncle and waited for the reply. That, however, was all he waited for. In two days he was off, promising to return within the week with fresh game enough to restore Geoffrey's health.

"We must try again," Joanna said to Geoffrey the night before Sir Léon left. "You are not strong enough We will think of something else."

"No," Geoffrey replied. "We will go."

"You cannot!" Joanna exclaimed.

"Do not be a fool. If I must, then I can. I will not take the chance that 'something else' will work. Sooner or later Louis will ask about me, and Leon will tell the truth—why should he not?—that I mend apace. Louis will not be led away again."

From this position Geoffrey would not be moved although Joanna alternately wept and pleaded and raged and stormed. He proffered no other reason. He could not because his real reason would merely have distressed Joanna more. It had occurred to Geoffrey that, if he were to be slain, it would be necessary to kill Joanna also. Obviously, his body could not be presented as that of a knight casually come upon and killed while trying to resist or escape when

513

his wife could, and would, cry the truth aloud to the world. For Joanna the only safety lay in instant flight. It would not matter if he died on the road; that, in fact, would improve her chances for safety.

It was a nightmare journey. For Joanna, mounted pillion behind Geoffrey, all sense of time disappeared, and yet she was horribly aware that time was important. The effect was heightened by Geoffrey's orders that they must not pass through any village or town. Because Joanna was not familiar with the territory and the land was flat and featureless, they seemed to move continuously on the same stretch of road and woodland.

When he was first lifted to the saddle, Geoffrey laughed in spite of his pain, saying it brought back memories of his early childhood to be so mounted. He talked a little to Joanna at first also, pointing out a place where he thought he had camped before they brought the army to confront Philip, remarking on the gait of her mare and how it differed from that of his destrier. He fell silent after that, thinking of the three horses he had lost and hoping they had found new masters who would be kind and appreciate them. Alarmed by his silence, Joanna asked if he wanted to stop to rest and Geoffrey told her rather sharply that they were scarce an hour on their way. That, too, contributed to her confusion. To her apprehensive mind it seemed they had been riding most of the day.

As time passed Geoffrey spoke less and less. When he had to answer a question, as when Sir Guy, who was ranging ahead to divert them from any town, asked for instruction, his voice was low and breathless. Later, Joanna saw blood seeping through his tunic from the hip wound. She wept softly, knowing there was nothing she could do for him. To stitch the flesh again was useless; it would only tear anew. Later still, his body began to sag against hers, but when she cried out that they must stop, Geoffrey roused himself enough to countermand the order.

Joanna might have overborne him—the men were hers and would obey her—but Geoffrey said softly, "It will only serve to lengthen my torment. I cannot suffer more, but I can suffer longer. Dear heart, if I should fail and you are strong enough to hold me, ride on and ride faster. I will not feel it then. Better still, let one of the men mount behind and hold me.''

There was good sense in what he said, and Joanna yielded except that she would let no one else hold him. Her arms ached and her body screamed with pain because she held herself all twisted so as to avoid rubbing Geoffrey's torn shoulder. To compound her misery, it began to rain on the second day. Geoffrey shivered, but he constantly threw off the cloak with which Joanna tried to cover him, muttering that the rain was good—so cool. And when Joanna touched his face she found he was burning with fever.

Despite her weariness, Joanna did not sleep at all that night. Geoffrey tossed and moaned and called pathetically for her, but he did not know her when she soothed him. She did not think they could go further, only toward morning his fever dropped and he begged hoarsely to continue.

''I cannot bear to get a little better and then begin again,'' he sighed. ''I want to go home where I can rest.''

Again Joanna yielded, not only because of Geoffrey's pleading but because she could do so little for him in a woodland camp, because she knew he was so near unconscious most of the time now that he suffered less. It was growing colder too, especially at night, and they had nothing really dry and warm. To let Geoffrey lie cold and wet might be his death as easily as traveling onward. Throughout the day Geoffrey slipped in and out of consciousness, in and out of delirium. He would not eat at all that night, and did not recognize Joanna again.

Edwina consulted Sir Guy and then, trembling, confronted her mistress. ''You must leave him to me,'' she said. ''He does not know you anyway, and you must sleep or you will not be fit to help him.''

''Yes, yes,'' Joanna agreed absently, ''I will sleep. Let me be, Edwina.''

''If you stay here, you will not sleep. You will hear him call and run to him even though you know he does not know you. The rain is over. You must go out of here and sleep away from Lord Geoffrey. My lady, you have the right to flay me or even kill me, and you can order Sir Guy to be punished also. Nonetheless, if you do not go of your own will, we will drag you.''

There was not strength enough in Joanna for rage to come. She wept, but when Sir Guy picked her up and carried her out, she did not struggle. She lay, wrapped in three cloaks, sobbing softly and listening for Geoffrey's voice. He seemed much quieter, now that she was gone, and she wondered guiltily if she had violated one of her mother's maxims and allowed her own anxiety to make her patient uneasy. Exhaustion did not permit guilt, or any other notion, to torment her long. It was just as well because, if she thought about it she might have guessed another reason for Geoffrey's silence. Edwina, far less tender than her mistress, was muffling his cries with a firm hand over his mouth.

Not everything was bad. At least they were not pursued. Sir Guy continued to avoid towns and villages because there was more likelihood of French being there, and the French might ask awkward questions. As they came deeper into Flanders, the country folk were less to be feared. In spite of sporadic enmity over the question of who should grow and who weave wool and where the greatest profit should be, the Flemish preferred the English to the French. Besides, just now the outrages of the French were freshest in their minds. They would give no voluntary information to the conquerors even if they did guess that an English knight had passed.

This was fortunate because as they came nearer to Oostende there were many people and villages. True, they looked aside as if they saw nothing, but Sir Guy was aware that the port city must be full of French and that, if they did not actually guard the gates, they would have spies there. They would not be looking specifically for Geoffrey; their purpose would be to watch what goods came in and to whom those goods went so that the taxes would be paid. Nonetheless, it was unlikely that a man in Geoffrey's condition would not arouse curiosity. He would be snapped up as a bonus.

Sir Guy could get little help from Geoffrey or Joanna. Geoffrey was not rational, and Joanna thought her husband was dying and did not care in the least what happened to her or anyone else. Then they had a piece of luck. In a mean village where Sir Guy stopped to buy something—anything— to eat, the woman he had dealt with, taking him for French, cursed him in English as he paid. Stumblingly, Sir Guy replied in the few words he had of that tongue, rode back in haste to bring Knud, who explained in his native tongue their case and their need. The woman agreed to hide her compatriots.

A place to rest, filthy and odorous as it was but at least warm and dry, sparked a little hope in Joanna. She remembered the name of a merchant from Oostende who had done business with Roselynde and might take a chance and help them in hopes of future favors. In the city, the good luck held. Sir Guy found the merchant cursing the French who had confiscated his merchandise and were generally making business impossible and his life miserable. He was very willing to transport the party to Roselynde. Sir Guy was sure he could trust the merchant. Wars with France might come and go, but trade with Roselynde was not a sometime thing. That would go on for many years and yield a rich profit—but not if the merchant betrayed the daughter of the house.

The trust was well placed. The merchant went himself with a horse litter to fetch Geoffrey—a sick friend for whom he vouched at the gates—and he did not wait for cargo but sent off his ship with the first outgoing tide. He did not ask for payment either or even for surety; he knew the lady of Roselynde of old. He trusted, he said, to God to reward his good deed; one must cast bread upon the waters sometimes.

His faith was fully rewarded, as he doubtless expected it to be, and the bread he had cast out returned to him, after Geoffrey had been tenderly carried into Roselynde, in silver and gold and jeweled armlets and necklets. Three full cargoes could not have brought an equal profit and the good-will he gained would increase his future profit through favors and reduced excises for many years.

It was as if the place itself, the great stone walls, the murmur of the sea, the smell of spice and roses in the sheets, was curative for Geoffrey. Within hours of being bathed and laid in his own bed, his fever began to drop. For Joanna, the weight of mountains seemed to fall from her when her mother's arms closed around her. For a little while, as long as she needed it, Joanna could be a child again, all responsibility shifted to other shoulders, with no need to think and plan through a maze of fatigue and fear.

The one thing she would not yield was her watch over Geoffrey, and Alinor did not try to draw her away. She offered instead a comforting assurance that everything Joanna had done for him was right, and in every case where a decision had to be made Alinor made it so that her daughter's tired mind was relieved of all fear of mistake or blame.

They did not come away completely scatheless. By the end of October, Geoffrey was free of fever and gaining strength again, but too much sloughing of torn, dead tissue on his hip had taken place. The wide scarred area would never be as flexible as whole flesh. Geoffrey would be lame. Joanna told him as soon as she was sure herself. He said nothing much about it while he was very weak, but one day when he was stronger and alive enough to be thinking about fighting again, he asked if Ian would come and look at the hurt. For Geoffrey, Ian was the fount of all wisdom where fighting was concerned.

"How will it hamper me?" he asked, when Ian was finished with his examination.

"You will be less eagerly sought as a dancing partner," Ian replied.

Geoffrey looked blank and then began to laugh. "Is that true, my lord?"

"Of course it is true. Do you think I hate you so much that I would lie about what might cost your life, not telling you of a weakness of which you must beware? That is a stupid, dangerous thing about which to lie.'' Then he shrugged. ''You will not run or walk evenly or as fast—but you know that already from what Joanna has told you, and an armed man does not run well in any case. It might a little affect your jousting. I will need to try you before I can speak as to that—but for a jouster such as you,'' he added with loving contempt, ''who could tell the diffcrence?''

''At least there were few men who could unseat me before this,'' Geoffrey protested. ''Will I be less firm in the saddle?''

''No, not that,'' Ian assured him. ''It is in the forward thrust that you might be limited, but, of a truth, I do not think so.''

Geoffrey's mind was relieved; he was not really a vain young man. So long as it did not impede his ability as a fighter, he would not have cared much if he walked like a crab. Now that his personal anxiety was over, however, there were other matters he wanted to talk about.

''I am almost glad of it,'' he said, ''because it gave me occasion to ask to see you alone. Joanna will tell me nothing of what is happening in the world. Or, if I demand an answer, tells me what I greatly fear are falsehoods.''

''So?'' Ian said, ''She is not unwise in that. What purpose can there be in fretting you over what you cannot help?''

''Then there is trouble,'' Geoffrey said tensely.

Ian could have kicked himself. He knew his wife and stepdaughter would be fit to flay him alive for his awkward answer. Only now he realized that Geoffrey's opening gambit about being kept in ignorance was a trap for his unwary tongue, and a trap he should have recognized. Geoffrey was too clever by half. Ian knew Joanna would not be so crude as to refuse to answer or to tell obvious falsehoods—not Alinor's daughter. Probably what she had said to Geoffrey was very convincing; Geoffrey had almost been deluded into believing all was well. Still—too clever by half—there had been a doubt in his mind raised by the memory of the disastrous defeats. If only, Ian thought, I had said all was well now because John had given up the idea of more expeditions to France, he would have believed me. Now I have overset the fat into the fire.

"My father?" Geoffrey urged anxiously.

Ian's brow cleared. On that subject he had good news. "Safe and soon home. He would have been released sooner but that he himself did not like the conditions."

"What conditions? What more can be asked of him than ransom?"

"Curse my loose tongue," Ian exclaimed. "Geoffrey, I had better leave you. If you are in a fever again when Joanna returns, I will not be allowed near you for a sennight."

"It is more like to put me into a fever to be left hanging than to know a bad thing."

That was true. "The conditions had nothing to do with your father," Ian said. "It is only that Philip will not accept ransom for Dammartin or Ferrand. To do John credit, he offered to pay and swore he would not haggle. Philip will have none of it. He was willing to exchange your father for Robert of Dreux—no ransom being taken for either—but he said Dammartin and Ferrand were *his* vassals and traitors to him and that he would make example of them." Then forgetting himself in his anger, "It is said they are held like beasts in filthy stys, loaded with chains, even that Dammartin is allowed no freedom and is kept chained to a huge log."

"God pity them. Mary have mercy. They were good brave men both." Geoffrey's eyes filled with the easy tears of convalescence.

"For God's sake, do not weep," Ian begged. "My loving daughter Joanna will rip out my arm and beat me to a pulp with it, and Alinor will spit on what remains if you make yourself ill over this."

Geoffrey laughed and sobbed at the same time, then wiped his face impatiently. There was much good sense in Ian's jest. It would do no one good and him great harm to grieve over the fate of his battle companions. He must thank

God for his own and his father's escape and try to forget the rest.

"What does the king?" he asked next.

Ian looked uneasily toward the door, but no one came to rescue him. Suddenly, it occurred to him that this long interval of privacy must be deliberate. Alinor would certainly know, even if Joanna did not, how long it would take him to look at Geoffrey's wound and give his judgment upon it. One or another of the women would have been in the room very soon after that if they were opposed to his talking freely with Geoffrey. He had visited him often before, and either Joanna or Alinor stood at his elbow to be sure he spoke little and that little in the right words.

That meant that they wanted him to give Geoffrey the news, that they would have told it to him themselves, except for fearing he would think the truth even more horrible than what they related. Ian looked at Geoffrey and bowed to the judgment of his womenfolk. Geoffrey was excited by the opening of his prison of sickness, but even after the effort of taking off and replacing part of his clothing, it was clear it was doing him no harm. His eyes were bright, his color good, and his gestures easy, displaying none of the slow, leaden character of fatigue. He was too sensitive still, too easily moved to tears, but that would wear off. Ian dragged a chair nearer the one Geoffrey was sitting in, sat down, and stretched his long legs.

"Have some wine," he said, smiling and filling two goblets.

He then did a swift look and look-again at the goblets and flagon, which Geoffrey did not notice because he was now looking nervously toward the door. Ian chuckled. The women were right. Geoffrey was eager to start living again. He was looking at that door like a prisoner, fearing the arrival of a keeper who would put to an end a deeply desired visit.

"Be easy and have some wine," Ian said, grinning more broadly.

Geoffrey's eyes went to the flagon and goblets at which

Ian was pointing. He looked puzzled, then as their meaning came to him, his color suddenly rose and his eyes brightened dangerously.

"No, no," Ian warned, laughing even harder. "Do not demean yourself by losing your temper. Is it not a tactful way to give us permission to talk—a little sign, a flagon of wine and two cups? You would like it even less if Joanna said in words you had her leave to hear the news. Now, now, Geoffrey, do not turn that color. It is useless and ruins the digestion." Suddenly his laughter cut off and his face grew older. "Besides, I have that to say to you that can sour your stomach for a worthier reason."

"I feared it. I feared it. All the honeyed words, all the sober tales of how the king was chastened and all was now smooth as silk—told so—so surely! So easily!"

"Geoffrey," Ian said softly and soberly, "you believed because you needed to believe, and Joanna lied because you needed those lies. Yet I dare swear they were not really lies. Our women do not lie to us; they leave things out or place the emphasis on the wrong word so that the thought is bent. You were very sick, Geoffrey. Your body needed peace to mend itself. You were given that peace. Now you are strong enough to carry it, a part of your burden is handed back to you. Do not mistake how hard it is for Joanna to yield you up to the struggle of full life again—so near to death as she has seen you, and after believing you dead already."

There was a silence while Geoffrey digested that. His eyes rested all the while on the two goblets and, finally, the frown smoothed off his face and he reached out and took one and chuckled. "Perhaps, but it goes against the grain to think that I have got my own way for once, and then discover that it is her way after all."

"You will grow accustomed," Ian retorted drily, and sighed. "As for your question about the king—Joanna did not lie, at least not by John's seeming behavior. It is quiet and modest. He does no ill, but—curse him and rot him, what a fool! He comes home a whipped cur—although it is true enough that was no fault of his. He bore himself right manly and planned the battles full well. We would have swallowed all of western France but for those treacherous Poitevins. Nonetheless, no matter whose fault, we came home worse than empty-handed—beaten—and he scarce sets a foot upon the land before he demands scutage.''

"Well," Geoffrey said doubtfully, "it is his right. The lords owe him knight-service, and if—''

"I do not deny it is his right," Ian snarled. "It is your right and mine to beat our wives silly for amusement. What would that get us?''

"Likely a knife in the ribs," Geoffrey answered, grinning, although he knew the question was both rhetorical and made a most unfunny point.

"And likely that is what John will receive. Think of it! Who was it who did not answer his summons? The faithful came; even the doubtful came, thinking to have some loot and some sport where it would do no harm to their own lands. Who remained sulking behind? Only the rebels and those who adhere to them. And of them John demands scutage of *three* marks.''

Geoffrey rubbed his hand across his face, rasping along the fair beard that had been shaved only yesterday but was already a stubble. "Have they flown to arms already?'' he asked.

"No, and I do not think to see that yet, not this year. They are growing cautious and clever. To speak the truth, I detect a steadying hand carefully hidden. You remember what Langton was preaching last year? He does not appear in this, not openly after the reprimand he had from Innocent, but instead of a call to arms by that hothead Vesci and that greedy boar FitzWalter, there is a call to a meeting. It will be held at Bury Saint Edmunds the third week of next month to consider the matter of the scutage and other things.''

"A meeting, eh? Do they seek to draw you in? Will you go? The scutage is nothing to you, and when John hears of this—''

"Draw me in, they cannot, but these 'other matters' that are to be considered interest me greatly," Ian said. It is not to be named in the invitation, but there is a strong purpose to bind the king to sign a charter. Langton believes, and I also, that this can save the realm. In any case, John cannot love me less—'' Ian shrugged.

''Nor me either,'' Geoffrey pointed out, ''I know well enough who would have paid the double ransom Isabella offered. I do not think he will dare accuse me of treason, however. I will go to Saint Edmunds.''

''We must see how you heal,'' Ian temporized, but he obviously thought well of the idea.

Once over the hump of infection, Geoffrey healed with the rapidity of youth, which was fortunate because Ian had to rush north to quell a totally unexpected rising on his own lands. He had not been worried about the scutage because his men had gone with him to serve the king. However, he had obtained quittance for certain of his vassals for varying reasons. The king conveniently ''forgot'' these quittances and levied scutage. Promptly, even eagerly, Ian's vassals armed themselves to resist, after informing their overlord of the despite done them. First, Ian confronted John with the signed quittances, wrung from him a written, signed, and sealed pardon of the scutage, and then went to calm his seething men.

This, of course, did not endear Ian to John, but Salisbury had returned from France and was showing his brother such a black countenance and such icy reserve that the king did not even frown at any man Salisbury loved. First, it was necessary to convince Salisbury that the price offered for Geoffrey's body was offered *after* it was known he had not been taken alive and that the intention was only that Geoffrey should not be buried in an unmarked and untended grave. John was shocked when this reasonable explanation was not snapped up with relief. He withdrew himself with wounded dignity, but he suffered more than Salisbury from the chill between them and he was very careful not to exacerbate his brother's suspicion by attacks on any of Salisbury's friends. Nonetheless, it was thought best for Ian to remain in the north.

Geoffrey went to Bury Saint Edmunds. He was quite well, except for an odd gait—one short step, one long—and for the fact that he still tired easily. To provide him with an active and reliable pair of hands and feet, in case violence broke out or much running to and fro was necessary, Adam went along with his brother-by-marriage. They returned frankly enthused both over the idea of a charter and the moderate behavior of the men. Nothing was to be done in haste, Adam reported at a family council. Alinor stared unbelievingly at her son, so much the man now that he understood the purpose and importance of political maneuvering.

The terms of the charter would be presented to the king and he would have sufficient time to consider before any pressure was applied, Adam continued. Geoffrey concurred with Adam's description of the proceedings, adding only that he thought there were some who were not too well pleased with the moderation. For them, he feared, this talk of a charter was only a device to draw in the uncertain until they were in too deep to withdraw. Perhaps the more rebellious hoped to drive the king into a rage, Geoffrey suggested, so that many would despair of reaching a settlement and join the more radical element.

If that was true, it did not show at first. Possibly, that was because the king also behaved with great moderation. He attended calmly to the complaints presented to him by a delegation on January 6, 1215. He even agreed that these were matters of grave importance, that there might have been injustices done. Finally, he said that he would consider what was owing to his lords and to his own honor and give them a reply after Easter. The family was dispersed by then, but Salisbury was back in court; he had not been able to resist John's urgent invitations with their note of pleading, only his eyes were clearer than they once had been. He wrote to Geoffrey at Hemel, and Joanna wrote to Adam and her mother that John was not as passive as he appeared. He had written to the pope for support.

Innocent's first move was as conciliatory as the king's, which implied either that he had attended to Langton's analysis of the situation or that John had actually written a fair account of the case. Both of these expedients seemed so unlikely that it was simpler to credit Innocent with divine perspicacity. First, the pope had been sadly disappointed in Stephen Langton, who was a man of strong independence and a fanatic devotion to true justice. Thus, Innocent was at daggers drawn with the man he had forced on John in the belief he was inserting a faithful tool of his own into the government of England. It was most unlikely he would attend to anything Langton wrote.

Joanna and Alinor also dismissed the idea of John's being fair out of hand. They took comfort in the thought that the pope was a man of great wisdom and had seen through John's demands. Oddly, Geoffrey did not agree. As much as he loathed his uncle, he believed John did want peace at this time and was anxious to be conciliatory. Since John's best hope for peace was if the pope acted as mediator, it was not impossible that the king had stated the problem honestly.

Whatever the reason, Innocent did not blast the charter or those who proposed it. He offered instead that if there were differences between the king and his barons that he would himself, or through an impartial legate, arbitrate the differences. It was at this point that Geoffrey's predictions came true. The hard core of real disaffected showed their purpose. They neither accepted the pope's offer nor reiterated their demand that John sign the reasonable charter that had been written. What they did was to publish a new set of demands that were, frankly, outrageous. John refused with dignity and calm. On May 3, Eustace de Vesci, Robert FitzWalter, and their kinsmen and adherents formally renounced their homage to the king and moved to besiege Northampton.

Joanna had the news by May 5. She was in Roselynde, Geoffrey having refused to take her to court with him because at last there was a hope that she was breeding. She did not weep when she heard that civil war was at hand, but she did not dare look in the mirror for she knew what kind of eyes would look back at her. Grimly, she told old Beorn to choose out a party to accompany her within the next few days. She was sure she would need to ride out to urge men to answer a war summons they would rather ignore and to gather supplies. The ugly task fell upon her shoulders because Alinor was in the north again. Ian had no hope of bringing men to the king, but he was making a last-ditch effort to keep them neutral.

The summons did not come, however. Joanna had a half-hopeful letter from Geoffrey to say that John had taken no notice of the hostile act beyond announcing that he was ready to accept the pope as arbiter of all the differences between his lords and himself. In addition he promised, without urging or pressure, not to take those who had declared against him as enemies, not to disseise them, nor attack them, except as allowed by law or by a court of their own peers.

This nearly took the wind from the rebels' sails. A number of lukewarm adherents deserted and, what made the rebels look ridiculous, they could not take Northampton. To save face, they abandoned that siege and moved upon Bedford. That stronghold fell to them, but it was known to be held by a sympathizer who had put up only a token resistance. It seemed as if John had the kingdom in his hand again and that it was time to close his iron fist upon the rebels.

Again, Joanna prepared to summon men and gather supplies. Geoffrey's next letter stopped her, asking her to send money instead. "I do not know whether the king is right or wrong, but he has bought troops of mercenaries instead of summoning an army out of his own realm. There is some reason for this, as you know, John having little reason to trust armies made up of those who owe service, yet I fear that it will work ill, breeding resentment in the people. The rebels are all, whatever else can be said of them, men of this land."

"As to the news you wrote me that our hope of a child was over, your flux having begun again," he continued, "I can truly say I am sorry only for your sake, as I know you desire a little one. We are young yet, and there is time in plenty. Also, I take too much pleasure in the effort to get a babe on you to grieve much over the need for continued effort. Mayhap I should not jest, knowing that you are disappointed, but if I do not I must say to you that I shudder with fear when I think of bringing a lamb into the pack of wolves among whom we live.''

Geoffrey's fears were immediately proved valid when London, crying her fear of rape by the foreign mercenaries, opened her gates to the rebels and prepared to defend herself stoutly against Salisbury and the Flemish troops he led. An enormous army with numerous siege engines and endless supplies would be necessary to break London, and the city could not be besieged because of the river. Salisbury withdrew. The beating heart of the kingdom, from whence flowed a good part of the gold and goods that kept it alive, was locked away from the king.

Stalemate. The rebels could not come out. The king could not get in.

On June 10, John came to Windsor. Negotiations began anew. Because Geoffrey was known to be faithful to the king and yet to dislike him heartily for good reason, he was considered the perfect intermediary. Many who feared to go directly to Langton, who was serving as spokesman for the rebels although he dissociated himself from them, and others who feared to receive any messenger from the king, were all willing to talk to Geoffrey.

Back and forth he went between Windsor and London. Geoffrey rode the track so often that he could soon sleep on his horse while it found its own way. That was just as well because he had little other time to sleep. It seemed to him that he no sooner took off his clothes and lay down in either place than he was summoned by another stealthy messenger who led him to a nervous overlord with still another suggestion or complaint. His hip ached unmercifully, but not nearly so much as his jaw ached from being clamped tight over expression of his own convictions.

Too clever by half, Ian called Geoffrey, and it was true. He was observant and thoughtful, and he saw more than those intimately concerned noticed. They were absorbed in details. This word was changed and that phrase. The barons were convinced to yield one small matter; the king yielded another. Langton grew gaunter, his burning eyes like beacons in his tired, ashen face. Some feared he would fail physically, but it was not at him that Geoffrey looked when he was called to be told of the answer decided upon for a complaint or suggestion he had transmitted. Geoffrey looked at the king. That barrel body grew no thinner and, although from time to time he would rant and roar, to Geoffrey's ears there was something false in John's display of rage.

Ian rode down from the north and arrived on June 14. He was tired, for he had ridden through two nights, but he was very happy because a dream that he had held for many years seemed near to fruition. Geoffrey kept his jaw clamped shut. What was the use of moaning of vague disquiets and spoiling Ian's joy with forebodings? He rode back and forth between London and Windsor, opening his mouth only to repeat as near word perfect as he could what other men had bid him say.

Late that night, he was summoned for the last time, now to his father's apartments where he was shown a copy of the completed document. Politely he scanned it. He was familiar with most of the sixty-one articles, particularly with those of which every word had been picked over until both sides agreed it was bare and strong as bone. He looked a little more closely at the other articles, those which had been left as mere suggestions because they did not sear men's souls, things like the measures by which goods should be judged. There was nothing in those that could account for his uneasiness, Geoffrey decided, until he came to the very last. He had heard nothing of this, and he read it with starting eyes.

Having done, he cried out to Salisbury that it was madness, pacing the floor as he expostulated. Salisbury, who still winced inwardly at Geoffrey's uneven gait, looked aside. The king had always had a council, he pointed out in a dead voice. This was only a formalization of that.

"Formalization! Papa, have you not read this? This council has the *right* to rebel against the king and to call up the country to force the king to its will. I have my differences with my uncle, but he cannot agree to this. No king can agree to this."

"I am not blind or deaf," Salisbury remarked indifferently. "I have both read and heard that article. Without it, the barons will not accept the charter, and John says he desires peace. He says he is tired of war and grief—"

Appalled at the tone and even more at the phrase "John says," which implied that Salisbury did not believe his brother, Geoffrey stared at his father. Cold settled inside him. Salisbury did not care. He had seen that he had loved a lie all his life, but he could not break the habit.

"Besides," Salisbury continued reasonably if still without much interest, "you know—and I, and John—that twenty-five men, all of equal importance in their own eyes, will never agree on anything, much less anything worthwhile, such as what is just cause for rebellion. I tried to have the mention of the four responsible for summoning the others taken out, but Langton outmaneuvered me there. Without that, the article might as well not be written. Even with it—oh, what does it matter!"

On June 15 in a great meadow called Runnymede, King John signed and sealed the Magna Carta. Geoffrey did not witness the signing. He went to bed. No one missed him in all the excitement, until after the feasting and celebrations were over when Ian, Adam, and Salisbury gathered in the earl's chamber for a last drink and a little quiet conversation. Then it appeared that no one had seen Geoffrey all day. Anxiety leapt into Salisbury's eyes. A messenger was sent hastily to seek him and ran him to earth, still sleeping heavily. Wakened and told he was wanted in his father's chamber, Geoffrey dressed hurriedly and went without asking why.

"Come have a drink with us and celebrate—" Adam hesitated. He had been about to say, "celebrate the curbing of the king, but in deference to Salisbury he changed it to, "the new peace."

"Bah!" Geoffrey exclaimed furiously, and began to swing around to return to bed.

"Wait, Geoffrey. Tell me what is wrong." Ian was plainly distressed. Geoffrey usually had a very sweet disposition. He had even been good natured and patient to a remarkable degree all the weeks he had been abed. This irritability was not at all like him; it was unnatural.

"He does not like the sixty-first article," Salisbury said, his voice distant.

"But Geoffrey," Adam cried, leaping in where his elders were too cautious to tread, "how else can there be surety that the king will keep the other articles? If the sixty-first article was not written in, Magna Carta would be as worthless as all John's other promises. Oh—I beg your pardon, my lord." Like his mother, Adam blushed readily, and he retired into his goblet of wine in some confusion.

"In any case, the barons would so believe," Salisbury remarked.

Ian turned and stared at him. His lips parted, then he swallowed. He had not been alone with his friend since he had returned from France. Salisbury knew John for what he was, Ian realized.

"I think the king intends to abide by the agreement," Ian said hearteningly. "I am not sure I agree wholeheartedly with the sixty-first article, but it will serve to stimulate John's memory if he should sometimes forget. It is not meant to be used, only—"

Geoffrey looked from one face to another. "I hope to God you are right," he said less violently, "But I tell you, I do not believe it. To me, the fact that John signed a charter with such an article in it says one thing only—he has a way to overturn the agreement."

Salisbury said nothing. He looked down at the wine in the goblet between his hands. Ian looked at him, looked back at Geoffrey who drew breath sharply but continued doggedly.

"And if any of you thinks signing any charter or any ten charters will silence Vesci and FitzWalter, you are either deluding yourselves or are much stupider than I have ever believed. That article is there only to give them the *right* to prosecute this rebellion." His face set and bitter, Geoffrey walked to the table—short step, long step—and seized the last goblet. "I will drink to peace, but I tell you, gentlemen, you had better look to your weapons for what is coming is real war."

CHAPTER THIRTY

On June 19, the barons of England, rebel and loyal alike, repeated their oath of homage to the king. Geoffrey swore with the others and then asked leave to go, which was readily granted. Since Alinor was at Roselynde, Joanna rode out and met Geoffrey at Hemel. She soon came to the conclusion that she had better have stayed at home. His mood was black as night, and nothing she did seemed able to lighten it. Often, even when they made love, instead of falling asleep after a few drowsy, loving words, Geoffrey would get out of bed and pace—short step, long step; short step, long step.

If Joanna asked what troubled him, he usually came back to bed and pretended to sleep, but one day he turned on her, snarling, ''You wanted me to hate war—well, you have your desire. I hate it!''

After that, Joanna asked no more questions, believing that Geoffrey's sufferings had marked his spirit as well as his body. She found to her own amazement that she did not despise his fear. Love encompasses all things. She was only agonized because she could offer him no comfort. She prayed for peace with a fervency that her own fear had never brought to her. Her voice trembled with tenderness when she spoke to her husband and she said ''beloved'' to him with her heart on her lips. That, which he had so dearly desired, brought no light to Geoffrey's eyes. Perhaps the love, naked at last, made him look more haunted.

Joanna's prayers were not answered. The news was hesitantly good at first. John really seemed to be trying to right the injustices brought to his attention and keep the letter of Magna Carta. But soon the rumors turned as ugly as Geoffrey's scowl. The hard core of rebel barons began in July by displaying open insolence to the king and went on in August by refusing to leave London or to allow John and his men to enter the city. Geoffrey made no comment on the news. He gave his time to drilling his men-at-arms in the techniques of battle and to refining and completing his mastery over the three gray war stallions that Alinor had given him to replace his own lost destriers.

He did this with a bleak, grim intensity that wrung Joanna's heart. Geoffrey had always enjoyed every aspect of the art of war and, in particular, he loved training horses. Now, nothing seemed to give him pleasure. Certainly the news that he had even been right about John's intention of overturning Magna Carta drew no spark from him. They learned of that in September, although the first hint of it came at the end of August with a letter from the pope that strictly enjoined the barons to obey the king and give him his due in whatever he demanded.

Appalled by this intrusion into what he believed could still be worked into a basis for a permanent peace between the king and his vassals, Langton set off for Rome to explain the situation to Innocent in person. On the way he found he was too late. Even before Magna Carta had been signed, John had written to appeal to his overlord, the Holy Father, to annul the agreement forced upon him by his disloyal subjects. The letter that fulfilled John's wish met Langton before he crossed the Alps.

That was all that was necessary. When this information burst upon them, the rebels cried aloud of betrayal and flew to arms. They took Rochester, a key point. The same letter that Salisbury wrote to give this news also requested that Geoffrey come with about one hundred men, but no vassals. The king would not call levies, Salisbury wrote, being too much in doubt as to the loyalty of his subjects. He would use mercenaries. With a face of stone and dead eyes, Geoffrey went to make ready.

If Joanna had felt fear for her husband before, it was nothing to what she felt now. It was useless to beg Geoffrey to refuse. From his looks and his manner, Joanna could only conclude that his fear had bred a self-loathing and that he went out to seek death as the only cure for his inability to face life. Near mad, Joanna wrote to Adam, spilling out her grief and terror and pleading for help. Perhaps Adam could think of some reason or some device accepted as honorable by men to prevent Geoffrey from joining his father. She confessed all except the core of the problem. It was impossible for her to admit to another man—even to Adam—that Geoffrey was afraid.

The answer she had to her letter nearly tipped her right over the edge. "Be at ease," Adam wrote, "I will not let any ill befall Geoffrey. I will go also and guard him."

That was all. Adam had learned to read and write and cipher as his mother insisted, but he still did not love the work and kept his missives down to the bare essentials. Frequently, as in this case, he even omitted a few essentials, such as where and when he planned to meet Geoffrey. Joanna had no idea where to send a letter to stop him. It was useless to write to Salisbury. By the time Adam came to him, he would have committed himself to Geoffrey and nothing any woman said would affect any of them.

Instead of helping Geoffrey, Joanna thought, she had endangered Adam. Obviously, Adam believed that she feared Geoffrey's injuries would make him awkward. He would not realize that Geoffrey was seeking death. He would follow where Geoffrey led without thinking of danger and they would both be killed. At that point, a flicker of sanity returned. However Geoffrey felt, he would never lead Adam into disaster. Joanna's heart stopped pounding in her throat. Perhaps she had not done so ill after all. Caring for Adam's safety might teach Geoffrey to live with himself; in fact, Adam might even accomplish Geoffrey's cure. It was very hard to resist that gay and loving nature.

Those were comforting thoughts to which to cling, and a sudden spate of activity also helped dull Joanna's terror. Geoffrey had hardly left when Alinor wrote asking Joanna to return to Roselynde if it was possible for her. Ian was going north again. Joanna wrote to her husband at once and received an immediate reply with his permission and the information that Adam had arrived safe and well in time to enjoy the assault upon and reconquest of Rochester. Now, he said, they were encamped near London doing nothing.

After that, Geoffrey did not write again, although Joanna sent a messenger when she was settled in Roselynde. She could only assume that Adam had been unable to conceal his reason for appearing where he had not been invited. Geoffrey was probably so furious at her interference that he thought silence preferable to what he would be driven to say if he took pen in hand to write.

This did not grieve Joanna much. It gave her something interesting to think about. She could plan ways of assuaging Geoffrey's anger and, on the whole, it was better to think of him in a rage than heavy with unspoken and unspeakable misery. She had plenty of time for thought. December passed and then January. Alinor wrote that Ian's lands in the northwest were quiet, but that they had heard the king was in the northeast burning and pillaging. She did not know the truth for as yet they had only rumor from a few common serfs who swore they had escaped after everyone else was dead. Of course, runaway serfs would say anything, but Alinor was afraid there was truth in this. Joanna did not pay much attention to that. She assumed Geoffrey was with his father and she knew there was no fighting around London.

Besides, Joanna had some disquieting rumors of her own to worry about. Soon after she arrived in Roselynde, she learned from a merchant who docked ship in the harbor that the rebels had appealed to Philip and Louis to invade England and depose John. Thus far it seemed that Philip was disinclined to listen. The king of France had a clear memory of the reaction to a threat of invasion in 1212. It was said also that Philip realized that John had become something special to the pope—a jewel in his crown, like a prodigal returned to the fold. If Philip moved to invade England, papal anathemas would soon be flying around his head. However, Louis felt differently; he was certainly interested.

As late as February, Louis had done no more about this interest than send a small contingent of knights who soon became a laughingstock. They sat in the rebel stronghold of

London and complained because it was necessary to drink beer—the wine had run out. Toward the end of that month, the most dismal of winter, when freezing rain lashed the battlements and the breakers roared on the beach and exploded against the rocks of the low cliff, a ship struggled into Roselynde harbor, near sunk. They had put out from Le Havre when the weather seemed to be fairing up, intending only to run a little way along the coast and the storm had come up suddenly and swept them away.

The master of the ship, brought up to Roselynde keep, told Joanna without the slightest hesitation that Louis had convinced his father to support him and was gathering ships and men. He would come in the spring, in April or May, the master said, smiling. It was so very apparent that he expected Joanna to greet this news with pleasure that she made an effort to do so. It seemed that the French were now convinced that England would welcome them with open arms. Philip had letters containing oaths and promises from more than half the barons that they would join his son and make him king if only Louis would come. This was a far cry from the promises of one single lord, even a powerful one, and Philip now felt it was worth a chance.

Joanna listened until she was sure the man had no more to tell. Since he was not a regular trader in Roselynde port, had never been there before, she ordered that he and the crew be put to death, the ship and cargo impounded. She sent word of what she had heard to Alinor and to Geoffrey. By now she had given up hope of receiving any reply, so she was surprised when her returned messenger handed her a letter from Salisbury in the first week of March. Her father-by-marriage thanked her for the information, although he had heard it from other sources. He had taken the liberty of reading her letter, he explained, since he did not know exactly where Geoffrey was at the moment and he feared, because the letter was sent to his camp, that there was some emergency that required immediate response. Salisbury had sent his own messenger on with her letter to Geoffrey, but it might be some time before the man caught up with his son.

Unbelievingly, Joanna reread what was written. She

knew Salisbury was not well skilled in reading or writing. Could he have written the wrong words by mistake? That was a brief reaction to disbelief. Joanna knew Salisbury had not written the letter himself. It was a fine clerkly hand, free of blots, waverings, and blotches. What could he mean? Where *was* Geoffrey? Where was Adam? Could Geoffrey have been so angry that, when his father gave him leave to go, he went to Hemel or some other keep rather than join her? In that case, Adam must be back upon his own lands. She would write and ask Adam where Geoffrey was.

Another rereading of Salisbury's letter eliminated that notion. He said he did not know "exactly where Geoffrey was at the moment" and that it might take the messenger "some time to catch up with Geoffrey." That could only mean that Geoffrey was moving around quickly. Where? Why? She forced a little calm on herself by insisting over and over that it must be some business of Salisbury's Geoffrey was engaged upon. She read the letter yet again. It must be. There was no hint of anxiety in what Salisbury said. That was ridiculous. Salisbury would never permit such a feeling to show; he had long training in hiding such nuances from Ela.

Before Joanna could drive herself distracted, she had a response to her news about the possibility of invasion from her mother. Alinor had had positive confirmation from other sources. Louis would come. It was now useless for her and Ian to remain in the north. What John had done between York and Berwick had so frightened and sickened Ian's men that it was useless to talk to them any more. The vassals would initiate no trouble—that was sure. They would sit quiet if they could. However, if Louis came into the area, they would not resist him. Much as they loved Ian, nothing could now hold them for the king. Thus, it seemed best for Ian to come south and fight Louis there. A few weeks more they would stay to tie up all the loose ends of the administration; then they would return to Roselynde. Joanna could expect them about the middle of April.

Meanwhile, there was much to be done, Alinor continued. Joanna must go first to Portsmouth and see what preparations were being made in the king's stronghold against the invasion. Then Roselynde must be stuffed and garnished. They should be able, counting on fish from the sea, to hold out for a year of siege. There must be pitch and tar and oil for the walls. There must be stones and leathers and timbers for the catapults. There must be shafts and feathers for arrows, metal of all sizes for swords, arrow heads, bolts for crossbows, axes, pikes, rings for mail, bands for helmets. There must be hides for shields and corselets for the men and for all other uses for leather. And there must be food, and food, and food.

The young men of Roselynde town who could fight must be warned to be ready to come up to the keep with the valuables of the town; the women and children and oldsters must have carts ready and be prepared to flee to the woods. Doubtless spring came to England sometime in late March or early April. Joanna did not see it. She rode and counted stores and added up figures until she could not see, and then she slept. Over all she did, however, was a black pall of doubt and fear. Where was Geoffrey? If he had held so great an anger against her all these months—since early November—was it possible she would ever redeem herself in his eyes? Worse yet, had his knowledge of his own weakness ended by killing his soul so that, even though the body walked and talked, Geoffrey was a dead man?

All was ready in Roselynde. Joanna waited only for Alinor's coming, which she expected that day or the next. Then she would leave for Mersea on the excuse that Sir John was by no means convinced that Louis would be a worse king than John. Actually, she did not think she could endure to stay and see the love between her mother and Ian. For want of something better to do at the moment, Joanna was going over the clothing she would take to Mersea. She had found that she dared not sit down to sew or embroider. A task must have something to it that would fix the mind, like counting.

"Lady!"

She looked up at the manservant who had interrupted her and made her lose count. Harsh words rose to her lips—they did so too frequently these days—and then she saw the man was all excited.

"What is it?"

"Lord Geoffrey and Master Adam are here. They—"

Joanna leapt to her feet and ran toward the stairs. Before she started down them, she froze. If Geoffrey was still angry, she did not want all the outdoor people to see. She drew back and drew back again until she was in the area by the great hearth reserved for the family. No servant would come near unless called. She stood there, trembling, looking at the entry from the stairwell, then tearing her eyes away and fastening them on her hands. She heard them. Her breath stopped. With her last bit of will, she kept her eyes down, fighting tears.

A heavy tread. That did not sound like Adam, who for all his bulk had a light, lively walk, and it could not be Geoffrey's uneven gait. Who—? Her eyes flew up. Breath rattled in her throat as she gasped. Adam? Long step, short step — Joanna's eyes retreated from shock only to find horror. Her heart froze. Surely, although he was walking, Geoffrey's face was that of a dead man.

"What has befallen us?" Joanna cried.

Geoffrey winced. "Nothing ill," he said, with a heartiness that frightened Joanna still more. "The king has now retaken most of the rebel strongholds in the east. He prepares now to stop Louis's coming. I must see to what ships are in harbor and have them fitted for war."

"Yes," Adam said—his voice was high and unnatural—"I must do the same."

Joanna looked wildly from one to the other. She knew disaster when she saw it. She knew men pushed beyond endurance. She knew personally what it meant when it was necessary to cling to things like counting barrels of salt fish or, for men, fixing the mind on the details of the next physical task to be done. What Joanna did not know was what the disaster was.

"I only wondered—" Adam was still speaking. "I only wondered," he repeated, his voice suddenly shaking, "is mama coming? Ian? I need to see them. I need—''

"Beloved," Joanna whispered, taking his hand. It was the most horrible thing—almost worse than Geoffrey's walking death—to see that face, which had grown the lines and the eyes of an old man, and to hear the voice of a boy who needed his mother. "Sit here, beloved," she urged, pushing Adam into a chair. "Mama will be here soon, any day now, very soon." She turned to call across to a maid. "Bring wine, strong, sweet wine."

Her eyes fell on Geoffrey who was looking around the hall. He saw the baskets used to carry clothes on pack animals half-full.

"Where are you going?" he asked conversationally—as if he had not heard Adam, not as if he cared, only a polite question.

"I thought since Sir John is so uncertain in his loyalty and my mother will be here, that I would go to Mersea," Joanna replied mechanically, not really thinking of what she was saying, her mind still busy with what could have happened and what could be threatening them.

To her amazement, those innocent words made Geoffrey turn toward her with starting eyes. He opened his mouth, but instead of speaking gagged, clapped his hand over his mouth, and staggered hastily toward the alcove where the waste shaft lay. A swift glance showed Adam sitting quietly, his head sunk into his hands. Joanna ran after her husband to brace his body against her own and hold his head while he vomited. After he straightened up and wiped his mouth, she drew him against her.

"Are you sick, dear heart?" she asked tenderly.

"No. It was what you said—about going—"

All Joanna's inbred sense of possession leapt to life. "Mersea!" she exclaimed. "What has happened to Mersea?"

"Nothing, nothing. Mersea is safe and quiet. But I will not have you ride over the lands between here and Mersea—not for any reason."

"No danger threatens Mersea?"

"No, I swear it."

"Then I will not go, if you do not wish it," Joanna assured him soothingly. "Come and sit down. A little wine will settle your stomach. Tell me, Geoffrey, please tell me what is wrong."

But Geoffrey told her nothing. He sat and drank his wine as she directed, but when she asked where he had been, he said, "With the king," and looked so sick she thought he would bring up the wine he had just swallowed. That path was closed. She asked then if he or Adam had been hurt. Geoffrey closed his eyes and took a breath and then "made" a horrible travesty of a smile. A few bruises and scratches, he said, nothing that merited the effort of undressing to be tended.

It was Adam who finally answered her. The wine had put color back into his face and, when Joanna turned to him, unable to bear either Geoffrey's numb despair or false good cheer, Adam saw her fear and confusion.

"I am sorry we frightened you, Jo," he said, sounding more natural. "There is nothing to fear, really. It was—" he passed a hand across his face. "The whole east," and his voice shook again, "the whole east is a burned-out wasteland full of stinking corpses. First we took Rochester." His eyes brightened momentarily. "That was good fun. They held out fiercely and the walls would not yield to the catapults and mangonels. We had to set the men to mining under a tower, and then we burnt out the timbers shoring up the tunnel and the tower fell, and so we breached the walls."

The light died out of his eyes. "Then Salisbury settled to keep the rebels in London," Adam continued slowly. "I was just thinking that I had better get back to Kemp because—" He glanced toward Geoffrey, looked at Joanna, and mouthed "later," "—because there were already rumors of invasion. But the king came and," his voice faltered, "and commanded that Geoffrey and I come with him. He said we had well-trained troops and would be useful."

There was a short silence. Joanna looked from one to the other. Geoffrey was staring down into his wine, the goblet clutched so tight in his hands that the knuckles showed white. Adam had lost his color again and his eyes were black pools in his chalky face.

"Tell me!" Joanna insisted.

"It was like nothing I have ever seen." The words spewed out as if Adam could no longer hold them in. "Where we stopped, the world burned. Nothing and no one was spared. I do not think a hundred women and babes came out of Berwick alive, not to speak of men—I think not one. He let the French dogs loose upon his enemies. God knows, our men-at-arms are not gentle, but—but they do not spit the babes on their pikes and roast them while the mother is held down where she can see and hear it and be raped. The woman's convulsions lend a spice one of them told me. I killed him." Adam blinked and swallowed.

"But surely," Joanna quavered, "you could control your own men—you did not need to permit—"

"Oh, no." Adam sighed, sipping the wine again, "that was not our part. We were used to prevent the mad dogs from running completely amok. John is not crazed." He swallowed again. "I almost wish he were, but he is not. Those who were faithful to him and who offered large enough bribes were spared. It was our part—Geoffrey's and mine and a few other men with their own troops—to keep the *routiers* off those who yielded."

"Then there is no shame to you," Joanna urged. "Why are you so heavy of heart?"

Adam looked at her with a touch of bewilderment. "I—you know, it is a strange thing. At first I was sick, but then, except for a special thing now and again, I grew accustomed. It was not until we rode away from all that, when I saw the land green and the new lambs leaping and the colts and calves all legs, that I—" His eyes widened. "When did you say mama would come?"

"Soon," Joanna soothed, "soon. Come with me now and let Edwina take off your armor and bathe you."

"Edwina?" Adam's voice dropped back to its normal depth and he grinned. "How many little bastards does that one have now?"

In spite of her awareness of Geoffrey sitting and staring in just the position she had left him, Joanna could not help smiling. All would be well with Adam, she thought, if he could evince so great an interest in Edwina. She signaled the maid behind her brother's back to let him tumble her if he showed a desire for it. Ordinarily, Edwina regarded Adam as a "child" and would have refused him, but she looked at Joanna as if to say she was no fool and knew as well as her mistress when a man needed such warmth and soothing. Tears rose and stung in Joanna's eyes. Geoffrey was beyond such ministrations, she feared.

Alinor and Ian arrived with the dusk that very day, and one could see Adam's spirit healing as they spoke, explaining and comforting. Geoffrey, however, did not change. He was perfectly sensible and, owing to wider experience, not nearly so distressed by the excesses of the foreign mercenaries, but his eyes were the color of mud and there was no life in his voice. He had given no response to Joanna's overtures when she bathed him, and she desisted, her own passion chilled. When they went to bed she tried again.

Although Joanna succeeded in rousing her husband, it was a dreadful mistake. He said all the right words; his hands and lips did all the right things. He was patient and considerate, waiting and waiting for her because she was very slow to reach orgasm. She came at last because the stimulation of her body blanked out the sorrow of her mind. Geoffrey was not there—not Geoffrey. This was someone remote and indifferent, cold even in the moment of climax.

The next day, Adam dragged Joanna out into the garden to tell her that she need not worry about Geoffrey. "He is as able as ever. The hurts he had do not hinder him in any way. God knows, he needs no guarding from me. I may be a little the stronger, but he is quicker and much more subtle. I had enough to do to keep up with him."

That was not, of course, what Joanna feared, but it was impossible to explain, so she thanked Adam and kissed him and said she was sorry that he had come to harm through her. If she had not begged his help, he would not have been dragged on John's murderous campaign through the east. Adam's mouth hardened, but he replied that *he* was not sorry. He had learned a few things.

What he had learned came out that evening as they sat before the fire. "If Louis comes, will you hold by your oath to John, Ian?" Adam asked.

Ian looked startled. "You know I will—and it is not through fear of what you saw the king do. That is an ugly and a terrible thing—but it was not wholly undeserved by those who suffered it. Whatever John is, he is the rightful king and he will stray abroad no more. When Louis is cast out, will the pope, nill the pope, we will bind John to Magna Carta and have peace in this land and a right rule."

"You will never have it with John," Adam replied steadily, "charter or no charter. Even those who follow him and are loyal to him hate him. It was not for what he did. You have said, and I have seen, that these things are necessary. It was because he took pleasure in it. *I* hate him, Ian, and I have never hated any person in my whole life."

Ian opened his mouth as if to give a sharp order, and then swallowed. Adam was beyond being commanded. He was not knighted, but there could be no doubt that he was adult and master of his own.

"So?" he said bitterly. "And you, Geoffrey, what do you say to this?"

"I? There is nothing I can say. Adam is quite right. There will be no peace as long as John reigns. If he continues to be king much longer you will see father pitted against son and brother against brother. But it will not help if Louis wins. There will be no peace anyway. First, he will kill John's heirs so that we will have no rallying point. Then he will set foreign masters over us who do not know our customs. He will find excuses to disseise us and give the land to his own men. And those of us who remain, by his grace and our humbling of ourselves, he will drain to the last drop to pay for his wars in France and Flanders, and Savoy. . . . There will be rebellion again."

"But what will you do?" Adam asked, not completely convinced, but certainly shaken.

"I will do nothing if I can. If I am summoned by the king, I will go and fight for him. My oath is given—and Ian is right in that—John is the rightful king. What can I do beyond wishing and praying I were dead?"

"Oath or no oath—I cannot fight for him," Adam cried passionately.

But Joanna hardly heard him. She was aware suddenly that, although Geoffrey did not seem to be looking at her, his attention was fixed upon her. Very briefly his eyes flashed to her and away. Joanna sat still, very still. He hated her! Why? Why? Because she had fought for his life when he could have died?

The single glance was all Geoffrey could bear. She was so beautiful, so warm, so loving, so alive. Every question he had ever had about Joanna's feelings had been answered when Adam appeared before Rochester. Because she feared for him she had been willing to thrust her adored "baby" brother into danger. There could be no doubt who came first in Joanna's heart and mind. Geoffrey wished passionately that he were not such a coward, that he could stiffen his spirit enough to plunge a knife into that exquisite white throat or through the sweet white breast into Joanna's heart.

He would never do it, no matter how driven, yet it was the best and kindest thing he ever could do for her, the ultimate act of love. And he was not capable of it. Instead, he would see her torn to pieces with fear for him and grief for her people and her family, and in the end, she might be torn to pieces literally. He had seen. . . . No, he would not think of that. Before that, he would find the courage to kill her. He would!

Adam, Ian, and Alinor talked long that night. Joanna could not tell whether Geoffrey listened or not. He sat and looked from one to another, but her flesh crawled and she knew that he saw only her. She crept from her chair and up the stairs and into bed, and she cried and cried until she was so exhausted that she overslept the next morning. Adam was gone by the time Joanna woke, and so was Geoffrey. Her blank, stricken expression did not need explanation to Alinor.

"Geoffrey has only gone down to the town to see about the ships," she said. "He will be back to dinner."

Joanna's body stiffened as if to resist a blow, but her mother did not question her or offer her sympathy. She began to speak about certain problems, which Joanna had left unsolved for Alinor to settle, explaining in detail to her inattentive daughter what decisions she would make and the reasons for these decisions. Ian was slower to see Joanna's misery. It took him another day or two to determine its cause. Then Alinor had to drag Ian off to Iford before he murdered his son-by-marriage. Mercifully, the ships Geoffrey had chosen were readied in a short time, and he sailed off to add them to the fleet the king was assembling in Thames mouth and the Dover roads.

There were a few weeks of quiet, not expectant and eager as the period of waiting for invasion had been in 1212, but sullen and ominous. On May 18, a new disaster struck. A violent storm swept in and destroyed the fleet. England lay naked to the invaders. Four days later they came. John's army was in the right place. The trumpets sounded, the troops were drawn up—and the king ordered them dismissed and rode off to Winchester.

Geoffrey returned to Roselynde. With a face of stone, he told Ian that his father had parted company with the king. He gave no reason for it, only said that he would go and see to his lands and stay upon them. Joanna went at once to pack her things. He had kissed her when he came in and called her "sweet heart" and somehow she had choked down the scream in her throat and prevented her body from shuddering and shrinking away. It was no light thing to be embraced by a corpse.

Ian followed her into the women's chambers and begged her to let her husband go and to stay with them. Numbly, Joanna shook her head.

"I love him," she said simply. "I never wanted to. I knew that love is only suffering, but it is too late now. I love him."

They did a round of Geoffrey's properties and then went and shut themselves into Hemel. In their travels they had seen that the scars of John's campaign were healing rapidly under the new growth of early summer, but all the other news was bad and grew steadily worse. There was hardly any resistance to Louis. Keep after keep opened to him. By August, two-thirds of the barons had yielded. Then, there began to be a hint of change.

Some, of course, had remained loyal from the beginning. Dover had shut herself tight and resisted all Louis could do, although he came himself to oversee that siege. Engelard held Windsor, hurling taunts and insults down at the attackers. Barnard Castle stood firm against the Scots, and Eustace de Vesci died in an attempt to storm it. Nicolaa de la Hay leaned out from the tower of Lincoln keep and spat down at the commander who ordered her to yield. By God's grace the wind carried the spittle right into the man's face. That was her answer and God's. Lincoln did not fall.

Ian, after considerable discussion with Alinor, went to the king at Winchester. With Salisbury and his brother estranged, Ian was determined to give John no excuse to name him, or Geoffrey, or Adam traitors. A small force of French did come to Roselynde when it was known the lord of the keep was gone and called upon Alinor to yield. They thought a keep, no matter how strong, would be easy meat when ruled by a woman. Alinor's answer was no less rude than Nicolaa's—except that she used words. The French looked at the walls of Roselynde and at the sea, tasted a few yard-long arrows from Ian's Welsh archers—and passed on to softer prizes.

Kemp lay tight shut also, with Adam prowling the walls like an angry lion. One of Louis's men had seized a smaller stronghold of Adam's and had butchered the garrison and the castellan and his family, even though Adam had offered ransom for them. That ended Adam's brief desire to flirt with a foreign king. Geoffrey spoke true. Only Louis's own Frenchmen would be favored. Other barons who had yielded were discovering the same truth. They received a very cold welcome from Louis indeed and, even though they were willing to fight for him, discovered that their lands were not safe from Louis's men. The French knights in Louis's tail were poor men. They had come to England to seize lands for themselves, not to rid the English of an unwanted king.

Men who had changed sides once, changed sides again. John *had* signed Magna Carta, after all, and he had tried to live by it—at least more than Vesci and FitzWalter, who had brought this plague of Frenchmen down upon England, had done. Of course, John had betrayed them by asking the pope to annul the signing. But that was John. Better the devil they knew than this new devil, who had all the hungry maws of his own men to fill and nothing to fill them with but the land of Englishmen. Feelers were sent out and were well received by the king.

By mid-September, John felt it was worthwhile to begin a campaign. He marched out and down the valley of the Thames, drawing the besiegers away from Windsor and then, with the help of the garrison which poured out to support him, drubbed them soundly. The king then turned north to Lincoln and relieved the siege of that castle, where Nicolaa had held out valiantly after her defiance. By October 8, John had moved across eastward to Lynn. There he was welcomed without any battle, and the royal forces paused to consider where next to strike. On October 10, the king was not well. He had a severe flux of the bowels. They waited one day more, but even though he grew no better, John was impatient to move south. They moved on to Wisbech.

On the twelfth of October, a catastrophe befell John and his supporters. The baggage train with the entire treasury, the crown jewels—everything—was overtaken by an unusually swift incoming tide as they crossed the Wellstream estuary. Everything was lost! Everything!

The king and his suite rushed in on their more powerful horses, thinking to save something of the treasure. A few men were drowned, all were soaked through and plastered with the mire of the swamp. They saved nothing; they nearly lost the king, dragging him away by force when his horse was near helpless in the quicksand. Even after that, John would not leave. Racked with dysentery and chill, he insisted upon waiting until the tide went out again. The carts were so broad and heavy that he hoped some at least would not have been swept away or completely swallowed up, Ian and a few others had thrown off their furred cloaks before they rushed into the water. Anyone who had a dry stitch contributed it to warm the king. The wind blew sharp across the marshlands. Ian crouched against his destrier, shivering until he thought the flesh would shake free from his bones.

Before the tide had even run out again, they were back in the icy water, groping and tugging. The king had been right insofar as the carts not sinking completely, but they had all tilted or overturned. The small, heavy items had slid off and sunk deep—deep beyond recall. The treasure was lost forever. A few broad plates were saved, but none of the gold; that had sunk.

When they came forth from this second wetting, Ian was numb. His head felt huge and his chest tight. Weary of body and stunned with the magnitude of their loss, they struggled on to Sleaford. There, a distant cousin of Alinor's gave them shelter, and they stayed over the fourteenth and fifteenth. Ian heard the king was worse. He was not well himself, coughing continuously and finding difficulty in catching his breath. The weather was horrible. It poured rain, and the wind howled so that it could be heard even through the enormous walls of the old keep.

Unbelievably, on the sixteenth of October, John insisted on moving again. Whoever had influence with him begged and pleaded, but he would not listen. Alinor's cousin looked at Ian when the word came that the king would go.

"You should not," he said. "Stay here. You are more than welcome. He will not miss you."

The eyes said more. They said the king would miss no one and nothing any more, and when Ian saw John it was plain that this was true. Death was on his face and his flesh seemed loose on his bones. Ian knew the king would not realize that he had remained behind and that, even if he did, it would not matter. Nonetheless, he could not do it. Hate and duty had bound them together through all the years. Shivering and coughing, Ian mounted his own horse and followed the master he had never loved but could not leave. They struggled on a bare twenty miles until John collapsed.

It was plain now the king would not live. Ian was not sure he would live himself. Each breath was a torment and his limbs were not willing to obey him. John survived the night of the seventeenth, but as the dark ebbed, so did the spirit. Before dawn, the king was dead.

Ian could not believe it. It was inconceivable. All his life John had been there, a threat, a force to circumvent. Hate is as strong as love; Ian felt as if his life had been broken. A terrible need seized him and a terrible fear. He feared he was dying and he needed to be with Alinor. Even though he could barely walk and could not speak at all, Ian gathered the men of his personal guard and rode out of Newark.

They traveled through the day, although Ian became so weak that his master-at-arms Jamie had to mount behind him and hold him in the saddle. During the night, he was worse, but he signed to be lifted to his horse in the morning and they rode on again. By afternoon, it was plain that whatever Ian wanted he would never live long enough to reach Roselynde. In these times, however, a man could not simply ride into the nearest keep and expect to be welcomed. Jamie sent a few men south and west to ask the names of the holders of keeps in the area. He nearly wept with relief when he learned that Hemel was only five miles ahead, due south.

For Joanna, the past five months had not been as dreadful as she expected. The agony of pity and fear had receded into a dull misery, although Geoffrey had not changed. She was accustomed to the deadness under his smile and loving words. Only once in a while, when there was word that French troops were moving in the area, he looked at her in such a way that a cold sweat of fear broke out on her body.

Self-preservation aroused in Joanna a lively and unavoidable interest in what was going on in the country. Hemel was a substantial keep, but nothing like Roselynde or Lincoln. If Louis or one of his powerful supporters turned his attention to Hemel, it might not be able to resist for long—and Hemel was the nearest of Geoffrey's keeps to Louis's main stronghold. Joanna could not help wondering, when Geoffrey's eyes rested so strangely on her throat, why he had chosen Hemel above one of the other strong places. Was it habit? Hemel had been the home of his childhood. Or was it because he almost hoped they would be attacked so that he could end his living death in true peace? It was a fear that sharpened Joanna's interest in the news and in every act of every day.

Thus, when word of a troop of men headed for the castle was called down from the wall, Joanna set aside her work and ran down to hear the exchange of challenges. Instead, she heard Geoffrey cry for haste in letting down the bridge. This must be a welcome, yet there was something in her husband's voice—Joanna took to her heels and ran, arriving just as Geoffrey and Tostig received Ian into their arms.

"My lord!" Geoffrey gasped.

"Ian!" Joanna echoed.

Then she heard the sucking, rasping breath, the cough like that of a half-drowned man.

"Bring him to bed," Joanna cried. "Geoffrey, listen! Strip him naked and strip yourself and Tostig too. Do you both get into bed with him and keep him warm until I can bring hot sand. Prop him high so he can breathe. Cover yourselves with everything you can lay hands upon— feather quilts both above and below you. Be quick! Be quick!"

It was the maddest day Joanna had lived since she heard Geoffrey was not dead. This kind of illness did not permit quiet. The bags of hot sand must be changed continuously; braziers to heat water so that Ian would breathe steam fragrant with aromatic herbs had to be tended. Ian had to be lifted and shifted so that his coughing would bring up the phlegm that clogged his lungs. Servants came and went; medicines were compounded, trickled down his throat; maids with warmed hands thrust under the covers massaged his legs and arms to make the blood flow better.

After the warmth of his body was no longer necessary, Geoffrey was useless in the sickroom. He hung about anxiously for a while, but soon realized that there would be no change, either for good or ill, for many hours. All he could do was send off a messenger to Alinor. She would be in some danger traveling in these times, but if Ian should die— After that, not knowing what else to do, he went to ask Jamie when and how Ian's illness came about. Naturally, the most important news came first. The king was dead. Geoffrey could not believe his ears. He asked Jamie again and again, and was assured with more and more detail, which eventually described the whole of what had happened, that John was, indeed, dead.

He galloped up to the sickroom, but was unceremoniously shoved out of the door by Edwina. If Ian should happen to regain his senses, the last person anyone wanted him to see was Geoffrey. Three days followed in which Geoffrey had plenty of time to digest the news and consider it in all of its ramifications. He kept coming to the sickroom and being driven away. Although Joanna was sure that Ian no longer wished Geoffrey any harm, she had no intention of permitting him to be exhausted by man-talk now that he had regained consciousness. On the morning of the fourth day, Alinor arrived, shaking with tiredness and terror, to be greeted by the happy news that her husband was out of danger. He was weak, but he was able to smile at her and whisper her name before he drifted off to sleep again.

In spite of her fatigue, Alinor would not yield her right to sit with her husband. Remembering how she had felt the same when she brought Geoffrey home from France, Joanna did not protest. She was strangely reluctant to leave the sickroom, however. She could hardly endure to turn away from the reawakening life there to meet her own husband's deathlike despair. Perhaps news of Ian's well-doing would wake some spark in him.

To Joanna's amazement, Geoffrey leapt to his feet as soon as she appeared in the stairwell and came across the room nearly at a run. "Joanna, Joanna, did Ian tell you?"

His eyes were blazing, golden as the sun, his breath was quick and his color high. Joanna's mouth fell open with surprise. Her heart began to pound. Here was Geoffrey, re-

turned to her. She was almost afraid to speak, afraid to
move, lest something she should do or say would throw him
back into the pit in which he had lain so long.

"Tell me what?" she faltered.

"The king is dead," he said breathlessly. "John is
dead!"

"Yes," Joanna replied, "I think he did, but—"

Geoffrey laughed, seized her around the waist, and began
to whirl her around the room in a wild dance, which was
made even wilder by his limping step. Joanna could not
help laughing also, but she was frightened too.

"Are you mad?" she cried, and there was a note of genuine question under the laughing protest. "Will this not destroy us utterly?"

"No! No, it is salvation."

"Do you mean that now all resistance to Louis will die?"
Joanna asked hesitantly.

Ian had had little strength and Joanna had done her best
not to let him talk, but he had muttered something about
Prince Henry—no, poor child, he was King Henry III now.
Joanna knew without being told that Ian would fight for the
prince's right to the throne.

"No, of course not," Geoffrey laughed.

"But Geoffrey," Joanna said fearfully, "that the king
has died will not discourage Louis." She kept watching his
face, dreading to see the light die out of it. Nonetheless she
had to continue. It would hurt more if he glowed longer and
then faded. "The war will go on."

"Yes, of course," Geoffrey agreed with enthusiasm.
"Yes! Yes!" Then he began to laugh again. "How very
glad Roger will be to be rid of us—or, at least, of me. Poor
man. He knew when he accepted this place that this would
be my home and he little more than your Sir Guy, a hired
knight. Still, he has had it to himself for so long. And then I
came to stay—and in such a mood! Joanna, Joanna, we are
saved!"

Joanna stared at him. One thing sure she had been wrong
about, Geoffrey's injuries had bred no fear in him. He was

ready, even eager, to fight again. But what was this sense-less excitement? "Geoffrey, be quiet," she said. "What has put you in this fever?"

"Keeping my joy to myself. I came to whisper it to you, but you cast me out, and I did not have the chance—"

"Geoffrey," Joanna protested softly, "I did not love John either, but—but he was your uncle. It is not decent to crow like a cock on a dung heap just because he is dead."

He saw at last that she did not understand, and he took her and kissed her and drew her to sit in the window seat beside him. "I have frightened you. I am sorry. As to John him-self, as a man, I did not care whether he lived or died. He was not a good man. He was cruel and lecherous and treacherous. Let that go. He is dead now. As a king, the matter stands differently. As long as John lived, there could be no end to war—never. If Louis were beaten, new rebels would rise and draw in more pretenders to the throne."

"But why— Surely—"

"Because of what John himself was. He could not stop alienating men, even when he wanted to. There was some-thing that ate him and drove him. Perhaps he was possessed. I never told you why my father left him because I was not sure myself. But he may have discovered that John asked me along on that ravaging of the east to do away with me. Your brother has a keen eye for an assassin's knife and for an attack from behind—and I had grown pretty sharp to see such also. Papa said to me that, when they were together just before Louis came, John had attempted Ela."

Joanna had made no comment when Geoffrey confessed that John had tried again to kill him. While there was still danger of it, neither Adam nor Geoffrey would have told her such a thing. Now she need no longer worry. Decent or not decent, she began to taste the joy that Geoffrey had ex-pressed. All she said, however, was, "Ela? But he could never endure her."

"Who knows," Geoffrey sighed. "There was something sick inside the king. Perhaps it was true. Papa went back to him when things looked so very black, and I do not think he would have if—" Suddenly, he smiled again. "It does not matter any more. Now we are free of John's vices and treachery. We can begin again."

They talked all morning and all through dinner, and Joanna began to let her hope take root. The febrile excitement had died out of Geoffrey, but he was warm and alive, his eyes bright and intent as he spoke of the future. The prince was young and he had about him fine, strong men— Pembroke, Salisbury, Langton—men who would teach him honor and justice. John's oath to the pope had died with him, so that England was no vassal state any longer and the annulment of Magna Carta was meaningless. With that as a guide, the prince would know from his youth what were his duties and his rights.

Joanna agreed to everything, more with the joy of seeing hope in Geoffrey than with understanding, although she knew what he said was important. She was so happy that it was only some hours later that she realized she had not offered to relieve her tired mother, nor even arranged to have a meal carried up to her. She ran up, Geoffrey following, and found Alinor and Ian, hand in hand, also with peaceful eyes full of hope. Joanna turned to thrust Geoffrey out again, but Alinor smiled and said he could come in.

"Ian has promised to say just two words, and then go to sleep."

"He does not even need to say one," Geoffrey put in eagerly. "I know about the king, and I am ready and more than ready to take up arms for the prince. I will go now, this very night if you think it needful, to swear for myself and for you. Then I am ready to call up my levies. I know they will answer without hesitation now that John is dead. Adam too will come and swear."

The expression of anxiety faded from Ian's dark eyes, and his lips twitched into a faint smile. "You need not leave this very night," he said slowly and with effort but also with pleasure. "You may at least say farewell to your wife."

Geoffrey laughed aloud. "Do not fear me. I would have spared a few minutes for that."

"You had better take more than a few minutes at it," Ian advised.

"Ian, do not waste your breath on nonsense," Alinor remonstrated, but she could not help smiling. No preoccupation could blind her to her daughter's glow.

He nodded, still smiling, gathered strength for a minute, and said, "I do not know what will be asked of us, but my levies will answer also, even those in the north. Louis will never sign nor acknowledge Magna Carta, and all know it. I will give you a letter so you can summon them if they are needed before I am strong enough."

The last words were a bare whisper. Joanna and Alinor both said, "Enough!" with one voice.

"Wait—" Ian whispered.

"He does not go tonight," Joanna said firmly. "Tomorrow you can tell him what else is necessary."

With those words, she propelled Geoffrey out the door. She withdrew herself, but only into a shadowy corner, waiting the few minutes while Alinor soothed Ian and his eyes closed. Then she drew her mother away and insisted that Alinor sleep also. It was late, far later than Joanna expected when her mother woke and returned to watch beside her husband again. She hugged Joanna hard but quickly.

"I am sorry, my love, to sleep away so many of the last few hours you will have with Geoffrey," Alinor murmured hurriedly. "He is whole again, I see. Thank God for it. I will not ask you to tell me now how it came about nor waste more of your time to thank you for my Ian's life. Go now. Go to your husband."

Because there was nothing else she could do, Joanna did go, but she was torn between eagerness and fear. To watch a sleeping man breathe, alert to help him if he should seem to be in difficulty, does not occupy the mind. As dusk slipped into night, Joanna had grown less and less sure of the continuation of the miracle she had prayed for for so long. If Geoffrey had changed, slipped back again, she thought she could not live.

That fear was nearly swallowed in disappointment when she found Geoffrey fast asleep, but enough was left to make her undress very quietly and slip gently into bed. If he did not wake, she would not need to know. However, as soon as her weight hollowed the mattress, Geoffrey's arm slid out to draw her close. His lips found her and he began to fondle her body.

Had Joanna suffered less, she would have realized this was the proof of his cure. In all the months since the ravaging of the east, he had never once approached her for love. When her craving was too strong, Joanna would make the advances. Then he served—or perhaps serviced her would be the better words—with a pretense of a pleasure that was more dreadful than refusal. At times, the ultimate horror, he had withdrawn when she was finished without completing the act of love himself.

Geoffrey knew her body well. He knew just what would bring it to fever pitch, even while her heart was breaking. As Joanna's passion rose, so did her fear. Geoffrey's face was blank; those mirrors of his soul, his eyes, were closed.

"Open your eyes," she cried. "I cannot bear it—open your eyes."

They were wide at once, shining in the dim light of the night candle. "My heart," he whispered, "did I hurt you?"

"No," she sighed, "no." He was whole; he saw her True desire, not merely the fever of the body, flamed up in her.

"What did I do? What is it that you cannot bear?"

"Later. I will tell you later. Love me now—love me."

He followed Ian's advice and took more than a few minutes over it. He brought her to moaning acquiescence and then eased her back to quivering expectation, each time building her heat until at last she cried as she had that time in France, "Hurry, oh hurry, please hurry." And he brought her with him, both heaving and singing aloud in their joy. They slept at once, still joined, only turning to the side so that Geoffrey's weight would not crush her.

Morning brought conviction to Joanna at last. She woke, still wrapped in her husband's arms. He was already awake, gazing at her seriously but with absorbed, loving attention, his head tilted back to see her face better.

"Poor Geoffrey," she murmured, "you must be so cramped, holding me all night."

He did not answer that, except for smiling a little to show he had heard. "What is it you cannot bear?" he asked.

Joanna had hoped he would forget, but she knew it was better to speak the truth than to let him depart wondering. "I thought you were—I do not know how to say it—serving me to give my body ease although you hated it and hated me, as you have all these months past."

"Hated? You?" There was horror in his voice. "You are my life. You are the breath of my body. God knows, this last year I would have thrown myself on the first sword shown to me if it was not for you."

"That may be true, but then you hated me for binding you to life."

"Not you—never. I foresaw only endless years of fear and pain and, in the end— I saw what happened to the women, even gentlewomen. I dared not speak of it, comforting myself that when I saw we were overmatched I would kill you myself. I tried so hard to hide it from you that I did not see I hurt you worse by my silence. Beloved, forgive me."

"One does not forgive a person one loves because there is no—no anger. Tell me only this. If what you say is true, why were you so—so indifferent when we coupled?"

"Indifferent!" He laughed awkwardly and flushed. "Oh, God! That was true idiocy. I knew it, and yet I could not control it. I did not wish you to bring a child into this world. I saw such horrors before us, if we lived at all—flight, prison, starvation—and the babe to suffer and fear for. I would have left your bed entirely, but—but, Joanna, I was *not* indifferent."

Joanna could not help laughing. Now that he had said it, she saw it clearly enough. She had misread him. It was only Geoffrey, always overanxious, always feeling that he must be the one to lift the world on his shoulders. She felt light as a feather. If Geoffrey had not been holding her, she thought, she might float right off the bed.

"Will you do something for me?" she asked.

"Anything, I will do anything." Then an expression of extreme anxiety came over his face. "I mean—"

"Do not spoil it," Joanna warned, laughing gently. "Even if I am the breath of your body and your life, I know where my influence ends. I will not beg you to stay with me, nor even beg you to take me with you. My mother said to me once, and it is true, that when you love a man you do not bend his soul all awry. I only wished to ask—will you play and sing again for me, Geoffrey? You have not done so in a very long time."

"This very day," he said joyfully, "as soon as—"

The lightness passed. This very day they would be parted again, only God knew for how long. Love remained, confidence in each other, but joy was gone. They rose, dressed, heard mass, ate breakfast, and went to see if Ian was well enough to give Geoffrey orders about his men.

They found him somewhat stronger, although still rasping in his breath. He said what he needed to about the men, and Alinor handed Geoffrey the letter she had written and Ian had managed to sign and seal. Then he looked from one to the other as they stood, handfast, facing again the sorrow of parting.

"What I wished to say when you all overbore me, was that I do not think any large armies will be on the march in the next few weeks. Many who hated John do not hate young Henry, and many have come to realize what Louis and his men really want here. I doubt there will be any hard fighting until the lines are drawn clear again and the sides are sorted out." His voice was weakening.

"Let me finish, love," Alinor interrupted. "The west will be hard for the prince. He is known there and that is where Pembroke is strongest. In fact, the worst danger will be around London where Louis's strong points are. Ian thinks this is no good place for Joanna."

Geoffrey's hand tightened on his wife's and his eyes lit. He would not ask, but if someone else suggested it— "I agree. Hemel is not really strong enough and it is too close to London."

"Then what will be best," Alinor said gravely, although her eyes were sparkling with laughter, "would be for you to take Joanna with you to the swearing. It is proper also that she swear for me, who cannot come because of my husband's illness.''

So there was joy again, as well as love and confidence. Neither Geoffrey nor Joanna had delusions about what was coming. Well-entrenched, Louis would fight hard to win all. There would be war, and partings, and fear—but not now. Whatever else was said, neither Geoffrey nor Joanna heard anything very clearly except Ian's breathless chuckle, as he said, ''Go! Alinor will write what is needful.''

As soon as the door closed they were fast in each other's arms. ''So I will sing to you this day—this very day,'' Geoffrey murmured. ''That is, if you are a good, careful wife and remember to bring along my lute.''